At the Coming of Of Darkness

BY

MARK HARRINGTON

i

In loving memory,

Vera Johnson, Lesley Cook, Richard 'Chunky' Whyte and Rachel Plowman

Nan, Aunt, Uncle and friend.

I miss you.

ACKNOWLEDGMENTS.

This book very much started in secret. After all, it seemed such a ridiculous idea to tell people that I wanted to write and publish a book. We all have dreams, but many of them go unfulfilled. I am so guilty of that! The guitar in the corner of my living room being a prime example of such an abandoned idea, as it continues to gather dust.

But something about this idea was different, and as time went on and the project grew, I knew I needed support, after all, writing can be a lonely process. More than that, I needed to bounce my ideas off of someone and see if they worked. To that end, I want to thank my twin brother Stuart who bore the brunt of my conversations about this book over the last few years. More than that, he was very candid in his observations (as I knew he would be) and told me quite plainly if something wasn't working (an abandoned section about Fitzgerald's drive to Ashmarsh springs to mind!)

I also want to thank my test readers in the order they received it. Liz, Jenny, Gary, Stuart (again) and Kelly. You all gave me confidence that I could put this book out into the world and that was invaluable to me.

I want to thank my two editors, Alex and Will for their work and insight into the project and making me see things I hadn't before.

Thanks to Lenny for his proofreading, and tracking down those rogue apostrophe's (amongst other things!). Thanks as well, to Iain for his time and effort in producing a fantastic cover design.

Finally, thank you dear reader for picking this up. I really hope you enjoy it and it gives you a scare or two along the way.

Now let's get started...

THE BEGINNING

Beaumont-Hamel,

The Somme.

09:10hrs, Saturday, 1st July 1916.

With a small gasp of fear, Alistair Giles awoke from his dark dream and into a darker reality. The fading nightmare had been of an all-consuming pain; a fire set deep in his core that burned through him, turning him to ash. All the while, two dark disembodied eyes looked on, and the sound of soft laughter washed over him, revelling in his torment.

At first, his sleep-addled mind struggled to come to terms and make the leap between the fading horrors of that which he had escaped and his new surroundings, but a glance from under his low Brodie helmet, placed him on familiar ground; a narrow warren of mud cut from French soil and pressed full of the men of the Newfoundland Regiment.

Here was St John's Road, a reserve trench affectionately named after the harbour town some 2,500 miles distant, that he and most of this regiment called home.

How he had found sleep, he could not know. Exhaustion and fear were not natural bedfellows, but the former had won out somehow, despite the uncomfortable incline beneath him and the hard press of his pack at his back.

Through the sound of explosions rending the earth both near and far, came the familiar voice of his friend John Phillips. "Back to the land of the living are you?"

Alistair smiled as he pushed his helmet back and ran a hand through his matted hair. "What did I miss?"

John opened his mouth, but Sam Benfleet leaned forward and interrupted. "Oh, not much. The Kaiser came down personally and offered his surrender when he heard the Newfoundland boys were in town."

"He better had," Alistair said as he dug his friend in the ribs with his elbow.

1

"If only," John interjected, "Word came down the line nearly half an hour ago, we're to go on soon and take the first German line."

"Shouldn't it have been taken already?" Alistair replied, his humour quickly running dry.

"Mixed messages my friend. Whispers have been coming down that the 86th and 87th brigades are taking a hammering. Jackson got word half an hour ago that we are to go up and make good on their gains. Your guess is as good as mine as to what's going on over there."

Alistair looked up and could just about make out the sight of the Battalion Commander, Lieutenant Colonel Jackson, some thirty yards away. An ensemble of officers crowded close around him and were seemingly in fierce debate as several of the company's sergeant's awaited direction.

"It's bloody carnage out there," came the timid voice of Charlie Watson, the youngest of the group at only 19 years of age. "The way up is full with wounded."

Charlie, or Chappers as they had quickly dubbed him in homage to the comedian and screen idol Charlie Chaplin, had only joined them after the regiments ill-fated campaign and withdrawal from Gallipoli earlier that year.

The veterans exchanged a quick glance and Sam said cheerfully "Come on Chappers, chin up. Our artillery boys have been working overtime and softened them up nicely for you. This time tomorrow we'll be halfway to Berlin! And the men of the Newfoundlanders will be knee-deep in bratwurst, beer and skirt!"

Sam or 'Bully' as he was affectionately known was the joker of their pack, quick-witted and with a very dry sense of humour. He served the morale of the platoon well and had taken Charlie under his wing from the moment of his arrival.

Alistair could hear Charlie's soft laugh despite the commotion of war about them. Even so, Sam's bravado did little to ease his own tension. The offensive along the front was now pushing two hours old, and the rumour that surrounded the men of the 86th and 87th brigades sat heavily upon his heart. To think, it had only been a few short hours ago when each of them to a man had quaked at the sound of a momentous blast that had signified zero hour.

That had come at 07:15hrs and talk had long since filtered back to the Newfoundlanders that the explosion had been set beneath a German fortification at Hawthorn Ridge where the 86th and 87th were making their attack. The news had been greeted with much excitement, but now his companions had suggested the advance was not going as planned.

Alistair thought on Sam's words as the myriad of shells continued to fall upon the ground above. It was indeed their own artillery in which they must place their faith, for the battle plan had been in full effect for a week now; a seemingly never-ending tirade of shells volleyed at the German lines — designed to break the enemy defences and so clear the way for the impending advance. It was hard to believe that anything could survive such an onslaught, but over the course of the week, he and others had heard the faint echoing shouts of defiance drifting back toward the British trenches.

"Look, something's happening," Sam indicated with a point of his left hand as his right elbow nudged Alistair in the shoulder to grab his attention.

Alistair followed his direction and could see that the assembly of officers on the Auchonvillers Road was quickly breaking up and orders were being barked down into the trench, as the waiting men found their feet in preparation of what was to come.

Like a domino effect in reverse, the wave of standing men moved in their direction, and as one, Alistair and his friends likewise found their feet. And as they did so, Alistair heard the first whisper that served to twist a small knot of fear in his stomach.

"We're going over the top."

He turned as a voice came from his left, and he was in time to see the Company Sergeant, Cook, jump down into the trench.

"Listen in lads. We've got our orders and we're going over the top of St John's Road." The soft murmur of discontent that followed was palpable. If he heard it, he did not let on, for Cook continued, "the communication trenches up to the front lines are blocked. We have our orders that we are to press on immediately."

"It's as I said," Charlie whispered. "It's all going to hell over there, the way up is rife with those dead or dying."

There was no time for a response for Cook was quickly making his way down the narrow line in their direction.

"It's as we trained boys," Cook went on, "A and B companies over first, C and D to give them forty yards grace before they make off."

"Christ, this is it boys," Charlie said. Alistair could see the look of abject horror in the boy's eyes.

Alistair reached past John and grabbed the boy by his shoulder. "Look Charlie, just remember what you've learnt and that you'll have your friends around you. Just look to us and stick close."

Charlie nodded and let out a deep breath. Alistair could see the first stirrings of resolve in his friend.

Cook was nearly upon them now, and so as a group, they fell orderly into the line to allow the sergeant to make his pass. Alistair could see that the man was taking his time as he went, as he offered words of encouragement. Stopping here or there to tighten the chin strap of a soldier's Brodie helmet or inspect the rifle of the man holding it.

3

Sam nudged Alistair, and they smiled as they beheld the man playing his part to the end. Cook had been a stubborn and hard influence on the men, but it was in moments such as these you could see the effect he had on the company, as many would stand taller at his approach or following his words of optimism and comfort. In that instant, he felt stronger himself.

But something was out of place. Cook had stopped suddenly in the middle of his inspection of the line and appeared to have frozen before whatever or whoever he beheld before him, his eyes riveted at some fixed point between the men.

The sergeant was only some fifteen yards or so away from where Alistair stood, and there were at least ten or so soldiers stood between him and whatever held the sergeant's attention. He craned his neck forward so as to see better, and he was able to detect that there was some small break in the line and that break was right in front of the sergeant.

His curiosity got the better of him, and he stood forward a pace, and as that did not help, he took another. He was taking a risk in breaking the line and Cook would not look favourably should he turn and see him. A quick hard prod in his ribs from his left-hand side reminded him of this. He shot a quick glance back at Sam and met a pair of inquiring eyes that he ignored, for now, his angle of sight had opened up in the narrow width of the trench.

From where he now stood, the division in the line was all the clearer, and in front of the sergeant stood one man. Alistair looked upon the men on either side of this apparent stand off and was surprised to see them shrink away from this lone figure before Cook.

Who is that man? Alistair thought to himself, but the profile view and the low worn helmet gave him nothing but the protrusion of the man's nose and his right eye. And that eye seemed fixed upon the sergeant, as the sergeant was fixed upon him.

The confrontation had roused the curiosity of those around him, judging by the unsteady shuffling of feet and the soft murmurings of speculation. Ordinarily, such behaviour would cause the sergeant to bark, but not so now and Alistair had to crane his neck forward all the more, as a few more men began to lean forward from the line and try to observe what was happening.

In the midst of the murmurings that surrounded him, he heard one word come through, "Searle."

Searle? He racked his brains to try and associate the name with the visage of the man he now beheld but found that he was unable. It was all too clear though that he was also of the Newfoundland Regiment. He knew most of the men by sight, and those he did not know directly he might recognise at least by name or reputation. Not so, this man Searle.

The seconds stretched on and the uncomfortable moment lengthened. Alistair tried to find meaning in what he was seeing. Had this Searle character broken the line? Uttered some disobedience? Or worse still was refusing the company order to go over the top? That drew an involuntary swallow from Alistair, and at that moment, he thought that must be what had happened. What else could cause Cook to come to such a halt? The punishment for such desertion of duty or cowardice was summary execution.

But now Alistair was pushed back a step as Sam joined the throng of men distancing themselves from the two. Rather than follow suit, Alistair stepped forward so as not to be caught among the retreating group and was quickly stood alone and facing them. The gap surrounding the two widened as the men retreated past where he now stood.

Another whisper came to his ears, "has he injured himself?"

This might be the truth of what he was seeing, but the man Searle was stood before the sergeant and did not appear to have suffered any self-inflicted wound.

Alistair knew from his time in Gallipoli and the short time he had spent in France that some men had chosen the release of their rifle rather than the release of the enemies. But many more had instead inflicted injury upon their own person, be it by bullet, bayonet or contrived accident, all in the hope of being shipped back home.

His instincts kicked in and he stepped forward toward the two men, trying to remain oblivious to all the eyes cast upon him as he did so. Whatever he thought he might do was quickly lost though. A slow deep dread began to build in the pit of his stomach as he edged closer and he realised the sound that came to his ears was the muted sobs of the men who had been closest to the epicentre of this disturbance. Somewhere deep in his mind, a tiny voice appealed to him to stand back, that he wanted no part of this, for what could make him and those closest to him feel such raw terror, as he now knew he was feeling?

And so his footfalls shortened the closer he got, his feet reluctant to obey his commands and he cursed himself, for he had put himself forward in front of the company with the intent of intervention. He did not know the source of the feelings that rose within him, or of the retreating men, but it was clear it surrounded the two isolated soldiers who continued to stand off in silence. Now, every slow foot forward intensified his trepidation.

Christ, does he have his weapon drawn? Does he mean to do it here? He thought, his mind returning to thoughts of suicide or worse still murder. With relief, he quickly saw that was not so. The character Searle, stood with arms by his sides, his rifle stood safely by his right leg in the order arms position. Then what was this? If this man intended no harm to himself or any other, then what the hell was going on?

And so Alistair drew at last to a stop before the two, not a single word had been uttered between them since the sergeant had stopped suddenly in his tracks and thus drawn the attention of the whole company. Alistair was now oblivious to the presence of those behind him, who either continued to sidle back or look on captivated in nervous anticipation of what was to come, as all of his senses were drawn only to the two men before him and to something else that now nagged at him.

A dry heat emanated from his left and the man Searle. Alistair swayed backwards on his heels such was the intensity of the heat that greeted him. It came through as if in waves, and

5

his mind began to slow. Comprehension began to evaporate as a fugue-like state threatened to overwhelm him. What was clear was that this swelter beat from Searle like a pulse. Some other force was at play, and he was now caught in its lure as was Cook.

Slowly he forced his gaze towards Cook whose face, though ashen and white, poured with sweat and Alistair recoiled when he saw tears stream down the cheeks of the hardest man he knew. The sergeant's gaze was fixed unwaveringly upon the man before him as if in some kind of spell and Alistair knew that to follow suit would result in losing himself to an unknown horror that he may not rouse from.

With all the courage and strength he could muster, he stepped forward, placing himself between the two men, so as to be face to face with Cook, his back to whatever danger this man Searle held. Although he was immediately aware of how exposed he was, he felt the spell over him diminish, though the dry heat continued to assault his person from behind.

And for Cook, this had a similar effect, for he blinked hard and shook his head as if trying to clear a persistent fly from bothering him. Whatever power had held him was broken, and recognition came to his eyes as he breathed Alistair's name as if seeing him for the first time.

"Giles?"

"Sarge" he whispered back. "The time…"

Cook again blinked hard and nodded. He turned his head to the sides, quickly rolling his sleeve over his wet cheek and brow.

"You men there!" he bellowed. "What do you think this is? A mother's meeting? Fall in there quickly!"

Whatever had happened was over, the men quickly fell back into their positions along the trench wall.

"Giles, you as well." The sergeant followed more softly. This was followed by a short snicker of laughter from behind him, and Alistair's blood ran cold as the man Searle was quickly remembered. Perhaps sensing his unease, Cook put his hand out onto his shoulder and pulled him along as he made his way down the trench to where John, Sam and the rest of the men now stood straight and in order along the trench wall.

For now, there was to be no truth or understanding to what had happened, as the voice of the approaching Captain Frost washed over them as if from afar.

"Damn you, men!" he shouted as he approached the throng of Tommy's that lined the wall of the trench. "What the hell is going on here? We'll be off in minutes! You men, fill that gap, bring up the ladders!"

"You heard the captain, Giles. Back in line!" Cook turned and spun off toward the approaching captain, and Alistair did likewise to return to his comrades, his recent fear all but forgotten at the coming of the old.

They were going over.

The spell that had been cast upon the group was instantly gone as discipline overcame them all and they remembered their duty. Each fifth man placed a crude wooden ladder against the high trench wall and returned quickly to position as the cry from Cook rang out.

"Fix bayonets!"

Alistair removed the long thin blade of metal from it's sheath and smartly pressed it home close to the end of his rifle's barrel. He looked as both Sam and John did likewise, and he could not help but see Charlie's hands shake as he followed suit.

The only sound now was the continued whistle of artillery arching and falling from the skies above, as the crowd of men below nervously anticipated the moment of release. For Alistair, such feelings were coupled with the strange fear that had only recently overcome him. His stomach lurched with butterflies, a sensation he knew well, but was oh so different from only moments ago.

This he relished, for it was well known to him. He had felt this same unease on many occasions, from the trenches of Gallipoli to the very first time he had spoken to his sweetheart Alice and later asked her to marry him. And so he clung to that in those few short moments, as it served him better than to recall what had just happened between himself, Cook and that man Searle.

He could now see that Cook and Frost had separated, Cook was advancing down the line toward them, while Frost was stood high upon a ladder and looking through a pair of periscope field glasses into no man's land.

"Right you men!" Cook began. "Step forward, one man at the ladder, four more to follow! No gaps, no waiting, you hear?!"

The men shuffled slowly forward; it was John who came first to the base of the nearest ladder, Alistair second, followed by Sam. He did not see who his fourth and fifth were, such was his focus on what was in front of him, but knew Charlie would be close by.

"On the whistle, you go!" came the next cry from the sergeant.

"Jesus, what are we waiting on?" whispered John back toward his friends. "They've got to know we're coming!"

Alistair was in silent agreement. His tension was at its peak and sweat began to trickle down the nape of his neck as he imagined what was to follow.

"What kind of plan is this?" came the sound of Sam Benfleet behind.

Alistair's eyes searched the trench and quickly picked out Captain Frost. The man stood, whistle in mouth, eyes cast downward at his watch. Tick tock, the seconds passed and still nothing. Alistair realised that they would be waiting all down the line. The attack when it came must be coordinated.

He looked up and down the line, and he could see and sense the fear of those around him, and he wondered if the reality of the battle ahead could be worse than the anticipation of it.

As this thought crossed his mind, his eyes once again moved toward the waiting captain, to ascertain the exact moment they would go over. But his eyes did not reach that far, for only three ladders down he saw Searle once more.

He willed his eyes to carry on and meet their intended target, for he did not wish to recall whatever spell had previously taken him, but they would not obey. Now he had an unobstructed view of the lad.

Searle stood high above the others, number one on his ladder and only inches from the top. He was surely little more than 18 years of age, a skinny wretch that stood 6' 0 tall. His Brodie helmet was so large that the rim almost fell to his eyes. His webbing and pack looking so heavy as to almost overwhelm him.

The men around him had seemingly forgotten their previous terror of him and crowded close by, the reality of what was about to happen surely more pressing than this pathetic streak of a person. What could have caused him and Cook to have reacted as they had done toward him?

But it was with the meeting of their eyes across the crowded trench that brought it back to him, and his jaw dropped as he saw a fierce savagery within. Searle could see he had him in his gaze and flashed a wicked smile, making it appear that he relished all that was about to come above ground.

And at that moment, Alistair lost all hope as he gazed into the eyes of this twisted soul. Eyes that burned with latent savagery and a fury that he had never before witnessed. As Cook had been, he too was now locked upon this male and could not turn away, his continued unease now toward the boy and not for the surrounding war.

Suddenly Frost cried "That's it! Go! Go!" He then put his whistle to his mouth, and a single shrill blast emanated from it and was echoed up and down the trench line as other whistles combined. That was all it took for the men of the Newfoundland Regiment to stir into action, and a fierce battle cry went up as they attacked the ladders and forced their way up onto the French soil above.

The legs of John Phillips disappeared ahead of him, and Alistair shot Searle a grin of his own. His, he felt was weak and had none of the malice that the other mans had held. But he realised it had been done in relief as the whistles had broken the hold on him and finally allowed him to move and escape the eyes of the boy who emanated such hate.

His eyes moved to the rungs above, the stupor that had threatened to overwhelm him was broken, replaced instead with anger.

Alistair roared his defiance toward the enemy as he broke the surface and quickly straightened his eyes, focusing quickly to the broken and savage terrain before him, already the previous lull and quiet before the storm was gone as his companions and brothers did likewise and rose into the morning sun of the Somme.

He was greeted with a keen buzzing noise that defied interpretation. That was until only a second or two later as he witnessed the form of John Phillips go down before him. The machine guns of the German army taking the first bite of an impending banquet of death.

"No!" he screamed and brought his weapon to the enemy as he ran toward his fallen friend, quickly falling to his knees by the man's side.

"John? John!" he shouted as he hauled him to his side to reveal his broken and bloodied face. And with the world going to hell around him, he could not comprehend what he saw, for only moments ago, this man had been John Phillips. Now though he could not see, nor recognise what lay before him. A firm tug at his elbow brought him to his senses, and he looked up into the eyes of Sergeant Cook.

"He's gone lad, come on."

And Alistair did. His mind spun, and he could find no rational thought as to what was going on around him, but the objective was clear and easy to follow as he saw the long line of men continue to descend the muddy slope toward their own front line some one hundred yards away.

Already, the battlefield before him was awash with bodies, as pinch points had been identified by German machine guns where the regiment was using small boards, laid the previous night to bridge their own barbed wire.

Christ, we're not going to make it. We're not going to make it.

The echoing thought was reinforced as he witnessed the bodies of the fallen about him. The decision to go over the top at St John's Road had robbed them all of the cover they so desperately needed to make the British front line, and with their position on the high ground being highlighted against the bright sky behind, the German defenders down below had no problems finding their targets.

In the few seconds he had taken by his friend he had already lost Sam and Charlie amongst the crowd. He fell in abreast of his comrades as they moved ever onward, the buzzing of the machine guns was all the clearer now, and quickly, all too quickly, he found that the men who once stood at his shoulder were no longer there. Cook was nowhere to be seen, and the line was now sparse as the rest stumbled and pitched their way on the broken and ruined surface beyond the wire and on toward the expanse of no man's land.

Somehow, he made the front line trench and was appalled at what he found. Here before him were the dead and wounded of the first wave of earlier that morning. As he fell to the floor, the sound of bullets bit closely to the wall where he had entered. It was only a small respite, for quickly he saw some of his regiment already clawing their way back toward the surface, while a distant cry of 'advance' came from afar to his ears.

And so he went onward, heaving himself up once again into hell, as the German guns trained themselves upon the closer threat.

As he continued, his mind at last began to rebel at the insanity of what was happening. The few moments since he had been beside his friends already seemed like hours, and he realised that the anger that had driven him on was now expired. He looked around himself and could not see one man standing, while the buzzing of the bullets was an ever-present reminder of the danger he was in. But his mind now felt like a fog had settled over it.

The slope before him was littered with bodies, and he saw a single broken tree in the expanse of no man's land ahead of him. He lurched onward as it was the only cover the barren slope offered, and already several prone men could be seen cowering beneath its thin trunk.

He was not to make it. Both thought and action seemed to come sluggishly, and it was as if in slow motion as he watched the trail of bullets snake steadily toward him, spewing small clouds of mud into the air as they homed in upon him.

The first bullet took him in the stomach. Alistair fell to his knees and watched in fascination as the earth around him became alive with gunfire. The second bullet took him in the shoulder, and the momentum threw him backwards. He felt glad, for all of a sudden, he felt so incredibly weary that he just wanted to sleep.

He fell in a crumpled heap, and despite the heaviness of his eyelids, he watched as the dancing mud moved off to his left and in search of another target.

Touching gingerly near his stomach, his hand came away red. Already there was too much blood, and his belly was wet with it. Perversely he felt no pain from that wound. It was his left shoulder that screamed at him.

There was surely little time, and with his one good working arm, he delved into his jacket to recover his pocket watch. Quickly working the clasp, it opened to reveal a photograph of his beautiful Alice.

"I'm so sorry," he whispered to her picture, as the fantasy of returning to her was replaced by the reality that they would never see one another again.

His arm though was weak, and the watch fell into his lap. His eyes could seemingly no longer hold themselves open, and so he let unconsciousness come on and so fell into darkness.

Time passed. He couldn't tell how long, but something was very different around him when he woke. He gazed high above him into the clear blue sky and could see that the sun had moved on. It was surely no more than mid-morning, but here he was barely alive and in furious pain.

Suddenly, he heard a soft shuffling sound and his eyes shot open as panic gripped him. His arm shot up to his brow to block the light and there from the direction of the German lines approached a single man.

Alistair screwed his eyes tightly, but he could make no more of the silhouetted figure that stood against the sun. He did not know the reason for this sudden anxiety, for he had already accepted both his pain and his impending death. If this was surely some German scout, what difference would it make if he was here to end his life only minutes prematurely?

But there was something about this figure of a man, the way he just stood there surveying the battlefield before him. To Alistair, it seemed that this was somehow right, that this was his field and his to do with as he pleased. He seemed to have no fear that his life might be taken in much the same way as Alistair's would soon be.

As he looked on, he saw the man begin to turn his head, as if looking for something. Alistair felt frantic. For whatever reason, he did not want himself to be that something. Slowly though the man turned and faced him. Alistair could not breathe, and his eyes widened in horror as the man took his first step toward him.

Only some twenty yards away now, the pace of the figure quickened as it latched onto him. He wished to close his eyes but found that he could not; a silent scream failed to break the surface of his parted lips. Although he could not yet recognise the approaching figure, he did recognise his terror, as it was the same that he had only recently experienced in the trench. That was all it took to know that this man was called Searle and somehow that spelt a worse end than he had already accepted for himself.

Tears rolled from his eyes, and a long-rattled breath emanated from his lungs that wished to be heard but could not. Searle stood before him, blocking out the sun. Seemingly larger now, he knelt toward him, and Alistair found himself looking into two bottomless black wells that were the man's eyes. And as Searle slowly reached out for him, he again felt the rabid wave of heat that poured from his being and felt his face begin to burn and the moisture in his eyes run dry. Here was the end that his nightmare had surely foretold.

He had not known real fear it transpired, not even back in the trench during their first encounter, for back then he had not yet gazed into the black depths of this man's haunted eyes.

Hand met hand, and in that split-second, Alistair felt the savage fire that seemed to dwell in this man course through him; an agony which his inflamed wounds only paled in comparison to. A slow whine finally broke his lips, and he watched as the corners of Searle's mouth twitched and slowly began to form a smile. Fire now seemed to burn inside of him, but mercifully his Lord must finally have heard his silent call, for darkness took him at last.

CHAPTER 1

Tuesday, 18th October 2016.

Iain Fitzgerald rubbed his aching eyes, as his car wove its way in slow formation on a laboriously long hill that seemed to have no end. Stuck behind an articulated lorry that incessantly coughed black smoke back at him, Iain watched on as brake lights filtered through the sheen of running water that his wiper blades struggled to clear.

His eyes flitted nervously down toward the digital clock on the centre of the dash for the umpteenth time. What he saw caused his brow to furrow and gave him cause to contemplate the meaning that he should be tardy in arriving for his meeting with his predecessor Father Liam Shilling. It was nearing 11:45 am. He had been due to meet at St Peter's Church at 11:00 am.

Mercifully, the antiquated lorry turned off with a final billowing cloud of exhaust fumes, and the road both levelled and opened out before him. Soon he found himself in a built-up area once more as the steady stream of isolated farms he had passed, gave way to footpaths, street lights and terraced housing. And there before him at last, he read the sign 'Welcome to Ashmarsh'.

Ashmarsh in the county of Eastland. His new home and parish.

A second road sign quickly reminded him that he was now in a thirty mph zone. Relieved to finally make the town, he eased his foot off the accelerator and watched the needle of the speedometer fall.

"Here's to us, Ashmarsh." He breathed quietly to himself as he went.

The road hit a sharp decline, and there ahead of him, high above the horizon at the opposite end of a valley, was the tall clock tower of St Peter's Church. His car made its way slowly down the hill, and he let his eyes wander upward, taking in the tall, imposing sight of the church that seemed to cast a watchful vigil high above the streets and buildings of the town below.

The sight of the church was quickly lost as the road flattened out at the floor of the valley. His route began to twist and turn before him, and he was afforded quick views of the local police station and the town park, before coming to what must have been the high street proper.

It wasn't long before his car was ascending the long hill of the other side of the valley. He glanced around and could see that the adverse weather was taking an inevitable effect upon the day's trade, as he could only see the odd umbrella-laden person here or there. The additional sight of a couple of teenagers with their hoodies pulled tight to their faces, shoulders hunched against the cold wind and rain gave testament to the awful conditions outside.

As the duo receded in his rear-view mirror, his car reached the peak of the hill, and with it, the grounds of St Peter's Church opened up before him. Checking his mirror one last time, he flicked the turn signal and turned the car in through the gates and into the small car park.

The time was now 11:58 am. Nearly a full hour late, and to top it off he could see by the multitude of parked vehicles in the small lot, that the mornings Parish Communion was already well underway.

Bringing the car to a stop, he allowed himself to lean back and run his hand through his hair. A small sigh escaped his mouth, and he closed his eyes. Tiredness was threatening to overtake. But having little time to rest, he instead glanced about himself for signs of life but saw none, finding only a small path which lead from the car park into the yard of the church itself.

Pulling his jacket tight against himself against the unrelenting rain, he quickly bolted from the car and onto the path. Following it quickly, it took only a few short steps until it curved lazily around into the wider grounds of the cemetery, and toward the protrusion of an entrance porch. Quickening his pace, he soon crossed its threshold and found shelter.

Iain turned and looked back into the rain-sodden day and beheld the sight of the cemetery. Before him were lines of grey tombstones, and there, a statue of a shrouded woman, a monument almost lost to the creeping ivy that entwined itself around her like a second skin. Her forlorn gaze made him feel oddly ill at ease, and so he quickly turned away from it and back toward his goal.

Making the large oak door to the church, he reached out to twist the iron ring which would work the latch on the inside. The mechanism made an approving noise from within, and so he pushed lightly on the door. He was greeted with the low monotone of a male voice which echoed down the nave from the as yet unseen lectern and the service in progress.

As he pushed further on the door, he looked up and saw several sets of eyes snap over to his direction from the back most members of the congregation, and with that, a sensation of guilt washed over him as if he had been found out for some indiscretion. This was hardly the entrance that he had hoped to make, but perhaps he could just slip in quietly and find a quiet pew at the back so that he might go unnoticed.

But just as the thought occurred, so did another. A strange far off voice in the back of his head telling him that maybe he should simply back out and shy away from this place. The thought had surprised him to the extent that he hesitated at the door, caught in indecision as to go onward or back away.

He was startled from this involuntary reverie as the sound of the bell tower above began its hourly chime signifying it was now midday. Mind made up, he took a deep breath and hoping that his indecision had gone unnoticed, he pushed through the door into the church, allowing him his first view of his new charge.

Quickly making the back most pew, he felt relieved as the sermon continued ahead of him without pause, and those curious eyes that met his intrusion had clearly found him of little interest and so reverted back to the service.

Grateful for some anonymity, he allowed his eyes to wander the high arches of the vault above him and down toward the chancel at the head of the church where he saw a solitary figure that stood before the lectern at its end.

Ah, Father Shilling?

And though he squinted hard, he could not make out much of the man who addressed the somewhat meagre crowd before him. The fact was the church almost seemed to be in darkness; such was the small light that the high chandeliers cast, coupled by the drab day outside, which offered no light to the large stained glass windows that adorned both the north and south transepts of the long nave.

Fitzgerald had long since been used to the sight and feeling of an unused church and so would not allow feelings of darkness overwhelm him, for he knew that with light, warmth and the sound of song, the room would come alive, and as he looked on, he tried to picture such a thing in his mind.

His attention was quickly drawn back to the sermon though, as the words of Father Shilling echoed down toward him.

"And so at last, we come to the end of my time here with you at St Peter's. It is a bittersweet moment for me and perhaps for some of you as well. I say this because as I look out over the diminishing numbers that attend here in the Lord's house, I see some of you that I hope I have been of comfort to in your hour of need. When I started my time here all those many years ago, it was with such a belief that I could serve this congregation. That I could spread the good word and love of Jesus Christ and that in part, I hope I gave to you."

Shilling paused as several heads could be seen to nod their agreement.

"Gave some of you that is. For as I look out at you all today I see many I have failed. And I don't just see it in the faces of those I see before me; I see it also among the empty pews around you, each of which is indicative of another stray soul whom this church has failed to touch. So yes, bittersweet. For some, my impending retirement won't have come quickly enough, and for those, I hope that my replacement can give you what I so clearly could not."

Iain swallowed involuntarily at the reference to himself, and as he did so, he could see Shilling's eyes trained down the nave in his direction and locked upon him. He quickly knew he had failed to enter the church without Shilling's notice. The priest's next words left no doubt.

"I will say this to you, Father Fitzgerald..." Shilling's voice raised now to reach him, and seemingly as one, all of the congregation turned to look at him.

"...the people of this town are sinners."

Addressing the room once again he went on "yes, you heard me. But is that not the human condition? Is that not the vicious cycle of life and Catholicism? Sin, guilt, redemption, and so the wheel turns, and in our complacency, we begin the cycle anew? Well, I tell you now, we have danced this merry dance for too many years."

"You are weak and jealous. You are hypocrites and gossips, and yet still you return here weekly. Your small penance, your meagre atonement for a life led in sin."

Fitzgerald could now hear the small crowd murmuring in discontent at what they were hearing from their parish leader. He shifted uneasily on the wooden pew as the previously quiet voice in his head reminded him that it had warned him of entering.

Ridiculous.

Of course, it was, but what should he do? Should he stand and interject somehow? Turning his head, he met the eyes of an elderly lady and could see that her lips were pursed as if biting down her anger. Her demeanour seemingly implored action upon his part, but doubt descended quickly. He was out of his element here. What had meant to be a simple meet and greet with Shilling, followed by a friendly introduction to the congregation had turned into some kind of admonishment, one that he neither understood or was in any position to interrupt.

As he thought on this, his attention was quickly shifted as he saw that several people had got up from near the front and were quickly making their way toward him and the exit.

What in God's name is happening here?

He had no answer, but some resolve stirred into him at last. He must act, knowing that if he did not show strength in this moment, that his term at St Peter's might be doomed to failure from the off. He shuffled forward in his seat, ready to stand, but Shilling seemingly anticipated such interference and quickly and firmly pushed his open palm outward in his direction, indicating that he would not tolerate any intervention. He raised his voice now as he addressed those fleeing from the back of the church.

15

"Cowards as well? Well, that is no surprise, either. You see Father?" he said, addressing Fitzgerald once more. "This is your flock, and these are the souls you would save, and yet they would not save themselves."

Turning back toward the nave and the people, he now grabbed the lectern before him with both hands, and his voice began to rise. Fitzgerald had uncomfortable visions of the evangelist preachers he had seen on the high-numbered TV channels, as he prepared for the full extent of Shilling's outburst.

"I see that some of you would not hear the truth. No matter, I am sure word of my final sermon will reach all before long. But it is for your own good that I give you these words. For, have we not between us, satisfied our parts by simple lip service all these years? And to do so in the house of God? That is why I tell you these things before I leave, for who would hear my confession?"

Those that remained were now transfixed upon Father Shilling. The mood in the church had altered, and it was clear that they would hear his final passing words. Fitzgerald knew that for some, they wished to see the man implode so that they could pass testimony to that fact later that night on their social media networks. For others, he could see nodding heads and those who seemingly relished the reprimand they were receiving. He also knew that there was no stopping this now. The audience was captive, for better or worse and whatever would unfold, and for whatever damage it would do, it would be his to fix when the dust had settled.

"I have married you, and I have buried your dead. I have baptised your children and so been a full part in the circle of your lives. I have heard your confession and watched as you repeated your sin, only to ask forgiveness for the same. And what of the rest of you? For this is a small town, and many of you have not taken confession of your wrongdoing. Many of your names are mentioned in the confessional and many for such wickedness and depravity, and still, you take the Eucharist free and aware of your mortal sin, that goes unrepented."

Several heads nodded in agreement, while several bowed themselves to the floor.

"But how have I let this pass? Have I become comfortable and complacent as the representative of Christ? That is my confession to you before we part today, for I have allowed the evil that shrouds this town overwhelm and exhaust me to the point of failing my sacred duty to you. There are those among you who will know of what I speak. The dark days of this town are still a shadow that blight its future and spiritual growth. I heard the stories when I came. That a devil dwells here among you in Ashmarsh, a black shadow casting its net wide from the doors of Thoby Hall. Yet still today there are those that believe that shadow remains and would use that as an excuse for poor moral fibre and the poor choices that are made."

A devil? Is he serious?

Fitzgerald couldn't know. As for the reference to some place called Thoby Hall, that meant nothing to him either. None the less several more heads nodded their agreement at Shilling's words.

God only knew what he had walked in on here, but despite the lack of context, he had also become transfixed with the priest's rhetoric.

"We know that for the nonsense it is. There are those who want to believe that the town is cursed and our fall from grace is an inevitability of that. But those people are not taking responsibility for their own choices for which God gives them free will to make, for right or wrong. We must come together to fight such superstition, and all unite and bask in the light and truth of our Lord. Will you not lift your heads from the sand and allow Father Fitzgerald to do his work as he should? For he is only a conduit to God and Jesus Christ and though you may hide your sin from him, you cannot from the Holy Father and his Son. The gates of heaven will surely be barred to those who do not repent!"

Shilling's voice had elevated almost to a shout as he concluded. Now, he looked exhausted and was breathing hard. The congregation beneath him were quiet, casting nervous glances between themselves. Mercifully the moment passed quickly as Fitzgerald observed a previously unseen man, a deacon undoubtedly by his dress, rise from the area of the chancel at Shilling's back. A comforting hand came to rest upon his shoulder, but Shilling shrugged off the gesture and stormed off toward where Fitzgerald knew his sacristy would be located behind the pulpit. Shaken and bewildered, Fitzgerald shook his head as if to negate everything he had seen and heard. It had been some welcome to St Peter's Church.

CHAPTER 2

"Father Fitzgerald? I'm very pleased to make your acquaintance. I'm Colin Morris."

Iain had observed the deacon from a short distance and saw as the man had ably pacified the departing members of the congregation with no small degree of charm and diplomacy.

"Pleased to meet you," Iain returned, "I am so sorry I was late, the traffic…"

Morris dismissed it with a wave of his hand. "Ah, if only it had been worse, we might have spared you that little display."

An awkward smile broke on Iain's lips. "Erm, is everything okay? with Father Shilling, I mean?"

Morris beckoned him back over to the pew where he had been seated. "Oh, nothing your arrival won't fix. Father Shilling has become somewhat frustrated with his lot of late. This retirement can't have come soon enough."

Fitzgerald nodded his understanding.

"I am sorry you had to see that. That is hardly the welcome we had prepared for you."

Fitzgerald judged Morris to be in his late fifties. A full head shorter than his own six feet, but surprisingly broad for someone of his age, and with his tightly shaved head, Fitzgerald could easily picture him without his white collar, working a door at some night club.

"I hope I'll have no such problems with you, Father Fitzgerald?" Morris continued with a sly smile upon his face.

Fitzgerald was very quickly warming to Morris's affable nature and was glad to find a degree of normality following the strange sermon he had seen delivered by Father Shilling.

"No, nothing of the sort. But I have to ask…I mean all that stuff he said of the parish and the congregation?"

Morris slowly nodded his head. "You'll understand that Father Shilling and I don't share certain views, and it would be wrong of me to answer in his place. However, there is some substance in what he said. The parish has suffered its fair share of trouble and no mistake. I don't doubt that Liam will fill you in on that side of things. Perhaps when the dust has settled, we can speak more openly about it?"

Fitzgerald got his meaning immediately; they would discuss it further when Liam Shilling had been packed off into his retirement. He could guess that there was little love lost between the two.

"Do you think it is a good time to go speak with him?"

Morris stood and seemed to consider for a moment before answering in the positive. "No time like the present. I'll take you down to meet with him."

Fitzgerald followed suit and quickly fell in beside the deacon who made his way down the nave.

"Now, don't mind his bluster when you get in there. He can be a surly one, but I always found it easier to stand my corner." Morris said as they made the door to the sacristy.

"Liam, I have a visitor for you," Morris said as he pushed the door inward. Standing aside, he gave Fitzgerald a short nod that told him to go in without further invitation. Holding his position by the door as Iain passed by, it was clear that Morris would not be joining them.

"Well come in boy, let's have a look at you," came the gravelly voice of Liam Shilling.

Fitzgerald's attention shifted now to the elderly priest who sat behind a sparse wooden desk in the centre of the room.

"Father Shilling?" he began, "It's very nice to meet you. I…" He was cut off as the old priest drew his chair back and with careful deliberation stood, before slowly sidling past him without so much as a glance. Making the door, he took it and pushed it firmly shut in the face of Morris.

Iain found himself shocked at the other man's appearance. He knew Shilling to be in his sixties and imminently close to his retirement, but his experience of the priesthood thus far, had afforded him visions of senior clergy reaching their advancing years with grace and vigour. Not so Liam Shilling who bore the grizzly visage of a man who might be more at place in a homeless shelter, what with his unkempt white hair and stubble. And more, as now he was sure he could detect the bitter stench of whisky in the room.

Fixing a smile, he extended his right hand in greeting, as the other man drew close by on his way back to his seat.

Again though he was ignored and he quickly dropped his extended palm, as he viewed what he could only surmise to be deeply arthritic hands on the elderly priest.

On his return, Shilling not so much sat in his seat as fell in it and Fitzgerald felt the stirring of genuine concern for his peer, who now sat with his eyes closed, while short ragged breaths whistled through gritted teeth.

19

Slowly he detected signs that the priest was returning to normal. Perhaps only a minute had passed by, but it seemed so much longer as he stood embarrassed, the silence having stretched on between them. His anger had begun to rise, but again his reliable Catholic guilt rose to the surface as he could see that Shilling was not at all well.

And so he opened. "Father, is there something I can get you? Water, perhaps?"

Shilling slowly shook his head and allowed his eyes to flutter open and replied as if angry with him. "No, no. I'll be okay in just a minute…just a minute…"

Guilt had now made way for worry for the old man. How was it that he had been left so long to fulfil his duties in this state?

"Sit down, boy, sit down." Shilling managed.

Fitzgerald looked about and saw a chair by the wall. Hardly a suitable place to promote conversation and the thought crossed his mind that perhaps that was the reason for its placement there. He stepped over and dragged it to a position in front of the desk where he decided it would live from now on.

"So, here you are at last, the new kid on the block. Thank the heavens, I won't be left here to rot after all."

"Father?" Fitzgerald questioned.

"Use your eyes boy," Shilling retorted, "look what this god-forsaken place has done to me! Twenty years of my life wasted, thrown away to those godless sons of bitches out there." He threw his arms wide, as if to encompass an unseen throng.

"And look what it has taken to have me removed! I've become an embarrassment. A cynical, drunken old fool, preaching the gospel faithlessly to an unrepentant flock."

Fitzgerald bit his lip and squirmed uneasily in his chair. Shilling though seemed oblivious to his reaction and Fitzgerald was afforded a brief glimpse at the man's tired, bloodshot eyes that were a window to the man's pain. But as to what that pain might be, he could not even begin to guess and so sat in silence, stuck as to how best to placate the aged priest. In the quiet that lingered between them, he thought back to his previous parish and the vehement passion of those he counselled who demonstrated similar pain; anger as well as sorrow, but he had not expected to find it so apparent from one of his own.

Now though, Shilling was quiet, except for his heavy, laboured breathing, brought on no doubt by his angry tirade. Fitzgerald looked desperately about himself, trying to find some inspiration as to how to respond. He opened his mouth to break the silence between them but quickly thought better of it, as he couldn't quite find the words to begin. It was Shilling though who spoke next.

"How have I treated you? This is no way to introduce a new priest to his parish. Please, you must forgive me, I'm so very tired you see. Twenty long years…" He trailed off.

20

Fitzgerald found his voice. "Of course, Father, you've worked long and hard in the service of our Lord. Your retirement is well earned."

Shilling looked up at the young priest, a quizzical look upon his face, Fitzgerald could see that he was trying to weigh him up, to see if he was genuine in his concerns. He met the priest's eyes with fixed determination and held them. And slowly a warm smile broke on the man's face.

"My retirement, eh? Bundled off to John Paul's?" Shilling said, referring to the retirement home named after the former Pope. Fitzgerald had a vague knowledge of the lodging as an old mentor of his had retired there only last year.

"Aye, I guess that will do for me. It wasn't the future I saw for myself when I was your age lad, but as the years have gone by, I guess I've had my eye on that as my salvation. Lord how this town has dragged me down and damn if I haven't petitioned them to cart me away!"

"There I go again, lad. What can you think of me? Some greeting, eh?" He finished.

Fitzgerald paused to gather his thoughts; so far, his experiences of Father Shilling had been unusual, even troubling to say the least. Something had been bothering the man, and clearly for some time. Perhaps if he was careful, he might shed some light on those issues.

"No need to apologise Father. It sounds like your pleas fell on deaf ears?"

"They did boy, and it wasn't for the lack of trying I can tell you."

"You made mention of the town there. But I don't understand, it seems of good heritage and has a strong Catholic base, doesn't it?"

"You've done your homework, eh? But I'll venture your internet or whatever damned contraption you use these days won't get near the truth of it."

It was true, Iain had done his research. In one sense Ashmarsh seemed to be blossoming, as the population level reached the twelve thousand mark. It had high ranking schools and had been very successful in the Eastland in Bloom Competition, that awarded merit for a town or village of particular floral beauty. On the flip side, the town was in decline in a commercial sense, falling behind to large shopping complexes and malls, much like other small towns across the country. Fitzgerald felt he knew full well the challenges he would be facing.

Shilling continued. "Ah that's enough out of me I think. Here you are only five minutes through the door, and there's me venting at the first member of the Church that had the poor fortune to turn up. Maybe we should start over? Tell me about yourself."

The old man's breathing was now back to normal, and the red flush of his cheeks had diminished somewhat. For that, Fitzgerald was glad. Now he might begin to tell his story and ask his questions.

21

"Well Father, I was ordained only a few short months ago. I was at the seminary in Guildford, and my formation into the Church began there. I also served at St Mark's, in Colchester for six years as a volunteer until my time came. I guess I'm surprised to find my new parish is so far from where I called home most of my life."

Shilling raised an inquisitive eyebrow.

Fitzgerald nodded, glad the conversation had turned in a different direction and happy to impart some of his story so as to keep it that way. "Well, I am an Essex man originally Father; Colchester in fact. My family were a hard-working lot. My father was a self-employed builder, and I worked alongside him when I was younger. My parents thought I would follow in his footsteps and take the business on…"

Shilling cocked his head.

A nervous smile broke on Fitzgerald's face. He had nearly taken the story too far in his attempt to appease the old priest. He had not found his calling to the Church until he was 30 years of age. The interim years between boyhood and priesthood had their own story, something that he wasn't ready to share here with this man.

"We were, of course, a devout Catholic family and strong supporters of the local church," he added to keep the old man genial.

The story he had told, all be it short would hopefully be enough to satisfy the old priest, and then surely Shilling would follow suit, taking the invitation to offer his own experiences. But the old man simply nodded, not taking the implied invitation.

"Well, lad, you'll have a relatively quiet introduction to life here. We'll get you settled at the rectory shortly. But tomorrow is coffee morning at the church hall. I hope to say some goodbyes there, and it'll be an ideal way for us to introduce you to some of our more devout parishioners. I had planned to introduce you this morning but…"

"I'm sorry Father, the traffic…" Fitzgerald cut in, keen to keep the focus squarely away from the sermon he had witnessed. In truth, he was still angry at how Shilling had called him out in front of all of the parishioners, something he knew he would remonstrate about if the conversation turned in that direction.

But as for a coffee morning, it was an ideal suggestion, and he was glad that there would be an opportunity to meet some of the flock before the following Sunday and his first service.

Sensing that the (few) social niceties were nearly spent and that within a few minutes he would be shown back into Colin Morris's hands and ultimately to the rectory, there would be no better time to voice his concerns and ask his questions.

"Father. I wonder if I might press you more regarding your time here? It would be wrong of me not to ask the benefit of your experience within the parish."

"Benefit? I would hardly call my experience here a benefit lad, but you'd be right to ask. After all, I can see it in your eyes. What's brought a senile old fool to such rack and ruin eh?"

"Father, I only meant…" Fitzgerald began. Shilling though dismissed the protest with a smile and the wave of his hand.

"Forget it; I know what you meant. I have to admit that I have been somewhat preoccupied and my thoughts never once turned to the poor soul who would follow in my footsteps here, keen as I was to escape. Ask your questions and don't hold back."

Fitzgerald considered for a second, trying to find the right words. "Well…as you said, you don't feel that your time here has been of value?"

At that moment, he could see Shilling's face drop and his strength seemingly evaporate. In the blink of an eye, it was as if the weight of another 20 years had been heaped upon his shoulders. Fitzgerald looked on in quiet anticipation. And as he did so, all that could be heard was the continued patter of rain upon the roof overhead and the first soft grumble of thunder from afar. In the unlit room, it served as if some kind of dark foreboding and he shivered as he felt the realisation of countless years to come, wash over him.

The spell was broken though as Shilling reached down to his right and pulled open the desk drawer, his hand returning to the surface with a large bottle of whisky. Quickly his hand disappeared again to produce two tumblers. He fixed a stare at Fitzgerald as he spoke.

"I pray you won't need this as I have. But you may find comfort in it by the end."

Fitzgerald opened his mouth as if to protest and quickly thought better of it. Instead, he gave a brisk nod as the golden liquor splashed the base of the first tumbler. He reached out and took the offered glass and waited for the priest to fill his own.

"St Peter's." Shilling toasted as he offered the glass. Fitzgerald met this, and they both quickly swallowed. The bitter taste quickly warmed his throat and belly. Shilling sat back and beheld him again.

"So how do I begin? Perhaps I should start where you are today? Things were slightly different when I was sat where you are for the first time. There was no cosy drink and believe it or not the welcome was no less cold than what I have offered you today. 1990?…" Shilling paused, and Fitzgerald could sense him thinking.

"…1996 it would have to have been. This wasn't my first parish; you see I have been a man of the cloth for some 40 years give or take." Fitzgerald sat back in his chair as he prepared for his story.

"I'd heard of Ashmarsh of course, based where I was in nearby Springmoor. I'd heard the scandal and the sordid tales of the town. But even in that day and age what was heard wasn't anything you couldn't hear about anywhere else in the world. Springmoor, after all, presented challenges of its own due to its size, there was murder, rape, domestic abuse, all in a day's work for a parish priest. But why was it that this little town of Ashmarsh was rife with such rumour?"

Fitzgerald knew the question to be rhetorical and so kept quiet, and as he looked on, he could see much of the earlier tension had left the old priest's face as he spoke. Perhaps all he had needed was an appropriate and avid audience, and Fitzgerald knew that he was it.

Shilling continued. "The call came as I said in the spring of 1996, after the suicide of Father Crosby. We'd all heard the news of course as well as sordid speculation as to why he would have done such a thing. Let me tell you now lad, whatever idle gossip you hear, remember, that man was no child molester. The problem was that Ashmarsh has suffered in that respect in the past and so, such gossip was rife."

As he spoke, Shilling reached out again for the whisky bottle, pouring another considerable measure into his glass. He offered the bottle out toward the lip of Fitzgerald's own tumbler and raised his eyebrows questioningly.

"No thank you, Father." Fitzgerald returned, the previous measure already glowed warmly in his belly, and he felt that to indulge further would make him all the worse for wear.

Shilling shrugged before taking his own glass and swallowing half the measure.

"There is, of course, a danger you'll take what I say and dismiss it as the ramblings of a tired old fool, and I can accept that. I think though that time might change your mind as it did mine. But I digress. Where was I? Oh yes, Father Crosby. Well, to cut a long story short, in the aftermath of his demise, I was told that I would be coming here as his replacement. For the ambitious fellow I was, I relished the opportunity to come to the town and reverse its ailing fortunes. I was proud you see and naïve as to the core of the problem. There had been scandal in the sixties when the serving priest was run out of town amid rumours of child molestation as I said. The Church doing its usual housekeeping. After that, the next serving priest fathered two children with one of the parishioners and likewise left under a cloud. There was a lapse then, in that men would come and go, none staying for long, at least that was until Father Crosby arrived in 1990 or thereabouts. From what I could make out, he was a proud and good man and in that early part of the decade did good work in the reversal of the church's bad name. But ultimately he was taken, be it dementia, insanity, your guess is as good as mine."

Fitzgerald began to shift uncomfortably in his seat. It was clear from Shilling's tale that the town had a chequered history with the Church and any such disgraces were not easily overcome or forgotten. There could be no doubt that there would be those amongst the faithful that would remember the events that were being described and as such, be keeping a very close eye on him. All the worse then, that this man before him had chosen to leave them under a similar negative cloud.

Fitzgerald now found his voice. "But how could such rot have been allowed to fester for so long?"

"Don't you see lad? The town was a lost cause in the eyes of the Church. They had done what they could to sweep things under the carpet. It was damage limitation in their eyes. They thought they had finally resolved the mistrust and apathy with Crosby's appointment, but that too ended only in failure."

"What became of him?"

"It's hard to say. At first, nothing at all. It seemed that the demons that haunted this town had been laid to rest. The town and the church enjoyed somewhat of a revival under Crosby. The man kept diaries, you see, and it was as if somewhere along the way someone simply pressed a button and so began the man's descent into madness or despair."

The old priest's eyes became glazed and distant as he spoke. Captivated, Fitzgerald brought him straight back into the conversation.

"Diaries you say?"

"What? Oh yes, surprising isn't it? After all, I thought as you might that the subsequent investigation into his passing might have had an interest in them. As it was, I did not find them for some years, but that was not to say they were hidden. Simply stored neatly amongst the man's personal effects that I did not wish to disturb."

Fitzgerald leant forward, "and these diaries, you still have them?"

"Oh yes," he replied, smiling. "I thought they might have been of interest to you, but I never expected it would be this soon! I believe they might offer you more insight than I regarding this town and its sordid history."

Why am I so interested? Fitzgerald asked of himself. He couldn't quite place his finger upon the answer, though. Perhaps it was just curiosity. But no, something about Liam Shilling and his story had fascinated him, and more, for there was something about this church and its history with Ashmarsh wasn't there? Stories of suicide and malpractice that would have embedded themselves in the local mindset and so never been forgotten.

For now, he felt somewhat placated, understanding coming to his mind as to Shilling's demeanour and the crude welcome he had enjoyed. Ultimately though, what mattered was discovering what ill the church was responsible for and the resentment that still lingered as a result. If he was to be a success here, then there were fences to be mended. Many fences, and the understanding as to the root of the cause would hopefully allow him to achieve this.

"You've read the diaries?" Fitzgerald inquired.

Shilling nodded in reply. "I have in part. I guess I was seeking my own answers at the time. For I to was brought to the brink of events here. And as if by magic, here were these diaries."

"And what did they say?"

Shilling looked long and hard as if weighing him up again. Fitzgerald knew he was questioning himself; deliberating whether he had said or suggested too much, and he found himself disappointed as he realised this was so with his next comment.

"Look, you must be tired. Perhaps I will show you to the rectory and get you settled? I've spoken far too much, and to someone I hardly know! What must you think of me, eh lad? The nonsense I have been talking. You shouldn't mind me, a senile old fool, taken up with the notion of bad luck and dark spirits upon the town. My time here has worn me down and so don't take any notice. The parish is yours now and yours to make what you will of it. It won't be easy, but don't let my failings and those that came before allow doubt into your mind. If you are of an honest spirit, you can achieve good things here."

And before Fitzgerald could protest, the old man raised himself off his chair and was heading back into the church.

CHAPTER 3

"**B**less me Father, for I have sinned."

The voice stirred Iain Fitzgerald from his reverie, and he found himself within the small confines of a confessional booth. His mind was groggy and he did not know how he had come to be in this place.

"Father?" The voice seemed to reverberate about him, and as a result he felt disorientated, as to where it came from. The dim light also playing its part to confuse him as to the voice's source and direction.

Reaching blindly outward, his hand met the latticed partition that served as a portal between this and the other chamber, now identified to his left.

"I'm sorry," he said, "please, continue."

"It has been fifteen years since my last confession. But you already know that don't you?"

The female voice was familiar somehow and sharp in its accusation. His mind was clouded though and no recognition came as to the owner of the voice or its meaning.

"I am sorry child, I don't know of what you speak. But please, go on."

"Oh you know all too well, Iain." His name was spat with loathing, and a small pang of fear made itself known in the pit of his stomach and in the accelerated beat of his heart. The voice went on, "You have forgotten me Father? How convenient for you, for I am undoubtedly an unwelcome reminder of your sin."

His fear blossomed from a slow thudding pulse into a crescendo of drum beats which made him sick to his stomach. Although he could not yet make the connection, he knew the voice spoke the truth. A truth that he could not allow himself to find.

He stood to escape the confessional and swiftly drew the velvet curtain back, only to be met by a smooth wooden wall. He spun quickly, desperate to find the way out, but each wall of the enclosure was the same, there was no exit.

He sat down hard and closed his eyes, trying to find some place inside of himself where he could retreat and distance himself from his terror. There could be no such sanctuary however, as the voice cut through his shoddy defences easily.

"There is no escape, Father. None can evade his watchful eye. You have sought to disguise yourself amongst men as a conduit of God, and for that he is vengeful."

"I have answered my calling nothing more." He protested weakly.

"Your calling? You are a fool, for your faith is weak, shrouded in doubt as to his being. You are an affront to his good name, and worse for you reek of your sin…"

"No!" he protested.

"Yes! you deny still, but I see through your charade Iain, as you know who I am and cannot hide your nature from me."

Slowly, recognition began to dawn on him. She did know him; knew what he had done.

"Emma, no."

He could not help himself, he opened his eyes to seek her out. The walls of the confessional were now gone, and all about him was darkness, he whirled in nothingness as he called her name, "Emma?"

He twisted frantically in the dark and became dizzy, until his eyes fell upon a distant shaft of light, penetrating the scene from above and enveloping the simple pine coffin that stood upon a metal bier. He had seen this before.

He approached, as he had no other choice; there was nowhere else to go.

Upon the lid was the same lattice partition of the confessional. Her voice reached him easily through it.

"You let me die, Iain."

He fell across the lid as his sorrow overwhelmed him. "I'm sorry, so sorry."

"There Iain. You need not be afraid, you need not be alone."

He felt the pressure on the lid beneath him, and drew back from it, and watched as it slowly rose. Her voice now came cleanly to his ears and he welcomed it.

"Come be with me Iain, there is no place above for one who doesn't believe, but here, here there is only darkness and the eternity of peace. Come be with me."

And so he did, he went to the open casket and looked within the dead eyes of his lost love. But there was no peace there as she promised, the stench of her death was ripe and he looked on in horror at the ashen pall of her skin, but none the less he went to her and watched as she raised herself from the decay of her stained bed, arms outstretched to meet him.

She embraced him and pulled him into the close space of the coffin. The lid fell slowly downward, the light diminished and he was in darkness once more. In the black space of nothingness, he heard her voice, but now from afar.

"Beware the shadow."

"Emma?" There was no response. Now he floated in oblivion, the press of her dead flesh and the coffin about them gone.

"Beware the shadow, Iain. A devil dwells among you…"

He craned his eyes upward and searched for the voice, which was louder now. He rose toward it.

He broke his dream, like breaking the surface of a lake. He gasped for air in the cold confines of his bedroom. Still all was dark about him, but his mind easily made the transition from his nightmare.

She had come to him again, as she had on many nights. But where many such dreams had been happy and of the good times they had shared, there had still been those dark ones, of which this had been by far the worst. She had tried to take him away into the darkness…But then, a warning?

And with that came the memory of Father Shilling's parting sermon of earlier that day.

'A devil dwells here among you in Ashmarsh, a black shadow casting its net wide from the doors of Thoby Hall.'

What did it mean?

And so he sat there wrestling with his thoughts, any hope of sleep long absent as he listened to the soft patter of incessant rain that fell upon the roof above, and dripped from the flowing roof gutters. He reached over to the bedside cabinet, a press on the keypad of his phone brought a harsh green light into the room, and he had to squint before his eyes could focus and see that the time was now past 01:00 am.

Sighing, he kicked the covers off his body and quickly swung his feet over the side of the bed and into his slippers. He was very quickly aware of how cold the rectory was at this late hour and in the dark of his bedroom, he wondered if his breath was making clouds of cold steam before him.

His mind would not rest, for his strange dream had brought back Liam Shilling's words during his final mass, which continued to echo through his mind as he wrestled to find meaning from the strange sermon.

'A devil dwells here among you…'

That had been the strangest part of all, and as he reflected on what had been a difficult afternoon, he knew his initial anger following the service had prevented him from touching on this, the most outlandish part of Shilling's ill-advised mass. But as the day had gone on, he found there was to be no further opportunity to discuss or question Liam Shilling, who had made himself scarce.

Ultimately, he finally had his introduction to the parishioners at the evening mass from Colin Morris, as again Shilling was still nowhere to be found, until that was, when he returned to the rectory and found the priest passed out drunk and sprawled across the living room sofa.

And so the evening had worn on, and there had been clues to Shilling's recovery as Fitzgerald had heard several loud thumps and crashes through the wooden floorboards, a testament to the fact that Shilling had woken. His instinct though warned him to avoid his rowdy housemate at that time. But now this nagging voice from his dream needed to be heard, and answers had to be sought.

He got up and fetched the dressing gown from the chair at the foot of the bed and made his way toward the door where he fumbled blindly for a moment trying to find the light switch. Again he was made to wince as sharp light flooded the room and stung his eyes.

Grimacing, he went through to the landing, where he quickly saw a shaft of soft light spill from beneath the door of the study that was situated at the far end of the short hallway he now stood in.

"Father?" he questioned, his voice loud and harsh in contrast to the quiet that enveloped the confines of the small cottage. He stopped and cocked his ear for any response, but all he could hear was his soft breathing and the continued soft patter of rain.

To his left, he saw the door to Shilling's bedroom was open, but the room was in darkness and clearly uninhabited. That left his destination and Shilling's whereabouts all the clearer.

As he made the study door, he saw it was slightly ajar. "Father?" He tried again as he gently pushed the door inward.

The light in the room was low, and he quickly saw that it was the desk lamp that shone within the room, casting long shadows over the bookshelves that lived on the wall to his right as he looked in. Peering around the partially opened door toward the desk, he saw two things at once. The deep swivel chair that sat behind was turned with its back toward him, offering no immediate clue as to if anyone was seated within it. The second thing he saw was the whisky bottle which was on the desk itself, giving likely answer to the first question.

Quietly he entered the room and made his way across the small space toward the desk. As he approached, soft snores could be heard, and he knew what he would see before his eyes met it.

Here was Shilling, his head tilted back at an uncomfortable angle, his right arm resting in his lap, while his left hung loosely over the side. He could see from looking at him that now was not the time to remonstrate with him, for he would have trouble it seemed simply to wake him.

With an audible sigh, he began to head back toward the door, his first thought to find a blanket for the old man to make him as comfortable as he could. Whatever needed to be said could wait until tomorrow.

But with that, he already knew that tomorrow would be too late. After the coffee morning where Shilling would say his goodbyes, he would be leaving soon after by car and into his retirement. What good would it do to question or remonstrate with him then? No, perhaps let things be as they are. If Shilling were to remember his parting words to his congregation, maybe he would have his own regrets.

As he turned to leave, he saw something from the corner of his eye.

On the desk at Shilling's back were a collection of what looked like journals. A small pile of perhaps four neatly jacketed volumes and there, two more books, only these two were open, the desk lamp casting a bright ring of light over the open book that sat closest to the man behind the desk.

He leant in closer for a look at the open page. The page on the left was adorned at the top left with a date.

Friday, 15th November 1995.

That was all it took to know that these were the diaries that belonged to the former parish priest that Shilling had mentioned to him on their first meeting. Father Crosby, the same man who had taken his own life no less.

He peered in closer and began to read.

"Another lonely visit to Thoby Hall today. This really is becoming too much to bear. Elizabeth was beside herself by the time that I arrived. She has the house to herself again, but for the servants. Robert, nowhere to be seen, another one of his business trips no doubt.

After my last visit, I implored her to talk to someone, a family member, a friend, anyone and maybe take time away from the house. She seemed in agreement, but I can't say I'm surprised such a thing didn't happen. She blames Robert of course, suggesting he won't allow her far from the hall and that her relatives are all but barred from the grounds.

As for this time? Her paranoid delusions regarding the staff are still in full flight; accusing Mrs Hodgson of stealing. That's all I need to know the truth of it. Hodgson would sooner cut her arm off than harm that house or family.

Elizabeth is lost in such a big house. It must have seemed like some big adventure when she married into such wealth and stature.

The truth is that I begin to fear for her sanity and I wonder if an intervention other than the Church's might be in order, and though she won't speak about it, we know the real cause of her pain. Poor tragic Lydia..."

As Fitzgerald read, he was at first oblivious to the fact that Shilling's ragged snores had ceased and the chair in which he sat had quietly begun to turn. His heart gave an involuntary leap as the elderly priest spoke.

"Iain? Is that you, boy?"

"Father...I..." he managed weakly, and he quickly stepped back, embarrassed, as if being caught with his hand in the biscuit barrel like a small boy.

He could see though that Shilling had not paid any mind, or maybe even noticed he had been looking in the diaries. The priest looked dishevelled as he came into view. The long shadows given off by the lamplight seemed to intensify the wrinkles around his face, making him look all the older.

"Father. I was worried when you didn't show tonight. There were those present at mass who would have said their goodbyes," he managed at last.

The chair continued its slow revolution, and now Father Shilling was directly facing Fitzgerald and the pile of journals in front of him. "You found the diaries then?"

Fitzgerald felt tested. Had he been asleep after all? He had been oblivious to his state as he read from the pages of the book and so felt to play ignorant might be for nothing.

"Yes, Father. I hope you don't mind. You made mention of the books, and I was curious."

Shilling nodded in return. "I will admit they are a difficult read in places. An exercise of routine and triviality on the whole. It seems that Father Crosby's version of this parish was much the same as mine and likely yours to come. It's been a long afternoon, and I have not yet scratched the surface of what is there. But what is certain, is that matters of interest seem to centre around this woman Elizabeth McArthur and that wretched place Thoby Hall."

That got Fitzgerald's interest and gave him his way in. "Thoby Hall? You made mention this morning during your sermon..."

"Aye, that I did. Thoby Hall, the residence of Mr and Mrs Robert McArthur, heir and squanderer of the Thomas Searle estate and fortune."

Father Shilling put his hand out, offering the seat across the desk.

Taking the opposite seat, Fitzgerald felt a sense of déjà vu as Father Shilling reached for the bottle of whisky on the table and poured himself a measure in the tumbler that was to his hand. He searched about himself as if looking for something.

Fitzgerald, knowing what it was, cut across him to get the conversation started "No, not for me, Father."

The old priest gave him a long look, seemingly of disapproval. Nodded and then drained his glass quickly. "What would you know then, boy?" He shot across at Fitzgerald.

Iain sat there for a moment gathering his thoughts. It had been a strange day thus far, made more so by the behaviour of the eccentric old man that sat before him. He reluctantly had to admit to himself, that he was glad it was only a few short hours until he was gone from the church of St Peter's for good.

But the memory of those nodding heads of agreement during the morning sermon came to mind, as he remembered Shilling speaking of this place Thoby Hall, and whatever dark curse it held over the town. And he knew better than to dismiss simple superstition within a small community such as this. It certainly seemed the place exuded some ill-feeling. Perhaps if he could learn more, he would be better armed and prepared to get the church back onto a better foothold in the community.

"That's the second time you've made mention of that place," he began. "Just what is it you think that gives it such a hold over this town?"

Shilling managed a weak smile in response. In the shadows of the room, it gave no comfort or warmth, instead, making the elderly priest look grim and deranged. "Do you believe in dark spirits lad? And I don't mean those of which we preach during sermon. I mean something real, physical if you like. A power that sits and festers like an open wound, whispering and subverting those of weak will and mind that are caught in its lure."

Fitzgerald looked into the dark eyes of the elderly priest and saw that for now at least the man was lucid, for the eyes, though haunted held his own without flinching.

Shilling continued. "I see it is not a question you are yet ready for, but I fear in time you will know only too well. Instead, know this. If such a power exists, then for the town of Ashmarsh it lurks in Thoby Hall."

Fitzgerald spotted the contradiction immediately.

"You aren't serious, Father? Your sermon this morning…you spoke of dispelling such superstition." Fitzgerald began.

"Never mind what I said, boy. Would you have them carry on believing such? It was for you that I said what I did, for you will have to likewise deal with their notions of ill-will at work. And is it so hard to believe? That perhaps something should happen, which was so bad that it leaves an echo or an imprint of itself thereafter? Something elusive… intangible maybe? But all the same very real."

"Are you telling me something bad happened there? Something which affects the community?"

Shilling shook his head. "I know I am not saying it right. But yes to an extent you have hit upon a part of it. A house like that has history. And there are those who like their haunted house and ghost stories all the more. Even so, you would do well to understand the place and the unusual hold that it has on the town and its people. Perhaps that was my undoing when I first came here. I did not give any credence to the superstitious minds and what that might do for the community's perspective and faith."

Fitzgerald nodded in understanding. It seemed he and Shilling's views were not so contrasting on this matter after all.

"I think you'll find your answers here." Shilling said, as he waved a hand toward the diaries. "Curious they would turn up again, so close to my leaving here. But the truth is I've not had the time or presence of mind to investigate them fully. Put simply, I am tired and defeated and think perhaps I am better off not knowing everything that lies within. Instead, my replacement arrives and takes such a burden. Well, good luck to you lad. You'll need it. But I guess you are a canny one, for you'd do well to mind Thoby Hall if you are to succeed here. That is why you asked, isn't it?"

"It is Father. If you are right and if such a shadow, or belief if you will, hangs over the people of this town, then I am keen to see that reversed and see such folks prosper at the church."

Shillings brow furrowed and he slowly started shaking his head.

"You'd do well to consider it more than some idle belief. I don't know how to explain it to you, boy, but the things that have happened…"

You'd have me believe this place is the cause of the ill-will in the town? It's no wonder you lost them, Father.

Despite the thought, he nodded, keen to continue the conversation. Shilling was a drunk, a broken one at that. But that did not mean he couldn't offer some useful insight into the church of St Peter's.

Shilling took the cue to continue.

"You may do well to start here then." He motioned at the open book on the desk before him. "From what I did read I can see there are intermittent mentions of the Hall and its residents. It seems Father Crosby's dealings with young Mrs McArthur are where things begin to take a turn for the worse for him and her."

Fitzgerald raised an eyebrow.

"I mentioned that Father Crosby took his own life, did I not? Well, many have formed the link between him, the McArthur woman and the Hall and see that as his undoing. You don't have to go far to see that most things go back to that damned place."

"It must have been a difficult time for all those involved. A Catholic Priest taking his own life? I can't imagine what that would do to a community."

"Aye, it is a touchy subject, and there are those that would press you on the Church's views on suicide while reminding you all the while of what Crosby did. They don't ever forget."

"As it is, you may have had a glimpse." Shilling continued, motioning to the open book again. "The McArthur woman it seems was his downfall. When I first arrived at the town, I heard all of the rumour and speculation. Some of it added up, and some of it didn't. But what was clear is that the demons in that house were very real for Elizabeth McArthur and she was party to their whispers for too long. I was to mark the page for you but if you begin where I have indicated you will see that Crosby believed her to be mentally unstable and questioned his ability to help her, rightly believing medication was a more appropriate answer. However, the McArthur woman sought his counsel, rather than that of doctors or psychiatrists. What led him from there to his demise I do not know."

"You are not curious?" Fitzgerald asked.

"Curious? Ha, oh my yes! But also scared of what I might find. That all this time, my despair and misgivings might be mirrored within, and that I am not far removed from a similar mind-set as that of Crosby. Suicide though? No, not me, lad." He finished as if answering an unheard question.

"But this house. It still exudes that kind of power?" Fitzgerald followed.

The priest sagged in his chair, and a pained look furrowed his brow. "Alas yes. That too is not so hard to find, and you will hear much that supports those theories. You see there have been incidents over the years, too many to count I am afraid and that, of course, lends weight. Parents will warn their children away, and the seniors will share their stories in the dark of a winter's night."

"It is abandoned then?"

"Oh, goodness no. It's owner remains, though his fortune flounders and disappears."

"It's owner?"

"Robert McArthur lives on yet. He was the sole heir of the Thomas Searle estate and though he has seen that fortune lost he clings onto the house still."

"How can this one house have such a lasting and damaging effect upon the town? Surely such matters should long since be forgotten?"

"Perhaps so," Shilling replied. "But the thinking of a small town is so much different from the normal. You see the people who these events and tragedies affect are intrinsically linked through generations and as such, so are any feuds, grudges and most importantly any beliefs, no matter how ridiculous an outsider may find them to be."

"You've mentioned tragedy again, Father."

"Yes." Shilling leaned over the desk and took his bottle and Fitzgerald could see how fragile the man was as he poured whisky onto the desk before it met the lip of his glass. "I have seen that tragedy myself over the years, and after a while, even one such as myself came to know despair at the tragic loss of young human life. Today's display? They will forgive me that on my departing because we have shared so much sorrow and pain over the years. You see, we partake in the key parts of their lives do we not? The happiness of birth and baptism. We bring them together in the holy union of marriage, and we bury their dead..." He trailed off, and Fitzgerald could see the pain etched upon the old face before him.

The conversation left him feeling uneasy and yet Shilling had only offered fleeting gossip, innuendo and worst of all suggestions of dark forces as any suggestion to the town's ills. Surely there could be no wonder at the man's failings as the local leader of the Catholic faith if he had made no attempts to subvert these childish tales of a curse, and more than that, seemingly given no mind as to local feeling following the suicide of their former parish leader Crosby.

"Father, what was it that brought you such despair?"

"No more lad, eh? No more tonight. Leave an old man to his pain and his memories."

You're not the only one to have known pain, Father.

The thought had blindsided him, and he quickly pushed it away, back to the recesses of his mind. He would not go there, not now, not in front of this broken mess of a man.

But as to Shilling and their conversation, Fitzgerald could see that he would get no more. He looked across the desk and saw that the spilt whisky had enveloped the corner of the open journal and turned the open pages wet and yellow. Maybe there he would find his answers, for at the moment his conversation had left him only more questions. Shilling was tired and miserable, the result of twenty long and painful years within the parish and he wondered now if a similar fate would be his own. He picked himself up and slowly backed toward the door, the old priest not once looking up in his direction to see him leave the room.

CHAPTER 4

Sunday, 6th November 2016.

The diaries of Father Crosby were soon to be forgotten as the next few weeks passed by without incident. In fact, Fitzgerald was quickly warming to his new parish, and though it was late in the year there were several happy events at the church including the baptism of new born twins and the renewing of wedding vows for a couple who had reached their silver wedding anniversary.

Inevitably, there were some sadder moments as well as he was soon conducting funeral services, sometimes as many as two a week. But for a town the size of Ashmarsh, this was no real surprise. And though Father Shilling had hinted upon tragedy in the area, the passing of those elderly citizens on the cusp of winters arrival, might well have been anticipated.

Occasionally though, he would lament his predecessor's departure, but only because he felt somewhat a stranger speaking of the lives of people he did not know at such services.

On the flip side, Father Shilling's departure had been to his advantage, for he learned that his predecessor had been a hard traditionalist and where Shilling might deliver a stern rebuke, Fitzgerald offered soft words and comfort. This it seemed was earning him some favour, which might soon be measured by the girth of his waistband as the number of dishes and desserts he was presented with on Sundays was quickly becoming overwhelming. Instead of politely declining, he would offer thanks and suggest that perhaps any leftovers might make their way down to the coffee mornings at the church, which was a suggestion readily agreed upon.

It was on the first Sunday of the month that the names Thoby Hall and McArthur finally came flooding back to him.

Having finished the Holy Communion, he stood in the porch of the church wishing the patrons good day. There was still some small activity, as several of the choir boys whispered conspiratorially in their small huddle close to the entrance of the car park; waiting impatiently for their parents to say their goodbyes to one another. And now the organist, a decrepit looking man called William, made his way out of the church. In his seventies, and of a somewhat cantankerous disposition, he made his slow way down to the car park. Seemingly glad to be free from the constraints of the church as he lit his rolled cigarette, as Fitzgerald watched him make his way.

Colin Morris was stood nearby and engaged in his own goodbyes with a group of older women that included a lady called Eileen. Fitzgerald had quickly learned that she had been the person who had looked to him to interrupt Father Shilling's parting speech all those weeks ago. Needless to say, he hadn't quite won her or her group of peers over as yet, and they still favoured Colin Morris by far. He smiled as he watched them surround the deacon and hang off his every word.

Fitzgerald turned back and entered the building once more, instantly feeling at peace as he looked back toward the altar. The church had been splendid in song as he knew it would on his first visit, and the tall candles now burned brightly before him.

His reverie was interrupted as he felt the presence of someone close by, and he turned to behold the sight of a well-dressed young man. He was instantly curious as he did not recognise him from his congregation of that day, or any other day for that matter.

He was perhaps only in his early thirties. His black hair was cut short and slicked back. He also sported a neatly trimmed beard that Fitzgerald knew to be the current fashion. Fitzgerald looked down and saw an eager right hand presented in greeting.

"Father Fitzgerald?"

"Yes?" he replied, finding himself surprisingly wary of this newcomer who had more the air of a salesman than churchgoer. "I don't think I've had the pleasure..." He tailed off as he accepted the man's handshake.

"Harvey, Frederick Harvey that is. I am very pleased to make your acquaintance. That was a lovely service this morning Father."

"Thank you. I don't believe I have seen you here before though Mr Harvey?" The man grinned nervously, and Fitzgerald had his answer before he could open his mouth.

"Well, now and again, Father. My parents, before they moved away and my grandparents before them, were regulars here for years before they sadly passed on."

Fitzgerald nodded, waiting for the man to get to his business. Such introductions weren't unusual for those of small or little faith he knew. But a glance at the man's left hand and the ring there told him that he wasn't here to petition the church for its wedding services. What was it then? A Christening perhaps?

"I apologise for the nature of my introduction today Father, and on any other occasion, I would have waited for a more appropriate time to approach you. But I am here on behalf of another party whose need is great. I wonder if we might have a moment in private?"

"You are right in respect of the time I'm afraid. I have another service to prepare for shortly. Maybe we can make an appointment for when we can better discuss your needs?"

He saw the furrow of the man's brow and the small bead of sweat upon his forehead. He could see that this man Harvey was nervous for some reason and that he wasn't seemingly about to take no for an answer.

"Perhaps so, Father. I do understand you are short of time but so is my…" Harvey hesitated before choosing his words. "…my friend… and he would not have it for me to have come away empty-handed. Father please, just a minute?"

Fitzgerald sighed inwardly. "Okay, but just a minute. I have other duties as I am sure you understand." He beckoned for the younger man to follow him, and made his way to the front row of the pews.

"Okay, Mr Harvey, what can I do for you?" he said as he seated himself.

"Well, as I said Father, it is not for my own need that I am here." He paused as if searching for the right way as to how to deliver his story or message whatever it should be. "Father, tell me. Have you heard the name McArthur since you began here at St Peter's? Robert McArthur?"

Fragments of old conversation with Father Shilling came flooding instantly back to him, but regrettably, he realised he had not followed on from that night and knew little other than the sparse ramblings of a drunken old man.

Even so, the name Robert McArthur was uncomfortable to his ears and immediately he was unsure he wanted to hear what business the man had that would involve him or the church.

Harvey looked troubled as he continued. "I can see from your reaction Father that you do know of him, but don't let the words of others twist your mind against him. Mr McArthur has been a staunch benefactor of the church here over the years and is himself a devout Catholic. More than that, his business interests over the years have been a boon to this town with jobs and investment."

Fitzgerald already felt at a loss. This man Harvey seemed to feel the need to advocate Robert McArthur's good points as if to negate any ill-will or negativity that he may have already heard. Also, it was though the other man knew he had heard badly of the man already.

Harvey continued, "unfortunately, there are those who would speak ill of him Father and sour his legacy."

Fitzgerald felt the need to cut through the character appraisal and get to the point of the matter. "I can assure you that your friends' reputation for better or worse will have no great bearing on what I may or may not be able to do. That depends on the nature of Mr McArthur's business with me."

"Of course, Father, of course. I am afraid to say that Mr McArthur has been housebound for some considerable time, else he would have met you in person. You see he is dying

Father, and we fear that his end is close at hand. He would ask that you take confession from him before he passes on. Then, of course, the matter of last rites and funeral."

This all now made more sense to Fitzgerald. Perhaps the method of the introduction had been unusual, but now he felt a small portion of guilt for his initial reaction on hearing the man McArthur's name for the first time. But given the circumstances, his duties were clear to him. Robert McArthur was dying and seeking last confession and rites to make what peace he could before passing.

"How much time are we talking?" Fitzgerald asked.

"Well, the more positive doctors would have us believe a month, maybe more. Mr McArthur though does not take with such ambiguity. He feels his need is more urgent than that. He would ask that you might meet with him as soon as possible."

"May I ask what he is suffering with?"

"Cancer, Father. He has fought long and hard against it and entered remission only a year ago. A small miracle for a man of 92 years I'm sure you will agree. He has always been a fighter, but now I am afraid it is back, and this time we are told to expect the worst."

"And you are…you said you were his friend?" Fitzgerald asked as the apparently large age gap between the two men begged the question.

"Well yes and no. I am Mr McArthur's solicitor, you see. But don't let that sway you. My family, particularly my grandfather and then father before me, have had the privilege of acting for Mr McArthur and his estate. He is a remarkable man I am sure you will see for yourself."

"Are you here though as his friend or his legal representative?"

"Both Father. You see for a man of Mr McArthur's standing there are…how should I say it? Certain issues that he would only speak with you. Of course, we know that the seal of confession is how you say…inviolable? But there are matters of a legal standpoint that must also be addressed."

"Mr Harvey I can assure you that the sanctity of confession is divine. There is no requirement for the Church to…"

Harvey nodded and quickly cut him off. "Of course, Father we don't seek any issue with the Church, the stipulations made by Mr McArthur are slim to be sure, but perhaps a matter to be discussed between the two of you? More than that though Father, can I deliver the news that you will meet with him and soon?"

Fitzgerald nodded his agreement. "How soon should this be done?"

"Would tomorrow be too soon? That is to say, to come and meet Mr McArthur and discuss his requirements?"

40

Fitzgerald raised an eyebrow in question. Harvey understood as he followed. "Mr McArthur is of reasonably good health at this time, well, as good as can be expected. He does not share the doctor's optimism, as we have discussed. But as I speak, I believe he has some time yet."

"Very well. Tomorrow it is. Shall we say 10 o'clock? And where?…"

"10 o'clock. That would be perfect. Have you heard of Thoby Hall by chance?" Fitzgerald nodded. "That is where you will find us." Harvey stood and stretched out his hand again. Only this time there was a business card to be found there. "Should there be any issues, Father, please don't hesitate to call me."

Fitzgerald looked at the card. 'Frederick Harvey. Solicitor', followed by a local telephone number and an e-mail address.

"Thank you, I will."

With that, Harvey stood, smiled and with a curt nod turned to walk away, leaving Fitzgerald to puzzle why the name McArthur and the proposed visit at Thoby Hall had left him feeling oddly at unease.

CHAPTER 5

Monday, 7th November 2016.

As Iain Fitzgerald drove through the iron gates of Thoby Hall he looked worryingly at the dashboard clock. Similarly to his first meeting with Father Shilling all those weeks ago, he was in danger of being late for his appointment with both Robert McArthur and the solicitor Harvey. The day had begun badly, and he had awoken at 09:00 am to find that he had not correctly set the alarm on his phone. Luckily though, he discovered that Thoby Hall was only a short drive away and he rushed through both his shower and breakfast in the hope of winning back some time.

Thoby Hall was not the picture postcard that he had expected, having viewed images of the house while performing his earlier search for directions. Of course, the view with which he was now confronted was not helped in any way by the drab grey November morning and the line of frail and skeletal looking maples that he passed upon the long driveway. The lawns that he saw were in stark contrast to the brilliant lush greens he had seen on the internet, instead matted with fallen leaves and having an air of neglect which would undoubtedly see the leaves rot long before the spring would arrive again and rejuvenate the bleak grounds.

The house itself did not appear in full profile until he had travelled the 1/4 mile or so of gravelled road, his view hindered by the long line of trees that stood silent sentry along the rutted drive. He had adjusted his speed after a sharp jolt on his left side told him he had found a pothole which had been obscured from view. But soon the house had opened up, and he saw the road split and circle a stone fountain he had previously seen in the welcoming website photograph of earlier that morning. He took the left branch and circled around so that he was in front of the porch and the large double door at the head of the house.

Fitzgerald climbed from his car and was quick to see there were no signs of life; although all of the windows were lit, nothing stirred and there was no sound to be heard than the occasional drip of dew, dripping down over the eaves and from the gutters.

The house was as grand as he could have expected despite the disappointment of the gardens. He craned his head and looked up at the two storeys above and could see that scaffolding adorned the left most of three chimney stacks. He counted quickly and saw that the ground floor had ten sizeable Georgian style windows, the second floor eleven and the roof storey another six. As he had only viewed the house from the front, he could not guess as to the depth of the building.

Burrowing his hands deep into his jacket pockets and dipping his head low into its collar, he crossed quickly underneath the pillared porchway and saw a pull cord that no doubt sounded a bell somewhere inside the house. He pulled it once but heard no corresponding sound from inside. The mechanism felt somewhat loose in his hand, and he wasn't convinced that anything had happened. Instead, he curled his fist and knocked hard on the wooden front door. There were no windows to be seen; either within the door or to the sides and so he was unable to see if his intrusion on the quiet had any effect.

As he waited, his eyes roved upward, and he saw that the door had a triangular pediment over the top of it. An intricately carved stone piece was at its centre point, and he stepped back to get a better view. The shape depicted in the carving appeared to be a gold-coloured pentagram within a circle.

The image was familiar to his eyes, and he tried to recount his studies within the seminary where he had touched on other religions and the religious symbols that represented them. There could be little doubt that a pentagram such as this was of pagan origin, but the real question was to why it adorned the doorway to such as Thoby Hall? Robert McArthur, after all, had been described to him as a devout catholic and a symbol such as this was not only at odds with that assertion, but also not at all in keeping with the aesthetic of the house.

His attention was quickly diverted though by the sound of footsteps, and the door was swung open before him. There stood Frederick Harvey who greeted him with a familiar outstretched hand and smile.

"Father Fitzgerald. I see that you found us okay. Please do come in and get yourself out of the cold."

Fitzgerald stepped past the man and into a large lobby. Immediately he had a better sense of the size of the house as the area was immense in size. Closed doors greeted him to his left and right and in front was a grand rounded double stairway; two flights curving upward so as to almost meet one another atop the large balcony that overlooked them and the hall below. A large bright chandelier hung low in the room and many more light fixtures burned brightly upon the walls, which he could also see were adorned with portraits along all sides.

As he took all of this in, one other detail could not be ignored, because there before him and set in the white marble floor was the pattern of the same pentagram he had seen above the doorway, only this one was fashioned of black marble. He stood now at the bottom, between the lowest two of the five-pointed tips of the star that stretched some five feet before him.

He shivered involuntarily, as strangely, the cold now seemed to press closer than it had when he had been outside. That and feelings of uneasiness began to encroach upon him as he viewed the expansive floor with its disquieting design.

His heart jumped suddenly as the quiet of the room was disturbed as Harvey closed the door behind them with an echoing thump.

"Father if you'd like to follow me?"

Fitzgerald hesitated, feeling flustered at being rushed into the lion's den. "Is Mr McArthur ready to receive me?"

Harvey looked surprised and stopped in his tracks. "Oh, goodness no. Not yet, at least. He is keen that we attend to our business first. But don't worry I am sure that you and the Church will be thrilled at what Mr McArthur proposes."

There it was again. Harvey had alluded to some legal proceedings on their last meeting, and despite his assertions, Fitzgerald could not help but feel trapped and a little out of his depth. Again he thought of Father Shilling and wondered what he might have to say about this pending meeting and what consequences it might have for him personally as well as the Church.

Harvey had already turned and started to walk off again, and Fitzgerald fell in behind him, trying his best not to step upon the black marble stones as he followed in the solicitor's wake toward the right wing of the house.

"That symbol," Fitzgerald began, so as to change the subject and fill the void of quiet. "I believe I have seen something like it before. Is it in any way related to the house or Mr McArthur personally?"

Harvey didn't reply at first as if considering. "The symbol? Oh yes, I can't say I know the full story behind it, but I understand it is left over from the previous estate owner who commissioned it. I am to understand that he was quite the superstitious type. That and many more like it adorn the house."

"Superstitious? "Then it is a pentagram?"

"Well, maybe. I am afraid that such things are beyond me, Father. I will let you into a little secret though. I am told there is real gold set within the stone above the door. How about that?"

Fitzgerald though wasn't concerned as to the possible value attached, but more the symbolic significance of such an item. Pentagrams or pentacles as they were also known were ancient symbols associated with both paganism and witchcraft. He certainly had not thought to find such things here where he was to do the Lord's work.

"Ah, here we are," said Harvey. They had taken a path that led to a long corridor to the side of the rightmost set of stairs. Many more doors were apparent on both sides. They had stopped on the second door on the right, and the young solicitor stepped into a large office. Another of the large Georgian windows stood behind the desk and peeking past, Fitzgerald could now see more of the gardens and hedges on this side of the house.

"Please do take a seat." Harvey motioned to the single black leather chair that stood before the desk and made his way around to the other side where he seated himself.

The office was sparsely decorated. A single bookcase held a collection of tired-looking hardbound books and on the opposite wall stood a solitary filing cabinet. The desk itself though looked like it was meant for work as a large collection of papers threatened to overload a sorting tray marked 'in'. Its twin compatriot marked 'out' on the other side of the desk was comparatively light with only a few papers visible. Other than that, only a laptop computer, a desk lamp and telephone adorned the rest of the large surface.

"So, Father. May I get you a drink before we begin? It would not be a problem?"

"Thank you no," Fitzgerald answered. He was keen to get to the point of this diversion ahead of his real business here.

Harvey's smile faded somewhat before he continued. "Ah yes, you will be keen to get to the matter at hand no doubt. I am sorry that I have not been able to brief you properly before now, but Mr McArthur is very set on how this business will be done."

Fitzgerald's patience was wearing thin. "As you say, Mr Harvey. Business. But what business would your client have with the Church that requires your instruction? Mr McArthur seeks absolution through confession does he not? That is our business. There is no room for a third party or any dissemination of what is said."

Harvey nodded his understanding. "Of course, Father, of course. And that is not my purpose here. If you will allow me?" He got up from his seat and walked over to the filing cabinet where he withdrew a number of papers held together in a violet-coloured envelope. He placed them on the table before the priest. "Here Father are the full title and deeds of Thoby Hall. Mr McArthur would bequeath them all to the Church on his passing."

Fitzgerald was stunned into silence. Harvey it seemed was enjoying his moment, for his smile was now etched halfway across his face. "Did I not say that Mr McArthur was a generous benefactor to the Church? I am sorry that I could not speak of this earlier, but I should also point out that there are certain conditions attached."

Fitzgerald looked up sharply.

"No, no, Father, you misunderstand. Mr McArthur, as you know, is very near death, though we cannot say exactly when such a day will come. He has requested confession and last rites which as a devout Catholic man he is assured, yes?"

Fitzgerald nodded his response.

"The estate here as you can see is dwindling Father. It is all that remains of what was once a thriving business portfolio that included steel and textile interests that were nurtured into national and international concerns. Times though have hit the family hard. Mr McArthur is not survived by any heir and what remains of those business interests have long since been sold on so that the estate here at Thoby Hall might remain. What he offers, is all that he has left in the world, and in return for such grand generosity; the only request, or clause if you prefer is that you might remain here at Thoby Hall until his end."

Remain? Fitzgerald was puzzled as to what was being asked of him. "Mr Harvey, what exactly are you asking?"

"Well, we know you will undoubtedly need to seek guidance from your superiors. Bishop Burrows isn't it? You may be glad to know that we have taken the trouble of addressing that hurdle and he awaits your call. You will find that he looks favourably on Mr McArthur's request."

Fitzgerald's mind was racing. A lot had been said and suggested in only a few moments. And it seemed that whatever it was that this lawyer, Harvey was asking had in fact already gone above his head to his Bishop. But what exactly was it that was being asked and supposedly agreed to?

"Mr Harvey. Please. Can you just spell out for me what exactly it is you are asking of me? You said to remain here, are you suggesting that I take up residence here until Mr McArthur's passing?"

"That is exactly it, Father. Mr McArthur is a god-fearing man and not knowing the moment of his passing is a great concern to him. He would have it that you are here in that time to hear confession. He will not have it any other way."

"I do not doubt that, but what you are asking is impossible. The parish…It requires me to be…"

He was quickly cut off. "Deacon Morris is a capable man, is he not? We do understand the difficulties this presents, please believe me. How can I say this? Mr McArthur's confession I understand will be somewhat difficult. You see he is in and out of consciousness and the high doses of painkillers leave him somewhat muddled and to be frank, stoned. At this point, his reliance on the morphine is beyond the control of him or his nurses. And it is for only for these medical reasons that we make this request. At his own choice, he wishes to be weaned off of the drug so that he might be lucid enough, to be frank, and honest in his conversations with you. Such a process cannot be arranged or managed by appointments Father."

This was at least now making sense to Fitzgerald. But Harvey continued. "And Father what of confession? What if he was not able to repent his sins before his end? Where does that leave him in the eyes of God?"

"If Mr McArthur is sincere in his wish to confess, then in the eyes of the Church, it matters not. It is only that he has the true desire to do so. It is our teaching that God works through the sacraments of the Church, true. But as you may well know that does not preclude him from working outside of such bounds."

Harvey again nodded through his answer as if impatient and Fitzgerald again felt another pang of irritation at the man. For him as a solicitor, the only law he seemed interested in was contractual and not of the Church. He seemingly only had one mandate here, and that was to fulfil his client's wishes.

"That is known to us, Father. But you see Mr McArthur understands his duty to confess while he is still able. Will you not grant him that? At the very least the matter should be discussed with the bishop should it not? I apologise for my candour Father. But you see time is short, and we will require an answer as soon as possible. I can assure you that it should perhaps only be a week in all, if that. The matter of last rites is for another time, and you would have satisfied this small contractual obligation once full confession is heard."

Fitzgerald was backed into a corner he didn't like. The request in its purest form was not beyond his capacity to grant. Colin Morris was more than competent to hold the reins at St Peter's for a small length of time; there was little doubt of that. The man had 17 years in the Church as a deacon and would no doubt be looked upon favourably for priesthood if the criteria were met.

No, it was not for lack of trust, or for the short amount of time that he questioned this matter. It was the seeming offer of reward in exchange that did not sit nicely with him. Having already expressed his reservations at the idea, he did not relish the idea that Harvey could have the right in this matter. But what was clear was that he and his employer had already gone over his head and sought the approval they needed from his bishop. He would need confirmation of course, but he could sense that the matter had already been resolved, and a quick phone call would no doubt confirm as much.

"Mr Harvey, I am not without compassion, and I do understand the urgent need for my answer, but you must understand that I will require to speak to the bishop."

Harvey stood, grinning. That was what he had been waiting for, and Fitzgerald knew the resulting few minutes would confirm his suspicions.

"Of course, Father, of course." As Harvey passed by the side of the desk, he picked up the telephone and turned it 180 degrees so that the receiver was facing Fitzgerald. "No time like the present. Can I get you the number?"

Fitzgerald didn't doubt it was somewhere close to hand, but his temper at this point would not allow any further victories, no matter how small to go to the solicitor.

"No, that is fine. Some privacy, perhaps?"

Harvey bowed his head in concession and walked straight to the door and left the room. Fitzgerald shuffled forward in his seat and reached out for the phone. Is this necessary? He asked of himself as he dialled in 192 for directory enquiries. But his inner voice had temporarily deserted him. Instead, a female voice from the other end of the phone asked what name or business he required.

He was on the telephone for less than a minute, and it was all exactly as he had believed. The arrangements it seemed were already in place, and Colin Morris had willingly agreed to take his place. There could be no argument then. Something did not sit right with him about this though, as he leafed through the paperwork previously placed on the desk.

A contract? Yes. It seemed that this part was true and that more than anything had him worried. He had quickly tuned out to the words spoken by the bishop on the phone as he flicked through the pages, such was the mimicry in the bishop's words, that it may well have been Harvey on the line from another part of the house. And it seemed clear that the two parties had long since come to this arrangement.

He placed the receiver back in its cradle and sat back in his chair, defeated. He had his orders from a higher power, only that power spoke without any semblance of masking its avarice of the reward that was to be won on signing the contract. This did not feel like God's work, and he wondered what his bishop's position would be for a man of more meagre means than McArthur.

Harvey ultimately sidled his way back into the room, but his voice and conversation were all background noise as Fitzgerald scrutinised the contract he was bound to sign. What was clear though was the simplicity of the arrangement, and for all the pages of legalese, it boiled down to two things. The inheritance of Thoby Hall and it's grounds to the Catholic Church diocese of Springmoor and Highbridge (of which Ashmarsh was part) in return for a confidentiality agreement and Fitzgerald's pledge to remain on the estate until confession had been taken.

On the very last page, he saw the shaky childlike scrawl of Robert McArthur as signatory. Witnessed of course by Frederick Harvey.

He looked hard at the face of Harvey as he found his own name in print at the bottom of the page. The man knew he had won his way before he had even arrived here at the Hall today. Feeling sick to his stomach, Fitzgerald signed his name so that he could leave the office and company of the serpent-like Harvey as quickly as he could.

CHAPTER 6

Fortunately, there had been some small grace allowed in the signed contract and Fitzgerald had been able to return to St Peter's and make his necessary preparations for his stay at Thoby Hall. Colin Morris, for his part, had not known the full nature of his departure, having only been told that he was having to go away on urgent Church business. The confidentiality aspect of the agreement had only referred to the matter of confession, and so he was keen to advise Morris of his destination and told him he would be available on his mobile if required.

The deacon did not seem surprised by the news.

"So Father Shilling did escape in time then?"

"Escape?" Fitzgerald had replied.

"There was no love lost there I can tell you. And Liam had mentioned such a thing. Said he would be damned if he bartered for a man's soul."

Fitzgerald felt both lost and embarrassed. "Shilling knew about this? Colin I…"

But the older man had given him a soft smile in return. "Oh, never you mind Iain. Don't you think the timing was a little all too convenient?"

Puzzled; he replied. "What do you mean?"

"That old loon McArthur nears his end and the very unstable Father Shilling finally gets his move away into retirement? With a prize like Thoby Hall in play? The Church would leave no stone unturned to get their hands on a piece of real estate like that and so here you are! Don't feel bad Father; if it hadn't of been you, it would have been somebody else. Don't let the thoughts of contracts or deals sway you. You are here to do God's work, and that is all that is required of you. Let the Bishop worry about the morality of it all. When you've been in the game as long as I have, you won't be surprised by what you see and hear." He finished with a wink and Fitzgerald was left thinking that he was somewhat naïve and inexperienced in the machinations of the Church's business model. He resolved he would learn, though and quickly.

It was past 2 o'clock in the afternoon before his car drove through the gates of the Thoby Estate again. He felt somewhat anxious, given how quickly things were going. That and

49

somewhat mistrustful of both Harvey the solicitor and his own bishop who had bartered this deal without his knowledge or input. Morris though, had put things in perspective for him regarding his duty, and it was true that despite the unusual arrangements he expected matters to be quite straightforward. If that was all true, then why did the butterflies in his stomach not settle?

As the stone fountain came into sight once more, he could see that the area in front of the house was now a hive of activity and he had no choice but to take the right fork at the fountain due to the left side being blocked by a builder's van. Three men with high visibility coats and hard hats could be seen, and Fitzgerald easily surmised who was the foreman or boss, as the two younger men followed the pointed finger of the third man who directed them toward the scaffolding on the west wing of the house and the chimney there. Fitzgerald leaned forward in his seat and followed their gaze. Perhaps this building work had been the reason for the home's closure from the public he reflected, as he thought back on the web page that had not only informed him of his directions but also the fact that Thoby Hall had in years gone by been open to the general public.

Would the tourists ever be allowed access again? A quiet inner voice told him that once the diocese had claimed the building for themselves, the answer would be a resounding no.

His eyes wandered again over the house, and its large expanse of windows. Again nothing stirred and the building looked grim in the low light. He looked to the skies beyond the high roof above and saw dark clouds which threatened imminent rain. The image of the Hall and its surroundings served only to reinforce his melancholy mood.

Returning his focus to the driveway, he began to take the right bend, thinking he should park in front of the house, but no sooner had the thought crossed his mind when a small grey-haired lady came out of the double doors at the front of the house and immediately made a beeline in his direction.

A quick press on the electric window and he was face to face with her, and he could see how short this old woman was, as she did not have to bend to see into the car and talk to him.

"Father Fitzgerald? If you could follow the path to the right, you will find ample parking on that side of the house. I am afraid this area is going to be something of a circus today it seems." She finished, turning her head and appearing to scowl at the builders. Following her gaze, he could see the three men were oblivious to her implied recriminations.

"Very well. It is nice to make your acquaintance…"

He was cut off. "Park around the side Father. There will be time for introductions shortly." And with that, she turned sharply and made straight for the three men.

He smiled awkwardly, not knowing what to make of the short encounter but knowing he felt like a chastised schoolboy before a strict mistress. Well, he better not get on this woman's wrong side he thought and again put the car into first gear to drive off toward the side of the house.

Just as he was about to engage the clutch and set off, he cast his eyes over the house once more, and as he did so, he thought he detected a slight movement in one of the first-floor windows. Instead of moving off, he glanced back, trying to identify which of the panes of glass had attracted his attention.

Working his way along the middle row, his eyes settled on the last window on the left. This one window among many stood out, as unlike all the others, this window was in darkness. The realisation made him shift his gaze and take in the rest of the house again. Despite the early hour, every single window bar this one was lit, a detail he hadn't truly absorbed earlier that morning on his first visit.

He returned his gaze to the far left once more, seeking out that which had attracted his attention in the first place. As his eyes fell upon the pane once more, he thought he could just about make out the silhouette of a person, set back from the window. Squinting hard, he lost the silhouette against the dark background, but just as he was about to turn his attention away, another slight movement confirmed his initial suspicion. Someone was undoubtedly there and perhaps trying to keep a low profile as they looked down at the woman and the builders below.

Following suit, he looked down to what appeared to be an apparent altercation in the driveway beside him. For he now saw that the elderly woman, who stood no higher than chest height on the smallest of the three burly builders, had clearly begun to remonstrate with the group, over what, he did not know. But the younger two looked suitably rebuked as their boss seemingly fought a losing battle on their behalf.

The scene that had played out before him and the stranger at the window was quickly at an end though, and the builders were soon to start picking up their toolboxes and placing them in the back of the van. The woman turned about and seemed set to head back into the house, but stopped smartly, as apparently she to saw the figure in the upstairs window looking down at her. She glared up at the window and following her gaze; he saw the figure was still and made no motion to move now that it was discovered.

Fitzgerald wondered if this person was employed in some capacity at the house. Thus far he only knew of the solicitor Harvey, and given the bleak prognosis of the homeowner, it was very much unlikely to be Robert McArthur who he now gazed upon.

As for the old lady she certainly had the air and confidence about her to suggest she was in some way responsible for the goings-on here, what with her brief introduction to him and the stern way in which she gave the builders their orders.

Fitzgerald followed her gaze back upward in anticipation of some interaction, but none came, as the sun finally broke through the thick cloud cover, causing him to wince as sharp light reflected off the window, leaving red spots to dance over his pupils.

51

It was only but a fraction of a second, as the sun was quickly swallowed by the racing clouds. Fitzgerald retrained his eyes on the first-floor window, but saw the mysterious figure at the window had disappeared and the old lady had begun to walk back toward the house, giving no clue to if she had seen him observe the tense moment between her and the stranger.

Before she could revert her attention back to him and not wishing to have been seen looking on, he fed the clutch and hooked the steering wheel to his right.

At the side of the house now, the track followed round and then cut sharply to the right behind a high hedge. As he made the turn, he could see a collection of cars under an open-air carport and a set of closed garages. He had found his destination it seemed, and he stopped the car in the first available bay. The logical path was back the way he had come and so, retrieving his suitcase from the boot he made his way back to where the high hedge had begun and where the car had diverted from the side of the vast house.

As he returned, he found the elderly woman standing on a narrow pathway that led toward a small open doorway on what was the east wing of the stately home.

"Ah, Father, very good, if you would like to follow me," she said before quickly walking off.

He was curious as to the nature of the encounter he had witnessed only moments ago, but thought better than to bring it up, instead, resorting to small talk as he followed in her wake.

"Of course. You have me at a disadvantage. Ms?.."

"Mrs Hodgson," she cut back and again the thought that he was a schoolchild crossed his mind. "I am head of the household here at Thoby Hall, and it is my job to see to you during your stay here."

She had walked off ahead and was now talking back at him over her shoulder. "I am told you will be here the week, Father, maybe longer. I know little else than that, as its not business to know, but should you have to leave us in that time. You are to park here and enter on this side. We won't be advertising Mr McArthur's business to all and sundry I think."

He nodded his head in response even though she did not see it. Given the terms of their agreement, he wondered if he would be leaving the Estate at all until his business was concluded. This had not been an idyllic start to such a stay, and if it was her job to look after him during his time there as she suggested, he thought that he might be better off fending for himself.

She seemed a woman of few words for nothing else was said as they made their way to the side door. As they got there he could now see a stairway leading downward and just to the side of this was a large trapdoor. A basement or cellar no doubt, given the vast size of the building. That seemed a plausible theory because through the side door itself they found themselves in an expansive kitchen, where a dumb waiter was built onto the south wall, directly over the area he had just observed and likely employed to make easy work of carrying goods between the two floors.

Thankfully this seemed like the starting point of the tour with Hodgson as she stopped suddenly. "You'll no doubt soon know your way about Father but a few things of note. The kitchen here is open to you at all hours. The pantries are well stocked, and you're free to take what you want."

She looked somewhat downbeat as she continued. "I'm afraid we had to let the chef go some time ago. Poor Mr McArthur has little appetite for such things now, and visitors are all but non-existent. That said, fresh produce is still brought in from the town, you won't want for anything during your stay with us."

Fitzgerald nodded his approval. He knew that for a house of the size and stature of Thoby Hall, a large staff would no doubt be necessary, but it was only earlier that morning that the solicitor Harvey had alluded to the financial problems the Estate had suffered.

Hodgson continued with her briefing, which brought him back from his thoughts. "There is though a nurse here at all hours. You will no doubt meet them both during your stay with us. The doctor is Dr Stanley from the local surgery. He is on hand if needed, but that is nothing for you to concern yourself with, as either Melissa or Keira will take charge of those matters."

He raised an eyebrow questioningly.

"They are our resident nurses."

She went on. "After you are settled, perhaps I can give you a tour of the rest of the house. You might well know it was formerly open to the public and so very much open on the whole should you wish to explore. Be mindful though, that Mr McArthur's rooms are in the west wing. That man Harvey will no doubt keep you informed, but unless you are engaged with Mr McArthur there, I would ask that you be mindful to his privacy and keep the peace and quiet."

He again nodded his consent to her wishes.

"Also on the west wing, the library is unfortunately out of bounds I am afraid. You saw the builders this morning? Well, the west most chimney stack is unsafe and requires urgent renovations. The library has been closed for some considerable time as a result. Given the timing, I can scarcely believe that the work is to be done. But that is another story…" She trailed off, her eyes began to glaze and seemed far away.

"Come now. Let me show you to your rooms. They are most comfortable and among my favourites in the house. I hope you will find them to your satisfaction." She managed this with a smile, and he wondered if he had perhaps judged her too harshly in his thinking. The Estate was vast no doubt, and she had the job of seeing to its upkeep and care. Perhaps there was no wonder she was fiery. It certainly seemed to have an appropriate effect on the builders, but her smile when it finally came was warm, and the mention of his rooms made him realise that she was very proud of the house here.

They left the kitchen and Fitzgerald felt he was on familiar ground as surely they were on the same corridor as the office he had attended with Harvey only that morning. But instead of turning left toward the front of the house they went right and delved further into the east wing. Before long they came upon another staircase, much simpler in design than the elaborate cascading work of the entrance hall, but still no less impressive due to the intricate carvings he could see in the woodwork. The bannister itself though was a shock, for he went to put his hand down and quickly recoiled as his hand met the carved finial of a snakehead.

Hodgson stopped ahead of him, and he looked up and saw a frown on her face. He felt somewhat defensive and thought she had judged his reaction for some weakness when truth be told; it had been only surprise. But she shook her head, and a look of sadness came over her face.

"Not our finest work Father. I'm afraid for some time now certain elements have had a very unfavourable influence on the house and its décor."

Fitzgerald did not understand. He looked down and saw that the post to his left was splendid and adorned with small cherubs; he could see those who played the harp or flute and those who held flowers, but all for certain were focused above as if ascending upward and metaphorically toward heaven. It was though, the right-hand post he had placed his hand on. This seemed to depict serpents and lizards all of who appeared to be focused on descent. Their forked tongues protruding through pinched snouts, many of which showed rows of sharp teeth. The contrast between the two bannister posts was stark, but the message less subtle, for plainly one depicted the ascent to heaven while the other the fall into hell.

"Elements?" He questioned, responding to Hodgson's statement.

"Lady Elizabeth, among others," she replied, and quickly she turned about and continued up the stairway, Fitzgerald had seen the sadness still on her face and wondered if it was to Elizabeth McArthur to whom she referred. Father Shilling had alluded to McArthur's ex-wife and her involvement with Father Crosby who had taken his own life. He cursed himself for his ignorance and followed on up the stairway after Hodgson.

The corridor they now walked in was adjacent to the side of the building and was also brilliantly lit by a succession of light fixtures in the walls and the ceiling above. In fact every room and corridor he had seen of Thoby Hall so far, had been similarly lit and despite the drab Autumn day, the light succeeded in pressing back the bleak weather seen through the large windows that they passed. Here, he was offered a fantastic view of the gardens and hedgerows of the Thoby Estate. As they continued to walk, he could see the rooms had name plaques, he saw the Wellington Room and the Churchill Room, quickly followed by less ostentatious names such as the Maple and Oak Rooms and he wondered if those former rooms had once housed such noble and great men. It seemed though there was little time for a more elaborate tour as Hodgson ploughed onward to the end of the house and the last doorway. He read the sign 'Willow Room'.

The door was unlocked, and Hodgson entered. He quickly saw that it was not, in fact, a single bedroom that he had been assigned, instead, a large apartment, as he was now stood in a comfortable looking lounge with closed doors to each side and to the front. She opened each door as they went and he saw a large bathroom to his left and a study to his right. Hodgson though, did not stop and met the final door which opened up into a very large bedroom. Fitzgerald was overwhelmed by what he saw, having never been afforded such opulence in his time.

From his vantage point by the door, he could see a four-poster bed to his right-hand side and a dressing table against the far wall. He crossed to the large windows and as Hodgson drew back the thick curtains he was met with an astonishing view. Here at the end of the east wing, the bedroom windows faced the rear of the house and were opposite the west wing, which was perhaps some one hundred metres across what was a most spectacular garden. The upkeep at the front of the property had been disappointing, but here there were no such issues. Hodgson, it seemed shared his feelings for she came over to his side and took in the sight.

"Our pride and joy," she began. "Since Mr McArthur has taken to his rooms, it remains Dougie's primary focus."

"Dougie?" Fitzgerald questioned.

Hodgson looked momentarily lost as she processed the question as if the asking was out of context with their conversation.

"Douglas is our gardener Father," she eventually returned. "The upkeep of the Estate is well beyond the capacity of one man as I am sure you can imagine, but for now the garden below you is his sole focus, as when Mr McArthur is well enough he can enjoy the view from his windows. Ah, if only you could have seen it in the Summer. Oh, the colours!" She exclaimed. Fitzgerald had little doubt that it would indeed be something special to behold. But even now in the late fall, the greens of the high hedgerows seemed to exude a light of their own. He allowed his eyes to wander and could see that all of the hedgerows pointed and allowed access to a central point in the garden where a sizeable octagonal gazebo was situated. There about it, was a large rectangular pond and several benches. He could see as well that the lower portion of the west wing and rear of the house had a large cloister that no doubt extended to the side of the east wing below him as well.

"Spectacular," was all he could find in reply.

She smiled and slowly moved away. He turned and saw that she had gone to the left of the room where there was yet another door situated. She opened this for him as well, and he walked over to investigate, and saw that it was a large dressing room. Again he felt amazed as to the level of comfort he had been afforded.

"Thank you, Mrs Hodgson. This is beyond my wildest expectations."

She smiled in response and again he sensed the pride in her. Maybe that was why she had chosen a room such as this.

"Well, I'm afraid the house does not get its share of visitors any longer. Alas, we have not known the happy sound of tiny feet running around the house and gardens for some years, but since those days we have entertained many dignitaries or notable guests. I am glad the room is to your approval, Father Fitzgerald. All of the rooms on the floor are currently empty, and you may well find it quiet on this side. I'm afraid it can be a lonely place to be."

Fitzgerald nodded in response. He motioned over to the window. "Mr McArthur's rooms you say are opposite in the west wing?"

"Yes. The Queen Elizabeth Rooms are opposite your own."

"When might I expect to meet Mr McArthur?"

"That I am afraid I do not know, and I have been given no direction as to protocol. I expect you will be in conversations with that lawyer Harvey through the week. I am sure he will notify you of such things, but even then it is reliant on Mr McArthur's state of health and mind. Either Keira or Melissa will no doubt be able to advise you of any suitable window of opportunity to speak with him."

"How bad is it?"

Hodgson looked tired and defeated as she spoke. He could not guess as to how many years she had served here, but had there not been a mention of her in the pages of Father Crosby's diaries? That being the likely case, it was no doubt that she felt the sadness at the inevitable demise for her employer Mr McArthur.

"We seldom have good days now. He has little other company, and I am afforded some time where we will talk about the better days in this house. But all too often, he is under the influence of the drugs that control his pain. He is a stubborn man though, and I know he fights still and will endure what he can so that he might have some lucid hours among his day."

He wondered then if Hodgson knew the fate of Thoby Hall and what that might mean for her. He thought better of such conversation but instead thought it a better time to counter some of his ignorance.

"You said little company, Mrs Hodgson. Are there no other family?"

"Some, I believe. But very far removed. Mr McArthur has no children you see, and those women who went before have stripped the Estate bare." Fitzgerald could certainly sense the bitterness with which her words were delivered.

"Elizabeth?" he offered, hoping to glean a little more information.

"Elizabeth? oh, goodness no Father, poor child. She was the best of them by far. So sad what happened. But with her, we had high hopes for happy times in the house and for Mr McArthur. No, it was those other women who have robbed this Estate blind and left it in the poor state you find it in today."

"So Mr McArthur has been married on several occasions?"

"Three times in all. Elizabeth was the second. We did not think he would take another wife after what happened with her; such was his devotion."

Given his little knowledge, Fitzgerald was keen to know more and so pressed. "What did happen Mrs Hodgson?"

She looked up suddenly and blinked hard, she looked uncertain and surprised to see him. "Father? oh, I…such matters are not for me to discuss. I have already said too much of that which is not my business. You must please excuse me."

He was frustrated but could see the difficulty that she was in. He might be a man of the cloth, but he was asking her to give up private information on her long-time employer. She would feel that she had crossed a boundary by telling him or at least alluding to as much as she had and would probably be guarded in her reactions to him from then on. However, he felt that the information was important, so as to get a better understanding of McArthur and his history.

He was no counsellor or psychologist to be sure, and perhaps such information was immaterial to what he had to accomplish here. But the man required absolution before he was to pass on. It was certainly within his mandate to probe into such areas and facilitate a full confession through conversation, and so, such background information could prove undoubtedly useful. He had though crossed a line with this woman, and he knew it too soon to have won her confidence.

Perhaps that could change over the week, and if necessary, he would probe for more information as thus far he had little other than meagre suggestion as opposed to real facts about the man and his life.

"Oh please no Mrs Hodgson. I apologise if I have caused you to be uncomfortable. Perhaps I should say that this has all come on me very suddenly and I only wished to know more of Mr McArthur before meeting him."

"Very well, Father. But perhaps that is not for me to say. No doubt Mr McArthur will tell you what you need to know himself."

"Of course and we have all that to come." He smiled at her, trying to exude an element of warmth. It may only be a short week here at the Thoby Hall household, but he knew well that Mrs Hodgson would be a better ally than enemy. "Perhaps we will speak again soon?"

"Yes, Father, no doubt. Perhaps not today though. You should know that I am off the Estate by 06:00 pm. After that time, you will have the entire house almost to yourself," she said, seemingly happy at the change of subject; perhaps feeling awkward at what she had divulged. "You have everything you need?"

He looked about. "The room is exceptional Mrs Hodgson. Thank you, I am sure everything will be just fine."

The small talk had taken over and had the desired effect. He knew well that a simple compliment could play wonders and the surest way to win Hodgson's trust and respect was to pay homage to the magnificent house which she tended to. That was no issue as he was genuinely impressed at the beautiful home and gardens.

With that, Hodgson took her cue to exit, and he was left alone in the large apartment that was to be his home over the coming week or so.

CHAPTER 7

With Hodgson now long gone, Fitzgerald felt at a loose end and so explored the sumptuous apartment. Going back through to the lounge, he saw it to be very comfortable looking, and he could see he had both television and phone access. Perhaps the TV was a little dated, but it came with a set-top box which showed that Thoby Hall was at least up to date with digital technology. A quick press of the remote control though left him disappointed as try as he might, he could only find static on the screen as he cycled through the channels.

Well no matter, that was not what he was here for and though there would be many hours that he would have to wile away on his own, he could see he would have no lack of reading material, as a quick look through to the study, afforded him a look at a large bookcase which held many popular volumes.

This same study also came with a printed welcome pack; no doubt prepared in better times and for more sophisticated guests than he. Fitzgerald was also pleasantly surprised to find a key code for wireless Internet access, and though he doubted it was still in effect, he unpacked his laptop, placing it centrally on the study desk and sat himself down in the high-backed chair behind it. Very quickly, he found the wireless network and was able to log on seamlessly.

With little else to do, he thought he might make use of the time with some research. To date, he knew very little of Robert McArthur, the sole reason he was here at Thoby Hall. He couldn't put his finger on the reason, but he was somewhat apprehensive at the thought of their impending meeting. Also, he felt himself at somewhat of a disadvantage, after how he had been railroaded into his agreement to remain at the house.

Of course, both the names of McArthur and his home at Thoby Hall had featured occasionally during his short time in Ashmarsh, and not in any good way for that matter. But the rest of his time there had been very positive, and so he had allowed himself to put such thoughts to the back of his mind. However the hour would soon be upon him and they would meet, so it might serve him better to have some background on the man.

There was, of course, the additional tales of misfortune that surrounded him and the house and though Fitzgerald only believed them to be no more than local superstitions and old wives' tales, he knew he had been remiss in not following through on the words of Father

Shilling, by not reading the diaries provided by Father Crosby or by doing some simple Internet research.

I didn't bring the damned diaries.

Well, it was too late for that now, but before him, he had the means to learn what information he could, in the short time he had. But where should he start? The cursor blinked at him in the empty search bar of the Google page.

He thought for only a second before typing in the name Robert McArthur, doubting very much that his man had any kind of social media presence. Very quickly the page populated in front of him and he saw the list of various websites and pages that ranged from Wikipedia and Facebook entries to LinkedIn profiles.

Checking the list, he saw that first and foremost was a Wikipedia page for a Robert McArthur, a Canadian-born ecologist. Not what he was looking for.

He scrolled down to find a long list of different profiles and smiled as he saw that there was an Elvis impersonator with the same name. A quick click onto page two didn't bring him any nearer to finding his real target. He clicked the search bar at the top and added the word Ashmarsh onto the end of his named search term and again clicked enter.

Bingo.

The link was again for a Wikipedia page, and he saw in the right-hand side of the screen a small biography.

"Robert McArthur. Industrialist."

"Robert George McArthur is a British Industrialist who was born in Leytonstone, London on 12th December 1924."

Confident that he had his man, Fitzgerald clicked onto the link and read the lines of text that followed. There was no accompanying photograph with the very short article.

He was born on 12th December 1924 in Chelmsford Road, Leytonstone, London. The son of George McArthur.

Served in the British Army between 1941 and 1945 with the 1st Airborne Division and the 3rd Parachute Brigade.

Operation Biting in Bruneval, France - 27/28th February 1942.

Operation Freshman in Telemark, Norway - November 1942.

Operation Tonga during the Normandy Landings - 5th June 1944.

Medals - 1939-1945 Star.

France and Germany Star.

War Medal.

Distinguished Conduct Medal.

Former staff member of the Industrialist Thomas Searle and inherited his fortune following his passing in November 1979. Robert McArthur was married on three occasions and had one heir, Jonathan McArthur (1954-1975).

Only a short profile but Fitzgerald was suitably impressed with McArthur's War service record and medals. He clicked back out and could see that the next few links led to ancestry sites, and he frowned believing he would not turn up anything of any real relevance there. Quickly though, he saw a link to what appeared to be the Ashmarsh Gazette, the local newspaper.

The headline read 'Girl 7 drowns at Thoby Hall'. And in the lines beneath - 'A 7-year-old girl has died following a tragic accident whereby she was found drowned in the swimming pool at the Thoby Hall Estate in Ashmarsh…Robert McArthur was unavailable for comment…'

Fitzgerald quickly pressed the link but found the article to be sparse on detail. The news had still been fresh at that time, as the accident had occurred only the day before the report had been published. There was no name given for the poor child who had passed away, and the reference to McArthur was only the same as the preview text on the previous page; that he was unavailable for comment. Fitzgerald knew though that he had discovered some of the tragedy to which Father Shilling had alluded.

His, was a business of faith and healing but when the Lord saw fit to take a child there was often little comfort that those, such as he and Shilling could offer and quite often such poor souls who were left to deal with such loss would fade away from the Church and the support it might offer. And why not? He knew he would be at a loss, should he be confronted with such questions as Father Crosby would have met at the time of this terrible story.

Is this what led him to despair?

He clicked back to the website home page and making a few alterations he quickly found an updated version of the story from only a few days later than the first. The article was also from the same newspaper website and was accompanied by a file photograph of a building which he instantly recognised as Thoby Hall.

He read.

A 7-year-old girl from Ashmarsh died on Wednesday morning after being found unresponsive after swimming at the indoor swimming pool at Thoby Hall. An ambulance was called to the location, but the girl was pronounced dead at the scene.

It is reported that the girl was in the house in company with her mother on invitation from the Estate owners.

Police Inspector Deborah Joy of Eastland Police said there were no suspicious circumstances surrounding the incident and that all of the potential witnesses had been spoken to. "Sadly, this is every parent's worst nightmare and happened in a very small timeframe where a young girl has gone from her mother's side to enjoy the facilities the house offered."

Mr Thomas Harvey, solicitor and acting on behalf of the resident and Estate owner Robert McArthur said "This has been a sad and tragic day for everyone who is a part of the Thoby Hall family. Mr McArthur has expressed his horror that such a terrible set of events could have been allowed to happen. We offer our sincerest condolences to the family."

Robert McArthur was unavailable for comment.

Fitzgerald clicked back once again to the home page and changed his search parameters.

'Thoby Hall, Ashmarsh'

The resulting page was adorned with several pictures of the magnificent stately home, and he soon saw the link to the official website, where he had found his initial travel directions from earlier that morning. He idly clicked the link, hoping there might be further information among the pages of the website, that he had missed on his earlier visit.

Here was the page that gave a further history of the Hall and its construction, and several clicks later he found a page that said 'Visitors' he was disappointed to see a notice that reinforced the fact that the home was currently closed to the public. That entry was listed as far back as the 3rd February 2005 and had not seemingly been updated since. A comments section at the bottom of the page suggested that others shared similar feelings.

'A jewel in the English countryside. When can your public see you again?' From anonymous.

This wasn't what he was looking for. Clearly, a public website would not suggest to the homes more unfortunate history. He bookmarked the page though intending to read more on the history of the house at a later stage.

Another small amendment to his search parameters finally gave him what he was looking for as he added the name of the local paper to find what reports they had made on the house over the years. A whole host of articles flooded the screen before him, and he could see a variety of fetes and events that had been held at the house over the years. But a long look down the list suggested nothing further of any concern. Had Father Shilling been a little melodramatic regarding the homes chequered history? He leant back in the swivel chair as he pondered the words of the former parish priest.

He sighed and rubbed at his eyes. *What am I looking for?*

Proof of Shilling's paranoia? It was true that he had indeed found a very sad event in the history of both the house and the town, but could something such as this have led to the downfall of Father Crosby and to local superstition regarding the house? Maybe so, but what of Shilling? This event had predated his tenure at St Peter's, so what was it that had ground him down to the wretched mess that Fitzgerald had only recently come to meet?

An idea struck, and he typed out the name of Crosby alongside Thoby Hall, and it was quickly apparent that the two search parameters did not associate. A quick press of the delete key and he was left with only the blinking cursor once more.

There was something just under the surface that linked the priest to the Hall and its occupants; as well as the poor young girl who had drowned. In particular, there had been several clues to his association to the young woman Elizabeth McArthur with whom he had not yet satisfied his curiosity.

Knowing already that a vague search term would not aid him, he typed in 'Elizabeth McArthur Ashmarsh Gazette'. Perhaps the local newspaper would hold some relevant information about the woman.

The page quickly populated, and he was glad to see he had found what he was looking for. A whole row of entries with her name in bold; and there right before him within the first few lines, Elizabeth McArthur and St Peter's Church.

He clicked the link and was again confronted with the now-familiar web page of an Ashmarsh Gazette news story. The article was small and accompanied by a photograph of a very striking young woman stood in front of what he recognised as the same church hall he had recently attended for coffee morning with Father Shilling. The caption read.

'Fundraising events announced to raise money for Church Hall'.

'A series of organised events are soon to be held in the Ashmarsh area in aid of the ailing Church Hall at St Peter's church. The church situated on Market Hill is holding the first of four events, a brass band concert on Saturday 4th June in the public gardens. Stalls, food and games will also be available during the event.

'Elizabeth McArthur who chairs the fundraising committee for the church said: "Unfortunately our Church Hall has seen better days, but yet is a vital part of our community and is used for various social groups such as scout and girl guide groups, as well as art classes and dance. As such, we want to give those people the very best facilities that we can, that they can enjoy their classes and environment equally."

He could see the article was dated Friday 27th May 1994. He looked again at the photograph of the young woman.

1994?

How old was she? He was hard-pressed to believe she was outside of her twenties. And from remembering the Wikipedia entry on Robert McArthur, he knew him to have been somewhere in his late seventies at that time. Hodgson had made suggestion of previous wives

63

stripping the Estate bare, but not so Elizabeth McArthur. But as he looked at the warmth in her charming smile, he wondered what had motivated her to marry an aged man like McArthur if not for the money.

What was clear was that he had found the area he was looking for, and a few quick presses on several of the links delivered him to similar articles about fundraising work and church events. It seemed the young woman was a very productive member of her church, but what of her and Crosby? The time and dates correlated and he knew Crosby to have been at St Peter's at that time.

He punched the name into the search bar.

Again the page was instantly flooded. And one Father James Crosby came to the surface. The headlines though were much darker.

'Local priest takes own life' read the Gazette dated Friday 2nd February 1996.

'Parishioners of St Peter's Church in Ashmarsh are today mourning the death of their former Parish Priest Father James Crosby. News of Father Crosby's passing was delivered by Bishop Burrows of the Springmoor and Highbridge Diocese, who announced the priest had passed on Tuesday 30th January.

The news followed unusual and previously unreported events during the service on the previous Sunday, the 28th. The Ashmarsh Gazette has learned that Father Crosby's mental health was called into question on that day when it is believed he substituted wine used in the sacrament for his own blood. Father Crosby was removed from his position the same day.'

'Ethel Strong, 75, a member of the St Peter's congregation for over 70 years, had this to say on delivery of the sad news: "Father Crosby will be sorely missed. He was a kind and well-spoken man, and I am sorry that it came to this."

'Of events from last Sunday, she added: "There was an incident certainly. Father Crosby did not seem at all well, and his sermon suggested as much. I was in line for the sacrament, but my turn didn't come. I saw a commotion, and Father Crosby led from the church by the deacon."

"There were tears, and we wondered what had gone on. It was only after, that rumour had gotten out that the Father had injured himself somehow and used his blood in the sacrament. A nasty business, but given the news, perhaps the Church could have done more for him?"

'Bishop Burrows has refused to comment on these reports but did confirm that Father Crosby had been removed from his position for reasons of 'mental exhaustion' Chief Inspector Richard Stubbings of Eastland Police said that the death was not being treated as suspicious.'

Fitzgerald sat back in his chair. As usual, the reporting in the local newspaper was vastly underwhelming in its detail. He opened up his Internet search believing such a story must have gone national. The suicide alone was shocking news, but the use of his own blood in the sacrament? That was the kind of sensationalism that many tabloids thrived on.

As he searched he reflected on the story and knew the man must have been very ill at the time and he wondered if Ethel Strong, was right in her views when she suggested the Church might have done more for him.

He quickly saw that he was right and the nationals had covered the story as well in the days after the event. The Ashmarsh Gazette it seemed had the scoop, but perhaps not the resources to follow through on what was big news. For the Sunday Mail went with 'Catholic Church in Suicide Cover-up' in their headline which was printed on page three of the Sunday 4th February edition. The bulk of the story had remained the same and little to no detail had been released by the diocese. However, their reporter had it seemed found an anonymous source who did wish to speak of the events of Sunday 28th January.

'Father Crosby was a warm and gentle-hearted man. What happened on that Sunday was utterly out of character. But yes, it did happen. We were close by when Mary (Shields) took the sacrament. I was shocked when she spat it back out and thought of her sacrilege. She was visibly upset, and Father Crosby continued onto her husband who you understand was more focused on the welfare of his wife. She was in tears, and he took the cup before it reached the lips of the next person. It was then that I saw the red stains on the sleeves of Father Crosby's robe. He, (David Shields) stood, and there was a scuffle. It was only later that I came to understand what I had seen. Father Crosby had to be taken away by Deacon Morris.'

Colin? Fitzgerald was stunned. His own deacon had been involved with this?

The article had little else of substance though, and repeated attempts for comment from the Church had met with silence.

Fitzgerald was beginning to see why Father Shilling might believe the Church to be cursed. Such an incident as this was likely never to be forgotten. Additionally, Shilling's own performance during his last mass had no doubt reopened memories of Father Crosby and the expectant audience that day had perhaps anticipated a similar showing.

Damn you, Liam.

In the half an hour that followed, he clicked through several news stories, all of which pertained to Father Crosby and his suicide. None though shed any more light on the matter than the first. It seemed the matter was quickly forgotten in the press as the weekly editions had moved onto the release of genetically modified foods going on sale for the first time in the United Kingdom and the IRA breaking a 17-month ceasefire when they bombed the London Docklands.

For now, Fitzgerald had his answers, at least some of them anyway. The question was, would McArthur touch on these events at all? He still needed answers, and perhaps their conversations might touch on such areas. But with the suicide of Crosby, and McArthur's second wife somehow linked to the events, he knew he needed more, and if McArthur wasn't to be forthcoming, then perhaps Colin Morris would be the man to ask.

He stood from his chair and stretched, his work done. The time was now 04:30 pm, and his stomach complained to him that now might be the time to explore the kitchen's pantry.

65

Opening the study door back into the lounge of his apartment Fitzgerald instantly recoiled, as he was at once blinded by a brilliant white light that emanated from the open bedroom door and the far window that looked into the gardens.

He cupped a hand to his brow to shield his eyes as they adjusted to the unnatural light and stepped into the bedroom, which seemed to glow brighter than a summer afternoon.

What on earth is that?

He made his way to the window where he had only recently admired the view of the gardens below with Hodgson by his side. Fitzgerald could quickly see that the entire area below was fiercely lit by a succession of spotlights that hung below the eaves of the roof and that these spotlights were mounted along the entire circumference of both wings and the main house. More than that, he could see spotlights in the garden that were trained upon the upper stories, and one such light it seemed was trained upon the room where he now stood. He blinked away the imprint of the light that lingered behind his closed eyelids as he had inadvertently glared into the source of the beam.

It took a moment or two to adjust to the pillar of light that assaulted him, but before long, his sight had adjusted to the glare, and he was able to look out once more. Surely the house could be seen for miles such was the strength of the light and he was amazed as he realised it kept the very darkness of the late autumn night at bay.

All at once he felt vulnerable, outlined as he was against the window, and as his eyes shifted, he thought he saw a trace of movement on the opposite wing of the house. Had there been someone there? Perhaps stood as he was surveying the garden below? Or perhaps surveying him?

Feeling uneasy, he quickly shut the curtains and felt instant relief. He sat on the soft bed. Even with the curtains drawn, it was as if it was daylight outside and he frowned as he knew that the light would be a constant companion as he slept if it were to remain on.

Why would they light the house this way? He thought, thinking as well about the multitude of lit rooms and hallways he had also observed in his short stay.

With the house now closed to the public surely there was no need for such extravagance. And wasn't the house suffering financially? The electricity bills must have been extortionate.

Thoby Hall was certainly a strange place, and this latest development, coupled with the distressing news articles he had found made him feel ill at ease. He couldn't put his finger on it exactly, but the place, its reputation and the people who were connected here, either historically or currently, all contributed to this feeling he had.

And as afternoon gave way to the early evening, he found it more comfortable to stretch out on the sofa and close the door to the perpetual light of the bedroom. Time passed, and it was now well after 09:00 pm, and there had still been no word from McArthur or his nurses. Surely it was also well past time for the house staff to have left the premises and he paced the

66

apartment wondering what he should do next. Occasionally he would go to the bedroom and peer through the curtains at the rooms opposite him in the west wing. The distance though and the outside light made distinguishing anything there a virtual impossibility.

The house was quiet, and feeling restless he picked up the phone in one hand while reading the contact number for the office of Frederick Harvey from the business card he had been given, but perhaps as could be expected at such a time, he only got the answering machine.

CHAPTER 8

Fitzgerald felt listless. The last few hours had amounted to little more than pacing the few rooms of the large apartment over and over again, interspersed with frustrating attempts to pass chapter one on the novel he had selected from the study. Frustrated, he had finally given up and decided he would go and explore the house.

It was now past 11:00 pm as he slowly pushed the door of the Willow Room open. At once, he was quickly assaulted by yet another fierce beam of light, as there below in the gardens, he could see yet more spotlights trained upward so as to light this, the east side of the house.

"Really?"

The sound of his voice reverberated down the long corridor of the first floor, and he gulped involuntarily, fearing some reprimand for his indiscretion in breaking the silence. Of course, no such thing came, but that didn't stop him from steering to the centre of the floor where a long thin carpet stretched far into the distance. It would undoubtedly cushion his footfalls as opposed to the hard-wooden boards that sat beneath it and filled the entire width of the corridor to its sides.

Walking softly, he quickly came upon the staircase that led down to the ground floor. His brow furrowed as he recalled his earlier startled reaction to the carvings that were set within the bannister and Hodgson's lament regarding the 'unfavourable elements' that had taken their toll upon the house over the years.

And so, as he made the staircase, he stopped. The carvings before him were difficult to ignore, and he realised that his way would be downward as with the serpents. Such an idea was not a happy one, and he simply stood there, indecision rampant within him as what he should do; to press on with his exploration or retreat to the sanctuary and comfort of his rooms.

Get a grip man.

Yes, he was being foolish. After all, what was he going to do with his stay here at Thoby Hall? Stay locked away in his rooms, waiting for the few and probably far between meetings with McArthur? But despite this reproach, he couldn't help but let the thought cross his mind that he might do exactly that.

He blew a long sigh and shook his head as he instead took the first stair downward and toward the familiar grounds toward the kitchen and the corridor that led to Harvey's office, and in a few quick steps, he was back at the front of the house.

Here in the vast lobby, the temperature was in stark contrast to the comfort and warmth he had left in his apartment. More than that, he felt the first stirrings of solitude as he stepped deeper into the vast room. The house was creepy, and he could find no better word for it. The simple sense of isolation was in that moment almost overwhelming, even though he knew there were at least two others on the premises at this late hour; McArthur and the nurse that cared for him.

Additionally, there would be no respite from the light it seemed, as the heavy chandelier overhead was still brightly lit, as were the lamps that were set into every wall. The effect was spectacular as the contrasting colours of black and white, that was the marble floor beneath him shone. And more than that, as an odd trick of the light seemed to make it appear as if gold flecks hovered and danced above the black marble of the pentagram set in the floor before him. At least from this, he could feel some small comfort, as the effect was to give the room an air of warmth — something that the frigid air about him did not lend to in any way.

As he gazed about the room, he knew he was stuck in indecision as to where to go next. Hodgson had permitted him to explore the whole house, except for McArthur's west wing, where he undoubtedly lived and was being treated. But even with such permission, he was at a loss as where else to go.

A thought quickly struck, and he looked up toward the large balcony that run along the first-floor at the back of the vast room. It had been suggested to him that the nursing staff were in residence 24 hours a day. Perhaps he could tentatively go into the west wing and make his introductions, while at the same time garnering any knowledge as to how and when he might meet McArthur.

A small voice in the back of his head quickly piped up to tell him that if he did so, he would be breaking the only real rule that had been set, but given that his duty ultimately lay in the west wing he quietened the voice with assurances that everything would be fine.

Climbing the left most stairway, his view quickly opened up, and he saw that a long corridor stretched in both directions from the long balcony, likely giving access to the upper floors of both east and west wings.

He made his way to the left along the corridor and the route that would take him to the west wing and where he believed McArthur's rooms would be situated opposite his own.

All at once though his step faltered, as feelings of trespass began to wash over him. Doubt resurfaced in his mind, and he questioned the necessity in what he was doing. After all, what kind of time was it to go calling on some poor startled nurse in the depths of the night? He stood still, lost in indecision, his eyes searching to the west and his goal, and then back to the east where a persistently growing voice insisted he retreat.

As he took his first step of retreat, his eyes roamed about him and fell upon the artworks that adorned the walls. He could see at once that many depicted rolling green landscapes which he could well imagine as part of the Thoby Hall Estate. And as curiosity got the better of him, he took a step back toward the west wing as a watercolour depicting a fox hunting meet before the main house of Thoby Hall, caught his eye.

Intrigued, he walked back to the west side, to get a better look and though he did not consider himself in any way artistically inclined, he was quite taken with the contrast of colour within the landscape. The red coats of the riders and the hard blacks of their helmets, intermingled with the browns and whites of their steeds and foxhounds beneath them.

And now there before him, was another feature that begged further scrutiny, for high up upon the roof of the main house was a bell tower, something he knew was no longer a part of the building.

Peering in closely to the bottom corner of the painting he saw the flourish of the artist's signature and a date. The name he could not distinguish, but the date showed February of 1965. Satisfied, he slowly pulled back from the painting and decided at last that his rooms were to be his destination after all, and so began to turn back in that direction, but as he did so, he caught something in the corner of his eye.

It had been indistinguishable at first, but it was almost as if some movement had registered just as he had turned away from the painting. A movement that begged recognition.

Such a thing was impossible, of course, but something within the canvas begged further study. He scanned the picture idly, no fresh detail immediately apparent and then he saw it.

There, on the leftmost window of the first floor, a silhouette within the window.

Puzzled, he leaned in closer for a second look.

All of a sudden, his senses were assaulted by the loud crash of a door slamming. The noise was so unexpected and so loud that it caused Fitzgerald's heart to skip a beat.

Quickly he turned his head to his left and the west side of the house where the noise had originated.

"Hello?" He ventured nervously. There was no response, only silence.

In that instant, fear coursed through him, and he was frozen to the spot.

His eyes wandered slowly back to the painting. His train of thought was now broken as his mind wrestled with the violent intervention of sound, forgetting what he had seen there in the picture only moments before. That was until his eyes fell straight back to the first-floor windows, where now no silhouette could be seen. The first-floor window was painted bright and unobstructed.

What the hell?

Feeling immediately ill at ease he stepped quickly back from the canvas, keen to put as much distance between himself and the strange feeling that now sat within him, but it was not in the direction of the east wing that he went. The sound of the door slamming indicated a presence nearby, perhaps even the nurse he had hoped to call on. The loud slamming of a door had threatened to make his heart stop, but maybe it had been he, who had instigated the matter, by scaring some poor woman with his presence in the corridor at this late hour.

"Hello?" He ventured more confidently as he paced slowly toward the source of the sound. Quickly, he came to the end of the corridor and found that it met a large anteroom, where he could see a double door immediately to his left, and one to the front. A glance to his right, saw the corridor strike up again and he was met with a mirror image of the upper east wing, as he could see many doors stretching away into the distance on the right-hand side, and similar large beams of light from unseen spotlights intruding into the wide-open space.

Somewhere toward the end of this corridor, he would undoubtedly find Robert McArthur's rooms.

But for now, his attention was focused elsewhere. Here before him, were two closed doors, one of which had been shut very abruptly only scant moments before his arrival.

Fitzgerald stopped and keened his ear, hoping to distinguish which of the two doors had been so firmly closed. He shut his eyes to better concentrate, but as he did so, a chill breeze felt the side of his neck. He spun quickly in the direction of the draught and found himself face to face with the double doors to his left-hand side. His internal geography, instinctively telling him that the room behind this door would be facing the front of the house.

Surely, if that was so, was this not where he saw the figure who peered down on Hodgson, earlier that day?

The second thought came so quickly, and he had no time to bid it to be quiet.

The silhouette in the painting. It's the same room.

This caused a shiver to wash over him, and he took an unconscious step backwards from the door.

He let out a deep breath and was surprised to see that his breathing was frosted before his eyes. It had been cold for sure in the old house, but in what had seemed only an instant, the very temperature around him had dropped somewhere south of freezing.

But what could be causing such a thing? He took a tentative step toward the door and detected it at once. A cold freezing draught of air seemed to be emanating from that direction.

He held his hand out toward the long gap at the side of the door where it met the frame, believing that perhaps a small airflow might be detected there. None came, but as he eased in closer, it was clear that the freezing draught did come from where the two closed double doors met.

All about him was dead silent. Plumes of white fog continued to expel from his mouth and nose, and he felt fear. The cold and quiet washed over him, and he was caught there indecisive as what to do next.

Slowly Fitzgerald put his hand out before him so as to confirm what he had felt, and cold air met his hand. He took another step forward toward the double door.

Another step forward and he had to bring his hand down for such was the chill in the air that his fingers were beginning to feel numb.

Instead, he stepped to the side and found that he was no longer in the current of cold air. He was stood now before the doorway and still the silence held.

He waved his hand back and forth through the draught. Once, then a second time for final confirmation. He had detected the source alright, but what on earth was causing such a phenomenon as this?

Inching forward he allowed his hand to rest on the door and drew it back sharply as he might have done, testing a resting kettle for warmth. The doorway though was not cold to the touch as he had expected. But being this close, he could now hear the air current whistling through the gap to his side. He leant in slowly, holding his breath and lowering his ear to the door to try and hear what was causing such a thing to happen. All thought of any other persons being present, now forgotten.

He reached down with his right hand toward the handle and allowed it to rest there. Again he half anticipated the metal there to be cold, but it was only cool to the touch.

Slowly, he pressed down on the handle, but it resisted the pressure he put upon it. It was locked. He looked up toward the second door, as thoughts of another person quickly returned, and he was at once glad of the thought, as loathe as he was to admit it, he was now distinctly anxious. He was about to move away and try the second door, hoping beyond hope he could tell someone of the ill breeze.

It could be dangerous, some kind of leak.

The thought was barely finished when he heard the sound from beyond the double doors. He stopped in his tracks, frozen still, as he heard the noise repeat itself. He leaned in closer, almost close enough for his ear to touch the door. Had that been a footstep, perhaps falling upon a wooden floor?

He held his breath to listen as hard as he could, and yes there it was again a third solid tap on wood, only slightly closer this time and a little louder. The noise though was not of footsteps, he now thought, such was the slow, languid nature of their coming. He was though very conscious of the fact that it could well be a person inside and very quickly the door could be flung open to reveal him listening in and exposing him as some kind of voyeur or peeper.

He looked down. There was a keyhole.

Despite the silence and the unnatural cold that continued to stream to his right, it was not fear he now felt but uncertainty. What if this was some leak? Some toxic substance? He wasn't sure that he believed that, but certainly the draught was in some way ill and unnatural. Perhaps the noise was the source of what was creating it?

He began to squat lower, his left knee that he had hurt some years ago in a football game cried out at him as he put pressure on it. Finding his level, he allowed the leg to straighten and bore his weight on his right leg instead, while the left allowed him to balance. Checking around himself one more time to be sure that no one was about to intrude on him, he looked in.

At first, all was dark, and he found his eye wasn't at all level with the hole. He lowered himself ever so slightly, and a soft light met his eyes, and he knew instinctively the light he saw would be coming through the large window which faced toward the front of the house and the driveway there.

He saw nothing, though he leaned both left and right. The angle was of course too acute to see anything other than what lie directly in front of the hole, and seemingly nothing stood between that and the light at the far side of the room.

Frustrated, he began to shift, ready to lift himself when he heard it.

"Fitzgerald."

His blood ran cold, and he froze. The voice had come from inside of the room and seemingly close by as if only whispered from the other side of the door.

He was caught before the keyhole, and a black shadow passed quickly before the door. There was someone in there.

His fear was overwhelming, and despite willing himself to move, he could not. It was only when the door handle moved by his nose and rattled up and down that he fell backwards onto the floor.

The door handle continued to rattle, and he heard the voice, only louder this time repeat his name. The very sound of it seemed to tear at his ears. The tone of the harsh voice felt scratched, like nails drawn down a chalkboard, grating and yet somehow old and feeble. He sidled backwards as best as he could, expecting any second for the handle to come down and the door to burst open.

All at once, the handle ceased moving.

Fitzgerald's heart was galloping, and he could not register what was going on. He continued to crawl backwards until he felt he had enough distance between him and the door. He leaned forward and came up onto his knees. This time though he did not feel the pain in his left leg.

Fitzgerald blinked hard. The pulse that seemed to beat behind his eyes was still racing, as was his heart. But the terror he had felt was abating now as understanding returned in its place, someone was in there alright, someone who had wanted to play a cruel joke on him.

He picked himself up and looked around himself, to be sure that no one had seen his folly. He frowned heavily and wondered who might seek to play such a harsh trick on him. He did not know anyone in the household, but who else could it be but the night nurse? Surely there could be no one else, as Hodgson had described the meagre nature of the staff and the nature of the on-going care for her master. But what of the dry, cracked voice that had spoken to him through the keyhole? Well, surely that had been put on, to frighten him.

Angry and embarrassed, he pulled his robes straight and walked off to the front of the house. Using the rationale that he had been a victim to a nasty, childish prank, wishing as well that some small accident would befall whoever had played it upon him for their juvenile behaviour.

CHAPTER 9

Tuesday, 8th November 2016.

Tuesday morning dawned wet and miserable. The grey veil that hung over the Thoby Estate that morning seemed to reflect Fitzgerald's mood, as he had suffered a difficult night's sleep. His dark dream had found him once more before the mysterious door of the upper west wing. Only this time, as he leaned in closer to the keyhole to observe what was within; some sharp needle had been rammed forcibly through the hole, piercing his eye and inexplicably robbing him of his sight in both eyes. And as he fell to the floor, he was in darkness as the door handle rattled above him, only this time the door had begun to creak slowly open; the chill voice whispering his name all the time it crept closer and closer.

To escape such thoughts, he had gone to the bathroom, where he splashed ice-cold water over his face. It was at once reinvigorating and succeeded in dispelling the terrible nightmare which now retreated below the surface of his mind.

No sooner had his thoughts turned to the day's business when he was interrupted by the shrill ring of the telephone within the living room of the apartment. Grabbing a towel, he had walked quickly through to the main room where he caught the phone on its third ring. He was met with the sound of a soft feminine voice with a hint of an Irish accent.

"Father Fitzgerald?"

"Yes?"

"Father, this is Keira Morgan. I am one of the staff nurses here with Mr McArthur. I understand you were expecting my call. I hope I didn't wake you?"

"No, no Keira, I am glad you rung, I was hoping to make your acquaintance soon."

"Well Father, I had word from Melissa this morning as she handed over; Mr McArthur left instruction through the night that he would like to see you this morning. As such, she has lowered Mr McArthur's morphine intake in line with his instructions, so that he might better be able to talk to you as soon as possible. I should warn you that the window is likely only to be a small one for his pain threshold is limited and I will have to take steps to make him comfortable when we reach an unbearable level."

Melissa? So, she's the one who likes to play games, huh?

His anger, which stemmed wholly from embarrassment was quick to surface as he heard the name of the night nurse. He was surprised though that his voice didn't betray him and give away his feelings as he responded.

"Oh, certainly. Should I come straight over?"

"Tend to yourself first Father. Mr McArthur is still asleep, and I believe we have a two-hour window until I need to increase his dosage. The morphine takes very quickly and can play games with the mind. He wants to be himself when he does speak."

"Of course Keira. Shall I come directly over when I am done?"

"Yes Father, you understand Mr McArthur's rooms are opposite your own? The layout on the top floor is almost identical, and I am sure you will have no problems finding us."

No problem at all.

"Thank you, Keira, I will see you shortly." He replaced the receiver.

So, at last, he was to meet Robert McArthur. The brief conversation with the nurse had reinforced the reasons behind his stay at Thoby Hall, and for the need for him to be at McArthur's beck and call. The old man was in a very bad way and these windows of opportunity, when they could wean him off his pain medication, would likely be few and far between. He sighed as he remembered the conversation he had shared with the solicitor, Harvey, knowing that he had in fact been told of such things already, but in his anger and distrust for the man, he had been loath to hear such things.

That said, the nature of the agreement between McArthur and the Church still didn't sit right with him, and he questioned the need to be contractually bound to remain. After all, a sick man required his help, and he was certain he would have given such help of his own free will on his understanding of the full circumstances as he now knew them. But with a prize such as the Estate itself, such a decision had been removed from the equation by the Church and his bishop.

Shaking his head, he departed back toward the bathroom and made himself ready.

And so he left the apartment and began to follow the familiar route down to the main house. As he made the top of the carved stairway, he looked onward and saw that the hallway before him still stretched further down the first floor of the east wing, and he knew he still had plenty more exploring of this great house to do. As it was though, the familiar way was the best way and not realising it, he subconsciously steered his hand wide of the serpent bannister and instead ran his hand on the runner of the heavenly side.

He passed by the kitchen door and the only other recognisable room to him on route, that being Harvey's office. Soon he came back to the grand entrance hall and just as he elected to replicate his route of the previous evening, he saw a figure on the first-floor balcony.

Quite clearly, this was Keira, the nurse with whom he had only recently spoken to on the telephone. She was perhaps only in her mid to late thirties and had striking red hair which was tied neatly back into a ponytail underneath her nurse's cap. She stood, perhaps 5' 10" to his 6' 0".

Her uniform he could see was perhaps more traditional, being a white tunic and trousers instead of the more modern scrubs that might be seen in a hospital.

Keira had made the ground floor and crossed the marble floor to meet him, extending a hand of welcome.

"Father. We just spoke, I'm Keira."

"Good morning, Keira," he replied, accepting her hand and at once met her piercing green eyes which held his own without blinking. He quickly felt flustered and averted his gaze from hers as he scrambled to find his words. "Er, Mr McArthur, is he?…" He managed weakly.

She gave him a knowing smile which suggested she had met similar reactions in the past, but that did not make him feel any less awkward, and he cursed himself for his childlike response. Keira exuded natural beauty and grace, and though at close quarters he saw she wore no makeup, she was none the less a beautiful woman.

He had known and met many young women from his work and from his time before the seminary, but he had never in his time in the Church acted in such a way, and he could not deny that the feeling that had washed over him was desire.

"Mr McArthur is awake, dozing in and out, but that is to be expected given his age and the effects of the drugs on his system. He is very much looking forward to meeting you, Father." Her Irish accent was soft, and he guessed from the Republic rather than the harsher tone of the north.

"Very good," Fitzgerald said and went to follow her as she climbed the stairs again, his eyes fixed firmly on the back of her head as he did so. "You're from Ireland I can hear Keira?"

"Yes, Father, you've got a keen ear. Dublin as a lass, but my family moved over to Liverpool when I was only 12. I preferred the big lights of London when I was old enough, but I guess there is more than enough of an Irish lilt to give me away still." She laughed softly.

They had made the first-floor balcony now, and he was able to look down at the entrance hall below and the expansive marble floor, and there below was the same pentacle shape that he had observed when first passing the threshold of the doorway.

It had been Harvey who had suggested to him that such symbols were apparent all over the house, but this surely was far and away the biggest example he might see, for the floor below was perhaps the size of a basketball court, yet it was the ornate pattern of marble near

77

the entrance that drew the eye. The black marble in stark contrast against the white of the rest of the floor.

He found that he had stopped to take the sight in for Keira had also halted to look back to him.

"It's fantastic, isn't it, Father? What would that be now, a pentagram? Isn't that a pagan symbol?"

He turned to look at her and saw the same wry smile on her face. Was she teasing him? Knowing such a thing might be at odds with his religion?

"Maybe so, Keira. Many still use such symbols as an amulet or spell against evil spirits. I heard tell that the house is abundant with such as this. Left over from prior inhabitants."

The nurse nodded. "Yes, Father. Mr McArthur, when he has been well enough, has told me of such things. A fascinating history."

"The truth is though that the pentagram has roots in many other cultures and religions, including both Judaism and Christianity."

"Oh?" Keira replied, a look of curiosity upon her face.

Fitzgerald smiled, happy to impart some small part of his knowledge to her and channel his inner Robert Langdon.

"Indeed. Did you know that the Star of Bethlehem that led the three wise men to the manger was believed to be shaped as a pentagram?"

"I did not."

"What's more, early Christians of the middle ages used the pentagram as a symbol for Christ's five wounds, which were formed upon the cross. They believed the pentagram a protective amulet, and it was the primary symbol of Christianity back then, even more, common than the cross."

"I had no idea…that is to say my Sunday School teachings are some way behind me now." Came Keira's reply.

Fitzgerald laughed and was quickly overcome with the same surge of desire for Keira, as he saw the corner of her lips quiver and slowly break into a smile. This time though it was she who broke eye contact, tucking some stray red hairs back under her cap as she did so.

Fitzgerald felt himself begin to blush, feeling that he had become all too familiar with this nurse Keira in too short a time. He was grateful to her as she suggested they move on toward McArthur's chambers.

As she walked away, he paused a moment longer, taking in the view of the black marble below him. Despite what he had said to her, he still had his doubts regarding the placement of the symbol in a place such as this. There had been truth in his words to the nurse, but the pentagram had long been disassociated from its Christian heritage.

Now instead entirely adopted by pagans, witchcraft and Satanists and it was this that caused him greater concern, as from this fresh perspective of the first-floor balcony, the image of the pentagram below might now be seen as inverted, that is upside down. The topmost point of the star pointing toward him. And what he would not share with Keira was that such a symbol depicted as he now perceived it and with a goat's head at its centre was the official symbol of the Church of Satan.

Such a thing in a home as this was a disconcerting find and more, for it caused him to consider to what extent such beliefs were prevalent within the house. Keira's sly smile had suggested she understood as much and sought to tease him with it. He sighed and left the view of the symbol behind him. He would choose to believe, that pagan or not the real intent and design of the shape was to greet visitors into the Hall and not to be interpreted from behind and above as had been his view from up on the balcony.

Now walking on the west wing of the house they came to the large anteroom, which Fitzgerald himself had discovered in his late-night exploration. As it was before, the corridor opened to the right-hand side, and directly to his left were the double doors where he had his embarrassing episode. Curiously though a placard was now stood just before the door.

He could read the sign 'Construction Site' underneath a yellow triangle depicting a bold exclamation mark and underneath that 'Keep Out!'

Had he been right after all? Was there some kind of dangerous leak beyond that doorway?

Keira followed his gaze. "Oh, the library. That's closed I'm afraid Father, has been since I got here. The building work you might have seen outside is for the chimney stack above the room. I'm told it's unsafe, hence the lockdown."

He smiled as he recalled Hodgson and the telling off that she had given to the builders on the morning of his arrival.

His smile quickly dropped though as the image of Hodgson's unusual encounter resurfaced, coupled with the unsavoury incident of the previous night. The figure he had seen in the window looking down on Hodgson had been located beyond this door, and so too this nurse Melissa, who he had now convinced himself had been the one to frighten him.

The room, or library as Keira had described it, was quite clearly not so out of bounds.

They moved off, and Fitzgerald allowed the thought to fade from his mind, for now they were on route to the end of the corridor and McArthur's rooms. The name plaques on this side of the house were somewhat more regal, and he read 'King James Room' followed by 'Queen Victoria Room'. Here now they stood before the final door in the corridor. The layout had been exactly the opposite as the east wing, but the furnishings and portraits that had adorned the walls and floors were significantly more upmarket, making him wonder as he had done before if the rooms had ever met their illustrious namesakes.

Stepping through the door of the Queen Elizabeth Room, Fitzgerald soon saw that the layout was the same as his own rooms, though reversed, so that the study was to the outside of the house and the bathroom within. And if he stepped into the bedroom, he knew well that the room would have fantastic views of the garden, as did his own.

Keira bade him to sit down on a black leather armchair, and she took a place on the couch opposite, quickly crossing her legs and leaning forward to better converse with him.

"So, the ground rules Father."

"Go on." He had expected as much but thought perhaps Harvey might have shown himself or at least contacted him to give him such guidelines.

"Very simple. Our only purpose here is not the preservation of life in its more traditional sense. Only that I preserve that life as long as I am able, at the very least until Mr McArthur's business with yourself is done. As such, we have been given a certain degree of leeway of how that is achieved. Nothing unethical I can assure you, Father, but I can admit medications where I see fit that will allow me to accomplish that task. Mr McArthur also understands that the nursing staff have the final say in matters regarding his welfare. Where that relates to you Father, is that we may see fit to limit your visits and monitor them to some extent. I understand what you are here to accomplish, but I cannot allow Mr McArthur to overexert himself or get overexcited. Then, of course, there is the matter of his pain relief."

This was all pretty much to be expected, and Fitzgerald sat there half expecting that there was more to come. But Keira now sat back in her chair and allowed her crossed legs to unfold. He only just caught himself as he followed them as they did so. Instead, his eyes met hers, and the brilliant green seemed to glisten as her pupils dilated.

He gulped involuntarily and knew this woman was having a profound effect upon him, and he was having thoughts that had very much lain dormant since before his time at the seminary. His celibacy to date had not in any way proved difficult, but here was temptation in the form of Nurse Keira Morgan.

"That's it, Keira? Are there no rules as to the nature of what we can and cannot speak of?" He managed so as to keep the conversation.

She looked puzzled. "Father? I'm sorry, that is not a matter for me. I thought perhaps Frederick might have notified you of such." Fitzgerald did not like the way she addressed the lawyer by his first name with such familiarity.

"I can't speculate as to what might be said Father, and can't rightly forbid or prevent his confession. I only ask that if matters become difficult that you allow us to do our work and allow Mr McArthur any necessary breaks."

"Of course. But that leads me to ask how pressed for time we are? It is not my wish to rush him, but I also understand his desire, to be frank, and open. What time will I be allowed?"

"Well, as for his life expectancy, I cannot say. He is weak, you see, and the constant tampering with his medication cannot help. If I believe him strong enough, I think we can schedule two visits a day. As for how long each of those might be, is largely up to him and what he can bear. You understand, don't you that once the morphine is administered it will be some hours before he is rested and lucid enough to begin again?"

Fitzgerald nodded. The rules and expectations were straightforward for a man of McArthur's condition, and he knew that he had been given special dispensation to allow for even those two short windows a day. A hospital or nursing facility would no doubt refuse such access, but it was McArthur who was paying the bills here.

Keira stood, smoothing down her tunic as she did so. "I guess it is time. Are you ready Father?"

He stood also. At that moment, his nerves and anxiety rose to the fore. Again he swallowed involuntarily and could only manage a nod in his response.

"You'll give me a minute then? Let me see if he is awake."

Without waiting for an answer, she approached the bedroom door and opened it a crack, enough for her to lean her head through. He craned his neck but was afforded no view of what lay beyond and the way was quickly blocked as she opened the door a fraction more and squeezed her lithe frame through, shutting the door behind her. The sound of muffled voices droned through the door and seemed to hum in his ears.

Quickly though, the door reopened wide and Keira stood to the side holding it open with one hand and beckoning him in with the other.

At last, here was Robert McArthur.

CHAPTER 10

Robert McArthur had a story to tell. A story that in all the long years of his life, he had kept to himself. Many had sought to glean this information from him; reporters, historian's, biographers, and no small amount of money had been offered to him along the years to share his tale.

Money had been of little sway to him though. On the initial receipt of his fortune all those long years ago, he could easily have counted himself among the top ten richest men within the United Kingdom.

And though the passage of years had been cruel and his fortune dwindled; his Estate all but disappeared, he would laugh to himself as the occasional correspondence would still arrive asking him to give his story. But all such attempts had been futile. He would only tell this once and only to one man, and that time would be now as his time was now growing short. For Robert McArthur had been diagnosed with lung cancer some two years previously, and despite the best treatments of experimental drugs and chemotherapy that money could buy, he knew he was nearing his end. And because of this, he would finally impart his confession.

He lay now, in his expansive bedroom that resembled more a hospital room and slowly rose to the surface from a drug-induced slumber. Slowly he raised his right arm and beheld the numerous wires that protruded from a small bandage by his elbow, and traced the path from the clip upon his finger that wove to a small monitor that brought a tiny metallic beep to his ear with each beat of his heart.

He cursed himself for the state that he had been brought to. He, once one of the most powerful men in Britain. He, who had been a captain of industry and caused influential men to tremble in his wake, reduced to this. This pitiful mess.

But with time now being short, he would finally impart the words that he had shielded so carefully over many long years, of how he, a simple servant and butler had made his fortune.

Made his fortune? No, that wasn't fair. Such a thing suggested years of hard work or perhaps some innovation on his part when the truth was much darker.

Would his story be believed? He couldn't be sure. At 92 years of age, he knew he was already seen as an eccentric, delusional old man that had inherited his previous master's insanity as well as his money. For he had served as butler and only confidant to a man who had really held the power, Sir Thomas Searle.

He allowed his arm to fall back to his side and closed his eyes, to capture an image in his mind of his former employer, only to find that he could not. It didn't matter anyway. He knew the fate of Searle very well, and he fully intended to absolve himself of his own sins so that he would not follow suit.

McArthur truly recanted his sins, rather, his sin. For looking back at the trivial pursuit of lust and power that had been his life, did not hold sway in his mind. He would face his God as the man he was, for better or worse, with the catalogue of his life apparent for his maker to see and judge. All but for this one thing, as he needed this absolution, this pardon of his one major crime against another.

He had known this day was coming for some years, and so in preparation had spoken with the wretched drunk, Father Shilling. That had been a mistake. The man's alcoholism had reached a plateau at that time, and though it had slowly receded in the last year or so, he could not leave his spiritual prosperity in such lamentable hands. No, change was needed and so with the aid of the solicitor Harvey, they had reached out to the diocese and Bishop Burrows, the agreement made so as the Catholic Church would be the sole beneficiary in his last will and testament.

And so now he was ready to meet with this Father Iain Fitzgerald. The name did not matter and nor did the man. He would be someone malleable and convenient, and that was all that counted.

No, that's not right, what matters is that my confession is heard and forgiveness is given, no matter the cost.

Yes, that was all. He would soon recant his tale, and he would be absolved by the young priest in exchange for his signature and the Estate of which he had called home for nigh on 60 years. It was a small price to pay in the face of eternal damnation.

His train of thought was interrupted as from somewhere beyond the closed door of his chamber he heard the sound of movement and soft voices.

So, he is here.

McArthur allowed his eyes to close, so as to take in the sounds from the lounge room adjoining. Turning his head, he looked toward the doorway where the young priest would soon enter. In doing so, it gave him some small respite from the glare of the many strip lights that adorned the ceiling and walls of the room in which he lay. Such was their brightness; they made the painted white walls almost shine.

The white glare was now a constant in his life which he had come to loathe in waking but found comfort in during sleep. For there were dark places in the bottomless pit of unconsciousness that was sleep or coma, where his demons could find him. And should his confused mind wander into such dark dreams, he knew the light provided an anchor and a respite even during his deepest fall into slumber.

But it had not only been when he had taken to his bed with illness that had he bathed in such an unnatural glow. The real truth of it was that he had found such relief in the light for some years, ever since the night of his former masters passing and though the nurse's had not known it, he had slept in conditions much the same as this for decades.

Can it be that long? He mused.

There had been a time when he had the solace and company of his three wives as bed companions when night terrors had been soothed away with the soft caress of a hand and some gentle words. But the women were now gone, and he was alone; had been for many years now and though he had taken some lovers and in later life the use of escort services, these had never promoted any respite for his broken nights as his former spouses had provided.

And so he had turned to the light, exactly as his master Thomas Searle had done before him, so as to spare him the dread of simply closing his eyes to rest, lest he fall into darkness.

It had not been as simple as the placement of a bed lamp or night light switched on to placate his terror, no. For there were things that lurked at the edge of one's vision, wasn't there? There in the blind spots and shadows that darted away when you searched for them, leaving your heart to pound and fear to strangle you in its icy unforgiving grip. Such things had to be banished, and it was Thomas Searle before him who had found the method for how to accomplish this.

For at Searle's request the vast mansion in which he now dwelt was bathed in a never faltering torrent of light, and more, for at the coming of darkness there were the massive spotlights within the grounds, the light they cast engineered to dispel any shadow from the towering structure of the great home.

McArthur, in his day, had believed Thomas Searle to have lost his mind; such had been the man's manic fervour to the completion of the project. Ultimately though, he too would go on to share his masters fear of the dark. And so he would also live in a house of almost perpetual light and not know real darkness other than sleep in the years since his last wife had left him.

Such thoughts had been at the forefront of his mind in the last few days as he picked the bones of his memories and catalogued them in preparation to receive the young priest.

His thoughts were quickly disrupted, and his attention was diverted once more back to the present as the bedroom door opened and his nurse Keira stepped through.

Keira was handsome in her own way, but his taste had always been for the younger woman, something which his fortune had both helped and hindered. For though he had found love with Nancy his first and Elizabeth his second wife, the third, had all but broken

84

the bank with her divorce settlement. Of his two nurses, Melissa, an attractive 29-year-old was by far his favourite. But there was something deeper to this woman Keira, something he could not quite put his finger on, for at times he would see a sadness, deep-rooted, seeming to reach to her core that almost made him want to nurse and comfort her. But such moments were broken the moment he would touch upon the subject; a broad smile breaking upon her face with assurances that she was fine, making him believe he had only imagined such sorrow within her.

"Mr McArthur Sir, how are you faring?"

"As well as I can be. He is here?" He answered her.

"He is."

"Then please show him through."

Closing his eyes once more, he allowed the sound of the priest's footsteps to announce his arrival.

"Please, Father, take a seat." He said, opening his eyes and taking in the man for the first time.

Immediately, he could see that Fitzgerald would be everything that Liam Shilling was not. Where Shilling was old and infirm, Fitzgerald was young and athletic. Where Shilling was arrogant and stubborn, this priest would be docile and subservient and all it took to know that was to look into his eyes, where he could easily see the trace of nervousness and doubt. That was good. He would undoubtedly be troubled with the direction given to him from his bishop and so would be the puppet that he required.

A smile began to form but was quickly cut off as a series of racking coughs burst from his lungs, leaving him to feel as many times before, that a fire had been set there.

The young priest rushed quickly to his side so as to ease him into a more comfortable position. Eventually, the fit subsided, and the priest passed him a handkerchief, produced from his pocket.

He lay there for some minutes as the fire within him slowly quelled, all the time measuring the priest.

"I am sorry, Father," he managed at last. "This meeting has been long in the planning, but it seems my strength deserts me when I need it the most."

He gazed deep into the eyes of the priest and now saw there both strength and compassion.

"There is no apology necessary, Mr McArthur. I understand you have braved much to make this meeting a possibility. But if it all becomes too much…"

"I fear this is as well as you will ever find me, Father, so we must hasten. I will bear what I can so that we may talk."

"I understand, but you have only to let me know, and I will fetch you your nurse."

McArthur nodded his understanding. The priest would have been briefed along those lines by both Keira and Harvey. He would be damned though, if he would let his pain get the better of him.

"Forgive me, Father, it has been many years since my last confession. There is much that I would share with you, and I am not long for this world."

Father Fitzgerald returned his gaze, looking long into the brown eyes of the old man. Slowly he reached out and took his hand.

"Robert, I will hear your confession. Here in the sight of God, you will be forgiven your sins if your heart is truly repentant."

"Yes Father, oh you have no idea! I am repentant, and I must be absolved. I have worked strongly in the Lord's name and service. This money that came to me did so with a heavy price. But I have used it in the Lord's name, don't you see? I have tried to make penance for what I have done."

"I understand that you have truly been a great benefactor to the church here in Ashmarsh. A life led as a Samaritan. Your legacy for the town is a great one, I am sure."

"Yes, yes of course. Please don't find to placate me with such niceties. This is beyond legacy, you understand?"

A nod in reply.

"Tell me, Father, what do you know of Thomas Searle?"

The priest hesitated for a moment. "Thomas Searle?" he finally returned. "Very little, I'm afraid, did you not once act on his staff in some capacity?"

That was good, and it would suffice that the priest knew little of his previous master. The information he imparted would be both fresh and honest; Fitzgerald would not be sullied by any prejudice or opinion garnered elsewhere.

"To understand my confession, Father, you must understand him as well, for ours was a complicated relationship that went beyond that of master and servant. You would likely have guessed as much, given how his fortune was bequeathed to one such as me. That is for later though. For now, you need only know that Searle was a war hero turned industrialist. And that through recession, his wealth and power grew. A powerful man that had the ear of the Prime Minister should he need it."

McArthur watched as Fitzgerald nodded his understanding before delivering his verdict.

"That is what he would have us believe, Father. But there was something hidden beneath the surface, something darker that no one saw, no one but me."

He continued. "You may care to seek further information of course, and I'll not doubt you'll come up short. You see, the man was an enigma, and in that, as in other areas, you will find parallels with myself."

"Certainly in regard to your war records, I'll wager? I took the liberty of some research on your background. You are a war hero in your own right I see." Fitzgerald replied.

"Yes, yes" McArthur spat back at him as if impatient. "Very diplomatic, you tread very carefully, Father, but there is no need. Do not think that you will lose any favour with me. There is no need for soft words or compliments."

"I am sorry, I only meant…"

McArthur waved his hand to negate the apology. "Be as true to me as I will to you, Father. That is all that I ask. You should not make your opinion based on your research. Instead, reserve such judgement until I have told my tale to you."

"As for Searle, you should understand a half-truth. Yes, he was the powerful, rich man you would believe. It is in the telling of how he made and kept such riches and power that defines him though. I believed him a clever man, and many of the rumours of his life were true, but in ways in which you could not imagine or believe. He had ties with the criminal underworld it is true. He bought judges and persons of influence, rigged elections and should someone get in his way? I'll leave that to your imagination, for it plagues my own to think upon it. I said Searle was a clever man? I thought so too. But it was clear he left himself too open. On more than one occasion, the authorities came after him, but always he managed to slip through their hands. I had great respect for him for that reason. I believed him smart, one step ahead of the game. But that wasn't the truth at all; he was sloppy and carefree; it was as if he wanted to be found out for the things he had done. But no one got close. I couldn't understand it until the end, but now I do, you see Searle had someone watching over him. Covering his back, making sure that everything he touched turned to gold. And so it was, until the end."

McArthur lapsed into silence and closed his eyes for they felt heavy now. His mind felt so alive, but his body so tired. He had so much to say and so little time. This is not how he wished it to be. Everything should be said, nothing left out. But he was beginning to get tired, and he feared that should unconsciousness take him now, then it might take him forever. And so he forced his eyes open and began.

"I guess I should start from when I met him. I came into his service in 1954."

CHAPTER 11

Tuesday, 19th January 1954. 9:00 am.

Thoby Hall.

Robert swept the Austin Somerset slowly through the wide expansive gates of the Thoby Hall Estate. The car was on loan from his wife's father, who had been only too pleased to lend out his prized possession, on hearing that his son-in-law was to meet a man of great prominence such as Sir Thomas Searle. The tyres crackled on the gravelled driveway, and though the day was chilly, McArthur couldn't help be impressed by the magnificent hedgerows that bordered the long road.

It had been a whirlwind couple of days, that had led him to taking this long drive down from London in the hope of at last finding gainful employment. The conversation he had held with his former commanding officer, William Chambers, only two days previously still echoed through his mind. He had fallen on his luck of late, and it had been difficult to find work in post-war London. But having visited Chambers for drinks with his wife Nancy, it had been the Captain who had suggested the opening. He remembered the conversation vividly.

"Robert I do know of something going if you have a mind for hard work?"

They had retired to the Captain's parlour with drinks after dinner, leaving the wives so that they might talk alone. He remembered baulking at that comment, a mind for hard work indeed! How could his integrity be questioned? Especially after what the two of them had been through in Normandy together. But he would not allow himself to rise to such criticism. This after all was the very reason he was here. Hard times called for hard answers, and he regretted imposing on an old friend in such a way. But handicapped as he was with shrapnel wounds to his left leg he had found work difficult to come by. And the Captain was by far the most influential man he knew.

"Sir, of course I have such a mind. I find myself in difficult circumstances. Nancy is some six months pregnant now, and I must find work so that I might bring my child into the world with some dignity."

"Oh Robert, it was not meant as a criticism. I have known you for some 15 years or so now. I would not question you. I know that you have a mind and back for hard work. No, it was as a warning that I asked, as I have something in mind that might just be the very ticket for you."

Robert arched his eyebrow inquisitively, inviting the Captain to continue.

"You've heard of Sir Thomas Searle? Well, there is a vacancy available within his staff. That of butler as it happens. The reason I asked of you is that Searle is one of the most mean-spirited old bastards I have ever had the misfortune to encounter. I would not suggest such a thing ordinarily, as I would not send you to the lion's den without need. But you need this, yes?"

"Yes William, it pains me to speak of it but I have become desperate. We barely have enough to feed and house ourselves. A baby? My god man I don't know what I would do should this be allowed to go on without check."

Chambers nodded as if to himself and placed himself behind his large oak desk and withdrew a cigarette from the drawer within, offering the pack to Robert.

"Quiet now, Robert, Joyce doesn't approve."

McArthur smiled back and reached over and drew a cigarette from the pack of Chesterfields. Chambers lit his and reaching over offered the lit match for McArthur to draw on.

Clouding the air with white plumes of smoke, Chambers continued.

"I'll make the arrangements then Robert, of course I will. I just wish you would have come to me sooner, damn your pride. I will warn you though that Searle has gone through seven different people in the last three years alone. He is brutish, arrogant and rude. Of those seven, four walked from his service because they could take no more. The other three were fired. It will take an incredible effort of will for you to succeed there, Robert. But damn it all, I think the old bastard might just take to you."

The meeting with Chambers had quickly been followed by an interview with Searle's solicitor Gregory Harvey; he too had been quick to describe Searle as 'difficult' and McArthur could be left in no doubt as to the challenge this final meeting represented. To that end, he felt as prepared as he could ever be, as he needed this job so badly and was willing to accommodate whatever problems a man like Searle might throw at him.

As he approached the large building, he noted a large statue situated in front of the regal house, and slowly he followed the drive in a loop around the magnificent effigy, coming to a stop before the porch. He stepped out and into the cold, drab wind and pulled his jacket tight around himself. Despite the cold, he took a moment to take in the house and impressive stonework of the statue behind him.

The house itself was vast. He craned his neck from the tight angle and could just see beyond the third-floor windows to the bell tower that took prominence over the red-bricked house. He noted that the gravel driveway split from the loop of the statue and disappeared behind the house, where he guessed the garages must be kept.

Despite the inclement weather and the bite of the cold, he could not help feeling anything but awestruck by the magnificent home.

A quick glance at his watch told him that he was some thirty minutes early. He wanted to impress, as he was to meet the solicitor before going in. His approach to the house told him that no other car was on show and so he decided he might drive round to the side of the house and investigate further. Perhaps he would find Mr Harvey at the garage?

He was about to get into his car when his eyes again fell upon the statue that stood before the great house. He looked toward the building for any sign of life but at 09:00 am the house was both still and quiet. The lawn where the statue lay was pristine, and he was wary of offending his host. But rather than skirt the expansive circular drive, he casually stepped onto the lawn to approach the statue as easily as he could.

On coming up the driveway, it had seemed as ordinary as any, a memorial cast to the fallen men of the Great War he had presumed. He knew that Searle had served with the Newfoundland Regiment on the Western Front on that fateful day of the 1st July 1916, during the Battle of the Somme.

It had been the solicitor Harvey who had referred to Searle's war record during his initial interview and suggested the two might share their military histories in common. And so he had done his research, if there was any information that could get him across the finishing line in the job interview stakes, he was keen to pursue it.

And moving now to the front, he found the statue to be exactly as he had presumed. For here was the form of a British soldier, seemingly advancing on his enemy, rifle and bayonet before him, a battle cry on his lips. A single plate lay at the base of the cold-chiselled stone which simply read. Sir Thomas Searle, VC.

McArthur looked up into the battle-hardened face of the Tommy and felt a shiver run down him in spite of the cold that he already felt, for this statue was not in keeping with similar memorials that he had seen which had projected the Tommy as sad and forlorn at the loss and brutality of the war. This one seemed to exude hatred and yes, a blood lust.

The featureless eyes seemed to burn down upon him with such hostility and contempt, and on closing his own eyes, he felt that he could imagine the raw blood-curdling cry that the soldier seemed to exude. His eyes again fell to the plate, reading the name of the soldier depicted once more. It was not a memorial for the fallen as he had initially assumed, but more a monument to a man. That man being Sir Thomas Searle.

McArthur was now well aware of Searle's heroics and his award of the Victoria Cross for gallantry, but this seemed out of keeping somehow. He traced his footsteps back across the lawn, trying to shake the ill-feeling from his bones. The statue had exuded some kind of power over him and stirred feelings which he had long since tried to bury since the fall of his own war.

As he stepped back to his car; one of the great oak doors swung wide and trotting down the steps to meet him was Harvey, with a broad welcoming smile on his face.

"Robert, Robert, excellent. I see you have seen Mr Searle's statue. Magnificent, isn't it?" The lawyer began, "a gift you know; from Willaby Scott. A rare piece indeed."

McArthur didn't know who Willaby Scott might be and so could not find the words that would adequately satisfy the eager solicitor and so he began. "Ah, yes, but the house. Magnificent, 1700's I would guess?"

The lawyer did not seem to notice his manoeuvre from the statue and seemed happy to continue in Robert's direction.

"Yes, 1706, in fact. You do have a good eye, Robert. Field Marshal Arthur Wellesley the first Duke of Wellington himself was resident here for some time when he became Prime Minister in 1828. Did you know that? Apparently, he found Downing Street too small and his own house required extensive renovations. Three months in all but the Whigs soon forced his hand, forcing him back to London."

"It is a magnificent property; Mr Searle is a very fortunate man."

"Absolutely, one hundred acres of prime Eastland Estate? I should say so! Robert, may I trouble you to move your vehicle? Mr Searle is very particular regarding his property, just follow the path round. I'll find you at the side door."

Side door? Robert mused to himself. *Servant's entrance more like.*

He nodded his agreement to another wide smile from Harvey and settled back behind the wheel of the Austin. Nancy's father, George, would be crestfallen to hear that his pride and joy was not deemed suitable for such a grand landscape. McArthur felt his anger rise at the thought. He had only been here for a matter of moments, and thus far he had felt unease at the statue and now even though it was politely done he was reduced to the level of some working-class skivvy. He felt very small.

He put the car into gear and circumvented the rest of the circular drive, following the track around to the side of the house.

Harvey it seemed had made his way back through the house as by the time the little Austin had found its way round he was standing waiting at a small side door, indicating to Robert that he should follow the fork in the driveway to the right rather than straight on to the back of the house. He approached the end of a large hedgerow and saw the road disappear around it. Thereafter he saw a small building which was neatly tucked away from view, at least from the front of the house.

The garage was open plan and had three carports, one of which contained a black Jaguar Mark V Coupe with whitewall tyres and a white canvas roof.

McArthur was suitably impressed. The car probably belonged to Harvey, and he wondered, despite the impressive vehicle, if it to was not good enough for the showpiece that was the front of the stately home.

"Yours?" McArthur enquired as he alighted from his own vehicle. "Very nice."

Harvey seemed taken aback by the compliment. "Really? oh, thank you. It does me fine." He was straight to business. "Well Robert, Mr Searle is waiting. Just some advice for you. Please address him with his proper title. Do not speak unless spoken to. Just a formality you understand for a man of his position. But be mindful, he does.....well let's just say that he is very forward with his observations? Don't take it personally mind; it's just his way. He'll want to test you out some. See if you're of the right stuff and all."

Despite his disappointments thus far, this was certainly to be expected. Although a self-made man, Searle had amassed a personal fortune and was rumoured to have been on the Christmas card list of the former King, George VI and the new Queen, Elizabeth II. That he should be expected to behave to such a high level of decorum was no surprise. But he wondered and not for the last time, would he be up to it?

Harvey led the way toward the side door of the house and McArthur wasn't surprised to be led into the kitchen. The room was vast, and he could see a range of three stoves against the wall and a dumb waiter that led to rooms somewhere above and perhaps below. The pantries were all of oak, and as he made his way to the door, he fancied, he saw what was probably a walk-in freezer. It was certain that he would be spending a great deal of time in this room should things go well.

From the kitchen, Harvey led him down a narrow corridor that seemed to be taking him back toward the front of the house. And so it did, for through one more door, they entered the expansive lobby of the home where he immediately observed two grand stairways that swept up and around from each side of the room, meeting at a balcony above. Here on the ground floor though, he found himself looking at several portraits that hung on the two walls that ran alongside the staircases.

There directly in front of him was the large double door that was the front entrance. Harvey walked across the lobby, walking to the large door on the far side. He knocked once and waited, several seconds passed before a gruff voice replied.

"Come."

Harvey looked back at McArthur and extended his index finger showing McArthur that he required him to wait here for the moment. He then opened the door, went inside and closed it behind him.

McArthur took the time to admire the expansive room. It was carpeted with a thick plush rug that nearly touched all four walls such was its size. McArthur did not know such niceties but assumed it was Persian, after all, that was what the rich craved wasn't it? The exotic and the expensive.

He traced his eyes across the portraits, all of which depicted a different male in some regal-like pose.

McArthur could honestly say that he didn't recognise any of these men and assumed that they must be former owners of the house, Lord this or Lord that. Slowly he swung his attention to one final portrait that sat high on the wall between the two staircases, this portrait seemed to dwarf all others, and he was shocked to see that this portrait depicted Sir Thomas Searle.

Hadn't Harvey just stated that Wellington himself had resided here? A quick scan of the remaining portraits confirmed what he already knew. There was no portrait of the former Prime Minister and hero of Waterloo.

McArthur gazed up at the portrait and was met with dark menacing eyes. This was in stark contrast with the other portraits, that seemed almost placid and languid in their depiction of the men recreated. But this other portrait seemed to exude strength and doubly so from its position of prominence over the lobby and other portraits. McArthur was somewhat unnerved by this; that Searle wanted to show dominance over the room and other men depicted. It seemed like a show of strength as the viewer had to look up to the expansive canvas.

And of Wellington? Well, McArthur could only assume that any portrait, had it ever existed, had been removed at the owners' behest, as even Searle could not claim prominence over such a great man. Looking up now at the picture, an involuntary lump came to his throat. The painting, as well as the statue, had both served to exude a power over him and presumably any other visitor that came. The message was clear. Searle was Lord and Master over this manor.

He was interrupted from his reverie by the sound of the lounge door opening and turned to see Harvey beckoning him toward the door. Again he felt oddly nervous. He had served in combat in the fields of France and onto Normandy where he had sustained his injury. He considered himself tough-willed and graceful under pressure. He had held his own when men of greater years and supposed stronger character had baulked in the face of enemy fire. He feared no man. And so this feeling of dread that had settled over him had unnerved him somewhat. Maybe it was just the atmosphere in the place? The statue? The painting? All seemed set to put a man at unease, but that wasn't entirely it was it?

But it was too late for such thoughts for he came to the door and found the ample lounge beyond. His eyes were immediately drawn to the vast hearth and fire that burned brightly within. And above, the mounted head of a tiger. The feeling of disquiet grew as he stepped further into the room. Comfortable looking sofas backed onto every wall, but it was a solitary high-backed chair in red leather that his eyes were now drawn to as he could see an arm resting on the side with cigarette blazing.

Searle.

Harvey interrupted the quiet. "Mr McArthur for you, Sir." McArthur turned his neck and could see Harvey still standing by the door, the smile gone from his face. Harvey gave him a quick nod and backed out of the room drawing the double doors behind him. McArthur was alone, and he swallowed hard.

Remembering the advice given by Harvey, he decided to wait until he was spoken to. And so he stood there and stood there some more. He realised then that the room was almost unbearably hot; such was the blaze that was the only source of light within the room. For though it were a little after 09:00 am, all the plush velvet curtains were still drawn. Sweat slowly trickled down his brow and the back of his neck. And he cursed himself for the thick winter coat that he still wore, for he had not had a chance to set it down.

The silence continued unabated, and he simply stood there, the only thing interrupting the quiet, the occasional crackle of the fire and rustle of Searle's sleeve as he lifted his cigarette to his mouth. McArthur was starting to feel embarrassed now for it seemed an eternity had slipped by in mere moments and still nothing had been said.

Don't speak unless spoken to. His mind repeated over and over.

Finally, Searle broke the silence startling McArthur somewhat. "Hmmm, McArthur is it?"

"Er, yes Sir," he replied to the back of the chair, almost tripping over his words.

"Harvey there seems to think that you would make an excellent addition to the staff. Is that so?"

"Yes sir, I believe so." McArthur replied.

"Well, how is it then McArthur that you are stood here before me, pitching yourself to work on my staff, when you show me no respect whatsoever?"

"Sir?" McArthur was bemused by the comment. What could he mean? Searle slowly lifted himself from his chair and turned to meet him. McArthur was shocked by what he saw.

Here before him was a man, a man supposedly of 57 years of age. Was this some kind of joke he thought to himself? Was he being tested again? For the man in front of him seemed to have come fresh from modelling the painting he had seen outside. This man seemed to be in his late thirties, no more. The hair on his head was jet black and slicked back in long flowing waves that settled on the nape of his collar. He had a light golden tan, with barely a trace of age or wrinkle that you would associate with a man in his fifties. He stood tall and rigid at 6ft and seemed muscular with it to. McArthur could hardly believe that this was Searle, some younger relative perhaps; a son? A younger brother? But he had to look no further than the eyes to find the truth. For here again burned that latent savagery that he had

94

beheld in the garden and the portrait outside. The eyes were of pure blue and seemed to flash at him, and he found himself looking away from that gaze as he felt himself wither before him.

Searle continued. "What are you an idiot, McArthur? I take the time from my busy schedule to see you and how do you repay me? With no respect, that's how. I suggest you leave." Searle then turned back and sat back in his chair.

McArthur was floundering. What could he have done? He had followed the instructions given by Harvey. Surely there wasn't anything that...Then it hit him.

"Sir, I do humbly beg your forgiveness. I am not yet familiar with the ways of etiquette that would be required to work on your staff. But I can assure you that I am a fast learner and will endeavour to work to the highest standard. Despite that, I am aware of simple tact, and I apologise for stepping onto your lawn this morning. It is just that I was caught by the magnificence of the statue there. I have also served his majesty in conflict and only wished to observe your memorial. I again apologise for any lack of regard on my part."

Searle remained quiet. And so McArthur pressed on. This would be the making or breaking of him. He needed this job so very badly and if he had to kiss up to this pretentious upper-class idiot to get it then so what? After all, what did he have to lose? And should Searle continue to be an arse? Well, then he'd get it, both barrels.

"It is my understanding, Sir that you fought with honour with the Newfoundland Regiment in the Somme. It is my privilege to make your acquaintance."

McArthur drew to a close, hoping that it would be enough. That he had inflated the man's ego enough to placate him. Searle was a man of power, and the statue and picture had served as signs to the man's own high regard for himself. By playing up to that, McArthur hoped that he could turn the situation around.

Finally, Searle lifted himself from his chair again and approached the fire, stooping to pick up a poker and prod the fire into life once more. He turned, and McArthur caught the red blaze of the coals in his eyes giving the man a demonic look.

"Hmmm, perhaps you are a man of honour after all McArthur? I can tell you that first impressions count for a lot with me, you know? And so imagine my thoughts when I see this cripple walking on my lawn? To say I was not best impressed would be an understatement."

Cripple? McArthur bit down on his tongue hard. It seemed that Searle would forgive his indiscretion but not without making him pay for it.

"I'd heard that you were lame of course McArthur and so I wanted to judge for myself your handicap. You think you're up to this job on that thing?" He said motioning to McArthur's left leg.

"Yes, Sir. I'm certainly not as quick as I used to be, but I have no problem getting around."

"Hmmm, well I'll be the judge of that." Came the quick reply.

"Well McArthur, despite my better instinct I'm going to allow this. This display this morning will not go unforgotten. I will expect exemplary service in return for my favour, hmmm? And should that leg get the better of you, I will have no qualms in dismissing you from my service. You're a very lucky man McArthur; it seems you have friends in the right places. It is for Captain Chambers that I will allow this, as he has vouched for you, and so should you fail it is he that you will have failed, not me. For I believe it is only a matter of time before you let yourself down. Now go on, get out. Harvey will fill you in on what needs doing."

And with that, Searle turned his interest back to the fire that certainly needed no more encouragement. McArthur stood there for a moment, his mind reeling, his anger coming to the fore. He slowly opened his mouth to retort. How dare this pompous upstart speak to him in such a way! But as quick as it came, his anger left him as a vision of his pregnant wife came to him. Sure it would feel good to let rip at him, to vent his frustration and anger but where would that get him? And so he turned heel and left the lounge leaving Searle to his fire.

CHAPTER 12

Tuesday, 8th November 2016.

Thoby Hall.

Another racking cough came to McArthur, and he was slow to catch the thin line of blood that spilt from his mouth. Fitzgerald had remained silent during the telling of his meeting with Searle. His story was yet only in its infancy, and he felt that by introducing Searle and his mannerism's that the priest might have a better understanding of their relationship.

"So you see Father, Searle was exactly as I'd been told. Rude, arrogant and self-serving. Of course, I wanted to tell him, but as I said, where would that have got me? I went to work for him almost right away. Nothing changed at first, he was as cutting and venomous with me as the day I met him. Nothing was ever good enough. Either I wasn't quick enough because of my leg. His breakfast wouldn't be right, or the car wouldn't be clean enough. You name it; it would be wrong. The job was as Harvey had said, but what I didn't realise was that Searle didn't have a great staff. There was only the maid, the gardener and myself. Of course, that meant I made all of his meals and was at his beck and call 24-7. It was hard, but it wasn't without its benefits. Nancy fell in love with the small house we had upon the grounds and the wage was excellent. With no outgoing bills, we were able to start saving and felt good that our child would have the best start that money could offer. And so it went on like that for a good while."

McArthur fell into silence as memories of Nancy washed over him. They had been so happy back then, despite the work for Searle he had still managed to be a happy attentive husband, and he had loved her so. In his weaker moments, he had dwelt on such matters with regret in his heart.

"It soon became apparent that we were on a downward spiral though, over the years Searle became more and more introverted, he'd seen three marriages of his own fail by the time I'd joined his service, and I believe he resented me and Nancy for our own happiness. That was the thing with Searle, despite his money he certainly wasn't happy and over the years he left the grounds of his house less and less until at last he never left at all. He'd badger me and bully me and belittle me in front of guests, but I was used to it all by then as it became apparent that whatever transpired he would not dispense with my services."

This caused Fitzgerald to stir. "Really? Why is that?"

"It is simple Father, by this time I was his only company and confidant. His fortune was well taken care of by the business suits, and Harvey dealt with matters of law. Searle had built his fortune but no longer had control over its future or destiny. He was but a figurehead, and this frustrated him immensely." McArthur replied.

"So the rumours you mentioned earlier?.."

"Most were true, Searle became bored and listless. His companies were fronted by good and honest men. But in Searle's eyes that was their failing, for he believed that they should transcend right or wrong for the sake of the business. That was where Searle came in. And as I suggested to you, Searle would grease the hands of the Government for favour but as I said before it went much deeper than that."

"You're suggesting that he had people killed?"

"Yes, only that, for there was little to no evidence of such wrongdoing. There was rumour of course, and Searle threatened me with similar on a regular basis, and though I took such words with a modicum of disbelief, I soon discovered that other men who kept his company had gone missing over a number of years. Some were found, and stories of suicide or misadventure would reach the newspapers, but I felt I knew better, for I had heard the threats that proceeded."

"That's incredible, how could he have hoped to get away with it?" the priest returned.

McArthur laughed. "We'll get to that Father and soon, but at the time it was so implausible that he did. He'd grown bored and so became sloppy, and yet still nothing could touch him. He took greater and greater risks in the name of profit and laughed at the little man's attempts to stop him. As I said, Father, Searle had someone watching over him, making sure that he came up smelling of roses every time."

McArthur watched as the priest's brow furrowed.

"Father, you've taken confession before, but this is not for the faint-hearted. You thought my story might be tame? Ha!"

"I have Robert; I was prepared for such revelations. I just wonder what else you might say to me."

"This is only the beginning Father, remain strong."

"You say that Searle had someone looking over him? He was protected?" Enquired the priest.

"Oh yes, Searle was protected alright. But not in the way you might think. As I've said, he knew some shady characters, and bribery and blackmail were not beyond him to reach his goals. Despite that, a man leaves a trail, don't you know? There were trials of course, and lesser men served hard time. Searle's name was at the forefront of such enquiries. But they could never trace anything back to him. And that astonished me."

"Oh?"

"I'd heard phone calls of course and interrupted meetings that he might have with such men. In the early days, he was a lot more careful. I wasn't party to such talk. But as he became a recluse, these people would have to come to him. And if they could not, that was when he'd get the calls."

"You're suggesting that you listened in Robert." It was not a question. "So what sort of thing are we talking about here?" Fitzgerald pressed.

"I'll leave it to your imagination, for the most part, Father, after all, this is my confession, and not his. Suffice to say I have neither the time nor inclination to divulge such truths. I don't believe Searle departed this mortal coil, having told his sins. Therefore, it is not my place."

McArthur grimaced as he manoeuvred himself within the bed. Could it be his eyes were failing? The priest seemed distant and out of focus, and so he positioned himself higher on his pillow and blinked rapidly to try and clear the fog from his eyes.

"Father, I grow weary, and though I would tell you it all as soon as I was able, I fear our time today is nearly at an end. Would you be so kind as to tell Keira that I need her."

And with that, McArthur closed his eyes to a pain, that had begun during the telling of his story as a dull warmth, but was now reaching a turbulent crescendo of fire within him.

CHAPTER 13

Fitzgerald came away, feeling wholly unsatisfied. The time he had spent with McArthur had amounted to little more than an hour, and in that time the old man had spoken only of Thoby Hall's prior owner and how the two had come to meet. Perhaps it was true that there would be some significance in that fact as McArthur's confession unfolded, but thus far they had got nowhere fast and given Nurse Keira's prognosis of McArthur's ability to meet with him, he knew that this was going to be a slow, drawn-out process.

He was now back in the lounge of McArthur's room. Keira had gone through to see to his pain medication and comfort, but he waited on her as he had questions that he needed answering.

Finally, she came back into the room and seemed surprised to see him still waiting there.

"Oh, Father. Was there something I could help you with?"

"Keira, yes, possibly you can. You made mention that these windows of opportunity would be limited. I was wondering just how long we might have between sessions when Mr McArthur is under the influence of his medications?"

The nurse looked up at the wall clock and saw as he did that it was just after 10:30 am. "Well Father, I would not expect him to rouse again before 2 or 3 o'clock at the earliest, but even then he will not be fully alert. At that time, we must monitor his pain relief and be sure he is comfortable. He expects that he might wake to see you again early evening or perhaps tonight."

That was very much in line with Fitzgerald's own thinking, and it was already crossing his mind that there was a window of opportunity to leave the house if required. The contract that had been signed had been very particular in its terms, but he could not understand the necessity of being ever-present in the house if McArthur had no chance of consciousness in that time so that the two of them might speak.

This left him in somewhat of a quandary for he knew the terms were iron tight and to leave the house would surely invalidate the agreement.

But would they? The essence of the contract was that he was present to receive the last confession of the man. As long as he was here for that then what issue would there be? Particularly if no one knew he was gone. For now, he realised that such opportunities would also arise during the night when McArthur slept after their second talk of the day. The house was empty after 06:00 pm after all, and only one other person dwelt in the house after that time, and that would be the night nurse who would reside here in McArthur's rooms with him. Who would know?

Keira waited on his response, and he wondered if she read his mind, as her smile suggested she knew well the purpose of his question. The girl might have her suspicions, and so he thought better than to give those any confirmation. "Early evening then? Very good." He turned to leave, and a thought struck him. "You will be gone by that time Keira. Remind me, who might the other nurse be?"

Still, the smile remained, and Fitzgerald was beginning to feel uncomfortable now in the woman's presence. He did not know if she played some kind of game with him due to his position, but everything that she did seemed somehow overtly sexual. Was she aware of such a thing? Or was it him?

"Melissa. No doubt, the two of you will meet tonight."

"And is it the same arrangement? Melissa will call through to the rooms?"

"Yes, I believe that makes sense, Father. I am sure the two of you will get on famously."

Oh, I am sure we will. Fitzgerald was very much looking forward to the chance to meet this woman Melissa.

And with that, the conversation was over. Keira turned and went toward what he believed to be the study. Instead, though he could see through the door to what looked like some kind of stockroom or pharmacy, clearly the place had been converted to house whatever medical supplies that would be required in McArthur's ongoing care.

With her out of sight, he was glad of the respite from her eyes, which made him feel uneasy every time they happened upon him. He considered this and knew perhaps it to be unfair on Keira, for surely she could not help the feelings it invoked in him.

Even so, he happily made his exit from the room and began to walk the long corridor back toward the front of the house, and this allowed him to clear his mind and think back on what had been said in conversation with McArthur.

What had been prominent was the name of Thomas Searle. This very Estate had belonged to him, and interestingly it had been bequeathed to a man who became his butler. Surely there had been more to the story than that?

And they hated one another, didn't they?

True, but he knew there was more to come from McArthur and perhaps that puzzling detail would be imparted shortly. And was a man passing his house down to a servant any stranger than the circumstances in which he now found himself in? Probably not.

Fitzgerald was soon back in his rooms. His thoughts having turned instead to the nurse Keira. Was she toying with him? Every look, every smile seemed designed to taunt him somehow as to his celibacy. But it was more than that he knew, for his attraction for her was a real thing, a slow-burning fire deep inside of him that was stoked into life by every little interaction.

Was it any wonder she had such an effect? He had not been with a woman for a considerable number of years now, and even then those had proven to be hollow experiences. There had only ever been one who he ever loved…

Emma.

Her face rose to the surface of his mind. It was always the same picture, the two of them in bed together, him waking and looking over to see her on her side, her head propped up on her arm. A look of sadness in her eyes, belied by the breaking smile as she saw he was awake. It was to this image he retreated time and again, when the other visions of her at the end, tried to break the surface and beg his recognition.

In all they had only been afforded one year together back in his early twenties. He had been introvert and alone back then, until he met her that was. It had been she who pressed and urged him to take life by the scruff of the neck and for the first time live. But it had all been a mask, for beneath the surface he discovered she carried her own pain and her own secrets.

He pushed the thought away, as only pain dwelt down that road, and he knew himself well enough, that if he allowed it, that pain would consume him.

And so he willed the image of Emma to fade, and in its stead came the picture of Keira and picking up on his previous thoughts, he was quick to dismiss any notions of attraction or flirtation on her part. He had been in the house for only a day now, and it was clear to see how she might have innocently given off such signals to him. Hers was undoubtedly a lonely role; a nurse whose patient slept for 18 to 20 hours a day, so was it any wonder she had been so warm and welcoming to new company?

The truth was, he knew he was in a similar position, for his own role was also affected by McArthur's ability to remain conscious, and he had already felt the stirrings of both boredom and loneliness in the house. He knew he could seek out Keira's company but knew he must be more wary, for the feelings she invoked in him were those he had long since tried to bury.

It would be easy to dwell on such things, but as it was, he had several hours to kill and so decided that a walk in the gardens might be just the ticket to blow off some steam and put these intruding thoughts behind him. A quick look out of the window reminded him of the season, and he quickly gathered his coat and gloves before leaving the room. The route down was simple, and logic guided him to the end of the corridor on the east wing of the house.

There he found a large glass door that led beneath the cloister surrounding the garden he had observed from the first floor. He looked up and was suitably impressed with the stone archways that ran the entire length of the house. A lattice-like pattern of stone linked each column, and he saw that a figurehead or statue was carved at the top of the stonework of each one. This held his attention for the moment, and he walked along the stone pathway, neck arched upward as various faces or animals came to his eyes.

He quickly saw that the pattern of work would extend all the way around the house and though the work fascinated him, he had resolved to come to the garden, and here to his right and through the posts of an archway was another pathway heading in toward the centre.

And so he veered off from under the cloister and between two large hedgerows that both bordered and obscured the garden from sight at this ground level.

Low bushes prevailed within, and he saw that the path went both left and right as well as straight forward. His goal though was the wooden gazebo at the middle of the garden where he could sit and look upon the pond that lay there before it. As he went, he found the garden had a maze-like quality as some high hedgerows marked the boundaries of yet new paths that lay beside now derelict flower beds. From his bedroom situated above, he had not been able to gauge the full size of the area, but it was clearly vast.

He remembered Hodgson's comments regarding the colour that would be seen there of a summer, and he felt a touch of sadness that he would not see such a thing. Despite the intricate pattern of hedgerows, his path was straight and true toward his goal and as he found the centre of the garden he saw that there were three other straight paths, all converging at this same point which was undoubtedly the highlight of the garden when all about it was in bloom. Here at the gazebo beside the pond, he took a place on a bench within. He now had a magnificent view back over the garden and at the rear of Thoby Hall.

He sat back and blew cold mist from his mouth. It was bitterly cold, and the grey sky overhead suggested some future snowfall, as opposed to the constant rain that they had been receiving. Such thoughts drifted away, for here and now, and despite the cold, it was so very quiet and peaceful.

No sound could be heard in the world but for a small fountain that splashed water two feet high over the pond. The sound was very relaxing, and Fitzgerald closed his eyes so that he could take it in. Oh, what a wonderful escape this garden must be in the Summer underneath the gazebo, and in his mind's eye he could picture Hodgson fawning over guests as she barked orders to a staff of impeccably dressed waiters who carried trays of champagne and canapés throughout an assembled throng.

He opened his eyes and sighed. The contrast between his imaginary garden and this one was large, but that made sitting here in the peace and quiet no less pleasant. More so, for as he looked left and right he knew he was obstructed from the view of the east and west wing bedrooms by the large sloped roof that sat low on the wooden structure about him.

The feeling was short-lived though, for there approaching down the central avenue was a man pushing a wheelbarrow. He was some distance off, and Fitzgerald hoped that he had not been seen as he did not relish any interruption. The man came onward though, and Fitzgerald could see he was a large man or failing that, heavily padded with clothing against the cold.

He wore a green parka coat with a fur-lined hood which was down. Perhaps surprising for his age was the baseball cap that was worn low and gave the effect that his ears were pushed out too far. As the man got closer, Fitzgerald guessed that he must be in his sixties. A ragged snow-white beard hung from his chin, and thin wisps of white hair protruded from under his cap. His goal was clear, and Fitzgerald knew he was about to have company as the man raised a gloved hand in greeting.

"Hey there!"

Fitzgerald stood and walked over to the edge of the gazebo. He waved back as the man was still some twenty feet away and he did not wish to raise his voice and interrupt the quiet as other man had. Drawing close now, the man bent forward resting the wheelbarrow on its arches and leaning back, pinched the small of his back to work away the strain.

Fitzgerald could see that the barrow was heavily laden with gardening tools. He had not been previously introduced, but here no doubt was Dougie, the gardener.

"Father Fitzgerald, I presume?" He began as he made the short distance between them, blowing heavily as he did so.

"Yes, and you'd be Douglas?"

"Dougie to my friend's Father and I hope to include you among them."

Fitzgerald smiled. The man had an affable nature to him to be sure. "Dougie it is then."

"I'd not thought to see you out here, Father. It's bloody perishing it is."

"Well, I have to agree with you there. But I was going stir crazy up in the rooms and thought a walk would blow away some of the cobwebs."

Dougie nodded his agreement. "Well I might be biased Father, but you just found the best part of the house." Dougie walked past him and into the gazebo, sitting himself on the bench he withdrew a thermos from his jacket. "Will you join me, Father? A small nip to keep the cold out?"

Fitzgerald looked over and saw the man pouring steaming black liquid into the screw top cup. The aroma of coffee filled his nostrils. "Are we having our coffee Irish Dougie?" he said with a smile.

"Aye. All the best drinks have a hint of Irish about them," he replied with a wink.

Fitzgerald sat beside the man and took the cup from the man's outstretched hand. He sipped the piping hot liquid, and soon the warmth hit his belly. He passed the cup back.

"You look like you have some work on here Dougie. The upkeep must be horrendous."

The old man nodded. "Well, used to be that I had me some hired help. Of course, it's too much for one man, especially one of my years. But luckily for me, old Mr McArthur's only concern now is this here garden, so that he might see it from upstairs." As he said this, he raised his cup up in salute toward the west wing bedroom, out of sight to the right of them, before taking another sip.

"It's sad he won't see it in all its glory come spring." Fitzgerald said.

"Well, we had a good year of it. We had some beautiful late dahlias and chrysanthemums. The roses though, they are his favourites, and we had quite the bloom. Part of me wishes he hadn't held on so long, you know? The garden has the feel of winter on it now and no doubt Mr McArthur feels that."

Fitzgerald understood what he meant. The conversation had all too quickly become melancholy. But what other line of conversation was a priest to suffer at such times? The silence between the two began to grow, and Fitzgerald began to feel uncomfortable with the man's presence. More so, annoyed that his respite had been broken by the intrusion. Perhaps sensing these things Dougie began to stand.

"Back to it, I think, Father. The Devil waits for no man." Dougie stood looking down on him, and he could see he was searching his face and was perhaps waiting for some reaction, approval or comment that would satisfy the social etiquette. Fitzgerald could think of nothing and so likewise stood.

"Perhaps I better get back inside?"

He turned, ready to walk away when a thought struck him. "Dougie. Can you tell me who might have access to the library?"

The old man stared at him, unblinking. He looked like the question had frozen him to the spot. Quickly though Dougie came back to life and searched around himself, looking this way and that. He stepped up close to Fitzgerald and taking him by the sleeve drew him back down to sit upon the bench. Leaning in closely, he whispered. "The library, Father? Why do you ask?"

Fitzgerald was somewhat taken back by the man's reaction, and he found himself looking around to find whatever it was that Dougie was seemingly cautious of.

"No reason." He began, not realising that he had also lowered his voice. "Well, that is to say, I am told it is off-limits and yet…" He paused a second thinking on the best way to approach the subject.

"Well…I passed by there last night, and I am certain that someone was inside. I heard…Well, it doesn't matter what I heard, but I thought it best to say something as…it's hard to describe. I was worried that the room might be dangerous somehow, that is to say, I felt some kind of…leak? I don't know if I am saying it right…" He tailed off, knowing he was being vague and also too close to giving away an embarrassing memory.

Dougie considered for a moment and stared hard into his eyes. Fitzgerald held his gaze, though he found such scrutiny difficult.

"Dangerous Father?" Dougie eventually whispered. "You'd be right in what you say. That room is not safe at all, and you'd do well to stay clear."

Fitzgerald remained quiet, continuing to hold his stare and waiting for him to continue the conversation. Dougie nodded, perhaps realising he needed to fill the gap the priest had left him.

"I wonder what you already know Father?" He said at last. "It would help if you did know something about the house, else you think these the ramblings of a tired old man."

"I know the house has a history, Dougie. A tragic history in part."

"I am sure there are those in Ashmarsh who gave you fair warning and told you of dark spirits or some such. Am I right?" Came the reply.

Father Shilling came immediately to Fitzgerald's mind as Dougie spoke, but the old man did not wait for an answer before he continued. "You'd do well to heed those who told you of such things. I don't know how to put it into words but the house...the house has a dark energy about it, and from all I know, it stems from that library. Did you feel it, Father?"

Fitzgerald considered. What had he felt? His mind went back to his earlier experience, and the first memory was one of embarrassment and anger. But before that, had there been something? Well perhaps, but dark spirits? No. Certainly nothing more than a cruel trick played by this night nurse Melissa.

But that aside, the library door had been the source of that cold draught that had caused his fingers to go numb. That was the danger of which he spoke, and instead of taking fair warning, this character Douglas instead wished to invoke tales of dark spirits or energy. He would do well to end this conversation and perhaps bring the matter to Hodgson's attention instead.

As to Dougie's question. Try as he might, he could not deny that he had felt something. At first, it had only been as to the strange cold draught that emanated from behind the locked room. But then there had been that voice, dry and chilling, whispered from the other side of the door. It had been a troublesome and scary experience he had to admit, but he had rationalised that within his mind with the belief that someone was playing tricks upon him.

"I...I don't know what I felt." He managed. Dougie still looked long at him, weighing up his answer.

"I see you don't quite believe yet, but something happened up there, didn't it?"

Fitzgerald did not wish to impart the details of his earlier experience, instead choosing the rational conclusions that he had drawn to those events. "No Dougie, nothing like that. I did get a start, though." He tried a smile at that, but it felt weak, and he believed Dougie saw right through him.

"Is no matter if you don't tell me. Only know this, I haven't set foot in that house for three years now, and you'll not find me in there again. Maybe I was once like you and tried to find reason in all the things I saw and heard, but certain things can only be denied so long. Aye, you were right with what you said. The house does have tragedy surrounding it, but ask yourself how much bad luck can one place have, and when does a series of accidents and deaths become the work of something darker than mere circumstance?"

The conversation had taken on a whole new dimension. Series of deaths? Fitzgerald could not draw on any knowledge as to any other happenings and so referred to one that he did know of.

"I know of the young girl that drowned here Dougie. I understand that such a thing can have a profound and lasting effect upon a place. That said I have been hard-pressed to know where such a thing occurred. I read about a swimming pool in the local Gazette."

"The swimming pool Father? It is long gone, and so you'll not find that wretched place I am glad to say. I don't think old Mr McArthur ever really approved of such a thing in the first place, but young Elizabeth had a way about her. Full of energy she was and I am sure he allowed it to make her happy."

"After the accident, though? He had it filled in without a second thought. Did she object? I doubt it. For a long while afterwards she insisted that the whole thing was her fault, but what could she have done?"

"It's not uncommon for folks to want to shoulder the blame, Dougie. So many times, people will say to me if only they had done this or that. Hindsight can be a curse coupled with a tragic event."

Dougie though seemed vacant. Clearly, their conversation was touching on some painful memories and emotions for the man.

"And do they question God's part, Father?"

"Of course and I seldom believe I hold all the answers for them. How, after all, can it be God's plan to take away such a young life such as the child who passed here? But with free will comes responsibility also."

"I hear that, Father. I am a Christian man myself. But the story of that poor child drowning doesn't end there. But I can see you are not ready for a tale such as that one. It would be too difficult in the telling and more so your disbelief afterwards. I wonder if you don't have a purpose here Father, one beyond Mr McArthur and perhaps if I am right, you might yet come to believe what dwells here and then truly hear what I would tell you."

107

The conversation had taken a turn, and where he had initially objected to Dougie's intrusion, he had now become intrigued, for the man had hinted upon further tragic events within the house and here perhaps was an opportunity to get a preview of what McArthur might later confess. But somehow his words had only gone so far as to put the old gardener on his guard.

He would get no more from this man. And so it would be, for with a grunt of effort, Dougie got to his feet once more and began to make his slow way back to his barrow.

"As I said Father if you find a purpose here beyond poor Mr McArthur, come seek me out and listen to what I would tell you."

And with that, Fitzgerald was alone again. Only this time, he found no peace in the solitude and quiet of the garden. The old man's words, now coupled with memories of Liam Shilling's last sermon and subsequent conversation in the deep of the night reverberated through his mind.

CHAPTER 14

Fitzgerald didn't remain long in the gardens. The conversation with Douglas had left him feeling somewhat perturbed; the references the man had made to the library only added to the feeling. What peace and quiet he had enjoyed in the garden, had suddenly given way to a sense of isolation and paranoia, as in his imagination all the windows of the great house suddenly concealed numerous sets of inquisitive and unfriendly eyes.

But there was more. He felt very much that he was missing some intangible detail about the house and its history, and that those about him, were offering only hints and fragments as to a story he had little, to no understanding of.

As he walked the short path back to the east wing cloister, he felt a sense of relief as the glass door swung silently closed behind him, sheltering him from the seemingly countless windows that observed his exit from the garden.

Returning to his rooms, he made a beeline for the study and dialled in the number for the offices of Bishop Andrew Burrows with who he had only spoken to the previous day regarding the contract. The phone was answered by a female voice who bid him hold the line. There followed the sound of soft murmurings in the background before she came back to the receiver.

"I'm sorry Father, Bishop Burrows is in a conference at the moment. Perhaps I might take a message?"

Fitzgerald didn't believe that for a moment, but none the less left his details asking for the bishop to call him back at his earliest convenience. He hung up the phone. Frustrated, he paced back and forward between the study and the lounge. A thought finally hit him, and he walked briskly back over to the phone. He punched in the number and drummed his fingers on the desk as he waited impatiently.

"Come on." He whispered, imploring the other person to pick up.

"Colin Morris." Came the answer at last.

"Colin? How are you? It's Iain."

"Iain? How are you, man? Enjoying the noble life, while you leave the rest of us to our toil?" Morris chuckled.

"I wish Colin. Things are… shall we say a little odd here, to say the least."

"Oh?"

Where to begin? Fitzgerald knew what he was about to impart would sound a little crazy. His experience thus far in Ashmarsh and Thoby Hall had been rife with talk of dark spirits and bad luck. But the fact remained something didn't sit right with him about this place and its inhabitants. To date, his research had formed a link between the Church, Robert McArthur, his wife Elizabeth and the late Father James Crosby. A link which somewhere along the line had involved the Deacon Colin Morris.

"What can you tell me about Father Crosby and McArthur's Elizabeth?"

The line went quiet for a second.

"Colin?"

"I'm here, Iain. You've touched a sensitive spot there I can tell you."

He had felt as much. From the moment of his first arrival at St Peter's, he had heard Father Shilling try and dispel such local belief, that the town's misfortune and bad luck stemmed from this place Thoby Hall.

He was keen to rejuvenate his church and likewise reverse any superstitious beliefs that the townsfolk held. A task made all the more difficult when you combined the suicide of the former parish priest and linked it (rightly or wrongly) to Elizabeth McArthur who had resided here. Part of him wondered if McArthur might touch in such matters as his confession went on, but even if he shouldn't, Fitzgerald was loath to pass up the opportunity to learn and use what he could to his own ends and for the benefit of the parish.

"I'm sorry, Colin. I did some digging and saw your name mentioned in the papers from the time Crosby committed suicide. I tried the bishop's office, but I couldn't get hold of him."

"So you know about Crosby. Do you know what became of Elizabeth?" Morris returned.

"I don't. Shilling, or at least Crosby's diaries suggested she might be under some psychiatric care?"

Again the line was quiet for a second. "Yes, she was sectioned as a result of all that happened there, and still is for that matter. Be careful Iain. As I said, that is a difficult subject. I knew Crosby of course, not so much the McArthur woman but after it all happened our little church was the centre of a media frenzy. I was under very strict instructions that such matters would not be spoken of."

"Why though Colin?"

"As much as anything I guessed it was more the manner of his departure. You know of his suicide? Then I guess you know what happened at the sacrament. Those vultures from the papers couldn't get enough of that."

"But what could bring him to do such a thing?"

Another pause. "I don't honestly know Iain. Elizabeth though? That's a much easier one to call."

Fitzgerald's mind went back to the passage he read in the dead of night, in Father Shilling's study.

"The girl who drowned here? Her name was Lydia?"

"You are well informed Iain, but I believe that was only the start. You have to understand that this business up at Thoby Hall with Crosby and Elizabeth went mainly under the radar. James was a good man, but quiet on the whole. He did not speak to me until close to the end. I had my suspicions; the time spent up at that hall with that young woman caused me to wonder, and I confronted him with it."

"And what did he say?"

"Only so much to appease me. I don't know what I thought, an affair maybe? Ridiculous for one such as he, but it didn't stop it crossing my mind. No, spiritual guidance is what he called it. She was a troubled young woman and had come to believe that the house was cursed. She had suffered the terrible tragedy with the young girl, and Crosby told me she had…well, begun to start seeing things."

"Seeing things?"

"He wouldn't allude to what it was Iain, I'm sorry. He speculated that she was unwell and his visits there initially were to give her peace of mind. He hoped by doing so he could help her, after all, she had been such a supporter to the Church, and I think he felt a debt to her. He had also suggested that she seek medical assistance. She had assured him that she had, but I have my doubts."

"But how did it all go so wrong?"

"That's a question I have been asking myself for a long time. You see when I spoke with Crosby, it was only several weeks before he killed himself. He seemed confident and sure of his path with her, but I watched as he sank into despair. I confronted him again of course, but by then, his path was set before him."

"I don't understand."

"I think you would have had to see it with your own eyes, Iain. On the surface, he came across as normal, but the eyes? The eyes had a haunted quality to them. Then came the incident with the sacrament. In a way, I was relieved. He was removed from his duties, and I was sure he was going to get the help that he needed, but…you know the rest."

Fitzgerald felt wholly unsatisfied. He had confirmed the link between the McArthur woman and Crosby alright, but how on earth had the man been set down the path to despair as he had done?

"I just don't get it, Colin. I understand the McArthur woman alright, but I don't understand how he could do that."

"I have wrestled with that in my mind for many years Iain and I keep drawing a blank. I wonder if there wasn't more to it? Something private and unrelated to that woman? That's the only thing that makes sense to me."

Fitzgerald nodded, perhaps there was more to it, and maybe the answer lay with Crosby himself.

"Colin? The diaries that Shilling left for me, I would very much like to get my hands on them. I hoped you might bring them to me, stuck here as I am. They belonged to Father Crosby."

"Well, certainly but where would I find them?"

"You should find them on my study desk."

"Interesting. I didn't know he kept any diaries. Perhaps you will find your answers there. But I have to ask, of what relevance is this to your duty?"

"I don't know Colin. There is an undercurrent here, something strange I believe, but only in the minds and spirits of those who reside and work here. Shilling mentioned how the Hall has an effect over the town, and I am keen to find out why. McArthur has yet to impart anything of significance, but I feel that the history here will perhaps be at the heart of it."

"Iain, I'm sorry, perhaps I should have been more frank with you before you ever left for that place. Just be careful."

"I will Colin, don't worry."

And so ended their conversation. Resting the phone back in its cradle, he thought on what had been said. Secrets it seemed had been kept from him whether willingly or not he could not tell. Morris for one had held information back, but had he known Fitzgerald's interest in such matters? Perhaps not, the conversation with Father Shilling before his departure was for the best part of his knowledge, private.

Perhaps Morris could have volunteered more though, knowing as he did of Fitzgerald's impending work at the house. The answer to that was an unequivocal yes, and he couldn't help be disappointed with the man for not telling of such things before he came here.

Walking back through to the lounge area, he noted the time was now past 03:00 pm. He was surprised at the hour as time was now getting on. How much longer would it be until he was summoned once more to meet with Robert McArthur, and perhaps this other nurse Melissa who worked the night shift? The thought brought a picture again of Keira to his mind, and he dismissed it as best as he could. He did not have the resolve for such things, tired as he was. She would be off the estate at 06:00 pm along with Dougie and the others, and he felt better at the thought that he need not see her again that day.

For now, though he was tired. His day had been uncomfortable and troubling, and perhaps the way he now felt was as much down to mental fatigue than anything; such was the deflating and depressing nature of learning the history of the house.

He walked through to the bedroom and drew the thick curtains, shutting out the grey afternoon and knowing that within an hour, the large floodlights outside would intrude into his bedroom. He lay down and massaged his head as he tried to put together everything he had learned that day and how that might affect things going forward with McArthur. But slowly, his eyelids began to grow heavy, and he drifted off into a deep sleep. His last thought before giving in to unconsciousness was of Crosby, a man that he did not know and a suicide he could not begin to understand.

CHAPTER 15

It was now after 06:00 pm. Fitzgerald though had not been aware of the passing hours, having dozed fitfully through the afternoon. His time at Thoby Hall, coupled with feelings of isolation had served to drain his energy away. But what sleep there had been was broken by a series of dreams, that each in slow, deliberate turn had turned toward nightmare.

He lay on the bed at a loss as what to do, as he was now at the beck and call of the night nurse Melissa, who would inform him as to McArthur's health and readiness to continue in his confession. Raising himself, he was all too quickly aware of the bright light that intruded in upon the bedroom. Had he not the use of his mobile phone, he might well believe that he had not slept at all as the room was as bright as a Summer's afternoon.

Going through to the lounge, some small light followed him inside but did little to brighten the room, and he quickly turned the switches to dispel the long shadows within. He slumped down on the sofa, where he could view the telephone. He remained there for a few minutes waiting for it to ring, while at the same time bidding it not to.

He was tired. Tired of this house and tired of McArthur and his confession. He felt a prisoner, and it was a simple analogy to make, such was the binding nature of the contract that forbade his leaving, as well as a perimeter that was adorned with huge spotlights.

Such thoughts caused the stirrings of anger within him, as he knew they were the truth. McArthur's confession was going to be slow, and the moments in-between would, in truth, feel like a sentence. Well, McArthur be damned.

He stood and quickly moved off toward the apartment door and quickly left without so much as a look at the telephone behind him.

He strode off down the long corridor, with no particular destination in mind.

Fitzgerald soon found himself on the ground floor again and facing the front of the house. In this direction, he would find the kitchen, a large dining room (which he had earlier happened upon), as well as Harvey's office. There were yet more doors which had thus far remained closed to him, but an earlier glance at his visitor's handbook had alluded to what lay behind each, namely a large servant's hall, a morning room and butler's pantry. The house, of course, had no butler in it but for the owner, Robert McArthur, but his days of receiving guests and fetching meals were now long behind him.

Walking aimlessly forward with no destination in mind, it occurred to him, that he might stop off at the kitchens to prepare his evening meal. But his appetite was thin following his broken sleep. He was as if in a daze until that was, he stood before the door to Harvey's office where he came to a stop.

Without thinking, he pushed on the door. It swung in easily much to his surprise.

The room as, all the others in the house, was brightly lit. And due to its location on the side of the building it looked out toward the east and the garden there. Somewhere close by yet more spotlights were trained on the house, so as to cast the night away.

Fitzgerald walked over to the window and looked cautiously out. There before him on the ground was the pathway toward the kitchen he had taken with Hodgson on his first arrival, and hidden over to his right behind the large hedgerows would be the carport.

All at once, paranoia took over, as he felt framed, stood as he was in front of the large window, and though none were apparent, unfriendly eyes would easily see him trespassing in the solicitor's office. Quickly he drew the thick curtains, and some relief washed over him.

Turning quickly, he was at Harvey's desk. He sat, and pulled the string of the desk lamp. A bright yellow ring instantly pooled across the surface revealing the in/out trays which were now noticeably empty.

Fitzgerald leaned backwards, and the chair reclined slightly under the pressure.

Why am I here?

There was no answer in his mind. He had felt restless, and the clawing isolation of his room had driven him out. But the house offered no other refuge he might take comfort in, as it felt barren; as if no one had so much as stepped foot within for years. That, or like he was in some museum after closing, leaving only him and some ancient relics for company. Relics which brought on different feelings in the cold and quiet of the night.

Idly, he reached out to the topmost drawer on his right side and pulled. It did not budge. None the less, he tugged lightly on the two below and was met with the same. He nodded his understanding. It had been a surprise to find the room unlocked, but at least Harvey held with some security.

Rolling the chair back on its casters, he stood and stepped over to the filing cabinet. It would be locked, he was certain, but when he reached for the top drawer, it slid effortlessly forward in his hand.

Inside, were a row of perhaps ten dividers. His fingers nimbly danced between them and soon found that all of them were empty. Until now, he had not known any purpose in coming to the solicitor's room, but stood before the cabinet he realised it was the contract that he had been bound to sign back on his very first visit he was searching for.

Opening the second drawer, he was met with the sight of stuffed papers bulging the first divider to its very seams. A quick glance told him that the rest were empty. Plucking the first sheet to hand, he began to read.

At the top, he saw a company logo 'Eastland Electricity' and below emblazoned within a red box were the words 'final demand'. Fitzgerald had wondered about the potential for such exorbitant bills and here was evidence. Some £4,100 being due back in February of that year. Had the bill been paid? Tucking it back, he withdrew another at random, showing December of 2015, when the amount owing had been £3,220. The estate was indeed dwindling as had been suggested and it seemed that Thoby Hall was perhaps all that McArthur might have offered the Church, for Fitzgerald wondered if he had anything else to give.

Pawing his way through the rest of the invoices, he found a repeat monthly invoice for five hundred litres of diesel. Curiously though, this bill was met each and every month without fail. He could not even begin to guess at the need for such a large quantity of fuel. Surely McArthur's days of leaving the house were long behind him?

The rest of the invoices though were wholly mundane, and fitting with the upkeep of a large stately home. Some were paid, some were not, and clearly many were juggled to make payment one month and skip another (or two).

And so, Fitzgerald came to the last drawer. It too gave easily and quickly thumbing through the dividers it was clear to see that there was no trace of the violet envelope and the contract he had signed. That was quickly forgotten though as he plucked the first of a series of letters that all bore the same letterhead. 'St Luke's Hospital'.

It was addressed to Frederick Harvey and was dated 12th July 2014. He read:

Dear Mr Harvey,

Thank you for your letter dated the 25th of June. I am delighted to be able to tell you that a space has become available at St Luke's Hospital, and we very much look forward to receiving Elizabeth in the coming weeks.

The facility at St Luke's offers first-class 24-hour treatment for those suffering from extreme mental health issues. Our patients receive the very best in individualised care, therapy and treatment in a safe and warm environment, which includes very comfortable rooms, tailored to the individual and their personality, as well as beautiful gardens which we utilise not only for rest and relaxation periods but also therapy sessions. I have included a copy of our brochure and hope that it meets yours and Mr McArthur's approval.

At this time, we are liaising with doctor's at the Rodell Centre regarding Elizabeth's current treatment, to appraise ourselves of her history. This way, our staff will be in the best possible place to receive Elizabeth and make the transition from one institution to another as seamless as possible.

If you have any further questions, please do not hesitate to get in touch.

Kind regards.

Hilary Swan.

Fitzgerald flipped the letter and saw it was blank on the opposite side. As he turned it again, he read an address; Lakeside Road, Banfield.

Banfield was several miles away he knew. He didn't know where the aforementioned Rodell Centre was, but it very much looked like McArthur had brought Elizabeth as close to home as he could.

Picking out another letter, he began to read again. What followed was clearly an update as to Elizabeth's condition. Once again, feeling the voyeur intruding on another person's private business, he quickly stuffed the letter back into place. His fingers danced between the remaining papers, separating them so much that he could surmise the content of each. Following her initial admission, it was clear that these were monthly updates as to Elizabeth's health and wellbeing.

Sighing, he removed his hand from the drawer. This was not what he had set out to accomplish, and the feeling of invasion that now sat within him made him feel all the lower. He went to slide the drawer closed when he saw another sheet of paper, which had seemingly been dropped between the dividers. Without thinking, he tugged the paper loose and read the letterhead, which again denoted it was from St Luke's Hospital. The date on this page read Friday 14th October 2016.

That's only a few days before I met Shilling.

Opening the divider again before him, he was quick to see that the letters were filed as to date, he would simply put it neatly back in place…

Instead, he began to read;

Dear Mr Harvey,

I am writing to you to give an update as to Elizabeth's ongoing condition and welfare while staying here with us as St Luke's. You may well remember that my last few updates were wholly positive, Elizabeth making substantial progress to the point where we considering some community work with her.

I regret to inform you however, that things have taken a sudden and unfortunate turn for the worse. Dr Kapoor informs me that Elizabeth has retreated into a state of catatonia. This is described as being a neuropsychiatric condition that affects both behaviour and motor function, the result being an almost unresponsive state in someone who otherwise appears to be awake. Given her aforementioned progress, this is a huge setback. I can tell you that Elizabeth remains comfortable and the doctor's here are monitoring her medication while trying to identify the root cause and trigger for this episode.

I am very sorry to be the bearer of such bad news, but we hope that we can continue to work with Elizabeth to identify the issues and bring her back to the point of progress that we had mentioned. I understand that any and all updates are to go through yourself, according to Mr McArthur's wishes, but we are happy to answer any questions that he might have.

Given our long correspondence regarding Elizabeth, I wonder if we might talk further on the phone about this matter? Dr Kapoor has raised concerns that Elizabeth's set back may well be in part down to the very events that set her on this path many years ago. Given the excellent work done by the Rodell Centre before her transfer here, we have limited information as to those core events as Elizabeth had demonstrated a rational grasp of reality in her thinking about those demons she believes beset her household. However, as Elizabeth withdrew into her current state, it was evident that those matters involving Father James Crosby and his suicide were once again forefront in her mind and fuelling her paranoid state. I hope that through yourself, Mr McArthur might shed some light on these matters to better assist us and help us understand what Elizabeth is going through. Of course, we have the original psychiatric notes and are taking steps to contact the Rodell Centre and Dr Fisher to obtain what further information we can.

Kind regards,

Hilary Swan.

Fitzgerald closed his eyes as he processed what he had read. He had been trying to find some link between Elizabeth McArthur, Crosby and the Church and knew he had already tentatively pieced it all together. He had believed the matter would ultimately play some part in McArthur's confession, though there had been no evidence to that as yet. But this letter did more than reinforce the link he had found; it brought the matter to the here and now. Elizabeth McArthur had suffered some sort of regression on the very eve of his coming to Ashmarsh and beginning this business with McArthur. Surely it could not just be a coincidence?

The sound, when it came, did not register at first. He was overwhelmed with thoughts of Elizabeth McArthur and what she had suffered in the aftermath of the young child's death at her home. But on the repeat of the noise, he at once stopped breathing, and his head shot toward the door.

It had been a creak, so soft as to barely be heard. But his senses were alive to his environment, as adrenaline coursed through him. Adrenaline born of his trespass in the solicitor's office and the realisation he was about to be found out.

His mind had made the connection, and he knew that someone was outside the room. The low creak had been as foot met floorboard, and had been so delicate as to suggest that whoever stood beyond the doorway, was trying to keep a low profile.

This thought rang hollowly through his mind, and as panic grew, he could not think what to do. The letter dropped soundlessly from his hand as he frantically looked about himself; for what he did not know, a hiding place maybe?

What and be found cowering under the desk?

No. Reason came back, and he gently pushed the cabinet door quietly back into place, to hide any evidence that he had been snooping through papers that did not belong to him. If someone were to enter, he would say he came to use the telephone, perhaps?

No one entered, and he found himself holding his breath and straining his ears, for the slightest sound beyond the wooden door that would indicate that someone was still there. In any event, he was trapped. Though the large window behind him offered a potential exit, it was set so high that once through, he would not be able to reach back and close it behind him. And what if he was caught in the act of doing so? No, his best recourse was to be upfront, he would walk through the door and deal with whoever it was, face to face.

Forgetting the signs of his intrusion still lying on the floor behind him, he walked lightly to the door and taking a deep breath, pulled it open before him.

The corridor was empty in both directions. Had he imagined the noise?

The thought went unanswered and dropped from his mind in an instant as he beheld a puddle of water on the wooden boards outside of the office. His eyes snatched upward as he searched the corridor to his left and right a second time, but as he already knew, there was no one to be seen.

As his eyes came back to the puddle, he saw a multitude of wet patches stretching off toward the back of the east wing and toward the stairway that would take him back to his rooms.

"Hello?" He ventured into the empty void that was the corridor before him. There was no response and anger immediately came to the fore as he recalled his episode before the library door. There had been someone there then. Someone who had played a cruel trick on him and now it seemed that someone had been spying on him. He sat down on his haunches to better see the nearest puddle of water from the door. It could not be denied; it was a bare wet footprint.

He lifted his eyes to trace the next print, only inches beyond the first and was quick to track them off into the distance.

Melissa.

In his mind, he knew it was right. She had sought to embarrass him before at the library, and now she spied upon his movements and actions. Who else could it be? At this time, only he, McArthur and the night nurse shared the house, and there was no earthly way it could be McArthur.

Looking in close again, he viewed the small wet print before him and edged his size eleven foot alongside. The wet mark was tiny in comparison to his own foot. How small could this woman Melissa be?

He straightened quickly and headed off in the direction of the prints. His anger was a real thing now, and a small snarl unwittingly curled the corner of his mouth as he strode past the carved staircase, bearing down on his target, who it seemed was heading for the back of the east wing.

He could only surmise that the route she had chosen would take her out of the house and into the garden, from there she could follow the cloister around to the west wing, or she could cut straight across. Maybe if he was quick enough, he could cut her off, maybe…

The prints stopped suddenly, as did Fitzgerald.

He looked up and saw the glass doorway ahead of him on the left; the footprints stopped some twenty feet short. He searched quickly about him, already knowing there were no other doorways before the end of the corridor.

"She put her shoes back on." He mouthed quietly, but already his inner voice was asking why she would have taken them off, and for another matter how or why would her feet have been wet in the first place?

That's easy. She came in through from the garden. It must have been raining.

Yes, that was good. That was the easy answer, but the question remained as to why they suddenly stopped.

Slowly a wry smile broke on his face as he looked back over his shoulder. He had seen this trick before in some movie. *What was it called?* He couldn't remember, but an image of someone backtracking over their prints in the snow came to mind — someone who was trying to evade capture.

But looking back, he quickly doubted this farfetched hypothesis. For one thing, the prints back on the floor behind him were pristine and perfectly formed. No one could conceivably have tracked back in the same direction, which only led to the one rational answer he had come up with. Whoever it was, had put shoes on to continue their escape.

In his mind, it worked. He wholly ignored the reason as to why the prints would be wet, instead grasping the idea that someone (Melissa) had removed her footwear so she could silently come down the corridor and observe his actions in the solicitor's office.

With an affirming nod, he turned back to the rear of the wing and made for the glass door that led to the gardens. Only, as he reached for it, he saw a secondary door to his right slightly ajar.

Had he seen this doorway before? He had only made the journey to the back of the east wing on one occasion, and that was to go to the gardens. The glass door to his left marked the way to that route, but had he seen this before? He didn't think so, and what was more, he couldn't recollect having seen a further room this far back in his visitor's guide.

He approached quietly; his ear cocked for the slightest of sounds that would indicate the presence of the night nurse, over on this side of the house. The only sound that came though was beyond the glass door to his left, with the rustle of leaves being buffeted by the wind through the cloister.

Fitzgerald tipped his head to afford a view through the small gap in the doorway to his right but could see nothing as the room appeared in darkness. Cursing, he pushed lightly on the door and watched as the hallway light encroached within and afforded him a look at what lay inside.

His eyes roved immediately upward at the vaulted ceiling and the wealth of intricate timbers that crossed just beneath the apex. As he looked, he let his hand feel along the bare brickwork to his left for a switch and feeling relieved; his hand soon happened upon the protrusion of a panel and a set of toggles set within. Quickly he thumbed them all downward, which brought to life a series of lamps set in the walls of the large room.

The effect was to cast the room in a low light, which gave it a feeling of cold and neglect. Stepping inside, there was no sign of any other person, but several potential hiding places offered themselves as there were multiple packing crates littered around the expansive space. Cautiously, he walked to the nearest item, and lifted the corner of a large dust sheet, to reveal a wooden vanity unit.

"Look, if there is anyone there just come out," he ventured. There was no answer, and though he bid it away, he could feel his fear and anxiety begin to build. It was much the same as his experience outside of the library; only this time, it was anticipation that brought such feelings to the fore.

"Melissa? I know you are there." He tried again as he took a pace further inside the room. "Let's not play these games any more…"

He came to a quick stop, as he noticed a transition in the colour of the floor. His eyes traced to his right as he saw a line marked by the contrasting colour of new and old concrete, and as he followed it, he quickly traced the circumference of a large rectangle in the centre of the room. His mind had already made the leap, and he knew he was in the old summer house where the girl Lydia had died. The evidence being the filled-in rectangle, some five metres wide by twenty long that dominated the centre of the floor.

The gardener Douglas had alluded to such, saying that McArthur had filled the pool in shortly after the tragic events that had unfolded with the young girl. The knowledge of his whereabouts immediately intensified his insecurity, and he looked back to the door that he had come through to see that his exit was clear.

As he began to turn back, he caught the flash of movement at the very periphery of his vision, and his head snapped back to face the centre of the room once more.

"Melissa?" His voice sounded weak and scared. Swallowing hard, he followed with a deep breath to steady his nerves. The movement had been to the far right of the room, near to what looked like a serving bar.

At that moment he was torn between fight and flight. But to leave, would leave this behaviour unchecked and surely validate this game Melissa was playing with him. No, he must press on and have this out with her, and by god, if she jumped out on him, he wouldn't be held responsible…

"I know you are there, Melissa. Stop fooling around for goodness sake."

He approached the bar and could see a set of mounted optics on the wall behind, all empty except the last one which held an empty bottle of vodka.

There could be nowhere else to hide.

Taking another deep breath to steady himself, he stepped quickly around the side of the bar, hands raised in case the demented girl should leap out at him.

"Right…" he exclaimed as he made the turn.

The area behind the bar was empty.

But what followed, served to nearly make his heart stop. A loud crashing sound reverberated through the room and shook him through his very core. He closed his eyes to the sound, and at that moment, he was frozen to the spot, as his mind reeled from the sensory overload.

He was vulnerable, he knew, but he could not move. Whatever the sound had been, it had been close, and to turn now would be to meet some horror or violence. Instead, he bolted forward and simultaneously fell to the floor and turned himself so that he was behind the bar, with his back pressed up against the rear. As he did so, his eyes caught the stacked glasses that were neatly lined on the shelf to his left and instinctively he grabbed one, ready to throw it should someone come into view around the side of the bar.

His pulse beat heavily through his mind, and his rapid breathing was all he could hear. Moving, he put himself up onto his haunches. Sat back as he had been, he would be in no position to defend himself. He felt assured by that action, as he was now in a position of strength should someone come at him and slowly, he regained some composure and quietened his breathing so he could hear beyond the bar and detected the change almost straightaway.

A low draught met his face, and with it, he could hear the soft moan of the wind outside. This was nothing like his experience with the library for the variation of the temperature was slight, as was the draught that touched his face.

Instead of the fear that he had felt before, he now felt his anger course through him, and he quickly stood ready to confront his tormentor. The room was as it was before, only he could now see the source of the draught within the room, for an exterior door, only yards away at the end of the room now lay open and swung gently as it was pushed by the wind outside.

Whoever he had followed here had made good their escape it seemed.

He walked over to the door and caught it, just as the wind picked up and threatened to tear it out of his grasp. Instinctively he knew this was the sound he had heard, as whoever had escaped the former pool house had crashed through the door, most likely allowing it to smash against the outside wall.

Looking beyond the threshold, he could see long into the garden before him, an expansive open lawn that went some fifty metres or so into the distance, before it passed into darkness beyond the array of spotlights that lit this side of the house. No one could be seen, and he knew pursuit was out of the question now as his assailant may have gone in any one of three directions. That said, he fancied he knew the direction she was heading; to the west, through the central garden and to her duty in the west wing.

There's been no rain.

He quietened the thought and quickly closed the door behind him. He then saw it had a latch on the inside. He secured it shut behind him, knowing there could be no return in through that door.

Why is she doing this to me?

No answer came. But what did was the matter of his trespass. Thus far the nurse had made herself known on two occasions. The first when he made tentative steps to go into the west wing of the house, despite Hodgson's instructions. The second, being the more obvious of the two, as he rifled through the personal affairs of Robert and Elizabeth McArthur in the solicitor's office.

The realisation raised an unwanted thought to cross his mind; he was the one in the wrong, not her.

Enough.

He would deal with the nurse later as now something more pressing came to his mind. Thoughts of the solicitor's office brought what he had read back to mind.

The letter from St Luke's Hospital; and talk of Elizabeth McArthur and her troubling descent into some catatonic state, and all at a time when her husband was nearing his end, preparing to confess. What did it all mean?

He turned to go when he saw it again. There in front of him, in the middle of where the swimming pool used to be; a puddle of water, and leading away and to the right a set of tiny bare footprints.

He now knew them for what they were and followed them the few short steps to the west wall of the room where they stopped. There before him on the wall was a plaque of bronze. He read;

In Loving Memory of Lydia Bennett.

1988 – 1995.

There is a star in Heaven.

It comes out every night.

I know that star is you,

Who has come to say goodnight.'

He bowed his head before the message and whispered his prayer. "Jesus is the resurrection and the life; whoever believes in him even if they die will live, and everyone who lives who believes in him will never die." He reached out and traced his hand along the lines of the plaque.

"Rest well, Lydia."

He turned and began to walk away toward the exit, even as he did so he saw that the footprints that led to the memorial did not lead away. None the less his mind did not recognise the fact, for it had begun instead to think of Father Crosby, Elizabeth McArthur and a memorial to a little girl, whose death had set the two on a very dark road.

CHAPTER 16

Fitzgerald returned to his room and made a beeline straight for the telephone. He was going to have this out with this woman Melissa, and he was going to do it right now.

Picking up the handset, he looked quizzically at the keypad, realising that he did not know how to reach an interior extension in the house. Cursing, he slammed the handset down and began to search for his visitor's guide in the hope that would offer him some clue. If he couldn't find the damn thing, he would march himself over to McArthur's rooms and have it out with the woman face to face.

The telephone rang behind him as he made the study door. He turned, and as near as able in the short space; ran the few yards to snatch the handset up.

"Yes?" He demanded.

"Father Fitzgerald?" Came the startled response.

"Melissa?"

"Yes, Father…I wanted to call through and apologise that I've not been in contact before. Mr McArthur has had a very difficult afternoon, I'm afraid. I think we will have to postpone your visit for this evening, I think."

His previous purpose forgotten, his heart sank at the news. He was keen to see his business with McArthur and Thoby Hall done as soon as possible and given the erratic; almost non-existent nature of their appointments, he wondered again as to why he should remain at the house when a simple call out, with an hours' notice would easily suffice.

The line was quiet as he pondered the message. But there was no way he could see to subvert the news.

"Father?" Came the soft voice from the receiver.

"Yes. Sorry, …I…that is regrettable news. When might I see him again?"

"I…I don't really know…" The voice wavered, and he immediately sensed some insecurity from the nurse.

Taking a deep breath, he tried to summon back some of his previous anger to help fuel his accusation. But it all seemed spent; Melissa having stolen the wind out of his sails with her bleak news.

"Melissa, tell me. Have you been over to the east wing this evening?"

"Father?"

The response caused his anger to stir as he knew he was to be met with denial.

"I found my way to the old pool house this evening." He began, carefully sidestepping his intrusion into the solicitor's office. "There was someone else there." He let the line hang for a few seconds, allowing the implication she had been found out, sink in.

"Someone else? I don't understand Father. Who might that have been? The house should have been empty as of 6 o'clock."

Fitzgerald closed his eyes. "I know. Was it you, Melissa? Whoever it was served to give me a bit of a scare."

"No, Father. I have been here with Mr McArthur. My duty forbids me from being anywhere else."

"Really?" He could hear the accusation in his tone. "And outside of the library last night? That wasn't you? You didn't leave Mr McArthur if only for a minute?"

"The library? I don't understand... Mr McArthur's condition...he..." she stammered.

Instinctively he knew her nervousness was for his insinuation that she had left her post and not for the fact that she had stalked his movements through the house.

He sighed, knowing he had addressed the matter all wrong, and this was evidenced as he sidestepped the accusation with his next line.

"I'm sorry, Melissa." He grimaced at his apology. "I meant nothing by it. Someone was lurking out by the library last night. And again tonight, someone down by the pool house. Someone keeping a low profile."

"I don't know Father." Her voice was now so soft as to barely be heard.

He could sense tears were forthcoming and knowing the battle was lost; he tried to recapture the situation, by changing the subject.

"So Mr McArthur then? Is there any possibility during the night? I am at your beck and call and the hour doesn't matter...if he is fit and awake that is."

The line was quiet for a moment. "It is possible, yes, Father. But I don't hold out much hope if I am honest. His medication will keep him under for a good few hours yet, and you understand that it takes some time to come up from it?"

"I do. Anyway, please bear it in mind. I am ready and waiting, should you call."

"Very well, Father, I will let you know if anything changes."

"Thank you, and once again, Melissa, I am sorry if I came off a bit rough. This house it…"

"Good evening Father." There followed a click sound and the soft purr of an open line. He stood there with the phone pressed to his ear for a moment more as he finished his sentence.

"…It has a way about it."

When he slept again that night, he had given in to the deep plane of unconsciousness quickly and without fear. In his dreams, he smiled as he saw himself as if from afar.

His other self was sat in a lawn chair sipping a cold iced tea beneath a free-standing black parasol that shaded him from the glare of the afternoon sun. His watching eye knew this place to be at a place called Thoby Hall, and though that thought gave him a small chill, he could not reason as to why as he saw a beautiful young girl come into view. She skipped and laughed, and the distant fear he had felt simply fluttered away on the afternoon breeze. He saw himself put his drink down and pretend that he could not see the young girl as she ran behind him and poked the straw sun hat from his head.

It was a peaceful scene, and he yearned to be closer, to be a part of it but knew he could not as he already was. The Fitzgerald he saw seemed at one with the world, and to his own amusement, he saw that this version of himself had allowed a small beard to grow on his chin. There was something else as well, but he couldn't quite put his finger on the change he saw in himself. That element though, was soon made clear as the young woman came into view. She wore a simple white shirt and sarong over a pale blue bathing suit. She wore a large straw hat to protect herself from the afternoon sun, as well as a very large pair of sunglasses that covered most of the upper part of her face. She sat beside his other self and playfully knocked off his hat again, much to the joy of the young girl who giggled incessantly as the other Fitzgerald looked about himself to find the invisible culprit who tormented him so.

Emma.

And in recognising his lost love, he understood the difference he saw in his other self. Happiness.

From his vantage point just beyond their seeing, he laughed to himself but deep down there was a sadness too, for this was something he had striven for, but never reached in his own life. A fact that was cemented as he saw Emma take his hand in hers and the two of them joined in a loving kiss, much to the disgust of the young girl who knocked his hat from his head once more. This time though he saw her and roared fake anger at her and leapt from his seat as she screamed in nervous excitement. He grabbed her and hoisted her into his arms where he succeeded in planting several kisses on her cheeks and head, despite all of her squirming efforts to escape his grasp.

At last, he lay her down on the lush grass where she continued to laugh uncontrollably for a few moments more.

Their words were lost to him as he watched on, but Fitzgerald could sense the happiness in them. He watched as his other self, sat by Emma, whose radiant smile seemed to intensify the feeling of joy that the three shared. But despite their happiness, the scene that played out before him seemed all at once very different to him.

At first, he did not comprehend the nature of the change as it had been so subtle. The three beneath him went on as before and rather than identifying a physical difference to what he saw; he realised that the change was within himself. All was not well somehow, and he could not shake the feeling of anxiousness that had suddenly come over him.

He searched left and right and was amazed to find that he was restricted only to this one view as from twenty or so yards away, for when he shifted his sight, the picture of the three moved with him so that it was always central. The sensation was odd, and he was reminded of a time when he was small and was gifted a 3D view master for his birthday present. The toy came with a circular reel of images which could be changed at the click of the button, giving the viewer a supposed 3D view of whatever reel the user had chosen. He remembered that his favourites had depicted dinosaurs. This, from a time long before he got into the craze of Star Wars' figurines. But with the red contraption held up to your eyes, there was no movement of head or eyes that could shake the image from the centre of your view. The sensation of what he now saw was very much the same; only these were moving pictures.

What he saw demanded to be seen, it was obvious, but what was it that begged his attention? Despite his ill-feeling, the scene that continued to play out was one of happiness.

When he saw it, his heart sank, but he did not know not why. The building was at the very periphery of his vision, and though he sought to focus upon it, it was but a vague shape at the utmost end of his sight. It hurt his eyes and so he relaxed his eyes and instead looked upon the three frolicking figures that were the centre of his experience. All the while though his eyes strained to look back to the small building and each time they did so, it was as if there was something different.

Whatever it was refused to come into focus, and the flickering of his eyes back and forth did nothing to ease his frustration.

His attention was quickly brought back to the three people at the fore of his vision, for now, they seemed to be in conversation, and somehow he understood that the young girl had requested something of them. Perhaps it was within the body language, for he saw himself exchange a knowing glance with Emma who nodded her agreement. The young girl literally jumped with joy and ran off toward the building that had plagued him so at the corner of his eye.

His heart lurched, and he was immediately overcome with dread as he followed the girl's path. Still, though the building would not come into view for him and he knew that when she reached it, she would be gone. No, not just gone, removed. To go there, was somehow the end for her. He tried his voice and in his mind, heard his scream.

"Lydia no!"

Was that her name? He couldn't be sure. But what was clear was that his voice carried no sound for still, she ran onward to the (*swimming pool*) building at the edge of the small-windowed world.

"No! Come back!"

His other self, sat up (*Did he hear me?*) and looked about himself, but not after the young girl.

Lydia, her name is Lydia. But if that is so, then this is all wrong.

He knew it was true, because this image belonged to another time, one that he and Emma could not be a part of.

The scene that played out before his eyes had twisted, a pleasant dream come nightmare, and he knew what was about to happen unless he could reach himself.

"Iain!" he yelled. "Iain, stop her, don't let her go! She…she will be drowned. You must not let her go!"

This other Iain Fitzgerald continued to look about himself with a frown upon his face. Though he screamed the words, he knew they carried no weight and were delivered as little more than a whisper on the afternoon breeze. Even so, they were reaching him. He glanced nervously now toward Lydia. The perspective now was strange for she had become a blur herself as she neared the edge of his vision, he still estimated that she was only halfway to the building and so there was perhaps still time.

His other self, asked a question of Emma and though he did not hear it, he knew he asked if she had heard something. She shook her head.

Although he had no physical being in that picture-postcard world, his throat was raw as he screamed at himself. He looked desperately between himself and the retreating figure of the girl.

"Iain, please! Please look" he searched again for the tiny figure of the running girl all the while pleading with himself to make it stop and bring her back. "Iain, please…"

He stopped short. There at the corner of his eye, another change had come over the world, and he strained his eyes, oblivious to the ache as he made out what he believed to be a doorway at the side of the pool house. It stood open and from it poured a dark pool of shadow.

"Lydia! Lydia no!" He screamed, and for one instant it seemed she heard him, for she looked back. He was awestruck as he beheld her, unsure of himself of how to reach her and prevent the inevitable.

She began to turn once more, and now the dark cloud that poured from the room could not be denied. Still, it hurt his eyes to look, but this was not due to the strain of seeing that which would not focus. Instead, the pain was from beholding the smothering clouds of shadow that now held the entire left side of his picture and infiltrated slowly but surely toward its middle.

It was already too late, for she had turned back toward it and if she saw as he did, she gave no clue for she went willingly onward to her death. The black arms of the shadow reached for her now as she came close, yearning for her and all the while she was oblivious for she began to skip the last few yards happily before she was consumed in darkness.

CHAPTER 17

The following day dawned drab and wet as before. Fitzgerald felt low as his remaining sleep had been fitful; memories of Emma following him into waking and preventing any hope of further rest. As a result, he was already wide awake as the spotlights in the garden turned off as one at 07:30 am.

As time passed and he surveyed the high ceiling above, he heard the soft drone of a car engine growing louder, signalling the arrival of the first of the day staff coming to the house.

His mind went at once to the nurse Keira, who would be relieving Melissa of her duties. This, in turn, brought back memories of the previous night and his experience in the solicitor's office; still unresolved as the damned woman Melissa had denied her presence over on the east wing.

Why on earth would she follow me there?

His mind gave no reply and instead brought to mind a picture of the memorial to young Lydia Bennett. He shook his head and pinched the bridge of his nose to try and clear his thoughts. The image persisted though, and he kicked his covers to the foot of the bed as a final image of wet footprints surfaced in his mind, and he wondered again as to why Melissa should have approached him in such a way.

Soon though, such thoughts were washed away as hot torrents of water cascaded over his naked form. The shower, rejuvenating his tired body and mind. And so it was with a positive step that he left the apartment, intent to visit McArthur's apartment in person to check on the man's welfare and establish when they might pick up their conversations.

It was en route that he was intercepted by Hodgson, who surprised him as he made his way through the lobby of the house. A nondescript door to the right of the double staircase opened, the woman appearing and making a beeline directly across the lobby floor toward him.

"Father Fitzgerald, I was wondering if I might have a moment of your time?" Straight to business as usual it seemed.

"Of course. Erm, where shall we…?" he murmured in response.

"Just here, the Stewards Room." She beckoned with her hand, showing him the door from which she had just come.

"Very good." He said, leading the way into a small room that contained little more than a small desk and two chairs. Fitzgerald guessed that she did not meet many people here in this room as it was undoubtedly too cramped for comfort. He also wondered just how much time she might spend here, alone.

"Please take a seat, Father. I won't take up too much of your time."

He sat on the uncushioned chair and looked around while she skirted the side of the desk to take her own seat.

On her desk, he saw a very old looking computer monitor, such was its thickness. Similarly to Harvey's office, she also had the inevitable in/out tray. Hers though looked like it saw a lot more use as a bundle of papers and letters threatened to escape the out pile on the bottom rung. Also on the desk was a single photo frame; it's back toward him. He could only surmise that this might be some relative, a husband perhaps or maybe a child.

The frame was the only item that he might consider to be a personal effect and the idea troubled him, knowing full well how many years the woman had served here at the house.

"I'll get straight to the point Father." She had not so much as touched her seat before she began. "You've been upsetting the staff here, and it is to stop immediately."

His mind reeled, at a loss as to the accusation, but quickly he knew of what she spoke — his phone call to Melissa only last night.

The realisation might have brought some element of guilt at having been found out, but instead, he felt his anger begin to rise to the surface. He was at once returned to his former state; tired, drawn-out and stressed from his time here in the house. This was the very last thing he needed.

How dare she?! His mind protested. *She's the one who is stalking me!*

He was now in no mood for pleasantries as he answered. "I will stop you right there, Mrs Hodgson, whatever I said to Melissa was deserved…"

He stopped himself as he saw Hodgson's brow furrow in puzzlement. His sentence went unfinished as she spoke instead.

"Melissa? I don't know what you are talking about Father, but I hope you have not been upsetting that poor young girl? Mr McArthur's care is a lonely and thankless task. Both Melissa and Keira do sterling work in difficult conditions. No, I wanted to talk to you about Douglas."

Dougie? He opened his mouth to answer, but she clearly hadn't finished.

"Perhaps Father, you would care to explain why he phoned me at home, drunk, in the early hours and in tears over matters that occurred years ago?"

He was at once at a loss, her words bringing no understanding.

"You've been here but a few days and already you've contrived to damage that poor soul. I doubt you would know this Father, but Douglas has been on the wagon successfully for 6 years now, and whatever it was you have said to him has set him back…"

A picture formed in his mind, the time of their meeting in the garden and the sharing of his thermos.

"Will you join me, Father? A small nip to keep the cold out?"

"Aye. All the best drinks have a hint of Irish about them."

Six years? I don't think so, Mrs Hodgson.

He kept the thought to himself. If Douglas wanted Hodgson to believe he had been on the wagon, then that was his business and not Fitzgerald's to share. Being that he would not tell, he now knew full well that she had the moral high ground in this argument and nothing he could say would appease her without breaking a confidence.

"…and furthermore, what business is it of yours to go questioning as to the history here anyway?" she continued. "Those things, those sad, tragic things are best left where they are. In the past."

Lydia.

At last, understanding came to him.

"Mrs Hodgson, please. It was not my intent to upset anyone. If anything some of the information was volunteered. You are right on one aspect I agree. Those events are tragic and upsetting, but what else is a priest for than to share such sorrow and upset? That I might be able to help someone overcome what had happened."

Hodgson snorted her objection. "Oh please. By stoking up fires long dead? Dougie doesn't need spiritual enlightenment, Father. I wager you did not talk as long to know that he has little faith. That little girl's passing took that from him. And perhaps he was the lucky one, what with poor young Elizabeth and Father Crosby."

"And you, Mrs Hodgson? What of you? Is it fair to say that everyone has had closure from what occurred?" He knew the question was likely to win him no favours, but his anger was keen to push her buttons and see what reaction he might provoke. Instead, she just looked sad.

"It isn't me I worry for Father. That day in 96 was the last happy day I knew here. Robert and Elizabeth, so in love, the house alive and wonderful!"

133

"It was after that when the money started to go, and the assets stripped away. Robert I think was shellshocked by it all and was but a bystander as his wife was taken away from him and his fortune dwindled. Did you know that he donated the family some quarter of a million pounds for their loss? Nobody asked him to do that, but he did it anyway, no doubt knowing even then that his financial security was limited."

The conversation was taking a turn that Fitzgerald had not anticipated. She was a hard woman, no doubt of that, but the fact remained that this house and the McArthur family (what there was of it) belonged to her in a way, for her to safeguard and care for. And what would happen when he was gone, and the home passed over to the Catholic Church? What would she have to live for then, but to dwindle away her final years alone and unneeded?

His anger was softening now as she opened up to him. Perhaps she also needed counsel or maybe just his ear to speak of what troubled her.

"That was extremely generous of him. He is a remarkable man."

She nodded vehemently and quickly reached for the top drawer of her desk from which she produced a packet of cigarettes, a lighter and ashtray.

"Do you mind?" She questioned, seemingly none too worried about what his answer was going to be. "Filthy habit." She said as he nodded his agreement to her.

"Your business, with Mr McArthur. When is that likely to be concluded?" she questioned.

"I don't know Mrs Hodgson. I really don't know how much more he has to tell me."

"That will be the end of him, you know? I mean, he has only fought this long so that he can confess."

"I am sorry." And he was. He sensed the bond that she held with her employer. He knew as well that those feelings were unlikely to be reciprocated, such was the social and class difference between the two.

"What will become of me then, eh?"

Fitzgerald hesitated, hoping the question was rhetorical. It was, for she quickly filled the small silence she had created. "Ah never mind that now, but what of Douglas? That is what we are talking about. You know Mr McArthur's passing will affect him also once your Catholic Church has its clutches on the house."

So she knows after all.

There was no trace of bitterness as she spoke. Of course, she was right. What room was there for a drunken ageing gardener in this day and age?

"I don't know, but though you are sure I am meddling in matters that are not my concern, you should know that Dougie's spiritual health is of importance to me. Perhaps he has unresolved issues that I may be able to help him with. If he is drinking, I can try to help him and refer him to the proper support, but know I would be there to see him through all of it. If that is what he would wish."

"Would you, Father?" He saw hope on her face, and he felt guilty for how he had spoken to her. He had judged her a meddler, but the truth was that beneath the tough facade that she put on, that she did care about Douglas and his wellbeing.

"Of course. I assure you I had no idea that such matters still haunted him; it was never my intention to hurt him in any way."

She stubbed her cigarette on the ashtray. Returning to her desk, she returned the smoking paraphernalia to the drawer and out of sight. She sat and searched his eyes, and though he felt uncomfortable beneath her hard eyes, he held her gaze to give her the assurances that he was as good as his word.

"Mrs Hodgson," he said at last, "If you should wish it, I would be glad to be there for you to, should you need me."

Surprise filled her face and left him wondering if anyone had made such an effort to reach out to her in the last few years or beyond.

"I…," she stammered, "Well, thank you, but for now I think all is well, but when the time comes I may take you up on your offer. Perhaps when all of this is over, it will be time for me to embrace my Church again."

He smiled at her, and she returned with one of her own. For now at least he felt he had won her trust. How long that would last, he didn't know. Satisfied, he stood up.

"That sounds excellent. But please remember I am here for the foreseeable future. Should you have any need, please do not hesitate to come and see me," he replied.

He had turned the situation around marvellously. She was a woman of faith it transpired, and her harsh words had only been in the interests of Dougie and his mental health. Women such as Hodgson had a strong reliance on their faith, their Church and their priest and as a result of that, he hoped they would share a better relationship as a result.

He stood from his chair, waiting to see if there would be anything further. Hodgson, still smiling, came back from around her desk and opened the door for him. He stepped through. "Perhaps we will speak again soon?" he ventured.

"Yes, absolutely." She turned and allowed the door to fall shut behind her. In that small moment, a thought occurred to him. All their talk regarding Dougie had centred around the tragic passing of Lydia Bennett, but there had been other elements to his conversation with the aged gardener which now returned to him.

Though he had hidden the true details of his experiences outside of the library, Douglas had gone to no small lengths to warn him away from that room. And now that memory served to bring another detail to mind.

"Mrs Hodgson?"

She put her hand out to stop the door. Turning to him again, she answered, "Yes, Father?"

"Forgive me, but I was curious. I have so much time on my hands. I was wondering if the work on the chimney was nearly at an end? I was hoping to access the library."

He was hoping that his request seemed nonchalant and an easy way to introduce his question about the moment he saw her share with the stranger in the first-floor window.

Her face, up until that point, a simple mask of calm, turned in a split second and he could sense the anxiety beneath as she spoke and tripped over her words.

"No, no, no, Father. The library…it is out of bounds. It is dangerous there…the chimney…"

"But I thought I saw someone… on the day I first arrived…"

Her eyes grew wide as he spoke.

"You saw what?" An unexpected accusation in her tone; incredulous at his words.

"Why, yes…perhaps if others have access…"

He was cut off quickly. "No, Father. Forget what you think you saw. There was no one there. No one at all." Hodgson had found her resolve.

"But…"

"No buts. It is out of the question. The library is closed and will remain that way." She abruptly turned and went back into the Stewards Room, the door falling shut behind her. This time there were no words to call her back with, he was speechless.

Her reaction had shocked him, and he had seen the underlying fear in her eyes as he spoke of the figure at the window.

What was clear was that whatever trust he had built during their conversation had instantly been destroyed. But why would she react like that? Who was the figure at the window and why such a reaction?

Whatever the answers, it was clear that both she and Dougie had serious issues surrounding the room.

Perhaps they had something happen there as well?

136

He shut the thought down. He had reasoned his experience down to the night nurse Melissa and the games she was playing with him. He would not speculate as to Hodgson or Dougie or to why they exhibited such strange reactions to talk of the library.

Shaking his head, he began to walk back towards the east wing, forgetting his original plan to call on McArthur's rooms, as he had another thought. If Hodgson would not tell him what was going on, then Dougie would. The man had even gone so far as to extend the invitation to question him further.

And so he set off toward the rear of the house, his mind reaching back to the time he had arrived at Thoby Hall, and seeing the figure there in the library window. This, followed by the strange moment he observed between the stranger and Hodgson. But the real question was why would she deny such a thing? He needed answers and now.

CHAPTER 18

Having left the house at the rear of the east wing, Fitzgerald ventured across the expansive lawn that sat behind the former pool house. The morning dew upon the grass brushed the hem of his trousers as he went, making them wet and uncomfortable.

He was following the direction in which Douglas had gone following their conversation in the garden the previous day, in the hope that he would find some workshop or shed from which the man operated.

He zeroed in on one of the huge spotlights that sat flush in the middle of the garden and made his way toward it. As he came alongside, he could see that a thick power cable, protruded from the rear of the contraption and wound its snake-like way down to the ground and disappeared. Nudging the grass with his foot, he saw the slight protrusion of a plastic pipe that swallowed the cable and led it underground. Wherever the power source for the device was, he could not tell.

As he had looked out on this area last night, he could not see past this machine due to the darkness that had fallen behind its beam. But on his approach in the light of day, he was quick to see a large hedgerow only some twenty metres or so beyond, and in it, a large gap which had been cut, creating an arch and thus creating an entranceway to what lay beyond.

As he made the gap, the lawn began to fall away in a deep decline and there ahead was that which he was undoubtedly seeking.

The workshop was red brick and had a flat roof. To its west side, he could see that it had a large shutter, big enough to drive a small vehicle through when open. And to its front lay a single door and high narrow windows; enough to allow light in, but too high to look through. Beyond the workshop lay the border of the garden, for a barbed wire fence ran long into the distance in both directions, and beyond that lay a sparse-looking wooded area.

There were no signs of life as Fitzgerald made the doorway. He knocked hard on the wooden door and waited, keening his ear for signs of life beyond. All though was quiet, and he searched about himself, wondering if Douglas was elsewhere on the Estate tending to its upkeep.

His vantage point offered no clue as to where Douglas might be. From his low lying position, he could not see the house beyond the large hedge line from where he had come.

Douglas could be anywhere on the Estate, and he could walk around the circumference of the grounds for ages without happening upon him.

Frustrated, he turned to the door and knocked again. This time he fancied he heard some noise from within. It had only been slight, but in the quiet of the morning about him, it had been undeniable.

"Douglas?" He called, as he reached for the door and pulled it outward toward him.

Stepping in, he was met by a multitude of smells that immediately denoted the use of the space as a gardener's workshop; cut grass, engine oil, fertiliser. The scent was not unpleasant to his nose, and his mind was immediately cast back to his father's small wooden garden shed which had sat at the bottom of their garden.

It had held little more than a mower and a garden fork, but even so, his dad had spent many long hours there in the long summer months. It invoked happy memories, of time spent together while he had been still alive, as out there in the garden his father was unrestricted by his mother's overbearing nature. Out there, he had gotten a glimpse of the man who he really was, as opposed to the repressed quiet man of the house.

The room he now entered was dark, the high windows affording little light due to the grey November morning outside. Immediately to his front, he saw a long workbench, and in the centre of the room, a ride on mower, with its canopy raised affording a view of its inner working parts.

Douglas was sat with his eyes closed in a lawn chair over by the main shutter. Fitzgerald could hear the low snore that came in time with his breathing. He was dressed, much the same as he had been on their first meeting, wrapped up warm against the late autumn cold.

To the floor on his left and beyond the reach of his limp arm, was a metallic hip flask, and with the sight of it, Fitzgerald now fancied he could smell whisky among the rich blend of aromas in the air about him.

Oh, Douglas.

Hodgson had been right.

He stood there a moment, looking down upon Douglas's craggy-like features; caught in indecision. He had hoped to find answers here, but much the same as a night some weeks past, the man he would question was passed out. As on that night with Father Liam Shilling, he made the same decision; that he would let sleeping dogs lie.

He turned to go, and his foot made contact with a metal oil can that he had not seen. It had sat on the ground beneath the open canopy of the mower and now skidded several feet away, making a hollow ringing sound as it collided with the concrete floor.

"What?" Douglas stirred immediately awake.

Shit.

Douglas raised himself quickly out of his chair and rocked unsteadily on his feet.

"Father Fitzgerald? What on earth are you doing here?"

"Dougie, I am so sorry I woke you. I had hoped to talk to you, but I..."

Dougie's head lolled forward as he surveyed the priest from under furrowed eyebrows.

"Jesus, Father, that's no way to introduce yourself, I near had a heart attack!"

Fitzgerald looked down and saw the offending oil can on its side, a small pool of oil puddled about the now open lid.

"I..."

Douglas turned away from him though and with one lithe movement bent low and snatched the flask from the floor and deftly made it disappear into the inside pocket of his parka coat.

"You'll not be telling her highness I was asleep on the job now will you?"

Fitzgerald smiled, knowing full well he was referring to Hodgson.

"No, not at all. I'm sorry I woke you like that, I thought it best to leave you be when I..."

Douglas was already nodding as his eyes turned to the upturned oil can. "No matter Father. I'll get that in a bit. Now, pray tell, what brings you down to my little retreat, huh?"

Fitzgerald weighed up how he was going to best deliver his questions. He also wanted to address the matter of Dougie calling Hodgson in the middle of the night, in tears and turning to the bottle as his comfort. But that said, he could not open like that. Dougie had already snatched away the evidence of his drinking as if ashamed, so no, he would have to introduce that part slowly.

Instead, he could open with an invitation accepted.

"When we last spoke Dougie, you said I should come find you if I had a purpose here beyond Mr McArthur. Well...I don't know how to put it, but I have some grave concerns about what has transpired here. As yet, I have barely begun my business with Mr McArthur, but I am concerned that matters involving his wife, Elizabeth and the death of the young girl Lydia still take a difficult toll on the house and its residents."

A pained look came upon Dougie's face and all at once he rocked forward on his feet. Fitzgerald felt a panic and snatched forward a pace, believing the man might faint or fall. However, he quickly rocked back again on the balls of his feet, and as he did so let himself fall back into the garden chair, he had initially been sitting in. The chair legs threatened to buckle underneath him as his weight fell into it, but mercifully they held.

140

"Aye, I did, didn't I? And here you are. I guess that's why I've fallen back into my drinking of late, as I knew you'd be calling at some point. Could be no doubt about that, once you had spent some time up at the house and started seeing things there."

"Dougie…"

"Don't try and deny it to me, Father, you were loath to say anything yesterday I know. But up there by that library, something happened to you, didn't it?"

Fitzgerald began to shake his head but quickly stopped. He would have to be open with this man if he wanted to get answers.

"Yes, okay, there was something you are right. Things in the house are somewhat odd, to say the least. First of all, I get a fright up by the library and then last night, out by the pool house…"

Douglas's eyes became large, and at once, he knew he had touched on something.

"The pool house, Father. What on earth took you there?!"

Fitzgerald considered for a moment. He would tell all of it, trespass and all.

"I followed someone there, Dougie. I was in the solicitor's office last night. I don't know what took me there, but the truth is my stay here at Thoby Hall is somewhat forced."

"There is no need to be coy with me, Father. I know more than you might reckon. Tell me what happened with the pool house."

Fitzgerald looked deep within the eyes of the aged gardener. They were alive and lucid. If the man had taken a drink, he seemed coherent and alive to the conversation. What was more, he was hinting that he knew well the fate of Thoby Hall on McArthur's inevitable passing.

"I'll admit I was where I shouldn't have been. But it was clear that someone had followed me there. The girl Melissa…I haven't met her yet, but there outside of the library and again last night…it's like she is playing a game with me."

Dougie though, was shaking his head as the words flowed. Fitzgerald at once felt a pang of irritation toward the man.

"Games, Father? That wee night nurse? I don't think so. I thought you'd come to me because you were ready to tell me what happened up there."

Fitzgerald though felt triumphant. Dougie's words had reminded him to one of the stranger aspects of his experience of the previous night, one which he was keen to share to win his argument through.

"Wee girl, you say? Well, I had proof of that alright. It was the darnedest thing, I don't know why she is choosing to play these games with me, but she left proof. It must have been raining…"

His mind went at once to the moment he had stared out of the back door of the pool house in the hope of seeing his tormentor fleeing the scene. He had looked across the same long lawn he had only just crossed this morning to reach Dougie. There had been no sign of it having rained last night.

None the less he continued. "She took her shoes off so she could sneak up to the door without making any sound. She left her footprints there Douglas, her small wet footprints."

He looked on Douglas to see the man had understood his words and the evidence in them, that the night nurse Melissa was somehow stalking him through the house.

Instead, he saw that Dougie's pallor was as white as a sheet. His eyes wide again, seeming to bore through Fitzgerald's own. All the while, his mouth hung wide open.

"Dougie? What is it?" His concern was instant.

Slowly Dougie shook his head and closed his eyes. "Footprints Father? Small bare footprints?"

"Yes. She must have taken her shoes off. It's like…"

"Lydia."

The name hung in the air between them. Fitzgerald at once confused by the introduction of the young girl, while Dougie was silent, searching in Fitzgerald's eyes for understanding.

"L…Lydia?" He managed. "Dougie, what on earth?"

The old man looked sad. "Father, I said to you that if you had a purpose here beyond McArthur to seek me out. I don't think you've found that purpose yet, nowhere near in fact. I think you've felt what dwells in that house, though you rationalise it as something else. You've felt something in that library, Father. Something evil. And there, there in the pool house? Something altogether different. A stray soul perhaps…that poor young girl."

Tears were now welling in Dougie's eyes. And here, Fitzgerald knew, was precisely what Hodgson had alluded to him less than 15 minutes ago.

"Tell me, Dougie. I want to know. That poor girl's death impacted on this house and Elizabeth was lost as a result. I think you've suffered to, so please tell me what it is that has got you this way."

Dougie dabbed his eyes with his sleeve. "Right. I'll tell you. But I wager it's nothing like what you expect to hear. I hope when I'm done, you'll see things in a new light and understand what I am telling you about that house. It's not easy listening Father but bear with me to the end. Then ask your questions."

"I will."

"Good, then first of all, know that I was here the day it happened. The day that Lydia Bennett died…"

CHAPTER 19

Saturday, 19th August 1995.

Thoby Hall.

11:30 am.

Douglas Foster was getting frustrated. He heaved on the starter cable of the dilapidated old lawnmower for what seemed like the umpteenth time, and only got a small cough of acknowledgement from the machine in response. A keen sweat had formed on his brow and had begun to trickle uncomfortably down his chest making his t-shirt wet. The effort to start the mower was one thing, but the relentless glare of the August sun from the cloudless sky above made every movement difficult.

He had dragged the mower out to the east side of the house in good spirits only an hour earlier and had been full of the joys of the day. A hot summer's day such as this was no bad place to be when you were the head groundsman for a beautiful home like Thoby Hall.

He had begun here some five years ago, only a hired hand for the summer season, back when the flock of tourists was at its highest. But as the years had gone on and he had returned over and over, his patience it seemed had finally been rewarded because he had at last ascended to the top job. In fairness such a thing had been easy for him because most of the casual labour changed every year; most of the hired staff being in their late teens or early twenties, merely holding down summer jobs while whatever School or University was in hiatus.

But year-on-year he came back, and though the former groundsman, the late Mr Hodgson was a stern taskmaster, his hard work and enthusiasm had perhaps earned him some well-earned respect. So much so, that when Hodgson suffered his first heart attack, he was finally called upon to come to the house on a full-time basis.

The job was not perhaps particularly well paid, and the work could be hard and long. Budgets it seemed were on the wane as were the number of temporary staff he was allowed to employ on an annual basis. Okay, he had dealt with such problems, but what he couldn't deal with was this fucking lawnmower which he had spent most of yesterday servicing and replacing the spark plugs on. It had fired up like a dream yesterday, so what the hell was the problem now? He had petitioned old Mr McArthur by letter regarding funding for gardening equipment. Resigned as he was to doing the majority of the work himself. The toil he could muster, but he could not do so without the proper tools.

It had been Mrs Hodgson though, in her capacity as head of the household who had sought him out and refused his request — making it clear in no uncertain terms that any such applications must go through her. Mr McArthur was not to be bothered in any way shape or form. He soon learnt that this would be a waste of effort as time and time again all such requests were refused and more than that, budgets were subtly cut. He knew the answer, of course, and the answer was in the shape of the new Mrs McArthur.

He could not be angry though, and he wondered how much Elizabeth knew of the house's ailing fortunes. He wasn't party to the accounts of course, but you didn't need to be a genius to see the cutbacks that were being made to accommodate the young woman and her extravagances. The new swimming pool for one that had been dug into the foundations of the east sunroom was evidence of such excess, and no doubt cost old Mr McArthur several thousands of pounds.

There were years between the two of course and anyone that did not know them might take her for a gold digger. Douglas had thought along those lines himself until that was, he finally met her and saw how she was with the old man. She seemed to have a way about her that instantly made one at ease in her company and he had even seen her put a smile on Mrs Hodgson's face on occasion which was more than a rare thing after her husband's passing.

In fact, when she first entered the house, he had allowed himself a small fantasy that the two might have some illicit affair.

'Lady McArthur and her Lover'. That always made him smile at the thought. Such fantasy stemmed from his baser emotions and were built primarily of lust, for she was an extremely beautiful young woman. It was no wonder that Mr McArthur showered her with gifts and allowed such things as the swimming pool to be built, for he must have constantly feared that his young wife might someday leave him or perhaps have an affair (with some handsome gardener). But Douglas knew he need not have worried. You only had to see the way she looked at McArthur and how she behaved in his company to know she was deeply in love. Douglas felt sorry for the man and for the deep-seated paranoia that would undoubtedly consume him. Such a thing was easy to see, for as easy as it was to see the love in her eyes, it was doubly easy to see the mistrust and anger in his when he saw her talking or laughing with any man.

For now, such thoughts were melting far away and he was on the verge of a meltdown of his own, such was his anger at the mower. Well, he would be damned if he was going to stand under the unforgiving sun and cook for no good reason, and so decided that he would retreat to his workshop that was situated at the bottom of the gardens. He pulled the machine behind him as he began the long trek.

As he neared his destination, the sound of laughter drifted over the high hedgerows, and he smiled in spite of his bad mood. A large splash followed, and he knew that a party of children on their school holidays were currently enjoying the newly-built swimming pool. That was one of the things he liked about Elizabeth. She had a capacity for giving and sharing as he had never known before. On the other side of the hedge, he knew that there was a small group of housewives and mothers, all of whom Elizabeth had befriended in her short time within Ashmarsh.

He had seen them there as he passed by the first time. The mothers outside, underneath a large sun umbrella, downing cocktails while the children laughed and played, shouting to get their parent's attention to watch as they jumped into the pool. All the time a small CD player blurted out what he thought was perhaps the most annoying song of the year, 'Cotton Eye Joe'.

Elizabeth though had stopped to wave at him, and he thought he heard some girlish giggling as he walked out of sight. Not Elizabeth, but perhaps a few others held fantasies about gardeners? He could only hope as much, and he made sure to walk as close to the gap in the hedge as he could to afford the women there a view of his tanned, muscular body. Well, once he had sucked his belly in that was.

He snatched a glance as he went but saw that the women there were now engaged with their children who were out in the sun cavorting about the garden, as such none had paid him any more notice as he went. He looked for Elizabeth, but she was nowhere to be seen.

He reached his workshop and dragged the mower in behind him. The shade within was an instant relief, and he went straight to the bottle of water he had brought in. He gulped quickly, and liquid ran from his chin, making a dark stain on the chest of his shirt. The water felt good, and he upended the bottle over his head and allowed the last of the water to cool his brow. He blew the remnants away and ran his hand through his thick brown hair to smooth it back. His fit of anger was now gone, and he felt better being sheltered from the hot day.

Only mad dogs and Englishmen…

Turning his attention to the mower, he placed a booted foot on it once more and pulled heavily on the power cord. Nothing.

He frowned and bent down to the machine. What on earth could be the problem? He was wary of flooding the motor as he had several times pressed the fuel injection button which was designed to get petrol into the fuel chamber. The button though felt leaden and did not depress fully as he put his thumb on it. Perhaps there was a problem with the fuel line?

He leant in low and gathered the machine up in his hands. It was a very old model and predictably heavy. He strained as his legs straightened and managed to heave the mower onto his workspace in one clean, quick lift. That would afford him better access to its working parts, as he had no desire to strain his back by working on the floor.

He wasn't sure how long it was that he was tinkering away at the innards of the machine, perhaps only moments, but he quickly got a sense that he wasn't alone. He had not heard the door open behind him and quickly, a smile came to his face, for he thought that perhaps one of the women in the garden had followed him over. He allowed the smile to fall as he turned as he wanted to appear cool. He was glad he had tipped the water over his head as his t-shirt now clung to him like a second skin and made his pecs stand out against the thin material.

There was no woman though, only a young girl.

She could perhaps have been no more than 8 years old he saw. She wore a one-piece bathing suit that had pictures from the television show The Simpsons, and he could see that she was wet through as if she had just got out of the water.

"Oh, hi, honey. What are you doing down here?" Douglas asked.

The girl though remained quiet and a small puddle of water formed at her feet as she stood there. He did not know this child, and though there were a few familiar faces amongst the group in the garden, he could not guess as to who she belonged to.

"What's your name, honey? Won't your mum be missing you?" He tried again.

She shook her head, and he could see she looked sad. She was only a slight little thing; long brown hair weaved into two long plaits that fell down her back. She had light freckles on her nose and piercing blue eyes. Douglas was beginning to feel uncomfortable at her presence. It was one thing for a cute young milf to come over but a kid? This would not look good if one of the mothers came over to find them here like this.

In this day and age, there was an instant mistrust of middle-aged men no matter their agenda. Douglas could understand it of course. It had only been last year or so that he had seen the news reports; a 6-year-old girl who had made national news having been snatched from a holiday home on the Norfolk coast and been raped and murdered. These kinds of stories seemed all too prevalent nowadays, and he wondered what had gone wrong with the world when he read and saw reports such as these.

When he was a lad, he had been free to roam the town or countryside with his friends until all hours. As long as he was back by dark, there would be no issues with his parents who would have had no idea as to who he was with or what he had been up to. They had been simpler times, but he knew of course that he had been sheltered from such despicable crime, though certainly it had no doubt carried on. Imagination and paranoia could be a parent's worst nightmare he knew, though he had no children of his own and he knew if he was to be seen here alone with this little girl that the wrong conclusions might be drawn.

"Maybe we better get you back, hey?" Douglas said, stepping over toward her. He leaned past and opened the door to show her the way. Nervously looking out to make sure that there wasn't someone coming over to find them. At the very least they would be better off outside if they were seen.

The girl did not move though, and Douglas felt an instant irritation toward her. Why had she even come here?

"What's the matter, don't you want to go back?" He regretted the question instantly as it sounded like an offer to remain. "I mean aren't you having fun up at the pool?"

She shook her head slowly and bowed her head.

So what was he to do already? He was a confirmed bachelor and easing the woes of the under 10's was not his forte. He looked back through the single pane of glass within the door, desperately looking toward the house, where he knew the group of mothers to be, half hoping that one such mother would now be seen walking over in their direction. But alas no.

For the sake of his comfort he now stepped outside and held the door open, hoping that the message was clear for the girl, that his workshop was out of bounds and for that matter, so was he. He felt sorry for her that was true, but shouldn't the mum be dealing with these sort of things instead of getting half-cut on white wine or cocktails at just gone 11:30 am?

He was just about to reply to the girl, perhaps to tell her that it would all be alright when a high-pitched scream cut through the air from somewhere behind him. He started at the interruption and quickly looked back out over to the house.

What the hell was that?

Quickly though all became quiet again and he stood paused, holding the door and in that same moment the light grew dim, and he was surprised when he looked up to see a dark cloud had drawn itself over the sun. The effect on the scene was stark, and he watched as several partridges took to the air from a nearby copse of bushes. All had become quiet, and he hesitated as he could not comprehend from where or from whom the scream had come. The girl was forgotten behind him, and he simply stood there waiting for something to happen. At that moment, stood there by the workshop, was as if he and the world about him were in freeze-frame, as nothing stirred and not a sound could be heard. So intent was he on concentrating, that he found he had held his breath, so intent on some noise or action to break the moment.

It did quickly, for there was a tug at his hand and he looked down to see the girl was by his side. Silent tears now rolled down her cheek and she looked imploringly up at his face, and for a moment he was lost in her deep blue eyes. Another shout though from beyond the hedges and his attention quickly reverted to the scene that was being played out just out of sight up at the house. Unknowingly he dropped the girl's hand and took a tentative step toward the growing sound. Then, at last, he was stirred into action as one word, clearer and louder than all others could be heard over all else. "Help."

He turned back toward the girl. Whatever it was that had been upsetting her would have to wait for now, and he began to speak as he looked back for her. "Look, honey, I gotta…" He pulled up short though, for the girl was gone.

He snapped his head around behind him, half expecting that she had slipped behind his back as he had turned, but nothing, she was not there.

"What the hell?"

For a moment, all else was forgotten for his mind couldn't comprehend her absence. She had been at his side just a second ago, so where had she gone? He still had the workshop door held open, and he put his head back through the door.

"Honey?" There was though no room for hiding in the small workspace and the only sign that the girl had ever been there was her tiny wet footprints and a small puddle of water that had formed where she had stood. How had she managed that? He looked back out through the door, half expecting to see her little legs scampering up the lawn and toward the house, but again there was nothing to be seen.

He did not have time to dwell on such things though as another shout for help went up from the direction of the house, and this time he did not hesitate. The door snapped shut behind him as he went off at a sprint. He was quickly blowing as he made the fifty yards or so to the hedgerow where he knew the party to be.

A large chatter could be heard from the other side, and the radio had been snapped off it seemed. Breaking the corner, he came to a stop, for the scene before him did not make immediate sense. There appeared to be a division in the group, for some three or so women stood to the side and had their children pressed close to them. The source of the situation was not immediately clear, but he also saw that several others were crowded close to the door of the pool house. The atmosphere was muted now, and he saw that several of the children had been crying and were being soothed by their mothers, who held them close to their breast. He searched the faces of those present, looking for some direction as to what had happened, but none came. He saw that Elizabeth was not among them and so he walked over toward the pool house where the second group was gathered.

"What…" he began, as he approached. But his words fell quickly away for as he made the group, he was afforded a view of the pool room itself and there, by the side he could see the back of Elizabeth McArthur who was kneeling over a young child and doing what he could only surmise to be chest compressions. By her side was a young woman who Douglas did not know. Tears rolled down her face, and he could hear her words as she held the lifeless hand of the child that was lain there.

"Wake up for mummy. Come on, honey. Please wake up."

"Elizabeth?" he began. Slowly she turned her head as she acknowledged the sound of his voice. As she did so, the child's body was revealed beneath her. At that moment, things seemed to go in slow motion for him, and the slow cold hand of fear seemed to reach and work its way through his insides from his stomach, to his heart and then mind. He didn't need to see the girl's face to know, for it was her. It was the swimming costume he saw first and the picture of Bart Simpson seemingly taking aim with his catapult toward him. He willed his eyes not to look further, but there now was her still lifeless face.

No, it's impossible.

But somehow it was. He would look back at the moment in the months and years to come, and every time those same thoughts would come to him.

It's impossible.

And surely it must be. How could she have gotten back so quickly? She had been with him when the scream went up and then…then nothing. And despite every later attempt to find reason in what he now saw, he knew it was futile for there was no explanation but one. One that he would refuse to acknowledge.

"Dougie!"

The voice seemed to come to him from far away. His head felt like it was full of water, and any reason or clear thought was lost to him as he continued to stare down on that young face. The only thing his mind allowing him, a continued mantra of *it's impossible, it's impossible.*

"Dougie!" Louder now, and his eyes finally shifted and focused on the shape where the words came from. "Dougie look at me!"

"Elizabeth?" he mouthed quietly.

"Dougie. Quickly now we need an ambulance."

He nodded slowly, but his eyes wandered back to the form of the girl on the floor.

"Now, Dougie!" Elizabeth screamed at him. At that moment, it was as if everything exploded back into place in an instant. He was alive and alert and needed no further coaxing to action. Elizabeth meantime had turned straight back to her chest compressions, and Dougie quickly moved beside the three that dwelt on the poolside. Then he was in a run again and making for the interior door. He burst through and afforded himself one last look back and saw that Elizabeth was now administering rescue breaths. And though he tried not to think of it, he knew it was too late for the little girl whose name he did not know.

He made his way quickly down the corridor and could see that the furore had roused Mrs Hodgson into action as she was making her way down toward him.

"Dougie?" she began.

"No time." He said breathlessly as he crashed through into the solicitor's office. This is where he had signed his contracts year in year out, and so he knew there was a phone here. Hodgson came to the door and looked questioningly at him as he thumbed in the numbers, 999.

He shook his head at her and was about to speak, but the line was quickly answered.

"Which service please?"

"Ambulance."

"Connecting you now."

Hodgson remained at the door as he relayed the details of what had transpired at the swimming pool. The questions were frustrating him as he realised that he did not know any of the answers. No he did not know the girl's name, no he did not know her date of birth, and no he was not with the casualty at the moment and could not feed updates through the phone. The only thing he could give was the address of the house and affirm, that yes, CPR was being administered.

The telephone conversation was all the information that Hodgson required, and as he stayed on the line, he watched as she slumped lower and sadness filled her face.

Before he hung up, she walked off, and he followed her out of the door. Turning right toward the pool house, he expected to find her in front making her way there, but no, the way was clear. He looked back and instead saw that she had walked back toward the interior instead.

At last, he found his way back and saw that the scene had not changed. He did not know how long he had been gone, but there had been no change in the girl's condition. Elizabeth continued to massage the girl's heart, and the mother lay at her head and caressed her brow while whispering in her ear.

He moved over and knelt opposite where Elizabeth continued to toil. A keen sweat had formed on her forehead, and he could see that she was exhausted from her efforts.

"Here let me." He folded his fingers together and quickly continued the rhythm that Elizabeth had begun. Their eyes met over the chest of the young girl and out of sight of the young mother below, Elizabeth slowly shook her head. He nodded his understanding but continued the CPR. In the end, time was lost to him, and he was surprised when, at last, the green uniform of the paramedic gently took him by the arm and steered him away.

He looked down on the girl's face once more and in his mind asked her why she had come to him at the workshop as she had, and what it was that he was to have done. No response came.

Elizabeth took his arm, and the two walked out of the pool house into the bright sunshine. He felt numb, and the two took hold of one another in a hug. Tears came to Elizabeth as he held her tightly. Slowly, he allowed his eyes to roam, and he found himself looking out at the west wing of the house. And there in the first-floor window was Robert McArthur, gazing down at the scene and at the man who held and comforted his young wife. Douglas silently bade the man to come out, to take charge somehow but as their eyes met, McArthur simply hung his head and allowed the drape he held open to fall, thus shielding him from the scenes that played out below.

CHAPTER 20

Fitzgerald had drawn a second garden chair and sat silently through Douglas's tale. As the old man spoke, he could begin to feel his well-constructed rationale begin to unravel. His mind creating a vision of a sodden little girl traipsing, through the east wing of the house, leaving tiny wet footprints…

And as Douglas's story came to an end, Fitzgerald slumped forward elbows on knees and took his head in his hands. He felt stunned at what he had heard. Until now there had only been suggestion and hearsay regarding Thoby Hall, and it's turbulent past.

But here was a man who offered that much more. It was too incredible though wasn't it? He had heard ghost stories before, tales of departed loved ones showing in old film negatives and supposedly lingering in familiar and favourite places. But this? This was so much more specific and begged questions.

Instead, though he reached out and placed his hand on Douglas's shoulder to offer him comfort for the man was clearly upset on recanting his story.

"I'm sorry, Father. Would you believe you are the first person I have told in some twenty years or so?"

"There were others you told of this Douglas?" Fitzgerald asked.

The man's head bobbed in agreement. "Yes, but only to Elizabeth and that was only after a time. You see, we had shared a moment. A horrible, horrible moment together and I thought she would understand. It seems she did only too well."

"What do you mean?"

Douglas straightened and turned to look at the priest. "Surely you know Father? That was the beginning of the end for her. She wouldn't admit to it at first, but I know she saw things to, that little girl and worse. That led to her…her breakdown."

Things were beginning to fall into place at last as to why the McArthur woman had been sectioned. "She told you of this?"

"As I say, only after it was too late. You see, I think it was only a week after the incident that I broke down and went to her. I had sleepless nights and though I was trying everything I could to rationalise what I saw; telling myself that it was shock or some kind of mental episode I was going through. My favourite being to tell myself that I had been wrong about the timeframe, that young Lydia had come to me much earlier and that I had sent her away back to her mother long before the accident."

"But no."

"No, Father. This was no trick of the mind I can tell you. It was exactly as I have said. I have tried to find the right word for it. Premonition was wrong, as it was all too late when she came to me for I knew she would already have been in the water. Visitation perhaps? Some lost spirit? Perhaps I gave too much of myself away to you, Father. A horny old goat lusting after young mothers, as I was. But I need to say it all, exactly as it occurred. And the saddest thing for me is that I sent her away lost and alone."

Fitzgerald thought on how to react. The man seemed genuine and honestly full of remorse and sadness for what had happened. But had it happened?

"You mentioned Elizabeth there before."

"Yes. I broke down as I said, and so I went to her. She did and said what she could to comfort me, even though she suffered the same. And me? So selfish as not to consider what she was going through in that house alone. That said, I did go on to find out that she didn't sleep either. I guess that was the guilt."

"Guilt?"

"Well it was her party, wasn't it? It was her pool. An extravagance I called it. And I guess she felt the same, for truth be told I guess it was Elizabeth who had the say-so and had the thing filled in and built over. But it was after that when things changed, when I learned of her sleepless nights and strange behaviour. It was then that she became unhinged."

"But why, Douglas?"

"The house Father. The house. Don't you see? That is the key to all of this. Perhaps I had the easy part of it as I don't go in there so much."

"Why are you telling me all this?" Fitzgerald questioned.

A look of surprise crossed his weary face as he replied. "Is that not why you are here, Father? To cleanse the darkness away? Don't get me wrong, I know of Mr McArthur's predicament. But I warrant he'll have more to say on these matters than I have."

Fitzgerald considered this for a moment, but there had been no suggestion at all from McArthur that he wished to talk of such things. Thus far, his story had only gone so far as to explain his arrival at the house in the early 1950's. Their discussion had included reference to his former employer Sir Thomas Searle and mention of bribery and corruption. Sin certainly, but the supernatural? No.

Not knowing how to pacify Douglas, he instead chose to divert the conversation from his purpose here with McArthur. "Tell me more about her."

"What can I say? You'll know just from hearing my words; I was taken with her. But not in the way you might think. It's true I am no modern man, and I probably thought more with my cock than my head. But when I saw her. The real her that was, I had nothing but respect. She was true to herself and yet made those around her at ease. Of course, women being women they would talk behind her back, and I hazard a guess that wouldn't be no different, no matter who she was. But she cracked Father, and I didn't see it until it was too late. She threw herself in at the church after the accident, and that is when she took up with Father Crosby. That would be the end of them both after a time."

And here now was the link he had been looking for: Father Crosby and his unfortunate demise. "I know of Father Crosby, Douglas. Not so much Elizabeth."

"It wasn't long after the business with Lydia that the priest took his own life. He bought into whatever Elizabeth was selling I can tell you that."

"And what was that?"

"Dark spirits, poltergeists, phantoms, ghosts, you name it. It's my understanding that she suffered the same paranoia and fixation as that old man Thomas Searle did before her. She was not short of material I can tell you. Have you seen the library, Father?"

Fitzgerald shook his head, both to negate the question and express his lack of understanding.

"No, of course not, stupid of me. But the shelves there are wall-to-wall with books on the occult, and I'm to understand she would spend all of her time there, pouring over old books and whatnot. It seems she found a kindred spirit in Thomas Searle, though he was dead years before she was born."

"Thomas Searle? I don't understand. What has he got to do with this? Or Elizabeth for that matter?"

"You've seen the house, Father? The weird symbols and such like? All fitted at Searle's request and much more besides that. Though I don't understand the most of it, Elizabeth told me that there are wards, or spells, if you like guarding the place."

This did not sit at all well given the Church's vested interest in the house.

"And how do I know all of this?" Dougie continued. "Well, I went and saw her some years ago now. She is more of her old self up there where they can nurse and medicate her properly. The doctors told me that she suffers from 'paranoid schizophrenia' whatever the hell that is, and warned me what I might say. She was older, of course, but I could see the old Elizabeth under those eyes. She would have the doctors think she understands her condition and that her thoughts of supernatural occurrences are a part of her illness. Well, as I say, she might have them fooled, but she still believes all of it."

"And what did she say?"

"Well, she believes that this fella Searle knew the place to be cursed." He hesitated, a frown forming on his brow. "You'll forgive me; the rest was quite beyond me. Frantic she was in her desperation to be heard and give freely of herself without those doctors listening in."

"It's okay. Please, tell me what you remember."

"Well I thought her fixation might be toward young Lydia and what happened in the pool house that day, but no. It is the library Father, that is where she went to find her answers, and it was there that sent her mad. And though you won't say it, I know something happened to you up there to."

Fitzgerald though was still keen to avoid talk of his experience. He was already fighting back images of the previous night within the pool house. He couldn't allow himself to think back on the library and be subverted to thinking there was some other explanation for what happened to him there.

"Thomas Searle?" He tried to steer Douglas as far away as he could. "McArthur mentioned him in our conversations. I understand that he was the master of the house. You say he also felt the place cursed?"

Douglas considered a moment and nodded his agreement. "Yes Father, but perhaps not in the way you might think. You see, Elizabeth said that some of these wards that she called them, were in part, ones of fertility. I didn't for a minute understand the relevance or what that had to do with poor Lydia and what we had both been through."

Fitzgerald considered this against everything else he had learned. Pagan symbols, wards and spells and now fertility rites? What could it all mean? And where did Robert McArthur fit into all of this?

Douglas continued unabated. "It seems old Thomas Searle didn't have any lead in his pencil if you take my meaning. She told me that he was unable to father an heir, despite the fact, three women came to be Mrs Searle. I guess medical science wasn't what it is today and when that failed, they turned to more, shall we say unorthodox methods?"

"Fertility rites?"

"Amongst others. Elizabeth told me that there were shamans and witch doctors all practising their crafts within the house."

"That's incredible."

"Isn't it? She also told me that all such methods came to nothing, and that is when he began to believe the house was cursed. All that light you see around here of a night?

Supposedly that was him that started that. Among all the spells and like, the house was lit like a Christmas tree so as to ward off any evil spirits."

"And she told you all this?"

"Yes, Father. Don't get me wrong, it was all quite unbelievable to hear, but the conviction in her voice! And more, for I knew at the heart of it, my own experience was real and so I was an avid listener. In any event, Elizabeth picked up where Searle left off. She spoke of these wards or spells if you prefer being weak and that she had desired to protect the house once more. That is where Father Crosby came in."

The penny, at last, dropped for Fitzgerald. Understanding finally coming to him, as he threaded together the final pieces of the puzzle with Douglas's story.

"It was as an exorcism, wasn't it?"

The old man arched an eyebrow in surprise. "You know more of this than you are letting on Father."

"Nothing of the sort Douglas. I knew parts, of course. Just suggestion really. I have been playing catch up it seems, but it is starting to come together. I am curious though, what did she say of Crosby?"

"Alas, nothing, Father. I would not press her none on that, less she have some kind of episode. Once she touches on that subject, you can see the sadness in her eyes, and I don't doubt she blames herself for that one as well."

"But an exorcism took place?" He knew that such a thing was kept quiet within the confines of the Catholic Church, but to have performed such a thing, Crosby would have required permission from his bishop. These were all things he could check into, and at last, he felt he had a handle on the strangeness that surrounded Thoby Hall and it's people.

"It did, and by Elizabeth's reckoning, only a week or so before he killed himself. I guess you know the rest as I know it. Elizabeth went insane and was taken away. Given what happened, I came to believe that ignorance was some kind of bliss and so stuck my head in the sand. What happened to me was but a one-off, though I jump at my own shadow every five minutes. I've come to believe that my story is only a small part in a bigger picture I want no part of. I hope I am insignificant enough for that to be allowed."

"But you believe though Douglas?"

"Every word Father. I know my words aren't those of confession. Only those of one man asking another to look out for himself and be wary of what is at the heart of this house."

Fitzgerald nodded. He could not judge the words that he had heard. He often felt that to understand and believe such tales, you had to have an unequivocal trust and belief in their source, and as it was, he did not know this man. He was thankful though for Douglas's story, for it was true that he was at last beginning to understand what was going on here at Thoby Hall.

He stood to leave. "I guess I will bid you farewell now Douglas. I know those weren't easy things to say. Just know my door is always open to you, be it here at the Hall or back at the church."

Douglas though shook his head. "If you wish to be of service Father, I wonder if there isn't something you can do for that lost girl?"

"I…" he was lost. Not only could he not reconcile what he had heard, now he was being asked to do something beyond his power.

"Dougie…I…"

The old man looked defeated. "If not you, Father, then who? Think on what I have said to you and find the truth. If you do, maybe then you can do as I ask?"

Fitzgerald nodded his agreement. He would certainly think about what had been said.

Without another word, Dougie reached inside his jacket to remove his flask and took a deep draft.

Knowing now was the not the time to address Hodgson's concern, Fitzgerald instead took his leave.

CHAPTER 21

Fitzgerald was barely back in his rooms when the telephone rang. Expectantly, he snatched the receiver up, anticipating Keira's voice giving him news that McArthur was fit enough to receive him and continue their conversation. It was Hodgson though who spoke; informing him that he had missed Keira's call that morning and that the news was bad. McArthur having had a difficult night and as a result was not able to see him.

Part of him sank when he heard the news, and he remained quiet on the line as Hodgson went on to inform him that he had a visitor; Deacon Morris.

For a brief second, he was puzzled as to why his colleague had come out to see him, but his mind soon picked up the loose pieces, and he recalled that he had asked Colin to bring him the diaries belonging to Father Crosby. He held onto the phone silently as he contemplated what to say in response, for his first instinct was to tell Hodgson that he could not see him and make up some excuse as to why.

Douglas's story still reverberated through his mind, and he was no longer sure that he wished to view the diaries and all that they might hold, for fear they might further enhance the picture that Thoby Hall was somehow...

Cursed.

He chased the thought away without acknowledging it further. He was at a low ebb following everything that had happened during his short stay at the Hall, and the worst part was the realisation that he was nowhere close to resolving his business.

Hodgson though was not party to his thoughts as she quickly destroyed any hope he might have of avoidance. "Shall I bring him to your rooms, or will you receive him in the drawing room?"

"No, I will come down, save you both the walk."

"Very good." This was followed by a click and the soft purr of a disconnected line.

He made his way down to the vast lobby and unconsciously circumnavigated the pentagram within the floor. He hesitated for a second before the large double door of the drawing room which was situated to the right of the entranceway as he looked at it. He took a deep breath and decided that he would keep this as brief as possible.

He depressed the door handle, and with a gentle push, the door swung inward. The first sensation he felt was warmth, for where Colin was stood he could see that a fire had been built in the huge hearth before him. It was a very inviting feeling, and as he closed the door softly behind him, he looked deep into the yellow flames as they danced seductively; the blaze similarly captivating the house guest, as he warmed himself from the chilly November day.

The room was strangely dark though, and he saw that the thick drapes had been pulled shut and the low chandelier did little to brighten but more than a small circle beneath it. It was likely the curtains were drawn to keep the heat in, for the rooms here were much the same as elsewhere in the house, vast and notoriously difficult to get warm in the cold of winter.

His entrance had not so much as caused a flicker from his peer, and he thought that perhaps he had not been heard coming in. He stepped further into the room around a plush velvet chaise-longue, hoping to approach his friend from the side and not cause him to start when he announced himself. He could see already the object of their meeting, because there to the side on a low cabinet were the very diaries that he had asked Colin to bring, neatly tied into a bundle with string.

"Colin?" he offered softly, knowing full well the man was concentrated with the fire and so likely to jump, no matter how low key the intrusion.

Colin turned toward him nonplussed though.

"Iain? Are you alright? My goodness man, you look awful."

Fitzgerald was surprised by his friend's concern. "I'm fine, Colin. Or maybe it's just heat stroke? Goodness you have that fire well-stoked!"

The frown on the deacon's face suggested that he wasn't entirely buying into his jovial response, but fortunately, he did not give voice to his misgivings. "I have the diaries you asked for Iain." He said, stepping away from the fire and walking toward the small pile of books.

Back on topic, good. Let's get this over with.

Fitzgerald tried on a smile so as to deflect any further concern. He knew it was a thin effort though.

It seemed to take the desired effect as Morris took the bait and moved the conversation on. "How goes matters with McArthur so far?"

"Interesting shall we say. I can't divulge too much of course, but I can say he has had an interesting past. War hero did you know? World War 2."

Morris nodded. "Shilling always remarked on that, said he would always pull that one out of the bag, just to remind everyone who was superior. Those two, you know?"

Fitzgerald did know. The two were chalk and cheese. No wonder Father Shilling had done his disappearing act before it became time to take confession from McArthur, and he wondered how many letters and phone calls to the bishop had been ignored from Shilling before the single offer of this vast Estate brought him the exit that he had so desperately begged for without success.

Morris now stood by the books and placed his hand upon them. "Well, here they are, though I can't imagine what you hope to find in there."

Fitzgerald hesitated, taking a moment to weigh up his colleague and consider if he could confide what he had learned. As it was though he needed this outlet, someone from outside of the house, who could interject and tell him he was crazy. Crazy for harbouring such notions as lost spirits and exorcisms.

"I don't know myself until I look. It may be nothing, but I can't help feel there is some clue there as to unlocking McArthur. You know he has said nothing of Elizabeth or Crosby? Surely something such as what happened would have registered with him somehow. I feel he has said a lot to me and yet nothing at all. I am keen to get to the heart of the man."

"Be careful Iain. I don't know what you will find, but remember, Crosby was a tortured soul by the end. And Elizabeth? No doubt her as well, given the circumstances."

Fitzgerald nodded his agreement. The door to what he wanted to discuss had opened but a fraction, and he was keen to push it through and just unload his frustration and doubt. But no. Not here, not in the house.

There had been a feeling there from day one of being observed. Reinforced now by what had happened by the library and then again at the pool house. But it was more than that, the house had a nature to it, so old and quiet as to be watchful.

"I will Colin and thank you."

"Not a problem. If there is anything else, just let me know."

"Well, now that you are here how about a tour?"

Morris grimaced. "Thank you, but no. I don't know, but I can't say I care too much for this place. My association with the place is negligible. I hope to keep it that way."

Fitzgerald felt deflated. He had hoped to divert Morris toward his rooms, perhaps there he could have hoped to open up on the subject of Elizabeth and Crosby, but no. There was something about this place, wasn't there? Morris sensed it and he doubted that the man knew half as much of its history as he did.

"Very well, let me show you out though."

Morris nodded and took his hand off the books. The two walked over to the door and Fitzgerald opened it for his colleague, as he did so, he saw him reach out and take a long coat that had been folded neatly on the chaise-longue. In the lobby now, the contrast was immediate, for the cold still air of the vast room hit him like a slap to the face and in doing so waking him from the sluggish heat of the drawing room.

Here it was light as well, though he could see ominous dark clouds as he opened the front door to let Morris out.

"Best wrap up Colin. Looks like rain."

"I will. Now, are you sure you are alright? I mean you look tired Iain and in there, I thought you looked ready to faint."

Fitzgerald looked about him, and seeing no one, closed the door behind them. He took Morris by the elbow and stepped out toward the driveway.

"Iain?"

"Not here. Where are you parked?" Fitzgerald answered, already leading to the carport to the right of the building. He glanced nervously about as they made the side of the house. He could not say what it was that bothered him so about being seen together. But still, the feeling of being watched lingered, and he was conscious of the large bright windows that brooded above them as they walked.

Soon they made the carport and seeing the blue Ford Mondeo that Fitzgerald knew the other man owned. He slipped quickly into the passenger seat. Already he was lamenting the loss of the drawing room fire for he had no coat of his own. He crossed his arms and rubbed his hands over his shoulders before rubbing them together to generate heat as Morris got into the car.

"What is this Iain? You've got me worried now."

"You remember what we spoke of on the phone?"

"How could I forget? Father Crosby has been close to my thoughts since we spoke."

"I asked you what might have brought him to take his own life, Colin. I think I know the answer now."

"Oh?"

"I know what I have to say may sound crazy, but please hear me out."

Morris was silent.

Fitzgerald took a deep breath and closed his eyes as he spoke. He did not want to see the reaction of the other man as he gave air to his disjointed thinking.

"Crosby performed an exorcism here Colin. I don't know all of the details yet..." He opened his eyes, his confidence returning to him, now that he had surmounted the most difficult part. "He performed an exorcism at Elizabeth's request, and this all happened only days or weeks before he killed himself."

His heart was hammering in his chest as he watched Morris's face. There was not a flicker of emotion that gave a clue as to how the man might react. Fitzgerald swallowed hard, knowing how ridiculous his story probably sounded. He was disappointed though as slowly, Morris began to shake his head.

"Iain I am sorry, but what on earth is that to do with your duty here?" Came the response.

Fitzgerald began to flounder. "But Colin, you don't understand…"

He couldn't think straight. So many things all clamoured to be heard at once; Dougie, the pool house and Lydia Bennett, all of it leading to Elizabeth McArthur and her break down. That, in turn, to Father Crosby and his suicide. It was all linked, and he was desperate to impart all of it, to make Morris understand.

Morris though cut through, "something is clearly troubling you, I can see that. But whatever it is steer clear. I will say this. Whatever it was that Elizabeth McArthur saw, or believed she saw here, Crosby bought into it and bought in hard. You say he performed an exorcism? That doesn't surprise me Iain, but don't you see that he was a man on the edge? I'll not ask what has brought you to these conclusions, but remember, this is what brought Crosby down, and I'll be damned if we'll let the same happen to you. Look at you. Any fool can see you are suffering and for why? Digging into matters that don't concern you, when all you need do is finish your business and leave."

"I…I…" Fitzgerald was lost for words. Looking into Morris's eyes, he felt he could see the hurt for a lost friend and the concern for a new colleague. He was overwhelmed by it in that instant and quickly had to look away as he felt as if he were on the verge of tears. He had tried to mask his feelings from this man, but he had seen right through all of that. Perhaps that was the gift bestowed to his position or his compassion as a man, but he saw through Fitzgerald's defences as simply as if he had found an open window built into a tower built of stone.

"Finish your business and leave Iain," Morris repeated before diverting course. "I wonder now if those diaries are right for you. I don't wish to fuel the fire any further, but you are a rational man. So read them, find the madness in his words, find the moments when he falls from the path of soundness and rationality and follows her into her delusion. And when you do, take stock and look at yourself and ask yourself where you are on that journey. At that time it is none too late to turn, you understand?"

"I do, thank you."

"Very good. For now, I suggest you get back into the warm and maybe consider some sleep. You look terrible Iain I don't mind saying. Let me drive you around."

Morris fired the car and gently put it into gear. The journey back to the front of the house was short, and now Fitzgerald leaned down, holding the door as Morris spoke.

"You remember what I told you, Iain."

"I do." He then thanked him for what seemed the umpteenth time. Morris looked hard at him and seemed to satisfy himself with his resolve for he nodded and turned his face back to the steering wheel in front of him. Fitzgerald allowed the door to shut with a loud clunk, and the car went away slowly. It had been only moments but already the cold was biting hard and his shirt ruffled in the strong wind. Despite that, he watched the car go until it disappeared, a small dot at the end of the long driveway.

Morris's words resonated within him, and he knew that he had to be stronger to get through his ordeal at the house. He could be stronger though and he would. What had Morris said? *"Finish your business and leave."* Sound advice and yes, that is precisely what he would do.

His new-found resolve dissipated quickly though, as he turned back toward the house and the blank windows that stared down at him. Shoulders slumped, he trod slowly back to the door.

CHAPTER 22

Through the walls of his apartment, Fitzgerald heard the soft chime of a grandfather clock marking the hour. Four chimes in all, and likely coming from the rooms that were next to his own.

He had remained in his apartment since the visit with Deacon Morris, his time spent between the lounge and lying on his bed trying to get into a novel. Slowly though, darkness had encroached into the room until he was squinting hard to read the words before him. He sighed as he placed the book and his reading spectacles down onto the bedside cabinet beside him.

The truth was that he had struggled with the book anyway, having reread the same paragraphs over and again. He had been listless. His eyes, time and again lifting from the pages of the book to settle upon the diaries of Father Crosby, which he had recovered from the drawing room following Colin Morris's visit.

There was that part of him that wished to interrogate the books at once, but something deep inside of him told him he that he did not want to know what was inside of them. That the text of Father James Crosby might somehow reinforce all of the crazy notions that some ill power dwelt in Thoby Hall.

In the end, the light was not to be a problem as the large spotlights that covered the grounds turned on as one, at 04:30 pm sharp. He must then have surely fallen asleep for the next thing he knew was the chiming of the 6 o'clock bells. He keenly listened as he thought he heard the sound of departing motor cars leaving the Estate for the night.

Now he was again at the behest of McArthur's call, and it was something he was impatient for. He wanted to talk about everything that had happened or been divulged during his time at the Hall thus far, and so wondered at how far he could push the old man, in the hope of getting answers as to what had occurred with his ex-wife and Father Crosby.

The call when it came did so past 7 o'clock. The soft local accent of the night nurse, Melissa, only staying on the line long enough to tell him that McArthur was conscious and anxious to speak.

The route to the west wing was now very familiar to him, and he thought he might take an evening stroll through the gardens to get there, the idea being that the fresh air might rejuvenate him and prepare him for his duty. A look through his bedroom window before departing had put him off though. A keen wind had built up, and he watched as the hedgerows and trees swayed heavily, their shadows dancing off of the tall brick structure that was the house and cast by the large sentinel-like spotlights. The grim view, coupled with the knowledge that it would be so very cold outside made his decision all the easier and he left his room, following the familiar path he had learned.

He made the balcony at the front of the house and hesitated as he realised that he would have to pass by the library again. He had made a conscious effort to avoid such thoughts, more so now that Dougie had suggested some supernatural alternative as to what had gone on there. And try as he might he could not push that new connotation away for Douglas's story had been unnerving, what with suggestions of spirits or ghosts.

He frowned and he walked slowly toward where the front of the house met the west wing, half hoping that Melissa would have come down the corridor to meet him as Keira had done before.

Alas, there was no sign of the woman. And so eyes fixed firmly forward, he gathered his pace and rushed quickly by the library door. He was glad to be past it and felt foolish for feeling as he did. Nothing happened as he walked by and he was acutely aware that there was no cold draught as he did so.

Coming now to McArthur's rooms, he found that the door was open and there waiting for him in the lounge area was Melissa.

All at once, his previous thoughts of Dougie's story evaporated and were replaced with feelings of anger again. He had played those moments out at the solicitor's door and the library, over and over in his mind, trying to find one tangible detail to show that it had been this woman who was responsible. As yet, other than his gut feeling, he had not found that detail. But what else was he to believe? That the house was haunted as Dougie had suggested?

Melissa was a petite figure, perhaps only 5' 5" tall. He guessed her to be somewhere in her late twenties or early thirties, but it was difficult to be sure due to the heavy foundation and makeup she wore that served to make her skin flawless and so much younger than she might otherwise be.

Her smile of welcome was thin and in his mind, he questioned if this was for the accusation he had made against her. Without realising it, his eyes dropped down to her feet; as he quickly tried to gauge if she had left the footprints in the east wing corridor. Her feet were small. And in his mind's eye, he focused on the comparison of his own foot beside the tiny wet print on the wooden floor.

"Father Fitzgerald?"

As she spoke, he couldn't help but think of the contrast between her and Keira, as her demeanour was strictly professional and he knew he would have none of the thoughts or feelings that the seductive Keira had brought up in him. He took the offered hand; it was cool and took his limply and without conviction. She quickly let it fall away at her side and dropped her eyes from his.

He could not read her, and this served to fuel his frustration. However, now was not the time for his accusations; he had business to attend to.

"You must be Melissa?" Fitzgerald answered with a broad smile, trying to put the woman at ease. Her tone had been soft and he had found that he had to cock an ear and concentrate to hear her properly. She gave a curt nod in response.

"Mr McArthur? Is he ready to receive me?"

Melissa nodded her response again. Seemingly she was a woman of few words.

"Against my better judgement Father."

He was surprised at her. "Oh?"

"We had a difficult afternoon, it seems. Keira told me he was in and out of sleep. Delirious."

That was a disappointment and Fitzgerald groaned inwardly. This process it seemed would be like watching paint dry, such was the lack of progress, and he was again acutely aware that he did not want to be here at Thoby Hall any longer.

"And now?"

"A marginal improvement. He wishes to speak with you."

"I understand this must be difficult Melissa, at odds even with your duty, but I am told such windows of opportunity were likely to be thin and that Mr McArthur has much that he would say to me…"

He left the rest of his sentence unsaid, hoping the woman would understand the implied message he was giving her. He watched as she bowed her head, her hands clasped together in front of her waist, one thumb rubbing hard at the other. She would not put up any resistance he knew instinctively. She softly nodded her head, and he was again struck at the vast difference in the personality of the nursing staff. Keira, exuberant, flirtatious, extrovert. Melissa, the mirror opposite.

He took a step toward the door and then another, expecting some further line of communication or refusal from the woman, but there was none. Instead, she took a vested interest at a pile of sheets that he saw neatly folded up on a tall-backed chair by the wall. She went to them and gathered them up as he walked past her. He arrived at the door to McArthur's chamber and looked back to see her disappear with her cargo into the makeshift storeroom that had once been a study. He shook his head and wondered if such a woman as she was married and pitied her either way, for she was likely diminutive and subservient if married and lonely and afraid if single, a ripe target for the affections of sexually dominant men. He realised he had not looked for a wedding band as he now entered McArthur's room.

Everything was much the same as before, but now it seemed the glare of the strip lights was tenfold, such was the assault upon his eyes.

He quickly blinked away the spots that now danced upon his pupils as his eyes had directly met a row of lights that hung low on the opposite wall. His vision now adjusted he could see that the white in the room seemed to bleed any other colour from it, all but the black of his priestly garments.

"My apologies Father," came the brittle voice of McArthur from across the room, "Melissa might have offered you the dark glasses. I will have a quiet word with her."

Is he talking about sunglasses? He could see the need.

McArthur could perhaps read his thoughts, seeming to feel the need for some explanation.

"The light…it is a comfort to me."

"It's no trouble, Robert. I just needed a moment to adjust."

Fitzgerald ventured further into the room and grimaced as he saw the sets of strip lights adorned on the walls of the room, all of which shone inwardly toward the bed of McArthur. There would be no respite from their glare no matter where he went.

"How are you this evening?" Fitzgerald continued. "Melissa suggested now may not be the best time?" He took the chair on McArthur's right side as he spoke.

"Hmm, did she now? She would do well to remember who pays the bills."

Thinking that he had perhaps caused some trouble for the woman, he relented, "Oh nothing like that Robert, only that you had a difficult afternoon. Are you up to this?"

"I have to be, don't you think?" The old man grumbled, "I don't think I'm to be spared the time I want, so I will make use of what time I have."

"Very good. Then shall we begin?"

"In a moment Father, in a moment. Tell me first, what did old Douglas have to say to you this morning?"

That took Fitzgerald by surprise. *How does he know?*

"Come now, Father, don't be coy. I'll wager he was filling your head with his stories."

This old man was seemingly more switched on to events under his roof than Fitzgerald could have imagined. But at the same time, he had touched upon the very subject of what he had wanted to raise. He would have to be careful though.

"Perhaps it was more of my asking than his telling Robert. I had questions."

"About the house?"

"In part."

McArthur leaned forward from his pillows and took the priest's arm in his hand. "Very good Father, very good. You have an inquisitive mind I can see. I had hoped as much when Harvey told me of you and that you would be right for this. I don't think I'm going to be disappointed."

Fitzgerald looked back and was shocked to see that McArthur's eyes were wet. He had believed him a hard man, but the weight and understanding of what was happening to him was now seemingly all too real.

McArthur released his grip and collapsed back onto his pillows with a pained look on his face; even that small effort had cost him. He went on, "I can guess what he told you Father and I know that you have questions. I think though you won't be disappointed as I have all the answers you crave."

"He mentioned the incident. The tragedy with the young girl."

McArthur had closed his eyes and nodded along at his words in understanding. "Of course he did and I will tell you of that and more. But for now, you must be patient, for everything begins and ends in this house with Thomas Searle and that is where I must continue. It is long in the telling and I have no doubt you are impatient to hear of more recent events. But you will understand Father, you will understand in time."

Fitzgerald held his glance for a second, the wetness that had been there only a second ago had now disappeared; giving way now on a hard, unyielding stare, which felt uncomfortable to return. Whatever emotion McArthur had allowed, had only been for but a second and was now gone, replaced instead by who knew what feeling or motivation. Fitzgerald let his eyes drop and bowed his head as he heard the familiar words of confession wash over him. "Forgive me, Father, for I have sinned…"

CHAPTER 23

Wednesday, 10th April 1963, 01:30 am.

Thoby Hall.

Robert McArthur wearily trod the soft carpeted floors of the west wing of Thoby Hall, his eyes aching at the incessant glare of the overhead strip lights. Searle had woken him from his slumber just minutes ago, and now he paced the corridors without a sound as if like a ghost. His anger was a real thing and he felt his pulse beat inside of his temple. How dare he call! How dare he? He had only retired some four hours ago and was expected to start as usual at 05:00 am. He didn't know if this was some kind of game Searle was playing but it was beginning to wear pretty thin.

Such calls had been a new constant in his life and had begun soon after Searle had suffered his heart attack some three months ago. The man had become overly needy and would often call on McArthur late into the night. It had gotten to the point where McArthur had moved into the hall so that he could be close at hand, and at Searle's beck and call no matter what the time of night.

Not that it mattered much now anyway he mused. Nancy had taken their son Jonathan and left some six years ago now. The torrent of abuse that he had been subjected to by Searle had obviously impacted upon him and had ultimately spilt over into his own private life, resulting in their departure.

Nancy it seemed had grown bored and listless with their life at Thoby Hall. Despite the elegant home within the grounds and steady income, she had become resentful of McArthur and his work. The long hours, the out of hours calls and ultimately the degradation and abuse that Searle constantly threw their way.

McArthur had worked hard, both at his job and his marriage, but ultimately it would never be enough. Both sides had demanded more than he could possibly offer. And now as he walked the hallways, he asked himself how it could be that it had been his family that had come out on the losing side. It had been like they had been trapped here; a pressure cooker waiting to explode.

His days would be hard and Searle unforgiving as ever. But to return home and be subjected to the abuse all over again? The accusations, the tantrums. It had proved more than he could bear. The arguments had become worse and worse until one day it had culminated in him striking her. He stopped and closed his eyes to the light as he pictured her face at that moment. The shock and fear with which she beheld him. He had never resorted to hitting a woman in his life and the fact that it should be her? How a life can be ripped apart in only a moment. For he knew as he saw her there lying on the floor, tears welling in her eyes, that it was over for them. That she would not trust him again, that he had crossed a line.

And so it had proved. They had tried of course. He had doubled his efforts with her but all in vain. Until that day six years ago when she finally left for good. And now here he stood, at the beck and call of the man who had been responsible for it all. He hated Searle, for it had been the unrelenting pressure that he had placed him under that had made him snap.

And yet, here he was. He opened his eyes to the glare and moved on, grimacing at the light. As if things weren't bad enough, there was this damned light to contend with!

McArthur couldn't fathom the reason why, but shortly after Searle's heart attack, he had commissioned for this work to be undertaken. Thoby Hall had been torn apart. Many of its antiquated chandeliers and lamps ripped out to be replaced with garish modern strip lighting that hurt the eyes and drained the soul. McArthur couldn't begin to understand why such a change had been instigated. He had long thought his master strange, but this? Barely a shadow fell within the home or upon its lawns for that matter, as vast spotlights had been erected in the gardens. A backup generator also fitted should the power fail.

Searle was as unpredictable as they came.

Things were very strange and yet he soldiered on. There had been a moment back when Nancy was still there when it all opened up before him and it seemed clear what he must do. That he must choose his family over his work. But she had ruined that for him. Damn her! A man of his stature could not be told what to do, so how dare she put him in such a position.

It was a decision that he was coming to of his own accord, but she had demanded that he pick between her and Searle. How could he choose otherwise? He was a man of principle and honour, a fact she knew well. But the fact remained she had given him a choice, and his stubborn pride would not allow him to consent to leaving his post at her desire, especially as he felt that it should be a man's own decision to do so.

How could he have been such an idiot? Damn his pride! And so here he was, still within Searle's employ, despite his hatred of the man and the man's hatred of him. He could have left still of course, but what did he have? Where would he go?

But it was too late for such thoughts as he'd arrived at the library. Searle had spent a great deal of time here in the last three months. Pouring over his old books and getting drunk.

McArthur had tried to impress upon his master the need for self-control in his drinking habits, given his health scare, but Searle had simply laughed in his face and continued to exude a youthfulness that belied his 65 years. McArthur believed that his master, despite his uncanny youthful looks, was on the road to self-destruction. The heart attack that he had suffered only a few months ago should have served as some kind of warning. That the rich fatty diet he enjoyed, combined with a lack of exercise, the drinking and a forty a day smoking habit must be put behind him. McArthur had learned the hard way that Searle would not be changing his regime though, as the steamed vegetables he had prepared in the wake of the heart attack had been returned to him at speed through the air.

Searle had thrown many a tantrum and food had been thrown in his direction many a time, but this was different somehow. Surely the old bastard must know that he was screwed if he kept on? But no. With the exception of the fitted lighting system, things went on seemingly as before.

Despite his now apparent fear of the dark, Searle had initially continued to gorge himself on the finest things life had to offer. Beautiful young escorts had arrived on a nightly basis, and he would lavish expensive jewellery and gifts upon them for their favour. The once quiet halls became alive with the sound of orchestra music as he began to entertain the social elite and rejuvenate his business interests. But Searle's mood quickly changed, and the social climbers soon found themselves unwanted and Searle retreated into his library, seeking only the solace of books and alcohol.

McArthur reflected upon this as he stepped inside the vast library. He shielded his eyes against the glare as he entered, for this room was more brightly lit than any other. The vast array of bookshelves meant many potential shadows could be cast and Searle certainly would not have that, at least in part, for every aisle was lit with a succession of lamps fixed upon the vast stacks.

In part? Yes, that was the strangest thing of all, for there was one exception. Toward the middle of the library, there was one aisle that was partly in shadow. This had puzzled McArthur for it was the only part of the great house and Estate that was not lit. All the more intriguing then, that this was the very row where Searle had had his heart attack.

And as he approached, here was Searle yet again as he expected to find him, his chair pulled close to the row shrouded in darkness, drink in hand.

He sighed. The truth was that he had contemplated leaving a case of whisky here for his master. After all, that was what he required wasn't it? But it was not his job to assume, and so he would return to the cellar night after night and procure yet another bottle and fetch it to Searle.

How Searle's heart had not given out, McArthur did not know. Despite his often drunken demeanour, Searle still looked unbelievable for his 65 years. His hair still as black as the day they had met and his frame as stout, his eyes still burning with the same intensity and fire. The only thing that had begun to hold sway was the fine pot belly that had started to take shape and the fine crow's feet that crept from the corner of his eyes.

Even so, for a man of advancing years, Searle looked remarkable and McArthur couldn't help feeling somewhat in awe of his vitality. And here he was again, gazing down the aisle of books as if he might behold his own fallen form, clutched in the throes of a heart attack that he could not escape. It was clear that the man was trying to come to terms with his own mortality. He had faced the worst that the German Army could throw at him in the most tragic day in the history of the British Army. He had survived recession and then a second war. He had built his empire and been untouchable. Until now that was, and it was this fact that McArthur believed the man was trying to come to terms with, that he might not be invulnerable after all.

He stood there, waiting for the command. In all the years that he had served Searle, he had not presumed to speak out of turn. He knew that this was something that irritated Searle immensely and so he clung to it. Despite the brutality of the behaviour toward him, he would not give this old bastard the satisfaction of believing that he had gotten to him, no matter how hard he tried.

Finally, Searle stirred from his reverie. Without breaking his focus from the aisle, he spoke.

"Robert? Thank you for attending me. I am in need of a bottle, I think."

Robert?

What was this? In all his years of service, he had never once called McArthur by his first name. Was something the matter? Despite this McArthur knew his duty, it was not his place to impose or ask of his master and so he would continue and deal with that which was requested.

"Yes Sir, at once." McArthur replied, turning on his heel.

He was stunned into place by the next comment that was uttered from Searle's mouth.

"You know Robert; this very aisle is where I died for the second time."

The room was quiet, and McArthur simply stood there, slowly turning his head back toward Searle. His mind scrambled and confused. What was the drunken old fool saying?

He knew as he glanced back at the man that whatever had been said should be addressed, but if he quickly walked from the room now, he could ignore the words that were spoken.

And so he stood there, hesitant. The question though, was did he even want to hear an explanation? To leave now, would result in this moment never happening. His relationship with Searle would carry on as it had and he would be none the wiser. The never-ending repetition of hatred and abuse at this man's hands would continue unabated to the point where they would both forget such a moment had happened.

But there was something more. Searle had never before uttered his first name, that whatever was about to be said was man to man and not a master confiding with his servant.

172

For a man of Searle's disposition that would be a humiliation he knew. Searle could never talk to him as an equal. Never. And so this appeal to his real self? To Robert McArthur? That was different, that wasn't breaking the rules in Searle's eyes.

Already it seemed that time had stopped, he realised that he had stopped breathing as he stood there, as these thoughts plagued his mind. Finally, the step he took was not of retreat.

And so he turned and faced his master, for the first time as an equal and for the first time it was he who would command Searle.

"Tell me."

Searle continued to look mournfully down the long aisle of books and raised his glass to drain what remained of the whisky. McArthur traced his eyes downward and saw the bottle that he brought his master only five hours ago was now empty. But looking back at Searle he could not detect a single trace of drunkenness. The man's words had been firm, and his eyes shone with the same intensity and purpose as they ever did.

Searle turned his head in McArthur's direction, fixing him with that stare. And for this time McArthur knew that he must meet it and show him that he was equal, that he was not submissive within this encounter. He had made the choice to stay and listen, he alone. He had not been ordered or harassed into doing so; he did so of his own volition. A decision he would come to regret for the rest of his life.

Finally, Searle spoke, "He taunts me Robert, he taunts me," and slowly he turned his gaze back toward the long line of books that stretched out in front of him and once again fell into silence.

McArthur simply stood there.

He taunts me? He thought to himself. *What does he mean?*

Maybe the old bastard was drunker than he let on. Suddenly though, the silence was broken as Searle threw his glass down the aisle into the darkness, shattering it on the floor into a thousand shimmering pieces and screamed.

"That's it, isn't it you bastard!? You taunt me and ridicule me, but you won't have me, do you hear me? You will never have me!"

McArthur jumped at the sudden ferocity of Searle's words, causing him to step back involuntarily. Quickly though he fought to regain his composure. Searle hadn't seen him start and he cursed himself for showing such weakness. The old man had clearly lost his mind, unless...

McArthur moved forward. A sudden fear came over him, as he realised that the two of them might not be alone and that there was someone in the aisle, just beyond his line of sight. That this third person might do Searle harm, perhaps even himself. But within a few steps, taking him around behind Searle, his angle of sight widened and he felt relieved as he beheld nothing but shadow down the long aisle of books.

McArthur didn't know how to begin, and he groaned inwardly even as he spoke the word's, despite his pledge that he would meet his master as an equal.

"Sir?"

He moved outward and onto Searle's left-hand side and joined the old man in looking down the aisle.

"I don't understand," he continued.

Searle turned suddenly and shot him a glance, fury erupting on his face. But within moments, it withered and disappeared. Searle closed his eyes and sighed heavily.

"I'm sorry, Robert, I am very sorry. How could you know? How could you even guess? I suggest you might bring that bottle after all. I believe we will both need its comfort by the time I finish my tale."

McArthur said nothing and simply stood there, weighing up the situation. He was torn with uncertainty. He could see now that the fire had gone from Searle's eyes and the man was resigned to some explanation. And as to confirm it, Searle gave a simple nod of approval that he might leave and return with a bottle.

And so McArthur left, his mind ringing with Searle's words...'this is where I died the second time'. He had never been on conversational terms with Searle and to try and guess at the meaning of his words was impossible. One thing was for sure, thought McArthur, Searle's heart attack had certainly affected him more than he could have ever believed. In viewing him from afar and bringing him his nightly bottle, he had believed him to be questioning his own mortality. But it was more than that wasn't it? Had Searle's mind become unhinged?

As he went, McArthur searched Searle's words for meaning...'he taunts me Robert, he taunts me' and then quickly followed by that explosion of anger toward an empty row of books. What could it mean? But try as he might he had no answers and realised that only in conversation could the answers be gleaned. But did he want that? What had already happened tonight would have a fundamental effect on their relationship. What else might the old man say? And was he ready for it?

These thoughts plagued him as he descended the cellar steps and all through his journey back along the long halls to the library and by the time he returned he half-convinced himself that he might have imagined the whole thing such was the absurdity of it all.

None the less, he was going to go through with it, and Searle certainly wasn't about to change his mind as he could see that he had drawn up a second chair that lay with its back to the shadowed aisle and slightly to the side so that Searle could still be afforded an unobstructed view of his obsession.

He sat and faced the old man who offered him an outstretched glass to fill. McArthur uncapped the bottle and poured a long draft, quickly followed by another for himself.

Searle took his and quickly drained his glass. Reaching out, he took the bottle from where McArthur had placed it on the floor and poured another. This time though he simply rolled the glass between his hands. His eyes searching the depths of the vessel as if for some hidden truth or answer. And so he remained for some short time. McArthur simply sat there and sipped occasionally from his own glass. Eventually startled from his reverie as Searle finally found the words to begin.

"What must you think of me, Robert, eh? A drunken old fool, given into flights of madness no doubt." He looked up and gazed into McArthur's eyes for confirmation but on finding only his hard inquisitive eyes, he smiled and looked back into his glass.

"You are a hard man Robert, a very hard man. And that is to your merit. How you must hate me. But never a flicker, eh? Never a sign or word of emotion? That is good Robert and that is why you are still here. All those others?" Searle continued, flicking out his palm in a submissive gesture. "They do not hold a candle to you, oh and I have made it hard for you for that reason. Tested you, pushed you and still that professionalism and never-ending restraint. You would have made a fine ally in the trenches of the Somme."

Searle went on, "I guess that's why I kept you on, damn that busted leg of yours. You have stared hard into the face of your own demons and are stronger for it. You know the hardship and strain of war, and yet you held your poise when all around you lost theirs and you remained proud. And that is what got you through isn't it? You could not be seen to lose face on those bloody beaches at Normandy, nor could you lose face with your wife and so you chose to let her go, and you cannot allow to lose face with me, isn't that right? To lose control? To scream into my face your hatred? Your loathing? That would be a defeat for you wouldn't it? And so, here you still are all these years later, despite everything, still in my service."

McArthur said nothing; the old man was surely testing him again. Or was he? He detected no hint of malice, could it be that Searle knew him better than he ever would have imagined? That he knew his pride and knew that his pride ruled him? And so he sat there and continued to sip from his glass.

"I think Robert that we are more alike than I would ever have cared to admit as I am also a proud man. Proud of everything that I have accomplished. Everything that I have fought for, both in war and in business. But now...to know that it was all a lie? That I am not a great man and was not destined for such a life. That I should not even be here and that my fate should be the same as those wasted souls in the fields of France all those years ago. I think that is the hardest thing of all to bear, that my accomplishments were not my own, that it was all a gift, a twisted, cursed gift, delivered to me by the hands of a devil."

Searle looked gravely into McArthur's eyes, seemingly looking for understanding. But McArthur was mystified at the words being spoken and as to what they might mean. As he sat, he became more and more aware of the stillness and quiet of the room. He continued to say nothing for to utter any words would break Searle's spell for he had not the right questions to ask or direction to take with the man. All he could do was let Searle's tale run its course.

Searle gazed past McArthur down the long line of books into shadow.

"I'm sorry Robert; I am ranting aren't I? But look for the truth in my words for the truth is there. I said to you that this very aisle is where I died the second time, did I not?"

McArthur simply nodded his reply and again sipped whisky from his glass.

Searle nodded and went on.

"To die a second time, a man must die a first. But for that, I should start over. The beginning then…I don't know if you know this or not Robert, I am actually of mixed parentage. My father was originally from Newfoundland and my mother was of British descent. After they wed, they moved back to Newfoundland, which was my father's birthplace and at that time still a part of the British Empire. As such, I grew up in St John's, and in August of 1914 the government recruited a small force that would serve with the British Army in the Great War. I was only 17 years of age at that time and let me tell you I had no hesitation in enlisting. This was long before conscription and the men who joined, did so gladly. A chance to fight for King and Country."

McArthur reflected on Searle's words; it seemed that he would be party to some sort of history lesson. He was aware of many of these facts of course. Being in Searle's employ and dealing with the vast amount of correspondence and visitors to the house, meant that he would have to be in the know regarding certain details of the man's background. Especially as many would question him on Searle's rise to prominence. Despite this, he did not interrupt. This was the first time that Searle had ever opened up with him and to interrupt the flow now might irritate the man, and so he drained his glass and reached for the bottle.

Following McArthur's lead, Searle smiled and drained his glass, then offered it out for a refill. He pressed on with his story. "You see, my mother had always told me stories of what life was like back in England and the fact that I should be very proud of my heritage. I think life in St John's was very slow for her considering her East End upbringing. I would lie awake in bed for hours as she told me wave after wave of stories, and as such, I made it my resolve to finally make my way there. So when war broke out that year, I was one of the first five hundred or so to sign up. I'd lied about my age of course, albeit by only a month and it wasn't long before I became one of the famous blue puttees."

McArthur smiled at this. It was well-known to him that the Newfoundlander's had adopted the blue puttee rather than the traditional olive colour due to fabric shortages at the time.

"Ultimately we were shipped over to England for our training. I'm sure you can imagine my excitement. It was a whole new world for me. I was mixing with real men, men with honour and I was made to feel a part of that. I was so proud. Soon though we would be called into action. Shipped over to Suvla Bay on the Gallipoli Peninsula with the 29th British Division to support the campaign there."

McArthur knew of the Gallipoli campaign only too well. His own father had been a sergeant in the Royal Hampshire's which formed part of the 29th and had landed at Cape Helles on that day. His father had never told him what transpired there, but he had learned the details over the years as he made his own way in service of his country.

"On September 20th 1915, I stepped into hell." Searle went on. "We were subjected to artillery fire, snipers you name it, but that wasn't the worst of it, it was those damned trenches, you know? I guess this was just the prelude for what was to happen to me on the Somme."

Searle looked up, and McArthur could see genuine pain in his gaze. He wasn't prepared for that at all. He had served his time and had come under heavy enemy fire many times in his own service, and he knew that look all too well. It was the sick underlying fear that lived with every soldier of every minute of every day — never knowing when your moment might be up. Watching as old friends and comrades lay down in the dirt and never got up again. Yes, he knew that look all too well, as he had worn it himself.

"Before the retreat on 9th January 1916, we had lost some thirty or so men. But that wasn't the worst of it, for those men died with courage in the wake of enemy fire and battle. The real problem was the damn cold that we had to contend with — pressed in amongst muddy walls. Sometimes ankle-deep in mud and water. It drained your soul, you know? What with the constant crash and thunder of artillery firing and landing nearby it was enough to drive a man insane. And yes, I include myself in that. I always imagined hell to be a hot place Robert, let me tell you it is not. Hell is a cold, cold place where a man might lose his mind."

McArthur nodded in solemn agreement at the harrows of war. He had also felt the pull on the threads of his sanity. He knew that his father had come back from the war changed and introvert. And he had seen it in the eyes and character of his comrades who had survived the Second World War.

"So there I was, young and naïve. I had believed that one man might win a war, and I thought that man might be me. I was stupid; I was fighting for a country I didn't know in a place I didn't care about. My early life patriotism had all but dried up in those festering fucking trenches. I wanted out. I wanted out badly but looking back now I could not believe the lengths I would eventually go to escape. You see Robert, Gallipoli was bad but it was nothing compared to the Somme. In the aftermath of our retreat, I had forgotten my fear, for as a unit we had served and fought well. The objectives were never met of course and the whole thing was a damn disaster. But we were given the final task of covering the retreating lines and we patted ourselves on the back for a job well done. Then came the fields of France."

Searle lifted his fresh glass to his lips. McArthur watched as his hands trembled as he did so. As the glass found his lips, he lifted the glass and poured the entire contents down his throat in one go. McArthur couldn't guess as to how many drinks he might have downed to this point, but now in the short respite from the story, he could see that the old man was very drunk after all. And for the first time since he had known him, he looked old and defeated. Whatever was to come, would not come easily, he guessed. Even now, thoughts of Searle going AWOL in the face of the battle of the Somme were beginning to press on his mind. How else might the man have survived in the face of such carnage? On a day when his entire unit had been virtually wiped out? And with that thought, he did likewise and drank the rest from his own glass.

He also was beginning to feel a little light-headed from the alcohol and he believed it a good thing. For how else could he deal with this tale should Searle speak of cowardice and betrayal?

His mind reflected back to the statue that stood in the driveway of the great house. The fierce Tommy, battle-hardened and determined in the wake of overwhelming odds. Looking at Searle now, he could not recognise the face as being the same. This haggard old man and that frightening fierce soldier.

But suddenly it came to him...the plaque at the base of the statue read, Sir Thomas Searle VC. VC, Victoria Cross. The highest honour of gallantry that can be bestowed upon a member of the Royal armed forces. So with that being the case, surely Searle could not have absconded? He felt confused suddenly for what he knew of the man did not equate with the words spilling from Searle's lips.

"The 1st of July 1916 was officially the first date of the attack." Searle finally continued. "The French were being hammered in Verdun, and it was our intent to make major inroads in the German lines to alleviate that pressure. We were again with the 29th, at Beaumont-Hamel and took our positions in April of that year. There had been no moves by either side during that time. The Germans in fact had dug in since October of 1914 and had greatly fortified their positions."

"The plan was simple enough. In the week leading up to the offensive, we would unleash an artillery bombardment upon them. The shells would cut the wire that protected the front lines and beat the Hun into submission. It was Haig's plan that as a result of this, we could virtually walk into the German trenches unmolested. What can I tell you? It was a farce from the bloody beginning. "

McArthur finally decided that it was time to contribute to the conversation. They had been sat there for some fifteen minutes now, and Searle was settling into his tale. He knew events of the Somme well, for it was those events that largely dominated the progression of modern warfare, through World War 2 and on to the current day.

"Was there any confidence in Haig's plan?" He questioned.

Searle looked up, brow furrowed.

"Yes, at first. The front on the Somme hadn't bloody moved in years, and we believed that this action could finally make some ground into winning the damn war. But it wasn't until the reconnaissance teams went into the field later in the week that we found the shelling wasn't having the desired effect, and that is when I felt we would be walking into a massacre."

"Why is that?" McArthur replied.

"I saw it for what it was. The German's were bunkered deep in a ravine just beyond their trench lines; the shelling wasn't touching them. And despite the constant thunder of explosions, I saw in the eyes of each man the dread of going over the top, of walking into the German machine guns. I could see the dead, barren plain that opened up between the lines of German and British and saw no cover but the ripped, ravaged earth. That was when I became scared, that was when I tried to find a way out."

McArthur swallowed hard and quickly raised his glass to hide any emotion that he might have conveyed. Here it is, he thought. This old bastard is going to tell me that he ran, that he ran and he didn't look back. He could feel his anger rising at such a thought. That for all these years that he had taken this man's abuse, this coward, this traitor...

But Searle quickly cut into his thoughts.

"I know what you're thinking Robert. I did not run." He paused before continuing. "God help me, I thought about it, I wonder if there wasn't a man among us that didn't think about it. For I think the worst thing was the anticipation, you know? A week, after all, is a long time isn't it? You begin with thoughts of gallantry and bravado, but slowly, slowly, doubt begins to eat away at you. The cheers of your mates die away and slowly morale fades away until you can see it in the eyes of every man you pass. The week counts down and the seconds pass and it becomes all too near. As every man there knows the time of his destiny and it is at 07:30hrs on the 1st July 1916. It all became too much and I did what I had to do."

McArthur held his breath for it seemed the moment was upon them, that Searle was going to invoke his great secret upon him. But what could it be? If he didn't run, then what?

And at that moment he felt a chill at his spine and fear seized him, and he realised he did not wish to know. He suddenly felt uncomfortable with his back to the row of books that held Searle's attention for hours at end. It was as if some small draught had come from behind, chill and evil whispering words of doubt, telling him that once told, he could not unlearn what was about to be said.

He also realised that things between him and Searle would be changed forever. And for a man of Searle's prominence? How could he cope with the sharing of such a story? But ultimately he was captured. The position of his chair in the mouth of the aisle of books, confronted now by Searle only a few feet away, there was no escape, there was no excuse. He had faced Searle as an equal, and now he would have to cope with the fallout of that decision.

But it seemed Searle wasn't yet fully ready to impart the ghastly details of his war, for he continued.

"You have to understand the pressure, Robert. I'm sure that you do, for have you not felt it yourself? You are a man of courage but did you not have the same thoughts run through your mind in the days, hours and even final seconds before you stepped foot on those beaches at Normandy?"

And McArthur knew that he had. The knot of fear in your stomach, the unbelievable tension of waiting and imagining the worst, only to find that your mind could not do the scene justice when it all unfurled.

Searle continued, "It was in the early hours of that morning of the 1st that I made my decision Robert, that was when I struck my deal."

CHAPTER 24

Saturday, 1st July 1916, 02:30hrs

Beaumont-Hamel,

The Somme.

Thomas Searle was enduring a nightmare without end. One that had taken him from the sanctuary of his home in Newfoundland, and transported him to the living hell that was the trenches of the western front in France.

He was standing guard, taking his shift by a fixed machine gun that looked over into the vast expanse of no man's land. His nerves were frayed, and he felt tired throughout his body.

It was not the physical exertion of the long march his regiment had made from the billets in Lovencourt earlier that night, and nor was it the watch to which he was now assigned that caused fatigue to envelop him. No, it was the impending action scheduled for later that morning that consumed him. The big push the General's called it. The advance designed to finally break the German lines and so bring about the end of the war. An advance that meant going over the top of the trenches and facing the Germans head-on.

He had felt a man alone as they made their long march, the surrounding men of the company singing a rousing rendition of Keep the Home Fires Burning, as they made their way back to the front. As a unit, they had seen such action before, but something that sat deep in his gut told him that the first ray of light on the new dawn might be the last for many of them.

As these thoughts consumed him, he unwittingly allowed his Enfield rifle to drop, the barrel coming to rest on the sandbag at shoulder level before him. His vision clouded as tears came to his eyes.

I don't want to die! It's not fair!

"Searle!" came the whisper. "Point that damn gun up, how many times have I got to tell you!"

Searle turned and saw Sergeant Cook making his way down the line toward him. Quickly he dabbed at his eyes, to dismiss the tears and refocused the barrel of his rifle toward the German lines.

"Ah, leave him be sarge," came the voice of Paul Ladder who manned the machine gun beside him. "I don't think the Hun are coming out to play tonight."

"Be that as it may corporal, I will not have my line slacking off, is that clear?" Cook said as he approached. "Look, son, I know it's hard, but we'll do our jobs to the end, eh?"

"Yes, sarge." Searle whispered so as not to let the emotion in his voice get the better of him.

"Good lad, only thirty or so minutes, okay? Then try and get some sleep, you'll need it for the big off." Cook replied, slapping Searle hard on the back. "You'll do just fine."

As the sergeant made his way further down the trench, Ladder whispered back at Searle. "Sleep? Who's he fucking kidding?"

Searle knew he was right. The knot of fear in his stomach would preclude any sleep that night as it had done on many nights past. Had anyone the inclination, they would have seen that his nerves were shot and that he was strung out. He hoped that they would. That they would see that he was just a lad after all and that this was no place for someone as young as him. But nobody had noticed. He was not the only one suffering, and nobody had time for this one soldier amongst many. He would be expected to do his duty as a man.

And now the clock was ticking. In a few short hours, the artillery bombardment of the enemy's positions would recommence. Six full days of firing so far, something in which he could place little faith. Any resistance should have been obliterated, but Searle knew otherwise, as reconnaissance missions undertaken in the darkness of the last few nights had returned with grim news, the German positions very much intact.

Time wore on. He stood there 'standing too' as it was called, looking out into the deserted plain ahead and his mind wandered to his Regiment's time in Gallipoli and how on arriving in France earlier that year everything seemed so different. For one, the debilitating cold of the Turkish lands was gone, and morale was high as men sang and laughed. But ultimately a malaise had set in. The days on the front were now a mixture of menial tasks and boredom. These spells alleviated every third week when the unit was allowed to retire for a week's leave.

Suddenly his concentration was broken, and he was startled as something darted narrowly in front of his face. He gasped, and his finger began to tighten on the trigger of his rifle. A rat made its way along the sandbag just in front of his nose, and he was instantly repelled by the vision.

And though he willed the picture away, the image had already formed in his mind of his old friend Alfie Drake; whose abandoned corpse had been nearly picked clean by these damnable creatures back during the Gallipoli campaign.

A night-time sortie into enemy territory gone wrong; Alfie had been picked off by a sniper's bullet only yards short of the sanctuary of the Allied trenches, his body tantalisingly out of reach in the days to follow in the wake of Turkish aggression and so left for the vermin.

And it was with memories of his friend prevalent in his mind that Searle's watch came to an end and he at last found himself back in the support trench of St John's Road, walking past the huddled forms of his comrades, a hundred pairs of eyes glinting back at him in the low light of the makeshift stoves that were cut into the walls of the trench. He saw fear in every face that he saw.

In no mood for company, he turned out of the crowded trench and onto the road that fed the front. It was closely defended by a high bank that shrouded it from the high fields above and beyond into no man's land. Here he found only isolated groups of men. Some had found the release of sleep. Others were huddled close, deep in whispered conversation and sharing cigarettes. And so he walked and walked. But he could not outwalk the memories of Alfie or how for days after he looked out at the unrecovered body of his friend. And how he and several of the company's men had gone against orders to recover the body under cover of darkness.

"I won't think about that; I won't." He whispered to himself. But it was already too late. On returning to the safety of the British line that night, they had seen by the low light of their trench lighters the deep exit wound of the sniper's bullet where Alfie's left eye should have been and how that wound had provided easy access to what was inside for the rats.   Searle hated himself that he could no longer picture the face of his friend, as now all he had been left with was this terrible vision. The gaping wound, the remaining eyeball feasted upon and the multitude of bites that covered his cold grey skin.

He'd walked some mile or so now and was long out of sight of the last group of huddled Tommy's. He drew a cigarette from his pack and lit it with trembling hands. It was a habit that had stayed with him in the wake of Alfie's death.

"Alfie," he whispered into the night. "What can I do?"

But the night had no reply for him.

Searle looked out at the cigarette in his hand and could see that he was shaking quite violently. He threw it down and fell hard to the floor, pulling his knees tight to his chest and allowed the tears to come. He regretted it all, and he hated the world for it.

Come on now, Tom, self-pity?

It was his mother's voice that resonated now in his mind, and though he understood that his subconscious brought her to the fore in moments of difficulty, it still caused the heaving of his chest to subdue and the tears in his eyes to dry.

That's my good boy. What good is crying, eh? How's that going to help you?

She had been an exacting influence in his life. Born to the hard streets of the East End of London she had left that life behind to be with his father and return to his native Newfoundland before the turn of the century. What dreams she may have had of a better life there, were quickly in tatters as Searle's father passed from typhoid only two years into his own infant life. He to had been a sickly child, but it seemed as much through her force of will than anything that he had survived.

I didn't raise you to quit Thomas. Find a way.

Find a way? He answered her. *It's because of you that I am here at all.*

That much was true. It had been his mother's stories of England and home that had elicited a pride in him that had made him proudly answer the King's call to arms. But where had that pride got him? He was on the brink, and in only a few short hours, his life would surely end in the muddy fields above.

Find a way.

There was no way, couldn't she see that? If he ran he would be shot, if he did his duty he would know only the same end but instead be called hero rather than coward, what other way was there?

You know the way Tom. It is why you are here after all.

He stopped breathing as an age-old memory began to encroach upon him — his mother down upon her knees, blood gushing from an open wound in her palm. Him, a sickly child rejuvenated somehow and rushing to her side as she repeated the same words over and over again. *They can't have you Thomas. They can't have you to.*

Something dark had happened in the depths of that lonely night in Newfoundland, something forbidden that he had observed through the veil of a fever that should have taken him. But that was not all; there had been something else seen through that veil, something or someone…

Suddenly he was interrupted.

"You going to let that go to waste son?"

He raised his eyes above the line of his elbows in time to see the round green circle of a Tommy's helmet bend in front of him. A hand reached out and picked up the cigarette on the floor.

Suddenly, Searle felt cold. It was as in the darkest coldest nights of his nightmare in Gallipoli. His breath rose in a plume before his mouth as he exhaled, and whatever sorrow he was suffering was instantly evaporated as an all-consuming fear flooded his mind in its place.

It felt as if a slow hand climbed his legs, drawing paralysing feeling within him as it went. His stomach rolled, and he felt the skin on his body shrink and his scalp freeze. His eyes were locked, and he realised that he hadn't been scared, had never been scared in his life until this point. He did not want this man to stand. He did not want to behold the vision of this man's face. But slowly the figure began to stand upright before him.

It was, as he thought the figure of a Tommy. As he straightened, he made out the three stripes of a sergeant on each arm of the man's tunic. He wore no other kit that Searle could see and somewhere within the back of his mind a tiny voice went unanswered when it asked how the man's uniform could be so clean.

And now, slowly, the man's Brodie helmet began to rise, first revealing his mouth where Searle briefly glimpsed a flashing maniacal smile. He shook his head to negate the vision, and when he refocused, the man was at last upright before him. His first and only instinct then was to run and if he should have to run the fields of no man's land to do so, then so be it. Surely it was better to face the guns of the German lines than behold this vision.

But it was too late; the sergeant was now upright before him. His smile gone, he appeared a simple man, and yet Searle still felt the same raw fear and knew this person was the heart of it.

The man took a long draft on the cigarette and sighed his pleasure.

"Hmmm, you know son these things will kill you, don't you?" He then smiled before taking another drag. "On second thoughts I think that's the least of your problems right now?"

"Stand up son and let me see you." The figure continued.

But Searle found that he could not move, his arms were locked in place, and he felt that he had no feeling in his body. Everything was frozen around him and all there was in the world was this man. He looked deep within the stranger's eyes as he found that he could not look away, and it was there, there in the eyes that he found the source of his fear. The eyes seemed to glisten despite the dark that surrounded them, and they emanated such a hatred that he could almost feel it.

The man spoke again, only this time with venom and Searle found that the very sound burned his ears.

"I won't tell you again son, stand up."

And despite his paralysing fear, he found that he could get up, that no matter how things might be, that he did not wish to anger this man any more than he could. For he guessed that he did not generally ask twice for the things that he wanted.

He placed his palms flat beside himself, and despite the offer of an outstretched hand from the stranger he pushed on by himself, for he felt that to the touch the hand, would be to find it cold. Dead cold. And despite his rational mind, that was all that he could think. That here before him stood a dead man.

185

"That's better son, now stand to attention!" The sergeant snapped.

The order got through, and Searle snapped to attention, smartly slapping his heels together and firing his arms straight beside him.

"That's good son, very good. You look a little perturbed. There is no need for that, for us to have a little talk; I'll need you with a clear mind. When I call stand at ease, you will do just that. You will stand easy."

And with the call, Searle did feel at ease. His fear evaporated from him as if taken on the gust of wind. So he stood there calm and relaxed and somewhat confused. Why had this sergeant made him so at unease before? He felt somewhat ridiculous all of a sudden. Maybe it was just his nerves getting to him. But for whatever reason, he did now feel very comfortable. His previous fears were gone.

"Now that's better." The sergeant continued. "I have a busy night ahead of me, so go ahead. Ask me."

"Sergeant?" Searle replied.

"No games, eh son? Do you mean to tell me all is well in your little world? That I should find you here snivelling like a little girl?"

All of a sudden Searle resented this interruption. With the release of his fear, he felt invaded by this man's intrusion. He had come here to seek solace and not to be belittled, especially in the wake of the new day and all that it would bring.

The sergeant looked long and hard at Searle, "Hmmm maybe I misread you Searle, no matter, there are plenty more like you, it will be a prosperous night."

And with that, the sergeant turned away and began to head back into the shadows from where he'd come.

"Prick." Searle whispered to himself and turned to face St John's Road again.

Suddenly he was aware of a flash of movement and turned in time to meet the sergeant's fist connecting with his chin. He immediately saw a flash of white as unbelievable pain met his jaw. He felt disconnected somehow, that was until he came to earth and skidded to a stop. His pain was unimaginable, and he rolled onto his front to take in his grazed bloody hands. He looked about and saw the sergeant approaching from some twenty yards away.

Impossible. How?...

All to quickly, the sergeant was leering over him, and he crawled into a ball, arms outstretched to fend off any further attack.

"I'll teach you to waste my time you pathetic cunt."

A boot lashed out, catching him in the stomach. This time he glimpsed the ground sail beneath him as he flew through the air. He landed squarely, and the air exploded out of him. He was rocked and his mind grasped for reality.

It can't be! Was all it could muster in his confused, injured state. He looked up and saw the sergeant approaching again.

"No, please," he whispered as he made his way onto his side and began to drag himself in the opposite direction.

"Are you scared now, Searle? Are you really scared!?" The sergeant bellowed.

"Yes, yes, please...please. No more." Searle replied.

"Oh, tonight is your lucky night Searle. I don't think you are scared. At least not scared enough. A man meets me of his own free will and makes his own free choice. I came because you made that decision, but it seems you changed your mind. But I am going to give you this opportunity. This one chance to take it back. I will show you your future, what there is of it and you will beg me forgiveness and show me the respect I deserve."

The sergeant stood over Searle a second time; again he rolled to protect himself, only this time instead of violence the man offered only his hand. And Searle knew that he must take it to preclude any chance of more injury.

The man pulled hard, and Searle was on his feet. His pain and the cold of the flesh he had touched, both instantly and inexplicably gone.

"Now that's better, don't you think? Now, let me show you as I promised. Your future."

Searle was bemused at what was happening. The fear, the pain. Was this a dream, some bad dream?

The sergeant turned and headed back the way he came with but one word. "Follow." And Searle did.

It was clear they were headed back in the direction of the St John's support trench. It was all Searle could do to keep pace with the man ahead. This whole experience had been so weird, and here he was following this man to his 'future'. What could he mean by that? Taking him back to the front line was kind of obvious after all; there was no doubt that his immediate future lay there. But it was more than that; there was also the underlying feeling that something else was amiss. He felt as if in a daze, more like walking through a dreamscape than anything else. There had been that terrible fear that had vanished as quickly as it had come and then the blow to the chin and the boot to the gut. The pain there, gone as quickly as it came and now this, following this stranger back to the front line.

As he walked the feeling of disquiet grew greater as he realised the lines of huddled Tommy's he had previously observed were no longer there. Although the long bank that shielded the support road was long, there were always many resting soldiers here. It was so quiet...

And that forced him into a halt. It was quiet..., it had in fact been quiet since his encounter with the mysterious figure, it had just taken his mind this long to catch up and recognise the fact. But why and where was everybody?

He looked up and saw that the sergeant had stopped at the entrance into St John's Road, where the earth had been cut away and slowly arched upwards into the two sides of a trench. Searle, eager not to upset him a second time, hastened on to catch him up.

"Don't worry son; we now have all the time in the world." The sergeant said as Searle finally caught up to him.

Searle looked through into the deserted trench puzzled. "Where is everyone?" he asked quietly.

"Oh, never mind them, they'll be back, they've got a big day ahead of them." The sergeant replied before turning and making his way on through the trench toward the front line.

Searle pressed on. His mind turning over and over. The support trench was empty, and now here he was making his way through toward the front line, and this to was empty.

This can't be. He thought. *This must be a nightmare, or I have lost my mind.*

But surely no dream had ever been so vivid. As he walked everything seemed so alive and real to him. And to confirm this, he allowed his hand to reach out and touch the sandbagged walls and the wooden support beams to feel their rough exterior, their touch and the continued cold about him could not be denied.

Such thoughts were quickly forgotten as he saw that the sergeant had stopped before the guard post of his earlier sentry watch. The machine gun, now unmanned continued pointing out into the night. Warily he approached the sergeant. Whatever he wished to show him would happen here, maybe...

"Squad, stand ready!" the sergeant bellowed in his direction, before turning and facing the thick wall before him. Searle observed, as from nowhere, the sergeant produced an Enfield rifle.

"Fix bayonets!" Came the next cry.

Searle was confused and somewhat scared; the cry of the sergeant hurt his ears in the dull quiet of the night. What was he saying? Why was he doing this?

The sergeant turned to him and shouted "Do as I say boy. Ready your rifle!"

Again those hateful eyes were upon him, and he felt panicked as he turned. Relief swept over him as he found his rifle swung over his shoulder. He proceeded to draw his bayonet and fix it to the end. Why was this man making him do this?

"Sixty seconds!" came the sergeant's shrill shout.

Sixty seconds? What did he mean? Searle looked up and down the trench line, hoping beyond hope to find someone else. Someone who could interrupt this bizarre display.

This can't be! This can't be! His panicked mind recited over and over.

"Are you ready son? Are you ready to see your future?"

"What? No...no." Searle's pleading reply came. This man was crazy! He meant to go over the top! They would be killed!

"Thirty seconds." Came the next shout.

This was a dream. No, a nightmare. And in his desperation, he clung to that idea. That he had simply fallen asleep and this was some wretched scene playing out for his eyes. That was why there was nobody around; that was why the night was so quiet and still. But despite that, the situation still held a terrifying reality to it. He was going to go over the top, and yes, there before him was the trench ladder that reached up into the unknown blackness above.

He looked over at the sergeant, a plea on the tip of his lips. He didn't want to go! It was as before. He was scared. But his argument would not be heard for the sergeant simply watched over him with that maniacal smile stretching his mouth wide. A whistle in his hand, he drew it to his lips and blew one long piercing note.

"Go, go!" he screamed, insanity in his voice.

And Searle did go, despite his fear. He would face this nightmare; he would face his demons. And so he attacked the ladder and hauled himself up onto the fields and brought his weapon to bear, the sergeant only scant seconds behind him, into a silent ravaged land.

Searle stood on the lip of the trench and surveyed the horizon. Before him, the land fell steadily away and led to the first line of barbed wire that guarded the forward trench. All about them were the muddy craters where German shells had fallen and exploded.

Here in the open, the light was more pronounced, so much more so that he looked above him and saw a multitude of single starbursts that seemed to shimmer in the air, casting long-reaching shadows to fall on the ground before them.

"Are you ready?"

Searle looked over at the sergeant and nodded his agreement, and they slowly made their way forward.

The going was surprisingly easy at first, although cut up, the ground was firm underfoot, and he made his way with confidence on toward the horizon. Every so often though he would allow his eyes to drift skyward at the shimmering light in the air as it begged understanding.

He turned and formed the question in his mind, but it was as if the sergeant had already read the thought, for his reply was brief.

"Flares."

And with that came understanding. Time it seemed had stopped after all, as the fiery lights simply hung in the air above them, their usual tell-tale streams noticeable by their absence. It also explained the deathly quiet and the fact that they were able to make their way onward unmolested toward enemy lines. It did nothing to quiet the unease in his heart however. For despite his repeated thoughts of a dream, it was all still too real, too vivid an experience to deny.

They walked ever onward, on the still declining fields. It seemed that some minutes had passed. Just how far were the German lines?

He pitched forward as his foot fell into a low crater at his foot. He caught his balance and looked on after the sergeant who seemed to glide across the landscape ahead of him unmolested.

Searle gathered himself and continued. The only way it seemed was forward, and he pressed on despite the difficulty of the terrain. He pitched and fell in the shadowed craters many times and as he looked onward, he found he could no longer see the sergeant. Panic again threatened to overwhelm him. He was all alone in the vast desolation of no man's land and despite his fear of the man; he did not wish to be alone.

Soon however, a strange silhouette came into his view. He was shocked as he found the sergeant again and as he did so, his fear threatened to take over him once more. The man stood some twenty yards ahead and it seemed that some huge antlers had grown from his head. It was only when Searle fell and gathered himself; he saw it for what it was. The sergeant now stood before a single skeletal tree that marked the midpoint of no man's land, its twisted and gnarled branches had appeared as some terrifying appendage adorning the mans silhouetted form.

At a tired shambling walk, he fell in beside him. Searle held his hands on his knees and breathed deeply, his eyes searching upward to follow the man's gaze. He saw it, and in his shock, he stopped breathing.

Before him and stretching each way into the distance in each direction was line after line of barbed wire. The land it sat upon was blasted into a million holes, and the lines lay at odd angles, many intertwining and thick. He had heard the reports, but here with his own eyes, he saw the truth.

The enemy barbed wire was intact.

And there just beyond, was the first pencil-thin black line of the first German trench.

Searle stumbled forward. "No. This can't be!" He looked back at the sergeant hoping for some kind of reconciliation, that things might not be as he saw. But the man simply stood there and watched on as Searle returned his attention to the wire. It seemed the recon patrols had been accurate, that despite the constant shelling of the area there had been no gaps created. The German lines were fully protected, and when the British troops advanced they would find the line impenetrable and all in the line of sight of the German machine guns.

Searle collapsed to his knees. The impending advance was doomed to failure; they could not hope to win through against the German defences.

"What can be done?" he said, looking up into the dark eyes of the sergeant.

"There is more, come." Came the reply.

The sergeant moved on into the thick tangle of wire and somehow managed to appear on the other side. Searle stood and approached warily.

There was no way through; how could he possibly? As he blinked, he suddenly found the pathway clear before him and he was able to walk by as the sergeant had done before him.

They walked until the blank line of the first German line came into view and slowly began to substantiate and become thicker. Searle could make out the beginning of a long line of machine gun nests lining the parapet to the trench below. And, turning he could make out the long slope behind him, back to the wire, and toward the British trenches. He knew that it was impossible to see in the dim light, but he found that he knew exactly from where they'd come. He also knew the Germans would have an unobstructed view of the advancing soldiers in the light of the new day.

The sergeant had come to a halt above the first trench and with a sweeping motion of his arm indicated the long line of machine guns.

"As you can see, the German lines are intact and will be found as such when you arrive. Though few if any will make this far."

"What can be done?" Searle repeated at a whisper.

"Done? Nothing can be done, Searle." The sergeant cackled. "Don't you understand that this is your future? There is nothing more for you beyond the dawn of the new day. That is why you summoned me, is it not?"

"Summoned? I don't understand!"

"Oh, I think that you do understand Searle, I think you understand very well. But before you choose, I will impart this final gift upon you. I will allow you to see the field as I see it."

And with that, the sergeant turned and beckoned outward with his outstretched arm. Searle looked beyond and gasped at the sight which his eyes fell upon.

Where there had been nothing but an empty, destroyed plain, now lay the scene of a massacre.

Searle's eyes widened in horror as he beheld the sight of thousands of bodies lying in the mud. Thousands of bodies wearing British uniform. The very field in which they lay ran with blood which pooled over the many craters it met as it ran slowly through the fields and toward them. And more, for as he looked, he gasped in horror as he found that as he scanned the hill that he knew the names of each man as his eyes passed over. There Sergeant Cook, there Private Ladder. And so it went on and on, wherever he lay his eyes he found a new name and a new victim until he could take no more and he closed his eyes to the terror and screamed, "no!", as he fell to his knees once more.

But there was no respite in darkness for the sergeant went on. "Can't you feel it? The carnage? The slaughter? I can taste it in the very air that I breathe. Open your eyes Searle and look."

And Searle found that he must, he opened his eyes and looked out onto the field once more. But this time it was as if his eyes saw everything. He could see along both directions of the front for miles and miles, and this time it was worse than he could ever have imagined. For now, he could see all of the dead of the war. In every direction, lay row upon row of bloody carcasses, stacked twenty high. But it was not just those of the British. He could see German, Russian, French and all other nations that had been blighted by the foul touch of the war. He saw male, female, adult and child and his blood ran cold at the sight.

"No, no...." Was all he could whisper as tears came to his eyes.

But it seemed the sergeant had not yet finished with him.

"Come, Thomas. There is but one more gift I would impart to you tonight."

"Gift? gift? You call this a fucking gift!" He raged. He found his feet and supported his weight upon his rifle. "Why would you do this to me?"

The sergeant softly laughed to himself. "Do this to you? I did not do this to you. Are you so naïve? This folly was commissioned by the Governments of Europe, this death toll to naïve and idiotic generals and politicians. Why would you accuse me? I have given you this insight, this glimpse of things to come. You cannot change it now Thomas, don't you realise?"

Searle looked up for a change had come into the sergeant's voice all of a sudden. It had become softer somehow, calmer, more recognisable. He looked across the darkened field, and he knew a change had come about for the voice with which he was now greeted was that of his old friend.

Alfie Drake stepped forward.

"Tom, can't you see? This is above you. It is too late now. These events have been set into motion; they cannot be undone. What would you do? Go back? Go back and tell them the folly of their ways? Tell them that they walk into disaster? They would not listen and you will have accomplished nothing with your remaining time. Come." Alfie finished, beckoning Searle to follow him back across the battlefield.

Searle was stunned as he turned though, for all of the bodies that he had beheld had simply vanished and in their place was row upon row of white crosses in neat, orderly lines as far as the eye could see. He stepped forward; puzzlement on his face, for his feet now inexplicably touched a soft plush lawn that stretched to the horizon in all directions. Gone was the blasted and ruined earth of the war from moments ago.

His eyes searched frantically but all around was the same — row upon row of white graves.

Alfie led the way back to where he knew the British trench to be, and nothing was said between them. Until finally they came to a stop.

Searle pointed to a spot on the ground and traced his arm off into the distance. "Here. This is where the trench should be...shouldn't it?"

But Alfie said nothing; he simply stood, head bowed, beside one single cross. Searle twisted his head sharply as he found that all of the other white tombstones had now disappeared, leaving only the lush green grass beneath his feet, and this one solitary cross that Alfie bowed reverently before.

Searle knew what he would see before his eyes met it. Despite this, he allowed himself to his knees and took in the name upon the cross.

Thomas Searle 1897-1916.

And with that, he knew his fate. He was to die here on the Somme on the morning of the 1st July, only yards away from his own trench line. He would not even make the German lines that he had witnessed first-hand, for the positioning of the cross so close to where their own front lines lay, told him that he would surely be amongst the first to go.

"Alfie, please...what can I do?"

"What?" Came the reply, "you know what you must do. Surely you understand the value of the gift that has been given to you? You have seen what will come to pass; the rest is for you to decide." Alfie replied.

"Decide? decide how?... you said..."

"What I said was that the future cannot be undone, all of what you have seen will happen. You cannot change these events for these people. But you can change them for yourself. But that as I have said is a free choice that must come from you, and you alone."

"My decision is made; how can I make it true?" Searle replied.

"It is time to stop lying to yourself and finish this as you began it. You know the way."

And he did, he knew in his moment of weakness the decision that he had come to before the sergeant's interruption. He had, of course, been kidding himself all along. It had not been an interruption at all. It had been the answer to his dark prayer.

"Alfie, please answer my call. I have nothing to offer other than my mortal soul in payment, but please spare me this torment."

"Alfie? Who is Alfie?" came the fierce reply and Searle looked up again into the cruel, unforgiving eyes of the sergeant.

"It will be done, Searle. You will fight tomorrow but you will not fall."

"Fight?" Searle questioned.

"Yes, but you shall not be harmed. You will have your life and make with it what you will. But you must know the cost of this bargain. For it is not a choice made lightly. Where you go, what you do, I don't care. But you must know that one day I will come to claim my prize and that day will mark an eternity in hell for you."

"I understand" Searle replied.

The sergeant laughed. "You do not, but you will. There is but one small formality that remains before the deal is sealed. But know this, even now you are free to choose. You can meet your fate as you were meant to, or you can seek my salvation. But when the choice is made, you will remember no more. For it is not kind fortune to ask a man to live with such a choice. How might you find happiness with eternity hanging over you? No, you will not remember. You will leave me and tomorrow you will fight. You will not fear and you will survive a hero. The choices that you make from there are your own."

Searle nodded. "You said but for a formality?"

"Ah yes, it is but the signing of the contract. Take your blade and do as I do." The sergeant removed the bayonet from the end of his rifle and pressed it against the palm of his right hand.

In a long fluid motion, he cut deep into the flesh of his hand. Blood quickly poured but he held his hand out as Searle cut likewise. The sergeant held his hand for Searle and motioned for him to touch with his own bloody palm.

Searle approached cautiously, there was no pain to his hand, but a new fear plagued him as he must finally accept a long-buried truth about his mother and what she had given him at the highest of costs. God, circumstance or bad luck had taken his father from this world, but she would not allow her ailing son to be taken. What he was about to do, he had seen before as a child and somewhere deep within himself he had always known it.

The part of him that also believed this a dream had long since evaporated and despite the impossibility of what he had seen he knew he had no choice, as the vision of the grave still held fast in his mind. And so he held his arm out to touch the hand of the Devil, for he could kid himself no more as to this thing's identity, and with that, he entered into the contract that would save his life and cost him his soul.

He shook the hand of the devil, and the contract was completed, signed in blood.

"Finally, Searle, there is one more thing. As I have said, you will remember no more until it is time for me to collect. But on that day you will remember. For a deal done in darkness must be completed in darkness. At that time you will be mine. Now go, go and sleep, and when you wake, you will do your duty and you will not fear the German guns. Be gone."

And with that, the sergeant turned and walked back out into the expanse of no man's land, again returned as it should be to darkness and brutality.

Making his own lines, Searle quickly jumped back into the trench and made his way back toward St John's Road, and as he did so, he noticed a change coming over the world. As he walked, he could see shadows moving in the trenches and a soft keen buzzing in his ears. And as he went on the shadows grew more substantial and the buzzing louder, and he knew then that he was coming back into time. That for a short spell he had been removed and taken a stroll with the Devil to see his future and now that it was done, things were coming back in to place.

And so he ran. He ran past the now substantial form of three Tommy's huddled over mugs of tea and though he saw them, he knew he was invisible to them. He ran on and on until at last his lungs threatened to burst, and he fell, exhausted where he had originally sought the anonymity of the night. But now there was no more fear, he lay down closed his eyes and fell into a dreamless sleep.

CHAPTER 25

Wednesday, 10th April 1963, 03:30 am.

Thoby Hall.

Searle had come to the end of his story, and now an uneasy silence had fallen between him and McArthur. He sat still, looking into the eyes of his servant, trying it seemed to glean some sort of reaction or response from the tale that he had told, for McArthur had not uttered a word during the telling of the story.

And now here it was, out in the open. Searle had confessed of selling his soul to a devil so as to prevent his own death. McArthur's mind reeled at such a thought. Had the man gone insane after all? Surely the evidence had been gradually manifesting itself over the past years; the seeming neglect of risk or danger in his business dealings, his increasing agoraphobia, he had undoubtedly displayed symptoms which would certainly lean towards a mild case of eccentricity. But now? And over the last three months? His apparent fear of the darkness came immediately to mind, as did the ripping up of Thoby Hall to accommodate the mass lighting system which should never be switched off. And now this confession? Were these the actions of a man in control of his own mind? McArthur became increasingly aware of the ever-stretching moment between them and knew he must speak.

"This is ridiculous of course." Was all he could ultimately manage, "surely you know that? I don't know, maybe it all got to you perhaps? The stress? The shock of it all? Maybe you snapped and dreamed this all up? I could understand that given the pressure you were under. Perhaps it was all just some vivid nightmare?"

But Searle was already shaking his head to negate the response. "No, no, Robert. If only it were. I asked you to seek the truth in my words. Do you think me a liar? Or perhaps this a story of a confused man? You can see beyond all that bullshit, Robert. I know you can."

"But it doesn't make any sense!" McArthur appealed. "You have even gone as far as to contradict your own story! By your own words, you said that on making the deal that you would remember no more! There! What more do you need? Surely it was a dream after all."

"Oh, Robert," Searle replied. "I did not take you for a stupid man, so do not act like one! I have said far more this evening, have I not? Have I not hinted at the truth? That here in this very room I died a second time? Perhaps I have short-changed you; perhaps I have not given you the fullest of accounts to make your true conclusion? I have told you of my distant past, and perhaps I should tell you of my more recent past eh? Three months ago in fact in this very room."

"No, no" McArthur interjected with a wave of his hand. "First, I must hear of the battle. Were you not honoured that day? Did you not win the Victoria Cross?"

"What? Yes, yes of course, but don't you see? It was exactly as the beast had promised. I did take my place in the line that morning, but all fear was gone from me. At that point, I did not remember the events of the night before and couldn't reason at my new-found vitality. I still knew the dangers of course but death held no fear for me. The knowledge that had been imparted upon me was also gone. I did not know the impossibility of the task ahead. I only felt...at peace. I have no other way to describe it. I looked long down the lines and was surprised by the looks of fear and worry that I beheld. I felt that it would be a glorious day and we would all fight valiantly for our King and Country. I didn't understand the thinking and demeanour of my comrades."

Searle reached out for the bottle and found it empty. "Hmmm, no matter. I think I no longer need the courage of alcohol. It is as if a weight is lifted from my shoulders with each word that I speak, for I think you will see the truth eventually."

McArthur nodded in reply and looked mournfully at the empty bottle of whisky. Searle may have felt that he'd had enough but McArthur felt that at least another bottle would be needed for him to come to grips with the absurdity of the situation.

"With the blowing of whistles, we went over the top and into the field of death. The morning had played out as it should, the ceasing of artillery fire and the explosion of the mine beneath the German positions. But all we did was alert the German's into our coming attack. It was they, and not us who deployed quickest, rushing to the vast hole created by the mine, taking up defensive positions there as we had planned to do. So how could we have known the futility of our actions? The High Command had ordered we advance at a walking pace. Can you believe that? They felt that the common infantryman could only comprehend the simplest of instruction and that by running the line would become separated and disjointed. And so we walked. And quickly, all too quickly those around me fell. I felt my anger begin to rise and my hatred overcame me. Tears formed in my eyes and I could no longer see the line beside me, for it had simply fallen. And I walked and I walked until my hate overcame me and with a fierce cry I ran at a German machine gun crew that had taken up a position to effect maximum carnage upon us."

"You made the German line?" McArthur replied astonished.

"Yes, Robert, can't you see? The impossibility of the act? Advancing into the German guns alone? I made the position and my fury consumed me. In the close quarters and unsteady footing of the floor, my rifle was no good to me, and so I took to them with my bayonet. Time was lost to me and I do not know how many fell beneath my blade. But all too

197

quickly it was over. My insatiable blood lust had not been satisfied, and I cried in fury as the German's ran from me."

Searle stood at last and stepped over to McArthur, looking hard down into his eyes. "Is such a thing not impossible Robert hmm?" And with that, he stepped past McArthur and walked into the aisle of books. With arms folded behind him, he spoke as if to the shadow at the end.

"And you would have me think that it was all me? That by my heroics alone, I made the German position. You called it a gift? A gift, pah! There was no gift! To take that from me? To show me my cowardice and take from me my pride? That is surely the true cost of my sin, is it not?"

McArthur craned his neck to look at Searle. *Who does he think he is talking to?*

Indeed he had gone insane. And McArthur was glad, for the story that Searle had told was very unnerving. He had begun to believe the words that were spoken, for they were told with such volition and honesty. But for them to be true, that would mean....no, that could not be. To believe in Searle's words would be to admit in the existence of an evil that he could not bear to utter the name of. He was a god-fearing man, but the other? No, he would not allow himself to comprehend such an idea. And so he clung to the idea of Searle's insanity. For surely the heart attack that he had suffered had affected his mind. And as he sat and thought on, this made all the more sense. For what more proof did a man need when his master lived in a house of perpetual light in fear of the darkness? He would humour Searle and his words.

From his vantage point, Searle looked defeated as he now stood, head bowed before the empty row. Slowly he turned to look at McArthur. "Don't you see Robert? Such things could not be! How could one man hope to stand where tens of thousands fell? The 1st day of July 1916 was to be my last. I too was to fall in the fields of France. But no, I signed a deal in darkness, a deal signed with blood. Look Robert, look!"

And Searle rushed forward, his palm outstretched. McArthur jerked backwards; such was the man's intensity. He felt that he might strike him with that hand. But he did not, Searle drew short, arm outstretched, hand on display. And McArthur beheld the single long line of scar that ran diagonally across the skin.

"You see!" proclaimed Searle triumphantly. "You see! It is so. And it all came back to me Robert; it all came back to me on the night of my second death. For as the beast promised, I would know all at the last! And there!" He shouted, pointing back into the aisle with his right hand. "That is where I fell, that is when he returned to me and revealed all!"

McArthur suddenly felt very vulnerable. Searle had become maniacal all of a sudden. And he was somewhat anxious as to what he might do next. He was clearly very excitable and so to placate him, he stood from his chair and turned to face the old man. Leaving the wooden furniture between them as an obstacle.

"I think I understand" McArthur uttered. "So tell me, tell me what transpired that night."

Searle seemed to calm at the suggestion. He had been so animated and vehement in his arguments. But it seemed that McArthur's seeming acceptance had calmed him.

"Yes Robert, yes of course. It was but three months ago when the natural course of my life came to an end. I know that sounds contradictory, given all that I have said. But on that night on the Somme, my life was renewed. I was given a second chance, and I took it. In the aftermath of the battle, I was flown home a hero. On the retreat of the German defenders at my furious attack, I was spent. My rage had subsided, and I was alone. As you know, I was not aware of my deal, and I didn't even stop to think how I might have come to be there alone. I searched the battlefield from the relative safety of the crater and could not find one advancing Tommy."

Searle walked forward, pushing past the chairs that stood between them and into the expanse of the library. Somewhere in the building, McArthur could hear the soft chime of a grandfather clock chime the hour. Other than their conversation, it was the only sound in the world.

Searle continued to pace and McArthur could see that his mind was stewing, that his previous display of exuberance might be repeated. He had the chair in front of him still, but he was worried what Searle might do in this mindset. And so, did the only thing that he thought a civilised Englishman should do. He sat back in his chair and turned his attention from Searle. If the man wished to continue with this charade, then he would have to do it on McArthur's terms, quietly and rationally.

And as Searle turned, he saw that McArthur had reseated himself. He stopped and McArthur could see tension almost lift from his visage as reason hit home. Searle walked calmly over and sat back opposite McArthur, and Robert could see the intensity diminish in his eyes. It wasn't perfect but it would have to do. A man, after all, must conduct himself with a certain dignity should he not? And by his example, Searle had followed suit. After all, how could he allow his servant to demonstrate the ideals of etiquette to a man of his position?

"Ah, where was I? Oh yes. So...there I was a man alone in the depths of no man's land. Still, the sound of machine guns tainted the early morning air. I was torn, to press on or to retreat? I still felt my savage fury but I did not think myself invincible, how little I knew. But reason, it seemed won through for it was back to my own lines that I retreated. It was then I was struck with a strange déjà vu on which I could not quite recognise. For as I retreated, I found the bodies of my fallen comrades. My experience of the night before was lost to me and yet this was all so familiar somehow. And as I walked, I found no more men advancing, and the German's too felt the stupid waste of life, for the machine guns droned no more that day. The senseless slaughter it seemed had worn heavily on them and some of those crews allowed the retreating injured to return unmolested."

Searle continued. "And as I walked back, I found that I could recognise the names of the fallen, for they were the men of the Newfoundland Regiment. Some were unrecognisable but for the blue puttees, such were their horrific wounds. And soon beyond I found Ladder. He had been beside me as we had advanced and had made it this two hundred yards or so before

199

a bullet had caught him to the abdomen. He was though still breathing and I had no hesitation in gathering him onto my back and bringing him to our lines."

"Did he make it?" McArthur enquired.

"Ladder? Yes, thank God. That some small good might have come from my sin is all I have to hold onto and I am at least thankful for that. You see Robert; it was not for the attack on the machine gun nest that I won my cross, no. I never told anyone of that, for I do not believe they would believe such a story. I had advanced long ahead of the furthest Tommy and no one made it as far as to recognise the fact. I'm sure there were some mighty scared German's who might adhere to the fact, but in the wake of the carnage, I was certainly not going to suggest that I had made such ground and killed a few of them. No, it was for the fact that I was able to deliver Ladder back to the trench safely, and more, for five more times did I leave in search of the injured, bringing back four more men. My last trip though was in vain, for I found no more alive."

"So it was for this that you were honoured?" said McArthur. "Don't you realise then that your honour is preserved? For whatever deal you feel you may have made, you risked your life and saved those men."

McArthur though could see that such an appeal had not won through, for Searle looked desolate and broken still.

"No Robert, don't you see? I could not die that day! Where is the gallantry in that? I had made my deal and as such I made the German lines! I might have gone out and rescued more of the fallen! If I'd but known! But my mind told me no, that I had done enough, that I had risked myself unnecessarily. My own sense of self-preservation and selfishness finally kicked in when I could have done so much more!"

"But as you have said you did not know, did you? You made a conscious decision to go back, time after time. Whether you could die or not, you did not know that truth. And so to risk it all again and again, that is truly honourable." McArthur replied.

Searle smiled at McArthur's reply. "Your words are very kind Robert and I thank you for them. But it is more than that. I bargained my soul for my own life and my life alone. I did not barter. I did not think of the lives of other men. Could I not have asked for more in return in the face of my damnation?"

"I see that you will not find redemption in my words alone. But what of the men that you saved?"

"They are all lost, Robert, all lost. Of the five, only Ladder and one other survived the operating table. Both were shipped home. Of the two, Ladder could not bear the strain of what he had witnessed and took his own life in January of 1917. The other, Alistair Giles, lived on. But the poor man survived one war but to die in the next. He was killed as German bombs fell upon London in the blitz."

"So you see in the end it was for nought. None of us should have made it back, don't you understand? The beast has a way of making all things right in the end, for those men would not have lived but for me. And so with my curse, they were tainted. And ultimately they could not survive in a world that had no place for them."

"And though I did not know it, I bore the same in my own way, for I could not father an heir. And it is only now, after the beast's revelation that I finally see that such efforts had been in vain, for no child could be delivered for he who has no place in the world. The additional cost of course, being the waste of three good marriages. This despite all of their efforts. Damn me for how I treated them! Not once looking to myself or my own shortcomings!"

McArthur was beginning to feel his anger rising. This was getting out of control now. Searle's capacity for self-loathing could not be stemmed it seemed. Whatever he might say to placate the man would not be enough. He wanted out of this charade now; it had gone on too long.

"So, you would have me believe your story? That despite your heroics, you would negate the saving of two men's lives? This is pathetic; I don't think I wish to hear any more!" And with that, McArthur stood to leave. Searle immediately bounced up from his own chair and grabbed McArthur by the lapel of his shirt.

"Pathetic! pathetic, you say? How dare you! Do you think I would wallow in such self-pity? No, it is he, he who torments me." Again Searle motioned toward the shadow at the end of the long line of books. "How do you think it feels huh? To know that your life is not your own? That your achievements were for nought, as they were bought and paid for by your soul! He told me that I would have the gift of ignorance until my death, but I did not die Robert, I did not die!"

And with that, Searle pushed away from McArthur and walked into the centre of the room when his emotion finally overcame him, and he collapsed to the floor in a ball and began to sob uncontrollably.

"I didn't die, Robert, as I should have. My heart failed me three months ago in that very aisle. And he came to me, and he told me all. And in that instant, it all flooded back. That night on the Somme, what I'd seen, and the deal that I'd struck. And now it was time for him to collect and I would follow him into the very pits of hell for eternity! He came to me in shadow Robert, in shadow. For as before he told me that a deal done in darkness must be completed in darkness. And as my heart gave in, he reached at me from the very aisle you see before you! I screamed and crawled away. For I was scared Robert, all the fear that I had felt that night was back and more! I crawled away from the monstrous vision of the beast; for now, I could see his true face. And I crawled into the light. And somehow, he could not reach me."

McArthur simply stood there stunned as Searle pressed on. "And so it is that I live on, the natural passage of my life ended three months ago and he came to collect but he could not, for now, he cannot reach me in the light."

Understanding finally came to McArthur, he looked high above him at the rows of strip lights that lit the hall constantly and he finally knew why the house was not permitted to fall into shadow.

Searle's sobs seemed to diminish and he lifted his arms from his head and turned to face McArthur. "Can you see it now Robert? Can you? I am doomed to an eternity in hell. The price for my cowardice is my just reward, but he cannot take me, he cannot! I have expelled every shadow but one, for the aisle that you gaze upon cannot be expelled. For whatever reason, he is there still. Trapped? Or simply waiting for me. And I am so afraid! I cannot give myself to him. I won't! He promises absolution in return but I know in my heart he lies. I gave of myself willingly and now I have made him angry. And he waits, he waits and he taunts me. I plead my case, night after night but all I see is that maniacal smile and those dead hateful eyes and I know there is no escape for me, for I know he will wait an eternity if need be. And all the while I make him wait the angrier he becomes. He promises fresh torture and because of this, I cannot go to him, I cannot! I will not deliver myself into his hands."

McArthur simply stood there stunned. *He believes this,* was all he could think of. *He actually believes this.*

Slowly the sobs died down, and McArthur could see that the fight had gone out of the man, and so he brought himself to his side. He knelt down and gently gripped the man by the shoulder and picked him up.

"You won't deliver me to him, Robert, will you?" Searle whispered into his ear.

"No, never. I must get you to bed. I think we both need to rest."

And so Searle allowed himself to be taken to his chamber and laid down. McArthur returned to his own bed, and on expelling the light, he found that he could not sleep for the conversation with Searle plagued him so. Finally, he got up and turned the light back on. It was only then that he could finally drift off, for visions of dark creatures hiding in the shadow had plagued him and only in the light could his mind find ease.

Both he and Searle slept in long after the usual 05:00 am call.

CHAPTER 26

McArthur had spoken for well over an hour, but for now, Fitzgerald could see that he was struggling and that as a result, this night's session was coming to an end. He had listened without interruption, fascinated by the words that had fallen reverently from McArthur's lips, and such as it was with good storytellers, Fitzgerald had allowed himself to be drawn in and become absorbed by what he had heard.

But now, as McArthur lay before him; eyes closed, the silence stretched out between them and his mind began to go into overtime as the rational fought against fantasy.

He had to concede to himself that there were elements of the story that rang true at least: the spotlights and the array of lighting within the Hall for one. The story told by Douglas the gardener, suggesting that the previous estate owner Searle was the one who had commissioned the project. The reason behind such a decision now laid bare by McArthur's story. But the rest? Deals with the Devil and the selling of a man's soul?

Does he expect me to believe this? Was chief among his thoughts even though he knew such an idea was redundant. McArthur did expect him to believe every word and what was clear was that even if he could not accept it, that McArthur himself believed every part of it.

That brought further things to mind, but these were easier to dismiss, for what he had heard from McArthur did not evoke any belief that the man had become delusional or was in any way suffering the effects of some dementia, such had been the power and belief in his words. But where did that leave him? Still, they had not come to the conclusion of the man's confession and he couldn't help but wonder what more was to come.

He looked down to see that McArthur's eyes were set upon him, perhaps waiting on some kind of response. But when no words came to him, it was the older man who filled the void.

"You think me a fool Father?"

Fitzgerald slowly shook his head to negate the suggestion. His issues were nothing like that, but he simply could not find where to begin or what questions to ask.

"Speak to me, Father, please."

"I…I don't know where to begin Robert. Your story is so incredible."

McArthur nodded his head. "Perhaps that is why I asked you here, Father. I know my words are difficult, and I, like you, had more than a few doubts regarding what I had heard. By that time, I believed Searle little more than a drunk trying to come to terms with his mortality following his heart attack. Certain things did fall into place of course, he did serve with honour on the Somme and was awarded the Victoria Cross for his heroism."

"But the rest Robert? Could this be some level of post-traumatic stress? After all, such a thing was unheard of back in such times. If something like that went unchecked, especially given the horrors he would have seen?"

"Yes and that would still have been the case in 1963 when he told me. But you do not need a doctor to tell you how we suffered after the war, and I include myself in that. Men would still exhibit all the same symptoms even though they had yet to come up with a fancy name for it. There were flashbacks and nightmares, as well as stress, sleep disorder, alcoholism, self-harm and suicide. Shellshock we called it in our day and in some men, it lasted only as long as the battle. In others, it lasted the rest of their lives."

"And in Searle?"

"Needless to say, I thought long and hard on that. You must remember that this Thomas Searle was nothing like the man whose employ I came into in 1954. You might wonder if he simply hid these things from me through the years, but I doubt it. Though I did not believe him at first, I quickly came to decide that he believed it, and it was with that information I acted."

"What do you mean?"

McArthur's eyes dropped once more. "That Father, I am not yet ready to say. It is late, and I must soon have my medication. You have been patient thus far. I only ask your indulgence a little further for what comes next is the key to my confession."

As if on cue, there was a light knock on the door, which was quickly followed by Melissa's entry into the room.

"Excuse me, gentlemen, but it is getting late. Mr McArthur, you must surely be ready for your medication?" her voice once again, only just a whisper which he had to strain to hear. McArthur though heard very well or understood well enough the timing of her entry.

"Melissa, yes."

The nurse made her way to the side of the bed and gave Fitzgerald a quick glance from the corner of her eye. He understood well enough, it was time to go, but he still had so many questions to ask.

"Robert I...I must ask you, please..." His mind whirled as he fought for clarity. He had still to ask of Elizabeth, Crosby and the girl Lydia. They were all pieces to the puzzle he knew, and though he could not reason as to notions of dark spirits, he knew the fate of the three lay closely tied with McArthur and his story. There had after all been an exorcism, a rite conducted at the behest of his wife Elizabeth.

"Robert…"

"Please, Father, no more. Soon, I promise. You will have answers to all of your questions."

He watched then as Melissa withdrew a packaged syringe and vial from a pocket by her waist. This was no doubt the morphine that McArthur relied upon. He had thought her a frail and nervous woman, but as a nurse, he saw that she was practised and confident in her duty. Her hands were graceful and calm as the syringe broke the seal on the vial and drew liquid into it's chamber. A small press on the plunger allowed some of the liquid to spill out in a small arc. Fitzgerald watched fascinated as she approached the far side of the bed and quickly took an arm and administered the injection.

Peace at once came to McArthur's face, and he was astonished at how quickly the morphine took effect. Already it seemed, McArthur had gone into a painless sleep.

"Until tomorrow then, Robert." He whispered.

He stood to leave, and as he went to turn toward the door, an arm shot out of the bed and grasped him by the elbow. With surprising strength, McArthur pulled him toward the bed and such was his surprise that his feet tangled themselves and he near went down onto the floor in a fall. The old man drew him in close and it was all he could do to quickly put an arm to the frame of the bed to support his weight and stop himself falling onto it.

A whisper emanated from McArthur's lips, and as it did so, the strength left his arm, and it fell limp on the blanket before him. Fitzgerald leaned in closer as he had not heard what had been said. It came once more before the man drifted off into his sleep and Fitzgerald quickly recoiled from the bed at what had been spoken.

"Beware the library. The shadow remains."

CHAPTER 27

On leaving McArthur's chambers, his first thought was that he should march right on up to the library door and force entry, so as to confront McArthur's delusion and negate it there and then.

Shilling had been right in what he had said all those weeks ago. The house did indeed have a power, a power evidenced by McArthur and Dougie's far-fetched tales of devils and apparitions. A power he was keen to remove. For if the whole town believed in the same stories, what hope could there be for them, and what chance then that he could rejuvenate his parish as had been his plan?

Such thoughts though quickly evaporated as he met the corner of the west wing and the front of the house, and stood before the door again.

Are you sure you want to do this?

Good question, but in his current frame of mind, he was feeling bloody-minded and wanted to confront the feelings that the room brought up in him. But yet something held him back. He stood there undecided, the silence about him seemed suddenly oppressive and he was quickly aware that his mouth had run dry and that his heart was beating that much faster.

The library door was closed before him, and he closed his eyes as he allowed a deep breath to escape from his lips; scared that he would see the same plume of cold mist form before his mouth, as he had during his previous ill experience. As it was, he found that the fear of seeing cold air before him had now been taken over by a very real fear of what he might actually see when he opened his eyes again. For one brief moment, it occurred to him that he should run, just as he was, eyes closed and quickly past the library door. He wouldn't see anything; he wouldn't hear anything. But what if he was to fall? What if he should hear the soft sound of the door handle begin to slowly turn? Wouldn't fear then overtake him and he be rooted to the spot, when some dark apparition cast in the shape of a First World War sergeant come from the door, bayonet in hand?

His imagination was getting the better of him. And he slowly opened his eyes. His heart climbed back down to nearer its normal rate as he saw that the door was firmly closed before him and that no white mist formed as he took a breath. This place was getting to him.

He took a step forward. The lights flickered, and his heart galloped once more.

It's nothing, he told himself. An old place like this does that all the time.

Gathering his resolve, he strode forward, eyes fixed firmly on the door handle of the library. If it moved, he would run. He reached out for the handle and quickly snatched his hand back to his side as it felt the same cold draught before the door.

In the depths of a November evening, the house was always chill outside the comfort of his rooms, and it was something he had gotten used to. This was more.

He slowly raised his right hand in front of his face and could see the hairs there standing on end. It was then, the faintest of draughts touched his face. He knew whatever the cause that it was not Melissa. At least not this time, for he had left her tending McArthur back down in his apartments.

Then who?

He would not have his answer, for as the cold draught intensified, he forced himself to move. It was though for the expansive landing at the front of the house he went and not to the library door, his heart racing as he quickly made his way, and though the sound was soft, he fancied he heard the sound of a footfall upon a wooden floor from behind the library door — much the same as his first experience there.

Remaining on the first-floor, he took the path back to his own rooms, where he quickly shut the door and locked it behind him. Charging manically between the rooms, he switched on all of the lights, relief coursing through him as the dark shadows that had lingered there were instantly dispelled.

He fell to the sofa and placed his head in his hands. What the hell was happening to him? How had he allowed the delusions of others to subvert his own thinking to the point where he was acting like a frightened child?

Lowering his hands from before his eyes, he was greeted by the sight of Crosby's diaries. The vision made his stomach lurch, but he fought the feeling back, to get control over his frail nerves.

Before seeing McArthur, he had avoided the books, worried that they would somehow validate the notion that Thoby Hall was rife with some dark power. But now, he needed to regain control. He was a rational man and by reading the books, he could see them for what they were and read the madness in their words. Additionally, he knew that McArthur was soon coming to some revelation, and if he were to read the books, perhaps he would be better prepared to deal with the fall out. He wanted to be ahead of the game and with whatever time he was to be afforded ahead of his next summoning call, he would use to scrutinise the diaries.

Gathering them up, he walked to the study and locked the door behind him. Setting them down on the desk, he looked long at them and wondered what secrets they might tell. He did not write a journal or diary and thought to do so was foolish somehow. To write down one's

207

thoughts and feelings, to forever immortalise them in black and white gave them credence and finality. So what then to time and experience? How might they affect one's previous prejudices and assumptions? No, better to take stock moment by moment than to give life to abject opinion that might ultimately, influence some future action. What's more, he knew the fickle nature of human nature meant that any such recorded material would ultimately prove contradictory; love one day, hate the next. What was the point?

But now he was going to pour through the private thoughts and experiences of a man long dead in the ground. Maybe that was the reason he was beginning to feel paranoid, for he was undoubtedly about to intrude into private matters. He felt like a voyeur, and that feeling had been reinforced tenfold when he had shut himself away behind closed doors to indulge in another man's personal affairs.

He sat himself down at the desk and drew the pile toward him by pulling on the neat string bow, tied by Colin Morris. Seven books in all, and even before unwrapping them he could see that they had been well used, for the spine of each book saw wear having been folded back over and over. Each volume was red in colour and was embossed with gold lettering denoting the year of each book. In descending order, he saw 1996 down to 1990.

Surely that's going too far back?

How long had Crosby been at St Peter's for? And for that matter, was that at all relevant? Surely the only things of interest to him would be between August of 1995 when the young girl Lydia had drowned, until January of 1996 when Crosby had taken his own life.

He pulled the string and took the first book into his hands. He read; 'Collins' (the brand) followed by the year, 1996. He flicked the book open somewhere in the middle and was not surprised to see those pages empty. The book was A4 in size, and he could see that each page was given to a whole day. He flicked backwards, March, February, January, where he stopped. He had rested on the 30th of January. Had that been the day he had died? Something in the back of his mind told him that he had, but the page itself was empty.

He sensed the discrepancy before he got to where the pages should have been, for the pages to his left hand were unduly thin. And yes, here was the rough tear in the margin where several days had disappeared.

"Damn it!" he cried into the room, his frustration all too palpable. But in the quiet of the room, his voice sounded unnatural and harsh to his ears. He sat up as if expecting some reaction from somewhere, but all remained quiet. He resolved he would not give voice to his displeasure in such a way a second time.

He returned his focus to the book. In all, eight days were missing. From what he had learned thus far from Father Shilling, his own research and the stories gathered from the house, that these missing days were relevant to the supposed exorcism that Crosby performed as well as his meltdown during sacrament at St Peter's Church. But who had removed the pages?

A simple candidate came quickly to mind. Bishop Andrew Burrows. He had been the Bishop of the Diocese at the time of Crosby's demise and it had been he who was keen to smother any press interest. The diaries would have made interesting reading if they had turned up in the wrong hands, and the bishop or someone acting on his behalf had perhaps decided to remove any incriminating material. He couldn't know this for sure, but in his heart, he felt he had hit on the truth of the matter.

But the question remained. What use were the books now? He read the entry on the first available page and groaned inwardly at the banality of what he saw, a single paragraph which read:-

DP attended service for the first time today since her mother's passing. It has been a difficult couple of months for the girl, and I was so happy to see how the congregation welcomed her back into their bosom. I believe with such shared compassion; she will again see the virtue of faith. It was difficult enough to bring her back to the fold, such anger that she had at her mother's cancer and none to blame but God for bestowing it upon her. Would that I could simply reply and tell her that the forty cigarettes a day may have played their part!

Fitzgerald smiled in spite of himself. *Humour?* These did not seem to be the words of a man who would take his own life shortly afterwards, no, these were more the words of a busy Catholic priest about his day-to-day business.

And so it went on, for as he tracked backwards, he saw similar entries all relating to the parishoners of St Peter's. Always careful that a person was only denoted by their initials, and certainly no hint as to their confessed sin. As a result, no judgements by Crosby as to their virtue or otherwise. This did not look like a book written by a man who planned to take his own life.

But would it? Fitzgerald asked himself, *these entries all predate the exorcism. That is the key, and that is what set him down the road to despair.*

He had no doubts about that, and he lamented the loss of the missing pages.

He tossed the book aside, frustrated and without any real interest picked up the next volume, marked 1995. He rifled through the pages and saw to a day that there was an entry for each. Some taking as much as a whole page, others just a sentence or two.

(Sheila's birthday coming up, don't forget!)

Here though in this book, he began to find newspaper cuttings. All of which were taped neatly into the pages. All of the said articles related to Church business and a quick scan saw that Crosby was often quoted in the now infamous Ashmarsh Gazette.

Pride? Perhaps, but it was easy to see that Crosby had engineered a thriving community Church and the articles reflected that, as they referred to fundraisers or events, similar to those articles that he had previously seen on the Internet.

A thought struck him, and he quickly leafed back to August of that year.

Let it be there. Let it be there. His mind repeated as he skimmed the pages backwards with his thumb.

And it was. Whoever had censored the book had not it seemed had a mind to delete the event that had pre-empted Crosby's suicide and Elizabeth being taken into care. The first thing he saw was the cutting, dated Monday 21st August 1995. This was almost the self-same article he had read online following on from poor young Lydia's death in the swimming pool. This wasn't though what he was looking for and he skirted back two pages, to find the same Saturday as the tragedy had happened.

It read; *Such terrible news. I have just come off the phone with Joyce Bennett. Oh, the poor woman was in pieces and what tragic news she had passed. Her young niece Lydia, only 7 years of age, has passed away at Thoby Hall only this morning. Drowned. And yet there were other adults and children there! How could such a thing have happened?*

Seemingly there was a gap in time; no doubt created as Crosby went to tend the grieving family, as the next paragraph continued.

The family are torn apart, and there was little I could do to ail their grieving hearts. The house was like a circus, what with extended family and well-wishers constantly phoning or visiting. Poor, poor Alice and Michael. He was putting a brave face on it for the rest of the family, but drew me aside and asked me to go to her in their room where she had remained undisturbed. He told me that she was virtually catatonic and could not come to terms with what had happened. I finally got to see her, but there were no words, no words at all that I could say and there was no need, for all she did was hug me and cry. We sat there for I don't know how long until Michael came in to take my place as he rightly should. I left the two in an embrace as they cried together. I bid Joyce that they remain undisturbed and she heartily agreed. I believe the woman near went and set watch on the bedroom door to protect their privacy.

I have offered what help I can. For now, the furore has died down and the family are alone. I have bid them that I will return tomorrow so that we can discuss funeral arrangements. Michael, thanked me for what I gave to Alice, but truth be told I was helpless. I feel my work there would have been done equally if she had hit me and screamed at me, whatever it took for her to release her pent-up emotion. Anger will still yet come no doubt. Neither Alice or Michael are regulars at St Peter's, it is Joyce who bade me to come and I am glad that she did. I hope I can give whatever help the family need and if they can be drawn closer to the Church all the better.

There appeared to be another time gap in his writing for the next passage began.

Elizabeth has rung me from Thoby Hall and I am to go to her at once. She was barely intelligible on the telephone such was her anguish and grief. She blames herself.

That concluded the entry for that day. Scant perhaps, but he understood that Crosby's motivation would have been in visiting those parties affected by the tragic events and not updating his journal with his thoughts. That he hoped would be reserved for the days and entries that would follow. Certainly, the diary could not divulge the most relevant part of his story but perhaps it might, after all, give an insight as to his relationship with Elizabeth in the aftermath of the child's harrowing death.

He turned the page and was not entirely surprised to see that there was no entry for the date marked Sunday the 20th and he could well imagine what a difficult and busy time Crosby had most likely had during those two days. So, he came back to Monday 21st and the newspaper cutting. He pulled the page from the book and there underneath in Crosby's flowing hand was a full-page entry for that day.

I am torn in my duty to both the Bennett family and young Elizabeth. Michael has stated that he has instructed solicitors to become involved regarding his daughter's death. Instead of grief, it is anger that now consumes him. He has distanced himself from Alice, who refuses to leave her room. Despite my best counsel that he should be with her and that doing this might help with his own feelings, having been wholly ignored. I think part of him blames Alice and I think blaming the McArthur residence is his way of avoiding questions about his wife and her conduct. I know he has chosen the wrong path but he is openly expressing that 'they' will pay for what they allowed to happen.

My conflict stems from Elizabeth's reaction to what has occurred. She is not the same woman as I knew only last week. She tries to put a brave front on things, and I do not doubt that Robert has had some bearing on this. In company, her smiles are forced and she is withdrawn, as if in some dream world of her own and you might need to repeat her name before she finds you. It is in private though where I can get to the truth of her feelings as neither Robert nor that damn solicitor of his can coach her as I have no doubt they have done so far.

She blames herself for the incident, can you believe that? That if she had never had the thing installed that such a thing could not have happened. She tests me with that, and I had little to say than there was some truth to it. But hindsight is a terrible burden and I have told her so. More than that, for when I dug a little deeper and worked my way past the tears, I believe I understand what has happened. I alluded to it earlier but the fact is, Michael is setting himself up for a fall, for what happens when his lawsuit is dismissed? And the true story hits home at last? Indeed there should be no blame attributed to poor Alice, for is it not every parent's worst nightmare that in the one moment they allow their guard to slip then some terrible thing must surely happen?

Only it did. Elizabeth, as I understand it had left the group to take one of the little girls into the house. She had seemingly cut her hand, only a tiny nick but for sure there were tears. I see the maternal instinct in Elizabeth whenever I am in her company and I could almost see it as she no doubt put the child at ease with that natural charm and smile of hers and led her to the house for her first aid. But who watched the children while she was away? There were several women there, who I understand were very happy to let the children do their own thing, after all, the noise of the group could easily be heard from the pool room as they laughed and screamed in happiness. Elizabeth had fussed back and forth, entertaining her guests and checking the children, but there were elder ones in the group. 11 or 12 years, and as a group, she believed them safe enough.

It happened when she came back out to the garden. The young girl all patched up, making a beeline for her mother, proud to show off her little plaster. All of the other children were now outside towelling off and she was just in time to hear the scream from within the pool house. Lydia had not exited after the other children, maybe enjoying herself too much who knows? But when the others came out, she had remained behind.

211

Alice spoke of how she was such a strong swimmer and how she had won her ribbons from her after school club. Oh, how could such a thing have happened? A momentary lapse in care and attention? Of how long? Seconds? Minutes? And poor Alice will take the burden of that to her own grave.

There will be more, of course. The other mothers present will feel both guilt and relief simultaneously for thanking the Lord that it was not their own child that was taken. Deacon Morris has been busy also in consoling those other family's that were affected by this terrible event. Would that I could separate my feelings and duty to the Bennett's and Elizabeth, but as the Senior Parish Priest, it is my place to be with the family at their hour of need. I also feel a huge debt to Elizabeth, without who this parish would not be so fortunate. Without who, I would not be so fortunate.

Fitzgerald sat back in his chair and allowed the book to fall closed over his fingers which bookmarked the page for him, as he thought on what he had read. The entry had alluded to blame, but the whole thing spoke of little more than a horrible accident. He wondered then what had become of the Bennett family for he was certain that no such family attended his Church. He made a mental note that he would check this detail with Colin Morris. But the book hinted at more didn't it? Feelings of debt or obligation to Elizabeth for example. Perhaps for the work, she had done for the Church, or perhaps more? For the very last line of the entry hinted at personal feelings from Crosby toward her.

Returning to the book, he read the requisite pages for all of the remainder of that week. There was no further mention of Elizabeth, or to events at Thoby Hall, instead, Crosby wrote of Alice and the slow progress he was making with her. She had, at last, come from her bedroom and Fitzgerald was glad to read that there had been a reconciliation with Michael, who now tended his wife's needs. Fitzgerald noted that there was no further mention of the lawsuit. Plans were being made that week for the funeral and the body was to be handed back to the family shortly, following the coroner's very quick announcement of accidental death by drowning. The service would be held on Thursday 31st August, for which Crosby was very glad for he believed that would aid the healing process for the family.

A few reminders were penned in for the week beginning the 28th August, such as 'Lydia Bennett service Friday at 10:00 am' but no other thoughts or feelings from Crosby as to the whole matter. Time it seemed was a quick healer even for Crosby and after the hectic few days that heralded the aftermath of the event, things were perhaps now slowing down for him and getting back to normal. That was until he saw the day after the funeral, the 1st of September.

And so yesterday went as well as could be expected. There was a huge turnout at St Peter's as might be expected and the floral donations were marvellous. Alice was of course in bits the whole time, but there were moments last week when I questioned if she would be here at all. Michael broke down during his speech and was led away by his brother, but he was oh so brave and there was no hint of blame or recrimination in his words. I hope at least he is coming to terms with that part. There followed the service and little Lydia was taken away to her favourite song which I understand is by the band Take That. That drew some fond smiles.

At first, I did not believe she had come.

(Elizabeth?)

I was disappointed for we had spoken on this very matter only a few days before. She did not feel that she could face the family. It seems she had not entirely come to terms with that, for when I did finally spot her in the back pews, I could see that she was attempting a low profile. She had to be there of course, but such is the depth of her character she did not want to upset matters further with any grandiose public gestures. If I know her well enough, she would already have reached out to the family before attending.

In any event, she anticipated the closing of the service and made a discreet exit, for I lost her between the Lord's Prayer and the lifting of the coffin. I thought that would be the last I saw of her, for when I attended the cemetery to lay the body to rest there was no sight of her.

I did not have to wait for long though, for it was on my return to St Peter's where I found her again. Seemingly she had waited on my return and surprised me as I made my way into the porch.

Can I write what was said?

The words spoken were not done so in the sanctity of the confessional, and so I am not duly bound, nor are these writings for anyone else's eyes but my own, but still.

Fitzgerald felt a small prick to his conscious when he read the last, the books were not meant for him he knew, and he could already see by the length of the continuing writing that Crosby had undoubtedly written what was spoken between him and Elizabeth McArthur. It was an intrusion he knew, but this was perhaps what he was here to find.

She has come to life once more, but not for the good I am afraid. She told me first of the medication that Robert had suggested for her, valium. That explained the lethargy and lack of focus that I witnessed in her on visiting Thoby Hall. At first, I was glad, but I mistook the fire in her eyes for something else, for now, she was her old self, quick-witted, vibrant, beautiful.

She spoke like an express train for fifteen minutes. I could not have interjected if I had wanted and oh how I did want to, for I felt to listen uninterrupted was only fanning the flames of her delusional beliefs. And how to respond? Oh goodness, when she stopped, and I saw the doubt in her eyes as she likely saw the doubt in mine. I wanted to reach out and hold her and tell her that it would all be okay, that it was a natural reaction to a tragedy such as she had suffered. I did not hold her, though. I instead tried to rationalise her words. She spoke of demons and curses in the matter of fact way that the bible would tell us they are among us in our daily lives. And how can I negate that with her, when my own sermons invoke the idea of a literal devil whispering doubt and temptation into the ears of my flock?

She had pressed Robert on the subject and whatever he said only served to reinforce her belief in this idea. The idea that the Devil himself resided within the walls of Thoby Hall. Bound by spells and witchcraft no less!

The words seemed to sear their way through Fitzgerald's eyes into his mind, and the effect was magnified as his eyes watered, thus blurring the characters on the page as if he had glanced too long at the sun. McArthur's last words to him, reverberating through his mind.

"Beware the library. The shadow remains."

And as the thought echoed, he became aware of the stillness and quiet of the room about him which was at odds at the racing of his heart and mind.

No! no! He shouted inside of himself to quiet the voice that was so insistent.

There is a devil within the library...

He closed his eyes firmly shut and pinched the bridge of his nose as hard as he could, that the pain itself might overshadow the words that demanded to be heard. Slowly but surely, it took effect, the thoughts diminishing and his mind coming to rest.

The sting from his nose was sharp, and he opened his eyes to find that his fingers were still clamped hard on the bridge. He released his grip and saw the book before him. Disgusted he snapped it shut and threw it on to the desk where it hit the stacked pile of other diaries, spilling several over the desk and onto the floor behind where they made a low thudding sound.

He stepped up quickly, unsure what to do, but keen to take some other action to prevent his mind from returning to its former state.

(The shadow remains...)

But what action? He went to move from behind his desk, and as he did so, he watched as if in slow motion as a small red bead of blood fell from his nose and landed on the closed diary beneath. The year he saw was 1995, the same book he had read from. His eyebrows lowered and he watched confused as the small red dot was quickly joined by another and then another. His nose had begun to stream and finally understanding he brought his hand up and wiped his fingers beneath the nostril. It came away bright red and already more red tears streamed down, now onto the desk and floor as he recoiled from the sight of his hand.

Pinching his nose quickly, he bolted for the bathroom where he slammed the door behind him. The diaries now forgotten as thick warm blood spattered the white porcelain of the sink before him.

CHAPTER 28

It was now past midnight and Fitzgerald lay sleepless on his bed. His thoughts circled his mind like prowling tigers, sizing one another up before fight. One thought rational and balanced, superseded by the growl of its darker counterpart that demanded to be heard.

Robert McArthur's story had been implausible, to say the least, but he knew the tale he had been told belonged to another; Thomas Searle. In telling it, it was clear that McArthur had bought into his dead master's account of the Battle of the Somme and the deal he had made to save his life. But what proof did he have? And why should he expect him to likewise buy-in without evidence?

But try as he might to cling to such an idea, the words of the departed James Crosby intruded and were reinforced by memories of what he had been told by Douglas. That some magical power or spell had been cast at the Hall to contain some ill power. That power now had an identity; Thomas Searle's devil that was apparently trapped within the library.

But each and every time his mind made this same inevitable connection, he veered away, for what followed was memories of his own recent experiences outside of the library door. It was one thing for the residents and townsfolk of Thoby Hall and Ashmarsh to believe in such a thing, but quite another for him to give credence to the impossible.

"Fitzgerald."

He could not though silence the cold, dry voice that had emanated from behind the locked library door on his first night within the house.

And so it went on as the minutes ticked past. He reached for his phone over and over again as sleep evaded him, cursing as the night made its way quickly toward morning. All the while, the light from the outside spotlights intruded past the edges of the large curtains of the window. It was both a continuing nuisance and comfort, for when he had earlier gotten up and tried the sofa in the lounge instead of the bed, he found that his imagination ran riot in the darkness and every creak of the house and gust of wind from outside set him on edge and so now here he was again...

03:35 am, damn it.

...back in the bedroom.

Sleep when it finally came brought no escape from the fear that had stalked him thus far through the night, because with sleep came dreams.

At first, he did not know that he was asleep. The dreamscape that took him was dark and featureless and knowing that he still lay in his bed, he felt frustration. As is the way with dreams, the transition to understanding was slow. For now, though, he simply blinked his eyes as he looked up and beheld the stars above.

The roof has gone.

But it was such a beautiful night, crisp and clear and from where he lay he could watch as shooting stars fizzed dramatically overhead. He followed one particular star, hoping it would not disappear until he had time to make his wish.

Keira

But what should he wish for? The star began to fall to his left, and he craned his neck, as it disappeared from the night with a boom in the distance. Now it seemed the walls were gone, for as he looked horizontally to himself, he found that he now lay outside. That to was fine with him and he reverted his eyes back to the heavens as a hundred more stars all crossed the skies crossing from right to left.

So many wishes!

He watched on for what seemed like an age, all the time the sound of the stars disappearing from the utmost limit of his view went with a loud boom. Understanding, though, did not register until his eyes found one star. So much brighter and closer than the others. He gasped at its beauty and he looked hard within its pulsating heart that glowed brighter than the sun.

This was the star on which to make his wish! But before his mind could catch up and seal the deal, fear came to him. The star was growing, becoming brighter, so much so, he had to shield his eyes away from it as it grew. He could now hear that it made a keen whistling sound as it approached. Frozen and captivated by the vision, he watched as it came lower still, all the time from his right to the left as the others had done and in one brief moment of clarity he was afforded a view of a thousand other stars beyond the first, all travelling in unison and coming ever closer.

At the last moment, he cowered. The whistling sound was intense and the pitch so high it threatened to shatter his eardrums. He pulled his arms over his head as the star missed him by feet and landed some ten or so yards away. It did so with an earth-rending explosion and mud and grass were thrown high into the air, showering him as if he had stepped out for a stroll on a wet winter morning. He looked now to where the star had landed but was afforded no time to comprehend as all of the time the remaining stars fell to the earth, and he watched and listened as the sound of explosions were met with each fatal descent. The ground was now torn and ripped wherever his eyes fell and he felt such overwhelming sadness that the night sky had come to fall in such a way.

Now though, the shining lights were all too close again, only feet over his head once more and he, at last, understood his danger. He was pelted with more soil as he at last turned and ran from his bed in the direction of where the stars came from.

The ground that had been lush and green beneath his feet quickly became rutted and difficult, and he found that several large craters had appeared within the landscape. He crested one and quickly fell within, tumbling helplessly over and over, the fall seeming to go on forever.

He landed face down, and the wind was taken out of him. For now, all was dark once more and his breath rattled through his teeth as he gasped for air. Somewhere ahead, he heard the sound of voices. Far off, and unintelligible from this distance, but instinct told him that they were meant for him and the urgency in their cries made him believe he was not out of danger yet.

Placing his hands flat at his sides, he pushed himself upward as if performing a press up, quickly he swung his legs beneath him and was glad that they took his weight. He looked down and saw that one of his slippers was missing.

Emma is going to be mad if she found out you lost her Christmas present!

There was no time to think about that now as he realised the danger that he was in. He made to set off toward the urgency of the voices, but as he did so, he looked upward and quickly stopped in his tracks. The night sky was dark and there were no more stars.

How will I tell them there are no more stars?

For one moment, he despaired, such was the overwhelming feeling of loss that he felt. But slowly, hope came for a tinge of light slowly grew behind him and he saw his shadow lengthen in front of him. The voices now were quieter, as if further away and he knew that soon they would be lost to him if he did not follow their beckoning call. He began to turn, slowly, as the light grew in the crater and he found that the lip that marked the surface was some twenty-plus feet over his head.

The light in the sky began to rise, and he wondered if dawn was, at last, coming to the land and that its warm embrace would touch him at the bottom of the hole in which he found himself. Surely then he would be happy and safe.

But instead of warmth, he felt bitterly cold and quickly grasped his dressing-gown close to him. It was no good though for the cold plumes of his breath were so clear they seemed as if they might freeze in the air and fall, shattering on the ground beneath.

Again the sound of the voices came to him as if from far away and he keened his ear to try and listen and somewhere far away he heard the word, "run."

His eyes went wide with fear. He did not know what it was, but the rising of the light and the coming of the harsh cold were as some prelude to some new terror. He wanted to run, but found that he could not, he looked down and saw that his feet were now buried in wet mud. He lifted his left leg and felt the cold ground take his other slipper. He fell backwards, his balance now lost, such was his desire to move away from the coming light.

He landed hard on his rump, and cold brown mud flooded his pyjama bottoms. He did not feel the cold though as his eyes were fixed steadily on the lip of the crater above, willing whatever thing was there not to appear. He could not imagine what horror 'it' might be, but he knew that when it came, it was the end of him.

He dragged himself backwards, to where the voices still implored him to run, his feet loosened and broke the surface of the clawing mud. He gasped with joy as tears fell rapidly down his cheeks.

I can run, I can run!

But hope quickly gave way to despair. All at once, the sound of the voices stopped as a shadow fell down into the crater from above. He knew that whatever they had warned him of had finally arrived and though he begged himself to keep his eyes closed, he let them rise slowly to the silhouetted figure on top of the crater.

It was a man. Somehow, he had known it would be and wondered how such a thing could instil such terror within him. The question would remain unanswered though for the figure demanded all of his attention.

He could not tell his height (he assumed it was a he) for the distance between them, but the unmistakable outlines of a Brodie helmet could be seen on his brow and webbing upon his back. In the right hand, he could see the outline of a (*Enfield*) rifle; the butt planted firmly into the dirt, the bayonet somehow terrifyingly sharp. He knew that to be so, even from this distance. He watched as the left hand brought a cigarette to its mouth, and in that instant, all that could be seen was the red fire of the tobacco, enlarged somehow over this distance and behind it the burning red eyes of a devil.

"No, no!" he screamed as he willed himself to move. He knew this demon somehow, knew his face though he had yet to see it. But oh god did he not want for that to happen. He pushed himself backwards, and he found he was on firmer ground.

I'm dreaming. Oh god wake up! Wake up! His head screamed these words at him, though his lips remained shut. He clung to the thought; *It's a dream. It's a dream.* Reciting it like a mantra over and over as he slowly edged his way from the figure that stood upon the lip of the crater.

This figure that resembled a British soldier, but was instead a monster, took the cigarette from between its lips and blew a fire ring instead of smoke. Fitzgerald saw it smile with satisfaction, razor-sharp teeth coming together in perfect symmetry and though he knew he could not possibly see from this distance, it was if everything it did was in slow motion for his sake and his sake alone. Such was the nature of dreams he knew, but try as he might, he could still not make that final transition of knowing, as it was all too real an experience.

He wanted to believe it was false; of course he did, and still, he begged himself to wake up. But the idea that this could be a dream was lost, buried below his overwhelming fear.

He turned onto his knees, facing away from the thing that stood on the crater, planting his hands under him now like a sprinter at the start line. He would run and he would never stop.

The voices came again. Closer now. "Run! Quickly it's coming!" He did not need to look back to know that it was so. His bladder voided itself, and warm piss warmed his thigh. No matter, he ran.

He never looked back but instinctively he knew it had made ground on him in an instant, and in his mind's eye, he saw the thing's hand reach out and grab thin air where his dressing-gown had billowed only a second before.

Reason was lost to him such was his terror, and it did not register to him that the crater he was in had no opposite side; instead he was on flat ground and there before him a thin cut began to open ahead. Slowly the ground ahead began to dip and he was on a slow decline that led directly to a hole in the ground. A hole, no. It was a trench, for it had no roof above. And there before him was the face of a young soldier. Similarly garbed as the thing that pursued him, beckoning him urgently on with his hand.

Here was safety, he knew.

The soldier ahead reached out for him. He was tantalisingly close and that is when he felt the hand on his ankle. The sensation was a strange one for it was as if he felt each cold dead finger slowly wrap themselves in turn and take hold before his progress was halted and he fell forward. He looked up at his lost saviour before him and recognition washed over him.

Here was one called Thomas Searle. A lad no more than 18 years old. His face etched in horror as it beheld the thing that stood above and behind where he had fallen.

He had been so close and knew that the boundary of the trench wall somehow offered sanctuary as the young lad dared not come beyond it.

And now he must meet his doom. He could not help it; the thing somehow willed him to turn and look. His ankle was numb with a cold that slowly spread through his left leg leaving it useless as it crept toward his crotch. Escape now was impossible and he saw tears fall down the face of the young soldier who was helpless to prevent this inevitable end.

The creature twisted its arm and flipped him so that he was on his back and now facing it. All the time, his mind shouted at him to wake. But the call continued to go unheeded. He looked on toward his doom and despaired.

The face was human and unremarkable, and whatever ill light had shone behind those eyes was now gone. But beneath the surface, something writhed as if trying to find a way out, it was snake-like and he watched in horror as it moved behind the left eye socket making it bulge impossibly outward before going on to form a trail along its forehead, before finally

219

disappearing. The smile, when it came was the same, and he saw row upon row of needle-like teeth. A long serpent-like tongue flashed out and subtly licked the end of one such tooth. The thing that posed as a man was surely the Devil himself.

Fitzgerald reached for his chest, and his hand anxiously grasped the crucifix which he found hanging there. He began to whisper the Lord's Prayer. The thing frowned down at him, but quickly its attention was drawn to the young man behind him.

Its voice was ice cold and Fitzgerald shuddered as he recognised it from a library door which seemed impossibly far away in both time and distance.

"You?"

Fitzgerald craned his neck back to the young soldier; a fierce, determined look was upon his face.

"You won't have him beast as you had me!" he roared as he burst from the sanctuary that was the trench wall. He came rifle first, bayonet lowered and Fitzgerald watched in wonder as the beast's face turned from confident triumph to fear. The blade pierced its chest right up to the hilt, but still, the boy's momentum drove him on, pushing the beast backwards and down.

"Run you fool, run!" He screamed at Fitzgerald as he passed him.

Fitzgerald did just that, he scrambled quickly to his feet and made the short yards to the sanctuary of the trench, but he did not stop there. He ran on and on, and quickly an impossibly loud roar reverberated down the tunnel toward him, causing the walls to shake and spill mud to the ground around him. Such was the sound that he was forced to clasp his hands tightly to his ears.

He looked back as he went and saw that the walls fell inward behind him, blocking his exit. He was safe he knew, for the cry that split the night was of frustration and not that of pain. The lad had no doubt bought his life with his own, and for that, he was thankful.

The walls continued to fall, and with alarm, he saw they crashed closer and closer to him. There was nowhere to go but forward and suddenly the walls ahead began to divert and open. The trench was no more, and all that could be seen was darkness. A great hole loomed that stretched across his entire view. The lip drew close and still the walls fell behind him.

He went over into the void of darkness, reciting the same.

Wake up! wake up!

CHAPTER 29

A devil in the library.

The thought reverberated through Fitzgerald's tired mind. He had been woken from his difficult sleep only an hour ago, the shrill ring of the telephone slowly penetrating his coma-like slumber. He had woken to find his bed wet; the faint smell of ammonia giving no doubt as to the cause. He searched the furthest reaches of his mind, a picture quickly forming of a long shadow falling over him from the lip of a very large hole. The continued ringing of the phone quickly chased the vision away though, as he closed his eyes and tried in vain to find that which had plagued his night.

The call had been from Keira, and the news was grim. McArthur was beginning to fail.

The rest of the conversation had washed over him. He felt numb and emotionless as Keira continued, and informed him that McArthur wished urgently to see him to finish what they had begun. The idea left him feeling flat in his stomach, for he now lamented the curiosity that had led him to Crosby's diaries in the dead of night. For now, they were approaching the final hurdle, and McArthur must surely be ready to impart the key part of his story. But what could it possibly be?

His tired mind could not find the link. Elizabeth McArthur, James Crosby, Thomas Searle. The tragic death of a 7-year-old girl and finally some dark power that lived within the library, trapped within shadow. But what of McArthur's part in the story?

Despite Keira's news, he was slow in his actions as all the component parts of the story tumbled in his mind. She had bid him to hurry over, but instead, he collected the soiled sheets from his bed and threw them into the tub and followed shortly after with a shower which did little to invigorate him.

Feeling the weight of the world upon his slumped shoulders, he made his way once more toward McArthur's rooms and so came to the anteroom which marked the merging of the front house to the west wing. Here before him once more was the closed library door.

Here it seemed, was the root of the evil that had plagued Thoby Hall.

His mind willed his legs back into action and to ignore what was before him, but he was like a statue, focused as he was on the door handle before him. Unconsciously, he had taken and blown several deep breaths into the air, perhaps expecting to see and feel the same cold that had enshrouded him previously. His mind still turning somersaults, as it wrestled between the rational and irrational of all that had come before. The balance of that scale, though was tipping ever more to the irrational and perhaps with it his sanity.

He took a pace toward the door and then another, not knowing what he was trying to accomplish until he saw his right hand reach out for the door handle. He stopped himself. Was he really going to do this? His heart pounded, and his mouth had run dry. Unknowingly he licked his lips back and forth as he weighed up the consequences of what he was about to do.

One more step and he allowed his hand to filter out to the side of the door frame in an effort to detect the same freezing cold draught that had emanated from the door previously. There was none.

He watched as if in slow motion as his hand came down and curled gently over the handle on the right side of the two double doors, he pulled back quickly as if anticipating the handle would be hot or cold, but there was no variance on the temperature that he could detect. Everything seemed exactly as it should in ordinary circumstances.

And so he brought the hand back again to the handle and grasped it firmly. Slowly he began to depress it. He had stopped breathing in that instance as he craned his head forward, trying to hear the smallest of sounds from within.

He knew as before he was in for a start should something sound from beyond. But no sound came as the handle lowered by fractions, Fitzgerald, highly-strung was ready to bolt should the slightest noise be heard.

The handle was now fully depressed, and he stood there, perplexed as to why nothing had happened.

Idiot! Push on the bloody thing!

Of course. And slowly he locked his arm and pushed his weight onto it. Nothing. Quickly he stood back, relieved in some ways and disappointed in others.

There is no keyhole. The thought crossed his mind as simply as any other.

But that is impossible. I looked through, didn't I?

His mind whirled, and self-doubt crawled over him, for he saw it was so, there was no keyhole, only dark stained wood where he knew he had once kneeled so as to look within. How could he have missed such a thing as that?

Confused, he now put his hand on the left handle and simultaneously pressed it down and pushed on the door — still nothing. Something must be blocking from the inside, but how? Certainly, that must be the case if there was no keyhole to lock the door with.

Was there another way in perhaps? He thought, knowing that this line of thinking was better than to address the situation of a missing keyhole, for if he did, it might go as far as to promote all of the strange goings-on that he had both been told of and witnessed himself. He was not ready for such as that, so a diversion, any diversion would suffice.

The idea that it was blocked or bolted from within seemed the only logical explanation, but if so, how would someone get out? The room had not been so out of bounds as had been suggested to him, for he had seen a strange figure in there on the day of his arrival and this was despite Hodgson's denials to that fact.

So how had they got in?

The thought that crossed his mind though was unwelcome, for now he imagined the figure from his dream. A World War One soldier, trapped somehow, it's voice ancient and rank, spoken once from behind this door, and last night from his dreams

No!

He bid the thought away and instead turned his mind back to the barred door before him.

A secret passage?

The idea was fanciful but not beyond the realms of possibility, so maybe there was a way in for him yet.

For now, though there was nothing he could do. His heart rate lowered and not for the first time; he felt foolish at his reaction to this particular place.

There was a keyhole damn it. I know there was a keyhole!

Ignoring his thoughts, he instead fought to remember his duty to McArthur, he turned his back to the door and walked off in search of McArthur's rooms.

The door when he arrived was already open, and Keira stood before him in the lounge.

"Oh, thank you, Father."

"How is he?"

"A difficult morning. He has been in some pain and discomfort. Of course he refuses his medication so that he be alert to speak with you. I counselled him otherwise…"

Fitzgerald could well imagine what McArthur's reaction would have been to such advice. "And you were right to do so, but I guess he would not have such a thing?"

"An understatement," she whispered. "But Father…are you alright? You look terrible."

He offered her a comforting smile but saw that it had little effect and so chose instead to steer the conversation away.

"Keira?" He hesitated, trying to choose his words carefully, but realising there was no easy way to put it. "How long does he have?"

She paused for only a split second. "I'm amazed he is still with us now, Father. I have little doubt his time will come when your business is concluded. It is all he lives for now."

Is this it then? Am I free?

Something that felt oddly like regret overwhelmed him. An all to strange emotion given the rollercoaster of emotions he had felt while being here. But why should he feel that way? He knew too well though; it was that fucking library and everything that had been brought up in him since day one. With McArthur gone, he may not yet get to the bottom of what drew all of the pain and sadness to that one particular place. Perhaps he should be grateful? He could walk away after all. McArthur dead in the ground and the house and grounds successfully passed off into the hands of the Church and so free him back to his parish. But no, part of him knew it would not play that way because he did not want it to. He would get into that room for better or worse and face his demons whether they be real or not.

In response to Keira, he reached out and held her arm and nodded his understanding. It had been an instinctive gesture, one he had mirrored a hundred times, but the look within her eyes and the quick smile that flashed on her face were not of sadness for McArthur's imminent demise. He released his grip on her and averted his eyes. His desire for her was alive once more, and had he seen the same in her reaction to his touch?

He turned away from her quickly, believing she would read his feelings in his eyes. He did not like the person he was turning into here, and he quickly recalled the words of Colin Morris who had told him to get his business done and get out. That was likely the best way and so without looking back, he walked to the interior door of McArthur's bedroom for what he thought might well be the last time.

CHAPTER 30

Robert McArthur could feel himself failing. It was as if there were some kind of shroud being drawn over his vision, for everything that he beheld seemed shallow and out of focus. To date, he had found the strength to get through the few sessions with the priest, Fitzgerald. But now, and as his confession finally drew toward its final chapter, he knew he must find new levels of resolve, for confession was only the first part of his plan to absolution.

He was beginning to feel scared for the first time, scared of what might lie behind the veil that was to be his death. Such thoughts had plagued him from the moment he had finally taken to his bed for what would be the last time all the weeks ago, and even if his schemes were successful and he avoided the fate of Thomas Searle, then what else could there be in the void after life? Heaven? No. And why? For all that he had seen and known had been nothing but darkness, and there had been no sight of the divine in his long life. So why should such rewards wait for him?

Whatever his end, it was fast approaching he knew. How strange then that he had felt so alive only an hour before, and he mused at how reliant he must have been on the drugs that had stemmed his pain. He squinted and blinked rapidly, for a shadow now fell upon his bed, and his heart lurched involuntarily at the sudden arrival of the priest, he who would be his saviour.

He tried in vain to ascertain the features of young Father Fitzgerald, who now silently sat down beside him, but focus would not come readily to him, not even the damned lighting system it seemed could provide enough light to fight off the encroaching darkness.

He sighed and closed his eyes. Soon he would truly know the darkness again, and for whatever fears it brought up in him, perhaps he should instead welcome that fact, for at least it would finally end his reliance in this perpetual damned light! And he could well accept the prospect of oblivion should there be no paradise for him, oblivion and the eternal rest of nothingness, an easy trade over where Searle now resided.

But first this absolution. His body was failing, but he knew his mind was as alive and alert as it had ever been. It had been the right decision to wean himself off the medication after all, for he might otherwise be in a slumber from which he would not have awoken. He needed this chance, and he knew that he could find the strength to finish his story.

The young priest would grant him the salvation that he sought, for it was simple Catholic mandate he be forgiven. More than that, there was still the matter of the deeds of Thoby Hall to be signed over; his solicitor, Harvey, waiting on the call that would sign the last of his Estate over as soon as the priest had done his duty. All would be well in that regard, but there was more.

Would Fitzgerald buy into the last of his story? Would he believe as he must, if he was to do his bidding one final time? Now was the time to find out.

"Father, please help me up" McArthur whispered at last.

The priest stood and held McArthur forward, quickly bringing pillows to support his back. On laying him down, a fine sweat had produced on McArthur's brow from the effort it had taken.

"Thank you Father. The time has finally come, I am drawing near my end and so I must seek your blessing. But before I do, I must confess my part, for all you have heard thus far is of Searle."

"I am ready, Robert. I understand the efforts you have made to bring us this far."

"Surely you must have wondered if I was raving Father? But trust me, all I have imparted is of relevance as to what came next."

"Tell me then, Robert."

"Well, you might well wonder how a man like Searle could impart such a story to me as he had, and live with the knowledge of that. That is easy Father; he fired me the very next day."

The priest seemed surprised. "He did? How can that be? I thought you had been in his service for the duration?"

"Almost, almost. You see Searle needed to get that revelation off of his chest. And who else was there? He had no friends, no family. There was only me. But to open up to a servant? It could only lead to one thing. And let us not forget the nature of our relationship. He hated me and I hated him. This opening up? This one night? That was all there had ever been between us and for that, he felt weak. And for a man like Searle? Well, that could not be. I missed his 05:00 am call the next morning and for that, he fired me."

Fitzgerald replied. "He fired you for that?"

"What else, Father? Did you think he would admit to the sharing of his secret? That he could look me in the eye after what he had shared? No, the simple truth was I had neglected my duty and he leapt upon this and used it as his excuse. In actual fact, it should not be so difficult to believe. Despite my years of dutiful service, it wouldn't have mattered if he'd shared this information with me or not. I believe he could have fired me for that neglect alone; such was the man's spite."

"What did you do?"

"What could I do? I packed my bags and cursed his name. I was out and there would be no argument. Again I did not question I only obeyed. I still had my damn pride after all and I wasn't about to show him that he could get to me. I simply left."

"But you returned obviously?" Fitzgerald questioned.

"Ah yes, it was little more than six months or so before I got the call from Harvey. Things it seemed had gone on as before my employ. Searle had gone through another three candidates in the short spell of my absence. All fired. He needed me back. He wouldn't admit to it though. Harvey, of course, suggested that it was all his idea that the old man had protested. But in my heart, I knew this came from Searle."

"And so you relented and returned?"

"No, not immediately, Father, I wanted to make the bastard squirm first. It wasn't about the money of course; I'd done more than alright in my years of service. I told Harvey that I felt aggrieved at the treatment I had received and that I required an apology from the old man. Ha! Can you believe that?"

Fitzgerald was silent.

"It was never going to happen of course I just wanted to rankle the old bastard. I did go back in the end, there was no apology but my salary had nearly doubled. I was a very wealthy man at that point. My pay vastly exceeded the level of my service and I doubt that Searle ever knew of this. It was as before; I was on Harvey's payroll."

McArthur's voice resonated with strength as he spoke, but little else of him shared such vitality. He turned his weak head and again tried to behold the visage of the man beside him and found that he could not.

The darkness that now threatened to wholly engulf his vision encroached to the point where almost all detail was lost to him, and he felt new fear overcome him, for all he saw in the bright light of the bedroom was a ghostly white mask of the man before him, with but two dark portals where the eyes should be and the continually shifting black hole that was the man's mouth. And all around it, the darkness seemed to seep in toward the centre of what he could see.

"Father, before I go further, you must try and understand the man, and for that matter me as well. I worked at Searle's beck and call for some 25 years or so, on and off. That's 25 years of unadulterated hatred between the two of us. He bullied me, assaulted me and demeaned me but I took it all, for I am a proud man. On my return to service what had been imparted to me that night was long forgotten. Forgotten that was until the death of my son in 1975. That was when Searle was at his most hateful and that was when I resolved that I would get him for the misery that he had bestowed upon me and my family. For I still blamed him for the breaking of my marriage and surely if things had gone as they should, then we would have been together, I would have known my son and things surely would not have unfurled as they did."

"You lost your son? I am sorry Robert. How may I ask did he die?" Fitzgerald asked.

"Jonathan died in a car accident. He was only 21 years of age. I had long since lost touch with his mother. She had met another man and as a family had moved to America. And it was there that Jonathan lost his life. He'd been out on a date as it happened and had returned his girlfriend home when he was a hit by another car, a bright red Plymouth Fury that might well have been a tank, driven by a drunk who walked away without a scratch. I did not know my son as I'd have liked. The distance between us was huge and the hours I spent with Searle precluded any travelling time but an annual holiday. I went to see him of course, and after his 18th birthday, he came and visited while travelling across Europe. I am ashamed to say that I did not recognise this young man as my own flesh, for in our time apart, he had grown beyond me. I did not know my own son and for this, I blamed Searle also."

"Surely though you can see the folly in this thinking? Did you not make your own choices Robert?" Fitzgerald asked.

"Yes, Father, I know. I did make my own choices. But a man will always blame another will he not? It is easier to find fault in the behaviour of others and blame them for our failings rather than admit to the honest truth of it. And the truth of it is that I was to blame. I should have walked from Searle's employ when Nancy bade me to do so. I should not have been so proud. I could have kept my family, my son. And my life perhaps may have been a happy one."

"But I ramble on Father; time is short. I must press on and tell you of what transpired the night Searle died and I came into receipt of his fortune. And I must tell you of what made me do what I did. Why I sold Searle into the hands of the Devil."

CHAPTER 31

Thoby Hall.

04:00 am Saturday, 10th November 1979.

McArthur thrashed out at the sheets with his feet, kicking them to the foot of the bed. Sleep, it seemed would not come to him this night whatever he might try. But he knew he was fooling himself. It was not the room temperature or the softness of the bed, or the position in which he lay that precluded any rest this night. It was the fact that his mind was alive with anticipation of the day to come and the memory of the weeks previous of plotting and planning that had gone into place. Today he would make Searle pay for the years of abuse that he had been subjected to at his hand.

It was true that he had taken all that he could over the past 25 years. But as a man of honour, as he saw himself, he had always concluded that there was nothing that Searle could do to defeat him. That he would take the abuse that the old man could throw at him. However, in the months following his son's death, depression and regret had hit him hard. He had himself turned to the bottle as he lamented the passing of his only family and the regret that he did not even know his son at all. In his mind, he blamed Searle. He had spent 25 long hard years in his employ to the point where the loathing that the two had for each other was all that there was left for either of them.

Searle had of course never mentioned the night in the library and nor had McArthur, but it seemed the old man wished to punish his servant for his own weakness on that night. At first, McArthur had rejoiced in Searle's failing. He had been initially dismissed from the man's service, yes. But on his return, the old man had been skittish and could no longer hold McArthur's eye and for the first time in his long service, McArthur had felt a certain power over his master which he enjoyed very much.

He still did his duty of course, but it seemed that Searle was loath to call upon his favour unless he absolutely had to. No more the 3:00 am calls and for that matter, no longer the out of hours or Sunday duties that had plagued him so before.

That was until Jonathan's death in March of 75. It had hit McArthur hard and the spiral into depression had hit him harder still. Hardest of all though was Searle, for it seemed that he had at last found weakness in his steadfast employee. Searle had shown himself at his lowest ebb in that late hour in the library and in the face of McArthur's resolute professionalism, he had felt small and weak. But now the tables had turned. McArthur had begun to get sloppy. Late for work, unkempt, unshaved and stinking of alcohol. Searle, it seemed had finally found the chink in the man's armour, and with that, he rediscovered his confidence and hit McArthur hard.

And so now McArthur lay there, musing on these things. The last few years had been a living hell for him. Searle had tortured him unmercifully for his failings which had been many; among which was resorting to stealing bottles from the cellar, coupled with the now unprofessional level of his service. And to top it off he had broken his one rule that he would always hold his tongue.

That had been the worst, for that was when he knew he was finally defeated — 25 years of hard work and professional service blown away in an alcoholic fury. Searle as always had been pressing his buttons, such sloppy and inept work should have resulted in his dismissal years ago, but now it seemed that there was now no wrong that he could do that would result in his being fired from his job. He was a broken man, and Searle it seemed would rejoice in that fact.

Searle was making him pay tenfold for his weakness in the library that night and would press him until he broke and that night had come some six months ago.

McArthur had been lying in this very bed as it had happened. It had been a difficult night, memories of Nancy and Jonathan had hit him hard and he had resorted to the only escape he had known of late, the bottle. And so he had stolen into the cellar and not for the first time taken one of the vintage brands. Such was his drunken state at the time that he had not noticed Searle's passion for the drink had diminished.

As he had fallen, Searle regained himself, sensing the balance of power turning back in his favour. Slowly but surely, the flaws in McArthur's work became very apparent. And so Searle stopped his own path to self-destruction that he might better bear witness to McArthur's fall into despair. Of course, this was all unknown to McArthur who despite the struggle, had attempted to hide his fall from his master. But with each passing day, he fell harder and Searle stood taller.

Searle had begun simply enough, the odd comment here or there, a little put down, a little sarcastic remark. From the outside looking in it seemed he was testing the ground, finding his way back and gaining confidence. McArthur though simply did not register that the balance of power was switching back to where it had once been.

All until that morning when the first hateful shreds of consciousness began to filter through to his addled brain. He opened his eyes to find the shadowy form of someone standing over him from the foot of his bed.

"Ah, Robert! How the mighty have fallen eh?"

McArthur blinked rapidly for clarity, for it seemed that he must be dreaming. The voice held no recognition for him, with its stark, booming quality. His mind all the while was fighting a losing battle for perception as the light tore at his eyes and his head throbbed with pain. He put his arm across his brow to shield himself from the harsh reality of waking.

His mind would not register the words spoken, and so he turned himself away from the sound of the voice in the hope of escape, but escape it seemed would not come as the voice continued.

"Hmmm, a little worse for wear are we? What have we here? A Bruichladdich 1960 single malt? My, you do have excellent taste, don't you?"

McArthur groaned at the intrusion of the voice. There was something within those words that he knew he did not wish to address. That there was something ill and wrong, despite the almost jovial carefree tone with which they were said.

"Robert?" It went on, "what will we do with you eh? I always knew you'd let me down one day. It was only a matter of time. I guessed as much the first time I laid eyes on you. A useless cripple, walking upon my lawn."

And despite himself and the wish to escape into the furthest reaches that sleep could offer, the beginnings of recognition began to wash over his mind, and McArthur felt dread climb into the pit of his belly.

The voice now began to become harsher as it continued.

"But you know, it was for simple amusement that I let that go. To watch your pathetic form hop around my halls on my simple whim. Never a word of complaint. Don't you know that I laughed at you Robert? That I took the best years of your life and laughed? I watched as you chose my service over your wife and family. I watched as your stubborn pride ruined the one good thing that you ever had. And I laugh still as you watched your son die and you became this pathetic mess that I see before me."

No! no! McArthur's mind rebelled. *That is not how it was! That is not true, how dare you!* And suddenly his fear was gone, for anger took hold instead. His mind was now alive to the situation and he forced himself to the surface that he might retort to this evil, twisted excuse of humanity, this man, Thomas Searle.

He forced himself upward and beheld the smile behind the dark eyes of his master. He allowed himself to turn, to take in the room, only to find the sight of the alarm clock. 06:32 am. He had overslept and guilt came to him in a flash. And here in his own quarters, standing over him with a bottle of empty, stolen whisky was Searle, a vicious, satisfied smile playing at his lips. And that was all McArthur needed to behold to know that he was beaten.

Only once before; the night of Searle's confession had he overslept, and worse, for not only that, here was the evidence that he had stolen from his master's cellar. Regret washed over him and not for his broken pride but because he knew he was beaten. Searle had won; he had tortured him, ridiculed him and now finally broken him. And it was too much. But it seemed Searle had not yet finished revelling in his victory for he continued.

"Ah yes, your son. What were he to think if he were to see you now? A pathetic wretched drunk is what. And more? He would be ashamed. And how would that be Robert? That your own son should be so ashamed? That he could not even look you in the eye such would be his disgust. But you know what? Maybe I am a little too unkind. Maybe he would thank you Robert. Maybe he would thank you for beating his mother and forcing her hand, forcing her out of the door."

"No, no." McArthur whispered, heaving himself to the side of his bed, taking his head into his hands. But there was no denying the words as they poured over him.

"It is true." Searle went on, "that your boy died too young. I never knew him of course, but we have both seen men stripped of the lives they might have led, have we not? And that is the greatest crime of all. But here? I don't know; you see it was by your hand that he led a different life. That he and your wife moved away. 21 years is too short a time, but I bet he'd be glad for the life that was offered him."

Slowly Searle moved around the foot of the bed until he came in front of McArthur, slumped as he was on the side. McArthur sensed through his clasped hands that Searle knelt and was now face to face with him, better so that he could see his reaction.

"And what a life eh? A new country, a new father. And a young lady involved to. It seemed he was on the up and up. I wonder Robert; I really wonder what went through that young man's mind in his last seconds, other than that car of course. I bet he was glad, glad that you forced Nancy's hand, glad that for 21 short years he at the very least had the potential to live. And I bet that the last word that spilt from his mouth was a thank you. A thank you, to you Robert, that he should not have stayed and grown in his own father's pathetic image. Yes! You should be grateful that your son for a short time, knew life and would have welcomed his end, rather than have stayed and grown in your image."

And as Searle's words fell over him, McArthur felt his anger reach breaking point. How dare he? Yes, perhaps he was right, surely by his hand, his family had left him. But he had loved them and he loved his son dearly. So now? That Searle would try and diminish his memory? No, that was not acceptable, not acceptable at all. Slowly he opened his eyes and looked between the interlaced fingers that covered his face. There was Searle, a smile playing at his lips. He was enjoying this and McArthur knew it.

Instantly, he curled his fist and lashed out toward Searle's head. He had but one second to see the visage of the man change from mirth to shock as he rocked backwards. The old man tumbled back in a ball as McArthur's fist met nothing but thin air. In his delicate state and poor position, he had misread the distance between the two of them, and so quickly he began to rise.

Fuck it. He thought. *25 years, wasted!*

He should have walked the day that Nancy gave him that ultimatum, but no, damn his stubborn pride! Hell, he even remembered being on the verge of telling this rich prick where to go as he made him stand in silence during their first meeting, but again no. And here he was some 25 years later, his life ruined. But now it was all too late for regrets. And so he would do what he should have done a long time ago, but he would do it in the most satisfying way of all. He would show this man his hatred of him.

But in an instant, the tide had turned. Searle was already to his own feet and as McArthur began to advance toward him, his jaw was met with Searle's fist. Pain erupted and in his groggy state he rocked backwards, as quickly the second blow fell to his nose.

As if in slow motion, he saw his own blood as it sprayed outward into the air and fresh pain washed over him. In his delicate position, with legs pressed against the side of the bed, there was only one way to go and that was backward.

And so he fell back to his bed, hands coming up to nurse his surely broken nose. His head throbbed and his vision was robbed of him as tears streamed down his battered face. But Searle it seemed was not finished with him as a further flurry of blows caught him around the ribs.

"You would attack me?! Searle screamed at the top of his lungs. "How dare you!"

McArthur rolled himself as small as he could and flailed out with his left arm as he tried to ward off the savagery of the man's attack. And as he did so, he looked out at his master through wet eyes and fear gripped him, for through his tear-veiled vision he did not behold his master of 79 years of age, but instead he beheld the form that had caused him involuntary fear all of those years ago. For here, in the hatred of the man's flashing eyes was the Tommy that exuded such hate in the yard, and the portrait that took prominence in the hallway. And despite his pain, that was the worst thing of all, for those eyes were fixed upon him and in his confused, drunken state and through watery vision it was as if the devil himself stood over him, for all that he could see were the black menacing eyes and the flashing grin as blow upon blow fell upon his broken form.

Mercifully, unconsciousness quickly took him.

And so here he was some six months later, his revenge playing in his mind. The aftermath of the attack had been very strange, for he had awoken in the Hall's small infirmary, his arm in plaster and a broken nose, seemingly reset. He was there only a few days, but doubt clouded his mind. His memory of the attack was thin, but enough small fragments remained for him to piece the events together. And as the days passed and his embarrassment and anger raged, the words Searle had spoken came back to him, and there on his hospital bed, he vowed vengeance.

But would fate allow him such an opportunity? After all, had he not attacked his master first? Had he not stolen from his cellar? In fact, the only reason that he believed he was still here at all was that Searle had not yet had the satisfaction of firing him from his service. Where would his revenge be then?

His question was answered on his return to his quarters. At first, he felt it was as he feared, for all of his belongings had been removed and a note placed neatly across the neatly made bed. It simply read,

In view of recent events your service has been somewhat lacking. You are to move back to the house at once. The day begins at 05:00 am sharp.

And so it had been. Searle made no mention of the assault and things quickly got back to how they had been before. The after-hour calls, the weekends, all of it. If anything, things were, in fact worse than they had ever been. In Searle's eyes, McArthur was a broken man and so his tirade of abuse started over. McArthur was beaten.

Or so, he would have Searle believe. The stay of execution that he had been granted would give him the opportunity to gain his revenge on his master once and for all. And so what harm would it do in the meantime to let the old man have his victory? It had been a long battle of wills and Searle was revelling in his downfall. After all, what good would it have done him to dispense with his services if he couldn't rub it into his face?

So there he was with but one question on his mind. What form should revenge take?

McArthur looked over and took in the time from the alarm clock. 04:42 am. It seemed it was all too late for sleep now, for his day's duties began in but eighteen minutes. He would rise and begin Searle's breakfast. On the face of it, the day would seem like any other.

And so it was. But for McArthur, it seemed that the clock dragged slowly onward as he went about his duties, until at long last he found himself once more back in his quarters, worry starting to gnaw at him; for now it was gone 08:30 pm and Searle had not yet called upon his service.

If his plan was to succeed, then it was imperative that he do so. And so he waited, and he waited some more. Lying back upon his bed, glaring into the dazzling strip lights as if for answer, only occasionally turning his neck to see that little more than a minute had passed by since the last time that he had looked.

Worry gave way to paranoia and he took to his feet, pacing the room frantically, back and forth. Why hadn't Searle called? Sure it had been a long day for him, finishing some hour later than normal. But now it was 9 o'clock and Searle had not yet called for his evening drink and cigarettes. As ever, McArthur knew that this was something that he could easily attend to himself, but where was his fun in that? Especially when he had his servant on ready call to do it for him at any given time.

Finally, McArthur allowed himself to sit on the edge of his bed, reason eventually winning through. Of course, there was a reason Searle hadn't called. After all, when he knew that McArthur couldn't relax in the wake of anticipation, why keep a regular schedule? Why not make him wait and guess? And suddenly McArthur knew that it was true. Why hadn't he seen such a thing before? That in all the years he had served Searle that he had spent his time, exactly as he did now. Not being able to relax for a moment, waiting for the inevitable call at some god-forsaken hour.

And so he was angry, angry at himself for not having seen it. Angry at Searle for finding new ways of torture that he hadn't realised that he had been subjected to. And despite his plan, he cursed the old man, swearing his revenge for the millionth time.

Suddenly though, calm came over him and a smile played at his face. For what he had planned would make up for it all. And in some way it would make it all the sweeter, for the bill Searle had run-up was larger than he had imagined and the cost the man would pay would undoubtedly make this right again. He would be well compensated for his master's indiscretions. And with that, he looked over to his dresser and smiled as he beheld both the envelope that he would deliver to his master later that night, and the small metallic device that would ensure the success of his plan.

CHAPTER 32

21:35hrs.

The call had finally come some five minutes ago. And now McArthur found himself en route to the library. Searle's need for cigarettes and alcohol was predictable, but even after all these years, it was still unacceptable for the man to attend his own need, or to simply have the library amply stocked with the provisions he would need for the evening.

After his own fall from grace, McArthur had noticed Searle, slipping back into the old routine. Nothing as bad as before, but it seemed he finally felt that he had the upper hand over his servant, and he could let his guard down somewhat, as McArthur's rigid obedience and subordination had quelled the fire in the old man's belly. Not that he tired of the put-downs and verbal assaults on his servant though. Those were still delivered with the same venomous tongue that they ever were. But with the game between them seemingly over, Searle had gone back to his old routine of books and booze.

Searle's breakdown and confession to him was old news now and the man no longer drank himself into oblivion into the small hours. A more suitable retirement time of 02:00 am was more the course these days and McArthur had but one nightly trip, to deliver the bottle and cigarettes. This had been the pattern for the past six months now and that pleased McArthur no end for it was in Searle's predictability that he had plotted his downfall. And to be sure that his plan would work, he had carefully spied upon his master to ensure that his routine held to the same path.

And so here he was, standing in the entranceway to the library leaning heavily upon the walking stick on which he was now reliant; looking over at Searle, huddled over a large volume in the leather-backed armchair that he favoured. McArthur looked on and found it rather ironic that the small pedestal to the left of the chair still held a reading lamp, which shone no brighter than the strip lights that hung like watchful sentinels above.

And as his duty demanded, he stood and he waited his master's word, for as ever, etiquette precluded his speaking out of turn. Of all the abuses that he had taken at his Searle's hand, this perhaps rankled with him the most, for many was the time that his master would simply leave him standing, ignoring his presence despite being there at his behest. Oh, and how he would stretch these moments out! And so he waited and the only sound that intervened between them was the soft swish of the turning of a page.

Finally, though Searle barked at him without looking up. "Hmm, took your damn time! That damn leg getting the better of you at last no doubt. Time I started thinking of getting someone able-bodied on the staff. By the time you've fetched my damn bottle, I'd have died of thirst."

McArthur simply smiled, "But of course, what might Sir require of the cellar this evening?"

Such exchanges were commonplace between them now. Searle issuing insults and McArthur simply deflecting them away as if they'd never been uttered. But something must have given in his one, for Searle looked up from his book questioningly.

And all of a sudden, McArthur felt found out. Searle's eyes held him, looking him up and down, the moment stretching out between them as Searle looked his butler over, seemingly trying to size up his mood. McArthur felt his stomach roll. There had been something in his voice, something that had made the old man suspicious. He'd given the game away, damn it. Not now, not now he was so close! So he stood there, Searle's black eyes pouring over him, trying to probe and find the source of the change within him. Sweat began to form and slowly rolled down the nape of his neck, coming to rest on the rim of his tight collar, where it began to itch. And all he could do was stand there as Searle's questioning, unforgiving eyes fell upon him. The moment seemed to stretch on, until finally, mercifully...

"Hmm, I don't know what's got into you tonight boy, but it is no concern of mine. Get out and fetch me the damn whisky and be quick about it!"

McArthur turned quickly, pacing as fast away from the library as his injured leg would allow him, into the sanctuary of the hallway where he could finally expel the breath that he had been holding and wipe the sweat from his brow.

That had been too close. It was uncanny how Searle had that ability to eye someone up and seemingly read their innermost thoughts. McArthur reflected upon this as he slowly made his way back down the hall to the main stairway. It was as if the man had an inbuilt defensive mechanism that protected him from apparent danger and come to think of it, he could remember many such occasions when he had been under the scrutiny of that hard gaze. There was no doubt about it, the man could read right through you, perhaps that had been the secret of his success and the fact that he had walked unscathed from many potential scandals.

But now it seemed he had passed the test. How after all, could Searle recognise what he had in store for him?

At last, he made the cellar and began to scan the vast racks of wines and malts that stretched out before him. And there it was. Dare he? Could he? For right before him was the last bottle of Bruichladdich single malt whisky. And despite the fact that he had almost been found out, he knew it was right, knew it was perfect. For it had been this very bottle that had contributed to his downfall those six months ago.

But would Searle recognise the fact? Surely he would recognise the brand and perhaps the ill intent with which it was given. Yet he knew he could not resist, that it was the most apt of things. Searle would certainly raise a questioning eyebrow and that hard stare would surely fall upon him again. But he had withstood that glare once already and knew he could withstand it again. Searle would not see what McArthur had in store for him.

Plucking the bottle from its nest, he smiled for he knew his plan was perfect. Searle had seen something in him but had not the cause to question him further. And his keen eye would certainly flag the symbolism the bottle represented. He would stand and allow Searle to search him for malice, but he knew that he would find none. He had waited too long for this and tonight would belong to him. The tables would finally be reversed; he would finally have the upper hand.

The climb back up to Searle was a long one, for he allowed himself the pleasure of running things through his mind once more, what he would say, what he would do and ultimately the pay-off; Searle begging him forgiveness and mercy.

Soon he was back before his master, bottle in hand and he stood in the doorway waiting to be acknowledged as he took in the sight of Searle drawing long on a cigarette as he scanned the pages of his book.

There was no long wait this time for surely thirst had gotten the better of the man as he simply extended his right hand and beckoned McArthur entry.

McArthur did as he was bid and approached the man from the side, laying a large tumbler on the pedestal by his master's side. Swiftly he broke the seal on the bottle as Searle watched on and poured the first large measure within. This time though he did not feel ill at ease, even as from the corner of his eye, he saw Searle glance at the bottle laid by his side with a questioning eye. He stood tall and allowed himself to look deep into his Searle's eyes. Again that feeling of disquiet washed over him as he felt those black eyes stare deeply into his own. This time there could be no question about it. He knew that the man was searching him, looking deep into the pit of his soul for answers and despite his earlier conviction, he knew doubt and could quickly see Searle's brow crease.

But as quickly as it came, it was gone. Calm washed over him like the lapping tide breaking on the beach and he was able to hold that glance and see puzzlement come to Searle's face.

In all, it was but seconds but it seemed an age stretched on until Searle finally commented.

"You are in an odd mood tonight, for why I cannot guess. Well, never mind, I have all that I require, be gone."

McArthur replied with a quick bow of his head and made his way back to his bedroom.

The game was on. Things were in place and now it was just a matter of playing the waiting game. It would take Searle a little while to get through his bottle of whisky and though that wasn't necessarily relevant to McArthur's plan, he had decided that he would much prefer Searle in a melancholy mood for what was in store for him.

The problem was the waiting though and he paced his quarters relentlessly, checking his inner jacket pocket for the paperwork that he needed and more importantly his back pocket for the reassuring bulge of the metallic item that was now held within.

Time though did not want to play his game and it crawled slowly onward giving rise once again to his doubts. He realised that he was taking a chance, that his plan would be foiled, laughed at even for its simplicity and probable stupidity. After all, it was so simple it was laughable. Why he hadn't thought of such a thing years ago was beyond him.

Of course, he hadn't been planning something as sinister as blackmail back then, but it still bothered him that he hadn't done something similar out of nothing more pressing than cheap laughs at Searle's expense.

Suddenly he was shaken from his reverie as the sky outside of his room became alive with epic violence; lightning, almost instantly followed by a loud rumble of thunder. A storm it seemed was brewing and the quick flash held fast on the inside of his closed eyelids as he shielded himself from the graphic display that was building outside of his bedroom window.

Opening his eyes again, he beheld his alarm clock, only 10:15 pm.

CHAPTER 33

23:45hrs.

McArthur looked up through the large window out into the night and beheld the lashing rain, falling upon Searle's floodlit Estate. Still, the lightning pierced the sky and dark, ominous thunder growled with discontent through the heavens.

It was time.

Reaching his hand into his pocket, he took the small metallic device within and held it before him.

What if it doesn't work?

Nerves took him, for the reliability of the device was in question; the technology brand new. He hoped that the expense in obtaining it would not have been in vain. He shook his head though to negate his doubt, all of his test runs had been flawless. It would work. It had to.

But the device was for later; first there was work to do and so he slipped it back into his pocket. Collecting his walking stick he made his way toward the door, stopping only to collect the small satchel that often accompanied him on his nightly duty. As he did so, he caught sight of himself within the three-piece vanity mirror that stood atop of his dresser. His grim visage looked back upon him; old and grizzled, the years of his youth gone, stripped bare and leaving in its place this wretched soul. He shot himself a grin so as to break the picture but this only resulted in making him look maniacal.

Let Searle see the same and know I am serious.

Leaving his quarters, he found himself by the east wing kitchens and close by to the cellar. Such a position now made the stealing of Searle's booze all the easier for its close proximity, but he knew the real reason for the location of his quarters, as it was yet another twisted ploy of Searle's, who knew that his advancing years and worsening leg, made the long trek back and forth to the west wing an arduous task.

Making the kitchen, he made straight for the cellar steps and began the slow descent for what might have been the millionth time. It was not though for liquor that he came searching on this night, for another part of his daily duties lay well beyond the cellar, for a long concrete tunnel had been formed between the house and his destination. A tunnel that had been commissioned only a year or so ago at his master's decree.

Weaving his way past the wine and whisky racks, and stooping low to avoid the low timber beams, he found himself before the door to the tunnel. He pushed the door open and was greeted only by darkness that was only marginally dispelled when he pulled upon the cord that dangled near his head. Low light filled the space before him, and he shivered as he made his way forward. From his vantage point, he could not yet see the far side where another similar door as the one he had passed would be found. In all, his walk would take him some one hundred and fifty yards, beneath the kitchens and well out and beneath the grounds of Thoby Hall.

He had initially welcomed the construction of this subterranean channel, for previously this same task had taken him out of the house and to a lone brick building that was ill in keeping with the grandiose aesthetic of the grand house.

Such nightly trips had been a pleasure in the beautiful summer months, but a hard and difficult task during the long winters. As such, he had felt the building of this tunnel to a new facility would ease his burden considerably. But the fact was, he would rather brave the elements than this forlorn and depressing journey. For here under the earth in the scant light and damp air, he had come to detest and even to fear this long nightly walk. For why he could not be sure, but such were the acoustics, that even the slightest noise was amplified and echoed mournfully down the long underpass, so much so that he would quite often snap his head back, half expecting to find that he had been followed.

Not so tonight, for his single-minded purpose precluded any outside influences from intruding, and as he neared his goal, he could already detect the bittersweet smell of diesel fumes and the low rumble of an engine in the close confines of the passageway.

So he came at last to the end door. This he vowed, would be the very last walk he would ever take down this damnable concrete burrow. But for now, this nightly burden would be his means of salvation and as he pushed the door inward, his goal was now visible before him, a military-grade Fermont generator.

The device was virtually brand new and supposedly top of the line. The construction of this underground facility and its installation a genuine surprise, for he felt that Searle had always known and enjoyed his hardship in the long walk to the old brick building where the previous generator had been situated.

It had been an off the cuff remark that had instigated this change; made little over a year ago, when he had inadvertently let slip that the cold made the previous model difficult to start. That had brought Searle to a virtual panic, and that quickly began the process of constructing this new building that would supposedly protect the machine from the cold and the elements.

McArthur had not known it then, but that raw and surprising panic that had flared in Searle had sown the seeds for this revenge that he would take tonight.

He made his way to the control panel and viewed the gauges within. All in order as he knew they would be, the fuel gauge needle between three-quarters and full, the battery charge ammeter within the green and the frequency meter at an idling speed. Exactly as it had been on every damned night that he had made his way here and set the blasted thing in motion.

For now, the multiple dials did not interest him; only the switches his hand now came to rest upon. Quickly he depressed the two power switches to the off position, closely followed by the two circuit breakers. The machine before him whined and quickly became lifeless as the last of the processed gases exited its system like a death rattle, to be expelled up the long chimney and into the cold of the night above.

Thoby Hall was now without any backup power.

Moving quickly, McArthur now made his way to a side door, that was situated just behind the large expansive machinery.

He shivered as he went inside, only not this time for the cold, for his whole body was alive with raw anticipation as to what was to come.

He surveyed the switches before him until his eyes met the switch that was marked, generator. He depressed it and instantly all about him became dark.

There in the black and the cold of the room, he waited. Keening his senses for a sound that he knew would not come. The generator was dead and would not fire so as to fulfil its guardianship of the home's lights.

Satisfied, he pressed the switch again, and it was some seconds before the light was returned to him and he could see the row of switches again.

This is so simple; it's a joke.

It was, and how he had never contrived to come up with this before was beyond him. Maybe it had been Searle's reaction to his news of the old generator and his failings with it that had finally stirred this inside of him, but the fact was the man had been petrified of the dark ever since that night in the library when he had his heart attack and his supposed devil had come to claim him.

Ridiculous.

But Searle would come to regret his weakness. Not for his fear of the dark, but instead the weakness whereby he broke down and told McArthur his story, for it was with that knowledge that he would give Searle his comeuppance.

Do it.

He began flicking switches. east wing lower, east wing upper, kitchens…All to the off position and as he did so, he imagined the halls above falling into darkness.

West wing lower, click.

West wing upper, click.

He knew that was the one that may have got Searle's attention and his hand rested now above the switch marked library.

Should he? If but for a second?

No.

It was tempting, but when the time came, he wanted to experience Searle's fear with his own eyes. And so he continued toggling all the other switches to the off position. Now the main house was in darkness and if Searle had not yet been aware, he surely would now for McArthur had just extinguished all of the spotlights in the garden. McArthur tried to imagine the panic that now surely coursed through his master.

Back where he started now, he once again depressed the switch marked generator and once again all around him became black.

McArthur slowly moved his hand up toward his face and found that he could not see it. He was giddy with excitement now, for he knew the entire house but for the library was now in complete and utter darkness. A smile played at his lips as he pictured Searle alone in the library, panic beginning to take him, as he felt elation at the coming of the dark.

McArthur reached out for the satchel that hung neatly at his side and groped around until his hand met the smooth metallic tube within. He toggled the switch and quickly a circle of light formed on the wall before him, spinning now he traced the beam over to the door and quickly made his way back the way he had come.

The circle of light from the torch bobbed and weaved as he slowly made his way back down the tunnel, relishing and taking his time as he did so. Knowing that Searle would be beside himself as he waited for his butler to finally show.

As he got closer to the kitchen, he began to make out the soft chime of a bell. The sound was alien and weird as it echoed down the long corridor toward him and he was at pains as to its source. Understanding only coming when he finally made the stairs from the cellar back up to the kitchen, for there before him and situated high on the kitchen wall was a service bell, that clattered and danced furiously as it chimed its unrelenting cacophony.

Searle.

He had all but forgotten that the bell existed, such was Searle's reliance on the intercom system to plague his beleaguered servant. Certainly, it had been some years then since this summoning bell had been sounded and oh how it was music to his ears as it danced back and forward, a veritable window to Searle's overwhelming panic in the rooms above.

Although he had not expected this intrusion, he welcomed it, and he smiled as he cast the bell in the light of his torch. He was now giddy with fear and excitement all wrapped in a neat little ball that appeared to be rolling over and over in the pit of his stomach.

Walking now from the kitchen he found himself in the east wing corridor and there again he saw himself depicted in one of the house's large mirrors which stared back at him. Within that mirror, he found a new image of himself, shrouded in shadow and demonic-looking. His visage took him back somewhat. But he found that he liked the menacing picture that it showed and he hoped that he would meet Searle with such a look and the man would at last look into his own black eyes and finally feel the same fear that McArthur himself had felt at the old man's hand.

Moving on, the circle of light bobbed before him, casting eerie shadows along the walls as he went. He walked slowly, trying to anticipate Searle's raw panic at the house being cast into darkness. At this point, he believed that Searle would believe the storm responsible for the loss of power, but he would no doubt be also wondering why the backup generator hadn't kicked in. The reason behind that little quandary was simple. There was nothing wrong with the power. For the first time in god knows how many years, the lights at Thoby Hall had simply been turned off.

So now here he was, approaching the library. The smile on his lips was very wide and again, he was aquiver with expectation at the events to come. But for now, he forced the smile away; he didn't want to give the game away too early did he?

He stepped quickly into the library, to be greeted by a frantic Searle.

"Where the hell have you been!?" he raged toward McArthur. "I've been ringing you for ten minutes! The lights, what the hell has happened to the lights!?"

McArthur tried to remain calm. Even now, right on the brink of his grand moment, Searle still knew how to push his buttons and he could feel his anger and hatred toward the man begin to rise. He was going to enjoy this, oh yes.

"Sir, the storm. It must have blacked out the power grid or something."

"Don't you think I know that!? What about the generator? Why hasn't that kicked into life?" Searle shot back venomously.

"I don't know Sir, perhaps it has after all? I mean the library is still well lit, is it not?"

McArthur could see that Searle's eyes were wide with panic as he beheld him. Although the words he shouted were toward him, he could see that Searle was searching the darkness behind McArthur's shoulder for some unseen danger.

"Quickly man, come in, come in." Searle continued, quieter now. "Robert, quickly now, down to the generator, the fuse box, whatever. You must go and find the source of the problem and get it fixed, yes?"

McArthur could sense the urgency in the man, and knew that he was on the brink of panic and that he represented his only hope in this situation. A hope he would now take away.

Slowly he reached around toward his back pocket, and there as expected was the small metallic device. He drew it round and held it in his hand before Searle.

"What is that, Robert? What do you have there?"

McArthur looked down into his hand and smiled.

"This Sir? Why this is called a remote control. Surely you've heard of such a thing? They are all the rage nowadays. But this one is a little more special than most. Cost me a pretty penny it did. They call it infrared technology. Completely does away with the need for wires. Apparently, every home in the country will soon have one of these little gadgets. But for now, they are somewhat of a rarity. Marvellous, isn't it?"

Searle's brow creased as he seemingly tried to weigh up the situation.

"But why, Robert? Why the need for such a thing?"

"Oh, it's simple really. I guess I thought of the idea some years ago now. You see I hated this light, this damn unending light! Back in my quarters on the grounds with Nancy, it wasn't a problem. Your lunacy couldn't stretch as far as my private home. But moving into the Hall was a problem. Perpetual fucking daylight all the time! I couldn't sleep! I would wish for a device such as this so I might have some peace as I roamed the house and now it seems I have my wish. Well at least in part."

McArthur took a step closer to Searle and watched in fascination as the man stepped back from him. Clearly, he knew that something foul was afoot, but as yet, he could not be sure of McArthur's intentions. The power rested with him in this situation and McArthur was going to enjoy every moment of it and so he paced forward and walked in slow steps around the man as he continued his story.

"It was unrelenting though and I would have no peace. No, not with your damn obsession. The bulbs gave way to these damnable strip lights and there was no hiding from them. Ultimately I began to smash some of the damned things just to get some relief."

Searle simply stood, tight-lipped. Clearly, he knew that this was leading somewhere but McArthur was just easing into his stride. It would be a mistake to jump in too soon. To give his plan away without savouring these precious moments of uncertainty on Searle's behalf.

"So quite simply, I had to replace the damn things so as you wouldn't find out. But the question kept coming back to me. Why? Sure it's your house and you have the run of it. But in all the years of my service, I have never seen you set foot into the kitchen or for that matter the lower east wing. So why there? That's when it hit home with me. The reason you had me move into the Hall. So that you could keep tabs on me, how else would you know so much of Jonathan and Nancy? To glean as much information as you could to torture me so? That's why your damned strip lights found their way there, so as you could follow me there and watch me."

"Robert, I..."

McArthur cut him off. "Shut up!" All of a sudden his anger rose to the fore. "It wasn't enough for you was it? It wasn't enough to demean me, insult me, and work me all the hours under the sun. No. That wasn't enough because it wasn't working. You couldn't break me. And so you found new ammunition, my one regret in my life and you exposed it like a raw wound which you then poured salt onto."

"But no more old man, no more. I have had enough, do you understand? For all the years of hate that you've put me through you are going to compensate me for. Right here, tonight."

With that, McArthur produced the document from his jacket pocket.

"This Thomas, is a legal draft, signing over all of your fortune to me. I believe it will provide an adequate settlement for what you have put me through. It simply requires your signature."

McArthur could see the change in Searle's expression the moment he made his claim. The old man would not be so accommodating. *Good*, he thought, all the better for his little game.

Searle suddenly began to laugh and McArthur felt his control slip a notch. The old man it seemed wasn't nearly scared enough.

"Oh, Robert. You poor deluded fool. You had me going there. You really did — such an elaborate ruse. But you're serious aren't you? Oh my, I can see it in your eyes. Do you think that such a parlour trick would convince me to sign my wealth over to an inbred nothing like you? Look at yourself man. Crippled, old and alone! And for this you blame me? Perhaps you should look a little closer to home eh? Try looking at yourself. You'll not receive a penny from me. Further, your services will be dispensed of forthwith. Now get out of my sight!"

Searle stepped forward. Confidence blossoming on his face once more and McArthur felt himself take an involuntary step backwards. He could feel his face flush. He was embarrassed and he took a further step from the oncoming Searle. Stepping back, he made the boundary between the library door and the anteroom behind. He was again bathed in the shadow of the powerless hallway.

Searle came to a grinding halt, just yards short of the threshold of the library door. His face again a mask of fear and McArthur smiled, knowing that the power was his after all.

"I don't think you understand what is happening here Thomas. This is not a negotiation; this is a demand. Blackmail if you will. The night ahead is long and there is no means of escape from this. You will take this paper and you will sign it. You will sign it or I will deliver you to the darkness that you fear! Let me show you."

And with that, he re-entered the library. Searle backed further away from him.

Perfect.

He looked down onto the control and beheld the row of switches that as yet had remained untouched. The rest of the house had been easy, but the intricate nature of what he had planned next had required a great deal more subtlety. He pressed the first switch and the sound of a switch turning overhead came to his ears. He looked up as the first row of lights within the room extinguished, casting a gloomy shadow on the near wall and floor. Searle backed away further and McArthur detected the first signs of genuine terror appear on the man's face.

"Do you know how long it took to achieve this Thomas? It wasn't quick or easy, I can tell you. But ultimately your paranoia won through. The day I informed you of the difficulties with the outside generator. Do you remember? Of course, you do. It damn near frightened you to death. But luckily for me, as on the last inspection, I instructed the fitting of these switches and for them to rig this small device."

McArthur hit the next switch, and instantaneously the shadow around him darkened and the wall that was behind him became black.

"You see? Perfect is it not! Adds a little drama to our situation, doesn't it?" McArthur teased.

All the time Searle was backing away from the shadow that stretched across the floor. McArthur could see that the darkness behind where he stood was having the desired effect and so took another few steps forward into the light.

"Have a seat Thomas."

And with that, he pressed the next switch. This one, however, had the opposite effect for a spotlight immediately shone from above Searle's leather-bound chair which faced the row of books he so dreaded.

"No, Robert no. Listen, we can talk about this..." Searle began.

"Talk? No, there is nothing to talk about. As I said, this is not a negotiation. This is a demand and it will bear no scrutiny or argument on your behalf. Now, sit down!"

Searle did not so much as sit down but fall down into his chair. McArthur could see that his skin was a pallid white, that the blood that supposedly flowed beneath had somehow deserted him in his fear. He couldn't have hoped for such a reaction, but whatever was happening, Searle was clearly terrified.

A quick flick of two more switches and the room was quickly brought into complete darkness. Not entirely though, for now, only one light shone, a pallid spotlight that burned a circle of light around the sitting Searle and his chair. Searle's groan was as if music to his ears.

McArthur quickly placed the remote control into his top pocket and approached the man. Searle it seemed was shrunken somehow, for he had drawn himself as far into the chair as he was able. Again McArthur was taken by the mask of terror that he wore on his face.

Now, clasping the legal document he approached, grabbing a nearby footstool, he dragged it within the circle of light that he had created. That done, he simply lay the contract on top before withdrawing a pen from his other top pocket. That to, he lay next to the contract. As he bent back up, he allowed himself a smile to Searle but was surprised to see that he was no longer the focal point of Searle's attention.

As he beheld the man, he could see his eyes flailing wildly, left and right as he searched into the darkness, and he felt shock at the level of fear the man was obviously feeling, for now, his lip seemed to quiver and a small line of drool hung limply from the corner of his mouth.

In that one moment, it was all he could do, not to alleviate some of the man's pain by bringing back, at least some of the light. But he stood straight and took himself back into the darkness, where he could bear witness to Searle's descent into capitulation. Yes! For he had him now, didn't he? He couldn't have dreamed for such a reaction from the man, his plan, simple as it was, was brilliant and had deeply cut to the core of the man's psyche.

But as he watched on, he wondered if he had not been too successful. He paced around the circle of light and approached Searle from the front, making sure to hide himself in the darkness. Yes, it was as he had feared. The eyes that he now beheld seemingly held little shred of sanity, wild and roving as they were. The man that he had known and feared all these years was undoubtedly gone, given way to this pathetic whining wretch. For now, he could detect the soft moan that Searle uttered all the more.

Searle had met his greatest fear and it seemed that it had claimed him.

CHAPTER 34

This is no good!

Searle had seemingly gone to some private primal retreat in his mind to escape the fear that he now met. For McArthur could find little reason in the eyes that he looked into.

"Thomas? Can you hear me?" His voice reverberated through the high ceilings of the library and all at once he felt exposed, stood as he was in the sea of darkness; the island of light where he had marooned Searle now feeling like an escape that he too might share, such was the creeping fear that was beginning to rise in him.

He had little time to dwell on such things as he could see that his words had registered with Searle; his eyes quickly finding their focus as he snapped forward in his seat. Sanity had found him it seemed and he craned his head forward as if to distinguish the voice that he had heard.

McArthur simply stood there. Searle could not know it but now his eyes met his directly, and in them, he once again found his old fear. Those dead black eyes boring into him, causing him to freeze where he was.

Searle finally spoke. But it seemed not to him, but to his dread beast that he feared.

"So you have come to claim me at last! A deal made in darkness, to be kept in darkness? Ha! I am not yours yet! Come claim me if you will!"

McArthur began to open his mouth, to retort to this lunacy, some veiled threat on the tip of his lips when suddenly his blood ran cold. He stopped himself and held his breath. Had that been a footstep? A footstep behind him?

And as quickly as it came, it was quickly followed by another. There could be no doubting the sound in the quiet of the library. For suddenly all of his senses were attuned to the night. The storm it seemed was over, at least for now, for there was no other sound in the world but for his slow, ragged breath and that dull thud of a foot falling upon the wooden floor.

Slowly, ever so slowly, the foot fell again. And he instinctively knew that it came from the direction of the row of books directly behind him. He was instantly paralysed with fear, he could feel his scalp begin to freeze and his mind numb, his legs seemed as heavy as lead and rooted to the floor. And suddenly, the cold hit him. How could that be? Was the only coherent thought that his mind would allow him. This had been no incremental drop in the temperature; it had been instant.

But quickly there was another sound, Searle found his voice for he shrieked into the darkness. "Robert, quickly, the lights!"

But he found that he could not move, the remote control was lost to him in his fear, and he did not even know where he might find it. Slowly, slowly there was the renewed sound of footfalls behind him.

His panic was high now, and he felt the whisper of cold air on the back of his neck.

It comes. Searle was telling the truth, the Devil approaches!

There was no time to rationalise his thought, instinctively; intuitively, he knew it to be the truth. In that one moment, there could be no doubt; his fear all the evidence he needed.

He found what little of his strength that he had left and quickly found his pocket. Where was the damned remote control? He could make this go away; he could...

A hand clamped down on his shoulder and he screamed.

Hot wet liquid found the front of his trousers and in his state of terror, he could not even acknowledge what it might be as he wet himself. He screamed long and loud and all he could do was stare into the eyes of Searle, that had somehow lost their fear. The man simply looked resigned, resigned to his fate.

A voice spoke, and confusion took McArthur, his mind it seemed could not register events such was his fear, but the voice it seemed was almost recognisable.

"Robert, Robert, calm yourself man! Whatever is the matter? I didn't mean to give you such a start old boy!"

That voice! But it couldn't be. Slowly the hand on his shoulder shifted as the form came from behind him, the light was poor, but relief flooded him for it was only a man after all. A familiar man, for that voice had been...

"Well Robert, long time no see, how are you, old friend?"

The voice and the shadowed face that he now beheld were those of his former Captain and mentor William Chambers.

Relief flooded him instantly, his mind was a whirl, but all at once his fear and embarrassment disappeared and he welcomed the arrival of his old friend.

"William? My goodness, you scared the hell out of me! How the hell did you..." he began.

"It was Nancy; she asked me to come over and see you. She said that she was worried for you. I tried ringing through but it seemed the damned lines were down. Then I get here and find the place in damned darkness. Sorry for the scare old boy, but I didn't know what the hell was going on!"

"Nancy? Nancy called you?" McArthur replied. All other concerns evaporated, his thoughts now only of his ex-wife.

"Why yes Robert, you gave her quite a scare I can tell you, ringing her at all hours, not saying a word. She was worried for you, what with Jonathan and everything."

"Ringing her?" He questioned. Had he done that? Had he called Nancy? His mind was quickly trying to catch up.

"Yes Robert, she said that you had been drinking, that Jonathan's passing had affected you. Damn you man and your stubborn pride! If that was so, why didn't you call me instead? What could Nancy do for you all the way from America?"

"Robert, no, don't listen to it! It is not what it says it is. It is trying to trick you. Quickly now, the lights, send the beast back where it belongs, back to the shadow!" said Searle from his white prison.

"Oh?" replied Chambers sarcastically, slowly walking around the circle of light that spilt onto the floor "What do we have here eh? Sir Thomas Searle! You know I must confess Robert I did hear all from the shadows. I must apologise to you for bringing you to this. After all, was it not I who recommended you for the job? I knew this old bastard was hateful but I never believed it could be to such an extent. I think you have earned your compensation. I think he owes you that!"

"You think you can fool him with that voice devil!" Searle spat back at Chambers. "I hear you, I see you for what you really are! Robert! Look can you not see? Can you not see it for what it is?!"

"Shut up!" McArthur shouted back at Searle. Events had taken an unexpected turn, his mind seemed foggy and Searle's words somehow hurt his ears as he spoke them, as if the very sound of them was poison to his mind.

All in stark contrast to those of William Chambers. How or why he was here, McArthur did not know. But he knew that despite his initial fear, he welcomed the intrusion; that the words that he spoke promised justice for all that he had suffered.

Chambers continued to circle the entrapped Searle who never once took his eyes from the roving figure. McArthur could only remain where he was. His purpose momentarily lost to him. His mind a haze, for he did not know what to do next.

251

Chambers stopped in front of McArthur, obscuring his vision of Searle; he strained his eyes, for it seemed that to look at him hurt his eyes somehow. Finding solace in the floor, he asked: "What am I to do?"

"Oh Robert, you don't need to ask that of me! Have you not your plan? Are things not in motion? Why would you ask of me? You are a free man and as such, have the benefit of choice. You alone have put these events into being. It is for you to decide their outcome. But ask yourself this, do you not deserve your reward? Does Searle not deserve his comeuppance for all that he has put you through?"

McArthur nodded grimly, but Searle it seemed was not done yet.

"Robert no, I know I have done you wrong. I will gladly sign my money to you, but please, no more of this, please return the light and dispel this beast. I too hear its voice. For it is with the same voice that it spoke to me long ago. Speaking of free will and freedom of choice. I was put under its spell. It offered me my life but the price was too high. Do not deliver yourself to him as well!"

McArthur simply stood there, indecision plaguing him. It was Searle who acted next.

"Look Robert, look." And with that, he reached forward and took the pen from the stool and with a quick flourish, signed the paper that Robert had left there. "It is all yours Robert, all yours! Now please, the light!"

McArthur looked up slowly and beheld the two, Searle's eyes pleading with him, those of Chambers alive somehow, dark and terrible. It was time to choose. He stepped forward slowly, reaching out and taking the contract. There as expected was Searle's signature. The fortune, his compensation was finally his. Placing it into his top pocket, he turned and headed for the exit, his other hand reaching for the remote. Searle would have his light. After all, how ridiculous was his fear?

As he reached for the switches, Chambers was quick to interject.

"Wait Robert! Wait a minute. You would let him have this victory?"

This caused him to stop in his tracks. He turned slowly. In the darkened room, it seemed different somehow; Chambers' face seemed to hover in the darkness behind Searle. It seemed diminished somehow, fading into the shadows. McArthur blinked twice for it served as some form of illusion, for his head seemed detached, a floating free form, the body beneath seemingly evaporated. He guessed that it was just a trick of the light, but it seemed the man was fading back into the darkness from where he had come. And so it was, for quickly Chambers' face faded slowly into the background and was gone.

McArthur looked down and found his finger on the remote control; it was almost as if the threat of sudden light had dispelled the image somehow. But for now, his mind was tired and he bore it no heed. Later though he would have many hours, days, weeks and years to dwell on the happenings of this night.

He quickly toggled the row of switches and with the now familiar sound and blinking of the strip lights, the light in the library was returned once again.

He stood there, undecided. Looking up now, he saw Searle looking over expectantly at him and with that his other senses came back into play. He saw through the window that the rain did continue to fall after all, for the loud patter struck the windows with some force. The storm had not passed, for the night was lit brighter than ever with the coming of fresh lightning.

As the low rumble of thunder that followed quickly fell away, Searle spoke.

"Well done Robert, well done. The beast will not claim his prize tonight. You have played the game well and have been victorious. You have been a worthy adversary. You have continued to test and challenge me and at the last, you have bested me. Well played Sir, well played."

Well played? McArthur's mind raged at this comment as fresh anger exploded. "Well played? You think this has been a fucking game?! You have ruined me! You have taken my family, my pride and my life, and you think it was a fucking game!" He shouted toward the old man who was visibly shaken by his tirade.

But as quickly as it came it was gone, clarity came to his head and he smiled at Searle. "Oh, I guess you are right. Do I not have my compensation? Have I not bested you?"

Searle nodded vehemently for he must have realised that he had almost lost McArthur with his comment.

Now, with the savage light from outside spilling into the room, he could see that the old man looked wretched. His once youthful looks stripped away as pools of sweat ran from his brow. The shadows cast upon his face, making his wrinkles look deep; his eyes looked sallow and tired. He had beaten him after all. For there was nought but misery and failure written there.

But Robert McArthur was not finished yet for there was one more thing. One thing that plagued him.

"You really believe it, don't you?" Was all he said.

Searle looked puzzled and looked questioningly at McArthur and replied with a question of his own. "Do you not believe it Robert?"

McArthur paused and reflected on the night's events. Sure, things had been strange. But his plan had worked perfectly had it not? Searle's fear of the darkness had won through and because of that, he had signed his fortune through to him. Why would he believe it? The old man was undoubtedly crazy; there could be no doubt of that. Whatever he had been through on suffering his heart attack in this room had clearly affected his mental state to the point of madness. But why would he expect McArthur to follow suit?

Reason was quickly lost though as a picture came to his mind. The picture was that of his friend and mentor Captain Chambers disappearing into shadow. And with that thought came fear, because there was more to this than met the eye. Something had happened here tonight. But his mind could not grasp the missing pieces for just as understanding came close, it retreated and made his mind hurt to think on it.

McArthur looked over, long and hard at Searle. No, he did not believe. Slowly he raised the remote control in front of him. A smile came to his face and what happened next he would carry with him for the rest of his life.

Slowly he toggled the switches once more to the off position. Darkness instantly flooded the room, there was now only Searle, his chair and the spot of light upon the floor.

Searle screamed, "No! Robert, no!"

The events that played out before him then did so as if in slow motion. Lightning rent the sky and was followed by a terrible crash as if the sky itself was falling. In the scant second it took him to toggle the final switch and cast the room into darkness, he was sure that he again heard the heavy fall of a foot.

In the total dark now, he could hear Searle's screams for mercy, but he could not register them, for now, his fear and memory were back. He could not comprehend how the moments previously had been lost to him, how he could have forgotten the ghost-like appearance of a friend who had been in his grave for ten years. How he could have forgotten the fear that had crawled over his skin and how the beast had tried to sway his mind. And now, in that one final vengeful act, he had done as this devil had hoped.

Lightning continued to strike and the room became as if a montage of picture frames. Despite his fear he was reminded of the old-style peep shows that had been so popular during his youth. A collection of disjointed frames, playing out for the voyeuristic viewer. However, the scene on display before him was not one of any gratification. The frames seemed seconds apart. And within the light created by the lightning storm, he could only look on in horror as the form came from within the shelves of books that had tormented Searle for so many years.

His instinct had not warned him until the sight of the soldier lumbered into view, the sound had not been that of a soft shoe fall after all, but that of a heavy army boot instead. Despite the darkness, he sensed that the puttees of the soldier were blue. And when he looked back on events in years to come he convinced himself that this was the case. That this was the sergeant that Searle had described in his story.

And yes, he did believe. There could be no denying it now as the form made its way slowly from the shelves — a twisted look of pleasure on its face. McArthur could only be thankful the visions were fleeting for he beheld madness within the eyes of this being. And within that visage, he found the same look that Searle's statue in the courtyard portrayed. One of primal hate.

And despite himself, he was frozen. He knew that one flick of a button would dispel the creature, for now, a creature it surely was, as the terrible eyes became black and the jaw unhinged, creating a terrible void of sharp pointed teeth in the impossible space that had once been its mouth.

He could only stand and watch as the thing descended on Searle, finally though, mercifully, the lightning stopped. He could see no more. But the loud crash of thunder that followed was drowned out by the agonising scream that came from Searle as the beast fell upon him.

He didn't know how long he stood that way for. His fear was all-paralysing and he could not summon the strength to move. He longed for the light now for the slow, wet ripping sounds that emanated from the darkness painted far worse pictures in his mind that he felt his eyes could ever portray.

Searle had sold his soul to the Devil and had made him wait for collection. McArthur was in no doubt that the beast was savouring its meal. But that would be nothing compared to the eternity in hell that surely awaited him.

Finally, though, the noises began to subside and like a shot to his heart, a single recognisable voice came from the darkness. His son Jonathan.

"Thank you, daddy. I was so hungry."

What was left of his sanity must surely have left him as he sensed the dead thing that had been his son approach.

But as it approached, the voice twisted, became deeper, now that of Chambers again.

"You have done well tonight, very well. I have had to wait a very long time for this moment and I have you to thank. You have your reward and it is well earnt. But beware, as it has come at a high price. I spoke before of free will and you acted alone."

The voice that of his wife Nancy now, "You have sold this man to me; you did it of free mind. And as such, there is a high price indeed Robert."

The voice now, whispering into his ear, that of Sir Thomas Searle.

"I will see you again when the time is right."

Somewhere in the great house, Robert McArthur could hear the chime of the hour, midnight. And as the hand lay on his shoulder a second time he fainted, and this time there was escape in darkness for he knew no more that night.

CHAPTER 35

Tuesday, 10th November 2016. 11:55 pm.

Thoby Hall.

"So you see Father, I must be absolved!" McArthur pleaded, his voice but a hoarse whisper. His strength was all but gone as pain wracked his chest. The effort in finishing his story had been immense, but despite the sickness that raged deep within his core, he knew that there were still matters beyond his forgiveness to attend. The prognosis that had been delivered from the girl Melissa had been grim news indeed, but now was not the time to falter. First, there must be this absolution and then to somehow find new reserves of strength, for there was yet more he would ask of this Priest Fitzgerald before his death.

So he fought the darkness that clouded his vision, knowing that it was not some trick of the light, nor a ploy similar to his all those years ago.

Paraneoplastic retinopathy syndrome they called it. It held little meaning for McArthur but the root cause was plain enough, as were the symptoms. For through the fog, he could now only just make out the dull glow of the fluorescent lighting. Beyond that, little else got through.

"Robert, that is an incredible story. I do not know what to say." Father Fitzgerald finally managed, distracting McArthur from his thoughts.

"It matters not Father. Do you not hear my word of confession?"

"Yes Robert, although I cannot reason with the words you have spoken to me I do know that in your heart you are repentant for your sins. But..." the priest paused.

"Damn your sensibilities!" McArthur groaned. "What more would you have me say?"

"It...your story...you saw this thing? This apparition?"

"I did. Do not doubt my word. It is for you to show faith now Father and I understand how all I have said must be difficult to reconcile. I once thought as you do now. Thought Searle a fool; that his heart attack had somehow made him weak-minded and superstitious. But I saw with my own eyes the truth of it. You must believe also, Father."

Fitzgerald paused.

McArthur felt he could guess as to the man's thoughts; that he, McArthur was weak of mind and scared of his impending demise.

But the priest's next words were not born of disbelief; somewhere inside of himself, he had undoubtedly come to some level of understanding. Not yet enough by far, but certainly enough so that he could do his duty.

"I believe that you believe it, Robert and that in itself is enough. You have shown true repentance for your acts and I do truly believe you have suffered for what you have done. I have no hesitation in absolving you of your sin. What you did was wrong but anyone may have acted similarly in your position. Thomas Searle was an evil twisted man who in your words, sold himself to the Devil. Whether literally or metaphorically, it matters not. The debt he owed was always going to be collected. You are absolved. In the name of the Father, the Son and the Holy Ghost, I forgive you."

And with that, Robert McArthur finally knew relief. What had happened on that fateful night had haunted his every step for 37 years. He had not known rest or peace; only the same eternal light as Searle himself had found refuge in all those years ago. For the memories of that night and what hid in the dark places of the world had plagued him in both waking and sleep ever since. He had complained to Searle of the misery that he had to endure, but the simple truth had been that on his masters' death, he had also found such comfort in the light and though he had decreed he would smash every last damned strip light within the house, he had instead kept, maintained and improved upon them.

And so now, forgiven, he could finally welcome the coming darkness. So it was with surprise that he found the light growing stronger and that which he could see become more substantial.

"Oh my…"

Now the features of the young priest were becoming solid before him. It was as if looking through the viewfinder of an out of focus camera, the edges black, the centre hazy, but as with the slow rotation of a zoom lens, things were finally seen as they should be. It was as if a miracle, for his decline in the last few days had been vast as he neared his end. If so, then there was power in the words spoken of forgiveness, for the pain in his lungs, though not gone had diminished significantly. Is this what it was to be forgiven at the end? Had his time now come? Free of pain as he was of his sin?

But it was not the end, for there was no tunnel of light, no rising from his body. The quiet, dull pain a reminder he was still completely rooted to his bodily form.

"Robert? Are you okay?" Fitzgerald had risen from his chair and stood low before him, worry etched upon his face.

"I am…I am Father, thank you. I can scarce believe it, but I feel renewed somehow."

"Thus is the power of confession Robert. But are you sure you are okay? For a moment there I thought…"

McArthur nodded. Whatever had occurred had been noticed by the priest, and the change that had come over him was obviously not something Fitzgerald had expected. And though he would relish the change that had come over him, he still had more that he would ask of this priest.

"Your work is done Father and for that I thank you. I know the terms of our agreement were difficult for you, but I hope you understand now the reason that I asked what I did of you."

"I do, I know that time was of the essence. Might be I would have taken to it easier if it wasn't for that smug solicitor of yours."

McArthur smiled, knowing it was so. "He serves his purpose, but you have the right of it there Father. I see very little of his grandfather in him. A good man."

He continued. "I must ask of you though; for it wasn't only for you to be close to my hand that I asked of you to remain at Thoby Hall."

Suspicion crossed the priest's face in an instant. "Oh?"

"I must know Father and ask you, as Searle did me. Do you not believe it?"

Fitzgerald stepped back and sat once again in his chair. His eyes hard and unflinching, meeting those of McArthur.

McArthur continued, "do you not feel it's presence?"

Fitzgerald considered. The silence about them was tangible, the mood sombre.

"You would tell me it remains here still?" he answered at last.

McArthur nodded. "A shadow remains Father. I believe it waits on me."

What he said next would be critical. In truth, the priest had fulfilled his duty, all but last rites, but the terms of the contract had been met, the house and grounds of Thoby Hall would be passed over to the diocese as promised. What he now wanted of the priest he would ask of him voluntarily.

"Did you not wonder Father as what came next in my story?

"There is more?" Fitzgerald asked incredulously.

"Fear not. No, my confession is done I assure you. But there has been much, much more over the years that serve my assertion that the beast still remains. First, there was the matter of Searle and my fraud against him. How could I expect to have gotten away with such as I had?"

That piqued the young priest's interest he could see.

"My ploy had been simple but not thought through to all of its inevitable ends. For if Searle lived, could he not simply have reneged on the contract? So it is with that question I ask myself, did I really know what would happen once I dispelled the lights?"

"And so did you?" Fitzgerald replied.

McArthur considered for but a moment. "In truth? I do not know. My mind was fogged, and thinking had become difficult, such was my acceptance of Chambers' appearance. That was all but a game, a ruse by the beast and I know its goal was to confuse. So perhaps I could not have seen such an end for him, but in my heart, I think I expected something. Such was his fear; I hoped that something would happen. That his heart would give out, as it had tried those many years ago."

"And if it did not?"

McArthur was grim in his reply. "I know what you ask of me. Did I have murder in my mind? I cannot say… only that the lights would be enough…somehow."

"And it was, of course."

"Yes. But upon waking the next day, my first thought and fear was that I would be found out. The contract was post-dated and had been countersigned by his own solicitor Harvey, long before his death. It had been easy to cheat the man out of it, such was the level of dementia that would finally take him and then a simple task to place the document within Searle's safe. But that was not my fear; for when the papers were read, who would question his bequeathing of his fortune to me?"

"He had nobody else, of course." Fitzgerald filled the gap.

"Indeed. And so it was for the terrible and bloody death that I knew he had succumbed for which I feared discovery."

"Your beast…you say it fell upon him. Devoured him?"

"That is correct, Father. Those scant moments that I beheld in the storm were terrible, a brief window into a bloody and foul end. How could I hope to explain something away such as that?"

"What did you do?"

"I did nothing, Father. For you see when he was discovered there, it was not with the wounds that would be imprinted within my mind, for there were none. I was told that perhaps his eyes betrayed the terror he felt, but there were no visible injuries. The coroner passing a simple verdict; that Searle had suffered a major heart attack. And with his history? The knowledge of his smoking and drinking? It was easy to accept and so Searle's fortune came to me without question. I had won."

"That's well and good Robert, but I don't understand how that relates to the here and now. You say the creature remains yet? How does any of what you say fit in? After all, had the thing not won its prize?"

"Patience, please. I was coming to that. For one, Searle's body being found as it was, was a relief to me. Don't you see? It was easier for me to negate all that I had experienced that night. To put it to the back of my mind and tell myself it was some hallucination of some kind. And so the library was locked away for good at my decree. What was out of sight was out of mind, but somehow it lingered still and I believe I know for why. But in the long years that followed and as tragedy followed tragedy, I lied to myself, cursing our god above for such foul luck and circumstance, not admitting to myself the true course of such horrors."

"This thing?"

"Yes! Don't you see? My Elizabeth? Crosby? That poor drowned girl? And more, for there are matters here at Thoby Hall of which you do not yet know."

Fitzgerald shook his head as if to negate all that he heard. McArthur knew he was losing him. His story was incredible, it was true, but somehow he needed to reach this priest, for him to hear the truth in his words. Because if not, how could he be expected to submit to McArthur's as yet unasked request? The man must believe, it was imperative; he must believe or he was doomed to the same fate that met Crosby all those years previously.

"Look about yourself, Father. You have only been here but a few short days, but have you not felt some of what I say to you?"

A look crossed the priest's face. McArthur could see it. Yes, there was something there wasn't there? But what? What had he experienced? For if he could tap into the other man's fears and give them substance, perhaps then he might believe.

Slowly Robert, slowly. Don't push him away.

It was good advice; advice which he wished he had heeded all those long years ago when Elizabeth had come to him with the same haunted look within her eyes. At the time, he had believed her to be hysterical; such was the weight of loss she had experienced at the young girl's death. But that had not been fair to her, for he knew in his heart the source of her troubles and the things that she believed she saw within the house. His denials not only to her but to himself had been monumental and had oh so nearly cost her life. In any event, he lost her anyway and all for his pig-headedness and desperate need to keep his head in the sand; denying what he knew dwelt within the walls of his home.

But with Elizabeth's loss, there had been little else to live and hope for. What dwelled in the library became forgotten and ignored once more, and though he took the hand of another in marriage some 3 years after Elizabeth's breakdown, it had not been the same. He shared no love with this interloper who cared only for his money and status. For her, it had not taken a tragedy or the creeping horrors of the Hall to subjugate her, no. For the gold-digging little cunt had scarce begun their married life before she was suing him for divorce on the grounds of mental cruelty and in so doing, robbed him of half his fortune.

Focus Robert.

The memories were difficult; it was true, for the look in the priest's eyes brought back everything that he had seen in Elizabeth and thereafter his failing of her. Perhaps with this one final act, he could hope to make good some of the wrong he had done her. He had gained absolution, could he also hope to find redemption? And if so, then how to proceed? How to win the priest over to his way of thinking?

He knew at least to proceed carefully, as to try and press the man's buttons and unmask his fear might cause him to withdraw. So, then another way…

"You have observed the pagan sigils have you not Father?"

Fitzgerald looked blankly back at the old man.

"The sigils Father? At the front of the house? Upon the threshold both inside and out?"

Fitzgerald slowly started to nod. "Yes, yes of course, but what of them?"

"Hard to miss, aren't they?" he smiled. "Those and many other such symbols of power adorn this house. All remnants of the prior household. As well as the sigils, there are many more wards and spells, all cast long ago."

"Oh?"

"You may have taken care to analyse the story of Thomas Searle, Father. Goodness knows I did in the aftermath of what occurred there in the library. On the day he first recanted his tale to me, I did not take heed, and why should I? Were they not the rantings of a lunatic? That, or the articulation of his fears, now that he felt death's cold hand come close? So no, I paid his story no mind. Not until after the night he finally died that was, for try as I might I could not forget what I saw. You have heard me say, I took solace in the same light as Searle and for good reason, for my night terrors were fierce I can tell you, but still, I did my utmost to distance myself from the truth. It was only after Elizabeth was taken from me that I finally had to address what it was that she would say to me; that which I already knew. That the beast remained still."

"What was it that she told you?" Fitzgerald asked of him.

"You will think me a monster Father, for how could I not have seen her unravelling before my eyes when she told me that she had found her way there into the library. My heart near but failed me with such news and all my old demons came back to the fore. But I digress, Elizabeth's descent had been almost total. I employed the best doctor's my money might buy, beyond that counsellors and medication played their parts also. But none seemed to reach her. Believe it or not, it was that cursed room that gave her new purpose and rejuvenated her."

"The library? Are you kidding me? With all that you have told me of it?"

"Yes, Father and I allowed it, for I saw her coming back to me; to her old self, such was her passion. For when she explained I saw no danger in what she was doing."

"And what was that?"

"The books, Father. Searle's old books and documents. For all the long years between his first heart attack and discovering his 'truth' and the day I committed him to darkness he collected and poured over these tomes to find ways to prevent deliverance from the fate, the beast had promised him. Elizabeth became as he did. Obsessed, and with it she sank under the weight of her knowledge, and she saw the touch of the occult all about the house."

"The pagan sigils?"

"Yes, Father, and more. She told me of spells and wards of keeping and imprisonment. She didn't know why they were cast as I did, but don't you see? When the beast came for Searle on that night of his heart attack, it was beaten back somehow, trapped between light and dark. Searle kept it at bay by lighting the house into a bloody beacon that might reach the heavens! But of course, there was more. All those nights in the library, me at his beck and call; he was pouring over the same volumes, trying to find ways to beat the inevitable."

Fitzgerald nodded his understanding. "So you believe he commissioned these symbols of power as a means to defeat this thing?"

"I do. But in truth, he knew he was not successful. He was tortured by the one shadow that he could not dispel and so instead of trying to be rid of it, he thought instead to capture and imprison it!"

"But you allowed Elizabeth to buy into this madness?" Fitzgerald accused.

"Do not be so quick to judge a man until you have taken a step in his shoes Father. After the loss of that little girl, I had lost Elizabeth, and for all my money and love, I could do nothing to bring her back to me. Somehow, she found salvation among those books and my heart sang! Of course, I allowed it; welcomed it even, for it gave her a connection to that lost little girl somehow. But I was wrong wasn't I? For what came after with Crosby nearly destroyed her and it is for that you must open your eyes and see, for it was not just for Searle and me that this thing existed, it very much existed for Elizabeth as well, and through her Crosby. You would be wise to see all that this thing has touched and tainted before you casually dismiss the idea of its existence."

"But for why, Robert? Why would you have me believe at all? Are you not free now, absolved of your sin?"

"I am Father, but it is not only for me that I ask this of you. I do so for Elizabeth and every other poor soul this malignant beast has touched the lives of. I want you to be rid of it,

Father, once and for all. To do as Crosby could not and exorcise this demon and to do that I ask that you believe so that you do not fail where he did."

CHAPTER 36

Fitzgerald found himself in the sitting room of McArthur's apartment. His mind was clouded, and he was surprised to find himself looking upon Keira, who raised herself quickly from the sofa, a concerned look upon her face.

"Goodness Father are you okay?"

The words barely registered with him, and though he parted his lips, only a soft breath emanated. McArthur's story had left him bewildered. All along it had been building to this; exorcism.

McArthur had hidden it well initially, buried deep in his story regarding Thomas Searle. No hint at first in the man's tale that he, McArthur, bought into the madness of Searle, but all the time planting the seed and watching it grow inside of the young priest.

McArthur had also suggested that he had needed to come to the truth himself and had he now done so? For here finally was confirmation from McArthur's own lips that he had seen the said demon himself and now believed that it waited on him. And as he thought on this, Keira ignored, other parts of McArthur's plan were realised, for why else had he been contracted to remain in this damnable house to take last confession?

His thoughts, though were interrupted as Keira stepped before him. Her worry evident in her eyes, her perfume close, compelling and seductive and drawing him back to the real world.

"Father?" She repeated.

His eyes focused at last upon her brilliant green eyes and recognition came to him. "Keira?"

"Are you okay? You look as white as a sheet." Keira continued.

From out of nowhere, he felt the weight of all he had experienced come upon him in one. All the years of tension, anxiety and depression that resonated within the house were all piled upon his shoulders. It was all too much to bear, and tears came quickly to his eyes.

"Can it be true Keira?" Was all he could manage. He dabbed quickly at his eyes with his sleeve, loath to show this girl his weakness and surprised that he had been brought to such misery by all that he had seen and learned. Keira, perhaps fearing he was ready to collapse quickly came to his side and put an arm around his waist and led him to the sofa where she had been sitting. She let him fall softly before sitting next to him. She drew herself closer and produced a handkerchief from her top pocket which she gave to him.

He felt foolish for his reaction, the tears were already drying, but here now was Keira reaching out and rubbing his arm in comfort and he felt a familiar tingling in his loins for her.

"Thank you, Keira, I don't know what came over me."

"I think I might have an idea, Father. You are exhausted; you only have to look at you."

He nodded his agreement. He was indeed tired but knew well it was mental exhaustion more than physical. He was tested, and his faith was tested. Still, he wrestled with the impossible. Everything he knew and believed conflicted with the evidence before him. McArthur would have him exorcise a demon as Crosby had tried and failed to do before. But how could he if he constantly fought with what was real and what was not? He knew well that Catholic mandate decreed he must believe in such a devil if he was to exorcise it.

If that wasn't enough, he knew well that he did not currently have the mental strength and fortitude to undertake such a challenge. For him, the passages in the Bible that spoke directly of the physical incarnate of the Devil were but a metaphor for the evil that was within one man's being. So, the idea that here and now all of these beliefs were being challenged and that he must try and accept the reality of true darkness in the house were almost too much for him to bear.

"Thank you, Keira. I feel better already." He lied.

She surprised him then as she leaned over and gave him a hug, her full breasts pressing upon his arm, such was his sideways angle toward her. She quickly got up, and he was glad that she did not look upon his face, lest she saw the feelings that she brought up in him. He felt vulnerable and open all at once and the wrong gesture or word from him could lead to the truth of his feelings come spilling out.

She disappeared into what was the pharmacy and returned shortly holding what appeared to be a small plastic vial with a screw-top lid. She held her palm out to him and he could see within two small white pills. He looked up into her eyes, uncertain.

"Sleeping pills."

He nodded dozily, and reached out for what was offered, simply glad for the kindness that she had shown him. Reaching for the pills, he felt a light sensual touch as one of her fingers lifted and stroked his palm as he took them from her. Instinctively he looked to her eyes, to see if there was any recognition of what she had done. But no, she sat herself down opposite him again, this time at a safer distance he noted with some regret.

"They are very fast-acting Father, so not to be taken until you are ready for sleep, do you understand?"

He was ready now he thought, but already this simple human interaction had helped ease his mind. His senses now were alive to what signals Keira might give as opposed to his previous crisis of faith.

"Yes, and thank you."

"They will do the trick. Between you and me? I can't sleep without them." She smiled and gave him a quick wink.

Is she serious? He couldn't read her, that was the truth, and he had far too much on his mind than to worry if Keira was self-prescribing medication for herself. Wouldn't there be a register or something? Melissa would know, wouldn't she if stocks were low? Well, they were about to be by two pills and he wondered if she might doctor McArthur's records to show she had administered the pills to him instead.

Now though Keira continued. "Father, I know what is said in there is between only the two of you. But should you need me...to talk to that is, you know where to find me?"

"I'm grateful, Keira. The truth is it is more than what I heard in there." A thought then struck him. "Tell me Keira, what do you think of this house?"

Her brow furrowed, and he could see worry in her eyes.

"It's okay. Please tell me."

"Well I...I don't like it if that is what you mean. An old house like this and only that unconscious man to keep me company during the long hours?" She shifted, ever so slightly closer to him as she said this. He did not allow his eyes to flinch, though as he held her eyes.

"Have you seen anything, anything unusual?"

She looked at him, confused, and he sensed he was being too vague with her. Neither one knew the other very well, and he did not trust her enough as yet to impart what he knew of the house and his experiences within it. And that being the case, why should she trust him with the same?

"Seen anything?"

"Oh I don't know, perhaps around the library?"

There it was, he had put it out there as subtly as he could, hoping that she would not sense the need in his question. For whatever else he had learned so far, the one thing that did not sit right with him was regarding his own experiences at the library door. That, coupled with McArthur's tale of what might lie within...

As to what he had felt, he had believed it to be the nurse Melissa, playing some game with him. But the fact remained he had not seen her and could not prove her involvement, no matter how hard he wanted to. But where did such an idea sit now? What with McArthur's story? And with these thoughts came the memory of the forlorn, ancient voice whispering his name…

Fitzgerald.

With that thought came another, the mysterious figure that he had seen at the window on the day of his arrival. Nothing sat right, for he knew well that Hodgson had seen as he did.

She denied it, though, didn't she? Said no one had access.

True. But there had been something in the way she had said it, something in the way she looked. Could it be that Hodgson was party somehow to what was going on? Whether McArthur's story be fraud or real, could she know the answers?

But in the here and now, he hoped that Keira might have answers of her own, after all, she had spent much more time in the house than he. What might she have seen or experienced? And if she had a story to impart then what side of the scale would the balance fall? To the rational? Of which he tentatively still clung to. Or the irrational? And McArthur's monster.

He knew that he needed it to be the simpler of the two and her answer now could go some long way to restoring his crumbling sanity, for if his ill experiences of the room could be explained, then surely he could regain his mind and see the rest of it for what it really was, the delusional rantings of a dying man.

The look in her eyes gave it away before she spoke. Here was the haunted look that he had seen thus far in those who had shared their story with him; McArthur, Douglas, and the evasive Hodgson.

So it was with surprise he received her words, for they belied what the eyes had already given away.

"The library Father? What do you mean? The library is shut off, you know. I was told it is dangerous in there and that is why they are doing the building work on the outside."

"Keira, please. I must know if you have seen anything, be it the house or more specifically the library. I…I cannot say too much; my vows preclude me. But something holds this house, be it an energy or something more tangible. A dark energy that seeps into your very soul if you let it."

She nodded her head. "If that is what you ask of me, then yes I can feel it to. But this place is old Father and beset with a sombre mood that heralds from Mr McArthur's illness and descent towards death. It is easy to feel it, I am afraid. Melissa feels it; I feel it. Is that what you speak of?"

"I do. But I mean something more…I…"

"Yes, you do." Keira interrupted. "It is plain to see the misery it has brought you. You are exhausted Father, what you need is rest. Rest and perhaps a diversion from all the sadness that surrounds you."

"Perhaps…but."

She shook her head, negating any argument he might have. He looked long into her eyes, but she held his gaze without wavering.

"No buts about it." She reached out and took his hand, uncurling his fingers from the medication she had given him. "Here is the peace you need. Sleep, and in the morning, everything will look different. I promise you."

Keira controlled this conversation now, and he had not the strength or courage to challenge her. He could not press this further he knew, at least not at this time.

"Perhaps you are right. Maybe I'm just letting my imagination run away from me. Forget I said anything, huh? I guess I feel the same way rattling around that east wing all by myself at night. It is not a nice house…" His words drifted off and he saw a shine in her eyes, perhaps one of understanding. Whatever her motivations he could believe her in part, for to be up here all night alone was undoubtedly a stressful and lonely experience.

"Perhaps I should come and keep you company then Father?" Again that wry smile, but Fitzgerald was too tired to read any meaning in it. He got up.

"Best I get back I think Keira." He rattled the pills in the palm of his hand. "I think my bed calls me."

"Of course Father and remember what I said, if you should ever need to talk…"

He nodded at her. Grateful at least for the kind gesture of pills and conversation she had offered. He left the room and entered the corridor. He looked down at the pills in his hand and dropped them one by one into his mouth. If they were quick working, he meant to sleep as soon as he returned to his rooms.

They were sour in his mouth, and he gulped several times before he was able to produce enough saliva to swallow them both whole. Satisfied he walked off once more to the anteroom where he must follow the path back to his room. This time though his mind remained blank as he walked by the door, with not a care for what lay beyond. For now, the only thing he desired was a long dreamless sleep.

CHAPTER 37

Drowsiness had begun to overwhelm him by the time he made, what he had dubbed 'the serpent staircase'. His eyelids were heavy and made long languid motions as he blinked. Whatever Keira had given him was indeed very powerful. He was determined though that he would not be found asleep somewhere en route back to his rooms, curled up with only the warmth of one of the ornate rugs that were scattered throughout the house.

At last, making his apartment door, he all but crashed into it, using it to prop his weight up as he scrambled in his pocket for the key. His mind was now close to shutting down and he felt sleep tug at him as might the calming deep blue waters of an ocean to an exhausted swimmer; out too far, swept out by the current with no energy to make the shore. He was going under and like that figurative swimmer, he snapped back to waking, knowing he had to go on before the inevitable.

He pawed and missed the lock several times with the key, and he knew if he was careless enough to drop the key, he might not have the energy to go down, collect it and get back up again. Mercifully though the key and lock connected on the third attempt and he fell through the door, unknowingly leaving it open behind him.

Although the connecting door to the bedroom was open, it seemed as if miles away and his eyes narrowed on the couch before him. Without even taking time to walk around, he pitched forward over the armrest and his head hit the soft cushion. If he had been able to see it happen, he would have marvelled that it was possible 'to be asleep before your head touched the pillow' but that was exactly as it happened to him.

And so, he slept, all time lost to him.

Dreams came to him, but held no distinct forms. Leaving only raw emotions as evidence that they had ever been; fear, sadness and most overwhelming the bitter feeling of loneliness.

He was cold and alone, somewhere deep and dark inside of his own fragile being, but something came over him suddenly for where there had been cold, he now felt warmth, and instead of feeling alone he felt the presence of some being, elusive yet near, whispering comfort into his ears.

Grateful and happy at the intervention, he now welcomed the darkness that surrounded him for it no longer held any fears. No demons and no memories of loss or hurt. It enveloped him and he was at peace.

When waking finally threatened to intrude, he fought against it as he had found a place in slumber that the real world had not held for him since he was but an infant. This intrusion though was physical and could not be denied. His arm thrashed as some light touch caressed the hair on his head and whispered soft comforts to his ears. The voice was familiar, but far away. It reached him as though whispered on the breeze. Its soft tones soothed him, and he knew that the same voice had guarded him against dark dreams.

However, the soft touch that met his brow felt heavy somehow. Real. And that connection he knew was an intervention from outside of his sleep and it threatened to pull him to the surface of the waters he had now gratefully succumbed to.

He thrashed with his hand again and connected with something solid. Something outside and so he retreated from it, twisting in his sleep to find distance and keep the thing which threatened waking at bay.

But his action caused something to happen. He felt a weight aside of him and the voice, once so soft and distant, was now so close and loud as if shouted down to reach him deep in his wonderful sleep.

"There now, it is all okay. It is just a bad dream."

But it wasn't. It had been bliss until the intrusion and whatever sought to comfort him, only served to agitate and bring him closer to the surface of waking.

He was powerless though for the physical touch on his brow was to real a thing. Slowly his eyes opened, and he made the unwelcome surface of the real world.

He was on the sofa, covered in a thick blanket which he had no memory of having brought with him. The light in the room was low. How long had he been asleep for? Hours? Minutes? He could not tell, but what was clear, was that the light in the room spilled in through from the open bedroom door and the source was undoubtedly the spotlights from outside. Everything was a blur. He did not remember how he had gotten to be here. The last thing he remembered was…

Keira. She was here before him, knelt down low on the floor before him and caressing his hair. His mind was jumbled; the fog of sleep that clouded his mind not yet parted, and so he closed his eyes and let the comforting strokes continue. It wouldn't be long, he knew from somewhere deep within, that this would have to come to a stop. That there was some inherent wrong with what was happening, but for now that understanding failed to reach him and he was glad, because the peace he had found in sleep still lingered on after waking.

And so, for now, he gave in to the sweet caress and watched as if from afar as his own hand reached from under the blanket and took hers. Their eyes met and he saw he had surprised her. She did not take her hand away though and somewhere deep down; he knew that if she had, this peace would be shattered. Instead, she leaned in and before he knew it, he closed his eyes and waited for the sweet touch of her lips upon his. He drew her close with his other arm and raised himself against the side of the chair so as to free his arm that held her hand.

Their tongues met, and electricity passed between them. His hand was now free to search and touch her face and hair. Their kiss took his breath away and he withdrew to look deep into her eyes. She was beautiful and his passion for her had made him hard. He saw nothing of the Keira he had known in the last few days, flirtatious, overtly sexual. Here and now she wore no mask, she was vulnerable and afraid.

She held his hand and pulled gently on it. He yielded without hesitation and allowed her to lead him to the bedroom, where they came to stand above the expansive bed. Their passion overcame them instantly, and their mouths entwined again.

He was within the moment, and he banished the feelings of inadequacy that threatened to taint their intimacy. She reached down and held him through his robe and he gasped at her touch. It had been so long since he had been here and in his mind's eye, he saw the face of his lost love Emma. She had been his first.

The two of them had been social and sexual beginners. Experimenting, discovering one another's bodies. Their love a real thing for such a short window of time. But with her gone, his doubt and pain returned to him in all of his following lovers, as he tried in vain to recapture what was missing since Emma's departure and wondering why sex without love left him feeling so hollow inside.

But here and now he was rejuvenated, his passion reignited. This was not love he knew but a more primal need. He could see it in her as well for his touch enlivened her as he caressed the swell of her breasts through her tunic.

She stepped back from him, and he waited. He ached to go to her straightaway but instead, he watched as she unbuttoned her top and quickly discarded it. The tunic had been all the clothes she wore to cover herself and his heart raced as he beheld her in the black of her panties and her bra. He went to her and they embraced, her breasts pressing hard into his chest as they kissed again. They were hungry for one another now and she ripped the collar from his own black shirt and hurriedly started on the buttons of his trousers as he dealt with his shirt. As he clawed the shirt from his chest, she took him in her mouth and he gasped in pleasure.

Now all manner of thoughts pressed him, though he bade them disappear.

He reached out and stroked her hair as she pleasured him. Their eyes meeting and seeing the life and energy in hers made his heart want to explode. He touched her on the shoulders and lifted her gently bringing her to her feet. Hooking his fingers beneath the straps of her bra, he exposed her breasts and brought his tongue down to the nipple as he caressed the other with his finger. She groaned with pleasure with his every movement and soon they took each other down to the mattress. Their lovemaking was frantic and passionate; their combined loneliness lost for the moment when they came together as one.

Every touch, every caress was like fire, so alive they were to one another's affections. When he entered her, it was quick, though he willed himself to last longer. But even then they found their pleasure together and he collapsed to her side, ecstasy still rich in his blood. Their bodies glistened with sweat, and she drew close to him, her leg draped over his, her bosom pressed tightly against him. He could feel the stirring of arousal already, but knew such a thing would not happen again. He hated himself for the thought as he looked upon her, her head rising and falling on his chest with every breath that he took.

Here now was the guilt as expected. He had allowed himself this 'out of body experience' (as he wanted to consider it) his body's needs supplicating rational thought and oh how he had been so glad to let that happen.

But what now? He was no fool; he knew well that this was the coming together of two persons who cried out for the warmth and companionship of another, nothing more. There was no love, only lust for him; and what for her? He didn't know, for he did not consider himself a handsome man, plain perhaps, average. Not the sort of person who would ever be seen walking arm in arm with one such as her, no. But it was more than that, such a union in circumstances such as these was wrong and what if word somehow got out?

He willed his mind to be quiet. These were thoughts for a later hour. He had needed this, and so to had Keira.

She looked up at him as if reading his mind.

"I made good on my offer to keep you company," she smiled.

He planted a kiss squarely on her forehead. "You did, indeed." He stretched his arms wide. He felt so relaxed. Sleep was coming again soon he knew, but it would revitalise him as the lovemaking had. He reached down and took her in his arms again and held her close. Whatever the ramifications later, he did not care. For now, he did not want to let her go. Her closeness soothed and comforted him and all other troubles had retreated beyond reach.

"May I ask you something?" Iain looked down and met Keira's gentle eyes.

"Of course."

She shifted out from his embrace and lay beside him, propped on one elbow as the other hand gently caressed his chest.

"Who is Emma?"

For a moment he was lost, and could make no sense of her question. Keira likely saw the confusion in his eyes, for she went further, "in your sleep, you were having a bad dream and then you said her name; Emma."

Fitzgerald searched his memory and found nothing, the moments before they had made love were now gone.

"I did?" He questioned. "I'm sorry Keira, I didn't mean to…"

"It's okay Iain, I only ask as it seemed to upset you. I was curious that was all."

He closed his eyes and allowed the vision of his first love to come to his mind. Slowly, a smile broke on his face and he nodded. "Emma, was my girlfriend," he began, "long before I became a priest."

Keira arched an eyebrow. "I don't mean to pry…"

"It's okay." He paused, thinking how much he could share of her. The memories of their time were buried deep inside of him, and often only surfaced in times of depression, where he would dwell on guilt and relive those times in his mind when he should have turned her from her path. And yet there were those times she came to him in his dreams, many of which brought him only peace and happiness, for in those times she took the loneliness of his being away, and in waking from such moments he lamented her loss and wished he could stay within such dreams forever. But here in Thoby Hall, there had been only nightmares.

"I don't know where to begin. It's difficult, but I guess the real reason I am here is because of her."

Keira laid her head back down upon his chest. "Tell me."

Gathering his thoughts, he knew he should be open about her…open about himself and his part.

"I lost her to addiction 15 years ago. God, can it be that long? I guess you could describe us as kindred spirits, we were both lost in this world you see. Lonely and afraid, until that was we found one another."

"You lost her? I'm sorry Iain, what happened?"

"It was a different time and a different me. I was alone and introvert, and she brought me slowly out of my shell. I don't know what would have become of me if not for her. I thought her to be the mirror opposite at first, as she seemed so free spirited. It was only later I found out she had the same insecurities. It was how she surpassed those issues and faced the world that ultimately brought her down."

"Addiction?"

He nodded, and Keira's head raised and fell on his chest as he did so.

"At first it was cocaine. I was blind to it at first. Her moods would catapult between depression to euphoria and back down again. When she was high, she was a live wire and would do the craziest things. But always the crash, the crash back down to her despair. She couldn't mask that from me. In the end, I joined her, I wanted to reach the same highs as her, and show her I could embrace life, I thought to do so, might prevent her inevitable fall each and every time, and so I used, and we would prolong the inevitable as long as we could. And I dreaded the crash, for the higher and longer we went, the harder the fall would be."

"That's so sad."

"I don't want you to think that was all there was. Perhaps in the end, but before that she seemed to embrace life, we would party and dance long into the night, and then afterwards we would talk until the sun came up. She was passionate about so many things, she…"

An old memory suddenly filled his mind, and in his surprise he let out a soft laugh.

Keira smiled in response as she looked back up at him. "What is it?"

"I just remembered something, it was so silly, and yet we almost split up over it."

Keira's smile remained and she kept silent, waiting for him to tell the story.

"You know the film, The Mutiny on the Bounty?"

"Vaguely."

"I remember we were at our place in Colchester. Just a lazy Sunday afternoon, sprawled out in front of the TV. We were about an hour or so in when she asked me which of the two characters I identified with the most. Captain Bligh or Fletcher Christian. I didn't hesitate in choosing the former. You see it was all set on a true story. The Bounty's journey was beset by problems and they had to take port in Tahiti for four months, where the crew became lax and discipline was forgotten. Anyway, Bligh was a hard taskmaster on the men, and the mutiny came on the return voyage home. Bligh and many of his officers were put to sea in a longboat with minimal supplies. Miraculously Bligh managed to navigate them to safety, without any navigational aids. "

"That's right," Keira said, "I remember it now."

"It was for those reasons I identified with Bligh, as he saved those men on the longboat, and tried to instil a necessary discipline on a crew that would be months at sea."

"Let me guess, your Emma thought otherwise?"

"She did. She called me an authoritarian, and said she sided with Christian and being a free spirit. I didn't help the argument when I suggested that the mutineers actually kidnapped the Tahitian women who they would make their homes with on Pitcairn Island."

"Typical man." Keira dug him playfully in the ribs. "Ruin a good argument by introducing evidence into the equation."

"Well, I don't know if it was true or not, I just introduced it to tip the balance in my favour. I only tell you to show you how passionate she was, I thought I'd actually lost her as a result! She didn't talk to me for days afterward."

"I think I would have liked her."

Fitzgerald agreed. "I think so to."

They lay quiet for a few moments. Fitzgerald for his part remembering his past with his former love. Keira to, seemed to dwell on the subject for she soon asked.

"What became of her?" And when seeing the pain in his eyes, she leaned in closely and kissed his lips. "It's okay," she whispered.

"She turned from the cocaine, to heroin and I followed willingly. As I said, I would have done anything with her or for her and I wanted to show her I was with her in everything. But I wasn't… I couldn't be, for it was only then, in the lowest moments of her addiction that I learned what it was that she was escaping from. The abuse her father had subjected her to as a child. And though I used, I could never share what she was going through and I was distraught, so I instead came out of it and pleaded with her to do the same, but it was too late, she either would not or could not."

"And so you lost her."

He was silent.

"Oh Iain, I am so sorry."

"There's more Keira, I said I would not be where I was today without her? Well that's only half the truth, because I was lost without her…I…"

He hadn't intended the conversation to go this far, but he knew he must go on and tell all of it. This interlude with Keira, had been more than just the dispelling of loneliness, it had served to unburden him of his repressed emotions, and guilt.

"Go on Iain, please."

He nodded. "As I say, I was lost without her…" tears formed in his eyes. "I don't know if I meant it to happen or not, but I overdosed. It was years later and I used again to bring me back close to her, and I nearly died. I should have died, because there was no place for me alone in the world at that time. I was at my end, and though I didn't know if I truly meant to die, there was comfort in the idea during my recovery, and all I could think of was how I wanted to die and be with her. That's when I found the Church."

Keira's attentive eyes bid him to continue.

"I was at my lowest point and without realising it, all of my long walks took me past the Church of St Mark's in Colchester. I don't think I saw it the first dozen times, but then I did, and it took me another dozen passes before I had the courage to walk in."

"And you found God? You found your calling?"

275

"No, it wasn't like that. I found Father Daniels. He counselled me and led me through confession. It wasn't God I found, it was Father Daniels. He forgave me my sins, and through him I found the power of God, for though there was no intervention from the heavens, I found the Lord's love and forgiveness through one of his servants and realised it is through us that he works in this world, and I believed I could act in the same way, that through me I could make the world a better place. I got clean, I served the church of St Mark's as a volunteer and so began my journey to where you find me today."

"But can such a thing happen?"

He knew her meaning. A former drug user being accepted into the sacrament of holy orders as a priest.

"There are others who have followed a similar path. I had my doubts, but Father Daniels stood by me through it all. With everything I went through with Emma, I never came into contact with the police…so no record to disclose, but I had to be open with them about my past, and confront my own addiction, for that is what it was. I didn't see that without Father Daniels's help, simply believing I only used to bring me closer to Emma."

"I guess she was part of your addiction?"

"Yes." His voice was low. "She went with me everywhere, and it was so hard letting her go."

"Your Father Daniels, sounds like a remarkable man."

"He is. I owe him everything."

"Thank you Iain, thank you for sharing."

"No, thank you Keira. I don't know what it is about you, but I feel I can be open and honest with you. This place has tested me, but being with you…"

"I know Iain, I feel the same way."

She lowered her head again to his chest, and he allowed his head to fall back to the pillow.

Content. Yes, that was the word and if he could only stay here with her forever, then everything would be well. He watched as she drifted into unconsciousness and gently sought the duvet that had been kicked to the bottom of the bed. The chill of the night pressed close now and watched as she shivered. He ached for her all the more and so spooned in behind her to keep her touch and scent close and he soon followed her into unconsciousness.

CHAPTER 38

Slowly, slowly, he rose to the summit of waking. This time though he did not resist for there was something there that begged acknowledgement. It wasn't the form of the person that lay close, the warmth of her skin and the beat of her heart a reassuring constant. No, something beyond that. Something real.

Wherever the depths of his sleep had taken him had been dark and comforting, but now a bright red hue hung behind his eyelids and he raised his arm over his eyes to shadow them from the intruding light beyond. But all to no avail for whatever the source he could find no respite.

In an instant, he was alive and awake to the world and sat bolt upright in bed. Something had moved. He looked down to his side and saw that Keira still slept on, her breath light, her beauty magnified as her face wore not the guarded defences of life. He felt the cold above the covers immediately and soon saw both the source of the movement and the light that had been behind his eyes, for the curtains of the room had been drawn back allowing the glare of the outside spotlights to intrude within the room once more. He was relieved in an instant though, when he saw the curtain that had been drawn back flutter in the night breeze, for surely that had been the movement that he had detected and that had woken him.

He looked down again at Keira. Dead to the world, which surprised him because the thick curtains had been drawn when they made love. He guessed that she must have woken before him and gone to the window to let the light shine within.

Night terrors?

Perhaps so and he had suffered them himself. She had admitted to the feeling of loneliness while on the long shifts, and he wondered if she also took comfort in the light as he had done on several of his nights here. Perhaps it was true, he thought. Maybe they do ward off evil spirits.

The curtain continued to flutter, and though he could not see it, he knew the window behind to be open. Perhaps she had been hot also? That seemed unlikely and only a small moment in the chilly November night would be enough to remedy that problem, so why open the window at all?

He frowned down at her, irritation coming to the surface as he also saw by the light of the room that his phone told him it was 03:05 am. He was now very wide awake. He felt rejuvenated yes, but the morning was hours away and the irritation that he felt was the fact that he knew she would sleep on without interruption.

It dawned on him then that there might be recriminations for their actions. Keira had undoubtedly passed McArthur's care on to Melissa the previous evening, before making her way to him on the east wing. But what if she slept through? He did not know at what time the two nurses exchanged duties. However, there would be the other members of staff beginning their day in only a few short hours and so he thought to wake her at once, though he was reluctant to trouble that pure, simple sleep she so desperately looked like she needed.

The curtain billowed again and muttering under his breath, he climbed naked from the bed and crossed the short expanse of carpet to reach the window. Already the cold was biting into him, and he shivered violently as a further gust caught him full-on as he approached the window. Goose bumps crawled all over his person and the hairs that stood on his arms did little to capture any heat for there was none. He reached out quickly and pulled the window down. His mission done he would quickly jump back into bed beside her, set his phone alarm for another hour and hope that he could find the peace that he had so recently enjoyed in the depths of his coma-like sleep.

He turned back, and two things happened simultaneously that caused him to come to a stop. Both the internal door through to his lounge was open (he didn't remember closing it, but that was no problem) but beyond that, he could see that the apartment door was also wide open into the hallway beyond. And as he looked down to his bare foot, which had found a wet patch on the carpet, he also saw from the corner of his eye a movement by the door. Already he was too late for the time that his eyes snapped back up, whatever it was had gone.

Fear welled up in him, and he groaned aloud, though he didn't hear it. He looked over to Keira for reassurance and saw that she slept on. There was some comfort in that, as to see her was like some anchor to what was real and that which sought to tease or trick him. He took a tentative step forward and now his left foot found a second wet patch from which he recoiled as if shocked.

What on Earth?

He could make no sense of what was occurring. The bed, only feet away looked and served as sanctuary from whatever games his mind was now playing on him, and he thought to bolt there as quickly as he could and pull the covers far over his head — waking Keira if he should need to, so as to dispel whatever deception of the mind was occurring.

His feet had at least found a dry base on which to plant themselves. What could have spilt by the window? Had there been rain while they slept, perhaps blown in via the open window? He looked out and beyond the glaring light to the heavens above. It was no good though, so intense was the shining of the spotlights that the night air held no darkness, or dark clouds that could be seen for that matter either. No mind, the window was shut and he would just go to bed, he would just…

Not with the door open like that.

No, of course, he could not sleep with the door to the house beyond standing wide and inviting access to who knew what terror? His mind though brought no monsters, only the vision of Mrs Hodgson standing shocked in the doorway as she beheld the two naked lovers caught like a rabbit in the headlights. No, he would close the door and then he could seek the comfort of the bed. The alarm would sound in an hour or so and he would bid Keira goodbye so that she could return to McArthur and no one would be any the wiser as to what had happened between them.

Pulling his trousers on as he went, he crossed over to the dresser where he found his robe and quickly tied it as close to him as he was able. Twice more en route to the door, his feet found wet patches on the carpet, and each time he jumped as if shocked. As he made the apartment door from the bedroom, he was now tentatively placing a toe down on the floor before him, before allowing his foot to take his weight. What had caused such a thing as this?

Long shadows stretched before him as he made the apartment proper, the angle of light from the window behind him not penetrating full within. He had detected a pattern in the wet floor before him, and such knowing caused panic to start to climb from the pit of his stomach. The trail, although unseen against the muddy darkness of the carpet no doubt led directly from the window to the door or vice versa and the fact of the open window and door were inextricably linked. Doubt seized him and he looked back to Keira once more, but from the depths he had entered the room she could not be seen.

No matter. He would walk as wide around the unwanted path as he could, shut the door and scamper back to bed as quickly as he was able. So he made the door and took it in hand, he willed himself not to look beyond the door jamb's exterior but it was already too late for the pattern of water could now be easily detected against the polished wooden floorboards beyond. The small pools tailed off along the corridor toward the main house and sat but a foot apart from one another, as if…

No, I won't think of that.

…as if tiny wet footprints, and it was too late, for the thought had completed itself before he could will it away. Fearing to tread the same boards he craned his neck outward of the room and observed the prints *(not footprints, no!)* and saw how they disappeared and picked up again both before and after the large patterned rug that lined the approximate centre point of the hallway. He did not doubt that if he were to look, (which he wouldn't), he would find the same wet trail held deep in the fibres of the carpet if he were to touch it.

Whatever escape he had found with Keira was now lost, and the house, his mind or whatever it was that sought to overwhelm him with terror was back. He regretted looking down the hallway and wondered why he had allowed himself to do so when his plan had been so quick and easy to accomplish. Closing his eyes to the hallway, he began to pull the door shut and even if Keira awoke, he would run to the bed as quickly as he could. His need for her company now a very real necessity.

Just as the door was about to snap shut, he saw it. His arm stopped instantly and the thing was framed in a one-inch gap on the floor before him — a single daisy.

He shut his eyes to it and held them closed as panic threatened to take him. But the darkness held no escape for him, for now, he feared what might lurk outside of that veil, should even Keira approach and lay a hand on him at that moment he would scream he knew, and no doubt lose his mind with it and so quickly he snapped his eyes open again.

It lay there still.

Fitzgerald unwittingly began to kneel before it, his arm pushing the door open wider as it bore his weight as he settled down. His senses told him that there was nothing there beyond the flower, that whoever (or whatever) had left it there had gone. His mind reached for Melissa, and he clung to the idea that some further trick had been played upon him. Could Keira be a party to her games? Planting the thing there, all the while smirking behind her pillow in the pretence of sleep? The idea was a captivating one and as before his mind wrestled with reality and other endless possibilities to illicit a rational explanation for what was occurring.

Before he knew it, it was in his hand. He did not know how it had come to be there. It was too late in the year for such flowers, but yet here it was, all very real and beautiful in his palm. The petals, the pure white of snow and the floral disc the yellow of the sun itself. Strangely it felt warm to the touch and with a gasp, he found that he was not cold any more.

The thing in his palm exuded a warmth that radiated throughout his whole body. And with that, he became calm. Fear vanished and he stood, he pushed the door open further and stepped out into the corridor knowing what he was going to see before he saw it.

And there she was. She had not aged he saw, but was now dressed instead in a thick blue jumper that bore a picture of the Tasmanian Devil from the Warner Bros cartoons. Not the swimming costume of Douglas' story. She stood at the apex of the corridor, between the end of the east wing and the front of the house. She smiled at him from fifty yards and he could feel the happiness within her. Lydia Bennett waved at him, beckoning him to come and follow. And so he did. He was not scared any longer and he marvelled at the vividness of all he saw, for it was a dream surely? A black cloud of remembrance stirred at the back of his mind as he remembered his last dream and the evil he had seen there. That to had been vivid, but this? This was something else and so to affirm that he reached out and allowed his fingers to brush against the wallpaper, amazed at the roughness of the textures as he went.

The girl disappeared around the corner, and he jogged onward to catch up, passing now the staircase to the ground floor of the east wing. He came to a stop and marvelled as he watched the shapes carved within the bannister come to life; the cherubs floated and looped around one another. He felt it so real that should he listen closer, he would hear their laughter. All the while their opposite, the serpents were still and lifeless.

None of what he saw perturbed him in any way, it was only a dream after all and as with all dreams, it begged continuance. And so there was no time to watch the angels play among themselves. Lydia awaited.

He made the corner quickly and was surprised to see her again at the end of the long balcony that overlooked the front of the house. He thought he had been so fast as to catch her, but that was not what was meant for tonight. She was showing him the way to the library door he knew, and though that caused some small part of him to rebel at the idea, he knew that all would be well, for the serenity that her presence brought within him.

He crossed now the very centre of the house, and she waited still. As he closed within ten feet of her, she turned and walked slowly out of sight to his left, beyond the end of the hallway and toward the library. He was overwhelmed by sadness suddenly for the reality of her being could not be denied. He had come close and seen still that her hair and clothing were sodden as if she had only just climbed from the pool. The feeling was heightened by the presence of her small wet footprints. They brought no more fear to him now that he understood their source and as he closed the last couple of feet to take the turn and meet her, he zeroed in on the puddles that marked the way.

He turned the corner. She was nowhere to be seen, and the library door was open before him.

In an instant, the warmth and calm her presence had bestowed was gone, for he knew that she had left him. And as fear and cold muscled its way back, his first instinct was to turn and run back the way he had come.

Why did you bring me here?

But there was no answer, either from his mind or the world about him. Soft white plumes expelled once more from his lips, and he held his breath as long as he could so as not to register their being.

The room beyond the boundary of the wide double doors was vast he could see. The window that marked the far end, from which he had seen the mysterious figure on the morning of his arrival stood just shy of one hundred feet away. The light within the room was extreme and from his angle, he could see that the ceiling bore one central chandelier that hung low over the middle of the room, beneath its protruding branches was a single high-backed-chair and beside it a small end table. The light sources though went beyond the solitary centrepiece for there were spotlights embedded within the ceiling and rows of strip lights fixed high upon the walls.

To expel every shadow.

But one.

From this central area, he saw row upon row of book stacks to his left and right and he guessed there might be as many as twenty aisles within the room. He had taken a step forward.

What are you doing?

He took another. Had she gone in? Is that why she had brought him here? The message must be an unequivocal yes, for here, at last, was what he knew he was meant for.

All was quiet as he made the threshold and he looked about himself for assurance that he was in fact alone. Already he was opposite the first line of book stacks, and as he leaned in close, he saw hundreds if not thousands of books all neatly lined in alphabetical order — 1984 by George Orwell, A Doll's House by Henrik Ibsen. Many more titles met his eyes, many he did not recognise but many more classics soon caught his eye. He looked further down the row but all too quickly the print became too fine to be legible.

He brought his attention back to the middle of the room and the single solitary chair that sat there. Had this been the very chair that had been as a prison to Thomas Searle? He was soon upon it and allowed his hand to caress the smooth leather, but no insight came to him. The chair, though, and the end table beside it were somehow wrong. He followed the line of sight straight ahead to the wide window frame before it and knew that was not somehow the intended view.

It came to him suddenly. He had been a fool to miss it, and he groaned inwardly at his stupidity. He searched backwards for the sanctuary that the door offered, all the while avoiding the stacks to his immediate left and right.

A shadow lies within!

No. He would not look, and he would not think about that. But he was caught he knew and should something happen would he have time to make the door?

Only if you acknowledge it, he thought. Yes, that was the key, for to look was to seek what was there and to look would be to no doubt find it. He cursed the small child that had brought him there and head fixed forward he took his first step back toward safety.

He stopped. The light caress of cold air on the nape of his neck was sudden, subtle, but undeniable. Ice filled his veins and he swallowed hard. He had not begged the question of himself, as to which of the two aisles had been Searle's bane. But the cold draught emanating now from his left could leave him in no doubt and the thought that he had willed away returned in earnest with its answer. That the chair should be facing the east wall and a shadow would be seen therein.

His head was fixed forward, but his eyes strained at the very limits of their capacity as they tried the impossible act of seeing behind himself. There, at the utmost limit of his view, he thought he saw a shadow, long and thin but steadily growing, reaching out from the aisle so as to swallow the light behind him. And though the lights burned bright from the walls and ceilings in front, the reaching shadow dulled the light behind.

Fitzgerald was now rooted to the spot in pure primal fear. No rational thought came as the slow creep of cold fear finally reached his mind and took control. He was helpless now, and a lone tear escaped his eye, for now, something moved in the darkness behind him. Slow and deliberately it came and he did not have to train his hearing to know from where. The sound was soft and it was only the repetitive tone in keeping with its progress that gave him insight as to what it was — the fall and slap of bare feet on hardwood.

It was close now he knew, and he closed his eyes as he anticipated the things inevitable cold touch, as it surely wrapped long-dead fingers around his throat and stole the life from him.

Closer and closer until the soft sound came...whump! He flinched and quickly clasped his hands to his ears to ward off the strange noise. But through clasped ears, he could now hear the sound of ragged breathing and instinct told him what he had heard. Whatever it was had fallen into the chair behind him.

The voice when it came was both instantly recognisable and appalling. The self-same dry cracked croak that had reached him from beyond that same door he now yearned to reach.

"Fear...fear, not friend." It came. His instinct was to press harder on his ears and blot the sound out altogether such was the horrid nature of its dire speech. Its breathing came ragged again as if it was trying to catch its breath.

Don't turn around, just walk...just walk away.

What strength there was in such a thought quickly evaporated for it spoke again.

"Please, please don't leave me."

And in that plea, he heard nothing but anguish and misery. He turned to it and was greeted with the sight of the back of the high-backed-chair. Both regret and gladness overwhelmed him as he did so. Regret that his base need to respond to pain had won through and gladness for the thing that sat beyond him was obscured by both the diminished light and the chair it now sat in.

That was but for the terrible sight of its long bony naked arm that lay on the rest and the small protrusion of its head, where wisps of long grey hair on a balding spotted scalp could be seen. Fitzgerald felt revulsion in what he now beheld and averted his eyes from the man that sat there. The sense of age was immeasurable and he felt like he could even detect the sweet smell of decay on the air between them.

And as he continued to watch, captivated, he could feel the shadow grow and become stronger about the man before him. Threads of black poured slowly from the obscured aisle and made heavier the black shade that surrounded the chair.

Unconsciously he stepped back as the pool spread on the carpet before him like a spilt inkpot enveloping and tainting all that it reached. The shadow seemed now like a barrier between him and it and as if to validate that thought he saw the billowing tendrils approach him and bounce away as if meeting some invisible barrier.

Wake up.

But was he dreaming? All he saw, heard and even smelled was all too real. And if that was so, he knew it did not need this scenario to reach some awful conclusion to play out before waking. Summoning all the strength he could find he stepped back again. As he did so, he saw the tendrils of black shadow that danced before him seemingly reach out for him, only again to be beaten back by the invisible barrier before him.

It's the light.

And he knew it was so, for now, the contrast in the room between light and dark was extreme and though he couldn't quite see it, he sensed the black shadow was creeping ever forward as if yearning for him. The effect was all the more apparent now as the fingers of shadow swirled manically before his eyes and contorted into vague shapes, like clawed hands reaching for him, before breaking up again like smoke in the wind. He gasped as a face formed before him, recognisable from McArthur's account of Thomas Searle's end, with its long pin-like teeth and impossible jaw.

Beyond the dancing shadows, the shape of the man beyond was still as he became rejuvenated. His hair was now growing darker, the skin of the one seen hand became taut, firm and darker in tone. It was getting stronger and that was evidenced by the strength of the blackness that enshrouded it and advanced steadily out into the room. If it should reach him, he knew he would be in the domain and control of the thing that sat and grew strong by the second.

The man cocked his head suddenly as if listening to his thoughts, and Fitzgerald sensed it had the strength, at last, to rise and face him. Spinning now, he turned his back to it and was exalted when he found his legs moving beneath him. He would not behold this horrible twisted thing and so he ran for the door.

It was closed before him.

"No." It was but a quiet whimper from his lips as he ground to a sudden halt. His fear was now total for as he found the shut door, he sensed a subtle movement from behind him and somewhere deep in his tormented conscious he knew the man was whole and had begun to stand. His eyes became wide now as they roved in their sockets, seeing, sensing the darkness overtake him from above and the sides, leaving only a small path of light on the floorboards beneath between him and the door.

The sound of a footstep behind him spurred him into motion again as he raced toward the door, all the while watching as darkness ran down from the ceiling above it as if like a water leak from an upstairs room. It ran quickly from ceiling to floor, masking any hint of colour or substance as it ran, leaving only the perfect vertical and horizontal lines of the door in view. The only exit was now only yards away but seemed a mile as the tendrils of darkness began to snake past his eyes and threaten to block the view of his retreat, while all the time he heard the slow tap, tap, tap of footfalls on the floor behind him.

His legs felt like dead-weights as he lifted them slowly in turn, willing speed but feeling like he was trying to run while waist-deep in water. Panic was a very real thing now and should he fall short of his intended target he felt his sanity would leave him and he would perhaps be found here in the days or weeks to come when the library was finally opened to search for the missing priest and they would find him either dead by the hand of the thing behind him or instead a gibbering mess gone mad.

In his mind's eye, he sensed the man close behind him and with all the will he could muster he leapt for the door handle. Should it be locked, it was game over for him.

"You would leave me?" The voice was now strong and oh so terribly close and loud that it made him falter, his hand missed the door, and he crashed in a heap before it. Quickly he spun and shifted himself so that his back was pressed against the door. Quickly he drew his knees up to his chest and cradled his head in his hands so as to bury his face as deeply as he could.

It was too late. The darkness had swallowed the room and there before him, perhaps within inches was the devil that posed in the form of a man. Fitzgerald's eyes welled with tears while he mouthed an unheard word over and over. No, no, no.

With the all-covering darkness had come the familiar biting cold of his dream and his previous experience before the library, but from somewhere close by he sensed hot breath emanating from the man. From behind his arms, he peered into the shadow and found the glow of two fiery red eyes held in the air above him and just as soon as he found them the fetid stench of the thing's raw hot breath fell upon him.

The thing erupted in a fury before him as it screamed its previous words once more. "You would leave me!"

Two things happened in that single moment. Fitzgerald cowered as deeply into a ball as he was able. He both sensed and saw the thing raise its razor-sharp hand so as to strike him.

As he anticipated the strike, his fear-addled mind struggled to comprehend that a change had come about him. A long line of light spilt from the open door beside him, to cut a long channel deep into the darkness toward the centre of the room where he could now see the high-backed-chair once more.

In that instant, he saw its face. Both young and old at the same time and indescribably terrible as it recoiled from the shaft of light that for a split second had split its face in two, between light and dark and in that instant, Fitzgerald's mind flipped for it impossibly comprehended two entirely different faces in the same head.

The first, dark, fierce, angry and appalling. The light, withered, frail and scared, similarly as it had appeared in the chair only moments before the darkness held sway.

Mercifully though it was but a second for the thing cowered away as the shaft of light that stole into the room became wider. He gazed in wonder as realisation at last found him. The library door was opening wider, the light spilling forth, dispelling the blackness and creating a chance for escape which he readily accepted. Not trusting his legs, he rolled forward onto his knees and scrambled from the room on all fours. The hallway before him was beautifully lit and he quickly collapsed onto his back. The door beside him closing of its own will and Fitzgerald not caring for how or why, for now, he was free of the terror within.

He lay still for moments or hours; he could not tell, not daring to allow his eyes to close into darkness for a second. All of a sudden he was aware that he was not alone and he sat bolt upright. The anteroom which he now found himself in was empty though. Despite that, he sensed the presence of something close by. When she spoke, the words came not to his ears, but instead to his mind. The voice of a child. A young child who had only recently led him to that same place.

"You saw the monster didn't you?"

He answered in the affirmative.

"I am sorry that I had to show you. The man in this house wants you to let it go. But you mustn't, do you understand? You must not."

Fitzgerald did understand. Whatever lay within that room was abhorrent and evil to its very core, but why would she suggest he would let it go? If it were trapped within, he would never willingly go near ever again, be it in waking or dreams, as long as it was in his power to do so.

He closed his eyes now for weariness threatened to overcome him. He felt no fear at that moment for he knew the voice that spoke to him, and it held no malice.

"Lydia." He whispered as darkness took him. And as unconsciousness won through, he heard her soft voice echoing now from afar.

"Beware Iain. I cannot see with whom, but the beast has brokered a new deal."

CHAPTER 39

"Iain wake up."

He did so with a start and sat bolt upright in bed. Sweat poured from his brow, and he did not immediately recognise where he was or who the person was that spoke. He recoiled when she reached out and tried to touch his brow and through wide eyes, he saw the hurt in her reaction.

"Keira?"

She kneeled beside him; the duvet clasped tightly around her. "You were having a nightmare. It's okay you're here safe with me now."

He searched her face and relief flooded through him at her words.

A nightmare? Is that what it had been? His mind quickly conjured visions of a dark and terrible image; an ancient being whose visage was cut in two by the intruding light of an open library door. And then the words of a departed child, warning him...of what?

He could not remember, and he closed his mind from the thoughts as he looked into Keira's eyes and saw the concern there. He reached for her and rested his head in her bosom. She accepted him willingly and brought him into her embrace and gently stroked his hair.

"My god Iain, was it that bad?"

He only nodded, though in truth whatever it was that he had dreamt was now departing to an extent where he saw only fragments of what had happened. Taking his cheeks in her hands, she twisted his head so that he was looking up at her. "It's this house, isn't it? You don't have to tell me what it was, but just know I feel it to. I...really don't know why I came here tonight. I think maybe I just couldn't be alone anymore."

He looked at her quizzically.

"You think you're the only one that feels it?" She said in response to the unasked question. "There was more to your questions earlier tonight than you let on wasn't there? Only you don't trust me enough to tell me. What has shaken you like this?" As she spoke, Fitzgerald could see her eyes become wet with emotion.

And with that, she let him go and lay herself down with her back toward him. He was both shocked and surprised at her reaction and he felt ashamed for keeping his feelings to himself when it was clear that not only was she trying to comfort him, but that she had fears and anxieties of her own, which he had done nothing to address.

At that moment, it did not matter about the house, the library and the source of all his ills; what did matter was the fact that she shared his feelings. That he was not alone and that Thoby Hall did have a negative and fearful effect upon those who dwelt there.

It was his turn now to comfort her, and so he lay down beside her and placed one arm over her as he propped himself upon the other, so as to whisper into her ear. "I am sorry Keira. I didn't realise you felt that way. You are right the house…it does…it has worn me down I know."

She turned back to look at him, and so he lay down so that the two were eye to eye. "Tell me." She said.

"Where do I begin?" He searched himself and knew that this had all begun as soon as he had arrived within the town. The spectre of fear the house emitted seemed to have been with him from the very first moment he had met with Father Shilling at St Peter's Church and had grown and become more powerful inside of him as he sought answers to questions he had no right asking. And that was at the heart of it wasn't it? He had been given a task to do; albeit an unusual and particularly unpleasant one given the nature of McArthur's despicable tale of hatred, jealousy and revenge. But despite that, he knew that it was he that had pressed for more. For knowing what lay at the heart of Thoby Hall and the evil spirit that dwelt over it consumed him now. But was such a thing real as suggested by McArthur or something that dwelled only inside of him and the minds of others who came into contact with the place?

He sensed Keira's impatience and knew that it would not do to fob her off. They had been intimate together and had filled a gaping chasm which had been their loneliness. It would not do to lie to her now, for she would be lost to him. The fact that their physical interlude had no possibility of continuing beyond even that day did not matter in the here and now of their being together for he felt connected with her and would tell her the truth.

"I don't know how much of this you know Keira," he whispered. "This house, it's history, I mean. You know I can't speak of McArthur's confession but he alluded to something. Something dark here within the house. His wife…his ex-wife, Elizabeth knew and sought help from the Church."

"Father Crosby?" She returned.

He was taken aback by her words. "How do you know?…"

"Robert…I mean Mr McArthur has told me more of this than you probably know Iain. At first, I believed it to be his medication. You know, drug-induced fantasy or fixation. But after a time…"

"What did he say, Keira, please," Fitzgerald demanded. "If you already know, then this makes this a whole lot easier for me to speak of it."

She nodded. "Only fragments I am afraid, and of those, I took little notice. I believed him to be delirious or worse. He made mention of the library as you have done. You have to understand Iain, the pain he has been through, I believed what he said to be distorted by his condition."

"I understand. But what did he say?"

"He spoke briefly of a man named Searle and of some kind of monster that he had welcomed into the house. It was crazy Iain, but such talk put me on edge every time I passed by that damned room on my way to and from the apartments."

Her words trailed off as he reached out and embraced her. She knew, and that was all that mattered. He was not breaking the sanctity of confession if Robert had already elicited the same story to her, no matter how broken and insane it may have sounded to her ears.

He broke off his embrace, raw emotion through relief engulfed him. At first, he could not speak and just nodded over and over. "You know? You know all of it? Elizabeth? Lydia? And of Thomas Searle?"

She paused as she considered. "Yes, the little girl...all of it. But it's not true. I mean it can't be true."

So McArthur had told his tale to more than one, and he wondered who else might know the sordid story. Hodgson? Douglas? Maybe even the solicitor Harvey and his very own bishop? He had no way to know, but in the here and now it mattered little for he had found a kindred spirit, one who perhaps felt the essence of darkness that clouded this house, even if they did not believe in truth all that they had come to hear.

"I don't know Keira. What I do know is that a shadow hangs over this place, one that has the power to affect us. Do I believe that there is something real in that library though?" As he spoke a fragment of his dream *(It was a dream, it was a dream)* returned to him, an ancient and terrible thing rising from its chair, now over him, reaching, reaching...

"But I can tell you what I do believe, this house has a dark and tragic past behind it and do such things leave a trace? Perhaps so, and are there those persons who are more attuned to such things than others? Yes, I do believe in that as well."

"Could that be?" He saw something in her eyes as she answered him.

"I know that McArthur believes it."

"And what about you, Iain?"

"I..." he stammered.

"Iain please, there is no need to hold anything back with me."

He knew what she said to be right and thus far it had been a huge weight off of his shoulders to share his innermost thoughts with her, even then he was surprised by the revelation he heard coming from his own lips. "I saw her Keira. I saw Lydia, she took me there, and the door was open waiting to receive me. It…I saw…something, someone. I…"

He expected scepticism but saw none. "What happened?" Keira asked. Her breathing was shallow, and her eyes fixed on his. The intensity of her gaze was incredible and he felt himself shy away. But such was the gravity of what he was trying to say he knew he had to meet that gaze and not bat an eyelid.

"I saw it. That is all. But that was not the message Keira, she…Lydia, she told me…"

"What did she say?!" Keira demanded, and Fitzgerald recoiled at the ferocity of her question.

"She told me that McArthur wants me to be rid of it, but I was not to do so."

Keira's lips pursed, and Fitzgerald thought he saw anger flit behind her eyes. But just as quickly as it came, it was gone. The reaction puzzled him for he had opened up and told her of fantastic and ridiculous things. She had not laughed in his face as he might expect, but he had made himself vulnerable to her. What might she think in the cold light of day?

Her next words fell on him like a weight. "But why not?"

"Keira?"

"I mean if he should ask such a thing of you then why not do it? Is that not what a priest does? You mentioned Elizabeth and Crosby? Was that not what they were trying to achieve?"

"Yes but…"

"And if they felt it to, why not ease the suffering of a dying man and lift this cloud from this place whether it be real or not?"

He was reeling and on the defensive. This was all so sudden and unexpected from her. "Keira…" he stammered. But she was unperturbed by his weak protests.

"You said it yourself Iain, this place it has an aura about it. Something dark and perhaps stemmed from tragedy. Why would you not want to do it?"

At last, he gathered himself to make a response. "But Keira, it is not as simple as that. What happened with Crosby…the Church would never sanction such a thing."

"Well damn the Church Iain!" There was a fire in her eyes now which he had not expected. This subject was threatening to explode, he knew, for he had touched something deep inside of her. "And what of me Iain?" she continued. "Would you not do it for me?"

290

"You Keira? But why…"

She snatched herself away from him. Gathering the duvet close around her, leaving him naked and cold on the bed.

"Haven't you heard a thing that I have said? It's not just Robert I see the fear in; it's all of them! They all go to their deaths alone and afraid. I've seen the light disappear from their eyes and I see no redemption, no hope and no sign of what lies beyond. They go into darkness Iain! And so for this one man can you not make his burden easier by giving him peace of mind?"

He saw tears begin to well in her eyes as she spoke, and she quickly diverted her glance from him and found her discarded clothing on the floor before her. "I have to get back." She mumbled.

Fitzgerald searched the room and saw his phone on the bedside table where he had left it. It was 04:50 am, and he knew she was right. That thought had crossed his mind once already and he knew they could not be found like this.

"Keira look. I am sorry. Perhaps there is more than you are telling me? I didn't mean to upset you."

She stopped for a second, her arms stuffed with her underwear and nurse's tunic. "There is." She managed. "But now isn't the time, I have to get back. But Iain, please. Should he ask you, won't you do it? Erase the bad thing that lives here and let that poor man rest in peace?"

He was defeated and could offer nothing else. And though Keira could not have known the question had already been asked of him, he replied. "I will Keira. If he asks, I will."

A look of triumph came over her which for a second made him falter.

What have you done?

But the look was quickly gone and replaced by her brilliant smile, and he knew then he was lost to his promise. She turned from him and allowed the duvet to fall from her shoulders to the floor, giving him a glimpse of her beautiful form and perhaps promises of what was to come for a promise kept. This thought again caused his loins to ache for her once again. But before he could even contemplate what such a thing meant for him or his faith she had left the room and closed the interior door between the bedroom and the apartment, so that she could dress in peace.

He took the opportunity to gather the lost duvet from the floor for the room was now bitterly cold in the wake of her leaving, and he wished there was some excuse or reason he could have her stay, but he could think of none. □

291

CHAPTER 40

Feeling exhausted and paranoid, Fitzgerald was rudely awakened by the shrill ring of the internal telephone at 8 o'clock. His first thought being that his and Keira's night of passion had somehow been discovered and would be the talk of the house.

The voice on the other end of the line was that of Keira, and she betrayed no hint of their intimate liaison of only a few hours ago. Instead, she was straight to the point and requested his presence back in the west wing as McArthur was anxious to speak with him once more.

Fitzgerald felt deflated, knowing well the old man sought his answer regarding the exorcism he would have him perform. As it stood, he had fulfilled his duty at Thoby Hall and had McArthur passed away in the night; he would have done so with the absolution he had so craved. Yet he lived on, and unknown to McArthur was the fact that Keira had already extracted his compliance.

But for now, the memory of a promise made plagued him. A faraway voice at the back of his mind nagged and begged to be heard.

I will Keira. If he asks, I will.

And now it seemed the hour of reckoning had arrived for this may well prove to be his last meeting with McArthur. But even at this late hour, he was still torn as to the request that had been made of him. Could he instead abandon the house, and the commitments he had so foolishly agreed? No one would be the wiser, and the house would still pass to the diocese with no questions, as there could be no argument to attest that the contract had not been fulfilled to its fullest. That said, Fitzgerald himself knew he would carry any such abandonment with him for evermore.

But to do as he was bid and to perform an exorcism, he knew he had to accept McArthur's story without question.

Could he? Thus far he had fought against what McArthur and the others had told him. But it was his own experiences coupled with their words that now tentatively gave him that which he sorely needed, to go ahead with the plan. And for that, he cursed Robert McArthur. The man had somehow known that to keep him here would be to subject him to the same horrors of which he had been told.

Even so, he was still torn as to if something physical existed within the walls of that library. The story of Thomas Searle had been fantastic but surely spurious. Or so he had believed until McArthur had relayed his own experience of the demon that dwelt there. That had served to nurture the first delicate shoots of believing and now those same shoots with time, care and application had blossomed. And what of Fitzgerald's own experiences? The previous night's excursion threatened to rip away the veil of doubt that had shrouded him for so long, for it was all too real and now refused to fade into obscurity as a dream should do immediately after waking. And it was not the image of an ancient and terrible thing coming to life that threatened to overwhelm his thoughts. Instead, it was the library itself, for he knew to see it for himself would confirm his worst fears. For to recognise it, to see it again and know that he had in fact been in there before would surely unravel the last of his doubt, and if so he could no longer deny that there was some dark power emanating if not from Thoby Hall, then the room itself. A power that was able to interlope upon his dreams and had perhaps done likewise with McArthur. So yes, he did believe. Certainly enough in his mind that he could do McArthur's bidding with an honest heart and mind.

Such thoughts were at the forefront of his mind as he made his way again along the first-floor landing of the front of the house, and again approached the anteroom, every step of his short journey plaguing him with a twisted déjà-vu from this self-same walk as last night. So much so that he half expected to see the form of the 7-year-old girl who had enticed and led him this same way.

As he made the anteroom again, the voice came to him so quickly and succinctly it froze him in his tracks.

"The man in this house wants you to let it go. But you mustn't, do you understand? You must not."

A hot sweat came over him, and his head twisted sharply as if to find the speaker directly behind him. The room was, of course, empty, and he felt his skin crawl as he found himself facing the library door once more. Had the voice been real or imagined? He did not know, but the effect had been for him to stand and face what he was so desperate to avoid. Despite that, he had already taken an unwitting step forward and found his hand outstretched for the door handle.

He froze in his tracks as understanding of what he had been about to do overwhelmed him. Should he have followed through, the door would be unlocked he knew, and the layout of the room within would be precisely as it had been in his dream.

Dream? Yes. He asserted to himself for what seemed like the hundredth time already that morning, for whatever dark power dwelled in Thoby Hall, it was still easier to believe it only in his mind, than behind the door he now faced.

His mind made up, he turned, his duty lying elsewhere.

Immediately he became calmer without the door in sight, and his rational mind won through and as it did so, it was not the voice of a 7-year-old, nor the impassioned plea of a recent lover but instead the calming voice of a friend and colleague who had told him to get

293

his business done and get out. And as he strode off toward McArthur's apartment, he knew that this was exactly as he would do as matters were now approaching their end weren't they?

He made the doorway which he already found open and there before him was a beleaguered looking Keira.

"Oh, thank goodness you're here Father," she opened. "He has been in and out of consciousness; he speaks your name while he sleeps. I am afraid that it may soon be time."

The priest within took over. Here at least he could play his part, and he welcomed the opportunity to do so, that he might push all other thoughts aside.

He took her hand and cut her off as she was about to speak. "Be calm now. If it is so, then it is the Lord's will. You have done the best you can but be ready. I have no doubt, he has strength yet as our business is not yet at an end. But soon, you must be strong and be ready, do you understand?"

Keira looked long into his eyes and nodded her understanding.

"You will do it, Iain?"

He knew at once what she meant, and his heart sank. She continued to hold hard onto his hand and held his eyes unflinchingly as she waited on his answer. The intensity in her gaze was unnerving and he could not reason as to why she had acted as she had in the depths of the night, as to this question of McArthur's request.

Had she already known the old man had requested an exorcism of him? After all, she had known so much more than he could ever have believed and now he was feeling the first stirrings of regret for having opened up to her, for she had turned the conversation back on him and made him promise he would do as asked.

"I will Keira." Was all he could manage in response.

He felt trapped. There was nothing but misery to be found here. Sorrow and tragedy ran like an undercurrent in the house, but what brought it? A very true and real demon who dwelt here? Or the remnants of a pain and despair that lingered long in the aftermath of the events that created them?

"May I see him now?" he asked, keen to escape her penetrating eyes.

"You…you may have to be patient, Father." She stammered as he walked toward the bedroom door.

He soon saw the reason as to her words, for making the room he found McArthur unconscious. *What if I am too late?* A darker deeper voice answered before he could shut it up and told him that perhaps that would be all the better, for if not asked, he would not have to make good on his promises.

Drawing the chair to the side of the bed, he sat and watched as the heart rate monitor continued its eternal vigilance over the dying man - the LCD screen showing beats per minute dancing between 60 and 62. Fitzgerald was none the wiser as to if this was high or low for a man in McArthur's condition *(he's dying you idiot, how can that be good)* but he found reassurance as he watched the electrocardiogram spike every second or so. McArthur's heart was beating and rhythmically.

While the man slept on, Fitzgerald gathered himself for what was to come. He had delivered last rites on several occasions. That had been part and parcel of his time and training both at the seminary and after for his short stint at St Peter's Church where he had on occasion delivered the rites to the dying or departed; penance, the anointing of the sick and finally viaticum.

The ritual was well-known to him, but there was something so much more powerful for him in these ministrations than many others, for he believed those who it was bestowed upon were within touching distance of God. It was for this reason, he often felt at peace with the passing of the individual he was administering the rite to. For in those moments, he felt powerful, and almost as if his words were reaching the heavens. A feeling he rarely obtained through mass and regular weekly sermons.

The movement of the ECG was somewhat hypnotic, and soon Fitzgerald's eyes became heavy. Without realising it, he fell into a light sleep which was periodically disturbed as he shifted in his chair and jerked awake, only to see that McArthur's own eyes remained closed.

He had no concept of time in that short period, and it was only when a light touch upon his hand brought him back to the surface of waking that he became alert again, for now, McArthur was awake and his eyes were strong and probing, seemingly at odds with what Fitzgerald had expected following Keira's bleak prognosis of her patient.

Reaching out, Fitzgerald took the hand in his own and found strength in its grip. McArthur was either far from his end or a stubborn and proud old man who would not willingly show him any hint of his weakness.

"Robert. It is good to see you again."

The reply though was soft, and Fitzgerald had to strain to hear the words. "And you Father. I feel our time together may now be short and still, there is more to say."

Fitzgerald arched an eyebrow. "Is there more to your confession Robert?"

The old man closed his eyes and shook his head softly. "Maybe there should be Father, for I am not a man without other sins. But I fear that I don't have the inclination or time to dwell on the smaller matters. Should I have been a better husband to my wives? Yes. Could I have been a better man, a benefactor for the helpless and weak? Yes. But I feel I must face my Lord on my own terms as the man I am. I have told you of my biggest regret and it is that for which I craved absolution."

"Your demon." It was but a whisper from Fitzgerald in response.

"Yes, Father. And I wonder if at last, you have come to terms with such a thing? For there is yet the other matter of which I have asked you."

Fitzgerald's defences were now on high alert, for here surely was the moment he was dreading. Keira had paved the way for his compliance, though it was true she was not the beginning of it. And in his mind, he saw Father Shilling, Deacon Morris, Hodgson, Douglas, and the diaries of Father James Crosby.

It had been a neat set of stepping stones that had paved the way to this moment, and he envisaged himself back at St Peter's Church with Shilling and unwittingly taking his first step out from a shoreline of safety, onto a huge expanse of water. The metaphorical shore had still been in sight back then, but each step forward had taken him further and further away and now when he looked back neither the shore or the footholds he had taken could be seen. There was only one way now and that was forward.

"I know what you would ask me Robert, but before that, I must have answers."

McArthur shifted in his bed and with what strength he had, pushed himself back to be in a sitting position so that their eyes could meet at a more comfortable angle. The effort caused him to perspire and Fitzgerald watched as a small bead of sweat weaved its way from his brow to dampen the collar of his pyjamas.

"Ask then."

"Elizabeth," he said after his deliberations, "You told me that you knew of her obsession and yet you allowed her and Crosby to go ahead and try and remove that thing. That was the end of them both one way or another. How could you do that to her?"

McArthur looked sad. "I did not know their intent Father. I swear I didn't. But yes I should have seen it and put a stop. You won't know what it was like back then, but Elizabeth, all of it, it was like the darkness was lifted somehow and I was complacent in my happiness."

"What do you mean?"

"That night. The night I told you of, where I sold Searle to the hands of that filthy beast? I was in denial at first, and I think you would be to. I am not trying to excuse my acts, but everything that happened was impossible. I know what I saw, of course, I did, but I denied it to myself. The last time I entered that vile room was the following morning when we had Searle carted away. As I already said, it was not as my last vision of him had been. No creature had set about him and torn him apart as I had seen the night before. I saw the horror in his dead eyes still, but the coroner's verdict was that he had suffered a massive heart attack and why not? The man was old and reckless. He smoked, he drank, he had survived one heart attack already and led the lifestyle of a man in his twenties! And so I chose not to believe what I had seen. I shut and locked the library and told myself it was all but a hallucination."

"Yes. You have said as much. But what of Elizabeth and that poor girl Lydia?"

"Lydia? Yes…yes, that was her name. Don't you see that I was in denial then as well? This house, this damnable house was beset by more than just the tragedy of that little girl and I chose to ignore all of it. Put it all down to bad luck and circumstance, for not to, was to admit the possibility of something too big to comprehend."

Fitzgerald stood and circled his chair, resting his hands upon his back to take his weight. "But Elizabeth must have spoken with you of her plan?"

"No, Father. And that was heartbreaking in itself, for it was only after that I knew she was lost to me. She should have come…"

"But you would have sent her away? Comfortable in your fantasy?" Fitzgerald's anger rose as he spoke.

"You are quick to judge Father. But you did not know her as I did. And perhaps I did not know her at all given that she could not come to me with what she knew."

"And what did she know?" Fitzgerald demanded.

"That the beast resided there still. In the library, as it has always done! We have been here already damn it Father!"

The effort of McArthur's response caused him to go into a coughing spasm. Fitzgerald came at once to his side and was stopped at arm's length by the outstretched palm of McArthur's hand as he coughed violently into a handkerchief he had produced from his breast pocket. Fitzgerald sat again waiting for the fit to subside.

"I am sorry Robert…"

The outstretched palm was again raised, only this time to ward off the apology and allow him time to gather himself to speak. "No. You have every right."

"Tell me of her then."

"Elizabeth? Oh how that little girl changed her, and so we came to drift apart. She took her solace from the Priest Crosby and not from me. I should have done more, tried to reach her somehow. But men like me, men like Searle, we are not built for such things. My support for her came with my money and not my love, for I knew no other way. She went to counselling and I satisfied myself with that. Did it work? No, but instead she found Crosby and I believed her faith would be her crutch. How wrong was that?"

"Ordinarily?" Fitzgerald ventured. "Nothing. But this was something more, wasn't it?"

McArthur nodded. "Yes, it was. I was out of town when it happened, on business. I remember the call like it was yesterday."

"The call?"

"From Elizabeth. They had gone ahead and tried their…well, you know. What was to happen to Crosby was still some days off yet, but it had begun in him as it had in her."

"What?"

"The madness. You will know she was sectioned of course, and what became of Crosby in the long run? It was all there in the phone call and my years of denial were thrown in my face and I was overcome by shame as I heard her rant."

"What did she say to you?" Fitzgerald whispered as the atmosphere in the room begged no more.

McArthur closed his eyes once more, and Fitzgerald saw that he was searching his memory to find as close an approximation of all that was said and he knew it was with such memory that he spoke Elizabeth's words through his own mouth.

"She said that it had found her. That it was inside of her and she could not get it out."

"My God," Fitzgerald said, stunned as Elizabeth's words through McArthur pierced him to his core. "It…it is real." And at that moment he saw that he and McArthur were the same. He had similarly tried to fend off the truth with rational thinking and buckets of denial, but all of his experiences could no longer be refused as they flooded through him and overwhelmed him.

"You see it, Father? You see it now?"

Fitzgerald sat hard into the chair and clasped his head in his hands.

"You are now as I was. Awakened. I had denied it ever since the night with Searle, and though I did not know it then, I had lost Elizabeth to it as well. Like Crosby, she tried to take her life in the aftermath of what happened. That is not known Father. I had her sectioned for her own protection forthwith. Crosby found more success with his own attempt."

"But how?" Fitzgerald managed at last. "And why? Why does it linger? Had you not freed it as you described? These bonds you spoke of, these wards or sigils surely they were no more than a placebo for Thomas Searle?"

"No. Wishful thinking Father. I did not comprehend at that time, the power that kept it prisoner. I utilised the light to my own advantage, but it was trapped still, for there was more at play than I knew. Still know for that matter, but over the years I believe I know what came to pass."

The very air in the room now seemed still and heavy. Every movement and word by the pair of them seemed somehow complicit and tense, and it felt as if unseen eyes and ears strained to know what passed. For his part, Fitzgerald found that he now bent heavily over the old man whose words had become quieter and more confidential, spoken directly into his own straining ear.

"Pagan magic." McArthur continued. "It is inherent here in Thoby Hall Father. It has been since long before I ever arrived to serve at Searle's side. But you might be surprised to know the source of it all. Who brought it. What staved off the beast when it came for him the first time and what likely still holds it here today."

Fitzgerald was confused by the words he heard. His mind was close to reverting to its prior sensibilities and deny what he had only just accepted as true. It had been a rude and terrible awakening to acknowledge the existence of physical evil within the house, but now it seemed McArthur would have him believe in magic as well?

"Stay with me, Father. Had you not questioned aspects of my tale? I have had many years to do so. All since Elizabeth was lost to me, I have had time to think on the night when I delivered Searle and more of course, for there were other aspects which I did not tell you."

Fitzgerald's head was beginning to reel. "There is more?"

"So much more. But I will not burden you with it all. No, there is only one other aspect that you must learn for this perhaps is the most relevant should you rid us of that thing."

There it is at last.

McArthur steam-rollered on though as if the words had not been uttered and therefore not picked up, as if negating the words could somehow allow them to fly under his defences and take root within his psyche without question.

"The question is and always has been, what compels it or forces it to stay? More so considering Elizabeth and Crosby's ill-fated attempts to remove it."

Fitzgerald could not deny the validity of the question, and despite his reflex abhorrence to the idea of performing a ritual of exorcism, he longed to know more of the thing he had now come to believe was very real.

"And so you suggest pagan magic?"

"Indeed, yes. But as I said, the source is quite unexpected. You remember well no doubt Searle's tale of how he evaded the beast when it came for him first? A deal done in darkness can only be completed in darkness?"

"Of course."

"Well, his delivery from evil also lay within the same unknown contract. If you study his tale, the clues are there, and I came to know that his saviour was in fact his third wife, Joan. You see, by making his deal with the Devil also precluded other things such as any possibility of fathering children. He was a man out of his own time after all; he was to meet his maker at Beaumont-Hamel during the Battle of the Somme. I have come to believe that a man such as he could bear no children, for to do so would cause ripples in a timeline that could not be. I believe you will see it if you look hard enough. You remember how he won his Victoria Cross?"

"Yes, of course. It was for heroism after the battle, he went back into no man's land and saved the lives of many of his unit."

"And you remember what became of them?"

Fitzgerald thought hard. That element was sketchy to him. "One died in the Blitz during the Second World War did he not?"

"And the other? Remember, many he brought back did not survive their wounds or the operating theatre. There was one other, Paul Ladder. He committed suicide shortly after the war."

"I understand that, but what of it?" Fitzgerald questioned.

"Oh come, Father, you are an intelligent man! They were also men out of time, can't you see that? If Searle had not brokered his deal, who would have gone onto the battlefield to save them? Would it surprise you to know that neither Ladder or the other man, Giles, fathered any children between the end of the war and what was left of their lives?"

He did see it then, it was so clear, but one element was still not. "Yes, I can see, but what does that have to do with Searle and the thing that resides here?"

"Ah, I was coming to that. You remember also that with his heart attack came the insight of the deal he had made? He lived his life in ignorance of it until the moment came when he was to pass from this mortal coil and into the hands of the Devil. But up until that point he had lived in ignorance of his deal, not knowing that he could father no children."

Fitzgerald could begin to see the direction McArthur was taking. "That didn't stop him trying though did it?"

"Exactly, Father! Three wives and no children! And of course, he blamed the women, for was he not a virile and powerful man in his own eyes? It was Joan who pursued shall we say the more creative ways of dealing with what she perceived as her barrenness or his sterility."

"Pagan magic."

"Yes! You must remember that things were not as they are today what with fertility treatments and surrogacy. People then did believe in old wives' tales, and you can believe me when I tell you that we all used to believe such things — drinking cough syrup after sex? That was one. Ha!"

A smile began to rise on Fitzgerald's lips; such was the enthusiasm of the old man's words and expression as he delivered them. It was hard to believe that here was a man who was supposedly fading from life before him. His voice had become strong once more and all the while the shine in his eyes belied the disease within him that sought to destroy. As he thought on this, though, another thought intruded so quickly and sharply; he felt himself physically stagger as if slapped to the face. Whether McArthur had seen it or not he doubted, for he talked on without being heard, for the talk of sex and fertility made him realise that he and Keira had not spoken of protection, what if…

The thought went unfinished though for McArthur's interruption. "Father, are you with me? God knows it is a lot to take in, sorry if I ramble, but I hope you soon understand where I am going."

Fitzgerald tried to snap back to the matter at hand without success. The enormity of his mistake with Keira was compounded by the fact that they had not sought to address contraception. What had he been thinking? And what if she should become pregnant? That would undoubtedly be the end of him both at St Peter's and the Church in its entirety. But on realising that, an odd calmness overcame him and he was surprised to find that such an outcome was not only non-threatening but also perhaps welcome. Both Ashmarsh and Thoby Hall had ground him down to a nub and the thought of an escape, no matter the method was suddenly very appealing. As to was the idea that there may be some way he and Keira could share a future.

"Father?"

"I'm sorry. You were saying?"

"You have to understand Searle's burning desire to father an heir. He was a leader in industry and had amassed a veritable fortune. Joan felt the pressure; of course, it was going to cost her the marriage if she did not become pregnant. Ultimately that was how matters panned out for her, and in the end, Searle gave in to the inevitable and never took another wife. But before Joan was cast aside, she had tried everything at her disposal and that included bringing the wiccan to Thoby Hall. It was, I believe she who saved Searle that fateful day, though she did nothing to alleviate the curse of his contract, or bring him the heir he so desperately yearned for."

"A wiccan? You are referring to witchcraft?"

"You show your ignorance Father; you surprise me. Wicca is a new pagan religion after all. What you refer to harkens back to the dark ages. A dark day in the history of the Church; the vilification and burning of women as witches?"

"…"

"Let us not debate the established and clandestine nature of christianity Father, no. In any event, we refer now to the twentieth century, albeit the 1940's when abortions were illegal and practised by women, some of whom in other ages would burn for their acts. These women practised other crafts such as love spells, no doubt utilising powerful hallucinogenics. Then there were spells of healing and ultimately fertility spells. That is what Joan sought."

Fitzgerald ignored the slight against his religion as he replied. "How do you know of all this? Searle perhaps? Surely this woman Joan was long gone by the time you came to his service?"

"Harvey. You've met that whelp of a grandson of his? Well, the senior saw and heard more of Searle's business than I would ever care to know. But he liked to drink and when he did so, he liked to talk and what became apparent was that he knew Joan and knew of her fruitless efforts to give Searle his child. Long before he died, he shared what he knew of Joan and the wiccan."

"So tell me."

"You must remember that Harvey did not know Searle's sordid tale, but even so, he told me that this wiccan saw something within the house. We both know what. She was more in tune with such forces than perhaps we might ever be and mercifully so. She gave onto Searle and Joan the spell of fertility they were promised. It did not work, and Searle cursed her for the charlatan that he believed her to be. But Joan confided in Harvey, what the wiccan had seen, that the woman had cursed Searle's name; 'Djalli është mbi të' were the words that she used; the Devil is upon him."

"She saw such a thing?"

"I believe so. You must remember that this came to me third-hand, it was Joan that imparted this to Harvey before I was, in turn, told of it. He could never know the meaning and laughed of the story when he told it. But I saw beyond it."

"But what makes you believe this woman had something to do with imprisoning this beast?"

"Një magji e mbrojtjes; a spell of protection. Harvey was a brilliant man before dementia took him. His recall for the Tosk, the Albanian language, stood the test of time and it was all I needed to make my mind up. For if this wiccan had the power to see the Devil upon Searle's back then might she not also have the power to imprison it?"

"Incredible…" was all Fitzgerald could manage.

"It is Father. For it must have been this spell and this spell alone that allowed Searle to escape within the light. For it was only after the beast came that Searle finally saw the truth of his deal and did all in his power to protect himself further. But it is my view, everything that came after was in vain, for that which protected him was already in place."

"Then, the spotlights? The symbols and the rest?"

"All for nothing I believe, all but the lights. For there was something in the light that saved him and assures me still. As for the runes and magic markers you see strewn within the house today, they are all at Searle's behest, and that is where I came in, for I was party to his paranoia and obsession in those years after the event."

Fitzgerald found himself captivated in McArthur's story, for now, the pieces of the puzzle he had agonised over were finally coming together.

"So Searle's fascination with the occult was to find further ways to protect himself?" he asked.

"Yes, and I do not doubt that all of it was farce, charlatans that would moan and invoke ridiculous rituals of protection. But, something stuck and the beast remained trapped here. For all I know, it was only that one woman that saved him. That wiccan and her spell, something that Searle would never know of and so he sought his own protection from it."

"But what of after his passing? This spell of protection or defence as you call it? Surely it was broken?"

"As I say, something stuck and…I fear I may have been party to it myself."

"What?"

"I told you how I tried to rationalise and hide from what I had seen? Well, only so far. I would not admit to myself what I had seen. But that did not stop the nightmares and so the spotlights remained on, for they gave me comfort from night terrors. The library remained locked and has been bathed with light ever since. I am sure it is more, for no doubt the spell or ritual still holds, but the light is a part of it I am sure."

Fitzgerald had only to cast his mind back to what he had clung to as a dream. The dread creature in the chair, the divide between dark and light and how the beast was cast back at the last by the opening of the library door and the light that split it in two and caused it to withdraw. He did not doubt that the light was a part of it to.

McArthur continued. "But now I am near my end, and I fear I have angered it. It speaks to me now in dreams of the tortures it would subject me to. You will see now, why I seek both redemption and why I must ask you to cast this thing back to the hell from where it was spawned."

"Why…why me?"

"I put this off for too long. When I knew I had this damned cancer, I began to think about how things would end for me. The nightmares intensified and that is when I approached Shilling."

"He rejected you, though?"

"He did. I was to direct. Even a man of the cloth with all the years that he had baulked at such an idea. Of course, he had no love for me either; I was easy to refuse."

"So instead, you brought me here? Manipulated me by having me stay?" Fitzgerald spat.

"Manipulated? Oh, Father no, not at all. Yes, I sought certain guarantees for my time was short. The contract was one of course and the cost of the house is a small price to pay. But the rest? You need to wake up and look at yourself first, did you not enter into such unions willingly?"

"Unions?"

"Come now Father, don't play games, I refer to young Keira of course."

Fitzgerald locked eyes with the man and as they did so a veil fell from his eyes. The timing of everything now nagged at him. Keira. The flirting, the way she had come to him in the night.

Oh Keira, no.

In that instant he knew then he had been played, and with that went any lingering fantasy he held of being with Keira. For if a manipulation it was, it was surely perfectly formed. How could he now reject the request? They held all the cards, didn't they? If he refused, there was the matter of his infidelity and the same escape from the town and the Church which had only moments ago seemed like a blessing, now seemed like a gaping chasm on which he teetered on the edge.

All the while, he saw McArthur study him, searching to see if he had pieced it all together. No words had been said, but if he should shy away from what was asked, they would then. And what else, would they have gone as far as to have recorded it somehow? The thought beat him into submission, for he had little doubt that they would go to whatever lengths they needed to get him to submit to their will.

"But I…this house… I needed…"

"Yes!" McArthur exclaimed. "This house! Why I had you remain? So you could see it for yourself! So you could feel it! How else could I ask you to buy into something so incredible? I didn't know what you might experience, but I knew it would be something. How could I ask you to do this thing if you did not believe it?"

"And how can you be sure that I do believe it?"

McArthur paused, uncertainty now prevalent upon his face, giving Fitzgerald a moments satisfaction as his adversary undoubtedly wrestled with the prospect that his well-laid plans were all for nought. The feeling was short-lived though, for what won through on his face was the self-belief of a man who had unlikely never failed to get his own way.

"Oh, come now, Father, let's not play games here. How could you not have felt something? This place is so fucking haunted I could run tours for christ's sake! But please, no games. I know things about you. I have eyes and ears throughout the house and know you have been digging. Your visit from Deacon Morris for example?"

"Colin? What has that got to do with…"

"You've been digging around trying to find information on Elizabeth and Father Crosby, don't try to deny it, I know he brought you the diaries. Let me ask you, Father, would you like to see the missing pages?"

Fitzgerald froze. The revelation that he knew of the diaries was no surprise. What was though, was the fact that he had been so naïve to think his enquiries had been in secret and under McArthur's radar. For a fraction of a moment, he wondered who might have betrayed this information, but the truth was he had not gone to appropriate lengths to cover his tracks, but why should he have needed to? The diaries were there for anyone to see, should they gain access to his room and as such both Keira and Hodgson were likely candidates to have seen them there. Thereafter it was no issue to put two and two together and work out what he was searching for. But now this, McArthur had teased him about the book's missing pages.

"Impossible." Despite his refusal, he could already see the truth in McArthur's gloating smile.

"No, Father. I wager you know why they are missing and what they allude to, but it was not the Church who recovered them so as to protect themselves, it was me trying to protect Elizabeth and my own interests."

"You've left no stone unturned it seems."

McArthur looked sad once more. "No, it is not like that. You think me a cold, calculating son of a bitch. But this was never some game to be played. Had I known what that imbecile priest was attempting to do, don't you think I would have intervened? To protect my precious Elizabeth? He took her away from me, damn it!"

This outburst led to another spasm of coughing. Learning his lesson, Fitzgerald did nothing to intervene and instead waited until the loud hacks and barks whittled down to a soft wheeze. At last, he was able to continue, but Fitzgerald was alarmed to see the man had wilted following his last attack and sank lower into his bed. He seemed now not to have the strength or inclination to meet Fitzgerald on the same level. "I took those pages, but not with some master game plan in mind. I didn't know all those years ago we would be here today having this conversation and me doing all I could to ask you to help me."

"Help you? Through manipulation? Why not simply ask?"

"And have you say no as Shilling did? I have not the time to start over, use your eyes man, this is it for me. I mention the pages as I know you seek answers and I think they may yet aid you if you do as I ask, so as not to make the same mistake as Crosby."

"Then you have read them?"

"Of course. I had to know what befell my poor Elizabeth. You will make your own judgements, of course, Father, but for what I read, the man did not believe and was overwhelmed at the enormity of the task. I would ask that you would take heed and be ready."

"You assume a lot, Robert. You assume I will do this."

"Then it comes to this then. I beg of you to do it, but not just for me, but for the memory of my Elizabeth and your own Crosby. Do it for the little girl who died here and do it for yourself. I see more in you than you could know and I know this thing haunts you, it is written all about you. You would be giving me more than the absolution I craved, for in my last act I would send that devil back to the pits of hell where it belongs and undo the wrong that Searle set in place and I exacerbated. Please, Father, help me do so."

"I must know first what should happen if I do not."

"Really? I hoped you would make your judgement upon what was right, but so be it. I have had Harvey draw a second will, of course. The house will never go to the Church and for that, they will blame you. Don't be as foolish as to think they do not take such a thing lightly. We are talking about the bequeathing of some £4.5 million in property and grounds and furthermore, there is the matter of testimony of young Keira. You would be ruined Father, your safe little parish gone as quickly as it came."

"And what of your soul Robert, what of your confession?"

"What is but one more sin now if no other is to be forgiven? I do not wish it to come to this, but I must do all that I am able. I am desperate, don't you understand? I would give anything!"

Fitzgerald was defeated. And he knew for why. Not for the threats of this desperate mess of a human being, for all that had been threatened held no sway over him. No, it was for duty to his God that he would do it and for the person he was. He had been soured and embittered by his experience here, and what hurt the most was Keira's betrayal. What had she been promised for selling herself, he wondered?

And so the fact was that this elaborate subterfuge was all so unnecessary and that McArthur just could not comprehend such a thing was a travesty.

"Very well, Robert, I will do it."

The relief on the old man's face was palpable. "Oh, thank you, thank you." Tears began to form in his eyes. "You shall have whatever you need. But first, for everything that has been said, I ask again…

"I know," Fitzgerald said, "You know the words."

"I do. Please forgive me, Father, for I have sinned…"

McArthur would be absolved a second time.

CHAPTER 41

Fitzgerald was back now in the study of his apartment. He felt ill at ease following his conversation with McArthur and giving the man absolution a second time, only this time for blackmailing him into submission regarding the exorcism.

In a way, though it was an ending of sorts. He had delivered what he had set out to do here and despite the ambiguous morals of the Church's agreement with McArthur, the house, for better or worse would soon belong to them. At least it would when he had done McArthur's bidding.

He knew such a thing would have to be done as soon as possible for their long talk had been exhausting and had caused the old man to sink under the weight of his efforts. Finally, Keira had administered a dose of morphine that had sent McArthur into a deep and welcome sleep. For his part, Fitzgerald wondered if the forgiveness he had given would allow the man to dream any easier. He was not so confident that his own sleep would be, for what he had agreed to, and Keira's betrayal were paramount in his thoughts and though he was eager to speak with her, her duty to McArthur prevented any chance.

And so he returned to his rooms. The diaries of Father Crosby now strewn over the desk before him. Such had been his anticipation to read the relevant and missing chapters he had begun in earnest to try and elicit meaning from what he did have. However, after an hour of frustration and learning little other than the simple engagements of the Church, he was none the wiser.

What he was waiting on he knew, was Harvey, who McArthur had instructed him to call and offer a password of "Redemption", for McArthur was in no condition to request the documents himself. This gave rise to wonder how much more the young lawyer knew of their situation, but when the packet finally arrived, he found that it contained a single stuffed envelope, fixed with the personalised wax seal of Robert McArthur, denoted with his initials RM.

It had been Hodgson who delivered the packet to his room, and if she knew the relevance of its contents, she did not show it.

And so now here before him were the pages — four in all, double-sided and full of the now familiar scrawl of Crosby. Quickly checking the dates, he felt relieved to see that he had that which he had been seeking. He checked his memory and immediately went to the diary marked 1996. This was the volume from which the pages were missing and though he already knew they were genuine, he tucked the pages back into the book to compare the neat tear lines. The pages fitted perfectly.

The first of the ripped pages that stared back at him was marked Monday 22nd January 1996. He began to read.

Oh, Elizabeth, how you had me fooled. I simply wanted to believe that you had come to terms with what happened to poor Lydia. You had me think that therapy and medication were working, all the while entertaining such lurid fantasy. How has Robert allowed this to fester for so long, or were you so successful as to pull the wool over his eyes as well? How he missed such clues, I do not know, or maybe he believed that the so-called faith healers you employed were all a part of the healing process. Not so. And now that they have failed you, you turn to me and reveal your charade. What am I to do now? For your own good, I should have at least informed Robert but you begged me not to. Instead promising to embrace your therapy should I only do this one thing. You have me between a rock and a hard place, for I should not entertain your delusions. But if I do not, I know they will go unchecked and consume you. That is not to say they have not already, but were I to do this thing, can I break the spell upon you? Deliver you from your demon where everything else has failed?

What would the bishop make of this? He'd laugh me out of the room, that is what. Not before reminding me that I am enabling your psychosis by entertaining it. Has he ever dealt with such issues himself though? It is one thing to know what is right, and it is another to speak with you and believe that 'the right thing' is right for you. I mean what harm could it do, if you believe it done? A harmless house exorcism, if that, for I need not enter into such rituals if I can simply make you believe I have banished the curse from your home. Do I not at least owe it to you to try?

Crosby's words had filled the page, and already Fitzgerald could sense the man's undoing. Just as McArthur himself had suggested, he had not believed. And to have taken on such a thing lightly and without the appropriate preparations, it was no wonder his efforts had resulted in failure. But what of Elizabeth? The page had made mention of what Crosby had called faith healers. Fitzgerald had little doubt they were somewhat more. He could not know to what extent she ever knew of the house's curse and how a wiccan spell had imprisoned a demon within but had she employed such people with a view of cleansing the dark forces she perceived within her home?

The sad thing he knew was that her efforts were undoubtedly behind McArthur's back. What if she had engaged him? Would he have shared what he knew? And if so, could they together have banished the spectre of evil from the house?

It would never be known of course, for she had acted alone and in the dark. What divisions there were in her marriage at that time he could not know for sure, but knowing McArthur, he could sense that a distance had grown between them as Elizabeth's mental health had deteriorated. He had in fact alluded to such a thing, stating he had left her to her doctor's instead of being there for her himself. And so, she stumbled on blindly and alone, until such time and through desperation, she reached out to her friend Father Crosby, who no doubt wished to act in her best interests without knowing the gravity of the situation he was putting himself in.

He turned the page and continued to read. Within a sentence, he snapped the book shut for what was written. Anger coupled with confusion washed over him and he deliberately opened the book once more to read the line over and over.

Colin has agreed to assist me.

(Colin Morris?)

Colin has agreed to assist me. I went to him so as to voice my concerns. He is a trusted friend, and he would hear me better than the bishop ever would. It was not until we spoke that I actually ever believed I would undertake such a thing, but with his support, I can see that it can and should be done. He knows Elizabeth well and broached something I hadn't really considered. What if it was real? Such a thing now dominates my thoughts and I am thankful to him for his words and help. This should not be entered into lightly and between us, we can invoke the rituals of exorcism correctly as if such a thing did in fact exist. All the better for Elizabeth, for anything less than 100% commitment may not be enough to bring her round and end her madness.

Perhaps the place is haunted somehow after all. All such manors have their 'histories' do they not? I would be wise to speak with her further and discover what she knows. Thus far, she points to the library. I don't know why and had to question how that could be relevant. I assumed the crux of her angst would be centred on that damned swimming pool. Was it not enough to have the thing filled in and be done with? Apparently not.

Fitzgerald considered what he had read. He knew well that Colin Morris had been at St Peter's back when all this had taken place. The man had gone so far as to tell him so. But this was yet another betrayal for he had known all along, had in fact been involved all along.

How could this be? He had only known Colin for a short time but had quickly come to accept him as a friend and confidant. Morris had gone so far as to try and prevent Fitzgerald falling into McArthur's trap. Hadn't he?

Fitzgerald's judgement was now in question, Morris had also delivered the diaries to him and in all truth had likely been the very person who had recovered the missing pages in the first instance and delivered them to McArthur. But what did that mean? Was it self-preservation? Or was Morris another pawn in McArthur's twisted game, that's sole purpose was his manipulation into doing this heinous act?

The thought gave rise to another. For to what extent had Morris been involved in the original exorcism and what might he tell him? Up until now, Fitzgerald had considered that this undertaking was his to bear alone, but should that be the case? Even Crosby had shown the sense to involve another, despite the fact that he had not believed in their ultimate goal.

Could Morris be compelled to participate and remove some of the burden that he was facing? The idea instantly held weight for him, for the anxiety of acting alone was almost too much to bear. In any event, he would have this out with him, words needed to be spoken and the truth demanded from the man. Morris owed him that much at least.

The next entry held no further surprises.

Tuesday, 23rd January 1996.

We are on for tomorrow night. I understand that Robert is away on business and Elizabeth has made it so that the rest of the house will be empty also. I must say that I feel a keen sense of dread at performing the ritual during the night. Elizabeth though will have it no other way, she speaks to me in riddles and suggests that a deal done in darkness must be completed in darkness. (Fitzgerald felt himself shiver) *I don't know what that means, but again if we are to lift this sickness from her, then we must show her that we buy into it.*

Both myself and Colin have agreed upon the order of the ritual and deliberated long over the relevant passages within the Bible.

Ecce crucis signum fugiant phantasmata cuncta.

Fitzgerald knew the translation from the Latin. 'Behold the emblem of the cross. Let all spectres flee.'

Within the passages, there again appeared to be a break in time.

We have seen the library ahead of our mission there tomorrow. Curious. It was as expected lit brighter than the sun as Elizabeth warned, and no shadows fell anywhere just as she suggested, such was the abundance of strip lighting there, but I fancy I saw something. A trick of the light perhaps, a shadow?

I did double-take, and of course, there was nothing but it gave me goose bumps and I will be glad when this is all over. I am decided that whatever the outcome that Elizabeth must get the help she needs, whether she seeks it herself or not. Her fear in entering the room was so evident and I have to admit infectious. She must believe it done tomorrow for who knows what will become of her.

I hesitate to mention my concerns now, for Colin is bullish regarding the ceremony. He is young and speaks of these matters lightly. I wonder if he thinks of himself as some Lankester Merrin or Damien Karras? Would that our ritual goes better than theirs did!

Fitzgerald smiled, but it was touched as well with sadness. Although he had never met him, he found Crosby a likeable person, his diaries although masked with humour, showed his fears and that he knew the gravity of performing the exorcism whether he believed it or not. In the circumstances, he wished it was this man that he could call upon to aid him when the time came, not the untrustworthy Morris. But despite that, he knew he had no option and would approach the man as soon as he was able.

He glanced over at the telephone that sat on the right-hand side of the desk and contemplated making the call immediately. Such was his anger, though he was not sure that he could trust his emotions should he hear the man's voice so soon. And what if he should try to deny his part in the whole thing? That would only put a divide between the two and make it all the more unlikely, that Morris would assist him in what should be done.

But should it be Colin at all? Should he not go instead to the bishop with his concerns? He could certainly make his case without any problem, and the bishop's greed for the house and Estate should certainly secure his undivided co-operation.

As soon as he had the thought though he dismissed it, for he knew to do such a thing would be to sell such a proposition as the indulgence of a dying man's last wish, he who saw ghosts in his closets. That would not do. While it might be agreed upon, what would happen if McArthur should pass away before the rite could be undertaken? Nothing that was what. And should he approach the diocese and tell them the truth? That he himself believed there to be some malevolent entity within the home? That would be the end of him within the Church he knew, perhaps even more so than if McArthur made good on his threat to renege the transfer of the house.

What was more, it had to be him he understood. His experiences here had driven him to this point, and despite his distrust and his animosity toward McArthur for his scheming, he did believe the man on one salient point. To do such a thing, meant believing.

With his mind now made up, he felt as if a weight had fallen from his shoulders. Such a feeling was a relief to a mind that had been in turmoil as it had wrestled with impossibilities, fear and confusion.

The resolution to such strife would be to do the damned exorcism (preferably with Colin's help, but without it if necessary) and then put the memory of Thoby Hall and all that had happened as far behind him as he could. And knowing this was right, he resolved that it would be that same night if it were possible so that his resolve did not abandon him and that he could finally leave this damnable house for good.

He turned his head, his eyes trailing to the clock that stood watchful sentry upon the mantel behind him. The day was getting on for it was already 11:30 am. There would be preparations that would need to be done, and that decided him. He picked up the phone and dialled.

He hardly had the time to think about what he was going to say as the phone was answered on only the second ring.

"Colin Morris."

"Colin? It's Iain. I'm glad I got you."

A slight pause from the other end. "Iain? Good to hear from you old man. What can I do for you?"

"I need you to listen Colin. I need your help. I wonder if you don't already know what I would ask?"

"…"

"I know Colin. I know all of it now."

"Iain, I…"

311

"Please, Colin, just listen. As I say, you may well have known this was coming. My business with McArthur is all but at an end and would have been but for one further thing, he requests. You know what it is, I think the day you came to me and delivered the diaries you would have known. I have the missing pages Colin and I know what you and Crosby did together."

Fitzgerald paused so as to let the weight of his words sink in on the other side. His anger had dissipated as quickly as it had come, and so he was steady and knew what and how he wanted to convey to the man.

"Why bring this up now, Iain? I should have known McArthur would not have let such a thing rest. Does he blame me? The Church? For what happened to his wife? If that is it Iain, I will deny it. I will deny it ever happened."

"God, no. He believes it Colin, all of it. What he shared with me. His confession. It did not start with him, but he has known of what dwells here for some time."

"What are you saying?"

"He wants me to be rid of it."

"Say it then Iain. Don't beat around the bush. Say what you mean, so I know we are not at odds with one another."

"The Devil." He whispered it for fear of being overheard somehow. All he heard though was the steady tick-tock of the timepiece from the wall behind him. "The demon, whatever you want to call it. You and Crosby performed an unsanctioned exorcism here in the library. He wants me to repeat it."

The line was silent, so he continued. "The confession was part of it Colin, but not all of it. I have delivered that part, but now he holds the contract we signed to ransom. I can't deliver the house to the diocese without following through on his request."

"Is that all of it Iain?"

Fitzgerald closed his eyes. Morris saw through him quite easily it seemed, but he would not have the whole truth of it. "No. It is not all of it. The real reason I am here. The reason I had to remain in the house was so as to experience it myself. And I have Colin, I have. I will do this thing but not just to fulfil the damned contract. I will do it for Crosby, and I will do it for Elizabeth, but more than that, I will do my Holy duty and send this accursed thing back to where it belongs. You have experienced this before Colin, I ask you for your help."

The line again went quiet. Fitzgerald's pulse had begun to quicken, and he was on tenterhooks as he anticipated the other man's answer.

"I don't know where to begin Iain. I am not sure I could…"

"Is it what happened to Crosby?"

"No, no," from the other side of the line, Morris found the resilience at last to acknowledge the subject matter. "Look Iain; maybe we should meet and discuss this, yeah? What you are asking of me…I had long since put behind me. But not for the reasons you would think. The ritual? The night me and Crosby performed the ritual? Nothing happened Iain. Nothing happened. The room was empty."

It was Fitzgerald's turn to be silent.

"What happened afterwards? I was at a loss Iain. Crosby? Elizabeth? What happened to them? It was crazy…I…the room…the room was empty."

"Look, Colin…" Fitzgerald stammered into the line.

"I know what you would say, Iain. Of course, it wasn't for nothing. What happened to the two of them I mean. I can only tell you what I know. We performed the ritual with Elizabeth. You would know her presence was critical yes?"

Fitzgerald did know. One of the key aspects of ridding a house or building of a malevolent spirit was for the resident, in combination with the practising priest to bid such a spirit to leave. He had already considered such a thing, as McArthur's own condition presented problems for how he would deliver the ritual in due time.

Morris continued. "We performed the ritual, and nothing occurred. I don't know what one is supposed to expect in such circumstances. Television had me believe that the books would fly from the very shelves. But of course, no such thing happened. For his part, I think Crosby cared not if it had worked, only for what her reaction might have been."

"And what of that? How did she react?"

"At first? There was nothing. I suspect she believed there would be some physical reaction also. In a way, I wish there had been. It would have been all the easier for her to believe. So what happened next, for her at least? She was not a well person Iain. You have to remember that. We did nothing to alleviate her mental health issues, she relapsed and of course, was eventually sectioned."

"But that doesn't explain Crosby."

"No…no, it doesn't. Look Iain. You can't mean to do this thing. It is farcical. McArthur is a deluded old man. I told you to do what you had to and get out of there. But this? It is an affront to God to perform the ritual in such a way. Perhaps that is what claimed Crosby in the end? Damn the house. Let the man die and if he changes the nature of his agreement, then so be it. You have lived up to your side of the bargain, what criticism could there be of you?"

Fitzgerald felt deflated, he idly turned the pages of the diary before him and found further entries that begged investigation and with that, new resolve found him also. Morris wished to negate the happenings within Thoby Hall and distance himself from what must be done. That much was clear. Fitzgerald could not believe for an instant that everything that had happened was for nothing and though Morris raised a credible point regarding Elizabeth McArthur's fragile mental health, he had done nothing to explain Crosby's descent into despair. He would not get the answers he craved from this conversation he knew. The pages before him were where the truth lay.

"Iain? Iain are you still there? Look, just walk away. Do what is right for you. I can see that damned house has affected you. I told you so when I saw you. Whatever you think you believe, you must discount it. Walk away and breathe the air and look in the cold light of day. You will see what I am saying is right."

"Perhaps you are right Colin. I am so very tired of this place, and yes, it does have an effect upon you after a while. Forget what I said."

The relief on the other end of the phone was evident. "Look, perhaps I should come get you? Bring you back to St Peter's?"

"I can't yet, but thank you. McArthur is near his end, and there is still the matter of last rites. It may be as soon as today now that his confession is done. It has taken all the strength from him. I will speak with you soon though."

Fitzgerald could hear the doubt on the other man's voice. "Are you sure, Iain?"

"Yes, yes. It's as you said. Get my business done and get out. It is close at hand now. I will speak to you soon."

Following a cursory goodbye, Fitzgerald put the receiver down and ended the phone call. He had been too quick to call Morris, he thought. The man's denials were such that he wondered what evidence he would have had to present to get the truth from him. He had suggested that the library had been empty. Fitzgerald did not believe that, for he had his own experiences to draw upon.

Morris, likewise had suggested that they had conducted the ceremony and nothing had happened. Fitzgerald did not believe that either, for one person had died in the days following and another committed to long-term psychiatric care. And so the conclusion had to be that Morris was lying. His reasons? Perhaps only to cover his own back in the aftermath of the tragedy that ensued, removing the relevant pages from the diary to ensure he was safe. But was that all of it? Fitzgerald could not be sure. There had been an underlying tone of fear in the deacon's voice as they spoke and it was not through fear of his secrets being discovered, Fitzgerald thought. In any event, the man would be no use to him.

Putting aside any thoughts of Colin Morris, Fitzgerald bent his head and returned his attention to the diaries of Father James Crosby.

CHAPTER 42

*T*hursday, 25th January 1996.

It is done. For better or worse, it is done. I ask myself now if it has had the desired effect upon Elizabeth. Only time will tell. I can't say that I knew what would happen, for everything that she has told me I half expected some demonic presence to reveal itself and physically fight against its banishment. It was with relief though that we concluded without incident. Having no experience in such matters, I only told her that it was done and already I saw doubt in her eyes, but what more could I do? Have Colin go and hide in the stacks and toss some books liberally around the room?

I must keep her close now and observe how she reacts. If there is the slightest hint of her falling back into the same thoughts, then I must act for her own good. I realise now how entrenched she is in her paranoia, so much so that I nearly bought into the exorcism. I feel foolish for that, for the real reason in performing it was for her peace of mind only. I read over my first line, ha! What did I expect to happen? Such a fool I am, but I have to readily admit there is power in the words that I spoke and the library itself was a fitting location for the mind to run rampant. Whatever happens now, it would serve her well to take a long and well-earned break from that house.

Fitzgerald's first reaction on reading the passage was crushing self-doubt. The words written by Crosby were at odds with every belief he had come to accept about the house and what had subsequently happened to both the author of the words and poor Elizabeth. How could it be that nothing had happened? In only a few days from this entry, Crosby would go on to slit his wrists and serve his blood in the Holy Eucharist and not long after take his own life. If so, what on earth could have happened between the exorcism and those events if the exorcism itself was redundant?

He need not have worried long, for the next passage, Crosby's last it seemed affirmed everything he knew.

Friday, 26th January 1996.

Where do I begin? **SINNER***! I have failed you Elizabeth* **ADULTERER***! For I did not see. How complacent I have been! It came to me at first in flashes and followed me into my dreams. The ritual, it was real, but I did not believe! I must explain, for my every thought is consumed by its presence, it overtakes me, and where before it lurked only in shadows and the corner of my eye, I fear now that I see it everywhere I go. It is the reflection in my mirror. It whispers horrors into my ear even while I am awake. Its razor teeth grin at me* *in the smile of a small innocent child. Oh Lord, help me, for my reaction would be to stab at it wherever it hides.* **MURDERER!**

Sinner, adulterer, murderer. The words were not in keeping with the flow of the text, and each word was all but carved into the page and scribbled thickly as if drawn over many times. Fitzgerald contemplated the fact that madness was already overtaking Crosby as he wrote. Had he seen the words as he crafted them? He could never know. He continued…

My mind turns back to the exorcism. We believed nothing had happened, how wrong we were. As I say, I saw it first in flashes. Fragments of memory returned to me as if in freeze-frame. Only scant seconds and gone, leaving me to question my sanity. I write these words now to remind myself and keep myself grounded as to the truth for they may yet be my salvation.

I must take Elizabeth **WHORE!**, *Colin, too if he is similarly afflicted and go to a safe haven. The bishop will not understand but there will be those in the Church who do, there must be! Rumour abounds that the Catholic Church* **LIARS!** *Have a secret cabinet who deal with such as we. Am I possessed? Is this what is happening to me? It crawls within my brain and behind my eyes now and a very real and horrifying thought comes to me as I feel I should poke my own eyes* **YES!** *out lest I hurt someone I see the beast in.*

Fitzgerald realised that there was a passage of time in the writings and did his utmost to try and separate them within the entries. This was not so difficult a task, for Crosby's descent into despair and madness could easily be seen as the writing became more erratic in its script and littered with obscenities that he doubted that Crosby ever saw.

It becomes harder and harder to focus and separate what is real and what is not. There is a veil between what I saw there and what really happened. At first, the veil was drawn only slightly, but now I see all of it. The ritual failed. It taunts me and punishes me now **FRAUD! LIAR! BLASPHEMER!** *It came when summoned I know that now. Rank and ancient it appeared at first and we were nearly overwhelmed at the sight of it. I froze, for all my preparations had been only of what words I would speak, never, never that it should be real or those words hold power. It came and I shrank from it. Colin* **RAPIST!** *Saved us or so I thought, for it was he who found the words to begin, to stop the beast* **GLORIOUS!** *In its tracks.*

Tene ego praecipio tibi in nomine Domini.

In the name of the Lord, I command you to hold, Fitzgerald read.

It approached him, and I could see hatred in the black of its eyes. Colin shrank from him but it gave me the time to act.

I held the creature before me. I gloried in the power of my words! **FOOL!**

Fitzgerald was likewise captivated by the words. It came to them rank and ancient! His dream, it was all that had happened in his dream.

It was no dream, Iain. You already know you have been in that room, you have seen it and the Devil with your own eyes. It was no dream.

He nodded, for he needed the affirmation of all he had discounted. He would not fail as Crosby had done, for he did believe. Crosby's own failings were apparent in his words for he had not accepted Elizabeth's truth until it was too late.

The thing became human before my eyes: a man, strong, dominant, compelling. His voice powerful and alluring. His hatred a real and viable thing, it exuded from him and was red hot upon my skin. It spoke, not to me but to Elizabeth and I saw the horror in her eyes. The reality of its being is more toxic to her than any possibility of delusion which I believed she suffered. She would be better off with madness than truth. **YES! MADNESS!**

It was all over soon after it began. I shouted the words of expulsion to it, so as to drown its words to Elizabeth. I know only they could be poison to her and though I had not believed, and though Colin had not believed, we joined in unison to expel the creature. It departed, but not as we intended and only with a hideous laugh.

At first, all was still and we thought ourselves successful somehow **IDIOT! RETARD!** *We went to her then and asked her what it said to her. She told me we had angered it, for we were not worthy and not capable. It would sleep again until its time came. But we, we who had caused it to wake ahead of its time would be punished.* **DEATH!**

How we came to forget what we saw, I do not know — some power the creature had over us. I read my earlier entry and see that I was blind, but these things came to me but slowly. I must go to her. I must go to her now before it is too late, for if she sees what I do, it will be her undoing. It may yet be mine.

Fitzgerald turned the final page only to find the back sheet was empty. Crosby had no doubt succumbed to the madness that would take him within the following few days. Questions were left unanswered of course and he wondered if he had been able to do anything for Elizabeth. Given what happened, that was unlikely, but what did not add up was how Colin Morris had remained seemingly unaffected by all that had happened. He had denied to him even that anything had happened and from reading the initial words from the torn pages, Crosby had likewise believed the ritual to have been in vain. Had Morris been somehow spared the knowledge of what had really occurred? If not, how could he have gone on living his life as he did?

The question now for Fitzgerald was what answers the passages had given him. Had there been power in the words utilised by Crosby, or had the beast simply ignored them all? What difference would his belief be for him if he uttered the wrong verses of rite? Much was missing from Crosby's account as it only suggested at how he and Morris had attempted to tackle the beast. How would he do it differently? How could he be successful if he was to do it alone as he was to do? Time was growing short; for now, it was well past midday. He meant to conclude the exorcism that same evening but yet something told him there was some clue amongst all that he had learned that he had somehow overlooked. Something so near but yet so far, but what could it be?

317

Perhaps the answer lay with the one person in all of these events who had been present throughout. Had instigated the exorcism. Had been present and spoken directly with the creature itself. Elizabeth McArthur.

CHAPTER 43

Something happened to Iain Fitzgerald as his car splashed through the muddy potholes on the long rutted driveway and Thoby Hall became a small thing in his rear-view mirror.

It was as if a weight had been lifted from his shoulders and as he made the end of the driveway and the car sat idling before the quiet country road, he temporarily forgot himself as to his purpose and where he was going. The early afternoon was brightly lit and mild and he had allowed the cool air to wash over him as he drove by winding down the driver's side window. The feeling was invigorating and he felt truly alive to the day as he sat there in his car, contemplating what should come next.

Reluctantly, he knew his path lay to the left and east for that is where he would find the town of Banfield and there within he would find St Luke's Hospital where Elizabeth was being cared for. The idea of going to find and speak to her had been somewhat liberating for there he would finally find a kindred spirit, someone who had the knowledge and answers to his most searching questions. Even so, the urge to turn the car right and in the opposite direction was a temptation he had to fight against, and he had to shut down the voices that told him, none would be the wiser should he do so.

McArthur would pass away sooner rather than later, it was obvious, for Fitzgerald had called back to his rooms so as to get his permission to visit with Elizabeth. He thought he may have found resistance there, but through Keira acting as the messenger, permission was quickly granted, though she bid him to hurry as McArthur was now becoming very weak.

And though he already knew the name of the hospital and the town in which it was situated from his late-night excursion into Harvey's office, he listened patiently as Keira gave him his directions.

All that had remained was one more phone call, to St Luke's itself. There he ran into a roadblock, the receptionist on the other end citing data protection regulations and stating that she could not verify the fact that they had a patient called Elizabeth McArthur. And so he was patient, explaining who he was and that he was providing dying care to Elizabeth's husband and that it had been his request that she be informed of his imminent passing. He also suggested that she call the family's legal representative to check the validity of his request and confirm his identity. He would simply leave his phone number and await her call, stressing that urgency was of the highest priority as Mr McArthur may soon pass.

It had been a gamble he knew, for he did not know what Harvey's reaction would be. What was certain was that McArthur was in no condition to contact the man and give instruction.

The return phone call was made within five minutes, he had half expected the voice on the other line to have been that of Harvey, demanding to know why he was seeking to see Elizabeth, but no, it was the same receptionist who now confirmed that Elizabeth was resident with them and that he was very welcome to visit her.

And so here he was at the end of the driveway and the horns of a dilemma. Left or right?

Frowning, he engaged the left turn signal though there was no passing traffic to witness it and he pulled the car out into the road, his destination the small town of Banfield.

The silence in the car was oppressive and nagging voices of doubt pressed at him until he tired of them and turned the radio on. He scanned the FM bandwidth with little joy. A debate about the character flaws of the USA's president-elect, a phone-in competition with some prepubescent disc jockey, where you had to identify three voices mixed together. He settled at last for the music of the Rolling Stones and a long-time favourite 'Gimme Shelter' on the local station. Before long he was singing under his breath and had at last found escape from anything related to Thoby Hall or its nefarious residents.

The respite was all too brief though, and before long, he found road signs that ticked away the seven miles to his destination. The Rolling Stones had given way to the Carpenters and they in turn by a traffic report, news and weather. The words came to him as if from afar like white noise and he was jolted back to reality only by news of a storm front coming in from the west that would likely mean more rain overnight and with that the sun took its cue to disappear behind a cloud, leaving Fitzgerald feeling low once more.

Country fields and hedgerows soon gave way to the first smattering of housing and not far beyond appeared the sign 'Banfield' (Please drive carefully).

A google map search had reinforced Keira's very simple directions toward the hospital, and before he even had time to question his whereabouts for the first time, Lakeside Road, his destination was before him and to the left. He indicated again to nobody and took the turn.

The hospital when he found it was not at all what he had been expecting. Here was a delightful and bright new build with three floors where instead he had imagined the rotting monstrosity of a nineteenth-century insane asylum.

Such buildings had long been used for the care of the mentally ill, and he shuddered as he remembered excerpts from a documentary he had seen about the shocking level of care afforded to such patients through the 1970s and early '80s. Images of sterile rooms and cracked paint, damp seeping through the walls and patients left to rot in their own filth came to him and he took a moment to cross himself and say a prayer for the troubled and afflicted who had suffered through it all.

Things had changed now, albeit slowly, and institutions such as this were now becoming more commonplace, though he couldn't help but wonder if McArthur's money had afforded her care such as this. He saw that his arrival had already been seen for a young woman in her early twenties waved at him from behind a receptionist desk inside. He looked about to be sure it was him that she greeted before waving back, the familiarity of her greeting was slightly off-putting somehow. The friendliness in stark contrast to all he had suffered and experienced in the last five days at Thoby Hall.

He put it aside though, such thoughts were only of prior experience, it had been a long time since he had felt warmth such as that and so he fixed a smile as he approached the door, which emanated a buzzing sound as he approached, indicating she had allowed him entry.

He found himself before another glass door that was closed to him. He understood the security well enough to know he was in an 'airlock' and had to wait for the smooth mechanism on the outer door to close before he could meet his happy contact.

"Father Fitzgerald? Of course, how silly of me. Please come through and have a seat. Dr Kapoor will be with you shortly. I was sure to tell her the urgency of your visit as she knows you must get back as soon as possible. Can I get you a drink at all?"

His facade it seemed was running smoothly. "Oh no, I'm fine, thank you. Jill is it? The one I spoke to on the phone? I realise you couldn't speak of such things without verifying who I was, but before I see her, can I ask how she is?"

The young woman looked sad as she spoke. "I'm afraid it is not really for me to say, Father. Elizabeth has been with us for some time now. She has good days and bad. I'm sure the doctor will be better able to tell you than I ever could. Please, let me get you to sign in and I will give you your visitor's pass."

No matter. He would find out sooner rather than later. That said, he couldn't help but wonder what the difference between a good day and bad was. He again imagined visions both from the horrid documentary he had seen, as well as movies and television, whereby catatonic patients in straitjackets would be left to their own devices in rooms no bigger than a prison cell, left to slowly rock back and forth as medication overwhelmed them and drool spilt from quivering lips.

He signed his name and walked to a partitioned waiting area, where the sofas were plush and of bright pastels. Jill busied herself with his pass, and he looked beyond her reception area to see a set of double doors also secured with a pac tag locking system. Only those staff members with the correctly coded fobs would have access in and out. Whatever this place was, it was secure and for someone like Elizabeth and those others who were resident, he knew they were likely compelled to remain under the Mental Health Act legislation.

At last, he saw a face appear through the window on the other side of the double door. He guessed from her ethnicity that this was Dr Kapoor. The door opened and so he stood to meet her. She was a very meagre 5' 4" and slim. Her hair was tied back in a short ponytail. Her green smock was in keeping with the bright pastel tones of the hospital. She smiled as she

321

approached him and exuded warmth. He guessed she was little more than 30 years old and so not too many moons since she graduated with her degree.

"Father Fitzgerald? Sorry for keeping you waiting. I am Doctor Kapoor."

"Doctor, thank you so much for making this provision. It is a delicate matter."

"Please let us sit down and talk." She motioned back toward the seats at his back. "I will be honest with you Father; this was a close-run thing. You do understand that Elizabeth's wellbeing was paramount in my decision to let her see you?"

Fitzgerald nodded.

"As it is, she has not been in a good way and has withdrawn from communication for several weeks now. You have spent time with her husband? You understand her condition?"

"He did not go as far as to lay it in medical terms doctor. But from what I have gathered, she suffers from acute schizophrenia."

"Hmmm. It is fair to say in Elizabeth's case, it goes beyond as simple a diagnosis as that. Paranoid schizophrenia yes and multiple personality disorder. Coupled with obsessive-compulsive disorder and bipolar disorder. You may now see why I thought long and hard about allowing this intervention."

"My goodness. Will she even understand me?"

"Perhaps so, deep down." Dr Kapoor hesitated momentarily. "You understand that I am ordinarily bound by the patient's confidentiality? This is unusual…the solicitor that you asked Jill to contact?"

"Yes?"

"He is exercising Mr McArthur's legal power of attorney while he is incapacitated."

"Unusual yes, but…"

"He instructed that I was to give you unreserved access to anything you wish to know. But be warned Father, as I said, my only concern is for Elizabeth."

Somehow Harvey knew. But how? McArthur had been in no fit condition to relay such instruction. So, had they in fact anticipated such an act on Fitzgerald's part all along? If so, it was true that he had been following a long line of breadcrumbs the whole time.

"Given her condition then doctor, is it wise that I should speak to her at all of this?" Despite his previous determination to speak with her, he was now ready to give up on the idea having heard of the terrible difficulties that Elizabeth was experiencing. How could he put her through such a thing if it were to cause her condition to deteriorate?

"That was chief among my concerns Father. But I am hoping the news will bring her some kind of closure for chief among her delusions is that her home is somehow haunted and that the residents there are in constant peril. You perhaps know of the young girl who died there?"

"I do."

"This, we believe, was the instigating event in the degeneration of her stable mind. Despite many pleas to what rational part remains, she plays out horrible fantasies in her mind where some demon taunts her and describes the horrors it would unleash there. Although a terribly sad event, the passing of her ex-husband through other, more natural causes, will I hope break the cycle of dread within her. Perhaps not at first of course, but it gives us hope that our psychotherapy can at least begin to have some inroads."

Fitzgerald nodded his understanding. "What of the other matter though? Father Crosby?"

"That is perhaps more complex and undoubtedly my biggest concern in the two of you meeting. I should ask first of all, was this Father Crosby a colleague of yours?"

"No, not at all. I am aware of the situation, of course, but I have only recently begun my work at St Peter's in Ashmarsh."

"Very good, I did not wish to say anything that might be upsetting. The problem surrounding this Father Crosby is that she does not fault this demon, only herself for his death. It took some time, many years in fact, before we had any kind of breakthrough with her and that was to learn of an apparent exorcism at the house? Certainly, this event as with the death of the young child is paramount in her delusions."

I should have come here first. Fitzgerald lamented. It seemed that Dr Kapoor knew almost everything that he had slowly pieced together over his five days on the McArthur estate.

"She blames herself? How?"

"For instigating it. You see, I have come to the conclusion that the girl's death unlocked something within her and set her down a path. What I can't fathom is that she does not shoulder any blame for the child's death. That is uncommon, given her condition. So what set her on such a destructive path I cannot guess. It is true that some of the conditions apparent such as bipolar disorder can be triggered by a tragedy such as this, as well as other factors of course. But that alone does not explain the rapid decline into other conditions of the mind that we have observed here."

Fitzgerald could well understand the root causes of Elizabeth's condition, and it played on his mind that this doctor and the medical team here at the hospital might better be able to treat her if they understood that what she was saying was real. If what he believed was true, then she had been in institutional care for nigh on 20 years and in that time she had made little progress. Were the doctor's so entrenched in the logic and reason of science and 'the real world' as not to consider that such things as faith and good and evil existed in the world?

Now was perhaps not the time, but when this was all over, he decided that he would write this doctor a long letter regarding the very real subject of dark spirits and exorcism and how the Catholic Church regarded them as real and viable elements in the human experience. Should they take any heed, they might be on a road at last toward helping her.

Dr Kapoor shifted from her chair, and he followed suit. "I will show you through Father. Be warned though that your visit here today may have been for nothing. As I said, she has been extreme in her withdrawal of late."

They walked toward the double door where a swish of the doctor's electronic fob caused a loud clicking sound to be made, denoting the lock had disengaged. Having passed through, the hallway they were in, much more resembled the interior of a hospital as he would have expected. Overhead signs denoted directions to various named rooms and by peeking into these places, he found that he saw the same sparsely-spaced and ill-furnished bedrooms as he imagined, though these were cleaner and brighter by far.

His presence there did not go unnoticed, and several residents stopped and stared as he walked the long corridor. He guessed that these were residents through their casual clothing, whereas the staff members wore similarly bright tunics and name tags as Dr Kapoor. At last, they came to a stop before a nondescript door. By its side was a small white board with the name Elizabeth McArthur etched in black marker pen. Kapoor smiled at him and signalled to him to wait by raising her hand. She knocked, entered and surprisingly Fitzgerald heard the mumbled exchange of two voices. Surely not that of Elizabeth though as the second was no doubt masculine.

He had little time for doubt as Dr Kapoor returned to him almost immediately followed by one of the largest men he had ever seen. She introduced him as Gareth and stated that he was one of the mental health workers here at the hospital. Fitzgerald could scarce believe it, for the man appeared more suited to the wrestling ring than the hospital. He was perhaps in his thirties and stood at over 6' 3". It was the sheer bulk of his muscles that shocked, that and his totally bald head.

Fitzgerald saw his own hand swallowed as he offered it in greeting with an awkward smile. Gareth's own smile was welcoming and his voice surprisingly soft considering his massive frame as he spoke. "Hello there, Father. I've been asked by Doctor Kapoor to stand in and watch over you while you speak with Elizabeth."

And with that, Kapoor made her farewells. "I'll leave you in Gareth's capable hands, Father. If you should need me at all before leaving, just let Jill at the front desk know."

A hurdle he had not expected. He bid his farewell to the doctor as he contemplated how he could possibly speak to Elizabeth with this hulking man standing watch. There could be no doubt that his proposed line of conversation would not be at all welcomed. Little matter, for it seemed his visit was likely in vain considering her current condition.

"Shall we?" said Gareth. Butterflies came quickly and easily to his stomach. He had been so focused on obtaining the truth that he had not considered the person from who he would obtain it. His mouth suddenly too dry to speak, he nodded his agreement.

As with the other rooms he had observed in passing, the bedroom was small. A single cot hugged the left-hand wall and a quick glance showed him that it was firmly secured to the floor. In the upper right corner, a television was silently playing cartoons as a middle-aged woman with long flowing brown hair, speckled with grey watched unflinchingly on.

Elizabeth McArthur sat with her back toward him, and he stood at the door and watched as Gareth made his way past her to sit at her side on the bed. He whispered something close to her ear which was too soft for Fitzgerald to make out. It gained no reaction from her.

Gareth motioned with his head for Fitzgerald to come in and he could see that an additional seat had been brought in for his visit, for an unsecured plastic chair sat opposite her. He made his way past her shoulder and sat himself down.

"Elizabeth?" he began. Visions of her picture from the Ashmarsh Gazette surfaced in his mind as he spoke. Age had not faded her beauty and her eyes near but shone as they darted over the animated shapes behind him. Her hair fell over one eye and it was all that he could do not to reach out and brush a curl away. Gareth looked over at him again and gave him an affirming nod to suggest that his candour was appropriate and that he should just talk irrespective of response.

"Elizabeth?" he tried again. "I am Father Iain Fitzgerald," a response? An almost instant movement of her eyes to his? But all too quick and so fast as to believe there had been anything at all.

"I am very glad to meet you here today. I have come bearing news." He waited. Nothing, no response. "Bad news I am afraid."

Gareth nodded further encouragement toward him, and he took it to mean that his pace was fine, he should allow the words to sink in (if they sank in at all.)

"I am the Parish Priest from St Peter's in Ashmarsh."

Crosby was from St Peter's, Elizabeth. Do you recognise that?

Nothing.

"I am here today on behalf of your husband, Robert."

Nothing.

"I am sorry to tell you Elizabeth, that Robert is unwell." He searched her face; the eyes remained the same glazed orbs as they had before. There had been not so much as a muscle twitch thus far.

"He asked me to come and see you today to let you know…I fear his time is short Elizabeth; he wished me to convey how much he loves you." Those last words he knew were false but perhaps appropriate, for though he had not been instructed to say as much, every word spoken to date by McArthur had been of his love toward this woman. McArthur would never have the chance and so perhaps it was right that he passed such sentiment.

However, there was still no response from Elizabeth. Gareth looked over, and Fitzgerald felt his impatience. His feelings were clear; this was a waste of time. How to get rid of him and reach her? He must reach her somehow!

An idea came, so simply and elegantly. Without a skip in his breath, he said. "Gareth, I wonder if we might have a moment? To pray? You need not go far; you will see us through the door."

He was reliant on the power of his office and the potential embarrassment of the man. Should he prove to be Catholic? He might ask to stay and join the prayer, but Fitzgerald had little doubt the hulking mass had deemed the gym to be his Church and had unlikely ever set foot in the house of God. He was not disappointed.

"Of course Father, of course."

The bedsprings sighed their relief as he raised himself and left the room.

At last, they were alone, even though Gareth now intermittently looked through the window in the door at them. To keep up his act, he waited until he was observed and made the sign of the cross upon himself. He bowed his head and clasped his hands together before his face, knowing that to do so would block any sight of his mouth. Gazing up over his palms, he saw her. Gareth though could now not be seen such was the way she was seated between him and the door. It was perfect.

"Elizabeth?" he began again. All the time searching her for a reaction. "I don't know if you can hear me or not so I will just talk, I hope deep down some of this gets through because I need guidance. Robert, your husband, told me all of it and you have to know that you were right. That must seem the cruellest of punishments for I have no doubts that they've taken 20 years of your life and tried to make you believe the opposite, that it was all in your head. Well, you are not crazy. It exists I know."

Still, Elizabeth's eyes flittered and focused upon the television behind him. How could this be? Dr Kapoor had suggested what? That she had gone into this withdrawal-like state some two weeks ago, just in time and seemingly coinciding with his own arrival in Ashmarsh. But could it just be that? Coincidence? Fitzgerald doubted that. And to look at her now and the glazed far-off look in her eyes he wondered as well as to how much medication they had been feeding her. He glanced around her toward the door and saw that Gareth was now toying with his phone. He had time, but not much more.

How do I reach you?

Thus far, he had been delicate, slow and probing for a reaction. There was no more time for such subtlety. "Elizabeth, I know what happened in the library with you and Crosby. You have to hear me now. I must know what happened there."

Still there was no reaction from the woman, and Fitzgerald felt himself slowly descending into despair. There was no more time; he could not eke this out any longer for such a thing could not stand to wait for him to return day after day until she broke this fugue state. No, it had to be tonight and while he still had the will to confront what must be done. Tomorrow? Tomorrow also might be too late, for McArthur would not last much longer he knew and when that happened other intrusions would make themselves apparent.

Steeling himself for what lay ahead, he took her by the hand. "I am sorry Elizabeth for everything. I must go now and be rid of it. I hoped by coming here I could learn what befell you and Crosby so that I would not suffer the same. No matter, my mind is made up and when it is done, I will come back to you. I don't know that you will ever hear me, but if I am successful and I rid that damned place of its devil, perhaps that will go some way to ease your burden."

He began to rise from his chair, and as he did so, he whispered something softly under his breath.

A hand jerked out and grabbed him by the arm and pulled him back down into his chair. His breath was taken out of him as he fell hard back into his seat. The action had made him start, and in reflex, he snatched his arm back from her. He looked now back into alert and focused blue eyes that searched his face. A low voice emanated from her and he gulped involuntarily to get air back into his lungs so as to respond.

"What did you say?" she repeated softly, the tone of her voice was in stark contrast to the intensity in her stare. Fitzgerald looked quickly behind her to see if the small disturbance had alerted Gareth to Elizabeth's waking. It had not.

"I…I…" he stammered.

"Lydia, you said her name."

The suddenness of her demand had caused him to reel and lose understanding. Lydia? He had not spoken of…no wait. Yes, yes, he had under his breath.

He repeated. "Perhaps I should leave it be as you asked me to Lydia."

"Why, why do you speak of her?"

Is that all she heard? Does she not know the rest of it?

"The young girl who died at Thoby Hall," he said in response. "I saw her."

Elizabeth McArthur looked him up and down and searched deep within his eyes. He held her glance without flinching for she was searching for the truth within his eyes. After a few

327

seconds, her eyes dropped, and for a second, he thought he had lost her again. But suddenly her gaze was upon him again.

"Tell me what you saw."

And so he did without pause or hesitation. To speak the words and give them life was liberating, and Elizabeth sat in silence as he unburdened himself. He did not give it all. Not now, for now, was not the time. It could not help to tell her of McArthur's folly and Searle's before him. He only went so far as to tell her that he had delivered final confession to her former husband and learned of the happenings in the house, the devil in the library and what became of both her and Crosby. And more, for he had experienced it himself and had seen young Lydia in what he had first written off as only a dream.

"She came from time to time," Elizabeth said finally in response. "She came with words of warning but I did not heed them and I brought poor James into my folly." A single tear spilt down her right cheek.

"Warning?" Fitzgerald replied. "What warning? I must know for she came to me and told me the same. That the man in the house wanted me to be rid of it but that I should not."

A look of surprise came over her followed quickly by fear. "No, no, Father, don't you see it?"

"See what Elizabeth?"

"It! The creature! It deceives at every turn!" Her voice was growing louder, and Fitzgerald looked anxiously toward the door. For now, at least there was no sign of Gareth, but he knew he may be no more than only a few feet away.

"Elizabeth, please. I hear you, but we must be quiet..."

She raised her eyebrow as if in surprise, but thankfully she lowered her tone to match his own. "The beast wears many faces Father; you must know this and all of them designed to trick and entrap you. What you saw? What you say you saw? That could not have been her for the message was not the same. She knows well the evil that dwells within and it was she that drove me to act and rid the world of its wickedness."

Could it be?

Her words, though drove home, and he knew that they likely told the truth of it. His dream, what he thought of as his dream had begun with fear but had quickly transitioned toward seduction. She had come to him and bid him follow to the library where she wanted to show him this terrible thing. And yes, he had seen it, ancient and terrible in its guise and coming for him, until at the last moment she had come back to rescue him with the intrusion of heavenly light. Had it been a ruse all designed to deter him from his path when everything else had pointed him to the very opposite? Perhaps and probably so.

"Yes! I can see it in you, Father. You see it now and there is more. It knows! It has always known you were sent to open the trapdoor back to hell."

"It knows? What do you mean?"

Again she looked sad. "Oh, poor James. If only I had known but it was all too late you see. In my desperation, I reached out to the only man I knew who might help me, who could help me! We sought to expel the creature. James thought it done or so he said but I knew from him and that other one they had not seen what I had. They thought nothing had happened and that it was all in my head; they did not believe Father! And that was what drove him to do as he did in the end."

"I don't understand Elizabeth."

"I…how do I say it? It was as if I was out of body. I stood with it, and we watched together as James and the other one (*Colin*) spoke their words of expulsion. But all the while they did not see as I did. The beast was there and laughed at their futility. It came and whispered in my ear as they continued none the wiser, speaking foul poison which I ultimately saw come true, for James did finally see the same and sought the only way out that he could. The thing, it told me…it told me that he did not believe and so his actions were doomed to failure but the day would come when another would arrive, another who would succeed in driving it back to where it comes from. It spoke of you Father."

Fitzgerald was shocked at what he had heard. Could such a thing as this be true? His lips moved as he formed a response only to be interrupted by a light knock on the door, followed by the entry of the man-mountain Gareth.

"Father, I am sorry to interrupt, but I have other patients that I must see. Will you require much more time?"

"I…" his eyes trained back toward Elizabeth, his excuse forming on the tip of his tongue as he prepared to lie to Gareth and gain more time in which to interrogate Elizabeth.

However, she looked past him. Her eyes glazed and flittering once more over the television screen behind him, vague and unaware of his presence. She was gone once more.

"How?…" he began.

Gareth looked concerned as he followed Fitzgerald's gaze toward his patient. He stepped further into the room and to Fitzgerald's side, where he looked down upon Elizabeth. "Father? Is everything alright?"

For a second though he was lost in her eyes as he fought to find any form of life or recognition. Whatever had been, had gone and she had reverted to the same vegetative state as when he had arrived.

It was at an end now for something in his demeanour had clearly spooked Gareth. "Father, perhaps it is best you go now? I don't want Elizabeth upset…"

Fitzgerald arced his eyes upward and met those of Gareth. Had he sensed some impropriety on Fitzgerald's part? Perhaps so, for his glare was resolute. This was over. He had time to look once more back at Elizabeth before he stood and had time to wonder if anything had happened at all between them.

"Gareth?" He said as they left the room. "Is it possible she heard anything I said? I thought for a minute there was some kind of response?" He asked, testing.

The big man shook his head forcibly though. "It is possible, likely in fact that your words reached her deep down. But a response? No, and what is more whatever was said is swallowed in the junkyard that is her drug-addled mind. It is such a shame after all this time."

"What do you mean?"

"Why her regression, of course. Did Dr Kapoor not mention it? She had made such progress in the last years; we had even planned her first supervised visit off-premises. She was so excited. But soon after, this happened."

"Please Gareth what possibly caused her to go into such a state?" Fitzgerald asked, knowing the answer before it came.

"I don't know for sure. But her delusion was in full force once again. She regenerated to the worst I have seen of her, violent and screaming nonsensical gibberish. That is why she is as you see her today. Her medication…"

"I understand. Do you remember what it was…this gibberish I mean."

Fitzgerald's blood ran cold at the response.

"Not all of it. But one thing over and over. Something about a deal done in darkness? For the life of me, I don't know what it means."

Gareth continued, though Fitzgerald heard no more.

"You can understand given your interest in her why I was sceptical of Dr Kapoor, allowing you to see her. But I understand her faith was strong. I hope some good comes from your visit."

CHAPTER 44

The dark and angry sky over Thoby Hall matched Iain Fitzgerald's mood as he turned his car back onto the long driveway. The visit with Elizabeth McArthur had done little to reassure him of how he should proceed with McArthur's request, as all he had learned from Elizabeth had cast into doubt the true identity of the little girl who had appeared to him.

Had Lydia Bennett appeared as an apparition from beyond the grave, giving words of warning that must be heeded? Or had it instead been some other being wearing the mask of a child that only sought to conflict and confuse him, for that was indeed how he now felt.

Then there was the question, had the poor woman spoken to him at all. Her transformation from a coma-like state to full consciousness and back again had been so improbable as to be believed. Had he imagined it? In any other life he would not have believed so, but the fact was that the experiences from the time he had set foot upon these hateful grounds cast even the basest of memories to be called into question. If he had imagined it all, then the real question must be as to why he was not locked up in the room next to her.

He was breaking at the seams, and when the time came, he would indeed take the necessary steps to address his fragile psyche. But now the time was near and he knew that if he just did this one thing then everything could just go back to how it should be and he could put the whole experience in a locked drawer at the back of his memory and throw away the key. Okay, that wasn't the healthy way, but it was one way and something was better than nothing.

The digital clock on the car's dashboard told him that it was 16:30 pm as the first drop of rain splashed down upon the windshield. The light in the air was low and though he could not yet see the house at the end of the long driveway, he knew that the many spotlights had activated as they caused an unnatural glow to find its way through the weary-looking trees. Somehow he was glad of the light though. At first, it had caused him difficult nights in his apartment as he tossed and turned before seeking the sanctuary of the sofa and a closed door, but as time had passed and bad dreams had encroached, it had been as if a guardian to him and in the throes of night terrors he had found solace in their comforting presence.

As to why, he had to admit as to the real reason. It was this unnatural light that supposedly acted as a defence against the caged creature that dwelt in the library.

As his car again buffeted against the uneven ground, he cast his mind back to the story of Thomas Searle and how he had eluded the foul beast on the night he was supposed to have died. For his part, it was sheer luck that had delivered him from evil that night as he had not a clue as to what was to happen to him. Instead, he was protected all the while by some kind of magic masquerading as a fertility spell. Never to father the heir he so desperately wanted, instead, living a borrowed life that he had no right to.

What did that mean though for Fitzgerald? Must he somehow unlock the wards put in place well over half a century ago? No. That would be foolish, for surely to do so would remove the lock that bound the creature. He would have to trust to the rite of exorcism and the power of his faith over whatever fail-safes had been engineered. He could only hope that his belief would outweigh whatever had been set in place all that time ago; after all, he did not seek to release the animal from its cage. He sought to remove it from existence and return it to the hell from where it came and in doing so perhaps he could satisfy the part of his mind that could not resolve the question of Lydia Bennett's advice to him.

The ritual would be complicated of course, by McArthur's condition. Ordinarily, he knew that for an exorcism such as this, the proprietor or resident would be present to recant words of expulsion and so technically making them crucial to the success of the ritual as it is through their command that an unwanted spirit would be cast aside. Crosby and Morris had undoubtedly utilised Elizabeth for that role in their own ill-fated ceremony. He could work past that but would have to elicit some form of bond with McArthur that would give him the power to act in his name throughout the ritual. Somehow he knew that would not present a problem.

McArthur would not pass from this world until this was done he knew. He was a stubborn and strong man and had connived to make what Fitzgerald was about to do happen, as such he would be going nowhere until it was done and if Fitzgerald had to wait all night for his blessing then he would. In all truth, he would feel all the happier to attempt the rite during the hours of daylight, but deep down, he knew such a thing would not be afforded to him.

A deal done in darkness must be completed in darkness.

By the time he stepped from his car, the rain had begun in earnest, and he made a dash for the side door of the house. His first port of call must be to McArthur, or more specifically to whichever of the two nurses who would still be on duty ahead of the night shift.

He found Keira exactly where he expected to within McArthur's apartment. For the first time in seeing her, he was not in any way captivated by her beauty. He had now come to know she had been a part of the manipulation of him all along. That suggestion had come from McArthur of course, who had threatened to out their sexual liaison. If she knew the nature of their conversation, she did not show it, as she greeted him with the same warm smile he had previously grown fond of. Now though seeing it for the potential trap that it was.

"Iain? You are soaked through, here come sit down." She took him by the hand and led him to the sofa where he sat down. "Let me get you a towel." She scurried off toward the utility room as he called out behind her.

"Robert? How is he?"

She spoke from the recess of the room; her voiced dampened by the wall now between them. "Robert? There hasn't been any noticeable change for better or worse. Why do you ask?" she said as she entered the room once more, holding out the towel for him as she got close.

"I'm going to do it, Keira. I'm going to do it tonight." He watched as her face became a mask of surprise quickly followed by what he felt to be victory. Maybe he only saw what he wanted but in that small fraction of a second, he found that he hated her for her part in all of this.

"Oh Iain, that is wonderful news. Thank you. Thank you! You will need to speak to Robert…"

"I will. That's what I came to ask, whatever schedule his medication is on, stop it. I need him awake and alert."

She nodded vehemently in response. "Yes, of course, I think we can wake him by…"

He cut her off. "Why, Keira?"

"What?… I don't understand."

"Tell me what's in this for you? Him I understand, but why does all this matter to you?"

"I told you already Iain, I…"

"That's bullshit, Keira!" He shouted at her. "What was it really? What did he promise you? Money?"

"Iain, please you're scaring me."

He could see it was so but felt little for it. "Then tell me why you did it? Ever since I have been here, I have been forced into this corner and now he has won. I am going to do what he asks but not for the reasons you would think. Had it never occurred to you both that there were other ways I could be convinced without you having to sleep with me?"

He saw the pain in her face as his words spilled out from his mouth. Such was his anger toward her though he could not stop the flow of hate. "Was that it Keira? Sleep with the sexless priest, tie him up around your pretty little finger?"

She stood there, the towel forgotten in her hands as she looped it unknowingly into knots. Her lips quivered, but no tears came to her and he was glad for he knew his resolve was thin.

333

"I slept with you Iain because I liked you and because I was lonely. Don't you know that? Didn't you feel the same way?"

He was already on the defensive he knew. "Yes, that is how I felt. But did you use that against me? To get me to do as he asked?"

She walked over toward him and squatted down onto her knees before him. Throwing the towel aside, she took his hand and looked up into his eyes. "Is that what you think happened? Don't be so foolish Iain. Yes, we talked, what else do you think there was for me during these long days and nights? He told me what he feared yes and I told you what I thought about this house, remember? So what harm was there if I asked you to do a dying man's wish?"

"You're telling me he didn't put you up to it?"

"Of course not, no! Do you know how foolish I feel every time I walk out of this house? It seemed idiotic to have spoken of such things with you when I am far away from here. But every time I return it comes back. That same heavy fear in the pit of my stomach, and so yes, when I asked you, it was for me as well as I am tired of this house and tired of feeling this way."

"If that is true then Keira, how does he know? How does he know about us?"

Her brow furrowed, but she continued to hold his eyes. He believed her, thus far anyway. But how could she answer this question?

"He…he can't. He can't know about us Iain. I have not told a soul, I swear."

He dropped her hand from his and held her beneath her elbow. Standing, he ushered her to follow suit so that they were now eye to eye.

"How can that be Keira? He threatened me. Threatened me that if I did not do this, he would renege on his agreement with the Church and go public about you and me."

"That's impossible, Iain. I don't know; you must, believe me, I told no one."

He held her stare for a second longer. He was confused, but he did believe her it seemed. Something else was afoot or failing that, Keira was an accomplished liar. He had enough life experience and time in the confessional to know if a person lied to him or otherwise held something back. She, he believed, was doing neither.

"I am sorry, Keira. I did not mean to accuse, but what I am saying is true. I have been manipulated here, though I will do this thing for my reasons. It was with his own mouth he spoke of us and so naturally I came to the only conclusion that I could. I didn't mean to hurt you, I am sorry."

"I am sorry that he would use such a thing against you, but please believe me when I say I had no part. I am glad you are doing this Iain for I feel we are on the threshold of something.

When it is done, I know this weight will be lifted from you, from him and from me. Please be careful."

She leaned forward and kissed him lightly on his cheek. He engineered a small smile and stepped past her toward the door. "I must go prepare. Please call me Keira as soon as he wakes."

"It will be Melissa soon enough Iain. It is coming to the end of my shift. But I will stay if you want me to. If you want my support?"

"I would like that Keira. I would like that a lot." He said as he exited McArthur's apartments.

CHAPTER 45

As on a night some 37 years previously, the night sky surrounding Thoby Hall was oppressive and threatening violence. The rain shower that had welcomed Fitzgerald back to Thoby Hall that afternoon only a prelude for the real show to come.

Such thoughts were a million miles away from Iain Fitzgerald though as he stood before the library door once more. The time would be soon when he entered this room again and sought to finally put an end to the darkness that had held sway over this house for more than a generation. Idly he stepped forward and depressed the door handle.

Locked, as it should be. Digging deep into his pocket, his hand fell upon the long iron key that would fit in the lock before him. The fact that the keyhole was now here and apparent for him to see did not faze him in the slightest; it was but another unnecessary distraction.

As well as the keyhole reappearing, there was it seemed more at work than he could have guessed for late that afternoon he had been disturbed in his study while he prepared for the coming ritual he would perform. Only a light knock at the door, he had gone to answer it. Depressing his door handle, he thought he had heard a very soft thump from the other side of the door. The hallway itself had been empty, much to his surprise when the door was finally open. Empty, with the exception of this one long key and its fob that had undoubtedly been hung on his door handle to slide off when he opened the door.

His message it seemed had gotten through to McArthur who had instructed he finally be given the access he needed to the library. Who though had delivered the key and made such a quick disappearing act? If there were those who still wanted to play games and toy with him, then so be it. Tomorrow, for better or worse he was leaving this place behind for good and should McArthur linger well past that point then he would send Colin Morris to conduct last rites, it was the least that Morris owed him having held back so much.

Turning away now from the library, he strode the corridor toward McArthur's rooms once more. The key had been evidence enough that the man must be awake and that Keira had delivered his message. This though nagged at him, and despite her reassurances, he couldn't help once again but think she was somehow in McArthur's pocket.

How else could he have known about the two of them? And no sooner had he told her that he planned to go ahead with the exorcism than here was the key mysteriously delivered to his rooms. The question of her allegiance had plagued him for some small-time now, the facts as they stood painted her as a liar and as a honey trap so that he would do exactly as

McArthur wanted. But she had continually looked him in the eye and convincingly told him otherwise.

So which should he believe? That she inadvertently did McArthur's bidding? That seemed so unlikely, as the nature of her interactions with him had seemed so specific in nature as to directly influence him to act as McArthur had planned. And what was more, how else could McArthur have ever known about the two of them without one of the two of them giving away the secret?

It had certainly not been him that was for sure. So, as much as he did not want to, his mind edged slowly back toward its earlier thinking; that she had been manipulating him all the while. Her motives for doing so? He could not guess, perhaps McArthur held something over her as he did Fitzgerald?

Making the apartments, he knocked lightly on the door. It was answered almost at once by Keira who ushered him in.

"Iain? I was just about to call you and let you know that Robert was awake. I delivered your message for you, and he is ready to speak. I should warn you though he is very weak."

He walked past her and into the living area. The room was empty, but for the two of them. "Melissa?" He questioned.

Keira closed the door behind him and walked round to face him. "She is in with him now."

Fitzgerald removed the key from his pocket and produced it in front of her. "Do you know anything about this Keira? It just arrived via ghost mail at my door." His tone was light, but she could undoubtedly see that he again scrutinised her for her answer. He felt bad for it, for he had tested everything she had said to him and still stated that he had believed her. Her patience would be running thin by now, he guessed.

"What is that?" She inquired, reaching out and taking the key from his hand. She turned it over once and saw that the fob revealed the name 'Library'. She looked up and searched his eyes "So you are going to do it then?"

He nodded his response and took the key back from her palm. "It seems someone wanted to remain anonymous. This was left outside of my room a short while ago."

"That's odd. I've been here the whole time with Melissa and Robert. I thought the house would be empty at this time."

"No matter. I don't care for their games any more. I will have this done, and that will be the end of it. I have to get out of here."

Keira stepped closer to him and took him by the forearm, whispering softly to him. "Yes, you must. I must. Robert can't have much longer to go, I'm sure. When it is done, I will see the back of this place for good."

337

"Keira?…" He would ask her why she remained at all and what hold McArthur had upon her, but the question would have to wait as the interior door to McArthur's bedroom opened, and Melissa stepped through.

"Oh Father, very good you are here, he has been asking for you. He is very weak now and in a great deal of pain."

Keira quickly stepped back from him at the intrusion, exchanging a last glance and smile hidden from the other woman. Fitzgerald stepped toward the door but found it was still blocked by the small framed nurse.

"Melissa?"

He suddenly saw within her a resolve and strength that had been all to missing thus far. She had something to say.

"I don't like this Father whatever it is. Whatever your business make it quick. That fine man should not be made to suffer any more, and he resists his medication though his pain must be immense."

Her words surprised him for there was a depth of feeling that he had not previously anticipated or expected from her, this quiet diminutive woman.

"It will be quick, Melissa," he responded, "My business here will be done tonight I assure you."

She stepped aside from him, and he caught a glaze in her eyes that spoke of untold emotions. She, it seemed had all the while sensed the underlying current of anxiety and fear at Thoby Hall and associated it all with his presence. He could not blame her for that, for if she was truly unaware of what was happening here, her instincts were as close to the truth as they could be.

He looked back once more to Keira who offered one more supportive smile and then entered McArthur's chambers.

The scene was as all the times before. The glare of the room's lights attacked his eyes at once, and he blinked hard, as dark shapes danced behind his eyelids. McArthur appeared as if already dead, such was the stillness of his face, but the ECG monitor beside him showed that he clung to life still. And all the better that he did, for what was to happen here would be crucial to his success in the library.

Fitzgerald took his place once more in the chair at McArthur's side, and the old man's eyelids instantly fluttered into life.

"Father, you have come. Good." Despite the quiet of his voice, strength still resonated within his eyes. Fitzgerald understood at once from seeing him that his time was up, and he remained only to see Fitzgerald's task done.

"Yes, Robert, I am here. You will have received the message; I will do as you ask."

"I am glad. But do not do so with a heavy heart for what you do here is just and good."

"I have difficulty in believing that Robert, but no matter it will be done."

"You are alone?"

McArthur's words at first confused him, but the context of the question made him quickly realise. "Yes, I am alone. Deacon Morris would have no part. You need not fear though for his participation would be but a hindrance."

McArthur's understanding of the situation was uncanny. "So he still does not believe? No matter. You though Iain, you do don't you? Tell me please, what did Elizabeth say to you?"

How could he know that?

The answer though was simpler than most. Doctor Kapoor. She had spoken to Harvey so as to allow him access. It did not take a genius to work out that such information had been fed back already. All the while during his stay to date he had been astonished by McArthur's apparent ability to know that which he could not. It was no mystery he now knew; he did it simply by anticipation and keeping his network close to him. In all probability, he and Harvey had likely anticipated his visit to St Luke's and Elizabeth.

He would not have all of it, though.

"She said nothing, Robert. She was under a lot of medication you understand."

McArthur nodded. "Perhaps that was for the best. I considered informing the hospital of my condition so that they might be able to pass the news when she was well enough. You made that decision on my behalf, and I see she is still not ready. Ah, Elizabeth, if only there was more time. Perhaps I could find a way to deliver you from the beast as well."

"It strikes me we may help her by doing this tonight, Robert. You should understand that it is not only for you that I do this."

"It matters not to me. Only that you do it all. You undoubtedly think me a cold, twisted old bastard. Well-deserved I am sure but know; if this gives her respite, then I can go to my grave happy. Will you tell her? When it is done?"

"I will."

"Good. For too long, I hid my head in the sand and dismissed her. She saw and acted when I hid from the truth of my own folly. If this can give her the peace, she needs…As I say, if not for me, you do a good thing here tonight Father."

"No more Robert. I don't want to hear another word. It is time, and I require something of you to make this work."

"Anything, Father. Name it."

"The ritual I will invoke, Rituale Exorcismus Domus, I have modified for our purposes. I would guess you have no understanding of it, or your part?"

"None Father, I am sorry."

"No matter. There is a preordained manner in which it should be performed, but your incapacity means we must adapt. We will begin with prayers of preparation, filling of the spirit, of blessing and finally of protection. These prayers give us the strength and the divinity to go ahead and perform the exorcism itself. They are vital to preserve us and give us protection from the machinations of the beast. As the owner of this property, your part is vital, as it is through your command as well as mine that the beast be expelled."

"I understand Father."

Fitzgerald could see the resolve through excruciating pain that McArthur was exhibiting. The preparation for the actual rite itself was long and already fine beads of sweat poured down his pain-etched face. He was glad that both nurses were close as they would likely have to maintain his pain control to successfully see him through the ordeal, at least long enough for him to return and finish the ceremony.

"You must remain strong, Robert. The ritual is long but necessary. Following the prayers for strength and protection, there are prayers for the protection of the house and to break the curse that holds it. It is only when they are complete will I leave you to perform the exorcism itself."

"And my part will be done?"

"When I return, there will be final prayers of blessing. I...I can perform them with or without you." The two men locked eyes and a curt nod from McArthur acknowledged his understanding. He need only stay alive until the exorcism itself was done.

"I will wait on your return."

"Very good Robert, I don't doubt that for a moment. Time is of the essence, we should begin." Fitzgerald withdrew a printed sheet from the small satchel he had brought with him. "You can read this, Robert?"

"My glasses Father?" he motioned toward the bed high cabinet on the far side of where Fitzgerald sat. Picking himself up from where he sat, Fitzgerald walked around the bed and retrieved the glasses and offered them to the old man. His frailty until now had been well masked, but now his hands shook violently as he made what was undoubtedly an extreme effort to even lift them.

"Here let me." Fitzgerald said, taking the frames from his hands and lifting them to his face. McArthur smiled gratefully, and it was with pity that Fitzgerald now saw him as opposed to the coursing anger he had previously felt. The reality of his condition could not be denied

340

and he was facing up to the inevitable with as much strength and grace as he could muster. "You can read from this okay?" He followed, passing McArthur the printed sheet of paper.

"Big print Father? You have come prepared," he said, focusing on the paper before him, "I should manage just fine."

"I will give you your cues, Robert. As for the rest, you are a lapsed Catholic but…"

"I know the rest of my lines Father." McArthur replied with another smile.

"Very good. Let us begin then."

Fitzgerald took a deep breath and was not surprised that his heart was galloping. He was scared, no terrified for what he was about to invoke. The words he spoke held power, real power, perhaps even more so than those last rites he had conducted with the dying and infirm. These words held the power to dismiss evil incarnate itself. And before he opened his mouth, he had time to wonder how Crosby and Morris had so failed to appreciate the undeniable influence of their words as they performed their own ritual.

He made the sign of the cross upon himself. "In the name of the Father and of the Son and of the Holy Spirit."

"Amen." Came the whisper from McArthur.

"First, Robert, the prayer of preparation. Please read from the top of the sheet."

"Lord in Heaven, I humbly prostrate myself before you, that you might give me your blessing, and that you might bestow upon me the armour I require to shield myself from the Devil's nefarious schemes. I will stand before him with you at my shoulder, that you might deflect his foul words of subversion and malice. Such will be my defence. Before me, I wield a flaming sword that is infused with righteousness and truth, that I might strike him down. Such, will by weapon. In my heart, I keep my faith which guides me on the path to salvation. Such will be my promise to you. For these gifts, I thank you, oh Lord, for they will serve me in the battles ahead. Amen."

"Amen." Followed Fitzgerald. McArthur's speech had wavered during his delivery and ended with a wracking cough with took over a minute for him to subdue. This was going to push him to the limit Fitzgerald knew and possibly only speed up the inevitable. None the less, he continued, McArthur delivering the passage for the prayer of filling of the spirit, before Fitzgerald's own dialogue began in earnest. He led McArthur through the prayer of protection, and they then recanted the Lord's Prayer together, though McArthur's own delivery was weak and broken.

By the time he got to the prayer for protection of the house, McArthur had sunk back deeply into his pillows, his eyes closed and screwed tight against his pain.

"Stay with me, Robert; we are nearly there." He continued, "in the name of Jesus Christ, we come before you oh Lord and ask you to give us the strength to withstand our ordeal, and that with your divine grace we might become the vessel of your good word, that the Devil heeds our words of expulsion, for he is not welcome in the home that is blessed by you. Satan is the manipulator and the deceiver, but through the merciful will of God, we are not blind to his schemes any longer. Whatever ill force, invitation, spell, seal or hex that brings him is hereby revoked in your good name, oh Lord. Henceforth he is banished to return to the fiery depths of hell so that Robert McArthur and all those who reside here at Thoby Hall can do so in peace and harmony."

"Lord in Heaven cast aside the veil of shadow where the beast lurks, so that he no longer can hold form in our world, and instead bring forth the brilliant light of the sun that you provided us, which gives us warmth and sanctity from those evil spirits that would do us harm. In doing so, casting away the foul stench of evil that has blighted the lives of Robert and Elizabeth McArthur and also that of James Crosby, who is your servant. Where darkness has held sway, let there instead be peace so that all who remain can live their lives untouched by the subversive whispers of your enemy and instead let them bask in all that is good and created by your hand. Let them live under your protection and let peace reign here forevermore."

"Lord, we now commence battle with our enemies and do so with regret and sorrow, for they are but the fallen. They have become blinded to the righteous path and were swayed by the lies of the Devil. And so we ask you to look upon them with mercy and show them the way back toward what is good. Give them your blessing and for all those who been so troubled by the evil forces that torment this house. Amen."

McArthur's response was but the parting of lips. His strength was failing fast, and yet his part was still unfinished, he must see it through. Providence it seemed was against him and he cursed himself for the trials and doubts that had delayed him in finding this moment.

"Hold on, Robert." He said to the room as he rushed toward the bedroom door. Pulling it quickly open, two pairs of expectant eyes shot to him. "Quickly, he needs help. We are not yet done."

There was a silent exchange as the two nurses looked between themselves. It was though Keira who acted quickest — picking herself up from where she was seated on the sofa her fear palpable in her demeanour. She pushed past Fitzgerald without hesitation and made a beeline toward the ECG. Fitzgerald followed her actions and saw the machine indicating beats per minute dancing dangerously low between 60 and 50.

"He is borderline bradycardia. I will need to give him adrenaline."

Melissa had appeared at the door. "Keira no. His heart…his heart won't take it."

Keira stopped in her tracks, a look of scorn, bordering on hatred seemed to pass from her to the diminutive nurse. "His heart? Jesus Melissa, look around you, what the hell do you think is going to happen here? This is what he paid us for, to keep him alive until his business with the priest was complete."

Fitzgerald watched as Keira's words hit Melissa like a slap to the face. "What will his lawyers do if you didn't fulfil your duty? You'll never work again Melissa, now fetch me the goddam epinephrine."

Melissa disappeared quickly. Fitzgerald looked toward Keira and was shocked by the anger he saw on her face. "What? Don't look at me like that Iain; this isn't the time. You want him alive, don't you?"

A change had come over her that he had never seen, the anger was prevalent, but underneath that, there was only what he could describe as raw panic. The realisation was confusing as he could not fathom as to why she acted as she now did.

Melissa quickly returned, and he watched in wonder at the dexterous nature of how they worked. Within seconds, Keira had affixed the cannula to McArthur's forearm and he watched on as the ECG settled on a more stable average of 70BPM. He returned to Robert's side and watched for signs of life to return. He needed him awake and alert so as to finish what they had begun.

"I should stay." Keira offered. "We need to be able to manage him as best we can. I should never have left you. It was stupid."

He only nodded at her; his eyes fixed instead on McArthur.

Slowly but surely, life began to creep back into the man. His breathing, previously shallow regained its regularity and his eyes fluttered open after several minutes of waiting.

"Keira? Did I…" McArthur whispered.

"No, Robert, nothing like that. The effort of all this was too much I think so I…we have given you a small shot of something to keep you going."

McArthur's eyes moved between the two of them and onto Fitzgerald. "Father, are we done? I am sorry if…"

"Don't apologise Robert. We are close, there is but one thing more I need from you before I go. Can you read?"

"I am sorry, my eyes…they are not as strong as they were…"

"That is okay, Robert, then just repeat as I say and I will be gone to do what must be done."

And so McArthur repeated; "Lord in Heaven. I come before you today as the owner of this property. I ask you that you remove the foul touch of the Devil from this house and the people within it. He, who is the deceiver, has wandered the halls and rooms of our home and made ill-promises, that demand the highest price a man or woman can pay. Cast him out, and recant the contracts he has drafted. He shall have no prize that is paid for with the human soul, which is your gift to us and only yours to give or take oh Lord."

343

"Exile, the evil one who walks among us, for he is an uninvited guest. Touch the rooms and halls of this home so that they become clean and pure and not fit for one, such as he. Make it this way so that all who reside here can live and bask in your love and protection, that they may in return do your bidding and live their lives in your name."

"And last of all, oh Lord. We humbly ask that for the gift of sight and knowledge. That should evil darken our door again, that we can see it for what it is and turn it out into the darkness where it belongs, and in so doing give it not shelter, nor credence, that it's schemes and plots are for nought."

Fitzgerald followed, "In the name of the Father and of the Son and of the Holy Spirit. Amen."

This was duly followed by both Keira and McArthur in unison.

"What happens now?" Keira asked.

"Now? Now you just keep him alive. My work is not yet complete; I must go to the library and be rid of it."

She reached forward and embraced him, her action surprised him, and he fell back a step under her weight as her arms clasped around him. "Do it," she whispered into his ear. And as she withdrew, he looked deeply into her eyes and saw they were alive with passion, alive with something more. He could not read her at all he knew, everything they had been through and suffered together to date and he still could not read her for good or bad.

"Keira? What?…"

"Please, Father be quick." Fitzgerald's eyes diverted over toward McArthur on his bed. "I don't think I have much more time."

There was nothing more for him to say or do here. His path was clear he knew, and haste was of the essence. It was a matter for McArthur of spiritual transcendence and he, Fitzgerald, must dispel the evil to pave his way. Taking his satchel, he left Keira and McArthur without looking back.

CHAPTER 46

As Fitzgerald began the long corridor from McArthur's rooms to the library, he felt once again as if he was within the same dreamscape that had plagued him during his time at Thoby Hall.

Every sense that he had seemed heightened somehow. The smell of floor wax on the polished boards beneath him permeated throughout the long passageway, the tap of his heel on the wooden floor echoed softly as he glided slowly toward his destination. But there was more he knew. Outside, he sensed the dark clouds gathering with electricity, in preparation for a furious onslaught and inside, he felt as if the old house watched on with bated breath as it sensed the climax and conclusion of an age-old battle.

And so he walked. He now felt elevated somehow, on some higher level of understanding and existence. This was his moment; all paths had led here somehow. From the mediocrity of his upbringing, the death of his father and the constant battle of wills with his mother. Of how he had met and then lost his beloved Emma. Onward, to the decision to join the Church. He had not known it then, but it had been a calling, a destiny if you will. He had never truly believed in the physical incarnate of heaven and hell in the conventional sense of a white-bearded man sitting upon the clouds, while the red-horned Devil armed with a fiery trident tortured the weak and faithless for an eternity, no. It had been Father Daniels who had demonstrated the Lord's love, and so he had come to know that it was through one's own actions that both God and the Devil acted within the world.

More than that, his faith was that of there being something more than the human experience. Something just beyond reach, perhaps lurking behind the veil of death. And why? For he believed strongly in the human soul, a life force pure and untouched by memory, pain or the human condition. The reason he had believed in such was that he saw the journey through life for what it was, something physical, the body just a machine.

Was such a device the work of God? He was a realist and evolution was too real to ignore, but the life force that fuelled life? That was something more and had been the foundation of his belief system as long as he could remember. He had questioned himself long as to whether such steadfast conviction was at odds with his calling to the Church, but had quickly dismissed it, for the Church preached the same gospel, one of faith.

And so despite the fact that those core beliefs had been turned upside down by his experiences here, he felt no uncertainty, for if there was to be a Devil then there should so to be a God, and everything that had been instigated here had been done so for a man's soul a long, long time ago and that was at the heart of his belief system. That very same thing he had held close to his heart for all those years, was real and that it was so precious, it was something that had been fought over for millennia between very real powers of good and evil.

Whatever happened in that library tonight somehow paled in his mind now in comparison to the enlightenment that flooded his being. There was a God, he knew now, and that meant the awakening of a new man, a new Iain Fitzgerald.

His thoughts though soon came to a dead halt as did he. He had traversed half the distance toward the anteroom and already he could feel it. A cold icy draught billowed down the hallway toward him, it engulfed him and quickly extinguished all feelings of confidence that had dwelled within him, bringing instead the beginnings of a deep-seated fear he had known many times walking these halls. This time though the feeling fed his resolve. He knew his mission here and knew that the fear was designed to cause him to baulk at the task at hand. He set himself in motion again and quickly came to the anteroom and the library door.

Reaching into his satchel, he withdrew the crucifix and took a moment to check that his preparations were complete, despite the fact he had done so four times before now. It was all there, holy water, holy salt and eight medals of St Benedict, which he had already prepared by dipping in holy oil.

Releasing a slow breath, he raised the crucifix before him and repeated the words that had been written in the journal of Father Crosby "Ecce crucis signum fugiant phantasmata cuncta."

With trembling hands, he withdrew the single iron key on its fob and found the lock of the library door after the second attempt. It turned smoothly within the lock and his ear was greeted with the soft click of the lock disengaging. He knew before he opened the door what he would see. It didn't matter if it was a dream or reality but Lydia had given him a vision of things to come, the library and the terrible form of an ancient beast that was locked within. Even so, he closed his eyes as he swung the door inward.

Instantly his face was flooded with the release of cold air, and he gasped in shock of the cold. Quickly though it dissipated as if he had opened an airlock or perhaps more likely opened a doorway to an ancient undisturbed tomb. His eyes opened and with the instant recognition of familiarity, his heart thudded deeply within his chest.

Here was the library that Lydia had shown him. There before him, the single leather-backed chair sat centrally within the room, the chandelier hung low above it. But this was not the room of his dreams at all. This library was a scene of violence. The bookshelves to his left-hand side had been tipped, creating a domino effect that led all the way across the room. The contents of the shelves strewn upon the floor. Likewise, the books from his right, but the bookshelves there remained standing. There was more, for the smell of decay had hit him the second the cold breeze had exited the room.

He took a step inward and quickly pulled his foot back as a loud crunching sound came from underfoot. He found broken glass there and turning to look behind himself, he looked upward and saw that the strip lights by the doorway had been smashed, and as he looked deeper within the room, he saw the same, for now only a scant few lights remained on. The effect was to cast long dark shadows everywhere about him and the room beyond. This only intensified the feeling of desertion about it, for cobwebs hung from the ceilings and fixtures. Considering the broken light fixtures, something told him that the damage was new somehow and had perhaps been done since he had seen the room for the first time. This feeling of change was unsettling, for he saw the room as if with feelings of déjà vu as opposed to real memory, that, or the feeling that it had been an eternity since he had seen it or been here.

If anything this picture was all the more unsettling than his 'dream', and his eyes quickly fell upon the chair before him, for that is where he had seen the creature that had haunted the room for so many years. Despite the high-back, he was thankful that it appeared empty, that was only to say that no head or arm was seen protruding above or to the side of it.

He was now only a foot or so from the door and reluctant to step further in. Already he had cast several looks backwards to ensure himself of the sanctuary and escape that the door behind him offered. For now, all was well, but to complete the rite of exorcism, he would have to go further into the room. What was for sure, was that the door behind would remain firmly open at all times.

Fitzgerald crossed himself and began. "In the name of the Father and of the Son and of the Holy Spirit. Amen"

"O Lord in heaven, hear my prayer. You, who created the Heavens and Earth and made man in your image. You, who gave unto man your son Jesus Christ, who died for our sins. I come before you today and plead for your power and protection as I take up arms in your name against the ancient foe. He who now resides here within the walls of this home. He, who is unwelcome, for within this abode, resides your humble servant Robert McArthur who beseeches you to purge the dark shadow that infects these walls."

He paused. All was still around him, and he took a tentative step further into the room. Feeling his confidence returning, he continued, "Father, this house is in need of a cleansing. We remember the words of your son, Jesus Christ who promised us, that what we should ask of you in his name, you will deliver. And it is in that vein I ask of you now to banish the evil that besets and beleaguers this house, that it might never return. I also ask that your blessing endures for all those that reside here, both now and in the future, that they know only peace and your love. We ask you this, Father, in the name of thy Son Jesus Christ. Amen."

His voice fell silent once more and so to the world around him. Now, his nerves were like electric such were the power of his words. It was working and what was more it was uncontested. He did not know what he had expected to happen here, but thus far it was precisely as Morris had suggested. That said, he ached for such a companion that would undoubtedly reinforce his resolve, for he was on tenterhooks, meek and paranoid as to some hidden danger.

In the here and now, it was Morris's experience he craved. He would simply say the words, lay the medals of St Benedict and retreat as quickly as he came. All the while though it was Crosby and Elizabeth who flooded his mind. Him, unknowingly reciting similar words before falling into insanity. Her, speaking of dark whispers of another to come to rid the house and world of the dark demon. As much as he ached for peace and an uninterrupted rite, their experiences caused him to imagine much worse ahead.

"I now bless this house and home in the name of the Holy Trinity, and I ask that the sins of Thomas Searle that set in motion these dire events, be forgiven. That, all who acted for good or for ill, and did so outside of your holy blessings, likewise be forgiven. For we know that the events that have befallen all beneath this roof did so at the behest of another, and in doing so, a veil was drawn that your holy teachings could not penetrate, we ask that you now remove this veil and that a cleansing light fill these halls, so that he, who craves darkness, solitude and the whispers of the dread night be seen and removed forevermore. Father, I ask you to remove this domain of Satan that now rests upon the earth and send it back to the eternity of hell where it belongs, that the creatures that draw strength from its shadow, be likewise removed, so as never to return, for their poisoned ground has fallen from beneath their feet..."

Subtly the lights in the room flickered.

Fitzgerald blew his tension from his lungs and continued. "In your name, I take back the sullied ground before me, and in doing so, it is returned to your glory and purpose. As it is restored, so it is free from evil. You are the protector and saviour and the floor upon which I walk is now blessed. No foul beast may sully or taint it, for it is rejuvenated in your name. In the name of the Father, the Son and the Holy Ghost, Am..." The sentence went unfinished, for an ear-splitting crash reverberated throughout the room. For a moment, his heart seemed to stop and all sense of reason left and was instead replaced with terror. The sound was as if the earth itself had exploded. The crucifix in his hand forgotten, tumbled to the floor as he clasped his hands to ears.

The rest happened in a heartbeat. Fierce white light exploded outside of the window ahead, quickly followed by a cacophony of ear-splitting thunder. Fitzgerald fell to his knees, his hands torn between protection of sight and sound.

In the moment afterwards, all was still. The shock of the intrusion now gone, Fitzgerald understood at once the cause. The storm that had been promised that afternoon on the weather report had arrived only all so suddenly and seemingly had its epicentre right above Thoby Hall.

Gaining his feet, he quickly paused as the lights flickered, once, twice.

He could sense the movement behind him all too late. The door behind him slammed closed as it had once before, only this time the lights fell also. All there was in his world was darkness and the furious sound of rain beating down on the roof above.

CHAPTER 47

Terror had been almost a constant companion for him since the time of his arrival at Thoby Hall, but this feeling was altogether new. He took a single step backwards not knowing how far the door was behind him, the hard click of his heel on the library floor caused him to cease at once. He was caught like a rabbit in the headlights of an onrushing car, for it was his imagination that would be his enemy in the darkness.

The timing of the blackout could be no coincidence as he shuffled a further foot backwards, hoping beyond hope that it would strike the frame of the door. That wasn't to be though as his foot went unobstructed. In times such as these, he knew the body had a self-defence mechanism. Flight, fight or freeze. It was not a choice he knew but an instinct, but the idea of staying still, reverting to some inner child and curling into a ball was not an option and the reason why was for what now lurked in the darkness.

Imagination? If only it were as simple as that. He had begun something here which had gone unfinished. Long gone were any thoughts or feelings that suggested that the tale of Thomas Searle and his devil were merely ghost stories. He had seen things, experienced things here, though at the time they had gone misunderstood, as his mind had wrestled to come to the truth.

His left foot planted, he slowly began to drag his right backwards. All at once, his eyes were stung as fierce lightning burst from the heavens to leave a vision of the library before him.

It had been brief. All too quick really, but had there been a silhouette, there upon the chair? He gulped involuntarily and willed his foot back once more. The door, how far was the door behind him for God's sake?

Quickly another loud boom followed the light and seemed to shake him through his core. All the time though, he crept backwards, knowing somehow that something lurked before him and this, as it was in his dream was the only source of escape.

The immeasurable relief that swept over him as he finally backed into the door was quickly torn away as a soft sound could be heard from somewhere in front. He recognised it immediately for all of his senses were now tuned to the chair that sat in the darkness before him.

The sound had been as though a weight had been removed from the leather-padded cushions and in the darkness, he imagined the decrepit form of that which haunted his dream, rising, rising slowly, perhaps as in his vision to grow and become strong, but undoubtedly all the while to be focused upon him and the ritual he had invoked to banish it back to the hell from which it came.

If it found him, it would strike him with a savagery and bloodlust beyond compare.

Oh Lord in Heaven, please help me.

Fitzgerald reached behind him and scrabbled for the door handle only to find that it wasn't there.

A footfall, from within the room. Deliberate and loud.

Panic then rose up in him, and he turned away from the devil. His arm collided with something in the darkness, and at first, he didn't register what it had been as he pawed helplessly at the wooden frame without luck. Mercifully though something registered within him and he knew that he had his bearings wrong.

In the sheer black of the room, he had slightly veered off course. Initially believing, he had met the intersection of where the door met its frame. Believing that so, it had been impossible to find the door handle gone. But the reality was so much simpler; he had hit the door where it was hinged and had searched the wrong side. In the darkness, his hands now scrambled across the wooden surface and mercifully found the handle at last and he latched onto it with frantic purpose.

Up and down, it rattled, but it was no good. It was locked.

No! How is that possible?

But it was possible he knew, for he had left the key in the lock and the question was to who, as opposed to how.

But questions such as that would go unanswered for another strong footfall reverberated from the hard floor. He was not alone. That which he had tried to ward off was inevitable. He froze. Flight was impossible, and the terror within him had long since removed any semblance of fight.

As he had the last time, he sank to the floor. In that experience, it had been the girl, the girl Lydia who had delivered him from the vicious beast that stalked him now.

"Please, Lydia, please." He whispered at the door, hoping beyond hope that the same rescue was to be delivered. Such pleas fell silent, and nothing happened, rescue was denied to him as the thing in the dark took another pace forward and found him in the dark.

He did not know how, but with its discovery of him came the same biting cold that he had felt on his arrival at the door. The cold intensified as the footfalls became quicker. And all at once he felt its hot breath upon his cheek. This was it; it was all over for him now…

From somewhere close at hand, he heard a series of clicks. The hot plume of breath that was upon him ceased and he heard a grunting sound. A further click and a band of soft light spilt from a strip light at the far reaches of the room. And in turn, those lights that were not damaged slowly became alive. In that moment, he saw the silhouette of the thing before him. It was not a man he knew, for curled horns protruded from its skull and the shine of the low light was reflected in pinched reptilian-like eyes, as it turned its face from him to find the encroaching light.

The vision was for but a second, for another series of clicks came from above and before he knew it, the library was bathed again in the lowest of light. The thing before him was gone, and he searched about himself, confusion raging within.

Whatever was happening had banished the thing back to the darkness from where it belonged.

Seeing the door now, he tore at the door handles and pulled upon them with all of his strength. Nothing.

"Hello!?" He shouted through the door, his voice cracked and weak. "Please somebody help!" But not a thing stirred from beyond the door. He turned back and beheld the room before him, his crucifix previously lost was within distance, and he reached out to draw it quickly to him, where he clutched it to his chest.

He looked about, and the nature of the intervention was now obvious, for all of the lighting fixtures were lit with the same soft low light, that cast long shadows throughout the room.

These were emergency lights he knew. It was McArthur's account of how he had trapped Searle, that informed him of that fact, that somewhere deep within the house or its grounds lay some hidden generator that had eventually come to rescue him from the darkness and the beast within it.

The sudden lightning storm had undoubtedly caused the power failure, but thankfully there had been this backup as was the design of Thomas Searle all those years ago, only now they had fired into life and provided the protection that Robert McArthur had cruelly taken away from his master.

His panic now subsiding, he stood once more. His whole body was still on edge and his senses alive. The rain continued to pour, and occasionally the window at the far end of the room was lit with flashes, though the thunder that followed seemed far away now.

Is it over?

"No Iain it is not over."

His heart leapt into his mouth at the sound. She stood there now, before the window where he had been staring all the time. One split second, there had been nothing but the rain and the flashes and then there she was the vision or perhaps the ghost of Lydia Bennett.

"Lydia?" He croaked.

"There is little time Iain. This delay will not hold for long."

He understood well her meaning; it would be back.

"Then…then I must finish, I must complete what I have started…"

The young girl stepped forward and walked the distance between the window and the chair. She was different now he could see, for where she now stood he beheld two images in the same place, one the hard leather chair, real and substantive and yet somehow he saw it through her, it was as if…

As if she were a ghost.

"Have you learned nothing?" she asked him. "It has been hard to reach you, so hard, but yet I came and I warned you. I showed you the face of the beast that dwells here and implored you to do nothing, to let it rot here within its prison."

As before with her, his fear had elapsed as if it had never been. He stood now and took a step toward her, all the while marvelling at the way he saw through her being.

It was true, here and now was the spirit of Lydia Bennett. But she was different, he knew. The look deep within her eyes held wisdom beyond her age; her words likewise carried the weight of someone far beyond her tentative years.

"I don't understand." The strength in his words were a surprise to him as he spoke to her. "You warned me against this? Everything, I mean everything has pointed me here."

"How soon you forget. Did you not see its face? Feel its hatred? That was all I could give to you. Something stronger, something beyond guided me here to you Iain, before it was too late."

Had he finally lost his mind? The terror he had felt at the falling of the light was natural, given all that had been in the run up to this dark event. But this? This he could separate from any dream or experience he had previously had, there was no doubt that she was here and he was talking with the ghost of a girl who had been many years dead. But that was not it, that was not what gave him consideration of madness for it was the fact that his fear was evaporated now and he conversed now with her as if she was as real as McArthur or Keira.

It was with the words of Elizabeth McArthur paramount in his mind that he spoke back. "I heard you, Lydia. Your message was loud and clear. But how can I trust your message? How do I know that it is not you that I have been sent here to dispel?"

Her face suddenly became vacant, and she looked distant to him. "No…no!" she uttered as a noise came from behind him, a soft click as he witnessed the handle to the door begin to slowly depress. Somebody was coming into the library.

He spun around quickly to behold the unexpected intervention. At first, seeing nothing for the darkness in the anteroom beyond was total, the emergency lighting that had come into being in the library did not extend to beyond its threshold it seemed. It was all he could do to see the silhouette of the person who now slowly edged the door inward.

Despite the calm that had come over him at Lydia's appearance, some instinct begged him to back away from the intrusion. It was all he could do to hold his ground, and a quick glance of his head revealed that Lydia shared the same feelings, as the vacant look she had worn had given way to some baser emotion, one he could only read as fear.

The shape of a heavy set man squeezed through the gap in the door and quickly turned his back as he saw to the closing of the door.

Fitzgerald did now take an unwitting step backwards. He suddenly felt the calm that had washed over him begin to ebb away slowly and he knew that Lydia was the cause.

Slowly the man turned back toward where Fitzgerald stood. He could feel his heart galloping now as understanding was lost to him. Who or what was this thing that intervened at this late hour?

From the shadow that bathed the door came a familiar voice.

"Oh, Iain. Thank goodness, I thought I was too late. I am so sorry my friend, I was weak but I could not let you do this by yourself."

"Colin?" Confusion clouded his mind.

"No," Lydia whispered, "Beware Iain! The deceiver returns."

"Wow look at this place. It looks like somebody went to town on it since I was last here." Morris spoke as he tentatively walked toward Fitzgerald.

"Colin, what are you doing here?" Fitzgerald managed.

"I came to help Iain. I should not have abandoned you as I did."

Fitzgerald watched as Lydia shrank away from Morris as he drew close by.

"My god when the lights went out," Morris continued, "I could feel it again, the memories of this place and what we tried to do here."

The ghost that was of a 7-year-old girl retreated further and rather than walk he saw her float further away from where Morris now stood. He stood amazed as she moved, Morris though looked unperturbed.

"Iain, are you okay?" he said, looking deep into his colleague's eyes.

"You don't...you don't see her?"

A look of puzzlement came over his friend's eyes before he twisted his head so as to search the room about him. "See who Iain?"

Fitzgerald watched on as Lydia continued to move further and further away from Morris, she appeared more ethereal now, less substantial as if she was fading away.

Morris stepped close so as the two of them were toe to toe. "Iain? See who? What do you mean?"

"I..."

"It's happening, isn't it?"

"What?"

Morris spun round to survey the room and to try and see the thing he could not. Holding his arms wide, he exclaimed; "It is here isn't it? It has spoken to you!" Finishing his pirouette, he clasped Fitzgerald by the arms and leaned in close.

"Tell me, Iain, it is here, isn't it?"

Fitzgerald nodded slowly, but all the while, his eyes were trained upon Lydia. She was fading fast now and he could barely make out her form but for its very outline, the vision now held no earthly features and all that was real in the world could be seen straight through her.

Morris continued. "Oh Iain, what a fool I was for letting you shoulder this burden alone."

As Lydia finally faded from the room, Fitzgerald allowed his focus to fall upon his friend. "Colin? What are you doing here?"

Morris allowed his head to bow. "It is as I said, I came to help, and it seems, just in time. It was real wasn't it? Everything that Crosby and Elizabeth went through here? It was real?"

"Colin, you were here. You went through it with them. Why didn't you say?"

A look of confusion washed across Morris's face. "But I did say, Iain. Nothing changed I promise you. It was exactly as I said, nothing happened. Or at least not at first, but you can't think that I wasn't totally unaffected."

"Spit it out then Colin." Fitzgerald's frustration with the man was reaching boiling point. Here was the man who had lied to him, had said that the previous exorcism had played out with no effect, despite the fact that the conductor of that ritual had gone mad and killed himself, while the observer had likewise gone insane and had been forevermore committed to an institution.

Here was the man, who had sought to cover up any evidence of what they had done by securing the relevant passages of Crosby's diaries and gone on to deliver them to McArthur, who in turn had manipulated him to take Crosby's place. And here finally was the man who had abandoned him to this horrifying task and to act it out alone.

Morris considered Fitzgerald for a minute more, before walking toward the centre of the room and behind the leatherback chair where he placed his hands on its shoulders to knead the leather there.

"You visited Elizabeth, didn't you?"

"What difference does that make?"

"I thought so." He spoke this as if to himself before he continued. "You should know Iain that I did likewise. How could I not in the aftermath of what we had tried to do here? I was at odds because what I told you was the truth. Or at least it was the truth as I saw it."

"Don't play games me with Colin…"

"I'm not. Damn it, Iain, just listen will you! The ritual we performed was exactly as I described, as I said from my point of view, nothing happened. But after what happened with both Colin and Elizabeth, how could I not see some kind of link? I went to her and she told me what she experienced, what Crosby had experienced."

Fitzgerald was silent; at last, it seemed Morris was ready to tell him the whole story.

"She told me how, while we spoke our holy words, the thing came to her, unseen to our eyes and whispered into her ear. If it weren't for Crosby's subsequent suicide, I would simply have believed what I believed before, that the exorcism was only a show for her benefit and that her madness held irrespectively. Crosby saw that don't you know? He thought as I did, that should our actions not have the desired effect upon her, then she should be committed. I was torn, for it was the easiest explanation, but Crosby? It didn't fit and so I went to her and she told me what happened. That to which I was blind."

"Why now, Colin? Why bring this up now?"

"For you, you fool. I had put this all to bed years ago. I didn't want to believe her; instead it was easier to believe that Crosby was likewise unhinged and I had simply been dragged into their delusion. But you brought it all back, with your questions and your insistence on obtaining the diaries. When I knew you meant to actually go through with this, then I saw it was real and was obliged to help. And just in time as well it seems for she was right, wasn't she?"

"How do you mean?"

"You see it don't you? It has spoken to you?"

"It is here."

"Then we must finish and be done with it once and for all!"

"Iain, you must listen to me."

The voice he heard now was within his own head but was not his own; this was the voice of the little girl.

"I am weak in the face of its power. You must resist it."

"Get out of my head!" he screamed.

Alarm flashed across Morris's face. Pushing the chair aside, he rushed to Fitzgerald's side and took him firmly by the arm once more. "It speaks to you? You must resist it Iain! It will send you mad as it did Elizabeth and Crosby!"

"Iain no, I am the friend that showed you the face of the beast. But it wears many disguises; you must look upon it and see it for what it really is."

The sound within his mind was overpowering, and he grasped his temple with both hands for the force inside seemed fit to tear his head open. "Get out!"

"Iain resist it. Do not listen to its lies! You have begun something here, and you must banish it. If you do not, it will consume you, as it did the others!"

"The beast you seek stands before you. It is in the making of its father. Its words, lies and deceit. It would have you make it free once more to wreak its terrible works upon the world once again. See it for what it is and resist its words."

"Fight it, Iain, fight it!"

He fell to his knees, his head a throbbing agony. Rational thoughts were lost to him such was the pain he experienced. All there was in the world were the agony of the child's words and the strength of his friends to fight it. He knew well the price he would pay if he surrendered now. Realising that his crucifix was not lost to him, he clutched it tightly beneath his chin as his other hand tried to withhold the agony in his head.

"Diabolus esse abiit."

"That's good Iain, fight it!"

"Diabolus esse abiit." He pronounced again, only louder and stronger. Within his mind, he likewise found his voice and though the voice of the child clamoured to be heard he repeated the Latin, 'Devil be gone' and it was working for the pain in his head was subsiding slowly but surely.

"Iain, please. Fall not for the schemes of the Devil, remember even Satan disguises himself as a child of the light."

And with that, the voice was gone as if it had never been.

Hauling his weight up, he stood now before Morris. "Iain?"

"It is done, Colin. At least for now."

"You beat it, Iain? What did it want of you?"

"It fights still to prevent its expulsion, but we are close. Quickly before it returns to us and should you hear any voice but mine Colin, do likewise and fight it."

Morris nodded. "You must finish now what you have begun."

Fitzgerald still felt woozy from the mental onslaught but knew he must continue and he had his friend to thank for his timely intervention. The beast, desperate in its bid to stop the exorcism, had come to him inside the mask of a little girl and tried to sway him from his purpose.

Morris had come in the nick of time and saved him from such chicanery. He must continue he knew, but the feeling of exhaustion that overcame him now prevented him from finding any words. The feeling had been sudden, the mental anguish had ended only for this feeling to prevail, and it was as if every limb ached to be rested and his eyes became heavy with tiredness.

He yearned now only for rest and peered at Morris through half-opened eyes, the low glare of the emergency lighting giving his colleague a withered and haunting look as he stood in the shadows.

"Iain please."

Stealing himself against the fatigue, he traced back to where he had been in his service. It was clear in his mind that it had been the completion of the prayers of exorcism that had precipitated the arrival of the spectral child. He could continue where he left off; the ceremony was close to completion. He walked now, back toward the door, Morris close in tow. He turned to behold the room once more; Morris stood at his shoulder, his very presence a reassurance and comfort.

"God in heaven above, God who created the earth and made a gift of it to man, God who gave us his Son, Jesus Christ…" the words came quickly and easily to him, the crib sheet he had prepared a forgotten relic now in the depths of his discarded satchel, for the words resonated from his core as if they had been etched within his very being.

"…God of all that is good and right, God who teaches of forgiveness, God who loves us, God who gives us life after death and the eternal paradise that is heaven…"

And as he spoke a change came about the world around him. Indistinguishable at first but soon undeniable, the sound of the rain had ceased altogether and the cold plumes of air that he continued to expel seemed to hover and expand slowly in the air before him as warm air met cold. It felt as if everything was slowing down and he turned to see that Colin Morris was seemingly caught within the same effect for his eyes blinked slowly and rolled impractically slowly to meet his own.

His words though continued in a torrent. "…I ask of thee to cleanse this house from the machinations of Satan. He who would blight the souls of men with doubt and fear, and so subdued, that they enter into his graces. I say no more! For it is an affront to all that is good and right about the world. Remove this evil oh Lord and return this house and all that call it home to your loving side…"

And so it continued, and he marvelled as time itself seemed to slow around him, knowing it was the power of the words and power imbued by God himself that resonated within him. The power to undo the works of the Devil and so banish it back to hell.

"We ask you, Father, to make restitution and deliver Thoby Hall from the clutches of the serpent of old. You, who have dominion over all, and by your voice command such evil to flee before you and so back to hell, that no vestige of their being remains within this house."

Now he felt alive and awake once more for he was the vessel of God, and even when the discarded books on the floor began to vibrate and slowly dance and jump like silent firecrackers he continued unrelenting; "There is but one voice the foul demon must obey oh Lord. And with your blessing, I am the herald that commands in your name. The beast, as all other living things, bows to your words, for it was you who commanded Satan and the rebellious hordes to hell. They are compelled by your power and so must leave this place as I command them to do in your name."

The vibration of the books upon the floor continued, and he watched on as one by one they lifted from the ground and began to slowly rise into the air, the vibration itself had become alive in sound as a keen buzzing reverberated throughout the room.

"…Hear now, evil one and hearken the word of God. I bid you leave this place and return at once to the dark realm that spawned you…"

The books that rose came together and swirled as if caught in a typhoon, slow was their speed at first, but faster and faster they spun, the hum of the vibration becoming a high-pitched shriek.

"…as I command you in the name of Almighty God to leave this place. Whatever rituals or bonds tie you here are now undone. There is no other word or command, but my own, which I invoke on behalf of God Almighty, the shadow that holds you is broken, it binds you to this place no more, and as my words break your bonds, so to they must be obeyed as I command you to leave this place…"

Faster and faster they spun until they were but a blur before him and there, there in the centre, a face?

Fitzgerald thrust out the crucifix before him.

"Ecce cruis signum fugiant phantasmata cuncta"

The sound of vibration reached a crescendo, an ear-splitting whine. With his last spoken word, two things happened at once, the glass of the window behind the books shattered in an explosion of white reflection moving slowly toward him. He cowered as fragments came inward to rain upon him. The whirlwind of books fell to the floor and as they hit, it was as if time was renewed for he was gently buffeted with air before the full force of the flying glass hit him.

All at once, the room again fell into darkness.

He lay huddled on the floor, holding his breath and testing himself so as to know if he had been injured by the flying glass. His hand met his face and came away wet and warm, and he knew it was so, from somewhere behind him, he heard the voice of Colin Morris, cracked and raw.

"It is done." Morris's voice floated as if from afar.

"Is it?" He whispered, not trusting to his instinct. He was hurt, and the exhaustion of before fell upon him like a blanket. The words he had spoken had indeed had power but seemingly had drawn the strength from his very being, but it was not exhaustion that defeated him then.

The pain in his head returned at once a thousand fold it seemed, and he fell heavily to the floor where he closed his eyes and quickly, the darkness was deeper than he had ever known.

CHAPTER 48

Robert McArthur started awake, confused and terrified for he found the world he inhabited bathed with the eerie orange glow of candlelight.

Was this it? Had he passed over to the other side? At first, he could well believe that such an occurrence had indeed happened, for the indescribable pain that had been a constant companion for months had now completely disappeared. Recognition quickly dawned though, as a familiar face bent over him and shone a bright light into each eye. Black dots swam in front of his eyes as he blinked hard against the light.

"Don't worry; he's still with us." The voice was familiar somehow, soothing and caring. Was it Elizabeth? A sad part deep inside told him that such a thing could not be, and should his carer have lingered for a moment more they would have seen a tear fall from the corner of his eye at the realisation of that truth.

"Thank goodness, he can't leave us yet; he has unfinished business." He detected a soft Irish accent, but the identity of its source was also lost to him.

No matter, it was a relief for him to know there were others present for the strange glare within the room had startled him, making him forget his whereabouts at first.

That though came back quickly, his mind finding an anchor in the familiarity of his surroundings. He was home at Thoby Hall. Relief coursed through his being for the voice had been right, there was unfinished business of some sort. He closed his eyes to the putrid light and tried to picture what such business might be, but nothing came.

"What the hell was that?" Came the first voice.

"I don't know, feels like the storm hit real close." Followed the Irish.

"Scared me. Christ, I thought we'd lost him."

"Don't worry; this place is rigged up pretty tight with a backup generator."

McArthur smiled. Yes, that was right, a backup generator.

Something had happened while he was under, a storm by the sound of it and yes he could hear the soft patter of rain from behind the speaking voices. In all his time, he had never known the generators be required. It was a relief somehow for it had fulfilled some purpose beyond simply the emergency lighting, but what was it? Still, understanding was just beyond reach.

"Thank goodness, but shouldn't the lights have kicked back in by now?"

"I don't know. Perhaps I should go and look." The Irish voice.

"What about the priest, could he help?"

The priest? Yes, there had been a priest! The fog in his mind was easing and the picture of such a man appeared in his head. Fitzpatrick? Fitzgerald? It was hard but it was coming back to him.

"He has business of his own. Just keep him awake; it will all be over soon."

Footsteps and the closing of a door. The Irish woman had seemingly left.

Yes, it would soon be over; his time, at last, come to an end.

Despite his sketchy memory, this one inevitable truth was undeniable, for all the clues as to his existence for the last few months were immediately apparent. The hospital bed, the cannula in his arm and the ECG monitor which sat now dark and unresponsive and soon to be made redundant.

What was remarkable though at this late hour was the lack of pain. He had given instructions to the nurse (Melissa) that he was no longer to be medicated, for whatever his forgotten business, he knew he must be alive and awake to it when the time came.

Perhaps such a thing had been impossible for her, though, he surmised. Whatever had happened she had done her work stoically, for here he still was to finish whatever it was he was compelled to see through.

All too quickly though his eyelids grew heavy once more and he could muster no more fight to keep them open.

Time passed. He knew not how much but a noise, or rather a succession of them caused him to wake once more. Whatever it had been had ceased now and he could not place the source of the disturbance though it had been close by.

"Melissa?" He questioned to the vast room.

There was no answer. He strained his head as far to each side as he could, but to no avail, there was no sign of his nurse. Had she gone to deal with the lights? A vague recollection came to him of a conversation overheard. Yes, that must be it for the room was still bleached in the low orange glow of the few candles that burned intermittently throughout the room.

"Keira?" Had he heard her voice? Time had been lost to him, and he could not fathom as to which of his two nurses should be present. The fact was though that neither were here to...

The door opened and in stepped a familiar shape, who quickly closed the door behind them.

"Father? Is that you?. Forgive me; my eyes are fading."

Fitzgerald came to the bed at once and took his familiar place on the chair to McArthur's side. He took McArthur's limp hand in his own.

"Hello Robert, how are you faring?"

At once, McArthur found new reserves of strength and his eyes found focus to gaze upon the priest. "Please, Father, tell me. Is it done?"

"It is done."

McArthur let his head fall back on the sumptuous pillows and let out a loud sigh. "Glory be! Oh, thank you, thank you. I can finally pass and rest in peace."

"In peace?" The priest replied quizzically.

"All thanks to you, Father. I am sorry for what you had to go through to deliver me this end, but I am forever grateful for your help."

Slowly a soft laugh came from the priest's lips. "I'm afraid gratitude won't quite cut it Robert."

Fitzgerald still had a hold of McArthur's hand, and slowly his grip tightened, causing the old man no small pain. He tugged so as to try and pull his hand away.

"Please, Father, I said I was sorry. Won't you please forgive me? You have done a greater deed here today than you know. It is not just for me that you have acted."

A look of curiosity crossed the young priest's face. "Pray, tell me Robert, what have I done?"

The pain in McArthur's hand increased as Fitzgerald tightened his grip.

"Aargh, Iain please you are hurting me!"

A look of surprise crossed Fitzgerald's face, and he quickly looked down, realising what he did he quickly dropped the hand.

"Goodness, what has gotten into you? What happened in there?" McArthur asked.

Fitzgerald stood and walked off toward the window, which was to McArthur's left-hand side and gazed out into the rain-soaked night.

"What happened? Why everything that was supposed to of course. You should be commended for how you played and how you manipulated."

McArthur nursed his aching hand. This fool priest it seemed wanted his pound of flesh for what he had been through. McArthur though, would not be so indulging.

"We've spoken of this before. I have no regrets."

Fitzgerald spun around, his eyes gleaming coldly. "No regrets? What of forgiveness, Robert?"

"You've already bestowed forgiveness. What do you want? A fucking apology on top?!" McArthur spat.

Strength coursed through his veins, and he felt truly alive. So strange that he should feel himself this way before the end, whatever concoction coursed through the IV feed was certainly giving him a high he had not felt in a long time.

"Ah yes, of course, confession. And so your sins were recanted and you will rise among the angels?"

McArthur was bemused by the priest's strange behaviour. Something had happened of which he had not yet spoken. "You are not yourself, Father, tell me, what happened in there?"

Fitzgerald cocked his head to the side. "Does it show Robert? You are the insightful one. Yes, I saw it. It was a close call, but I won through despite the interference of others."

"Interference? I don't understand."

"There was another Robert, another that would argue a different path, one that would cage your demon here forevermore."

"I don't understand. Who are you talking about?"

Fitzgerald walked closer and leaned in close to the old man and seemed to measure him up, all the while McArthur tried to slide over as far as he could from the priest.

As he drew in close, McArthur watched as his own breath became ice in the air before him, the room having become bitterly cold.

And as the cold had grown so to had his fear of the man before him. Had the priest perhaps become unhinged as a result of what had happened, as Crosby and Elizabeth had done before him? Doubt gnawed at him for this was one potential outcome which he had not foreseen, and now he lay there unprotected before him.

"You don't remember Robert? The child. She who died here in the pool that your money bought."

"What of her? What has she got to do with this?"

Fitzgerald's voice became lower, his eyes narrower. "What has she to do with this?" He growled, "she almost ruined everything, that's what she had to do with this!"

He spun away quickly and battered the chair before him, which lifted off the floor and flew across the room. McArthur shied away once more as Fitzgerald leaned in closely again.

"Enough games McArthur, it is over and you have lost!"

How dare he speak to me this way.

McArthur's own anger now began to rise. "It's not too late priest, watch your tongue, I can easily have Harvey change our agreement."

Fitzgerald lifted and stepped back; he laughed loud into the room. "You still don't get it do you old man? You have lost here and you will be delivered to the hell you tried so hard to avoid!"

"Melissa! Get in here damn it, remove this imbecile at once!" McArthur cried in the forlorn hope that his nurse was within earshot in the outer apartment.

She must have heard the ruckus for goodness sake, why hasn't she come?

"Get out of here, priest! Don't think I don't still have influence. I can see it that you are thrown to the kerb boy!"

"You don't see it yet do you, McArthur? I had hoped my little game might have jogged something inside of you, but no mind. You don't see through this face, but how about this one?"

McArthur watched on in horror as slowly Fitzgerald's face melted away before him and the realisation of the truth was afforded him like the lifting of a veil.

This wasn't Fitzgerald, instead the terrible face of the beast he had once known from the darkest of his nightmares.

The transition from one face to another was as an abomination of life, as skin peeled revealing the underlying muscle and sinew that likewise cracked and fell. Blood pulsed freely from where eyes had once been and the thing that wore the face of Iain Fitzgerald laughed all the while, the sound fading to nothing as the larynx and vocal cords went through their own destruction, only to be remade and the laugh come back deeper than before.

McArthur could not turn away from the terrible sight that met his own eyes, seemingly powerless to avert his gaze, hypnotised and terrified as he was.

Now the thing's hair came out, and the creature encouraged it the more by grabbing vast clumps and pulling them away to make the transition all the faster, a leering grin stretching wide across a mouth now lined with razor-sharp pointed teeth. The new face was becoming all too familiar, as the visage of Thomas Searle neared completion.

"Did I not tell you I would return when the time was right?" The thing laughed.

"No, please, god no! It's impossible!"

"Impossible?" Searle sneered back. "You sold me to the Devil, Robert, and so, in turn, your time has come. We will spend our eternity together in hell!"

"No! It cannot be, I am absolved! I am absolved!" McArthur begged.

Searle drew back, paused and ran its tongue over sharp teeth, causing blood to run from its mouth.

"Oh, Robert, I am so hungry. So much more than before, it is all I can do to prevent myself from peeling back your skin and tasting the cancer infested flesh underneath. Oh, and I will, know that for you are damned despite your protestations. You are absolved you cry! And yes I feel it on you, the lurid words of your good book come off of you like a stench that makes me gag."

"Yes! yes! I am forgiven! You may put me in my grave, but my path leads to heaven and salvation!"

Searle considered. "Very good Robert, very good." The demon approached and knelt at his side, and McArthur could not avert his gaze from it, looking deep into the cavernous eyes he looked and found an abyss where his sight tumbled and tumbled like Alice down the rabbit hole. And there, there at the bottom, through darkness and pain were the fires of hell, which danced and reached up toward him.

He tore his eyes away, as the lights threatened to hypnotise him and he be lost in them forever.

"How you resist Robert! But it is futile. I have already won!"

Searle reached and grabbed his hand once more. This time the pain was explosive, and he screamed as he felt the soft popping and cracking of bone.

"You played the priest well as I said, but he did not forgive you all of your sin Robert, for you did not tell him all."

Tears streamed down his face. "No, it's a lie. I told him everything!"

"Only all that you remember. Don't you see it now? Don't you see it in the visage of the one that went before you? He, who all was revealed to at the time of his death? Don't say you don't know Robert, he told you after all. Let me show you."

In an instant, the pain in his crushed hand was gone, and his fear vanished instantly. Such things were the work of the Devil he knew for he saw it behind the thing's wicked smile; it had given him this moment free from fear to think, to think back and recall. But what?

It wanted to taunt him, to make him see something forgotten, but there was nothing, nothing! He had lied and cheated, but he had revealed all to Fitzgerald. And so his soul was saved with forgiveness, why did the thing torture him so? All of a sudden, he felt hope for he was certain in his convictions and the creature before him sensed it didn't it? For now, there was doubt in its cruel eyes.

Still, it grasped onto his ruined hand. That was no matter, what was such an injury in the face of eternity? This beast, this demon may well take his life but it would never take his soul.

An image then came to him. A picture of long ago and of the real Thomas Searle. Drunk, hopeless and afraid.

"You know Robert; this very aisle is where I died for the second time."

It was from that night so long ago, when Searle had told him his tale for the first time. McArthur closed his eyes against his transgressor and found he could see.

He was astonished at the depth of his vision as he beheld his library exactly as it had been all that time ago. It was as if he was back within himself as he beheld the pathetic drunken wretch of a man, as the two of them drank…what had it been?

In his vision, he was able to use his younger eyes and seek out the bottle on the floor between him and Searle. A bottle of Bruichladdich whisky. The power of the vision was compelling and though he ignored the words of his master, he found that he had control of his younger self and was able to look about himself at will.

That was until the soft hum of words that expelled from Searle became substantial and begged hearing, a conversation that had taken place 53 years ago and was as familiar as if it had been only yesterday.

"Pathetic! pathetic, you say? How dare you! Do you think I would wallow in such self-pity? No, it is he, he who torments me."

McArthur watched on for a second time as Searle motioned toward the aisle of books that had plagued him so "How do you think it feels huh? To know that your life is not your own? That your achievements were for nought, as they were bought and paid for by my very soul! He told me that I would have the gift of ignorance until my death, but I did not die Robert, I did not die!"

He recalled the words uttered so long ago, knowing this was an advanced stage of the conversation he and Searle had held that night. But what was the meaning? The scene before him disappeared and in its place, only a white void remained.

He had been shown something, a glimpse of his past and meaning in the words of a long-dead man.

"He told me I would have the gift of ignorance until my death."

The words resonated with him. Here was the message that was to be heard, but what did it mean? What did it mean…

366

He blinked hard, and the white void that had been his memory was gone. He was back in the here and now for the monstrous replica of the same dead master was before him still.

It spoke. "Look, Robert, look at what you have done."

Still holding his broken hand, the creature lifted it and turned it so that the palm faced him. At last, he let go and though there was still no pain he felt something move inside as broken bones shifted. But his attention was quickly subverted to something else. Something that was both known and unknown to him.

He had born the long thick scar on his hand for 20 years. It had been a part of him for as long as he could remember, but now, suddenly it had new meaning.

"No, it can't be…" was all he could manage before the fear and pain returned to him like water through a broken dam. He was submerged in knowing and remembrance, the scar a testament to a deal made long ago.

The creature stood; its mouth wide in a delicious smile of victory. "You see it now don't you? You are not absolved for not all of your sin has been heard! I present to you my gift! The gift of ignorance until death."

"But I…what?"

It was already clear in his mind, though. The night he had finally returned to the library. The night he had begged for Elizabeth's life and made his own deal with the Devil.

"Yes! All is becoming clear." Searle hissed at him. "You begged me for her life, and I delivered and still; still you imprisoned me so! It was through your own arrogance that she suffered at all, know that before you die!"

It was true; it was all true. There had been more that he had held back from Fitzgerald, some of it knowingly, some not. He had watched as his wife had unfurled in the aftermath of the child's death, but the memory that had been taken from him had followed her attempt to exorcise the demon in the library.

In his own way, he had banished the memory of that night in the library with Searle and how he came into his fortune, refusing even to himself the truth of what had happened. Crosby had come to him and spoke of his concerns for Elizabeth, but he had waved them away and told the priest that he should placate her if that is what it would take to dispel her madness.

And so it had been him, Robert McArthur that had knowingly pointed her toward the devil he had done so much to forget, and when she had taken her overdose in the wake of Crosby's own death, it had all spilled in on him, the real truth of what had occurred with Searle and the horror that she and Crosby had sought to rid the house of.

In his grief and his terror of losing her he had gone, gone to the library and made his own deal, sliced open his hand as proof of his bond and so saved the life of the one that he loved. And so in keeping with the deal, to forget until his time came.

Until now.

"No! Please." His terror coursed throughout his being as he watched once more as the beast transformed once again, only slower than his memory, its jaw becoming unhinged again to reveal two rows of razor-sharp teeth. The thing revelled in his fear he knew and slowly it approached for the final time.

"A deal done in darkness must be completed in darkness, Robert."

It fell on him and his scream pierced the night as his throat was ripped, in the low light of the room his blood arced, appearing black before him. It was the last thing he would ever see for the beast had grown sharp talons that first raked his face and then plunged deep into his eye sockets sparing him at least the horrifying sight of his end.

The pain though, the pain was all there was in his world and his end when it came, did not come quick, for this time, the beast savoured its meal.

CHAPTER 49

When Fitzgerald finally came to, he found the library still dark with shadow. For now at least, the storm that had erupted above Thoby Hall was at an end, and the dark clouds chased away on the night wind, for a low soft moonlight fell within the room from the broken window at its far end.

Reaching tentatively back, he touched his scalp and felt a large bump, a gift from an unseen assailant. With a groan, he tried to stand, but his legs gave way underneath him and he sprawled out onto the floor.

What happened?

From his low vantage point, he beheld the dark library before him and knew at once that whatever terror had dwelled here was now gone from the room; the atmosphere was at once different.

Testing, he blew out a breath of air and saw no cloud. Although November cold, the biting, freezing temperature that seemed to follow the beast was now gone. That in itself should have been a reassurance, but as he shifted himself into a sitting position, he felt no such thing. Something had happened, something bad.

Certainly, as his ritual came toward a climax, there had been a frenzy of unworldly activity, the books that he saw strewn once again upon the floor had flown and the window before him had shattered — had that caused his injury? He touched his head again, and this time saw the product of the blow that had rendered him unconscious, for his hand was dark with dried blood. No, not the ceremony, something else...

Morris? Morris had come at the final hour, and as the books had whirled and danced, he had stood behind him, he had...

His head ached at the thought, but surely there could be but one explanation, Morris had struck him knocking him out cold, but why?

"Because he is the deceiver."

Fitzgerald cocked his head upward and there she was before him again. He felt no fear and his heart sank at the sight of her. Deep down, he already knew. He had been manipulated into believing it was she who sought to trick him.

"Lydia." His words choked, no more than a whisper.

She approached only differently this time, at once he could see that she was more substantial and he could no longer see through her form, and more, for now, she walked the short distance as opposed to how she seemed to glide and float previously.

She sat in front of him and touched his chin, raising it so that she could see into his eyes, her touch warm and soothing.

"Am I dead?" he asked.

She smiled. "No Iain, you are not. And it is not yet too late to avert what has transpired here tonight."

"I am sorry, I am so sorry." Tears began to form in his eyes.

"Don't be Iain. You were deceived and I had not the power to help you further. Here in its den I was weak and I could not reach you, its presence was too strong. It is well versed in the arts of deception and it wore the face of one you know and trusted."

Fitzgerald considered all that had happened. Something did not sit right.

"No, there was more than that. Why would it want me to succeed when you did not? I don't understand."

Lydia nodded, and in her eyes, he saw wisdom beyond her years, it was as if she had grown in spirit and mind for all the long years since she had passed.

"Because it was trapped here, Iain. There are spells and incantations stronger than the force of its will. Thomas Searle did not know it all those years ago, but the protection his wife accidentally bought, both held the beast at bay and imprisoned it here also. Those bonds are both tenuous and weak and it has been as much through chance that they have held. It brought you here, it manipulated so that the word of God would break those bonds and so they did, but your rite was incomplete was it not?"

It was true; the ritual had not been completed. Quickly he looked about himself for his satchel. "No, you are right, the medals of St Benedict were not yet lain, I was fooled, fooled into thinking it was done."

Lydia nodded. "And so the bonds are broken, and it is released. Already I fear it is too late for Robert McArthur, but it is not too late for us."

"How?" he demanded, "How can that be?"

"The creature remains a thing of the shadow and darkness, and as yet other bonds hold it here still. You will have learned well that Thomas Searle upon learning his plight sought any means to protect himself from his fate. One such bond he created is upon the threshold; it is likewise weak but still holds."

Fitzgerald knew of what she spoke, the pagan symbol both upon the doorway and the grand hallway beyond it.

"What can I do?"

"The ritual can still be completed, but should it pass through into the night beyond then all is lost. If you can, then light must be returned to these hallways, and so the beast returned to what shadow it can find. Then and only then will you have a chance. But be warned Iain, it acquiesced so far as to be released. You must remain strong for it will not willingly allow itself to fall into the pit of hell again."

"I will do as I can."

Lydia stood. "Be wary still; the demon will seek to further deceive at every path. It may wear any face that it has seen. If you find it, it may appear once again as a friend."

"I understand. I won't fall for Morris once again."

"That ruse is played Iain, be careful."

Fitzgerald lifted himself. He was at once unsteady on his feet but managed to hold his balance. He towered over the young girl before him and was overcome with a sadness for what had befallen her. He had so many questions that he would ask her, but deep down knew the answers were not for his knowing as no man should have insight into what lay beyond his life. As it was, he may well find out for himself before the night was over.

"I should go, but where?"

"I have spent many long years here; that part is easy. The generators are located underground. You can access them via the kitchens. Something doesn't quite add up so be careful, the fact that the emergency lighting is activated is testament to their functioning, but the house lights and the spotlights outside should have kicked in by now. If you can fix it, it will revert to shadow."

Fitzgerald nodded and turned to go, but was halted by a tug at his belt. Lydia motioned for him to move in closer and so he bent close, quickly she planted a kiss upon his cheek. She held him there for a second more and whispered soft words into his ear.

Raising himself, he nodded his understanding at the instruction given and turned to retrieve his satchel. Picking it up, he turned toward her, words poised upon his lips but already she was gone, gone as if she had never existed.

He sighed heavily. He had been played, played for a fool. At first by McArthur into performing the ritual at all, and secondly by the demon itself.

It had wanted him to succeed all along, at least so far as to free it from whatever held it. Everything that had happened had brought him to this point, McArthur, Elizabeth, everything. But had they been likewise fooled into believing the lie it had sown so deeply? That it should be removed?

His mind turned back to Elizabeth and how she had recounted the night Crosby had attempted the exorcism and how it had been doomed to failure. Prevalent in her account had been how all the while the ritual took place, the demon had spoken to her...

"The thing, it told me...it told me that he did not believe and so his actions were doomed to failure but the day would come when another would arrive, another who would succeed in driving it back to where it comes from. It spoke of you, Father."

There had been such conviction in her words as she had spoken them to him, and so he had bought easily into his task, that even the demon itself had known of its impending banishment.

But that to had been a ruse, a carefully crafted lie meant for one as fragile as Elizabeth to hold for many years until the time came to beg that same priest to dispense with it forever. And how he had fallen for it, but no more. He had been given a second chance, one the beast could not have counted on.

Steeling himself for the trials to come, Fitzgerald raced from the library.

CHAPTER 50

Already I fear it is too late for Robert McArthur.

Fitzgerald made the anteroom and quickly ground to a halt as Lydia's words came to mind. His mission was clear, the path of which lay immediately to his right and the front of the house. Instead, though he ploughed straight on ahead toward where he had left the dying man, at what now seemed hours ago. Although it was true that McArthur was near his end and that such a thing may have already happened; the implication from what Lydia had said to him was that he was in danger from the demon that now had the freedom of the house.

The trickery and deception that McArthur had applied to manoeuvre Fitzgerald to his will was now irrelevant in his mind, what was happening here was bigger than the two of them, and the beast had already claimed one victory, it would not win another if he could yet help it.

What was more, was Keira. He had left both her and Melissa alone with McArthur, if the beast had made that his first stop…

And so he ran, and though his head swam from the blow he had sustained and his legs threatened to fold underneath him through dizziness, he continued along the upper corridor of the west wing which now appeared eerie in the soft light of the moon that fell within.

Finding the door of the apartment open, he burst through into the outer room. What he saw immediately caused him to grind to a halt and his legs again threatened to give way beneath him.

Melissa was dead.

She lay across the sofa as if she had gone there for sleep. In another world, he might well have believed so and gently tiptoed around her so as to gain the room beyond, instead though the impossible angle of her head to her neck told otherwise.

The demon had indeed made this his first stop and snapped the poor woman's neck like a twig. The shock of what he saw had taken the wind from him, and at that moment his mind was overwhelmed by the sight; the trickle of blood from her nose, the wide staring eyes, fixed in horror at the last thing they had beheld.

Keira.

The thought gave him the power to move once again, and he shouldered the bedroom door open.

"Oh, my God."

His stomach lurched at the twin visions that he saw, for impossibly, his eyes held both McArthur and the room as a split vision.

One, almost serene and peaceful. The other violent and sickening.

He blinked his eyes hard to try to dismiss the latter picture he saw but found that he could not, it was as if overlaid like a cell from a cartoon strip — one picture on top of another. The first, tranquil and placid, only the sad image of a dead man finally succumbing to the terrible illness that afflicted him for so long. The second, an overlay, a gruesome insight as to what had really occurred here. For no matter how hard he tried to block it out Fitzgerald saw the carnage of the demon's work.

The bedsheets he saw were both pristine white, and black with blood. McArthur's face was both serene and a ravaged bloody mess. His jaw was at once both as it should be and ripped from its socket, twisted horribly out of place, leaving his mouth in a wide unheard scream. His eyelids closed, did nothing to mask the empty sockets beneath from where his eyeballs had been punctured and torn, leaving blood to run as tears down smooth white skin.

Fitzgerald twisted his head away and shut his eyes to the appalling visions. He knew well what had transpired, the beast had fed upon his soul, just as McArthur had recanted in his tale of Searle's end. That raised more questions than answers, for McArthur had done all he was able to deliver himself from such a fate, most of all obtaining absolution through final confession. It had served him nought it seemed, and Fitzgerald had not the mind to seek the answers.

Keira.

By the light of the candles adorned about the room, he scoured the large bedroom, but she was nowhere to be seen. "Keira?" he asked timidly. Only silence and the soft patter of impossible blood dripping from the hospital bed to the floor below where it pooled. Ignoring the vision, he turned to the far side of the room and beheld the large wardrobe that had kept a lonely vigil on the traumatic events that had transpired in the room, both tonight and the many months before. Fitzgerald pulled the door open and found nothing. Tearing himself away from the bloody scene, he returned to the living room and quickly pulled open the doors to both the makeshift pharmacy and the bathroom that sat opposite it. Again there was no sign of her.

"Where are you?"

Despite what he had seen, he was touched with relief, knowing that Keira had somehow evaded the beast's clutches. For now, though there was nothing else he could do for her. He had been too late for both McArthur and Melissa and the only safety he could offer Keira was to end this as quickly as he was able.

Reaching out, he slid fingers down Melissa's face and closed her eyelids and shuddered as he saw the revolting break in her neck.

Why Lord? Why should she suffer as well?

But his thought went unanswered. Quickly he crossed himself and said a short whispered prayer for her departed soul. For McArthur, he knew such an idea was too late.

Running again now, he saw that his twin vision of the world was not yet over. A trail of blood-soaked footprints now led away from McArthur's room and back toward the library. Fitzgerald tensed as he approached that room once again, half expecting to find the demon in whatever visage it now held, instead though seeing the footprints veer off toward the landing at the top of the house.

He followed and was soon over the balcony that overlooked the lobby of the house. As before the sight that greeted him was of an inverted pentagram, cast within the stonework of the floor below. The surprise and mystery of its being was now known to him, and he took the time to both thank and curse the unknown wiccan who so long ago had the foresight to cast a spell of protection for Thomas Searle, as opposed to the fertility rite she was supposed to.

If it had not been for her, the beast would have had its prize that night so long ago and haunted the house no more. Instead, revealed to Searle, he had done all in his power to preserve his life, long beyond its natural end, imprisoning and infuriating the beast in so doing. After his eventual passing, McArthur had known and had chosen to ignore that same fact. That had cost him his wife, and in the end, his fate had been the same as that of his master Searle long before him.

But what fate had Fitzgerald himself bestowed on the world at large by releasing it? Following the line of footprints, he saw that they went down and to the lobby. And so he ran onward along the first floor and would take the staircase in the east wing and come to his destination that way, avoiding the creature entirely.

If it still remains.

He shut the thought down as quickly as it had come. The footsteps he saw had led down to the doorway and to the point where the wards that were designed to prevent the beast crossing were located. Had it known of their existence? He could well imagine its rage as it found out that its freedom into the dark night beyond was still prevented.

If they worked as they were supposed to.

He could not dwell on that, though. He must act as if the creature was still bound, and so, breath labouring, he continued to run until at last he reached the east wing stairway.

Placing his hand on the rail, he was already three steps down in a run when he felt something move against his hand. Aghast, he recoiled quickly and jerked his hand away from the bannister. The movement had been slow, almost...*(slithering)* the image that greeted him affirmed his thought for the bannister was alive as it had been in his dream

Only it wasn't a dream, was it?

He remembered the revulsion with which he had first seen these intricate carvings in the wood, but this was so much more, for those carvings of snakes and serpents now glided and climbed over one another. He looked over and saw that the cherubs depicted on the opposite bannister were still. It was the mirror opposite of his previous experience, and in his mind the message was clear, the demon he had released was still here, for the snakes writhed like him to be free of their bonds. There was time still it seemed, though the absence of life on the opposite rails faded what little hope he had. Had all that was right and godly abandoned the house he had to wonder.

Taking the rest of the stairs two at a time, he came into the lower passageway and ran for the kitchen door.

The room looked alien bathed as it was in the glow of the moonlight, the polished steel worktops reflecting his movement as he walked.

Looking about himself, it wasn't clear as to where the entrance he sought was located. His eyes darted and fell upon the door he had first used to enter the building, little less than a week ago.

He wondered then if the other exits were as protected as the front. Had there been such a device above this doorway and others as there was at the lobby entrance? In his harassed state, he could not think and instead chose to trust that such bonds were in place all around. If not, it was surely already too late.

He skirted the first of the large countertops. Pots and pans that hung from a large ceiling rack likewise reflected his passing as he moved and caused his anxiety to heighten at his advance.

There was nothing. No doorways, no cellar hatches nothing that suggested access to a basement. Had Lydia steered him wrong? No, surely that could not be. What was more, he remembered the story of Robert McArthur well. He had accessed the same passageway to instigate his plan against McArthur by turning off the old generators.

Even so, the only doorway other than the hallway entrance and outside exit was the walk-in pantry...

Grabbing the huge lever, he depressed it and tugged hard at the heavy door. It groaned in response, and he had to get both hands behind it to fashion enough grip to open it.

The inside was dark. He felt inside, and his hands instantly fell upon a switch. Grateful, he clicked it down. Nothing. As is the want of those who are afraid of the dark, he toggled the switch several times in denial of what he knew.

Fitzgerald stood frozen and cast his eyes over the rest of the room, but it was no good, the room was utterly black before him. The entrance to the basement must lay within the pantry; but how could he bring himself to go into the pitch black beyond the pantry's threshold and search for it?

Fitzgerald took a step in and immediately retreated as visions of the door being shut behind him washed over. But go in he must. What to do? Why had he not thought to bring a source of light? But the truth was that self-remonstration was pointless. How could he have predicted such a scenario as this? Quickly he backed away from the dark room, feeling all the safer for distance.

He needed light, but where to find it? A mental scan told him that he had not seen anything approximating a torch since he had been here. There had been candles back in McArthur's rooms, and he cursed himself for not bringing one on his journey. But now McArthur's rooms were too far and time was of the essence.

A brainwave struck. The large dining room down the corridor; the candelabras in the room had been plentiful and well-stocked with candles.

Quickly he moved over to the large stove and hobs above. Twisting the first of a line of dials he heard gas whistle through, soon followed by the strong sulphurous smell. Another ceiling rack was hung to the left of the stove, and there he found the gas lighter which he sought. Clicking it multiple times he watched as a tiny blue spark fired at its end. *Perfect.*

Switching off the gas, he went quickly to the corridor. He was hesitant at first and listened long through the crack in the door. His senses seemed in overdrive as adrenaline and fear coursed throughout him, and every little sound or movement sent his heart into frantic overtime. For now, though all seemed quiet and he edged slowly out of the kitchen. Time was against him, but his imagination was now his worst enemy. The bannister coming to life and all that he had seen in the library and McArthur's bedroom would haunt him for years to come if he were to get through the night, but first, he had to get through it and so had to rely on his instincts, he wasn't ready for the demon as yet and so if it should come suddenly...

Quiet as a mouse he walked as quickly as he could, casting nervous glances all about for fear that he was being watched and soon discovered. The dining room door was open before him, and thankfully there were the candelabras laid out on the vast table.

Suddenly and from somewhere deep in the house, he heard an unnatural roar. So loud and so full of frustration. Fitzgerald clasped his hands quickly to his ears to block out the sound. The sound was terrifying, and he had quivered in place. It was only when it stopped that rational thought came back to him, whatever it had been; it was not close.

He could guess no other source than the beast, and though it was impossible to know for sure, he reckoned that it was perhaps on the far side of the house. Had it found out it was trapped as it tested other doorways and exits? That meant that it could perhaps even now be on its way over to the east wing to try there. Scared as he was, he was not planning on being found should the creature come this way. Grabbing the large candlestick, he darted for the hallway, not caring for the disturbance he now made.

Soon he was back in the kitchen, and five candles burned brightly in the ornate frame in his right hand. Their light and warmth enriched him and made him stronger for though their glow was sparse, it did something to hold back the wretched shadows of the night.

He stepped into the pantry, and testing the back of the door for a release handle; he felt satisfied that escape was possible. He drew the large door closed behind him, hoping that should the beast find the kitchen, then it would not sense what was going on beyond the pantry door and the basement beneath.

By the light of the candelabra, Fitzgerald found that the walk-in pantry was a vast thing. Like the library before it, row upon row of high-stacked shelves opened up, both to his left and right. His eyes shifted nervously in both directions as he went, as shadows flitted back and forth in his wake revealing copious amounts of tinned and packaged goods. As he searched each aisle for some sign of a doorway or hatch, his eyes happened upon large cans of coffees, cereals and tinned meats, neatly stacked three or four deep in their expansive rows. It crossed his mind that there might be supplies enough to see a person out for years.

Each passing row did not bring him to his goal, and he felt his hope ebbing away, the further he went. What if it wasn't here after all? The idea of relighting the house and so sending the demon back to its prison within the shadows had thus far been enough to keep him going, but what should happen if such a thing were impossible?

It was bad enough that he was surrounded by darkness already, but what if the beast should stumble upon him in its rage and desperate to remove itself from the house? Given what he had seen of both McArthur and Melissa he could well guess, the unanswered question though was to why the creature had not killed him outright within the library after he had fulfilled enough of the exorcism to break its bonds. What would be for certain is that it would not make the same mistake twice if it found him here seeking ways to capture it once more.

The small arc of light generated by the candles reflected back off of what was undoubtedly the far wall of the pantry. He had come in some fifteen to twenty feet, and there had been no clue as to where the basement entrance was. The thought of the dumb waiter came to him, and he wondered if its location might offer some clue. As that thought crossed his mind, his foot came into contact with something hard, which rebounded sharply off of his foot and skated off into the darkness. His heart leapt at the unexpected sound that it generated. Quickly though the object hit the wall with a tiny thud sound and came to a halt. Lowering the light of the candles, he was quickly able to identify a large metal padlock.

Confused, he stepped forward and saw it at once to his right, behind the last row of shelves — a large trapdoor within the floor.

He breathed a sigh of relief and planted the candelabra onto a small space on the shelving that bordered it. The hatch itself was metallic and had two doors, both of which could be latched to the wall or the shelving to hold them open. He bent low and grasped the left door handle and pulled it up toward him. It gave easily and silently, and he quickly latched it open. There now before him was a wooden set of stairs.

The glow of the candlesticks did little to penetrate the darkness below, and his mind sought to bring images of where the beast might lurk in the shadows below. What he could see though was that there were perhaps no more than ten steps before him before they gave way to the black pit beyond. As such, he had no way of telling how deep the cellar might be from his current vantage point.

The passage down was thin, and so he began to take hold of the second door to lift it. Something gave though, whether it was a sweaty palm, a misjudgement through the possible concussion he had sustained, or just bad luck.

The door fell from his hand and slammed noisily back into place with a clang. The noise was deafening in the small space and he winced inwardly. At first, all was eerily quiet, and the only sound was that of his own laboured breathing.

His heart galloped as he listened as hard as he was able, holding his breath as best he could and feeling the pulse beat hard in his temple. At first, there was nothing, and he closed his eyes and finally allowed his nervousness to expel in a series of deep breaths.

But relief was short-lived, somewhere nearby a familiar whine could be heard. At first indiscreet, it was almost so low as not to be heard, but having heard it before he knew at once what it was. The noise grew steadily in pitch and volume, and he could not deny its source for it was the same sound as had battered him when he performed the exorcism and saw a typhoon of books whirl before him.

Quickly though the sound intensified, became stronger until it was now more a hum, then becoming a growl and then a roar.

Fitzgerald was frozen in place as the sound grew and grew. It was close he knew, closer than before and it was that realisation that made him move once again, for he understood it was not that it was louder, but that it was coming closer by the second.

He grabbed the candelabra and squeezed through the open side of the hatchway, removing the latch as he did so and softly lowering the doors above back into place. He could not know that he should be so lucky as to be undiscovered for much longer, but he did not want to give the game away so easily as to have the thing discover the light he brandished before him.

It had heard, and it was coming, it was unlikely that there was any other way of escape for him he knew and so he must be quick. He said a small prayer in the hope that the spirit of Lydia had guided him well, if he could at least make the generator before the creature discovered him, then he might have a chance and for now, at least he had a head start.

The steps he trod were narrow, and so with painful deliberation, he had to slow himself so as not to miss one of the narrow shelves of wood where his feet fell. It could have been no more than sixteen steps though, before he found the concrete floor as he entered an expansive and cluttered basement.

Cobwebs hung low and clung to his clothes as he walked the first few steps into the room. There was a sense of familiarity within the basement for tall wine racks adorned the wall immediately ahead of him; these had formed a part of McArthur's tale to him; of the night where Thomas Searle had imparted his story for the first time. The racks though were sparsely filled and for that, there could be little wonder, he readily knew that McArthur's drinking days had ended when his illness had begun and also because of that, the house had not seen its usual share of guests.

Fitzgerald glided between packaging crates and discarded furniture, looking all the while for the way forward. It quickly came though, for a long concrete corridor opened before him on his right-hand side. This was a new installation he could see for the concrete was in stark contrast to the look of the rest of the basement that seemed old by virtue of the wooden beams that traversed its ceiling and walls.

He knew as he walked the long corridor, that he was heading away from under the house and out into the grounds. The tunnel he was in and the room for which he was headed had undoubtedly been built well away from the house for safety reasons. The generator, whatever it's make or designation would give off dangerous carbon monoxide gas that would need to be appropriately ventilated, more than that for should it malfunction in such a way that caused fire, it could do no damage to the house.

Sensing his goal was close now, Fitzgerald hurried along, and before long he saw a doorway barring the far side of the passageway. As he approached, he was relieved to hear the monotonous hum of what must be the generator at work, and this was complemented by a yellow and black warning sign that was attached to the side of the door depicting a lightning bolt within a triangle and the words CAUTION. DANGER. SECONDARY POWER SOURCE CONNECTED. BACK UP GENERATOR INSTALLED. Underneath a second sign warned, NO NAKED LIGHTS.

He looked at the candlestick within his grasp and set it down on the floor. He loathed though to extinguish the light that had brought him such comfort and he wondered if such a thing might afford him protection from the demon should it find its way to this long aisle. He dismissed the idea and a long glance back toward the basement from where he had come, motioned him to press ahead before he glimpsed sight of the thing that had bellowed such a terrifying wail from the halls above.

The door before him swung in gently and he was at once relieved to find some small light within the room beyond. The door swung softly shut behind him and he saw it had no conceivable lock or barring mechanism, and though he knew such a thing was for safety, he couldn't help regret the absence of any means to protect himself inside.

He found the room beyond was vast in size, for the generator he had been seeking resembled the steel container one might find on the back of a goods lorry. It must have been 20ft in length and both 10ft in width and height. There was a tangible vibration in the room as the thing hummed like ten thousand bees dwelt behind one of its two wide doors. Here to was the source of the light within the room, for on the side of the vast contraption was a single light fixture.

What the hell do I do with this?

Fitzgerald had little experience of such things and craned his neck to look over the structure as he walked before it.

Clearly the thing was operating, such was the noise it made, and evidenced as well by the light it generated, but why then was the house in darkness if the thing was functioning as it should?

Looking over the rest of the room, he saw two enormous tanks in an area closed off behind a mesh gate and fence — a sign, again yellow and black depicting a fire and the words; DANGER. DIESEL FUEL informed him of what lay beyond. Both the large tanks he saw had both hose and nozzle and were undoubtedly meant to feed the generator for as long as they were able. Both of the large tanks denoted that they held 5,000 litres of fuel each. Understanding now came to Fitzgerald as to the invoices for fuel he had observed in the solicitor's office above.

The space he was in was well-equipped and looked after he saw. A long workbench sat along the wall opposite the generator itself and beside it a tall roller cabinet toolset, which he saw the bottom two drawers were pulled out and various wrenches and sockets had been strewn over the floor. The image of the discarded tools was not in keeping with the aesthetic of the rest of the room which seemed like a well-ordered workspace.

There also in the far corner, a small door. No sign was attached, and so he had no idea to where the door might go or to its purpose.

For now, he was lost. Lydia had directed him here to restore the power to the house, but the generator it seemed was purring away as it should be. How was it that full power had not been restored? Looking for answers, he looked for some kind of control panel on the outside structure of the vast machine. Coming to the end, he saw a metal panel in the wall of the steel contraption, a heavy padlock nestled against its side, firmly in place. What was odd was that the metal panel itself had seemingly taken damage for he saw that it was heavily chipped and dented and one of the corners had been only ever so slightly bent over as if someone had tried to pry it open.

He peered in close to examine it when he heard the sound behind him. It had been quick but unmistakable, the grind of metal on concrete. He was not alone.

"Who's there?" he demanded, his nerves once again set immediately on edge.

At first, there was nothing, no sound, no movement. His heart pounded steadily in his chest and then, slowly, he saw a shape emerge from behind one of the diesel tanks and make its way toward the mesh gate that separated the two of them.□

CHAPTER 51

"Keira?"

"What are you doing here, Iain?" she said, coming to a halt behind the fence.

"Thank god you are okay…" He motioned forward, the joy in seeing her safe and well, filled him in an instant, but quickly it evaporated into uncertainty as she spoke again.

"I asked you what you were doing here."

He stopped and searched her face but found no obvious clue as to her strange reaction to seeing him. Could it be that she did not know what happened? She pushed through the mesh gate and stood before him once again; her face fixed rigid and fierce. He backed up a step for this was not the woman he had come to know and immediately the advice he had only recently received set alarm bells ringing in his mind.

"I could ask you the same thing," he began, "do you even know what has happened up there?"

She craned her head backwards and closed her eyes. She took a deep breath before she answered. "I can feel it, Iain. It is free at last." The same familiar smile began to stretch wide upon her face once more.

"It is."

He pressed forward and grabbed her by the upper arms and drew himself in close so that he could look deep within her eyes. "Is that you Keira?" He pushed her suddenly, and in surprise she fell back, letting out a gasping sound as she collided with the fence which rattled as she hit it.

Quickly pulling on the strap of his satchel, he drew the bag from behind him to his side. He knew he must act fast for if this was the demon in Keira's form, then all could already be lost. His hand searched throughout the bag but did not come across what he sought.

Panicking, he looked up and saw her gathering herself. Surprise it seemed had taken the wind out of her, but that would not be for long.

"What the hell?" she spat at him.

383

At last, his hand fell upon the crucifix and he heaved it from the bag and produced it before him. Quickly he crossed himself with the other as he spoke, "Be gone spawn of Satan, by the word of our Father and his Son Jesus Christ, be gone…"

"You fool…" She leapt at him without warning, and it was only in the last second that he saw it, for her hand whirled from her right side brandishing what looked like a short iron bar. Instinct made him move but it was too little too late. She slammed into him causing him to lose his feet beneath him and at once the bar struck at the side of his temple. He had barely felt the beginning of pain before they crashed onto the floor, his breath exploding from him as her weight landed squarely on top of him.

The bar with which she struck him bounced away as they landed, for he heard it ring on the concrete and though other tangible thoughts were lost to him, he recognised the same sound that had disturbed him from behind the diesel tank as Keira had selected her weapon.

Stars danced in front of his eyes, and the room seemed at once darker. He felt a shift of weight as Keira rolled off him and began to scramble for her makeshift cudgel. He groaned and tried to turn himself over so as to scramble away, his danger very real to him despite the injury to his head.

He made all fours, but it was not enough for already she was back, her first blow, misjudged perhaps caught him square between the shoulder blades and he heard her grunt her frustration. The pain though was immense and his arms and legs went out from underneath him. That though was his saviour, at least in that moment for a second swipe met thin air where only his head had been a fraction of a second before.

Fitzgerald twisted, knowing at once what was coming. His focus was blurred, but he made his back as the iron bar whistled down through the air to meet his face. His arms flew up to protect himself and he sought to catch her arms in the arc of their descent.

Pain exploded, and he screamed as iron shattered bone in his left wrist, but he had not time to give in to pain. He knew then that to allow his body to take over would be fatal. To freeze was to die, flight was impossible and so fight was his only recourse, no matter the agony he felt.

She stepped forward between his legs and raised the bar once more above her head. "Oh Iain, why couldn't you have left well enough alone?"

Where he lay, he would be helpless to avoid another blow and the crowbar she held was so far out of his reach. He could deflect more strikes, but at what cost? She could wear him down, break his bones until the moment came where she broke his defence and met his skull, giving her free reign to shower him with blows until his blood carpeted the floor.

He had one chance, if it failed it was all over for him. At the moment Keira held her hands high at the top of their arc, he clamped his legs together around hers as hard as he could, pinning them together. She let out a small cry of surprise and pinwheeled to maintain her balance. He could not allow for that to succeed and so with all the power he could muster, he twisted as hard as he was able. He felt her fight to wrestle her legs free and she need only pull one clear and he was done for.

Instead, she fell as he had hoped, the bar she held clattered to the ground once more as she reached out to brace her fall with her free hands. It was not yet done though; he had to move quicker than her. Clawing at her shirt he heaved himself on top of her, a hand raked out and he felt the sharp claw of her fingernails upon his cheek. It was in vain though for now, he planted a knee on her stomach to pin her and as the hand came back a second time he caught it and allowed himself to fall on top of her. This time it was her turn to cry out as all fourteen stones of him landed squarely across her.

Immediately she squirmed, her other hand came round and punched him square on the jaw, but he barely felt it, his body was racing with adrenaline now, and though the pain would later be exquisite, for now, he fed off it. Her right arm came round again and he blocked it with his forearm. Pain reverberated through his broken wrist and he knew he had no chance to hold her on that side. Already he was close to losing her as she squirmed. If she should best him, he was done for and he was not ready to meet her level of violence on the same level.

Looking down at her now, he saw the hatred with which she held him. Her frustration also was evident and she was not ready to quit on him just yet. Despite the rush he had felt, his body was battered and bruised and she would soon have the upper hand once more, he could not pin her here for much longer. He had to take the fight out of her.

Shifting his weight, he edged forward, his right knee fell upon her, pinning the left arm. He might do the same with the opposite side but knew that her bottom half would be unrestricted and she could topple him easily if she thrashed her legs and torso enough. No, it would have to be enough as it was. Her left arm was now pinned, but still, her right was free and that was on his weakened broken side. He had little other choice.

"I'm sorry, Keira."

He had a fraction of a second to see her face go from surprise to alarm as he curled his right arm and slammed his elbow squarely onto her nose.

He had no doubt that it broke in an instant, underneath her scream the sound of cracking cartilage and bone was supplemented by an eruption of blood that sprayed over her face.

She was out for the count, at least for now. Fitzgerald rolled off her, being careful of his broken hand. Using the generator as leverage, he pulled himself upward; his vision swimming and head throbbing all the while and threatening to overcome him. In the short aftermath of the fight, he was already so very tired and it was all he could do not to lay himself back down beside her.

He looked down at her, the woman with whom he had made love only recently. It was her he knew at once, the demon might wear masks, but the subtleties of her look and mannerisms would undoubtedly belong to her alone.

What the fuck Keira? Why?

Why indeed? She had not hesitated on seeing him; she had attacked without provocation after demanding to know why he had come. Surely she should have been glad to have seen him? But deep down, he knew there was something darker at work. At first, he had believed her to be the demon that roamed above, but there had been truths to discover in the words she had spoken.

'I can feel it, Iain, it is free at last.'

There had been a look in her eyes as she had spoken, a look of joy that begged further understanding. He looked over at her now as she continued to groan and hold her face. She was not unconscious, and as yet, he might not have taken all of the fight from her.

Searching for the crowbar, he shuffled past her until it came into his view and then became his. Moving back now to the generator he put his back to it and felt vibrations along his spine as he leaned and rested himself upon it, if she came at him, he would not go to the floor once again.

"Keira?" He asked.

There was no response.

Twisting the crowbar in his hand, he had an idea and turned himself to his left to find the control panel of the large machine. With his back to her though he felt like a target and so moved to the far side of it, his back once more to the generator. From this vantage point, he could see both Keira on the floor and the panel beside him. Quickly and deftly, he raised the crowbar to the corner of the panel and was not surprised to see that the bevelled end fitted perfectly into the damaged corner of the control hatch. She had been trying to work it open, but why?

From across the floor, she spoke. "Iain." It was a whisper.

"Don't move Keira. So help me, I didn't want to hurt you but I will again if I must. Why did you do it?"

She was silent for a moment longer, before then; "Iain please, I thought...I thought you were that terrible creature come to kill me."

He paused as he deliberated on all that had occurred. What she said now was at odds with what he had already heard, and again the words she had spoken echoed through his mind.

'I can feel it Iain, it is free at last'.

But there was more than that wasn't there? So much more. This young and beautiful nurse had made a beeline for him from the moment he had set foot in the house. A picture came at once to mind, the moment he had first set eyes upon her, there in the lobby.

When understanding came, it was as if a bulb had been lit inside of his mind, casting light on the shadows that had been vague in shape and context. But the vision of her stood there, looking and smiling at him had held no meaning at the time, her light, flirtatious manner, but now the vision meant so much more, and so the light that gave meaning to that one instance now showed so much more.

"I should have known you were too good to be true Keira. You spoke of loneliness only to expose my own, didn't you? You played me."

The groans had stopped, and he saw that she looked at him now over hands cupped to nurse her bloody nose.

"You lied to me, Keira."

At last, it was all coming together. At first, he had believed that it had only been McArthur who had manipulated him and that Keira, for whatever reason had been on side with him.

But the terrible truth had been much, much worse. The relevance of her being here and her savage attack spoke volumes as to her purpose and true allegiance; giving away the identity of the real puppet master, the demon she had gone to unspeakable lengths to set free.

He had believed her to be a fragile and frightened young woman, but that was not the case. Instead, she had been the tool of the Devil all along. Both her goals and McArthur's had been parallel up to a point and so it had been easy to believe that she was under his spell, but here and now, the divide in what she had meant to achieve all along had become apparent and her ultimate aim had instead proven to be a gulf apart from McArthur's.

"What did it promise you, Keira?"

Her eyes became narrow as she measured him from across the floor.

"I see it now — all of it. At first, I thought it was McArthur who had bought you. You were just too good to be true and I, no doubt, was an easy and willing target. It wouldn't surprise me to know that he did indeed give you such instruction, but it wasn't for him though, was it?"

Silence. She was still measuring him, weighing him up to see how much he knew. When she saw he knew all of it, he would have to be very careful of her.

"You spoke of solitude and loneliness," he continued, "perhaps there was some truth in that. And then perhaps it called to you somehow? Drew you close and promised you…what?"

"You think you know it all?" she replied, at last, her voice muffled from behind her hands. "It seeks only to be free of the prison that was created for it. The natural balance is broken you fool! It is the giver and saviour of life. It brings peace and prosperity. When your last prayer is spent and the one that you would call good refuses to answer, it comes. When all else fails, it brings hope to the hopeless!"

"But at what cost Keira? Don't you know the price you will pay? Do you not know the price of its bargains?"

Slowly she began to lift herself, freeing one hand to prop herself onto her knee. Blood fell freely from her nose and onto the floor. Without thinking, Fitzgerald adjusted the bar in his hands, his muscles tense and ready to respond should she attack again.

"Not for me. You do not know what it is like Iain. It is more than long and lonesome nights as you put it. I have seen with my own eyes, been there many times over, as the old and infirm pass from life to death. And it is not with joy and rapture that they are delivered to the heaven you so righteously believe in, no. They go into the dark alone and afraid, and I will not follow Iain, I will not walk that path!"

"Keira? Tell me, what has it promised you?!"

"Life everlasting Iain, and for no other price than to free it from its prison."

He was overcome at once by pity. "Oh Keira, the price you will pay is heavier than you can believe. What of faith? Yes, you have seen the darkness; you have also seen the impossible. But by virtue of that, can you not see that there is another side? Your demon is all too real we both know, and so if that can be, can there not be a heaven and a God?"

For a second, doubt crossed her face. She was standing now and unsteady on her feet. She stumbled backwards and collided with the workbench which she held onto to give her support. Fitzgerald was aware of the discarded tools at her feet. It had in all probability been Keira who had ransacked these tools in search for the crowbar he now held. He measured the distance between them and knew if she went for one of them at her feet, he could probably get to her before she was ready to attack again. But for now, she showed no signs of aggression or awareness of the tools at her feet; her attention instead fixed upon her broken face.

"Faith Iain? Is that all there is for you? A life spent in servitude to a God that will never answer your prayers? Can't you see that you can have so much more?"

"At what cost? Life everlasting, you say? Satan is the deceiver Keira, can it make good on what it has promised you? And even if it could, what then? You spoke of loneliness, how will you watch all you have ever loved and known crumble around you as the long years of your life tick slowly onward and to know that the gates of paradise are forever locked to you? It is not too late Keira, help me. Help me to defeat it."

From somewhere nearby came a noise, a low growl of rage. The sound was different now; it was as if an echo that reverberated down the long underground corridor that led to the bunker where they now stood. It was close by. Perhaps as near as the kitchen or worse, perhaps the pantry and only seconds away from finding the trapdoor down to the long tunnel.

"Perhaps it is you who should reconsider Iain. It comes now, and it will not look favourably upon what you seek to do."

Fitzgerald searched about him frantically; he had wasted too much time with her already…It came to him then that she had been stalling all along, waiting for the beast to come close, if she were to scream or shout now it would hear them, know where they were.

"Keira…"

It was too late, her mouth arched wide and a shrill cry filled the bunker. Fitzgerald was on his toes. The look of triumph that had filled her face was gone in an instant and replaced by shock as she saw him raise the bar over his head as she had done only moments before. He didn't know what he meant to do, but he must quiet her somehow. She pushed against the workbench and came to meet him.

This time, neither fell. She caught his arm perfectly on its downward arc with both hands, and he saw in a split second that it had been her head he had aimed for. Whatever gifts the demon had promised her had likely not yet been invoked, for her broken nose was evidence of such. He did not know if he could kill her with the blow (nor did he think that was his true intention) but perhaps he could render her unconscious and out for the count.

Such thoughts were now redundant as he was quickly losing the battle. His right hand that bore the iron crowbar was being forced downward, and she had begun to twist his wrist so as to get him to drop it. His other hand was useless at his side as it burned as if on fire.

As this happened, his stomach sank for he heard a noise that held too much meaning. The metal trapdoor within the pantry had been flung open and the sound of it striking the wall now carried down to his ear.

"Keira please…"

But she was lost to him. The fire in her eyes still shone with hatred toward him, and he knew that there were no pleas that he could invoke that would reach her and he wondered for how long she had resisted the creature's tentative whispers to bring her to the library and to do its bidding. It had poisoned her mind and that was all too evident to see. If he should come out of this what possible hope could there be for her now?

A roar, closer now and Keira began to laugh maniacally in his face. His grip on the bar was fading and she would have it wrestled from him in mere moments.

In one last desperate act, he had no choice but to use his other hand. The pain was immeasurable as he grabbed onto his other wrist and jerked the bar as hard as he could. The shift in balance caused them both to take a step together and in a different time and a different place they might have looked like lovers dancing.

He anticipated her next move before she made it. She had nearly lost the bar to him as his move had been unexpected, and in reaction, she pulled back with all her might. She had the leverage, the strength and the balance to do so. She would win.

He let go of the bar just as she began to heave. Such was the effort she pulled with she lost her balance. He had counted upon it and came after her at once. He hit her in the midriff with all the power he could muster in the small few steps between them. If she gained her feet, he was lost for she would have free reign to beat down on the exposed target that was his head. She hadn't though, and with a cry, they tumbled down again, only this time she was on the bottom and had not the time or instinct to cushion her fall.

Her head met the concrete in a sickening crunch. Her arms fell limp by her sides, and the crowbar was free once more.

He lay upon her like a lover, his head cradled in her neck. He had heard the sound and now saw blood pool in front of his eyes. Already there was so much of it.

"Keira?" Pinning his good arm beneath him, he raised himself to look into her open vacant eyes. She was gone; he had no doubt. The force of his attack had fractured her skull upon the hard floor beneath.

"Oh my god, Keira!" He reached out and held her face; it fell to the side.

All at once, a cry went up, one of such force and savagery he felt his blood run cold. He knew that somehow the beast had felt what had occurred and was now roaring with rage. It was close now, too close and the sense that he had, told him that it had now made the long corridor.

He pushed himself up and looked about. What should he do? The pressure of the moment was immense, and he froze. He had no answer. Lydia's spirit had guided him here and yet all he had found was betrayal and death.

CLACK, CLACK, CLACK.

The sound from the corridor was ominous, and he envisioned claws falling upon the cold concrete as might a dogs on a hard wooden floor. Panic overwhelmed him and he spun for the only exit that he had seen, the small door by the corner of the room.

Thankfully there was no lock, and quickly he pulled the door open. Whatever was beyond was in darkness and his heart lurched in despair. But no, there was something there, a glimpse of something that gave him hope in the second it took for the door to fall shut behind him and plunge him into blackness once more.

CHAPTER 52

In the scant seconds afforded him, he had seen that which Lydia had unquestionably sent him here for all along. But the vision was quickly extinguished as the light at his back disappeared; the door falling silently shut behind him.

From this all to brief look inside he knew the room was both small and enclosed, perhaps only standing room for four people toe to toe, it would offer no hiding place or escape. Maybe he had known that would be the case all along, from the moment he took the stairway into the basement, that there was to be no way back.

Such thoughts were cast away as the sound of the outer door, at last, crashed in. There was no more time. The demon had arrived.

Fitzgerald reached up and outward until his hands came into contact with the large metallic box that had been set high up on the wall. A fuse box.

His hands roved over a series of switches, all of which were pushed up. Though he had not the time to see, he knew that all would be turned to the off position. Had the storm caused all of them to break or had Keira turned them all this way? He could not know for sure. Her whereabouts at the moment of the lightning storm were unknown, but could it be conceivable that the storm should hit at just the right moment to turn the house to darkness?

CLACK, CLACK. All too close by.

Fitzgerald raised both his hands and ignoring the pain in his wrist took as many switches in his fingers as possible and pulled them all down. Just as quickly, they snapped back into place. Quickly, his hands danced along the row and continued to pull them all down. All followed suit and snapped back into the upright position automatically.

CLACK, CLACK, CLICK, CLICK. The sound had changed and now seemed more like the tap of a shoe upon the floor outside which soon came to a stop, perhaps only yards away. It would see Keira, and Fitzgerald cursed himself for not removing her. Her body being all the evidence the creature needed to know that it was not alone within the bunker. It would all be over soon, for it would know there were few places to hide.

"Oh, dear Keira." The voice carried easily through the door to Fitzgerald's ears. "This was not to be your reward, but perhaps it is fitting after all for you have not done all that was asked of you. You should be delivered unto hell for your betrayal, isn't that right priest?"

Fitzgerald's blood ran cold, and he quickly clamped his lips closed to prevent a whimper from escaping. His hands were still raised upon the switches in a last-ditch attempt he toggled them down once more. Again, nothing happened. What had she done here? Scrambling in darkness, he felt as far along the metallic casing of the fuse box as best he could; there was nothing, no hope, only…

His damaged hand felt upon something, a slight indentation within the box and within that indentation several holes.

"What have you done priest? You have been clever; poor Keira here did not anticipate such from you and to my detriment neither did I. You sought confession didn't you? Before you performed your rite? It seems I have grown stupid in my long imprisonment. I sought to kill you outright when you freed me, but that wouldn't be playing by the rules would it? For you were without sin. But now? Ha, ha, ha!"

Its laugh was wicked and cut through him like nails on a chalkboard. It was toying with him he knew, building his fear. It was working though and Fitzgerald knew that it was right for he had committed the one true cardinal sin, murder.

No, no, it was self-defence!

He was only lying to himself, though; he had attacked her. Thrown her to the floor. He had not anticipated she would hit her head, but what would he have done had she not received the blow? At that point, it had been her life or his.

His hands continued to rove, and understanding came to him.

The fuses! The fuses are gone!

It was true, he knew at once. Someone *(Keira)* had removed them, and as a result the purring generator outside was made redundant. But where could the fuses be? If they remained on her person, then it was still all for nothing for he would be discovered in moments.

From outside, he heard the sound of mesh rattling. The creature's first instinct had been to go to the diesel tanks where Keira had hidden herself before attacking him. It was the logical choice and only afforded him a few seconds more.

"Come out, come out wherever you are." The thing teased.

Fitzgerald stood on tiptoe and began to feel along the top of the fuse box. Nothing…no wait, his finger brushed by something, pushing it further back.

"Why don't you come out now, Iain? Let's have this out like men." The voice was now changed, that of Colin Morris.

With every muscle stretched to its limit, Fitzgerald reached as far as he could. The very tip of his finger finding the hard object. It was still out of reach, and if he wasn't careful, he would push it further away. As it was, he did not know what it was, but his only hope was that it was a discarded fuse. Even if it was, it was likely discarded as it was burnt out. There had been nothing else in the small room he knew, it served only to house the fuse box and as far as his slight vision had given him, held no other tools or spare parts. Whatever Keira had done with the fuses they weren't here.

Sweat poured from his brow as he toyed the object and felt it continue to move fraction by fraction further away. "Please," he whispered under his breath.

As he did so, the satchel that still hung around his neck and rested at the small of his back fell round and hit him softly in the stomach. *You fool!* His mind cried, but more in relief for he had forgotten its existence. Quickly he lowered himself onto the balls of his feet once more and pulled the strap from his head and took the bag in his left hand.

The doppelganger of Deacon Colin Morris grew louder. "So this is the contraption that would seek to bind me still? How behind the times I have become."

Fitzgerald then heard the sound of metal being wrenched aside. There could be no doubt of the sound; the creature was at work on the panel covering the generator controls. Once it had access, it would all be over, for darkness would enfold everything, the basement, the house, the grounds and so touch the night sky where the demon would, at last, have freedom and dominion over all.

Time was of the essence now and reaching up he dragged his satchel across the top of the fuse box, dragging the item along to the end where he reached up with his right hand and swept it neatly into his palm. He turned it quickly and knew it for what it was for two prongs dug into his flesh. It was a fuse for certain, but what hope was there that it was not broken?

His hands trembled as he turned the box in his hands and brought it up to the panel. He had estimated that there were perhaps eight sockets in all. Each one would cover a different area of the house he knew, and he had to trust to luck and the providence of God for his scheme to have any hope. Raising the fuse, he pawed it over the surface, unable to see the prongs home.

"Come on." He muttered.

A loud clang rang through from only feet away. The creature had access to the machine; he could only hope it was perplexed by its inner workings. At last, the fuse fell home and he traced his hand back along the row of switches. It was the moment of truth. He depressed every one as quickly as he was able, click, click the first two switches jumped back into the off position.

"Please, Lord."

His hands flew along the row, and something finally went right. The third set of switches held in place but nothing else had changed. He envisaged light coming back to another part of the house but what was evident was that there had been no change here in the basement.

In part the plan may have worked, for depending where in the house was lit, it would now restrict the creature's access at least to that part.

He dismissed this idea quickly, though. It still only had to walk through the door, find him, dispense with him and rip the fuse from the wall. No, it had to be here, here in the basement.

He ripped the fuse from its socket and went to plant it in the next hole as the switch that had held flipped back to its off position.

The demon spoke, and he froze in place for he was discovered. His actions seemingly alerting the beast.

"What are you doing there, priest? What manner of trick would you pull now?" With a growl, he sensed it coming for the door. The feeling was reinforced instantly for the thing's foot met with the discarded panel door of the generator which rang hollowly against the floor outside.

For a split second, the fuse in his hand danced as his fingers trembled. He gasped as the fuse slipped from his grasp. In the dark room, all was lost to him and yet he closed his fingers and found it still within his grasp. Now, his second guess had to be correct or all was lost.

The door behind him burst open and, a dark shadow loomed large over him and the box before him. By what little light he now had he slammed the fuse home in the very last socket. It had not been a choice, only the reaction of wracked and twisted nerves.

Reaching up, he pulled at the switches once more. From somewhere far off, there was pain, excruciating pain as something ripped down his back. His fingers latched onto the last switch as he fell and with his descent to the floor, it fell under his weight.

Fitzgerald fell hard and knew that all was lost. The beast stood at the threshold of the door, and the low light of the generator permeated still, only affording a slight view beyond the hulking figure that now stood before him.

"You!" It bellowed, spittle falling from its mouth to fall upon Fitzgerald's face. The cold had at once returned with its presence, but he could only feel the fire in his back.

Before him, it wore now another face. More terrible than any he had seen in his dreams. But as before it was as if two visions held the same place, one human, one monstrous. For though he saw the features of his friend Colin Morris, it was the face it wore beneath that terrified him so.

It came forward, and Fitzgerald saw impossible claws beyond where its fingers ended. He closed his eyes.

CLACK.

This was not the sound of the beast's foot on the floor. Fitzgerald looked up and saw puzzlement on the face of the creature.

CLACK.

At once, the low light of the generator outside fell, and all was black. It was done and it had all been for nothing. The darkness that the beast craved had been returned to Thoby Hall and in the next moment the creature would unleash its savage attack upon him, it would…

In the next instant, he saw the beast before him framed in white. Quickly and suddenly a series of flashes came from its back as the strip lights beyond fired into life.

In a split second, it turned to him, fury worn upon its face.

Gone was any semblance of Colin Morris, it wore now its own true face, twisted and terrible and yet familiar as its jaws opened wide to reveal his doom as McArthur had undoubtedly met his.

It came forward, allowing the door behind it to close and dispel the white which now enveloped the generator bunker. Raising its talons (for that is what he now saw them to be) it lashed out at him.

CHAPTER 53

What can happen in only the blink of an eye? Or more specifically, your last blink of an eye? Iain Fitzgerald had time for this one strange coherent thought and that only. Then came the light and he was filled with awe, for in his last moment the faith he had held onto had been vindicated, and here now was surely the pathway to heaven.

He reached upward that he might touch the light with his fingertips, but as he did so his stomach lurched as the floor disappeared out from under him. He fell.

The descent was over in a fraction of a second, as his body hit something soft beneath him. Sound and light came back as if he had broken the surface of a deep lake.

He lay there for a second, his eyes seeing only a bright white ceiling above, while his hands twisted in the soft fibre of a duvet that stretched beneath him.

"What the hell?"

Suddenly something fell beside him, causing his heart to lurch.

Slowly, he turned his head to the left and what he saw caused his breath to stop and tears come instantly to his eyes.

"Emma?"

"Of course you big idiot, who else?"

Fitzgerald scrambled away and to the side of what he saw was a sofa bed, all the while his eyes stretched wide in shock as his back hit the wall only a metre or so behind him.

A look of concern crossed his girlfriend's face. "Baby, what's wrong?"

It can't be.

His eyes roamed the confined space that was his room.

"It can't be." This time he gave voice to his incredulity. But it was. In the second or so it had taken to survey the room, he knew it was his. Here was the bedroom on the first floor of a multi-occupancy house in Colchester, he had lived in over 15 years previously, and here also was …"Emma?"

She cocked her head to look at him. She was now up on her knees upon the sofa bed, a look of concern etched upon her face.

"Iain, please, what's wrong?" She said as she came off the bed to stand before him. Tears fell down his cheeks as he took his hands and cupped her lightly beneath the jaw.

"Iain?..." She was cut off as he embraced her and buried her head into his chest. His heart seemed fit to burst, as he quickly pulled back to look at her face once again.

"My god Emma, it's you, it's really you."

She pushed back from him, arms extended into his chest. Her smile was crooked as she beheld him. "What's going on with you baby? You're acting all weird."

Her smile was just as he remembered it, and he reached out to stroke the corner of her mouth. "Nothing, nothing's wrong...for a minute there, I thought..."

What had he thought? His mind was suddenly blank and he shook his head as he tried in vain to reason what had caused him to act in such an odd way. After all nothing was wrong was it? He was in the company of the most beautiful girl he had ever known and seeing her now, his heart seemed almost fit to burst for his love for her.

He stepped forward, her outstretched arms caved willingly as he kissed her.

All other thought was lost to him, all but the single thought that this moment was perfect. Emma pulled away, and placed her back leg upon the bed, drawing him down toward her and back onto the bed. A sense of déjà vu washed over him as he allowed himself to be drawn down by her. He looked about himself and took in the room about him, the long velvet drape was pulled tight across the window as it always was, shutting out the day, the remains of a Chinese takeaway was evident by the discarded containers on the floor, and there on the TV, the movie 'The Bounty' was in full flow. Nothing out of the ordinary...except the feeling he had seen or experienced this all before.

"You had me worried there for a minute," Emma said, interrupting his thought process, "perhaps you need something to help you relax."

No.

The thought came from far away, and he dismissed it, allowing Emma to push him back down on the sofa bed. She was again on her knees as she pulled his left arm out and across her thighs, and he was able to see the track marks in the crook of his arm.

"This will melt your cares away."

He closed his eyes, as she applied the tourniquet to his bicep.

This isn't right. The quiet voice intruded again. He willed the voice away and it went without question, but what remained was the question of its meaning. He knew the thought did not relate to the drug taking, he and Emma had long since abandoned any guilt in what they did.

Both of them had long since discussed their reliance on the drug and he knew that for her, it was to carry her far away from the pain of her childhood and the sexual abuse her father had subjected her to. For him, it was an escape from a world that moved too fast for him to cope. His self-esteem and confidence, virtually non-existent.

The two of them were co-dependent in loneliness and depression. They had often spoken of the fact that they could not survive on their own, and that suicide had been a very real get out for each of them. Until that was they found one another, and when that wasn't enough, the heroin melted the rest away.

Iain felt the sharp pain of the needle and opened his eyes to see Emma looking intently down on him. "Happy trails partner," she said as a wide smile broke on her face. He smiled back, he was exactly where he wanted to be…everything was perfect.

Already he could feel the soft tug toward the place between consciousness and sleep and it washed over causing this feeling of blissful oblivion. His head lolled to the side, and his eye lids dropped heavily.

From afar, he heard the voices from the TV set.

"William, about your decision to go around the Horn."

"William? Not Sir, not Captain; William?"

"I don't think the men will have it."

The words were familiar and intensified the feeling of déjà vu that had previously come over him.

"Oh, the men won't have it. Are they in charge of the Bounty?" He murmured softly in time with Captain Bligh.

He saw a small frown form on Emma's face as she turned to look at the TV. She turned back and looked quizzically at him. "You said you hadn't seen this one before?"

"I haven't," he whispered in return. Even so he knew Fletcher Christian's response before it came.

"They might be if you insist."

The soft voice in his head came again. *This is all wrong.* He shut his eyes and willed himself to fall into the comforting blanket of his bliss.

"Wake up, Iain." Emma's voice was strong and found him almost at the bottom of his descent into the peace of nothingness. He slowed himself as he waited on her next words to fall down to him.

"I'm so sorry Iain; you must come back up. This isn't right, this isn't how it happened."

Captain Bligh's voice echoed down behind hers as if from very far away. *"Again, would you repeat that please. The men might be in charge. What are you threatening me with?"*

"Will you be quiet." He moaned. It was meant for Bligh and not for Emma, because if he continued the two of them were going to get into a fight, they would…

"It didn't happen here Iain; the argument…we moved in together on the corner of Partridge Road, please remember."

That was right. William Bligh and Fletcher Christian would cause them to fight and when that happened they had very nearly split up. It was crazy, such a stupid thing to argue about, but they had both been so stubborn. Only…

The realisation came down on him like a crushing weight.

"Oh Emma, no."

He opened his eyes and looked upon her. She was right; this was not how it happened. These memories were mixed up; here in his Colchester room they had indeed shared happy memories. But the drug use and the damned film were later, much later and at a different address. But why were these visions of old events playing out as they were?

Her eyes were sad, as she took his hand and pulled him gently upward and into the warm embrace of her chest, where she held his head close to her and gently caressed his hair.

"You need to go back Iain, it is not yet over. The creature would use me against you. No, your loneliness. But it doesn't understand us. It uses what little it knows and weaved a dreamscape to entice you. Bringing me back to you, the pull of the heroin into a safe and deep place where pain can't touch you. It is all a lie. It's last illusion to subvert you from your path."

And though he now knew it, he wished only to succumb and remain in this place with her forever.

"Emma, please no. Let me stay here with you. I can't lose you again."

And with that, she turned his face slowly upward so that his eyes met hers. Her smile was soft as she spoke. "We will have our time again Iain."

Cradling him as she might an infant, she lay him back down onto the bed. He felt tired and his eyelids dropped heavily. He forced them open once again but already she was but a blur through tear-soaked eyes, he lay down but it was not the soft warmth of the duvet that he now felt, instead the surface was hard.

The vision he had been afforded was gone and the veil that the demon had drawn over his eyes was lifted. Instead, replaced by black spots which began to dance in front of his eyes.

The sensation was a strange one, and in addition, he all too quickly was aware of the pain in both his back and wrist, his head now only down to a dull ache.

He blinked his eyes hard against the piercing light and found that he had been looking directly into the strip light that hung overhead. Confusion washed over him, but his place could not be denied. He was slumped in the corner of the room that served as the power hub for Thoby Hall.

"Emma?"

There was no response. She had gone as if she had never existed, so to the creature that had risen before him. It had worked.

In the last instant before returning the light to the small room, the beast had sought to attack him, but when that had failed, it had taken him away to a place of seduction. A place where he was meant to have stayed with his beloved Emma and in doing so, perhaps succumb to the terrible wound the creature had inflicted, or instead to remain there forever while his body slept in a long coma. The seduction had failed though, and it had been she who had sent him back, breaking the spell that he was easily losing himself to.

"Why Emma? I don't understand." He spoke to the empty room.

Again there was no answer. Slowly a tear broke from his eye and ran down his cheek. The sense of loss was at once overwhelming and he clasped his head in his hands as a series of low sobs overcame him. It had been all he wanted; to submit and remain with her, so why had he come out of it? If it had been a ruse by the demon, then how could it have failed, why had she brought him back?

There was to be no answer, all there was here in this world was pain, but he could deny it no more.

Grimacing, he drew himself upward slowly, tentatively feeling the fire in his back and seeing his hand come back wet with blood. A look at the ground where he lay gave clue to the fact that the wound was deep, such was the pool that had formed where he had fallen.

Finding his feet, he looked upward at the fuse box and the one small device that had saved his life. It was remarkable to see that it had been placed in the far most socket, over which he read a handwritten note; BASEMENT.

The other empty slots likewise had such notes, and he found the first of which simply read WEST WING LOWER. In turn, the next two read WEST UPPER and HOUSE. Had it been blind luck in the darkness that had saved him, or divine providence?

Given all that had happened, he was very much leaning toward the latter of the two, that in his darkest hour a guiding hand had steered his own, thus saving his life and dispelling the creature at once from his presence.

But dispelled where? That was the question at hand. The fuse box in front of him and the humming generator outside very much gave him the answer to that, and that answer would be anywhere else in the house but where he was now.

What he needed to do, was to find the remaining fuses if he was able and see about restoring light to the whole household, only then would the beast be returned from where it came, the library.

It was immediately clear that the room he was in offered no answers as to the location of the missing fuses and so he began to step out into the bunker proper. He took hold of the door and began to push through, as he did so, he did a double-take.

There to the left of the door was a simple light switch. A minor and obvious detail of any room hidden away from natural light, but that was not the issue, and the thing that caused him to stop, for it had been on hadn't it?

Yes, the moment he had toggled the switch upon the fuse box, light had blessedly filled the basement level and also this little room where he had fulfilled his task.

What was certain is that he had not known of the light switch's existence when he entered the room through sheer panic. And knowing that, he had not pressed it on, meant that somebody else had done so.

Could it be? And in his mind's eye, he could see Keira stepping into the small room and through nothing more than habit depressing the switch even though it was her goal to remove all light from the house. Was it as simple as that? Had she inadvertently saved his life?

Keira. His heart sank for what now lay through the door, and not as much for her death as for where her soul may now suffer.

She was gone.

Fitzgerald froze in his tracks. How could it be?

The evidence of what had occurred here only moments before was still evident, the broken and bent panel from the generator control panel littered upon the floor, the crowbar over which the two had fought and with which she had surely broken his wrist, and there, there was the pool of blood from where her head had met the ground.

He had believed her dead, but the evidence of his eyes gave him new insight for perhaps she had faked what he saw. No, surely not, but even so his eyes might have tricked him, and given the fear and adrenaline that had coursed through his body at the time it was easily possible that he had made an error.

But for now, where was she? If she was alive, then she was still unquestionably injured and perhaps losing blood as he did by the moment. Worse than that, for if she was free, she was free to wreak more havoc if she wished.

Her absence though, did not correlate with her mission. He looked over at the exposed control panel and though there were switches and dials, the one prevalent feature was the big red button which was the emergency stop.

He shuddered when he realised how close the demon had been to simply reaching out and ending it all. Could it have known it was so close? Instead, it had felt his presence and known the acts behind the small door conducted by him were equally vital, for understanding of what he was doing had driven it instead to seek him out and destroy him.

And so Fitzgerald could understand the reaction of the beast, but if Keira had woken while all this went on and seen the exposed panel? Had she relented at last? Or could it simply be that she had been concussed? If so, she was still in danger as well as being a potential danger for him. What was strange, however, was the absence of any blood anywhere but for where it pooled beneath where her broken head had lain.

Enough, get moving.

His first port of call was successful. The missing fuses were located inside of the mesh fence and beside the diesel tanks. However, Keira had taken them and destroyed them somehow, perhaps working as she hid from him, as he made his way down the long concrete corridor. He cursed himself for he knew that he had announced his impending arrival when he had dropped the metal hatchway from the pantry into the cellar.

Regaining the main room, he went on hands and knees as he burrowed through the cabinets and drawers that were situated beneath the workbench. He pulled aside paint cans, aerosols, oil containers and pots containing various screws, washers, nuts and bolts but still no replacement fuses.

The drawers above furnished no reward either as he found everything but that which he sought with the exception of a roll of electrical tape which he would soon have a use for.

Finally, his last hope was the roller tool cabinet from which Keira had found her weapon. A quick glance reinforced what he already knew; the bottom two drawers were useless as they contained only screwdrivers, sockets, hammers and such. At last, he came to the topmost drawer and there, at last, he found what he sought.

God bless you, Douglas.

There in a neat row were eight dual-forked fuses. Somehow he knew they would be there and his panic had not gotten the better of him. It was another small victory in the larger battle. Thus far he had been lucky, but now he had what he required it would come down to more than that. He would banish the demon back to its prison and then the real fight would begin, because as before it would not allow him to complete what he had started. There could be no surprises this time though and he felt he was ready for what was to come.

Each new fuse fitted like a glove, and quickly he depressed the remaining switches. All held in their on position.

Although he could not see it, he sensed the vitality of light coming back into the house once again and the creature simply disappearing as it had before him only minutes ago. That was only half of it, for though it was gone it had retreated to the only place where it could, the prison that Thomas Searle had steadily built for it over long years.

It was almost time. Fitzgerald stripped off his bloody shirt to discover he could see the final flourish of the demon's work stretched round from the small of his back to his left side.

The pain was intense, but it was the loss of blood that concerned him more. During his scavenging, he had discovered the electrical tape for which he had designs and also some loose rags and a bottle of turpentine which he knew he could use as both antiseptic and styptic agent to quell the blood loss. Dousing the rags, he applied them as far around his back as he was able. Through clenched teeth, he snarled as a whole new level of pain assaulted him. It would do the job he knew and padding several of the rags together he wound them to himself with the electrical tape in an effort to stop or at least slow his bleeding.

He was ready. He cast one last look at the generator room and made his way for the exit; the thought all the while intruding as to what should happen if Keira should return before he was done. He had no immediate answer for that and knew there was no other help he could call on at this late hour to assist him. All there was to do now was to return to the library and confront the demon one last time.

CHAPTER 54

Fitzgerald made his way back through the brilliantly lit house but felt little comfort in the stark light as he went. It was as sterile as it had ever been, and even though it was all clear as to why the house was bathed as it was in perpetual light, it felt cold and empty. Of course, there was power there also, for though man-made it had dispelled a creature of unspeakable evil. But what he yearned for was the dawn of the new day and the sunlight to touch his face once more.

There had always been a fear of the dark. It was a primal instinct and one that all shared in the small hours of the night. As he walked, he found himself thinking about his mother, who had not allowed him such creature comforts when he was small, such as a night-light or even to go so far as to leave his bedroom door ajar so that the hallway bulbs could send their monster dispelling power over his sleeping form.

As he walked, he shook his head to rid himself of such unwanted memories. There was pain there back from those days, where his younger self, no more than 7 or 8 years of age, would hide beneath his blankets and recite prayers to keep whatever lurked in the wardrobe or under his bed away. There had been power in prayer he thought from that early age, for though the fear lingered for years, the monsters never came.

Perversely, it had been his adult self who had actually discovered that such monsters had existed the whole time. The thought left him feeling empty inside. He had argued with Keira, the danger of her path and had offered her the counter-argument that should her demon exist then so to surely did God. The emptiness though was for the fact that he had not felt the presence of what was good and right throughout his entire time here.

It was true he had found Lydia, but she existed it seemed as a trapped soul. Surely again reason to believe in the higher power, but he doubted also that she had felt the touch of God in this unholy place. Of everything that he had encountered, perhaps that was the saddest of all, for though she maintained the form of a child, she had become older in spirit and mind and had been alone for almost all of her time here.

He wondered what might become of her, and if there were something he could do that would ease her away from this terrible place and into the eternal paradise that she deserved. That would have to come later; for now, his mission was clear.

He found himself at the bottom of the staircase of the east wing, it had been a wholly unconscious thing to do, for the quickest way would have been through the house and the dual stairway in the lobby. He could guess though the reason he had brought himself here, for it was to see the stairway that had previously come alive as evil had coursed through it.

When he saw it again, he knew what his eyes had previously seen was real, for though it was now lifeless, the forms of the serpents and snakes that had writhed and crawled over one another were now frozen in contortions of what appeared to be agony. It was as if it this had been the original carved design, but he knew better as he saw mouths locked in silent screams. The return of the light had seemingly been agony to them as well as the creature.

His eyes roved to the other side and saw that nothing had changed there. The cherubs sat as they always had and looked at him with blank eyes. The thought remained, the household had not been touched by the hand of God.

He stopped for nothing else as he climbed the stairway and made the first-floor, though he was tentative at every turn for fear that Keira lurked behind some obstacle or corner, ready to press home her attack once more. But the further he went, the more he feared he would find her at the library and if so he wondered if he had the strength or will to deal with each of the potential dangers that lurked there.

The pain in his back flared and reminded him at once the strength of the beast alone, its power and size had been tremendous framed there in the doorway before it had fallen upon him.

"What have you done priest?"

The creature's words to him echoed through his mind as he went. It had taunted him.

"You sought confession, didn't you?"

He had.

He did not know of all his earthly sin, but before returning to Thoby Hall, he had happened past the small Parish Church of St Joseph's in a small village called Tarnstead.

The matter of sleeping with Keira had prayed heavily upon his mind and to seek such confession before performing the exorcism was a vital part in performing the rite so that such sin could not be used against him. At that time, he had not known he would physically confront the beast and for what was now looming, but his protection it seemed had only bought him so much.

"I sought to kill you outright when you freed me, but that wouldn't be playing by the rules, would it? For you were without sin. But now?"

The thing had believed as did he that he had killed Keira and as such he was open game. It had physically attacked him and rendered him unconscious back in the library, but the suggestion was clear, it could not kill him if he were free from sin.

Where that left him, he could not guess, for he had no idea of Keira's whereabouts or her condition. Perhaps she lived yet, but the blow to her head was dangerous and could yet claim her. What was clear is that he could not know and so going up against the creature once more was going into the unknown.

Such thoughts ceased as he finally made the library door which was open wide before him.

Cautiously he moved forward and surveyed the wide expanse of the room. It appeared almost as it had been on his first arrival which now seemed so long ago, the difference being that the room was now only partially lit and glass crunched underfoot as he edged slowly inward. He could see the chandelier that once sat high in the centre of the room was now a broken mess upon the floor and many more of the strip lights had been smashed beyond repair. He had long since come to associate the clawing cold with the presence of the demon, and though all seemed calm before him, he shivered as he felt the temperature drop significantly on crossing the threshold of the room.

In the diminished light, long shadows fell this way and that and Fitzgerald consciously moved only where the light fell. Such segments were small though, and he could not pass further into the room without crossing into the divide where the demon was caught.

Reaching into his satchel, Fitzgerald produced a small wooden bowl and the canteen which contained holy water, blessed only hours ago. He would now finish the rite that he had begun and this time nothing would sway him from that end but his own death, for his life, was all that he had left to give and if that was the cost, then so be it.

Gingerly and mindful of his damaged wrist, he unscrewed the cap of his canteen and tipped half the contents into the bowl which he held with his left hand. He turned to face the threshold of the library, and though he again felt ill at ease with his back to the larger expanse, he continued by walking the few short steps back to where he had entered.

"In the name of the Father and of the Son and of the Holy Spirit." He recited as he dipped his fingers into the bowl and then flicked the holy water over the entranceway. When it was done, he crossed himself. "Amen."

"Father."

He turned slowly back to the room and beheld Lydia as he had last seen her. She was stood only several feet away, and at once, he saw that she was whole. She was dressed now in white, a simple dress that trailed to the floor and covered her feet. Her smile was broad and welcoming.

"It is over. The creature has been returned to the hell which spawned it."

All at once, he felt his being flow with the comfort she exuded.

He felt warm once again, and the sensation eased the pain of his injuries. It was as if he were a vessel filled slowly with wellbeing, and he gasped as the touch of it reached his broken wrist, and the pain became numb at once. It crept up upon him until it flooded his mind and on doing so, all became bright around him and Lydia shone in her white gown as if she were touched by the light of heaven itself.

"You have saved me also, Father, for now, my time here is over. For many years I did not know my purpose until that is I saw you and understood what must be done. We have won and we can both rest at last. You are injured I can see and must have fought bravely, but now it is time to rest. Listen to my words Father I can ease your pain."

Her words washed over him and soothed him by their very tone, and all he wished for was to close his eyes and bask in their comfort. There would be no pain in submitting he knew, no darkness and no nightmares. It reached for him, and he yearned to lose himself in its sweet embrace.

Without knowing it, his legs buckled beneath him and he fell to the floor.

"Wake up Iain, remember of what we spoke."

These words were an intrusion, their very being a sacrilege within this most special of places. They were spoken as if from far away and as if from the very limit of what he could hear.

They drifted away, and peace prevailed once more. It was time to let go and allow himself to heed to their will for the words promised peace. Peace from pain and more so from the workings of his exhausted mind.

"What did we speak of?"

Had he spoken? Or was this the voice of his subconscious rising up from somewhere deep inside of him? Already the words were fading, and no response came back. That was a good thing, why had he invited such a thing into this place of peaceful tranquillity?

...of what we spoke.

The thought was now a prevailing entity that prevented him from succumbing to the rest for which he ached. The question begged an answer.

If he could find it, then perhaps he could allow himself to fall and so succumb to the rest he so desperately yearned for.

He summoned the voice back, and this time it was stronger.

"Wake up Iain."

"Lydia?"

It came flooding back and all at once the warmth that had filled him evaporated, the pain returned to course through his being once more. He lamented the loss immediately, but what had been remembered could not be ignored.

It was not the voice in his head that answered; instead, the vision of the little girl before him.

"Yes, Father. But why do you bring yourself back? Back to this world of misery and pain? I will ease your passage if you will only let me."

Her words were real once more and seductive in what they offered. Every fibre of his tired being cried out to submit once again, but first, he needed this one answer.

"Your name…the name your father gave you when he made your bedtime stories?"

"Iain no, don't be foolish. You are hurt, let me…"

"Your name!" He demanded.

"I…"

It had been the last thing she had said to him before he left her to seek out the generator and return power to the house once more, a secret kept between father and daughter and held close to her heart even after death.

The room became darker once more as he fought against his desire to simply succumb to her words. Every step closer to the surface of reality was a steadily rising agony, and in his mind, he begged to hear the name she had whispered into his ear. If she did that he would allow himself to fall once more, to allow her words to wash over him like the tide on the shore and steadily tug at him until they carried him away to some better place.

There was only pain left in this world, and she now held the key for him to escape.

But his rise from tranquillity to agony continued for Lydia remained silent. Fitzgerald now gained all fours and looked on as he saw his hands were planted in long shadow. Quickly his eyes snapped up to where Lydia stood above him, only feet away. He watched as her eyes grew big as if with bewilderment or confusion.

When it happened, it was quick, the only warning being the narrowing of her eyes. She lurched forward and reached out for him, panic overwhelmed him, and he pushed himself back as far as he could. It was close. Her fingers landing in the space where his hands were planted only seconds before.

His momentum caused him to roll over so that he was on his back. A quick look affirmed that he was laid wholly within the light and a shuddering breath escaped him. He was now free of the creature's bewitchment entirely.

How was it that he had so nearly succumbed? What a fool he had been not to see what was now obvious.

Turning, he put himself on all fours again and pushed himself backwards and rocked back onto his knees, where he could behold her once again. Her demeanour was as it had been before and she appeared almost angelic to him, but deep down he knew this was the frightful creature that had plagued the house for ages, the same beast that had claimed Thomas Searle, Robert McArthur and poor Melissa. It only wore the visage of Lydia Bennett for it was its very last gambit. It did not yet know it had failed.

"Your name?" He asked once more.

"Poor Iain, please, you are delirious. Will you not allow me to ease your suffering?"

"And how would you seek to do that? Will, you not come to me and aid me as you suggest?"

A deep frown crossed the child's face and all at once; she ran at him, a snarl of hatred fixed upon her teeth. Fitzgerald put his hands up in protection but watched in astonishment as the form of the girl rebounded back as if struck by some invisible wall.

His mind was quick to make the distinction, and he looked down at the floor where the line of shadow was little more than two feet before him. It marked the line by which the creature was bound. At once he remembered the story told by Robert McArthur regarding his master Thomas Searle and how he had contrived to rig a spotlight around him and so keep the beast at bay.

At the time of hearing those words for the first time, he had treated them with incredulity. But now his eyes were finally open. For Thomas Searle, the light had been a prison, for Fitzgerald it now served as a barrier.

He stood now, his body screaming protest as he finally found his feet. Irrespective of the offer of peace the monster had promised, he knew well that he must act fast less he simply pass out from loss of blood. What would become of him and the demon should that happen?

"You have failed to answer me demon and so revealed your true self. She told me you were the deceiver and that you would come masked as a friend. But you did not reckon on her insight, did you? That she told me this one thing that she had shared with her father and that you could not know."

"It matters not priest." Her voice deeper, an edge of low hatred whispered beneath its breath. "You think this over? All you had was your innocence that protected you from me, but that is now gone. How can he who is tainted with sin as you are, expect the word of your God to bid me gone?"

Fitzgerald knew at once of what it spoke. He had the foresight to enter confession before tackling the demon, but since what happened with Keira could he still be a conduit to the power of God?

"You know, don't you?" it teased, "and what is to come next, priest? Hasn't the pitiful Robert McArthur promised this place to your Church?"

"What of it? If I am unsuccessful tonight, then they will finish what I have begun."

The form of Lydia Bennett turned away into the darkness until it came upon the upturned chair that once sat at the heart of the room. Picking it up, it drew it close to the line of shadow before taking its seat.

"Once I believed that to be true. Should this house be turned over, how long would it have been before my presence was felt and I be cast out? You though have delivered me halfway, for you have broken the shackles of my confinement and released me."

"The light binds you still."

"It does. That much is true, but with you gone, how long do you think it will be before this house sits in darkness once more? I have spent many ages plotting my escape and to see the pieces fall into order so perfectly is exhilarating!"

"This is your plan? From where I stand, I still see a prisoner."

"The best-laid plans of mice and men often go awry priest, but you have brought me to the brink tonight, but for the trick you played below stairs I would already be free, but as I say you no longer hold the power to expel me."

"You speak of Keira."

"Very good. She was an all too agreeable pawn and played her part to perfection. Beyond those doors, I had little to no influence, but once the Celtic whore had contrived to glean his story, she soon found her way to me. McArthur toiled in his plans and when you began to back down, she showed you the way back."

"You talk of her sleeping with me? Such sin, if it could even be described as such is already forgiven."

"I speak of murder priest."

Fitzgerald stopped to consider. The demon was surely stalling for why else would it hold him in conversation? But the fact had been, it had literally leapt upon the opportunity to reach him when he had crossed the threshold of shadow that currently bound it, but when it had failed by only the tips of its fingers it had reverted to converse with him.

Several things came to him at once, first of which was that most of what it spoke was true. He had partially released it, for his initial rite was only half completed; only going so far as to break the age-old bonds and wards that had been laid in the home by Thomas Searle.

That meant that only the light now held it and in that, the beast spoke truly as well, for with McArthur now dead it was surely only a matter of time before the house was closed down and inevitably to fall into darkness that would allow the creature's escape. But why tell him all of this? From somewhere deep inside of him, he knew. The real voice of Lydia Bennett had warned him that the beast was the deceiver and so undoubtedly was continuing to try and confuse and deceive him further, but the question was as to what end?

He cast his mind back to the horror of the basement and what had befallen poor Keira. He found that he held no anger toward her and instead it was with pity that he now thought of her, as she had been misled by this creature that had made her promises that it could not deliver. She had been seduced by the promise of everlasting life instead only to meet her end in that cold lonely room.

But has she?

He stopped suddenly and spun away from the glare of the creature that sat in darkness, lest it should read his thoughts or the look upon his face. It would have him believe that he had killed her, but what if that was not so?

Fitzgerald shook his head so as to dispel the fog from his mind, and at once, his thoughts became clear. The creature's words were poison, and it was obvious that it was more than just the deceiver for it was also the seducer, for he had been held by its words and had believed them. But the truth was he did not know that Keira was dead, and if that was so then the beast to was unaware.

Quickly he searched his mind and was easily able to recapture from what he had seen and heard in the moments the beast had entered the basement. It had seen Keira as he had, lain in a pool of her own blood, no doubt believing as he had that she had died.

But clearly, that had not been the case for when he had finally returned the lights to the area and returned to the room where she had lain; she had gone as if she had never been. Though that was not entirely true for the evidence of their struggle was still there to be seen on the concrete floor. The beast, though, did not know, did not know as he did that when he had returned, she had been gone. And if she was not, in fact, dead, then surely he was not burdened by sin as this foul creature suggested.

He spun back to face the beast once more.

"You would have me believe my efforts are futile? Let's find out shall we?"

A look of bewilderment crossed the features of the girl, and for but a fraction of a second, Fitzgerald sensed that he saw fear also.

"Of what do you speak priest? I warn you not to stand against me any longer. You know you are doomed to failure, and what is more, your sin is of the most heinous form. You enter now my dominion and lest you back down you know well what that means for you." And with those words, Fitzgerald watched on as the creature's face morphed once more.

It was supposed to invoke terror in him he knew. Intimidate him so as to give up and walk away. The thing before him had seen something in him, some new confidence that had scared it and bound as it was now only feet away, was resulting to whatever tricks it could to prevent him from acting further.

411

The transformation was hideous to behold, and he knew that this was its purpose. The skin on its face began to boil as if a fire was set inside the skull behind.

Slowly but surely the skin cracked, peeled and fell away but Fitzgerald refused to bow in the face of such horror, instead holding the eyes of the creature all along as the pupils within began to liquefy and stream down the burning cheeks and creating a thin hissing sound as steam rose slowly into the air above its head.

With slow deliberation, he reached into his satchel and produced a handful of medals. The medals of St Benedict.

On seeing them, the creature seethed in fury and at once ran at him. Fitzgerald did not know what to expect but held his ground. He blinked when the beast met the wall of light and saw as it rebounded back as if hit by something physical. He let out a deep breath of relief as he now saw the very real limits of the prison that held it in check.

He turned away from the demon, and though his body complained with intense pain, he knelt and lay the first medal at the threshold of the door. Bowing his head, he crossed himself once more as was decreed by the rite and repeated, "In the name of the Father, the Son and of the Holy Spirit. Amen."

With some effort, he heaved himself upward and turned to the creature once more, which was now still before him. Its face was black and charred, the dress it wore also blackened and burned as to was the body it wore beneath, a fetid stench of burned flesh assaulted his senses as he approached the border between the light and the dark.

Hollow eye sockets stared uncomprehendingly back at him, and he knew that it saw him well. Finally, it spoke once more; its voice charred and dry.

"Do this and die by my hand, priest."

Fitzgerald ignored it, took the next of his coins, crossed himself and repeated as he did with the first. When he was done, he lightly flicked the coin past the shoulder of the beast and heard as it met the hard wooden floor and rolled out of sight into shadow.

"You have not the power fool! I shall be released, and it will be I that finds you and drags you to the hell that awaits you!"

A third coin. The sign of the cross upon himself. "In the name of the Father, the Son and of the Holy Spirit. Amen."

Again he flipped the coin into the darkness on the other side of the demon. It now stood within the boundaries of the three.

"Dear Lord, please hear my prayer. I am but your humble servant and seek only to do your will. This house is beseeched by a foul and ancient evil, which has subverted the lives of your children. Will you not cast this beast back into the darkness where it truly belongs? And place upon it such unbreakable chains that it never intrudes upon your beautiful world again. Through Jesus Christ, our Lord, Amen."

On completing the verse, the creature attacked again in a frenzy. All was to no avail though, as it crashed back once more. With fury, it came again like a caged dog, bated and furious rebounding over and over.

"You are damned priest! Damned! Your words are for nought. You are an abomination to the Church for who you speak!"

Fitzgerald continued none the less. "Oh God, omnipotent and merciful, grant me your favour that I fulfil your holy charge. The earth that you have created is great and beautiful but is blighted with that which stands before me. I implore you to put an end to this perversion that masquerades as a child of your creation. Its eyes are not those of your making. Its false lips spill lies and perversions for which were not of your design. Here stands, not a child, but a monster. With your will and with the intercessions of St Benedict, I will dismiss this foul creature back to where it belongs. Through Jesus Christ, our Lord. Amen."

The passage came to an end, and suddenly there was a sound as if of something breaking or cracking. It had been close, and both Fitzgerald and the demon stopped as one to determine the origin and nature of the sound.

"What trickery do you employ?" it gasped, "your magic has no power here."

Fitzgerald was at a loss for he could not perceive whatever it was that the demon had deduced. Were his words having an effect? The last he had spoken in this room, little less than an hour or so ago had caused the books of the library floor to dance and fly and caused the window to explode. All part of a show he guessed, performed by the very creature that he sought to send back to the hell it belonged to. But was this some new trick? Some final gambit designed to subvert him somehow? He was close now, the rite was almost complete, but beyond the last verses, he had nothing to draw upon that would assist him further.

It was this or nothing, and thus far, there had been no discernible changes other than the beast's new attempts at trickery.

"These are the words of God, demon. You are compelled to obey."

"Compelled?" the creature spat back. "Your words are hollow for you are damned. You think me a fool? You believe your crimes non-existent, don't you? I see you priest and know what you would shield from me. You believe her alive still?"

"Shut up!" Fitzgerald roared. His mind spun as the realisation of the demon's knowing hit him hard.

"Your words are poison, and I know you would seek to subvert me still. I know your game now creature for you are the deceiver. Your last gambit is as to whether my soul is pure? Well, you will find out soon enough. I will hold nothing from you for it is down to this now.

You believe Keira dead? Well, she is gone let me tell you. When the light came, and you were cast back here, I went to find her gone as well."

The creature grinned, and Fitzgerald knew he had made a grave error though he knew not as to what it was. The demon though had delighted in what he said. Fitzgerald continued"...It is of no matter. You think me a murderer? What happened did so in the heat of the moment, and I sought only to protect myself. It was an accident...It was..."

"Bargaining? Is that what you are resorted to now? How delicious this is and right at the last? Don't you see I have heard such like a million times over when the time is come, and the debt is due? You and your pitiful species are all alike. He gave you free will and freedom and what do you do with it? You piss and you moan not knowing the paradise that is given to you freely until it is all too late, and you think to recant and to beg forgiveness at the last will win you through? He is merciful, but you cannot hide the nature of your soul from him, none can. You are as doomed as the rest and this folly you now employ is an empty gesture, for though you speak the words, you have not the authority to speak on his behalf."

Fitzgerald was weighed heavy with self-doubt. He believed the argument that he shared was now the crux of his success or his failure. The demon knew it to, and the fate of each of them depended on his unknown virtue.

The monster before him had revealed something when he had made mention of Keira's disappearance, but what? He could not find the meaning in its knowing smile, and so it rested less on whether she lived and more upon his guilt for the injury he had caused her. Had he intended to kill her whether he had done so or not?

For surely the intent alone would blight an otherwise pure soul. But no, he had not, could not have intended for what had happened. He knew he could not have foreseen her presence down there in the basement and nor could he have anticipated her savage attack. They had been lovers, after all. It was also true that he initially believed her to be this beast in disguise, such had been Lydia's warning, but it was she, Keira, who had attacked first. It was she who sought to free this devil and seemingly would stop at nothing to achieve that goal and so claim her prize.

Fitzgerald thought back, and he could now see the struggle they had shared as they fought for the crowbar that had shattered his wrist, his only thought at that time had been that if she won it, she wouldn't hesitate to have beat him to a pulp and perhaps even kill him.

The stakes had been higher than simply his life though, and it had been only to prevent this creature's escape that he had attacked her. He had not anticipated she would hit her head as she had done and truth be told he knew that had she not done so, the fight would still not have been over, but would he have killed her? No.

It was so easy to see now. So simple. Of course, he had felt the responsibility for her, for it was through his actions that she had taken the blow. But it had been through necessity that he had acted and that alone. He could not allow himself to take the blame when it was through her actions and her abandonment of what was right that had caused such a thing to happen, and after all, that was what counted here wasn't it? He could blame himself and in so doing so taint his belief that his intentions and so his soul were impure. And if that won through, he could not win through here and now. But it was the opposite that was true. He had acted in good faith, had tried his utmost to prevent the evil that this creature represented be released, and it must be with that in mind that he must continue, for if he did not believe in himself then surely the ending of the rite was doomed to failure.

The demon watched on as he wrestled with these thoughts, perhaps deliberating as to if its words had hit their mark, to make him doubt himself and so lose the volition of his words as he ended the rite.

"Please Lord give me the strength I need in this hour of darkness," Fitzgerald began, "I am but your humble servant and come before you in my hour of need. You who are merciful and forgiving give me the strength to finish what I have begun."

He faced the creature once more.

"Oh God, you are guardian and protector, lead us into the light and place upon this house an everlasting blessing…"

As he spoke, there was another loud cracking sound. The demon turned away from him at the sound and stepped further back into the darkness. Fitzgerald himself did not know exactly where the sound originated, but was at once filled with hope for the sound was one of power and resonated through him as he continued to speak.

"…such that will be a sign of your healing hands…"

Again another cracking sound and all at once he felt another tangible change, the room had grown warmer all of a sudden and accompanying the feeling was a sense that the light in the room had brightened by a fraction.

"…and all that would join me in my plea shall partake of your protection and love."

The source of the sound was now undeniable. All at once, Fitzgerald beheld the floor beneath the demon begin to crack, opening minute fissures through which red light rose upward. With the light, the distinct aroma of sulphur tinged his nose. It was working!

The demon understood at once and rebounded back toward where Fitzgerald stood.

"Stop this!" It cried, coming to an abrupt halt as the floor before it broke and another pillar of red light pierced upward between them. "Priest no, have mercy upon me." The thing fell to its knees, the pillar of light rising before it and lighting its hideous features.

Fitzgerald would not stop though. The thing before him had already come close to corrupting his mind, coaxing him toward submission and the sweet release of a dark place within unconsciousness or death. A place where he and Emma could be together again. But it had been a lie. To listen to it further, would risk the same.

415

It's the deceiver.

He knew it, and knew he could not allow its words to register.

"I will give you anything! Anything! Don't send me back there, please!

He hesitated for a fraction of a second and the demon perhaps sensed it for it continued.

"Yes! I was a fool. A fool to try and subvert one such as yourself. I underestimated you. I have been trapped here for too long and I used only that which I have known for centuries. But I see you now, know you. You have known loss yes? The gifts I can bestow need not come at the high price paid by McArthur and Searle, no."

The beast surely knew his pain for it continued. "He created a lonely world for you Father, didn't he?"

"And you used that against me, didn't you? It was her wasn't it? Keira? She told you of Emma. You used what little you had and thought to trick me with it. But you did not reckon on her, did you? That even as a pawn in your twisted game, her virtue won through and warned me of your lies."

"No, it's impossible!"

"Then you reckoned without the power of God, for something reached me. Brought me back to finish what I begun."

"No please," the thing begged. "I only offered that which I thought you wanted, but you can have anything, anything!"

"I want only to return you to the hell that spawned you."

"No! Look, look upon me and have mercy." The thing began to claw at its face and pulled away the remains of its mask. Rank fetid flesh fell to the floor, and beneath, Fitzgerald saw a face old, haggard and familiar to him, for he had been given visions of such on Lydia's first visit.

 Here was the ancient and yellowed skin of one so old as to defy logic. Its bald head crowned with a whisper of white hair, the mouth toothless and the eyes glazed white with severe cataracts.

"Do you see me now, Father? Am I not pitiful? I was once a man as you are now. Look, look here!" The waif of skin and bones thrust out its hand. Its fingers almost skeletal and brittle with age. "Do you see?" It cried.

Fitzgerald did see. Thereupon its hand was a long thin scar.

"These are the gifts that the Devil would bring. I was like the Irish woman, conceited and vain. Those were my crimes and those alone. I watched as those around me withered and died, I could not stand the same for myself! It was an age of witchcraft and magic and so I

416

made my deal as those you know have done. I have worn a thousand faces and yet I cannot forget my own as you see before you. My immortality is a perversion, my soul is forfeit and I am but a pawn for the Devil. Please do not send me there, his anger at my failure will know no bounds. Would you deliver me to eternal torture and damnation?"

"Yes. yes, I would."

The creature began to shriek as Fitzgerald uttered the words; "Lord God, I believe it speaks truly of one fact. That once it was a man and so in your image. Take pity on him for the decisions he made, for they were made with avarice and vanity. Naught remains of that man; have mercy upon his soul, but dispel that which remains in his image and that which serves only one master who is an affront to your being. Through Jesus Christ, our Lord, Amen."

He crossed himself and all the while new cracks tore through the floor of the library. The red light was now abundant and reduced everything to a glaze of dark red. Sweat now poured from his brow for the heat was oppressive and he knew well the source below.

All at once, a section of the floor fell away and tumbled downward into a deep chasm. Red flame licked at the lips of the precipice that was created. The sight defied logic for beneath the library simply lay the ground floor he knew, but he saw something that was both real and unreal at the same time as he had seen the corpse of Robert McArthur both at peace and mutilated, a picture upon a picture.

The heat though was real, and Fitzgerald stepped back as he saw more sections of the floor fall away and a large crack work its way slowly toward him. Slowly it crawled as if pacing him in his back steps toward the door of the library. He looked up just in time to see the entire floor to his left give way and fall into nothingness. He made the threshold of the door, where the fault line ceased, split, and likewise fell into the pit below.

Fire reached up and touched the hem of his robe, which caught at once until that was he pulled back further on reflex and watched the fire die as the cloth crossed the boundary between the two rooms. The floor continued to tumble and he watched now as those books and shelves that had not yet fallen burst into flame. There was no doubt in him that this was real and no trick of his adversary that now skittled to the centre of the room as far away from the edges of an unbelievable sheer drop beneath it.

Fitzgerald gazed below, but the fire stung his eyes and he recoiled, he had not seen the depth of the pit that would claim the monster and he knew that he should not, for such a sight was reserved only for those who had earned it.

At last, the surrounding sections of floor fell away and Fitzgerald watched on amazed as he saw the last section floating on nothingness. An island in a sea of flame that surrounded it. He quickly saw the reason why it remained for the floor that remained was defined by the three medals that marked its borders, the medals of St Benedict. The ritual was not yet complete.

The damned creature looked over the abyss, and Fitzgerald sensed its fear and hatred.

Finding his crucifix, he raised it one final time and recited; "Ecce crucis signum fugiant phantasmata cuncta."

A piercing cry assaulted his ears as the creature screamed. The floor crumbled beneath the coins and each plummeted quickly out of sight and into the fire, which engulfed them with an angry roar, causing a fountain of fire to rise and engulf the remaining platform. The demon was instantly consumed in fire, its high-pitched scream cut off as its face was eviscerated.

The platform crumbled and fell and the beast fell into hell which greeted its arrival with another explosion of fire which erupted in a square column before Fitzgerald's eyes. The force and intensity of the blast so heavy as to take him off of his feet and throw him backwards from the library door which slammed closed as he flew through the air. He landed heavily inside the anteroom upon his back, his head striking the carpeted floor and pain exploding where he had already been struck.

Darkness raced up to claim him, only this time he welcomed it for he knew there were no monsters hidden within, and he might have the rest he richly craved and deserved.

His eyelids fluttered heavilyy, once, twice. There before him, as he gave way to unconsciousness was Lydia Bennett, her face grave and pure.

"Rest, Father. It is done. Rest."

His eyelids closed a third time, and darkness won through.

CHAPTER 55

Iain Fitzgerald hovered somewhere between waking and sleep, and he found that it was a good place. In sleep, the nightmares followed. In waking, he found himself under the glare of watchful nurses and intense looking doctor's.

"Nurse is he awake?" An unfamiliar male voice.

A large black woman loomed over him and spoke with a Caribbean accent. "Father Fitzgerald? Are you with us? If you are up to it, there are some people here who have come to ask you some questions."

He groaned in response and twisted within his bed so as to escape the intrusion of her voice.

"He's still very weak you know officer, go easy on him and no more than five minutes you hear me?"

"Yes, ma'am."

The noise that followed was the irritating squeak of a chair being pulled over the floor toward the side of his bed.

"Father Fitzgerald?" The same voice. It was no good; his senses were too alive as to what was going on beyond his closed eyelids.

"Hmmm." he grumbled.

"Father Fitzgerald, I am Detective Constable Scott with Eastland Police, I am here with my colleague DC Rudd. If you are up to it, we are very anxious to speak with you."

Fitzgerald rolled back squarely onto the bed and allowed his head to loll toward the sound of the voice. Detective Constable Scott, it was clear to see was the senior of the two. Fitzgerald judged him to be in his early fifties judging by the wisps of grey on his head and in his beard, his colleague, DC Rudd was an officious looking woman with tight red lips and a steely glare.

"Detectives, please, I'm not sure I am up to this…"

Rudd cut in. "This will only take a few moments. We need your help." Her insistence rankled with him and he had time to wonder if this was her bedside manner with everyone she dealt with, including victims of crime.

"I'm not sure I can tell you anything..."

"Father, please." Scott followed. "You have been the victim of a very serious attack and we are keen to apprehend the suspects as soon as possible."

Attack? Suspects?

Fitzgerald let the words roll around his head. Is that what they thought?

"Detective please, the control by my side."

Scott looking confused, glanced over toward his colleague. "I..."

"The bed remote Jim."

"Oh...of course." Scott reached, found the control and passed it over. Fitzgerald held the button on the remote, slowly the top half of the bed began to rise.

Keep your mouth shut and let them tell you what they think happened.

It was good advice he knew. The police had already seemingly decided upon a likely cause of what had occurred; this would be simpler the more they gave him.

"That's better," he said as the bed came to a halt and he was able to look at Scott at an even level. "Please officer, anything I can do to help, but please know it's difficult to remember, my head..."

"A severe concussion the doctors say," Rudd followed, "that, a broken wrist and most strangely what looks like claw marks down your back. Before I begin, I must ask you first Father, may we please record this conversation for our enquiry?"

No police caution? Then they are treating me as a witness. At least for now, be careful what you say.

"Of course, detective."

Rudd reached over and lay what he surmised was a Dictaphone on the bed between them. The device produced a small click as she activated it.

"For the record then. This is a tape-recorded interview with Father Iain Fitzgerald. The time is 12..." a check of the watch, "...03 and the date is Monday 14th November. I am DC Jim Scott and my colleague is?"

"DC Pamela Rudd."

Monday? How long have I been out for? There was no time for deliberation though as Scott continued unabated.

"We are both stationed at Springmoor Police Station. This is a voluntary witness interview, could you please state your name for the benefit of the tape please Father."

"Father Iain Fitzgerald."

"Thank you, Father. Just know I plan to be brief, but we must ask that when you are up to it, that you provide an in-depth statement regarding all that transpired. Is that okay?"

"Yes of course."

"What can you tell me about those injuries Father, how did you sustain them?"

"I will, but please. What of the others who were in the house? Please tell me that everyone is okay?" It was a gambit, but fortunately, one that was quickly bought by Scott, who exchanged a knowing glance with his female colleague.

"Father Fitzgerald, the matter at hand is more serious than you know. We believe what occurred is an elaborate burglary gone wrong. Mr McArthur I am afraid to tell you has passed away…"

Fitzgerald nodded. "Yes, I am afraid so. You understand that is why I was there? Mr McArthur was terminally ill and sought my service for confession and last rites."

"Of course. We spoke with a Mrs Hodgson. The housekeeper at Thoby Hall? She explained all of that. Mr McArthur will be sent for an autopsy but at this stage, you are happy to say that he died of his illness as opposed to any other outside influences?"

"Absolutely. But what do you mean by outside influences? What of the nurses who were there? Please tell me that they are okay?"

A second look between the officers. Fitzgerald detected the slightest of nods from Rudd toward Scott.

"Father I am sorry to have to tell you that as a result of what occurred at Thoby Hall, we are conducting a murder enquiry. The nurse there, Melissa Hardy was found dead at the scene by the housekeeper, Mrs Hodgson. It was she who likewise found you and called for assistance. Tell me…I must know what you saw there the other night."

Fitzgerald swallowed deeply. It was a reflex, and if either of them picked up on such signs, they might easily sense his anxiety. But he could not hold the question back; he had to know…

"And Keira? The other nurse. What of her?"

Scott leaned forward, and Fitzgerald knew at once he had triggered something of relevance to the police officers. He searched the faces of both of them, his anger rising as a silence grew between him and the two of them.

"Tell me, is she okay?!" He barked at last.

"Father Fitzgerald, please be calm. First of all, I need to know what you are saying to me. Was Keira Morgan present at Thoby Hall the night Mr McArthur passed away?"

"What? Yes, of course. You're telling me that you don't know that? I just need to know if she is alright."

Scott stood up and turned away from the bedside, a nod of his head indicating to Rudd that he wished to converse in private. Rudd, in turn, walked to the door and made her exit as Scott spoke; "Father please, just a minute. There are elements here that are…difficult."

"For God's sake man, just tell me!"

A pained look came over the police officer's face as he backed out of the door, holding a finger up indicating to Fitzgerald that he only wanted a moment. Exasperated, Fitzgerald lashed out with his fists and punched the top of the bed by his sides, dull pain flared in his cast wrist and he gasped as a low fire now burned under his injury.

What was it they weren't telling him? Had they found her after all? Dead? Alive? Either way, he could be implicated, for if she lived, she might have already given the police her story. If not, and they had found her dead, what then? Surely there was sufficient forensic evidence to link him to that event and if they should so make that link what suspicion would then be raised by his account of Melissa's violent death?

Beads of sweat began to form on his brow. Had he already said too much? Given everything that had occurred, he had never thought so far as to what the far-reaching implications might have been. But the fact was that a woman was dead, perhaps two, and he was at the centre of it all. It was no good that he had acted with goodwill and only with the view to eradicating evil from the place, for who, if anyone would believe such a story?

Within only a second or so, the two detectives entered the room once more, Scott taking his seat as he had done before, Rudd in her spot over his shoulder.

"I am sorry about that, Father, I just needed to clarify something with my colleague. You have to understand that some of the information we have is need to know only and what I am about to share with you is only because of your position and what you have been through, but it is not to leave this room is that understood?"

Fitzgerald nodded, his mouth suddenly too dry to answer.

"Very good. But first of all, please let me clarify. Miss Morgan was present at Thoby Hall during these events?"

"Yes…" it was but a whisper. "Yes." He said again, only clearer and louder, "Miss Morgan…Keira I mean, she had nursed Mr McArthur for some time, she…she wanted to be there at the end. But please tell me, you've told me that you are conducting a murder enquiry? A botched burglary? Is she okay?"

"The truth is we don't know Father. Miss Morgan is currently missing and very high on the list of people we wish to speak to."

Relief flooded through Fitzgerald's core. She had gotten out it seemed, the blow to her head had not killed her after all.

Scott continued, "Now, please. Tell us what you remember."

Fitzgerald let his head fall back and closed his eyes, allowing the officers to believe that he was thinking hard on what had happened when the truth was he was saying a prayer of thanks for Keira's wellbeing.

At last, he rocked forward, "I remember the power going out. There was a storm, a big one and there was an…an explosion I guess you could call it. Whatever it was the lights went down. I had been with Mr McArthur and was preparing to conduct the last rites. His machines, all of it just went down. It wasn't for long, though. I guess they had some kind of emergency lighting, for the place was soon lit up again thank goodness. Poor Melissa was distraught with what was happening with Mr McArthur and so I took it upon myself to fix the power somehow."

"Was there any sign of trouble or disturbance at that time?" Rudd cut through.

"No… nothing at all. It was eerie I can tell you that, but I made my way down to the basement…through the kitchen and found my way down to the generator room. I remember replacing some fuses and then…"

He stopped, the next part was important he knew, for their Scenes of Crime Officers would no doubt have discovered the disturbance and blood in the dank underground room. "… and then nothing," he concluded, "I can't tell you if I even felt a blow…my head…" he touched the back of his skull for added effect and screwed his face up so as to try and look confused.

"Is that everything?" Scott couldn't mask his irritation.

"I…I think so. You have to understand it's difficult to think…"

"I understand, but I need you to think hard on the next part. Did Keira Morgan follow you down to the basement?"

Fitzgerald took a second. "I don't think so…why? Is that important?"

"You took a blow to the back of the head Father, looks like you landed badly when you fell. The marks on your back though, they beg further question, have you any idea how you came by those?" Rudd took her turn.

"Honestly no. You say I fell? Did this?" he motioned with his cast. "What might have injured my back as you say?"

"We'll get to the bottom of that," Scott answered, "my next question is how you got back up to the anteroom on the upper floor in the east wing?"

Fitzgerald slowly shook his head. "I have no idea, officer. My next memory is of waking up here. You suggest that Keira followed me down to the basement? Could she have taken me? Why didn't she call the police if she saw me...or saw poor Melissa?"

"That's a question we would like answered." Rudd mumbled.

"Perhaps we have come at this too soon," Scott said, "to summarise what's been said you are telling us that you had no sight of your attacker. And that secondly, Keira Morgan was present in the house during these events. I guess that's a start..." he trailed off.

"Perhaps if I just had some time..." Fitzgerald offered.

"We will have to come back to you as I have said, Father. But perhaps in the meantime, you may have a chance to think about events. If anything comes back to you at all, I don't want you to hesitate, inform one of the nurses here and we will be back as quickly as we can. Your formal statement can wait until they have given you the all-clear to leave."

"Thank you. I will."

Scott looked over his shoulder toward Rudd, who shook her head. Leaning back, he retrieved the Dictaphone from the bed. "The time is 12:06 and this very brief interview is now concluded." A small click and the small machine disappeared into his jacket's inside pocket.

"We'll be leaving then Father. I understand you have a visitor so we shall get out of your way." Scott said.

The duo shuffled from the room, undoubtedly disappointed with the fruits of their labour.

The door to the private room had barely closed when it opened a crack, and a familiar and yet surprising visitor's head popped into the gap. It was the solicitor Harvey. Fitzgerald wasn't sure if his groan was inward or outward, but didn't care either way.

"You're awake?" he opened as he entered without further invitation, quickly taking the seat at Fitzgerald's side which the detective had only recently vacated.

"What did you tell them?"

"I am fine, thank you for asking." Fitzgerald retorted.

"This isn't the time for games Father. I am here to help whether you believe that or not. I wanted to get to you before the police, but they had someone on your door from the moment you were admitted, it would have looked...suspicious, probably still does considering who I am." He whispered conspiratorially.

"I told them nothing. There was a storm, a power outage. I didn't see my attacker. They seemed most interested in what I had to say about Keira. Now, what do you want Harvey? Please, I am in no mood."

The solicitor nodded. "That's all good. First of all, I don't need to know the finer details of what actually did happen. I had a version of such from Hodgson. I believe the poor old bat may well have lost her mind. But what I do need is for you to hear what I have to say, because this is the official line we are taking."

Fitzgerald was silent. Harvey had his attention.

"It was a burglary gone wrong."

"I know that, the police…"

"The police believe exactly what we want them to at this stage, and you need to be on board for that to continue to be the case Father. The truth is that Mrs Hodgson's first call was not for 999 but to me and thank goodness that was the case. Mr McArthur, shall we say had concerns regarding your business. He didn't go into full details with me, but what Hodgson suggested was…well, never mind. The fact is that the police are following a lead on burglary because that is exactly what we want them to."

"You're talking in riddles. Just get to the point." Fitzgerald's temper was rising.

"With Hodgson's help we…how will we say?…performed a little housekeeping before the police arrived. The reason they are so interested in Keira Morgan is that the contents of Mr McArthur's safe are gone and you were left for dead, and as for poor Melissa…"

"That's ridiculous, they…"

"Believe every bit of it, Father and why wouldn't they? What exactly was Keira Morgan doing there at that time when it wasn't her allotted duty time? More than that, with Mr McArthur on his last legs surely there was no better chance and her last chance to take what she wanted, only poor Melissa discovered what had happened and was…disposed of."

There was reason in his words. He had pretty much read the same between the lines of what little the police had given away and what with Keira now missing…

"What of Keira? Has there been any sign?"

"None that I am aware of, but understand this. They are unlikely to believe she acted alone. Jobs like this usually involve some lover or bad element on the outside. It's unlikely your power cut was any accident. I suggest the amnesia card is your best bet for now and evermore."

"But why? Why do anything at all?"

"As I say, Mr McArthur had concerns. Perhaps he had some foresight to a difficult ending. It was not mine to question his motives but he was keen that whatever the circumstances his passing should be...shall we say quiet?"

"To the extent that you would tamper with evidence? Pervert the course of justice?"

"That's not of your concern. It is merely a nod toward the real perpetrator here, why else has she gone missing as she has? You should be thankful, Father Fitzgerald. If it were not for Mr McArthur, you would undoubtedly be answering some much more difficult questions."

Fitzgerald could not deny the truth in Harvey's words and that it looked bad for Keira. He had a different version of events of course, but Keira's place in them made her equally culpable. And what if he did choose to share his story? He would likely end up in an institution much like poor Elizabeth McArthur.

But what played on his mind now was to who or what had killed Melissa. His first instinct after seeing McArthur's mutilated corpse had been that the beast had been responsible, but the demon had given some clue as to its bounds when it admitted to him that it could not have killed him outright, there were rules it said. And so what of Melissa, was she tainted with some unknown sin that would bring her within the bounds of the demon's rules? Or could Keira have acted on the beast's behalf, committing the most cardinal of sins?

In his mind, he could now admit that such was possible for the picture he beheld in his mind's eye was of her furious attack upon him, and murder had undoubtedly been on her mind.

As to if he could follow along with Harvey's ploy of some heist gone wrong he did not know, but for now the amnesia ploy would likely serve him best for there would be more questions and more difficult questions at that, especially if and when they caught up with Keira.

"I need to think. Perhaps you had better leave."

Harvey looked decidedly put out by the rebuke.

"Very well. But ask yourself what good does it serve to upset the apple-cart now?"

Fitzgerald was silent, and Harvey finally took that as a cue to go, leaving Fitzgerald to his thoughts.

His physical injuries would soon be healed to the extent where he would be allowed to leave the hospital, but what then? Back to the Church and the mundane? He had been given a front row seat into the real workings of both heaven and hell, the scars on his back which he would wear forevermore, were indeed a testament to the latter, but in truth, he felt somewhat empty as to any feeling of the divine.

He had felt alone almost all the time he had been at Thoby Hall, and though the spirit of Lydia Bennett had revealed itself to offer what assistance it could, it had seemingly paled in comparison to the power of evil that had held sway over the house. If anything, the soul of the little girl had seemed as lost as he had and he hoped beyond anything that she could now have the peace which she deserved.

He felt low in that instant for though the beast was gone, the cost had been high and he cursed the memory of Thomas Searle for inflicting such malevolence into the lives of Robert and Elizabeth McArthur, of Lydia Bennett, of Melissa Hardy, Father Crosby and of course Keira Morgan who had been swayed by promises of gifts not meant for man or woman.

Slowly he closed his eyes once again and allowed visions of those faces to wash over him, and he fell into a deep sleep.

CHAPTER 56

Several weeks passed by, and Father Iain Fitzgerald once again found himself back in the welcome arms of St Peter's Church.

Things had now quietened down following the initial intrusion of the police, who had been a frustrating and constant presence in those first days since his release.

Following the advice from the solicitor Harvey though, he had provided sparse detail in his statements, only going so far as to expand slightly on the scant detail he had provided to Scott and Rudd.

Keira Morgan had still to be found, and he carried thoughts of her everywhere he went, as well as in his prayers. In those initial weeks, he was informed only so far as to suggest that she had gone beyond a person of interest, to suspect number one in the murder of Melissa Hardy.

He could still scarcely believe it, but the picture he carried into his sleep with him each and every night was of Keira standing over him, crowbar in hand and ready to smash down and end his life. They had been difficult nights of broken sleep and disturbing nightmares, but his integration back into the Church had thankfully been his escape as he went about his duties once more.

Then there had been the discussions with Colin Morris. Such talk had at first been impossible; such were the memories of his face upon the beast. But slowly, Morris had drawn the story of what had really happened at Thoby Hall out of him. The man had been incredulous at first, for he had somehow found his way through those same events unscathed, but ultimately he accepted what he had been told without reservation, for Fitzgerald's words had been echoed by Elizabeth McArthur's before him. As such, Morris had been an important crutch as Fitzgerald regained his strength and his faith became renewed.

He reflected on these things now as he sat within the sacristy of St Peter's preparing his sermon for the coming Sunday.

Such was his attention to the passages in the Bible; he was unaware as the man delicately opened the door and made his way into the room before him.

His voice was soft and smooth as he spoke, but even so, Fitzgerald's heart galloped following the sudden intervention, as old horrors rose to the fore. As a result, he was quickly awake and alive to this new presence as he snatched his head upward to receive this stranger.

"Who are you?"

Fitzgerald surveyed the newcomer's features. The man towered over him, a beanpole 6' 3" and skinny with it. His long black overcoat seemed almost to devour him such was the ill fit. He wore a kindly smile, but Fitzgerald detected a steely resolve behind sharp blue eyes. It was difficult to age the man as his beaten and worn face was offset with brilliant black hair and polished white teeth.

"Are you another detective? I told you everything that I can remember, you will need to give me more time than that."

Something did not quite sit right with his guess. The man had an air about him that made Fitzgerald think that he was not from the police.

"May I sit Father?"

"Do I have a choice?"

The man sat, indicating that he in fact did not.

"You've had some ordeal, Father Fitzgerald."

"You have me at a disadvantage, Mr?"

"My name is Lawton, and I am here to offer you an opportunity."

"Well I don't know if you've noticed Mr Lawton, but I am hardly in a position to…"

"Let us skip past the posturing, shall we? You are in safe company Father so let me give you an indication as to what I know. It will make matters go more easily as you will find you need not take the defensive with me."

Fitzgerald was silent, Lawton nodded and took that as his cue to continue. "You, Father, have acted without the accord of your superiors and outside the bounds of the Catholic Church's remit per exorcism."

"I…" Fitzgerald began.

"There is no need to deny Father. We have known for some time the secrets of Thoby Hall, but in our ignorance, we had not foreseen such an ending as this. It is astonishing that one such as yourself and without proper training could defeat the demon that resided there."

"What?…"

Lawton laughed. "You don't have a clue, do you? Did you not think it wise to know your enemy before you battled? I wonder how much of it was down to luck?"

Fitzgerald's head began to ache, and he became instantly aware that his current pain medication had run its course, what was more this man Lawton was talking to him in riddles

429

which only served to bate his anger, which was beginning to rise. That had been all too common of late and he wished only to escape the confines of the room and avoid any further interaction with this man.

"Mr Lawton please…"

"I am sorry, you are tired, injured and undeniably confused. I am representative here today at the behest of the International Association of Exorcists."

Fitzgerald sat up. The conversation had just taken a very interesting turn.

Lawton's smile suggested he knew his reputation had preceded him. "You've heard of us." It was not a question.

With that, Fitzgerald's mind raced to catch up with what had already been said. Lawton had said they had known of Thoby Hall, but how could they know what he had done and what he had achieved?

"Fear not Father, your secrets are safe with us. In time I wish to discuss in-depth your experiences with the demon. But first, we should speak of why I am here."

"You said you knew of Thoby Hall."

"You have questions, of course, and all in good time…"

"Tell me." Fitzgerald demanded.

Lawton undoubtedly saw determination on Fitzgerald's face. He sighed, "Very well. I sensed you have heard of our little organisation which helps us cut through most of the crap. Officially we began in 1990. Six exorcists, all of whom had acted previously in isolation, came together to discuss what was the very real war against the demonic hordes of hell. You may well know the names of Father Gabriele Amorth and Father Jeremy Davies? Well, they were two of that number and they saw what the Catholic Church at that time refused to recognise. That the spawn of Satan had ruthlessly and efficiently circumvented the shackles of hell to walk amongst men and seek to break the seven seals."

The seven seals Fitzgerald knew, referred to writings from the Book of Revelations. Seven seals that if broken, would spell the end of the world and begin the judgement of all mankind.

"You speak of this as a real thing?" Fitzgerald questioned.

"And who are you to say that it is not Father? Have your experiences gained you nothing? You, who have faced a real demon and not yet questioned its motives? I told you that we were aware of Thoby Hall, did you not think to ask as to how and why?"

"Then tell me."

"You will have heard the story of Thomas Searle?"

"Of course."

"Then you will know that during a period of his life he sought various counsel so as to rid that foul beast from his home?"

"Robert McArthur told me all of that."

"Thomas Searle, like you, did indeed try to dispel the creature. Did you not think that out of all that he learned that he did not seek the help of the Catholic Church and exorcism?"

Fitzgerald was stunned by the revelation. "But how? You said your association began in 1990."

Lawton nodded as if impatient. "Slow down Iain, slow down. That is true; we only learned of such a few years ago. Thomas Searle did indeed petition the Catholic Church for exorcism but was denied. We have the records, know the whole story."

"They denied him?!" Fitzgerald was incredulous.

Lawton nodded solemnly. "Indeed, they did. Your look of disdain is not lost on me. It is for reasons such as this that the association of which I now form a part of came into being in the first place. Evil has very real roots in this world. It is we who see them and seek to pull them before they take hold."

"But why would they deny him?" Fitzgerald asked.

"I cannot answer that question. A war for the souls of men has been raging for millennia. A war which the Catholic Church will not give voice to, by papal decree. We are not that naïve as to dismiss centuries of hardship and battle. Such associations as ours have existed for all that time in many guises. Searle made contact with such and begged them to assist him in removing his curse and to exorcise the demon back to hell. He was denied and so instead the home in which he inhabited became awash with witchcraft and pagan symbols."

Lawton was close to the truth with his words. Could he know of the wiccan and the supposed spell of fertility that had instead been the likely cause of the beast's imprisonment?

Lawton continued, "and here you are, Father, all these years later. Successful where Father Crosby failed and yet so naïve as to the bigger picture."

"What do you mean?"

"Think on Father. Remember what I said. A battle was being waged for the souls of men, but to what end? Satan fills the ranks of his legions, but what use such an army?"

He knew the answer. "The seals."

"Exactly! The seven seals! And if broken so to shall be the locked doors to hell itself!"

Fitzgerald allowed the words to sink in, remembering all that he knew of those passages in the Book of Revelations. The opening of the seven seals was to mark the second coming of Christ and so begin the judgement of mankind.

These beliefs had been taught to him through the seminary. The futurist, the preterist, the idealist and finally the historicist.

Finally, he spoke. "But what of this demon that I fought?"

Lawton replied. "That is more difficult to answer and we can only speculate to it's origins. Our studies tell us of a demon called Bunè. He is the deceiver, the giver and breaker of promises. His only goal is to secure the souls of men so that the demonic legion grows ever stronger. I wager he who you battled was among his number, and charged with the task of securing such souls and collecting such debt when it is due. In doing so making such a legion all the stronger."

"But to what end?"

Lawton's face was grim. "You know as I do what the Book of Revelations foretells. The coming of the horsemen of the apocalypse, the judgement of man?"

Fitzgerald nodded.

"There are many through history who have interpreted the opening of the seals, and still the second coming is yet to pass. And yet the futurist version depicts a World War instigated by the Devil himself in which he will crush those who are Christian. It is for such a purpose the hordes of hell prepare themselves. I hear that the doomsday clock will soon read only one minute from midnight."

Fitzgerald could well believe it. The world about them was in turmoil, as conflict raged across the planet, as all the while new threats revealed themselves. His though had been the battle for one man's soul and it was that which begged further questions.

"Then he who I faced, does he have a name?"

"His name is long forgotten, he is likely to have worn many faces over centuries. From what you told Colin Morris, he sought life everlasting and regrettably received it. In doing so, he likely forgets who he ever was, that in part is the way of the Devil, and punishment for his folly."

"You sound sorry for him."

"I am sorry for the folly of man, Father."

There was one other issue that prayed heavily on Fitzgerald's mind. "Those people… Melissa, Crosby, McArthur and his poor Elizabeth. Why? How could such as that be allowed to happen?"

Lawton bowed his head, a look of sorrow washed over him as he shook his head. "As I said, we became aware several years ago, as our association grew, and we were allowed access to the Vatican archives. We approached Robert McArthur who dismissed us out of hand. We had not a clue that he had seen the error in his ways and was seeking atonement for such mistakes. It is only now that it is revealed to us what transpired, that, and what your Deacon Morris and Father Crosby attempted to do there. The Church attempted a cover-up, after Father Crosby's death. Somehow Colin Morris was unaffected."

"But what then?"

"Then nothing. We petitioned McArthur for access to his home, but he refused us without question as I said, the wounds of what had happened to his wife were perhaps too raw. I do not know. We didn't know until afterwards that he had employed your services to help him be rid of the demon."

"Morris?" Fitzgerald mouthed his insight.

Lawton nodded his agreement. "He was worried about you. For what you have been through. It was he who contacted us and asked us to come and give counsel."

"So, what now?"

"You fulfilled your service to McArthur, and so his Estate is passed to the Catholic Church. More pointedly, Thoby Hall will be assigned to the use of our association. It is fitting, don't you think? That it should instead become an institution dedicated to the word of God and so seek to defeat the minions of Satan?"

"This war of yours is all too real, isn't it?"

"It is, which is why I came to you today. This isn't a debrief, only an explanation before what is to come next. We want you to come and work with us."

Fitzgerald was stunned. "But what of my parish? What of…"

Lawton exploded into a hearty laugh. "Father, oh, please. The bigger picture?"

Fitzgerald couldn't help but smile himself. It had all been so much to take in. He had discovered that he had been a fool all along, he had not been alone and there had been help there if only he had reached out. There was a bigger picture, just as Lawton suggested. It had only been a short time ago that he had questioned the folly of returning to his parish in the knowledge of what really existed within the world.

He knew what he had to do and what his answer was.

"I accept."

Lawton looked surprised. "Father, please feel free to take some time over this…"

"There is no need. The last few weeks have caused me to question every aspect of my faith and left me feeling alone. I see now that there is so much more and it is through the workings of men such as you and I, that the Lord works upon the world. I did not feel God's touch upon me, for I did not realise the whole time that it was through me that he acted."

"Indeed, Father. There is of course much more to discuss, perhaps when you are fit and well?"

Fitzgerald shook his head. "Come see me again tomorrow. But for the pain, there is nothing else the matter with me. Perhaps we can discuss just what my participation might involve?"

"Very good." Lawton reached into his jacket and produced a small card which he placed into Fitzgerald's palm. He flipped it over and read the name, Simon Lawton, followed only by a telephone number and e-mail address, no grand gesturing of his affiliation to such an organisation as the International Association of Exorcists.

"Shall we say 2 pm?" Lawton suggested as he withdrew deeper into the room and closer to the exit.

Fitzgerald thought. "Better make it 4 pm." An idea had struck him, his first port of call tomorrow would be to a small hospital in a small village nearby and to fulfil a promise he had made to a dying man. He would visit with Elizabeth McArthur and give her news that he hoped might go some way to help her troubled soul. And after that…

"Lawton." He called out just as the man made the doorway. Lawton stopped and looked back. "Lawton, how soon can we get back up to Thoby Hall?"

The other man looked puzzled as to the query but answered without further question. "The police have it under lock and key for now, but once their business is done?… Soon anyway."

"Good." He settled back into his chair and closed his eyes. Lawton remained a second longer to see if there was anything else, but when nothing came, he edged quietly out through the door.

Fitzgerald now sat in the gloom of the late afternoon, the sunlight outside of his window now diminished and hidden by low dark grey clouds. The November air was as grave as it had been all the previous weeks, but the gloom that had held close to Fitzgerald's heart had finally lifted as he had purpose.

First, Elizabeth McArthur and then back to Thoby Hall, for he had also made a promise to himself, one, that he would do all that he could for the spirit of one little girl who had stayed with him and kept him true, so as to defeat an evil that might otherwise be loose again upon the world.

And after Lydia Bennett, to the International Association of Exorcists and an age-old war.

EPILOGUE

From the outside, the King's Arms, public house in Wanstead looked much like any other spit and sawdust establishment that Steven Fisher had ever seen. Situated in a back street, only a stone's throw from the underground station, it mainly catered to an early evening clientele of commuters who would sink a few drinks around tables fashioned from wooden beer barrels, before heading home for the night.

Steven though was not here for the aesthetic choices or his comfort for that matter as he shifted uncomfortably on the tiny padded barstool; his portly backside near swallowing the vinyl-covered seat and no doubt giving the impression to the now sparse remaining customers, that the seat was in fact embedded up his arse.

He grimaced as a wave of sharp pain shot through his belly, and he looked longingly down the bar, giving a curt nod of his head to get the attention of the middle-aged barmaid who made no secret of her irritation that he still remained in the pub. He ordered his fourth double Jack Daniel's and swallowed it in one as he sought to put out the fire in his gut, as he did so, he stared unashamedly at the woman's cleavage. It had been the only bright spot of his evening thus far as he waited for his cue to depart to the back room.

Perhaps he needn't have arrived so early, but here was a chance to view the competition before the game ahead. It was nearing 11:00 pm, and soon the waitress would call time on the last stragglers and he would be let through to the back room at last. In the meantime, he fancied he had clocked several other of tonight's players.

He did this, so as to make sure that none of them recognised him. It was true, his look had changed significantly since he appeared on the UK Poker Tour all those years ago, and though he used a different name in each of the backstreet rooms in which he now played, there were still those who eyed him up and down, suspicion prevalent in their eyes as he won the final pot.

As he dwelled on this, a doorway set behind the bar opened and a wiry man in his fifties appeared. He waited until Steven met his eyes and gave him the nod that affirmed that he was to come through.

Steven felt a sudden rush of adrenaline course through him, and his heart pounded in his chest. There was nothing quite like this feeling, and it was as much for this that he still lived, than the money that he would undoubtedly be taking home with him tonight. He heaved his massive frame up off of the stool and saw that at least three of his guesses had been right, as three other men stood simultaneously and headed for the hatch at the side of the bar, which would give them access to the back room.

As he sidled in behind the last of them, the last man turned to him. Already a fine sweat was forming on his brow. Steven smiled at him as the man asked his question.

"You feeling lucky tonight, pal?"

He did feel lucky. This night and every other night, he had played the game for that matter, and judging by the man's nervous disposition, he would be an easy tell in the hands to come.

"Oh, I hope so," he answered. "Just a bit of fun, eh?"

The man's brow furrowed, and he turned back toward the door. He knew his calm demeanour had already gotten under the skin of the unknown player. He had seen his type before, desperate and undoubtedly reckless. Here was the type that when the going got tough, would throw all in on a high pair. He would likely be the first to go tonight, penniless and ashamed back to wherever he called home. He pictured an imagined wife for this man, her hair in curlers, waiting impatiently into the night for his return, to beat him down with her fists as she ranted of how he had squandered the rent money.

He felt no sympathy. He had been there himself.

The back room was small and dimly lit. The poker table, was a rickety-looking trestle table with a worn green velvet sheet thrown over it, squeezed in between stacked beer crates of empty bottles and boxes of crisps. Steven had played in worse surroundings.

Around the table were six folding chairs. The man who had bid them to enter took his seat beside the last remaining player; a twenty-something with a thin pencil goatee and sunglasses. Steven smiled. It was an old trick, designed so that you couldn't read the eyes of the player behind the lenses.

The room was lit by a single dim bulb, which hung low over the table and cast a putrid circle of light that cast the features of the five other men almost into shadow.

Steven took his seat and extended an envelope stuffed with cash, to the wiry man who had now taken his seat. The count was soon done, and each player was afforded 1,000 chips for the £1,000 they had handed over.

"Alright gentlemen, the game is Texas Hold 'em. Blinds will be £2 small and £5 big. Only three raises per round. We don't have all night so the blinds will double after thirty minutes. There are no buy in's. When you are out, you are out, and as per tournament play, there is no cashing out. We play until we have a winner, who stands to take home six grand. Mary is closing up around front and will be in shortly to get your drinks. Smoke 'em if you got 'em. Any questions?"

There were none.

The cards flew quick on the deal and so to the chips as the players laid their blinds. Steven started slowly as he always did, throwing in some promising hands and allowing sunglasses to take the early pot. His attention not for the cards, but for the barmaid Mary, who brought him his Jack Daniels.

His previous insight into nervous man's game had proved correct, and after only five hands, he had bled half of his chips, having played a pair of kings against what had proven to be a three of a kind on the river card. He was now ripe for the taking.

It was another two hands until Steven saw the glint in his eye that showed him he was going to play his hand. Steven turned back his own cards; a seven of clubs and a nine of hearts. Far from the best.

Where it came from, he did not know, but something from deep in his core fired into life. Steven quite literally had come to call it his gut instinct, but depending on its strength, he knew it was a sign as to the strength of his hand. A seven and nine of mixed suits were far from ideal and at this stage did not offer much chance of the win. But Steven had come to trust this instinct. He could remember exactly where and when this sensation had first come to him, and how he had gone home empty-handed from the small casino that was situated in Soho. He hadn't recognised the feeling the first time it came and threw in his hand. He then watched, amazed as the game continued and his hand of a two and a nine had been supplemented on the flop by a further two nines and then a single two on the turn — a full house.

Perhaps it had been a fluke, but weeks after, in which he had scraped together enough of a stake to go back, the feeling had returned. A simple pocket pair of tens, and out of nothing more than curiosity, he continued to call the modest raises of his opponent. His gut instinct, telling him it was a bluff. And by the time the river card was turned, he knew it was so. This was more than just the feeling inside. This was also the experience of a twenty-five-year loser, who had his odd share of good nights down the years, for the shifting of his opponent's eyes and the sweat on his brow were all the tell he needed to confirm that his feeling was correct.

And now, as the betting went around the table, (sunglasses folding his cards on his turn) Steven dwelt on how his new instinct had propelled him from the seedy casinos and backroom bars to the UK Poker Tour, where he had pulled down some real money.

But there had been something missing in those experiences, and that was all it took for him to know it wasn't the money he had been chasing all along, but the thrill of the game and finally, the sweet feeling of destroying an opponent. He was now, of course, a very rich man, so much so that he didn't need this game tonight, didn't need the money. But it was here, here in these back rooms that he had known humiliation and despair, and so it was only here that he could exact payback on those who had robbed him of his dignity.

The air was now thick with cigar and cigarette smoke as the flop landed.

6♣ K♦ 3♥

On the laying of the king, he fancied he saw the faintest of twitches on the nervous man's mouth. He was undoubtedly playing a three of a kind. Steven checked as the betting went around and wasn't surprised when nervous man only raised £20. A modest raise to be sure and Steven admired him for his restraint. He might be a loser, but he was undoubtedly a seasoned player and didn't want to frighten off the other players with an extortionate raise.

As it was though it was enough for the other two guests to fold and Steven fancied he saw the disappointment etched on nervous man's face. Wiry man did not disappoint as he called, and Steven did likewise.

Down came the turn.

10♣

Nervous man raised the pot by £50. Wiry man folded.

Steven matched and raised him another £50. Nervous man eyed him warily, perhaps worried that he was seeking a flush. He was well-practised in the arts of the game though and diverted his eyes while simultaneously rubbing his brow. He was trying to make his opponent think he was bluffing, but in all honesty, he need not have. Nervous man's greed would win through as he was likely carrying three of a kind or at the least a pocket pair of aces.

The wiry man laid the river card.

8♠

Steven let his disappointment show for but a fraction of a second. Enough to show the nervous man he had not made the flush. It was a small pot at this stage and signalled a way back into the game for his opponent. He might try and tempt Steven with a moderate bet, but something inside him knew better. He was not surprised when the nervous man for one brief moment became a confident man and pushed his remaining chips into the middle.

"All in."

Steven would let him have this moment. He had been in the exact same place. Sure and confident of his imminent success. It was that moment he still chased by playing these backstreet games, so as to see confidence in his opponent just before he took it all away from him.

Steven pushed his chips into the centre.

"Let's see them then."

Just for a moment, there was a flicker of doubt in the face of his opponent, but the muted appreciation from the rest of the table on the turn of his three kings quickly brought the smile back to his face. A smile that Steven would now take away as he laid his straight 6♣ 7♣ 8♠ 9♥ 10♣

There was an instant when nervous man had even begun to reach for the large mound of chips in the middle, his smile breaking, to be replaced with a look of bewilderment as he looked down upon Steven's cards.

"Just a bit of fun, eh?" He repeated his earlier words, as he stretched out his arms and gathered in the chips.

And so it went on, the game was slow after that and his opponents hesitant to commit, but the blinds went up thus forcing the pace to quicken. Steven was in his element now as opponents began to fall by the wayside.

It was now past 01:00 am. All the other players had left, but for the wiry man, who was undoubtedly the pub landlord and sunglasses, who remained as his final opponent. Mary, the buxom barmaid, had even sat herself down on a beer barrel to watch the final hand after bringing Steven what was his seventh Jack Daniels. She had looked bored and listless at first, as she waited on home time, but now Steven fancied he saw her looking at him with a glint in her eye. He didn't fancy himself in any way as an attractive man, and it was more for the pile of chips he had sat in front of him that she looked at him with avarice, perhaps hoping for a sizable tip for her continued service and putting up with his leering looks all night.

Fuck handsome, rich wins.

Who had said that? Steven couldn't quite put his finger on the answer, but he knew they were wise words, and there had been many a night when the cash pot had not been his only reward for his victory. It was with that in mind that he now looked up and afforded Mary a quick wink as he laid his cards; two pair, queens and threes.

"Fuck man!" Sunglasses threw his losing cards down. Mary's smile was all inviting, and Steven's heart galloped that bit faster.

"You have a gift." She offered, as the wiry man, showed sunglasses through the door and toward the exit, leaving Steven alone with the barmaid.

"I'd be lying if I said it was just luck." He boasted.

Her smile was broad. "You'd be right in that."

Steven's own smile dropped, and he felt his mouth run dry as she stood from her position in the shadows and came close to him.

"How about one more game?" she asked seductively as she reached out and brushed an errant lick of hair back behind his ear.

"What did you have in mind?" he asked nervously as he tried and failed at not looking at her cleavage once more.

"A simple game. I draw a card, and you follow. Highest card wins."

His heart was now galloping, and he had to swallow hard to get his words out. "The stakes?"

She motioned with a nod of her head toward one of the cash-stuffed envelopes that sat in front of him. It contained one-sixth of the prize pot, £1,000.

"And…what will you be putting up my dear?"

Her eyes sparkled, and her grin stretched wider. She reached out and held his leg close by the groin, and he could feel the stirrings of an erection, something he could rarely achieve without the stash of little blue pills he kept in his wallet.

"Why anything you want."

Steven took a deep breath and nodded his agreement as he didn't trust his voice.

"The cards?" She followed.

Stephen reached over and took the discarded deck from the middle of the table and began to slowly shuffle the cards, before fanning them out between his large hands. Without looking at the deck, she reached out and took her card from close to the centre and flicked it neatly on the table where it landed face up.

10♠

"You've not made it easy for me," Steven said, as he closed the fanned deck and handed it over to her. Mary likewise fanned the deck open before him. Steven closed his eyes and reached out with his index finger which he allowed to rest on the cards on the right-hand side. Slowly he slid the finger across the deck, waiting for that familiar feeling from his gut to inform his choice. And so it did, for after only four cards, he drew to a stop and opened his eyes. He plucked his card as he looked into Mary's eyes.

"Just a bit of fun." She said.

Steven's brow furrowed as she repeated his own words back to him. At that moment, there was something in her gaze that he did not like, and he hesitated as he held his card before him.

"Turn it." She demanded.

He now did not like her demeanour, as the smile had dropped from her face entirely.

Fuck you, bitch. He turned his card without looking and placed it on the table before him, waiting for the inevitable reaction on her face as she realised she had lost. She held his eyes though without emotion and in that moment, he felt a soft pang of panic begin to build in the pit of his stomach. Panic? No, this was something else; his 'instinct 'was now burning like a fire. He doubled over and held both arms tight to his stomach, as a wave of pain rose within him. What the hell was this?

His head bent low, he looked up at Mary, but her eyes were not upon him. Instead, her head was cocked, and her eyes cast down upon the table to where Steven's card lay. His instinct now turned to dread, as his eyes slowly followed hers down to the table.

He stared dumbfounded at the upturned card, and quickly his head snapped back up to look at the woman next to him.

"What the hell is that? Are you cheating me?"

Slowly she shook her head. Reaching out, she quickly picked up the card and held it before him. A look of relief crossed her brow as her arm withdrew from the light.

His eyes fell from hers down to the card before him — a picture of a skeleton carrying a scythe.

Xiii was imprinted at the top and at the bottom the German words, Der Tod.

The Death.

He knew the picture well enough, knew it had no place in an ordinary pack of cards. This was the 13th tarot card, the death card.

"What are you…" he began, but another wave of fire coursed through his gut, this time causing him to cry out in pain.

"Oh Steven, you poor wretch. What use was your gift?" Mary said. There was something in her voice though that caused Steven to look up from where he had been doubled over. The voice was different, her accent had been local, but now he detected a strong hint of Irish, and with that, he noticed more, where her hair had been a mousey brown, it was now a vibrant red, her eyes…there was something about those as well.

They were brown before.

Now they were a sparkling green. This wasn't Mary at all. This was someone entirely different; the only thing was, this new woman occupied the same place as the barmaid had done only moments before.

"Who are you?" he managed between clenched teeth.

She smiled. "All will be revealed to you at the very end, Steven, and that moment is nearly upon us. Your gift is a kingly one and yet you choose to frequent shitholes like this dive. Long nights, drinking whisky and smoking cigars. You've not been kind to yourself, have you? And now you must pay the price."

"What? I don't understand you."

"No? Then understand this, Steven. Your appendix has burst, the fire that lies within you is nothing compared to the fires that await you, but the nausea and pain you have chosen to ignore the last 24 hours has heralded your death tonight."

At that moment, it was as if a switch went off in his head and his mind was alive with a truth and a horror that had previously been buried beyond knowing.

"No! How?" but he knew. She had hinted at it as she had spoken of his gift. He had bought his success at the card tables at a very high price indeed.

"You see it now, don't you? Ah, this is the hardest part and you must forgive me for I am new at my work. Unfortunately, I to made a deal, tainted as it is. But that is no matter of yours. The time is now come and time to make good on your end."

He had sold his soul for tonight. The realisation came crashing down and he saw the moment at which it had come, drunk, alone and angry in the basement room he had called home for all those pathetic years. Years in which he had lost his wife and his daughter as he put his own selfish needs first. Years in which he had lost the family home to his addiction and the years in which he had begged, stolen and humiliated himself just to make a measly stake to feed his vice. It was in those years he had hit his lowest ebb and so he had bought his success the only way he could.

"Please, I beg of you!"

The redhead looked sad. Slowly she began to shake her head. "This is not my doing Steven; it is yours. Begging won't save you now."

Slowly, he picked himself up and pushed past her and staggered toward the door that led back into the bar, "help me please!" he shouted.

He looked frantically behind himself and saw that the woman had stood and now walked slowly toward him.

He turned about as he made the door and hit it hard to push through to the other side. It did not give though, and he rebounded hard and back onto his rump.

"Please!" he cried, hoping beyond hope that the wiry man or the youthful lad in sunglasses were in hearing range just beyond the door.

"Steven."

He turned. She was already upon him, standing tall above.

"Somebody help me please!" he screamed. "Why won't someone help!" It was more a whimper than a cry this time and streams of tears began to run down his face.

"Look," was all she said next, and he raised his head to look past her and back toward where he had been sitting.

Was still sitting.

"No, that can't be! It's impossible!"

He could not deny what he saw though, for there back in the folding chair; he beheld his own body slumped forward over the poker table which strained to hold his dead-weight.

"He gave you what you asked for Steven," she continued, "you had no other want than to win at this game that had taken so much from you."

He was on all fours as he reached out and grabbed at the hem of her dress. "No please, I'll do anything…"

"You have nothing left to give Steven. Come, it is time."

With that, he looked up and saw fire about him. The small back room burned in a gulf of flame and as he held her dress, it to became as fire and quickly the flame touched upon his hand to burn there and quickly move down his shirt.

All at once, he was a human pyre, and though his screams reached high, they were not to be heard by a single living soul.

The red-headed woman pulled her dress away and turned from the sickly sight and smell of the man's charred and burning flesh. She had seen similar hundreds of times already but her stomach was no more the stronger for it.

She had made her deal, and like Fisher, it had come at too high a price. The depths of hell were not yet meant for her, not when there still remained so much outstanding debt to be paid.

She had chosen life everlasting, but she had failed in her end of the bargain. She could still see the face of Father Iain Fitzgerald, he who had robbed her of her prize. He, who had killed her and left her on that cold concrete floor. The thought burned in her head, as her fury rose, for at her own end she had known he had been right.

Keira had not felt the touch of heaven in that god-forsaken place, but as Fitzgerald had suggested, she must surely know there to be a God when she had so readily accepted the Devil. So yes, she had known, but it had come too late for her. Her gift had been bestowed upon her after all, but it had been twisted and warped. She would live an eternity, but all in service to a dark lord who was an abomination and to carry on the duty of the demon she had failed to set free.

For this, she cursed the name of Father Iain Fitzgerald for it had been his interference that had prevented her fulfilling her duty. She would have her vengeance against him, if it took an eternity and in his weakest moment, she would cast aside the masks she now wore and look upon him with her own real eyes and so see the fear and realisation in his as she dragged him down to hell.

The International Association of Exorcists are very much a real organisation.

Formed in 1990, the association was formerly recognised by the Vatican in 2014. As of 2020, they number some 800 members around the world.

Father Gabriele Amorth a founding member of the association, is said to have conducted over 60,000 exorcisms over a 30-year period before his death in 2016.

ABOUT THE AUTHOR.

Mark Harrington was born in Colchester, Essex in 1973. He is a serving Police Detective in the UK and has previously worked within the Police Departments of St Helena, and the Falkland Islands. At the Coming of Darkness is his debut novel.

You can visit him online at www.markharringtonauthor.com

The Journey so Far.

A friend of mine recently asked me how long it was going to be before this book finally saw the light of day. "It's been 5 years, and still we are waiting!" he complained.

The truth of it is, that it has in fact been nearer 12 years (a rough estimation). Reason being, that is when I first put pen to paper, or finger to keyboard and begun the story that you find before you. It didn't take me long to write and the original story amounted to some 20,000 words. I called it a short story, published it to a website and let some friends read it.

Back then it centred only on the conversations of Father Fitzpatrick (name since changed for some reason) and Robert McArthur. The core of McArthur's chapters were all there, the meeting with Searle, the revelation of his secret, the trip to the trenches of the Somme and finally McArthur's revenge. In the original story, we knew nothing of the priest who took confession and in the end, he duly stole McArthur's fortune, as McArthur had done to Searle before. As a result, McArthur was similarly taken by the demon, as he could not have been absolved by such a corrupt being as this reprehensible priest.

It was probably badly structured and littered with overly long paragraphs and bad grammar. But it was well received, and that made me happy.

However, other things were going on in my life back then, as I was in the early stages of my policing career which would take up all of my time and energy (and still does for that matter. You may have heard me complain about it?!)

And so the story was shelved. It probably had an audience of about twenty people all told, and I knew I wanted more.

Such a thing was not possible until 2015. Having resigned from my job in the police, I arrived on the British Territory of St Helena. What a wonderful place it was, and my time there still brings back many happy memories. In addition, I loved my work there, but there was a nagging voice at the back of my mind that told me it wanted to start writing again. But what? I had a wealth of ideas, and had already committed several other short stories to the same website. Perhaps one of those or something altogether new?

Write what you know, is a very common piece of advice I hear in the writing community, but in truth I did not think I could add to the overpopulated crime market. And there was more, because my passion lay with horror and I had always known there was more to the story of Father Iain Fitzgerald and Robert McArthur.

447

As memory serves, I may have tentatively written a few paragraphs while there on St Helena, but things did not begin in earnest until my return in August of 2016 when I took a year off. Why not? I thought. You only live once and this ambition to write a book had become a burning desire.

And so I moved to Colchester and began. In fact the flat that is described within the closing chapters of the book was mine, and oh god it was awful! Come to think of it a lot of what is written in the book is mine, certainly Fitzgerald's belief structure is loosely based on my own, and something else of mine is in the story - the segment about the Mutiny on the Bounty which did in fact contribute toward a very real break up!

My target was 2,000 words a day and I did it. Some days it went quickly and other days it was a chore, but I stuck at it. By the end of that year I had over 200,000 words and I was amazed that I had completed something of that scale.

In my naïvety I thought I was done. How wrong I was, and so began the painful process of rewrites and dang it all if I wasn't interrupted by work again! Money was dwindling and so I headed to the Falkland Islands and picked up again in the world of policing. I loved my time there also, but I wasn't about to let things rest with the book. A good friend of mine (up the Spireites!) will attest to the work I was doing in my lunch hour and back at home, and the disaster that befell me when about twenty chapters of rewrites disappeared from my computer. It was painful but I soldiered on and returned to the UK in early 2018.

Now it was time to employ an editor and unfortunately things began to drag. I was impatient you see, and expected them to work as fast as I was and I let my frustrations get on top of me, and let the original editor go. Things didn't go much faster with the second, but I learned to be a little more patient, because I was learning a great deal about my book and characters that I had not considered before. I am grateful to both of them for their work and patience.

That brought me into 2019, and with money dwindling again, I got my old job back with the police in the UK, and though it would again demand almost all of my attention (7-day shifts, who invented those since I was gone?!) I was still determined to see things out and finally get published.

Which brings me to the last delay.

It was a slow day in the work office, and I know I was the only one in that day. Feeling tired, I was walking up and down to try and wake myself up. There on a colleague's desk was a green stress ball and I bounced it back and forth off the wall à la Jack Torrance and when that was done, I saw her magic 8 ball just sitting there. I picked it up, gave it a shake and got my fortune…

"Dream Big".

I put the thing down and left it at that, no best out of three or anything like that. My fortune was to 'dream big' and so I would. I would go for traditional publishing and secure a literary agent!

Well six months down the line and that didn't pan out, as I got the steady stream of canned e-mails saying my story wasn't for them. Then hope! One agent asked to read my story and so I duly sent it in and waited.

And waited.

And waited.

Until I got to the point I could stand it no more, I sent them an e-mail asking for an update. By 09:00 am the next morning I had another canned response.

And yet I wasn't disheartened. My ambition for this book is a simple one, that it finds an audience and that those people enjoy it.

So that is the story so far, and my response as to why it has taken so long. If you have got this far, then thank you and I truly hoped you enjoyed it. If you did, then I humbly ask that you tell someone about it so that it goes that little bit further.

And to the people who have put up with me over that time and supported this dream, thank you.

And finally, if I should do it again, I will only say it won't take me so long next time. Another idea is burning bright at the back of my mind and wants to get out. It's entirely new, so the fate of Father Fitzgerald and Keira Morgan will have to wait for another day.

Mark Harrington

01/12/2020.

Printed in Great Britain
by Amazon